Too Much Trouble

a Double Trouble Adventure

First Printing: 2019

Kindle eBook ISBN-13: 978-0-9963040-6-1
Paperback ISBN-13: 978-0-9963040-7-8

Front cover image: Sunset, Tyrell Bay, Carriacou, Grenada
Copyright © 2019 S. Mia McCroskey

For Ruga,
my early morning writing partner.

Acknowledgements

Friends have told me they see much of me in Beth. I take this as a personal compliment. I am not Beth, but perhaps she is an alternative version of me who made different choices. For the most part, those same friends deserve recognition here, for they are my fellow members of The Sailing Club (www.thesailingclub.org) who, mostly unwittingly, join me on my research trips. Thanks to them and the Club's organized bareboat charter trips I'm able to explore beautiful, exotic locations by sailboat.

In 2017 I enrolled in a series of on-line writing courses through Coursera, offered to participants in National Novel Writing Month. The program, organized by Wesleyan University, put me through the wringer and spit me out a better writer. I owe every instructor in the program my thanks for sharing their expertise, and I am also thankful for the critiques of my work provided by my fellow students.

Too Much Trouble is the result of two different NaNoWriMo projects. I drafted the two novels during the month of November in 2008 and 2016. After completing the Wesleyan course, I knew that neither stood on its own. I undertook the difficult challenge of merging them into a coherent whole. It took two years and too many revisions to contemplate without tears. Some of those tears were inspired by members of the online writing community Scribophile. My thanks to participants there who provided honest assessments of early combined chapters and drove me to do it over. And over. I leave you to judge whether I did it over enough times to get it right.

Finally, my thanks to Terrence Daley, a friend and gun enthusiast who kindly reviewed relevant passages. I have a feeling Beth will be calling on him again in the future.

Author's Note

Beth and Terry's visit to Barbuda was before the fall of 2017 when Hurricane Irma damaged or destroyed almost every structure on the island and forced the entire population to evacuate to Antigua. At the time of this publication in the spring of 2019, most of Barbuda's residents are still living elsewhere, most on Antigua. The storm destroyed the mangrove trees of the frigate bird sanctuary and naturalists feared that the birds would abandon their long-time home. But it seems that instinct prevails, and the frigate birds have returned to nest in the sticks and stumps of dead mangrove trees. Nature carries on. The resilience and strength of the Caribbean natives, human and animal, inform and support Beth's adventures and growth.

While the characters and activity in this book are entirely fiction, human trafficking is a crime committed on a large scale in many parts of the world. According to the U.S. Department of State, in 2016, the government of Sint Maarten identified and aided almost one hundred victims of trafficking and prosecuted six traffickers (data is unavailable for subsequent years due to the devastation of Hurricane Irma). Sint Maarten is recognized as a transit state for trafficking women and girls into the sex trades. I hope that my portrayal of this heinous crime brings greater awareness of it to my readers.

Prologue

Marigot Bay, St. Martin

Sodium lamps flicked, on casting stark shadows around rows of stacked steel containers in the shipyard. Security lighting on the single cargo vessel secured to the pier, fought off the encroaching evening. The longshoremen had clocked out an hour earlier, leaving the vessel partially unloaded.

A cooling sea breeze rustled the palm trees as a striking black woman descended the exterior staircase of an office building adjacent to the yard. Her red sheath dress clung to her considerable curves and contrasted sharply with the loose dark trousers and white cotton shirts of the two men waiting on either side of the steps. She walked past them and on around the building into the neighboring shipyard. The men followed at a distance, their gaits a matching loose-limbed saunter that further enhanced the contrast between them and the woman.

The woman strode among the stacks of containers as if on a downtown shopping street, passing through patches of light without pause. The group approached one of a row of warehouses where a single incandescent light bulb shone over huge doors. The woman and one of the men walked on between the warehouse and the one next to it and climbed a steel staircase bolted to the outside. He opened a door at the top of the stairs and she entered the warehouse.

She stood on a catwalk above the warehouse floor. Below her were cardboard boxes stacked like the cargo containers outside. In the middle of the room a dozen people—men and women clothed in stained rags—stood at work tables. Each of them picked an object from a box on the table, removed a sticker from the bottom, replaced it with a new sticker, and dropped the object into a box on the floor by their feet. Half a dozen children circulated around the tables throwing handfuls of coconut fiber into the boxes on the floor. Four men dressed like the woman's escort walked slowly around the tables, automatic weapons slung over their shoulders.

The woman watched for several minutes; the corners of her mouth curled in a cryptic smile. After a while one of the cargo doors swung open wider. At the familiar sound the workers at the tables paused to look toward the wall of boxes between them and the door. One of the armed men struck one of the workers with the butt of his weapon. Each of the workers seized another object and went to work with ragged fingernails on the stickers. The children darted in under the tables, but they kept adding fiber to the boxes, their eyes fearfully tracking the armed men.

A wail followed by a cry of "please, where are you taking us," echoed in the enormous space. The woman in red fixed her gaze on a space in the wall of boxes. First another armed man appeared and then eight more people stumbling and blinking in the dim light. The last man carried a child in one arm and held the hand of a slightly older one, both genders indeterminate. The guards shoved the adults into a line in front of the wall of boxes. The hands of the workers at the table kept picking, peeling, sticking, and dropping. All of their heads swiveled toward the row of people standing in front of the boxes.

One of the guards stood in front of the first new comer, a woman in a dress, her bodice ripped to expose the bruised flesh of her bare breast. Her cheeks glistening with tears. The guard looked up at the woman in red, who made a curt nod. The guard reached out and grabbed the woman's arm, propelling her toward the worktables. Another guard intercepted her and brought her to a space there. She stood immobile, staring downward. The man next to her reached over and took her right hand, gently guiding it to the box in the middle of the table.

The first guard moved along the line, receiving a nod from the woman in red for each person and sending them to the worktable. When he came to the man at the end he reached out to take the child from his arms. The man wailed an animal sound of terror, and clutched the child tighter, releasing the hand of the other, older child as he did so.

The guard raised his weapon and the man cowered, protecting the child's tiny body with his own. Two more guards stepped in and grabbed his arms, hauling him to his feet while the first guard yanked the child from him. It was a girl, her face a fine skinned oval. She wept silently, her dark eyes focused on the man who, until now, had protected her. The guard's hands almost encircled her torso as he held her up. Her legs churned weakly. The woman in red's head shook side-to-side once.

The man continued to wail, struggling against his captors, trying to reach for the girl as the guard handed her to another guard who carried her away. The guard swung the butt of his weapon at the wailing man, smashing his nose and left cheek. From elsewhere in the warehouse came a much higher, terrified scream. But the man couldn't hear the girl's cry: he slumped in the other guards' grip, his head dropping to his chest. The guard who struck him looked up at the woman in red. She nodded once and turned away. Her escort opened the door for her.

On the floor far below, a boy inched from beneath the table back between the stacks of boxes, overlooked by the guards dragging the half-conscious man toward the tables.

S. Mia McCroskey

Part I

One

San Juan, Puerto Rico

*L*owering her book with a sigh, Beth glanced at her boyfriend's profile. Terry's jaw worked as he read his magazine and she wondered if he was grinding his teeth. Was this a habit re-emerging as he returned to "normal" life? She didn't want to ask, didn't want him to change from the sensitive, funny, adorable man she'd spent the last five months with sailing the Caribbean. Trying to avoid thinking about it, her eyes scanned idly around the gate at the other passengers waiting for their flight to Washington, D.C., and across the concourse toward the gate on the other side. The people in the waiting area over there wore shorts and sandals. Everyone on this side of the concourse, in the D.C. flight waiting area, was wearing trousers and sweaters and many had coats laying over their carry-ons. Beth and Terry had changed from their shorts and t-shirts in the restroom when they arrived from St. Thomas.

The monitor above the counter said the flight across the concourse was headed for Pointe-à-Pitre on the island of Guadeloupe. For a brief instant she wished she was headed for Guadeloupe—or for any tropical island, instead of embarking on this new chapter back in the chilly northeast. She sighed again, shoving aside thoughts borne of fear of the unknown, and refocused on her book.

A few minutes later the attendant at their gate began announcing the boarding procedure over the loudspeaker. Her recital sounded over-rehearsed, like she needed to board one of the planes to an island herself. Terry closed his magazine and tucked it into his carry-on bag.

"We'll be up in a minute," he said, standing. Beth rose too, trying to zip her daypack while holding her book and almost dumping everything on the stained carpet with its repeating airline logo. Frustrated that she let her nerves make her clumsy, she set everything down before zipping the bag and shouldering it, clutching her book with her ticket tucked between the pages.

Terry half turned to her as the gate agent announced business class and gestured with his head toward the line of boarding passengers. Beth followed, tugging her ticket out of the book to read it again. *Row six? That's pretty far forward.* She promised herself to pay Terry for her ticket when she got the money, so she would never have bought anything more than economy. Glancing again at the crowds around them she couldn't help being grateful for more space on a full flight despite the cost.

Standing in the boarding line she let her gaze wander across the concourse again. Her eye fell on an enormous man in dark grey sweat pants beneath a matching hoodie heaving himself to his feet to shuffle toward the counter servicing the Guadeloupe flight. As Beth's eyes followed the large man, she did not notice the woman seated next to him, now revealed after his departure. Beth didn't see the woman's surreptitious glance, followed by a relaxed stare, as Beth turned her attention back to the gate attendant for her flight. The woman continued to watch as Beth, and then Terry, headed down the jetway, her lips curled in a slight smile.

An announcement from the gate check-in counter disrupted her stare. "Paging passenger Chapman, Oregon. Chapman, Oregon. Please come to the counter at gate thirty-four."

She reached for her cloth tote bag and faded red duffel and stood up to approach the counter.

)

Nestled into an enormous seat on the plane, Beth shut her eyes and thought about the previous day—their last on St. Thomas. Standing with Terry on a marina dock they watched the yard crew steer *Double Trouble*, her 36-foot sailboat, into the slings of the boat hoist. Terry slung his arm around her shoulders for a quick hug, then stepped away with his camera, eager to memorialize the event. An unexpected rush of emotion overtook Beth as her boat rose from the water to reveal a streaked bottom and keel. Her depression at ending their cruise transitioned into embarrassment when she saw the beard of algae streaming from the lower keel.

"I cleaned it before we left Tortola!" she said to nobody in particular. Terry was on the other side of the hull snapping away. The other people in the boatyard were more interested in their own business than an old sailboat being hauled.

Shaken from her depression, she strode up the dock as the yard worker drove the hoist slowly backward until *Trouble* hung over the gravelly earth. At least the wash with the yard's high-power hose, included in the price of storage, would clean it off.

"Algae grows fast," Terry said, reading her mind as he joined her.

"That much since we got to St. Thomas?"

"We just sat here at anchor for two weeks," he shrugged. There was no complaint about their lack of activity in his voice.

"It's a reason to keep the boat moving, I guess." Beth said. Except she had been blissfully happy sitting at anchor, swimming, taking the dinghy ashore to explore, and being alone with him.

"Speaking of which," Terry reached for her hand. "We should go. We'll check on her this evening after they've placed her."

Traveling alone she would have spent the last night on board. Terry had convinced her that a hotel room with a real bathroom would be much more comfortable before their flight. Another example of her financial dependence, but she agreed because, after all, he was right.

As the jet engines started to roar Beth felt Terry take her hand once more. She opened her eyes and turned toward him.

"Okay?" He asked, giving her hand a squeeze. His loving smile warmed her and she felt her shoulders relax. She inhaled and caught a whiff of his aftershave. The scent meant security and comfort.

"Yeah. I'm good."

⟊

Washington, D.C.

"Please put your tray tables up, check to be sure your seat backs are in the fully upright position, and your seat belts are securely fastened. Flight attendants prepare for landing."

The familiar pilot's message roused Beth from her book. Beside her Terry felt around for his seatbelt buckle. He was one of those obstinate travelers who never wore it unless the flight attendant made him. She touched the buckle of hers and gazed out the window.

Autumn was beginning to encroach on the mid-Atlantic: an occasional golden or red tree stood out in the carpet of green. Having grown up in Southern California, the sight of so much green in the east still took adjustment. She missed the wide-open feel of Los Angeles and the inland desert communities. She also missed the view of snow-covered mountains visible from almost everywhere except on the worst smoggy days.

The clank of deploying landing gear disturbed her reflections and she glanced at Terry. He had returned to his magazine, a business weekly aimed at entrepreneurs—which he was. She was struck by this fact when she saw him buy it at the airport in Puerto Rico. How different would he be here on his own turf? A shiver of apprehension took her and he glanced up.

"Chilly?"

"Nervous," she admitted.

"Landings bother you?"

She shook her head. Too honest to agree to that answer and let it go, she said, "About—everything."

He closed his magazine and took her hand. "Beth, I'm going to do whatever I can to make this work. To make us work. Will you do the same?"

"I already am."

His stare was intense for a moment before he whipped his head around to stare straight ahead an instant before the plane touched down with a jolt. The g-force of deceleration pressed them into their seats, and he squeezed her hand. And then he looked at her again, his expression intent.

"You are. I know it. How can we go wrong? Why are you nervous?"

She shrugged, smiling at his kindness and encouragement. "I can't help it. It's more excitement than nerves."

"Promise me something."

"Sure."

"Hey, used to be you asked what before agreeing."

"I trust you."

"If I get buried deep, say something before it gets too bad. I mean, if you're thinking it's not working, say something before you give up on me. Will you do that?"

"I promise," she said, realizing he was leaning close not just to be heard over the whine of the engines as they taxied toward the terminal. She leaned too, and their lips met with a familiar spark.

"I'm looking forward to making love to you in my bed," he murmured as the corners of his eyes crinkled in a smile. She felt her face coloring. "It's a lot bigger than any of *Trouble*'s berths." Beth grinned at his wink.

⟅

They planned to to take a taxi from the airport, but at baggage claim they found a driver bearing a sign with Terry's name. His business partner Jeff had sent a limo with chilled champagne. Beth thought it extravagant, but enjoyed it nonetheless. Terry laughed it off as Jeff's way of welcoming her to Washington—expensive, showy, and without his presence in person.

The special ride seemed totally appropriate in light of her new accommodations. Terry's townhouse in a nineteenth century brick building was artfully renovated. Beautiful woodwork, much of it original Terry said, brought warmth to the interior. The furnishings were tasteful—he admitted to hiring a decorator, although he made a point of telling her that he selected much of the furniture and most of the rugs from among the decorator's suggestions. Beth read pride in his eyes, not the territoriality that his words might also have conveyed.

Not only was his king-sized bed bigger than a sailboat berth, but his bedroom was bigger than any she had ever seen. Heck, the bathroom was bigger than *Trouble*'s saloon.

The sunroom off of the kitchen, overlooking the back garden, must be a wonderful place to enjoy morning coffee. Three stately ferns seemed to be enjoying it too. Seeing her touching one Terry chuckled.

"They're real. Stanley, my neighbor, has been taking care of the place."

"Of course." She realized with a start that in their months sailing it never occurred to her to ask about his arrangements at home.

Their flight had arrived late in the evening, so Terry limited his tour to the main rooms. He urged her to explore the whole house at her leisure, with an emphasis on "whole" as if to clarify that he had nothing to hide.

"I'm starving and I think Stanley will have left us something," he said as they returned to the kitchen.

She excused herself to freshen up, stepping into the downstairs powder room rather than going back upstairs where she would have to choose between his bathroom or the one in the hall. Insert herself into his room right now? Or distance herself by acting like a houseguest? The fact that he would not know what bathroom she used didn't matter in her travel weary mind. It mattered to her and she deferred facing the commitment.

When she joined him in the kitchen a few minutes later he had set out a supper of chicken curry, bean salad, and a crisp white wine.

"Stanley picked the menu?"

"He must have stopped at Whole Foods—I recognize the containers. I told him not to go to any trouble, just be sure we had something to eat."

"I look forward to meeting him—to thank him. This is really tasty. I never shopped at Whole Foods. Trader Joes is my gourmet standby."

"Mine too, even though there are a lot of fancy shops around here."

She felt encouraged to have a grocery store in common as she enjoyed the curry. The wine was smooth and easy to drink, and soon the tension of coming here, along with the flight, weighed on her eyelids.

"Ready to call it a night?" Terry asked, taking her plate to the sink.

She swallowed the last of her wine. "Very ready."

"I'm going to have to clear a couple drawers and closet space for you," he said as they climbed the stairs. "I didn't want to presume the need before I left."

Beth chuckled and smiled back at him one step behind her on the stairs, but she could see he meant it.

"Not that I didn't hope," he said, his tone a sensual murmur. They stepped onto the landing and she turned, bringing her hands to his shoulders.

"You are utterly perfect," she sighed, touched both by his lack of presumption and his admission.

"Perfection can become hard to live up to," he said, pulling her close. "But I'll take it for the moment."

Two

Georgetown, Washington, D.C.

*T*he next morning Beth spent too long enjoying the multiple jets of Terry's fancy tile and glass shower. To make up for her excess she used the squeegee hanging in the stall to clean the glass before stepping out and wrapping herself in an unbelievably fluffy towel. After a year of alternating between rough, thin terrycloth and microfiber pack towels, the terrycloth felt oddly heavy and unwieldy. But she wasn't about to complain.

She found Terry by following the smell of frying bacon to the kitchen. He stood over the range monitoring a sizzling pan, a row of eggs and loaf of bread waiting on the counter. He half turned as she entered, his eyes alight with his usual morning energy.

"Good morning! Coffee's hot," he pointed with his spatula at a drip coffee maker on the counter. "Unless you want latte or espresso." He nodded toward the separate appliance beside it. The cheap espresso machine back in Beth's New York apartment was an infant sister to this one with its gleaming steam nozzle and pressure gauge. It intimidated her.

"I think I'll defer learning how to use it," she said, noticing a mug waiting for her, a steel pitcher hazed with condensation next to it.

"Stanley stocked you well," she said, taking the coffee carafe from the heating plate.

"Yeah, better than I expected. Maybe because I mentioned you were coming."

Beth paused in her pouring and refocused on the mug, then let the brown stream flow again. *He told all his friends? Exactly what did he tell them?* Beth shuddered at the prospect of people making over her, other than on the typical occasions like birthdays or graduations. Being made into some sort of celebrity just for coming home with Terry scared her.

As she took her coffee to the kitchen table the sounds from the range changed: Terry removed the bacon and dropped several eggs into the pan. He didn't need to ask how she liked hers, they had each cooked countless meals for the other over the past few months. Beth sipped her coffee, savoring the mixed aromas of food and drink representing comfort and home. There was no reason to be scared of attention from Terry's friends and family. No, that didn't scare her. But the reason for it did—Terry's enthusiastic announcement of her arrival. What expectations did they have? How could she live up to them? She was just an unemployed marketing copywriter and sometime sailor with an old, used boat. Here in the metropolitan US her accomplishments in the islands—solo sailing long distances, coming to the aid of a friend in need—were irrelevant.

She sipped her coffee while pondering these thoughts until Terry placed a plate in front of her. She smiled her thanks.

"Still waking up?" he asked, leaning down to place a kiss on her forehead.

"Sort of," she agreed, turning her attention to breakfast. "This looks wonderful. Thank you."

"I was hungry." His usual, humorous response when he cooked a large meal. He retrieved flatware from a drawer—Beth tried to make a mental note of which one—and sat down across from her.

"I'm meeting with Jeff this afternoon. If you want, we can take a walk around the neighborhood this morning. I can show you what's where. Or we can do something touristy. It's not far to the White House …"

Beth shook her head, "local exploration. I can find my way to the sites on my own, but I would like to see your favorite spots in the neighborhood."

"I'm sure you'll find your own soon enough," he said, but she could see her choice pleased him, he wanted to show her his world.

"And I know Jeff and Carole want us to come for dinner. If it's too much, please say so."

"No, it's not. It's very kind of them. Of course I'll go."

He appeared to be relieved, which made her wonder about the nature of his relationship with Jeff. Perhaps after his long absence he needed to please his business partner.

"I'll confirm with Jeff." He swallowed down the last of his breakfast and stood up. Her meal was only half eaten.

"I made this for you," he said, retrieving several papers and a ring of keys from the counter. "There's the passcode for the wifi," he indicated a long string of letters and numbers that she could enter into her laptop to access the internet. "The address, although you'll remember it, I'm sure. Or we can pin it to your jacket," he grinned playfully, and she smirked at him. "This is a list of the businesses I use—the dry cleaner, wine shop, that sort of thing. Like I said, you may find others you like—the one I care about is the wine shop."

Beth scanned the handwritten list. "It's good to know," she said, unable to express her feelings. Somehow his quick notes to share his lifestyle made her feel more welcome than anything else he'd done so far.

"This is the alarm code. I'll show you how to enter it on the way out. You do need to be sure you get it, because if it goes off it calls the police and that sucks. When it's a false alarm, I mean. Here," he held up the ring of keys, jingling them, "it's a full set. Front deadbolt, front lock, back deadbolt—it's different—back lock, back gate to the alley," he held up each key as he identified it. Beth noticed labels on each one and wondered if he had them made for her—presumption or not. Watching her expression, he paused.

"This is my spare set. There's a hardware store on the list. Why don't you get another set made? They sell these labels there, too, right at the key counter."

She took the keys. "Sure. Easy."

)

Pointe-à-Pitre, Guadeloupe

Ori got out of the taxi, tugging at the hem of her shorts before shouldering her tote bag and duffle on either shoulder. After months trapped in Connecticut her warm weather sailing clothes were not as comfortable as they used to be pre-baby. A few weeks on board would get her back into shape. She stood for a moment inhaling the aroma of seawater and diesel fuel mixed with something fried— probably chips from the restaurant down the waterfront. Those aromas were more like home to her than the fresh paint and simmering stews in her parents' Connecticut home. On the second story balcony of a waterfront office building she saw her target: A sign hanging from the sheltering eaves painted with the name of the yacht brokerage representing her boat, *Dream Catcher*, for sale.

Instead of climbing the steps, Ori turned toward the ramp down to the dock. A gate stood open at the bottom. Thanks to French laissez faire sailors, she thought as she turned right and made her way along the dock. She stopped at the sixth slip and eyed the plastic sign hanging on the sailboat's bow pulpit proclaiming it to be *à vende* and represented by the broker up on the second floor. She glanced at their office and saw no movement, so she dropped her duffel and dug into her tote, coming out with a pair of nail clippers.

She used the clippers to cut the plastic wire ties holding the sign and tucked it under her arm, then went around to the other side and nipped that one off too. She picked up her duffel and carried it out onto the finger pier alongside the boat's cockpit. She set the tote and signs on the dock and grabbed the lifelines to step up on the side deck and heave her duffel into the cockpit. Stepping back off the boat she picked up the signs and her tote and headed back along the dock.

Cool air rushed out around her when she opened the door to the brokerage office. She took in the blonde woman, her hair in an impeccable chignon, her nails blood red, seated behind a desk facing the windows. Took her in and dismissed her to focus on man at the other desk set further back in the office: white cotton shirtsleeves with fine blue stripes; thick brown hair and squinty eyes; in the process of standing up.

"Good morning. I believe these are yours," Ori strode across to his desk and set the signs on top of a stack of papers.

"Excuse me, madame?" His French accent was difficult for her to understand.

Ori reached into her tote and withdrew a sheath of papers. "I am cancelling this brokerage agreement." The man watched with widening eyes as she tore the papers in half, and in half again.

"Your services are no longer needed in the representation of *Dream Catcher*. We thank you for your efforts." She let the multicolored layers of the torn contract flutter down on top of the signs.

"Madame, I cannot release the vessel to you, you are not the owner—"

"You certainly can *monsieur*." Ori's hand went back into the tote and she withdrew a thin red vinyl binder. She opened it and held it up facing the man. "I have her documentation here. So again, thank you. Good day."

She smiled, turned, and strode out of the office leaving the cool air behind.

Her show of confidence was barely more than skin deep. After all, the documentation in her hand did not show her as the owner of *Dream Catcher*, but her father. She picked up her pace, trotting down the stairs and back down the dock, pulling the gate shut behind her. She paused to untie the two lines securing *Dream Catcher*'s bow and tossed them up on the deck and hurried along the finger pier to climb aboard.

Ori gambled on her luck, betting the boat was being kept in working condition so the broker could take prospective buyers sailing. Why else keep it in an expensive slip? But even if the engine was dead, or the key was missing, she could sail out of the slip.

She recognized the combination lock on the companionway and opened it using the familiar set of numbers. She carried the hatch boards down the companionway ladder and dropped them on a settee, glancing around the familiar saloon. It was spotless, with a basket of fake flowers on the table. Shaking her head, she lifted the top of the navigation desk and found the engine key on its oblong float printed with the name of a New England marine supply store. She climbed back into the cockpit and stepped behind the wheel, glancing up toward the brokerage office before bending to insert the key into the ignition. She imagined that *Monsieur* was on the telephone to her father. She checked that the transmission was in neutral and turned the key.

The engine churned a couple times and turned over. She peered at the gauges, watching the oil pressure rise and the fuel gauge shiver up to about a quarter tank. "Cheapskate," she muttered, glancing up at the office again. Still nothing to see.

Looking along the port side she saw a spring line running from the midship cleat to a piling off the stern. She couldn't afford the time to get it off the piling. She climbed out onto the side deck and uncleated the line, tossing it over the piling. She crossed over to the port side and jumped off on to the finger pier, holding the lifeline to keep *Dream Catcher* from drifting as she bent over and uncleated the stern line from the dock. She tossed the line into the cockpit and climbed back aboard. Back behind the wheel, she put the engine in reverse and eased the boat backward out of the slip. As she turned the wheel, angling the bow of the boat into the channel, she saw the broker standing outside the second-floor office with his hands on the railing watching her.

Grinning, she waved at him before putting the transmission in forward and throttling up.

)

Georgetown, Washington, D.C.

"You almost sound disappointed, Bethy. He's doing fine, all things considered," Trish said.

All the things to consider about Beth and Trish's father were substantial, but Beth understood her sister's need to focus on the positive: their father's steady decline was slowed by medication. Beth wanted to credit her father himself—his powerful personality striking back at the Alzheimer's Disease, fighting to retain control.

Their father's mental departure began a year before and continued to progress despite beginning treatment. When their Mom caught him tucking the costly pills into the potted plant on the kitchen counter she started monitoring to be sure he took them. Now his lucid periods came more often and lasted longer, and he did better at the mental exercises Mom and Trish learned to do with him. They agreed it was time to sell the family home so Mom and Dad could move to an assisted living facility. More than half a year ago they presented this to Beth as if it was an option, not a final decision. When she realized the choice was made, she resented it, but understood.

She spent several weeks in California helping with the move and working through her guilt for not being more present for them. She thought of her father as robust. When she stood face-to-face with him in the kitchen where she had done homework, eaten peanut butter and marshmallow fluff sandwiches, and known the love of two parents, she truly understood. She wept at his confusion over who she was, only later realizing she was mourning him even as he lived.

Moving him, sorting through a lifetime of belongings in the house, and making decisions on his behalf tugged at the last frayed threads of the little girl who snuggled with him on a patio lounge looking at the stars on summer nights. A few years ago she had rushed to shed the little girl trappings and moved across the country. Now she mourned the loss of what she gave up.

She expected her father's condition to continue to decline while she went sailing with her boyfriend: how could it not? He went from her robust Dad to a confused invalid in a few months, so she expected the ordeal to be over by now. But as she listened to Trish's superficially upbeat report, the depth of her conceit struck her hard. Her father clung to his diminished mental faculties, and she was disappointed. The guilt over her reduced role in his care rushed back in force.

"I'm not disappointed, Trish," she said, swallowing down the rush of emotion at her appalling reaction to her sister's good news so her next words sounded more even. "I think I should come visit."

"Of course—I mean, if you want to."

"You don't want me to?"

"No—Beth, you're not being fair. I mean, things are going fine, you don't need to feel guilty for not being with them. Of course, we all want to see you, if you want to come."

Beth's jaw tightened. Trish meant she was not essential. Not part of her parents' support network. A visitor.

"I have to discuss it with Terry. I mean, I need to find out his plans for the near future."

"Beth, I don't think less of you for conferring with him, especially if you're going to make a future with him—are you?" The gossipy note of the last bit made Beth smile in spite of herself.

"I would like to."

"But?"

"No 'but.' But—" Beth grimaced at the contradiction, "we've only spent time together cruising. We have to sort out our relationship here on dry land."

"Terry sounds like a dream, Beth. I'm sure you'll get along as well in his house as you did on your boat."

Beth sighed. "He is a dream, Trish. I just hope Washington in winter won't wake us up."

Her sister snorted. "One way or another, you're gonna wake up eventually. I get it, Sis. You think, so far, it's an extended vacation fling. But I think you're underestimating the situation. Five months is not a fling. It's too long a time to hide personality traits. You have to decide whether you can tolerate them. That's all."

"That's all." Beth groaned, remember Terry grinding his teeth over a business article.

"Nobody said it's easy. If you want to be single, don't bother. If you want him, learn to deal with him in all situations."

"Thank you, Dr. Phil."

"You know I'm right."

"I know. I'm not ignoring your advice. But I thought—" she stopped herself, reluctant to voice the crux of her turmoil.

"Dad would be dying, or dead, by now?" Trish's flat tone suggested she was working hard not to accuse.

Beth swallowed, tears flooding her eyes. She couldn't suppress the accompanying sob. Her sister knew her all too well for her to conceal her deepest thoughts.

"I'm so selfish."

"You're human. You want the grief to end."

Trish could have sounded bitter or angry, but she did not. Beth envied her sister's maturity.

"I do. I can't make a decision knowing he's hanging on—"

"What? Why not? Beth, Mom and I, and Dad in as much as he can, do not expect your life to stop until he dies. No more than I expect my kids to stop growing."

Beth considered it for a moment, wiping moist hands at her hot cheeks. "I have to think it through," she said after a noisy snuffle. "You know me, I think too much before I leap."

"But when you leap, you do it big." Trish's chuckle made Beth smile. "Look, I think you better come for a visit. It might help to see how well they're doing. Bring Terry with you."

The line went dead before Beth could summon a response. She stared at the phone for a moment before folding it shut and dropping it on the sofa.

♪

That evening Terry found Beth sitting on the bed with her bag—a faded navy-blue canvas duffle—spread open beside her. Her face showed a mix of contrition and humor.

"What's up babe?"

"I have nothing to wear!" she half laughed. He looked pointedly at the bag and the folded clothes. "I've been living above seventy-five degrees for a year," she said, holding up her "good" skirt—a blue and white cotton floral print. It would be great in Washington's humid July, but too light, both in color and fabric, for late September. "Not just for tonight. I mean, for a job interviews. I don't even have a warm coat, only foul weather gear."

Terry crossed to the bed and sat down on the other side of the bag, looking again at the folded clothes. They were all she had, having pared down to what would fit in the boat's confined space and be appropriate in the tropical climate.

"Didn't you say you stored some things in New York?" he asked. She frowned for a second before she realized what he meant.

"I nearly forgot. I think I did keep a few winter things. I should get my stuff out of Eve's Mom's garage. It seemed important at the time, but I bet I can toss most of it."

"Well, you should have a look. There might be some keepsakes. Like photos."

Beth shrugged a tacit agreement. "I can take the train up and ship what I want to keep."

"Or we can drive up for a weekend in New York."

"Will you have time?" She thought about her sister's invitation. How much of his time could she demand? "I spoke to Trish this afternoon. She said if I come to California to visit I have to bring you." She watched his face, fearing annoyance or flat refusal. But instead he smiled broadly.

"I would love to meet your family. When do you want to go?"

"Just like that? And the trip to New York, too? Can you take the time?" After months of leisure, Beth thought she heard the clock ticking faster on his business, even if he didn't say so.

"Jeff and the lawyers have scheduled the closing on the business for two months from now. I need to help with the due diligence and planning. But I have a little time. I would love to go to California. A weekend in New York is not a big deal either."

He smiled and patted a stack of shirts in the bag between them, bringing her attention back to her immediate dilemma. "Look," he took the top shirt from the stack, "you can wear this year round—it would be fine for work, wouldn't it? You have two or three like it. Don't you have a pair of jeans in there? And a sweater?"

"A sweater, yeah," Beth dug under the lighter clothes on top and dragged out her reliable cotton cable knit sweater. "But no jeans. Just the cargo pants I'm wearing."

"Wear those tonight and one of these shirts. You don't need to dress up for Jeff and Carole. Tomorrow we'll take another tour—to the mall. Do not," he raised one hand, palm out, to stop her inevitable response, "say you can't afford to buy a few things. You need an interview suit, and it's in my interests to see that you have one. You'll pay me back."

Beth took the shirt from him, holding it against herself above the cargo pants. "I know when to swallow my pride."

"Good," Terry stood up. "I'm sorry I'm later than I planned."

"Everything okay with Jeff?"

"Sure. He's just in his 'check everything, check it again, and recheck it to be sure' mode. They're expecting us around seven."

)

Beth met Jeff when she met Terry: he invited her to join his crew in a regatta in Annapolis when she stopped there on her way south. Terry was another recruit, a beacon of maturity amid a crowd of young men selected for brawn over brain. Although Beth had spent a single day in Jeff's company, and he was focused on the race they were sailing, she felt as if she knew him from all the stories Terry had shared since that day.

She realized as Terry introduced her to Jeff's wife Carole and their two children, eight-year-old Ronny and seven-year-old Megan, he had told her almost nothing about Jeff's family. A hair shorter than Beth, Carole's willowy slender figure, long, shining black hair, and long face gave her a hawkish appearance and an oddly attractive alertness. Nearly black eyes stood out dramatically against her light complexion. If she were thinner, she would look too severe. Beth thought the children might greet Terry with enthusiasm like an uncle, but seven-year-old Megan stayed behind her mother and Ronny, one year her elder, simply said his hellos and wandered away, portable video game in hand. At least he took one earphone out to speak to them.

She caught a hint of frustration on Jeff's face as he watched his son's rude departure. More curiously, he turned the expression on Carole with more than a hint of blame. Terry was focused on exchanging pleasantries with Carole, and Beth was sure he didn't notice.

Don't read too much into anything until you get to know them, Beth chastised herself.

Jeff guided them from the foyer into the adjacent living room furnished in the colonial style. The bookshelves were for show, with a few too many cute accessories among too few books. A goose in flight, cut in silhouette from a piece of wood and painted, caught Beth's eye. It soared over the fireplace mantel against a red brick chimney wall. It put her in mind of craft fairs and quilts. The living room led into a dining area delineated by a wood floor and the opening of a dark hallway leading further into the house. Beth thought she could hear a television or radio off in that direction.

Jeff poured red wine from a bottle after showing Terry the label, a brotherly interaction that made Beth feel like an outsider. *Intentional? Ridiculous.* She suppressed the notion. *Don't be so sensitive.* Jeff gestured to them to sit down. The heavily padded cornflower blue sofa engulfed Beth. Carole disappeared with a word about seeing to supper.

"Welcome again Beth. I hope you know we're all very glad you decided to come," Jeff opened.

"Yes, here's to a new chapter," Terry said, raising his glass toward Beth. She raised hers to touch it with a gentle clink, then leaned across the coffee table to touch Jeff's.

Beth sipped the dry, nutty wine. Terry must approve and Beth was sure Jeff, more of a beer man, bought it especially for their dinner. *Or, to entice his partner back to the business. No! Stop over analyzing!*

As they sipped appreciatively Beth noticed Carole come from the kitchen to the dining area. She set a pitcher on the table and retreated without looking into the living room.

"I am sort of curious who you 'all' are. Has Terry told everyone he knows about my coming with him?" Beth smiled to hide the seriousness of her question. Terry turned to look at her and she knew he could see her nerves.

"Let's see," he held up an index finger, "Jeff and his family, of course, and my family," he extended his middle finger, "and Stanley," his ring finger went up, "the mailman, the dry cleaner, the guy who sells tickets at the movie theatre down the block—hey! I'll spill!" Beth elbowed him, grinning.

"Let me read you his last email," Jeff said, pulling a Blackberry from its holster on his belt. The sight made Beth realize Terry wore his on his belt, too—he never wore it during their time in the islands.

"No, you wouldn't—" Terry started to protest, but Jeff grinned maliciously as he pressed buttons on the device. He cleared his throat.

"Jeff," Terry warned.

"This is to me, Carole, several email addresses I believe are Terry's immediate family, and a few others—is the mailman jacks at optonline dot net? Anyway, it says: 'She's coming she's coming she's coming! I know you'll all love her as much as I do'."

Beth felt her face turn crimson. She saw that Terry was a similar color.

"That's a personal message, Jeff!" he said, studiously not looking at Beth.

"It has a broad 'to' list for a personal message," Jeff said. "It goes on: 'And I know you'll all make her feel welcome enough to stay, at least until we can plan our next cruise.' Now there's an interesting point. When is your next cruise?"

"Terry has explained you'll need time to get things going," Beth said hesitantly, suddenly fearful Terry had downplayed the necessary commitment. She didn't want to sound naïve. "But it's okay. I need to find a job and build my savings back up. I appreciate having a place to live in a town where I'll be able to find work."

"I should think so. I mean, you can find work here," Jeff said, holstering the Blackberry. "Nothing to be embarrassed about in message, buddy. She does know you love her, right?"

Beth felt Terry's arm settle around her shoulders and instinctively relaxed against it.

"I hope so." He pitched his voice pitched just for her. She turned her head to peer into soft blue eyes.

"I do," she returned his secretive smile, almost not believing how wonderful it made her feel. She stared at the side of his face as she contemplated his statement. Months ago, in an off-hand comment, he told her he intended to marry her. She wanted to believe him, but in all their discussion of what she might do now—come to Washington, stay in the islands, go to California—he never said it again. She feared that his comment was unintended, or that he had changed his mind.

"Beth?"

She realized Jeff was asking her something.

"Sorry?" she winced apologetically.

"How's your resume? If you think it could use polishing, we know someone—used to work for us."

"Still works for the company we sold," Terry said. "But he'll have a look as a favor—we made sure he was taken care of in the deal."

"Yes, it could use work," Beth considered it, "Maybe an expert can figure out how to spin my year of absence from the workplace."

"You mean, couch it in terms of life experience?" Jeff smiled.

"Yeah. I can write sales copy, but resumes take a special skill." She nodded.

"We'll set it up for when we get back from California," Terry said. "By the way, Jeff, Beth and I are going to visit her parents for a few days."

"When?" Jeff asked, his smile fading.

"In a couple weeks. I'll let you know."

Beth thought Jeff had a lot more to say about it than his icy "please do." But before he could go on, Carole reappeared in the dining area, catching his eye.

"Dinner is ready—anybody need to freshen up?"

"If I could," Beth said.

"This way. I'll rouse the kids from their electronic diversions."

That answered Beth's unspoken question about whether the children would join them. Apparently, food counteracted both shyness and indifference, for they sat politely at the table and engaged in conversation with their parents and guests. School, Beth learned, had started after Labor Day weekend. At seven Megan was learning how it all worked. A year older and in third grade, Ronny acted like the old hand. Probably just like his father at his age, Beth thought.

Jeff was all salesman, the same as Beth remembered from their one day of racing. She found his type of personality compelling at first, but over time she lost patience with it. He concealed his true self under a genial, clever façade appropriate for social occasions, but discouraged friendly intimacy. Beth thought this type of person must allow a few people in—in Jeff's case Carole and, she hoped, Terry.

Carole served grilled lamb chops with mint jelly, red potatoes roasted tender, and a mixture of thin carrots and asparagus. Beth gushed over Carole's skill, secretly wondering if their hostess prepared it got it at Whole Foods like Stanley. But Carole mentioned how much she loved the indoor grill installed when they renovated the kitchen. When she offered a tour of her new kitchen Beth agreed, insisting on helping clear the table and get dessert in the bargain.

"Of course, it's a mess in here," Carole said as they passed through the swinging door into the kitchen. Beth took in the spacious, well-lit space. The walls were lined with white cabinets, some of them glass fronted to show off ranks of gleaming stemware. The countertops were a highly polished composite stone in bluish green. A matching center island included a second sink and the grill.

"I love the counter tops, they remind me of the Caribbean," she said, imitating Carole buy placing the dirty dishes she was carrying in the sink.

"Do you? I don't know. After we had it done, I read blues and greens aren't conducive to the appetite."

"What colors are?"

"Reds. That's why you see so many red dining rooms."

"Huh. Well, I love this shade," Beth patted the counter, and examined the grill—the excuse for her visit. She nearly panicked, struggling to come up with something complimentary to say about an absolutely ordinary electric grill. "Cool, it's vented." Wall all she could come up with.

"You're prepared for this business deal, aren't you?"

Beth was unsure of Carole's meaning for a moment, but at least the other woman ignored her dumb observation.

"Prepared?"

"For the months of long hours, the arguments, the cancelled social engagements ..."

"I know they have to work hard. But I have to get a job and put in some hours too."

"Well, you have the right attitude going into this. But I'm warning you, it gets old." Carole looked around the kitchen again. "It pays for this. But it gets old," she repeated. Her gaze landed back on Beth. "You may not realize, but Terry has been different since he first sailed with you. He's less driven than Jeff. Good for you, but it could create more tension between them than in their past deals. I'm glad you're here—Terry may need your support."

"Is Jeff really glad I'm here?"

Carole eyed her, nodding as if to herself. "Fair question. You can tell what he says isn't always what he means, not when he's 'on.' He's been 'on' for weeks now as he's brought this deal home," she sighed, looking down at her clasped hands, then back up at Beth. "I think he is, because it means Terry won't be distracted by missing you."

Beth nodded slowly, considering the ramifications. "Do you think he minds us going to see my family?"

Carole laughed, a short, high-pitched sound like a lap dog barking. "Probably."

"Oh no!"

"No, no, don't you think you have to live by my husband's leave. He'll get over it. He always does."

"I don't want to come between them."

"Honey, that will never happen."

Beth frowned.

"I mean, Terry is going to fit you into his life, no question there. He already has. He won't fail Jeff either. They'll sort it out and we'll stand by the ringside, arms out to catch them when they need a break."

"You make it sound like they fight all the time!"

"Yeah, I didn't mean it that way. I meant, don't expect to be involved with their business. Catch him when he falls, and he'll love you forever."

Beth pondered Carole's advice off and on for the next few days. Carole seemed to see herself as the proverbial woman behind the man. Beth did not aspire to that role. She loved Terry and wanted to support his goals, but she had goals of her own that Terry supported in return.

Carole made her marriage sound like a one-way street. Ultimately, as Beth and Terry repacked for their trip to California, Beth decided to consider the source, and the source's husband, in her evaluation of the advice. Terry was not a duplicate of Jeff. She could not imagine him become so wrapped up in his own project he would not spare at least a few moments for hers.

Three

Riverside, California

"*T*here's Trish, in the blue t-shirt. With the kids—they're all in blue t-shirts," Beth said as she and Terry entered the baggage claim area at Los Angeles International Airport.

"I see them," Terry said, waving as Trish caught sight of Beth. "And I can't believe it—our bags are coming out." As he moved to get closer to the baggage conveyor Beth's eyes met her sister's. Trish mouthed an elaborate "wow." Beth rolled her eyes and turned to help Terry.

)

"I can't believe you got t-shirts made," Beth said, rotating in her seat to look at eight-year-old Sammy where he sat beside Terry. Last time she visited, half a year ago, he'd sat in the very back next to his sister. Beth wondered what caused the promotion. Maybe the two inches he'd grown.

"Got them made? We made them, didn't we," Trish said, glancing up into the rear-view mirror to see her kids confirm her claim before focusing on merging with traffic on the San Diego freeway.

"Yeah Aunt Beth. We designed them on the computer," Eli said, rubbing her hand over her chest. "Mommy printed them out and ironed them on the shirts."

"I wanted skulls," Sammy said with a scowl. Terry laughed, gaining his attention.

"Skulls would have been cool," Terry agreed, glancing up to return Beth's warm smile.

)

Trish had prepared the guest room for them. In between showing Terry around the house and getting the kids settled with coloring books in front of the television she pulled Beth discretely aside and told her their mother had offered lengthy advice about sleeping arrangements including she and Beth sharing the master bedroom, Terry in the guest room, and her husband Mike on the couch in the living room.

"If you want to keep peace in this part of the family, don't disillusion her. Please."

"We will sleep wherever you tell us," Beth said quite honestly. Having privacy with Terry for a few days was not as important as keeping things on an even keel between her sister and mother.

"Are you kidding? You and I never shared a bed and I'm not going to start now! Mike hates sleeping on the couch. And you two have been living on a boat for a year—"

"Five months."

"Whatever—" Trish's eyes widened, and she took a deep breath, "— you do sleep in the same cabin on the boat, right? I just assumed ..."

Beth laughed and assured her sister that her assumption was correct, although on warm nights one of them often moved out to the saloon or cockpit. She promised to tell Terry about the minor deception as well. She thought to ask whether the kids were in on it, but decided not to. If Trish wanted her kids to lie to their grandmother she didn't want to know about it.

)

"You're awfully quiet Beth," Terry whispered into her ear. He sat beside her on the second-row bench seat in the minivan with Trish and Mike up front. Both Trish and Mike had taken the morning off to visit the Andersons after sending the kids off to school. "Nervous?"

Beth pursed her lips and stared straight ahead. "I—"

He wrapped her hands in both of his and squeezed them gently. "It's okay Bethy. However they are, I'm glad to meet them."

Beth took a deep breath and forced her shoulders to relax, shooting a quick smile at Terry before turning her head to look out at the Monday morning traffic on the Riverside Freeway.

"Every time I come here, I'm shocked at the development," she said. "This used to be orange groves, what? Twenty years ago?" She glanced forward at the side of Trish's face. Her sister nodded.

"And open fields. Every one of those houses means two or three more cars. The traffic is crazy."

"It's kind of sad. Growing up we felt like we lived in the west, with the rolling hills and live oaks. This could be New Jersey."

"Or Florida," Terry said.

"Remember how we could hear the fans in the orange groves on cold nights?" Trish asked.

"Yeah. They had heaters in the groves—'smudge pots,' we called them," Beth told Terry. "I think they burned coal—in high school guys would get jobs tending them and come to school with black smudges on their faces. They had huge fans to circulate the warm air. We would lie in bed listening to them humming in the distance."

Terry squeezed Beth's hands again, the skin around his eyes crinkled with a warm smile.

"You knew it was cold outside when you heard them," Trish added.

"What, fifty?" Terry teased, eyes locked with Beth's.

"Below freezing!" Beth said. "That was the point—to keep the fruit from freezing."

"I used to light the pots," Mike said. "It was dirty, tiring work and it paid badly. But we got to stay up all night, and we felt important."

Mike exited the freeway and followed a broad avenue through several intersections, finally turning in at a gated community.

"Here we are, exclusive Orange Grove Wellness," he announced, lowering his window. "We're here to see the Andersons," he said to the guard inside an air-conditioned booth. The man made a mark on a clipboard.

"You know where it is?"

"Yes sir."

"Go ahead."

The red and white striped barrier in front of the van lifted and Mike drove on through.

"This is nice," Terry said.

Dense green hedges lined the road at the curb. Cement sidewalks inside of them wandered sinuously across manicured lawns dotted with plantings of flowering hibiscus and bougainvillea and stately palm trees. They came to a raised crosswalk and Mike slowed the van to climb gently over it. To their right a woman pushed a man in a wheelchair along one of the paths. Beyond the lawns and gardens stood single-story stucco buildings with flat roofs and wide doors and windows.

"This is the nursing home," Trish said, indicating the buildings. "Mom and Dad are in 'Independent living'."

"I wonder if they have a graduation ceremony when you move from one to the other," Beth muttered. Trish shot her a sharp look, but Mike chuckled.

"More like a reverse graduation, I think," he said, then glanced at Trish and shrugged. Her pinched expression silenced him.

"There's a senior community for the most active, independent living, which is a euphemism for assisted living, and the nursing home," Beth said.

"Are your folks anywhere near needing this kind of care, Terry?" Mike asked.

"Not yet. But my sister and I have discussed what to do, eventually."

"Made any decisions?"

"Of course not."

"Yeah." Mike's tone suggested he faced the same decisions with his parents, which reminded Beth she knew nothing about his family. She felt selfish all over again.

⌡

"Hello Mrs. Reynolds. How are they today?" Trish greeted an overweight woman in nurse's garb when they entered the independent living building. The nurse smiled, bright red lips in stark contrast to her ebony skin. She was seated behind a counter with a computer and several monitors.

"Hello Mrs. Walker, Mr. Walker. And Beth?" the nurse asked, smiling at Beth.

"Yes, I'm back Mrs. Reynolds."

"Your parents will be glad to see you, I'm sure," the nurse's gaze moved to Terry.

"This is my boyfriend Terry," Beth said.

"Good to meet you Mrs. Reynolds," Terry said.

"Welcome to Orange Grove Wellness. I'll check on the Andersons." She tapped a few commands on the computer keyboard and watched the screen expectantly. "The morning aid administered meds and confirmed they ate breakfast. Your mother was preparing to visit the gardens and trying to convince your father to go along."

"She knows we're coming," Trish said.

"Maybe she remembered," Mrs. Reynolds said. "I'll telephone now, but you go on in."

They walked along a side corridor lined with the doors to apartments, each with a peephole and number. The walls were an inviting shade of light peach, and framed prints alternated with the doors.

"It does look like an apartment building," Terry said.

"Yes, we liked that about it," Trish said. "It's not so hospitaly."

"They do everything to help the residents be independent," Beth said, sounding to herself like one of the facility's brochures. But she needed to believe it. She desperately needed her parents to be the loving, functional people who raised her. Terry took her hand and gave it a squeeze.

"I hope your mom hasn't independently gone to the gardens." His toothy grin and his grip eased her growing apprehension.

"We'll just go find her if she has." Trish still sounded irritated. She turned a corner and made a beeline for a door further down the hall.

"We can go right in," she said over her shoulder, the information directed at Terry as she knocked on the door. "But I never do."

"That would contradict the independence idea," he said blandly.

"That would make our mother livid," Beth countered, smiling at her sister.

Trish knocked again.

As Beth felt herself slipping into mild panic two things happened: Terry squeezed her hand, holding her to rationality, and the door opened.

"Hi Mom!" Trish said. "We're all here."

)

"This is wonderful. Absolutely wonderful!" Mrs. Anderson said as she set a tray of glasses on the coffee table with minimal rattling. Beth scooted forward on the sofa to help her pour iced tea into them.

Terry turned from watching Mr. Anderson, seated across from him, to Mrs. Anderson, who went on speaking.

"We are so proud of our Beth. When she called to say her boyfriend was coming, well, I was walking on air for days. Right Patricia?"

"You were, mom. Scared the kids," Trish said, straight faced.

"Oh you," Mrs. Anderson chuckled.

"They allow the children here?" Terry took his eyes away from Mr. Anderson again.

"They encourage it," Trish said, taking her glass.

"Oh yes," Mrs. Anderson added. "Trish brings them by after school a couple times a week. We thought it would be too much this time." She held out a glass to Terry.

Too much for whom? Beth wondered as she took the glass. Terry, me, the kids, or Dad?

Beth's father's eyes followed the conversation moving from one speaker to the next with apparent interest.

"Sam," Mrs. Anderson held a glass up in front of her husband. An awkward silence fell, and Mr. Anderson slowly raised his hand and took the glass.

"Thank you," he said softly, his gaze drifting up to his wife's face.

Mrs. Anderson moved to the armchair beside his and sat down with her own glass.

"Terry, Beth tells us you're about to buy a business?"

"Um, yes—with my partner Jeff."

"How does that work? Are you buying the building? What sort of business is it?"

Terry slipped into a practiced description of his business dealings, certain his audience wouldn't find business and executive training, the focus of the firm they were buying, very interesting.

Everyone was surprised when Beth's father leaned forward to put his glass on the table and looked Terry in the eye.

"What sales model does a business like that use?"

Terry did not miss a beat.

"Funny you should ask. The business model is one of the weaknesses Jeff used in the negotiations. The company grew out of a maintenance provider but never restructured. We'll be making radical changes over the next few months to bring it into line with the top players."

Mr. Anderson nodded, so Terry went on, describing the organization they envisioned compared to what existed in the company today, pausing frequently to gauge whether his audience understood.

Beth's fear turned to elation as she listened to her father talk lucidly with Terry. Her eyes met Trish's and she saw the same emotions there.

Eventually Mike checked his watch and caught Trish's eye. *Better to end on a high note*, his expression said.

"Mike and I both have to work this afternoon," Trish interjected when Terry and her father's discussion reached a natural pause.

"Of course. Sorry to monopolize the conversation," Terry said.

"Not at all," Mrs. Anderson replied, patting her husband's hand as she smiled at Terry.

Mr. Anderson subsided into his armchair, gaze fixed on his wife. He seemed to be annoyed, like a child restricted from a favorite pastime. Terry saw it and glanced over to see Beth watching too.

"We should get going," Beth said, standing.

"You'll come back soon?" Mr. Anderson spoke up. Once again all eyes turned to him.

"Absolutely," Terry said.

"Yes—I want to hear more about your sail," Mrs. Anderson added.

"Tomorrow too soon?" Beth asked.

)

"Incredible," Trish said, her head shaking slowly side-to-side. They were back in the van, Mike driving. Trish half tuned in her seat to address Terry. "He hasn't carried on a conversation in months. It was amazing."

"Has anyone thought to talk about his work with him before?" Mike asked.

Trish eyed her husband for a moment, then shook her head.

"I doubt it," Beth put in. "He's retired—we try to talk about pleasant things that he loves, like gardening and the grandchildren."

She saw Terry nodding thoughtfully and waited, but he remained silent.

Back at their house, Mike and Trish switched to his sedan. Beth and Terry moved to the front seats of the minivan.

"So you'll pick up some things for Mike to grill—or, Terry, do you like to do the grilling?" Trish asked, looking through the driver's window and across Beth at Terry in the passenger seat.

"We both take turns grilling, But I'll be happy to stand by the grill with Mike drinking a beer."

Both women laughed.

Beth enjoyed taking Terry to the local supermarket, although it had been modernized and upgraded since her childhood. She remembered an uneven floor and heavy wooden shelving under incandescent bulbs, but they found shiny linoleum, bright lighting, and the same modern display units as the stores in Georgetown. They half-filled a shopping cart with steaks, Portobello mushrooms, peppers, and the makings for a tossed salad. After life in the islands, the supermarket's wide aisles and massive selection was overwhelming.

At the checkout, Terry worked his way in front and slid his credit card through the machine before Beth could stop him.

"My treat," he said firmly.

To make up for the lack of nostalgia in the supermarket, Beth drove Terry past a few other family haunts: the pizza place, the ice cream shop, the boutique that had been her favorite bookstore. The sight of slim manikins in the windows shocked Beth, but Terry's comment on the sad fate of independent bookstores helped her regain herself.

Back at Trish's house they worked together seasoning the steaks and skewering the peppers and mushrooms. When she and Mike got home, Trish asked pointed questions about their most recent adventures, and forced Beth and Terry to confess to some of the more dangerous aspects of events leading up to his getting a concussion and temporarily losing his hearing. After withholding the details in her telephone conversations and emails to keep her family from worrying, Beth felt a sense of relief to tell her sister the whole story. Telling it in person allowed her to see how her sister reacted and mitigate any over-reaction.

When Trish learned the explosion that injured Terry had also taken a woman's life, she went pale. Her hands froze, half-loaded skewer in one, slice of red pepper in the other.

"Terry, how awful. I can't even imagine. How hard is it for a boat to blow up?"

"It's not that—it's not—" Beth faltered, unwilling to lie and say it was impossible. Fire was far more likely than outright explosion. She saw Terry also struggling with what to say.

"It can happen, can't it?" Trish asked, tone growing accusatory, as if her sister's floating home was a secret death trap.

Inspiration struck. "It's no more likely than for a car to explode, Trish," Beth said. "*Great Escape* was sinking."

That seemed to placate Trish, and Beth was able to steer the conversation back to the treasure hunt they'd been on when it all happened.

♩

"What were you thinking in the car, about Dad's conversation?" Beth asked hours later.

Standing in the guest room in t-shirt and boxers, Terry's eyes narrowed as he studied her for a moment. "You said you tried to talk about gardening and the grandchildren with him because he loves those topics."

"Right."

"How long has he been retired?"

"Not long. Two—no three years."

"He loved his work. He misses it."

Beth grimaced, unhappy to hear it put so simply.

"More than his grandchildren? His garden?"

"Probably not, but his work is different. It was all his. He did it for a long time, and succeeded at it."

Sitting on the bed in the cotton shorts and t-shirt she wore for pajamas, Beth was quiet for a moment, contemplating this analysis and considering how to use it.

"We should ask his former co-workers to visit."

"What a great idea. You should record his conversations."

The notion made Beth gasp with excitement as an idea struck her. "You remember the article I did for the family support group newsletter?"

"How could I forget?"

Writing the article about her family's journey through diagnosis and care had been an emotional pilgrimage for Beth through which she experienced all seven phases of grief. Terry witnessed and supported her episodes of weeping while they sailed together aboard *Trouble*. Even in that tiny living space, the project left Beth feeling isolated and emotionally bereft. Somehow, he'd provided the right amount of support, without intruding on her grief, to help her keep working. The result, Terry, Trish, and the newsletter editor all assured her, was magnificent.

"I wonder if I could find a way to use his conversations in another article."

She wondered if Terry shared her other thought: it might be a eulogy. He nodded enthusiastically.

"I was thinking about preserving his voice and his stories for yourself and the kids. But I should think you could get a lot of material to work with. Reflections on his life."

"Now I wish we thought of it today," Beth sighed. "Do you mind seeing them again tomorrow?"

"Of course not. It's why we're here."

)

The next morning they visited again and attempted to take her parents for a walk around the grounds, but her father was obstreperous. They got him to venture into the lush interior garden, but once there he sat down on a bench and refused to go on or speak. Beth's mother urged her and Terry to take a walk, so they did. But when they returned from a circuit of the garden she was at the end of her patience with her husband. He sat stiffly, stony gaze fixed on a fichus tree across the path, mouth a hard line.

Terry tried mentioning his work to Beth to see if it would trigger the same sort of response as on the previous visit, but it didn't work. Beth held back tears as they followed her mother's instructions and went to the reception desk to ask for staff to help bring Mr. Anderson back to their apartment. Then they left, also at her mother's request.

Four

Phillipsburg, Sint Maarten

*V*irgine Guesnon blotted perspiration from her forehead with her handkerchief, careful not to touch the eye makeup she'd labored over. Squaring her shoulders, she strode to the door of the modest office building on a quiet Phillipsburg side street and drew it open. Although the interior was not air conditioned, cooler air wafted out as she stepped inside. Plaster painted as dark green faux marble and dark paneling contributed to the effect. Virgine walked along a central corridor past several closed doors and climbed a staircase rising parallel to the hallway on the left side. It brought her to a similar corridor on the next floor. She turned right and walked half way down. A plaque on a door described this as the office of Elvis Rink, Esquire. Below the name it said, "Personal and Legal Business Matters." She stood squarely in front of the door and knocked.

"Come in."

She opened the door and stepped through, facing a utilitarian desk and a man who looked barely out of primary school. His white button-down shirt was in need of a pressing, but his hair was freshly trimmed.

"Yes?" He spoke with all the attitude of a youngster given too much praise.

"I am Virgine Guesnon, here to see Mr. Rink."

"Ah yes. Madame Guesnon. One moment." He picked up the handset of the black telephone sitting on his desk and pressed the first in a row of transparent buttons on the base. Virginie wondered whether the rest of the buttons were connected to anything. He murmured into the receiver so quietly, even standing right in front of his desk Virgine could not hear what he said. He replaced the receiver and stood up. "This way please, Madame Guesnon." He gestured toward an inner door.

He opened the door and Virgine stepped through. Elvis Rink, Esquire, reclined in his chair with his feet on the corner of his desk.

His black ankle boots gleamed with fresh polish, and Virgine wondered if the boy took care of them for him. His trousers matched a suit coat hanging on a hat tree by the door. The top button of his light blue shirt hung open, and his necktie lay loose around his neck. He made no move to rise as she walked into his office, which was furnished with slightly higher quality furniture than the outer one.

"Madame Guesnon," he said, his eyes traveling over her navy blue suit jacket and skirt. They settled on the soft folds of her silk wrap blouse. She resisted the urge to adjust it or glance down to gauge how much cleavage it revealed. "How long has it been?" he added. She got the distinct impression of a judgement, as if her feminine attributes had deteriorated since their last meeting. Which was ridiculous. She forced herself to reject his implied criticism.

"Four years, Elvis." She took a seat in one of the chairs in front of his desk.

"Not long enough?" His grin revealed his oversized, upper teeth. His beak-like nose made the expression all the more sinister, almost comic. Except Virgine knew very well there was nothing comical about this man. She declined to acknowledge his statement, which was true.

"As you may know, I am developing a promising product line for the American market. I have consultation lined up to make the distribution arrangements to guarantee a high level of sales. But in the near term I am in need of a bridge loan."

"No chit chat? I'm disappointed." Rink's feet dropped to the floor and he sat up, leaning over his desk toward her. "Very well. How much?"

"Twenty-thousand."

"Euros?" his grin widened and she hated not knowing why.

"Yes, Euros."

"And when do you anticipate these large sales?"

"Six to eight months. But I will be able to repay the loan sooner."

"Good. What is your collateral?"

"My business assets. You are familiar with my holdings."

"I am. Very well. I will offer you your twenty thousand euros at twenty percent interest, due, say, at the end of December?"

As Virgine nodded her blood ran cold. His agreement came too quickly. Her island handicrafts business was not very valuable, her office leased. She expected to haggle and accept a lower amount. Did he know something about her other business dealings? *No. Impossible.* She was careful, and her partners even more so. He watched her, eyes locked with hers, for a long moment. She showed no reaction other than her unwavering polite smile. Finally, he reached for the telephone on his desk. It matched the boy's outside. He spoke to the boy and once again Virgine did not understand despite her proximity. It was uncanny. He hung up the telephone and leaned back in his chair, hands clasped in front of his chest.

"Henri will bring the papers and the money. Can I pour you a rum?"

"No, thank you."

He looked disappointed.

"How is your brother?"

"Very well."

"No thanks to me?"

"Please stop putting words in my mouth."

Rink laughed, a dirty, grating sound that made Virgine's skin crawl. She hated that he got to her. Soon she wouldn't need him, or his kind. Soon she would deal exclusively with men who respected her authority.

The office door opened and the boy, Henri, came in and placed two sheets of paper on the desk in front of Rink, then turned and left. Rink scanned the first sheet, rotated it, and slid it across the desk toward Virgine. He took a pen from a holder on the desk and scrawled a signature on the second, duplicate sheet, then handed her the pen. She read the document more carefully than him, noting the hand-entered amount and dates. She took the pen and signed it, traded sheets with Rink, and signed the other copy. As they completed this ritual Henri returned with a nylon tote bag—the type used by peasants on market day—that he set on the desk. Rink put one signed copy of the document into the bag and stood up. Virgine rose too. Rink picked up the bag and extended it to her.

"Twenty thousand Euros and one agreement for repayment."

"You don't mind if I count it?"

"Be my guest."

He set the bag back down on the desk, shooting Henri an amused smile. Bristling, Virgine reached into the bag and removed four bundles of bills. She confirmed each bundle contained five thousand euros in one-hundred Euro bills, then replaced them in the bag.

Thank you. I will see you at the end of December.”

“Count on it, Virgine.”

Virgine picked up the bag and offered a curt nod to Henri, who wore a distasteful grin similar to his employer's.

Five

Riverside, California

*T*he next morning Terry looked alarmed when Beth, driving Trish's minivan, burst into a string of blue language because four other cars boxed them into the center lane as they approached their exit. Beth realized this was his first ride as her passenger in heavy traffic. Before she could contemplate that, a driver in the right lane courteously opened a gap in front of her so Beth could change lanes and take the exit.

"The traffic may be bad, but the drivers are nicer than D.C.," Terry said.

"She's probably not from around here," Beth retorted.

Their greeting at the reception desk was not as warm as the previous day. Mrs. Reynolds was not on duty, and the nurse who was did not know them. They gave their names and waited while she called Beth's parents.

"Hello, hello," Mrs. Anderson greeted them in almost a whisper as she ushered them into the entry. "Your father's watching golf and he can get testy. I reminded him you were coming."

They could see Mr. Anderson seated in an armchair with his back to the door, facing the modest television set in the corner of the room. Tiger Woods was about to hit a drive.

"It's all right mom, we'll visit. If he joins us that will be great." In truth, Beth was deeply disappointed. She glanced at Terry and could see he knew it.

"Let's sit in the kitchen."

"Should we at least say hello?" Terry asked, nodding toward the back of Mr. Anderson's head.

"No, any interruption sets him off when he gets like this," Mrs. Anderson said, guiding them through to the kitchen. She offered them more iced tea and set a blue tin of butter cookies on the table. Those cookies were a staple of the Anderson household all of Beth's life, and she pried off the lid with a metallic pop, inhaling the buttery aroma.

"Isn't it late for golf? Terry asked. "I thought the pro tours ended last week."

Beth studied her boyfriend, surprised at his awareness of the golf season. He mentioned playing with Jeff, but she did not realize he was a fan.

"I don't know, it probably is. I noticed earlier in the summer it soothes him, so I recorded a few hours. He doesn't realize he's watching the same match over and over. Or if he does, he hasn't mentioned it. Now, tell me more about the treasure hunt. Last we talked about it you described almost being run down by a ship." Mrs. Anderson mentioned this alarming event in matter-of-fact tones.

Reassured that her mother could handle the details, Beth picked up the narrative from yesterday morning, imitating the natives of Union Island in their cryptic warning "de mailboat, mon!" making all three of them laugh.

"Susan?"

Mr. Anderson's call from the living room punctured their levity. Mrs. Anderson head snapped up and she rose.

"Yes Sam?" she said, moving to the kitchen door. "I'll be right back," she said to Beth and Terry before heading for the living room.

Terry selected a cookie from the tin.

"Umm, those are ginger," Beth said.

"Which is your favorite?"

"The ones with chocolate, of course," she said, taking one.

"Of course," he grinned, bit his cookie, and took a sip of tea. The cookies had a commercial taste and texture—Beth had never thought to check, but some desert bakery probably mass-produced them. "They only have the one door, to the inner hallway, right?"

"They have the door from the living room to the garden. They're under more security than they realize. Or maybe they do realize it. But it's discrete."

"Are there cameras in the apartments?"

"No, it's not that extreme. At least I don't think," Beth peered up into the corners of the room, eyes stopping on a vent high on one wall.

Terry followed the direction of her glance and chuckled, making her look back at him with a sheepish grin.

"Here, see? You forgot Beth and Terry were coming," her mother's voice interrupted them.

Mrs. Anderson guided her husband into the kitchen with a hand on his left elbow. He walked with tight, shuffling steps.

"His arthritis is acting up," Mrs. Anderson said. Terry's surprised expression matched Beth's internal reaction.

"I didn't realize it was this bad, Mom," she said, a hint of accusation in her voice.

"Only sometimes," Mrs. Anderson replied in a tone that stopped further complaint from her daughter.

Mr. Anderson looked from his daughter to Terry and smiled.

"Hello again. You came back!"

"Yes Mr. Anderson. We wanted to talk more with you," Terry said, rising and pulling out a chair for the man. He sat down and reached for the cookies, pulling the whole tin in front of him and laying both arms on the table on either side of it like a fortress.

"His favorites," his wife said, moving to her seat. "Sam, we're sharing the cookies."

"They can't be good for him," Beth said, still annoyed with her mother's failure to reveal her father's true condition.

"They aren't good for any of us, him no more than the rest," her mother said sharply. "But I should have mentioned, you're looking well Beth."

"We don't keep cookies on board," Beth spoke more tartly than she meant.

Terry's brows furrowed and Beth realized she was being unreasonable. But she didn't care. No, she did care. But she hated feeling left out.

"Well, I'm sure being out on the water doing things all day is a healthier lifestyle than sitting in an office. You don't miss that at all, do you Bethy?"

"You're the fellow with the business," Mr. Anderson interrupted, bit off half the cookie in his hand and began chewing.

Terry glanced at Beth and her mother, who were both watching Mr. Anderson.

"Yes I am, Mr. Anderson. We had a fascinating discussion yesterday."

"Call me Sam. We're Susan and Sam." He looked at his wife. "S and S. Always wanted to set myself up and call it S and S Sales. Nice alliteration."

Terry smiled and nodded, surprised at the man's knowledge, or recollection, of language. He shot Beth a wide-eyed look, prompting her to remember her plan to record her father.

"Yes, that has a nice sound. But you never did it?" Terry prompted.

Beth reached into her bag on the floor and took out the micro-cassette recorder Mike had loaned her. She set it on the table and switched it on.

She leaned close and whispered to her mother, "I want to record him, do you mind?"

Mrs. Anderson nodded. "What a good idea."

As the day before, Mr. Anderson spoke lucidly with Terry about his work life. Terry continued to prompt him to tell his own story, limiting his contributions to direct answers to questions. Once again Mr. Anderson's period of lucidity ended rather abruptly when he waved a hand across the table knocking over his plastic cup of iced tea.

He jumped to his feet yelling incomprehensibly. Beth rose and grabbed a dishtowel from the counter as Mrs. Anderson went to her husband. Terry righted the cup and moved everything else on the table away from the spreading puddle.

"It's all right Sam. Don't worry. Beth will take care of it," Mrs. Anderson stroked her husband's back, gently lowering one waving arm. The other arm quieted as well and she turned him away from the table. "Let's go see how Tiger is doing," she said as she pushed the door open and guided him into the living room.

Beth finished mopping up the table and floor and squeezed the towel out in the sink, laying it over the faucet.

Terry had shut off the tape recorder when he rescued it. She put it into her bag with a heavy sigh.

"We should go," she said.

"This went very well, Beth. You realize that, don't you?"

"It's a matter of context Terry. He's my father, not a three-year-old. But he just acted like one, shrieking over spilled tea."

Terry stepped around the table and wrapped his arms around her, sheltering her from the grief and worry. She welcomed his support. Somehow the stoic loner sailor she'd been while writing the article was gone—perhaps by the very act of writing.

"He'll never be the same. I'm losing my Dad." She said, close to a sob.

"Shhhhh," he pressed her head to his shoulder with a hand on the back of her head. "You can handle it love. You're strong enough. You love him enough."

)

Saint-François, Guadeloupe

"I will put you on late shifts this week to try. We shall see." Monique, the bar manager at Casino de Grande Terre, was all business and immune to Ori's charm. But Ori's luck still influenced the situation: two of Monique's bartenders had quit—some nonsense about getting married—and she needed replacements fast.

"Thank you. What time do I start?" Ori asked. She concealed her excitement as best she could, but in truth, this was just about her last chance. Her cash was about gone, and the island cash machines were not cooperating with her bank card.

"Return at eighteen hundred. We will issue you a uniform before you start. Payment will be in cash. Gratuities are pooled."

"Fine. I'll be here at eighteen hundred. Should I ask for you?" Ori knew the manager might be too busy to take care of her later.

"*Oui*, I will introduce you to the others then."

"*Merci. Au revoir.*"

Ori gulped out her rusty French before threading her way back through the casino, where a few gamblers sat slumped at slot machines feeding in coins and pulling the handles. Three patrons shifted chips around the green felt of the one operating roulette wheel. It was mid-afternoon. Ori hoped things picked up in the evening.

Back out in the bright Caribbean sun her mouth spread into a happy smile. She strode across the parking lot and on across the street toward Les Arcades, an open-air shopping center. She'd visited all of the businesses in it and found no work available. It didn't help that she lacked a work permit, although it sometimes didn't matter on other islands. *Damn French bureaucrats.* She didn't know why Monique and the casino could overlook regulations, and she didn't care. She would soon have cash to refill *Dream Catcher*'s fuel and water tanks and buy food.

The other day, once she got the boat away from the marina and anchored out among the hundreds of other similar sailboats she discovered the nearly empty tanks and bare galley cabinets. Unwilling to leave the boat unattended for fear the broker called the authorities quickly enough for them to see where she took it, she got by on the last of the water in her bottle and two granola bars the first night.

Early the next morning she hauled the anchor and sailed along the coast past Gosier to Saint Francois, a community to the east along Grande Terre's south-facing coast. She anchored *Dream Catcher* in the open anchorage outside of the marina. She prepared the dinghy and lowered and installed the outboard motor using the block and tackle system she had designed and rigged two years ago during a maintenance stop in Long Island Sound. She'd first met Beth Anderson in that dreary City Island marina. As she secured the motor she wondered whether Beth was giving up sailing for the guy. When she saw them in the San Juan airport they were heading to Washington—she vaguely recalled he was from there.

But now, with employment secured and the bright Caribbean sun on her face, what Beth Anderson was doing was the last thing on her mind.

J

Riverside, California

Beth slipped into an emotional decline over the next days of their visit. They returned to Orange Grove Wellness each day so Beth could record more of her father's words. He ranged from uncooperative to confused, mixing events from various times into a single narrative. Her mother tried to sort it out, verbally unweaving the tangled threads and looking to Terry to see if he understood. Although he did not follow any one chain of events in Mr.

Anderson's story, he enjoyed every word for the picture it painted of Beth's childhood.

It didn't matter that the puppy's haircut was years before the party where Beth tripped and fell into Trish's birthday cake, or the pony party when Trish broke her arm. The swirl of mental images described by Sam Anderson was closer to the way all memories are held. Terry thought Mrs. Anderson's attempt to impose the organization of a healthy mind on them detracted from their appeal.

When Beth played back the tapes for her sister, they both laughed as they recalled the events on their own and added to them for Terry's benefit. Trish found photo albums in the den and they poured over them. It pleased Beth that Terry didn't lose interest in the faded pages.

After a final, unsatisfying visit during which Mr. Anderson spoke briefly with Terry, they packed their things as well as the tapes and the drawings made for them by the children. Beth begged her sister to continue recording their father's lucid periods. Trish agreed, but made Beth promise to have the first tapes copied.

"How you doing?" Terry asked when their airplane was in the air.

Beth sighed, settling back into the uncomfortable seat. "I don't know. It's not what I expected."

Terry nodded slowly, waiting for more.

"I thought he would be sicker by now, but he seems, physically, almost the same. Except for the arthritis. Now I think he could go on like this for years."

"Isn't that what you read about it?"

"Yes. I didn't believe it. Not of Dad. When he first started to decline it seemed like he went so fast."

"Didn't he avoiding taking his medication at first?"

"Yes. Then they put him on an experimental drug. Trish pushed hard for it. The thing is—" she sighed again, mouth tense, eyes downcast.

"Go ahead."

She looked up at him, familiar guilt in her eyes. He felt himself tensing in anticipation of whatever confession was to come.

"It feels like postponing the inevitable. So much of him is already gone—you saw it—and slowing the decline seems cruel."

"To him, or to you?"

Terry regretted the harshness of his question as Beth winced and turned her face toward the window. He thought he had lost her, or at best might be in for an angry fight. But after a moment she spoke again without turning from the window.

"Me. I feel like my father is gone, but I'm left with dealing with this stranger. It's unfair. I'm a selfish pig to want it to be over, but I feel like I can't move on until it is."

This was the admission Terry had hoped to hear for months as he watched her struggle with her emotions. He suspected she had constructed this artificial barrier to her future, but until she openly admitted it, he had to reason with her from other perspectives, trying to steer her around the emotional wall without acknowledging it. With tremendous relief that they now could discuss it, he freed her tightly clasped hands from one another and held onto the left one, stroking it slowly.

"Why do you think that is?"

She sniffed loudly. He realized there were tears running down her cheeks—maybe that was why she refused to look at him.

"I don't know." She glanced at him, before looking away again. "I don't. I can't focus on myself knowing he's hanging on, half himself—less—mostly gone, but not. I don't know when I'll have to drop everything and go. I can't get too involved in something else with it hanging over my head."

"Something else, meaning us?"

"God no. Terry, I need us. I need you so much. But—" She sniffed again and shook her head.

"But what love? Tell me. Let's work this out."

"Do we have to do it now?" Fatigue and sorrow etched creases under her eyes. His heart went out to her and he relented, even though he knew he might not have the chance again if she closed back up. He loved her too much to put her through such pain. He released her hand and wrapped his arm around her, pulling her close despite the awkward airplane seating.

"No, we don't. Why don't you relax? We'll get home and get some sleep and talk about it later."

)

Georgetown, Washington, D.C.

But they did not talk about it the next day, nor the next. No sooner did they reach the townhouse in Georgetown than Jeff called to dictate a tight schedule of meetings for the next few days. Feeling guilty, even though he did not regret the trip to California, Terry agreed to every meeting.

To Beth's surprise, Jeff had already contacted the former employee and lined up a meeting for her to review her resume with him. Her plan to work on it herself during the trip hadn't happened, so she spent the day after they got back sitting with her laptop trying to focus on it.

She knew she had opened a door with Terry and he wanted to step in. But she pushed it closed again and cowered behind it, wishing he would forget and knowing he would not. On one hand she wished she could reach her own decisions before opening herself to hear his thoughts, but she knew she should allow his advice to influence her choices. Relationships were about that. Unlike all the new places she took her sailboat in the last year, exploring this new emotional territory was terrifying.

Six

Georgetown, Washington, D.C.

*B*eth was to meet with Tom Biffle, her resume coach, at lunchtime near his office. This arrangement emphasized that he was doing a favor for her and his former employers, which made her want to be as prepared as possible. She searched the internet for suitable job openings and printed out many of the descriptions. She highlighted words she thought might be key, using green for the ones in her resume and orange for those that were not. She wasn't surprised that the jargon had evolved in the almost two years since she last ventured into the job market. She hoped Tom really did keep on top of it and could help.

He was not what she expected. She stepped into the Starbucks he selected for the meeting and looked around for a man with a Dell laptop. She mentally slapped her hand on her forehead when she saw three such men—*I should have known!*—but one of them caught her eye and stood up.

"Beth?"

"Yes. Tom?"

"That's me."

His bushy salt-and-pepper beard reached the third button of his shirt. His thinning hair matched it in color if not density. His girth was substantial enough that she hoped the restaurant's delicate cane chair could handle him. She guessed he was in his fifties. He wore a light blue shirt. A darker blue tie hung to a fashionable length above his navy blue light wool trousers—part of a suit, she thought, although he'd hung a light nylon jacket with a Washington Redskins patch on his chair back. As she reached him, he extended a hand and she shook it with a smile.

"Good to meet you. Thanks for seeing me."

"Not a problem. Jeff and Terry took care of me, and in those last few months before the sale Terry talked of nothing but you."

"Well, I'm sure he talked about business too. Can I get you a coffee or something?"

"Already got one," he glanced down at the table where she now saw a venti size lidded cup next to his computer. "Do you have your resume? I can review it while you get yourself something."

"Um, yeah," she unslung her bag from her shoulder and took out a copy of her resume printed on Terry's printer. "I'll be right back."

He took the paper and sat down, and she went to join the line waiting to order.

)

When she got back with her latte—she refused to pay the exorbitant prices for the sandwiches and pastries—he was making notes on her resume in bright red pen.

"Uh oh." She forced a smile, sitting down across from him and setting her bag on the floor. She waited to take out her laptop—Tom might be more comfortable working on the hard copy.

"You last worked in New York City," he said, not a question. "We'll need to make this a D.C. resume. There's a different emphasis here. Less financial, more political."

Beth thought she knew what he meant, but didn't let herself jump to conclusions. She took the printed job descriptions from her bag and set them on the table. He glanced over, cocking his head to one side to read them upside down.

"Job openings? Good instinct. Let's start with what kind of job you want, though."

Over the next hour he dissected her skills, interests, and experience and put it back together in a new form. He wanted her to interview with political consulting firms—another word for lobbyists, he explained. He did not care about the sales and marketing aspect of her writing. "It doesn't pay." He wanted her to reposition herself as a technical writer capable of preparing proposals and research documents. The way he adeptly reworded the descriptions of her publishing and corporate experience to support this aim amazed her.

"You should get one of these jobs," she said. "This is amazing. Nothing in here is a lie, but it says something totally different than before."

"I have one of these jobs," he laughed. "Skill at turning a situation to your favor through words is very valuable around here. Get into the right firm and you can write your own ticket. Literally."

An hour after they met Beth walked out of the coffee shop with him, her bloody resume in her bag. She thanked him again and they parted ways, Beth toward the metro and he back to his office. She paused half way to the subway stop and looked back, identifying him from his waddling walk.

This is the neighborhood where Terry used to work, she realized. On a whim, she skipped the subway and took a stroll around the neighborhood. She tried to imagine Terry picking up a paper at the newsstand in the morning, going to the deli for lunch, stopping at one of the local bars for a beer before going home. But it was an ordinary business neighborhood with few unusual features to make it special for Terry. After a half hour of wandering she found the metro again and headed for Georgetown.

Beth was deep into making Tom's revisions to her resume fit on a single sheet of paper when her phone rang the following afternoon. The caller ID said it was her sister, or she might not have answered it. After the usual greeting and status update on their father, Trish paused.

"Trish?" Beth said, wondering if the connection had dropped.

"I didn't say anything while you were here because I had to see the doctor after you left," Trish said.

"What is it?" visions of complications for their father swam through Beth's mind, even as she realized Trish said "I" not "he." Trish banished her confusion with two words:

"I'm pregnant!"

"She said they're both very excited, even though they're surprised," she told Terry over dinner. He had picked up a pizza on the way home at the amazingly early hour of seven. "She was annoyed at first, but when Mike was so excited, she got over it."

"The other kids aren't so young—I mean, at least they're out of diapers. I think Carole would have a conniption if this happened to her."

"Yeah, Trish mentioned potty training. I remember her saying, years ago, she was glad to never deal with that again. Oh well," Beth grinned. "Their real concern is financial. They've got to set up another college fund and cut corners."

"Do they contribute to your parents' upkeep?"

"No. We—well, Trish and Mom—set up their finances so the sale of the house covers their expenses. It will last for almost ten years. Mom could out live it. But Dad ..."

"Could too." Terry said simply, watching her.

"I can't imagine."

"Beth, you are not selfish for wishing you did not have to deal with your father's illness."

"I didn't say that."

"Not now, no. But you're acting like he's not going to be around much longer. You're waiting for him to die so you can move on."

"How can you say that? How can you say I want my father to die?" Beth's anger flashed so sudden and hot it shocked her. She stood up and strode to the refrigerator. Just to do something she yanked it open and stared inside. Behind her Terry swiveled in his seat to watch her.

"Don't run away from me Beth. Please."

She shut the refrigerator door and pressed her forehead to the cool brushed stainless-steel surface. The faint vibration of the motor resonated in her head, oddly comforting. She heard Terry's chair scrape on the floor, and a moment later he stood behind her, hands on her shoulders.

"Please," he repeated. "It's all right to be angry, but consider the target carefully."

"Not you," she whispered. She pushed away from the refrigerator and leaned against him. He accepted her weight, slipping his arms around her.

"Not me. Not yourself. Not your father, nor your mother. Not God."

"Who?"

"I don't know. Fate. Chance. The disease."

"What good does it do to be angry with the disease?" she heard a hint of whining in her tone and grimaced. She was tired of herself, sick of these tantrums, afraid Terry would get sick of them too.

"What good does it do to be angry with your family, or me? None of us is at fault. This is life."

"I know," she sighed, turning in his arms to lay her head on his shoulder. He stroked her back, soothing her. After a moment she lifted her head to see his face.

"I have to do it. I have to move on, regardless of what's happening with Dad."

"You can take baby steps at first. Find a job here, with me."

She smiled at that, at his self-interest coming through and how it meant he was not sick of her. Then he added, "And you can meet my family. On Saturday."

)

Westlake, Texas

An unseasonably hot breeze rolling in from the hills to the west rustled the rows of potted fichus trees that defined the wedding reception area on a much larger artificially green lawn. A few wedding guests fanned themselves and frowned at the inconvenient zephyr, but most didn't notice. The champagne had been flowing for an hour already. Standing next to his brother Parker in the reception line, Hunter Green realized an unforeseen benefit of rehab: an expanded tolerance for dull social obligations. But he was desperate for a smoke. As the last of the guests at his little brother's wedding—an elderly couple distantly related to the bride—finally worked their way along, Hunter heard his brother emit a quiet groan.

"It's not over yet," he chided, nudging Parker in the arm.

"At least this part is. My feet are killing me."

"You sound like a girl."

"I'm sure Becca's feet hurt worse than mine—did you see her shoes?"

Hunter glanced down toward the bride's hemline, but her enormous confection of a white dress concealed her feet. He didn't know Becca well, but he suspected that right now they might be bare. He hoped so—hoped his brother's wife was not the uptight Texas socialite everyone expected him to marry.

"I think we're about to be released to get a drink," Parker muttered, watching the elderly couple amble away into the crowd. Indeed, the wedding planner was striding toward them in her sensible heels, her well-practiced smile plastered over an expression of utmost seriousness. Hunter rejoiced that after another couple hours he'd never have to take direction from her again.

"All right, wedding party, let's circulate now for thirty minutes before we move inside to the high table. It's time to mingle!" She delivered this with a finger in the air and ringing tone that reminded Hunter of the wrestling announcer on TV. He muttered "let's get ready to rumble" to himself with a grin as he reached into his jacket pocket for his cigarettes and followed his brother toward the bar situated in the shade of a white marquee.

"Where ya goin', bro?" Parker half turned a concerned expression toward Hunter. Hunter frowned, empty hand dropping to his side as he stopped. Parker took another step before stopping as well.

"Just following you," Hunter said with a half shrug. It was true. He didn't crave alcohol. Alcohol was not his problem. "I could use a Coke and a cigarette."

"Just cola?" Parker asked, his concern remaining evident in his eyes.

"Yes. Geez Park, I'm good. I got back weeks ago, and I haven't slipped up yet. I'm thirsty. Let's go." Beyond Parker, Hunter could see the bride talking to someone, accepting a glass of champagne from a waiter in the process. He took a step closer to his brother so their conversation could be more private. No one around them appeared to have noticed yet, but it was a matter of time before someone came to congratulate the groom.

Parker looked suitably guilty. "I'm sorry bro. Sometimes I'm not sure how to handle this. It seems very black and white to me. I want you to be healthy and happy, so no drugs, no alcohol."

Hunter nodded, accepting his brother's misguided concern.

"And you're basically correct. But I can't go through life not being near alcohol. It is possible to order non-alcoholic beverages at a bar. I realize you wouldn't know about that."

Parker made a mocking scowl and lightly punched Hunter on the upper arm—exactly the reaction Hunter had been aiming for.

"I get it. I'm a nag. But you gotta' realize this is as hard for me as for you. I feel responsible for you."

Hunter inhaled a short breath and let it out. His younger brother's proprietary attitude was not out of line. Parker had rescued him from a dark place and stuck with him through a lot of months of anger, unhappiness, and withdrawal. Telling him he intended to go back to the islands would be tricky.

"I know you do. But it's time to set me free. Your wife insists on it—no pets in the new house."

Parker frowned, his head slowly shaking, "She's bringing her Dalmatian—Oh! Damn, I do need a drink. Come on."

Hunter's head shook side to side as he resumed following his brother. Parker wasn't stupid, but he could be slow on the uptake. That might make it take longer for him to understand about Ori. Better find a moment to tell him before the end of this marathon party.

Seven

Virginia Beach, Virginia

"*Y*ou look beautiful!" Terry said, looking up from his chair in the living room as Beth came in. She wore a dark green corduroy pencil skirt, lighter green cotton blouse, and low-heeled black shoes. She'd bought the outfit during their shopping expedition before the California trip. She expected to wear it to work, but when she thought about how to dress to meet Terry's parents and sister, it seemed like her best choice. Somehow blue jeans and a sweater didn't seem right. She had taken time to blow dry her hair into a semblance of control and put on eye liner and lipstick. The appreciative look in Terry's eyes reassured her.

"Ready?" he asked, setting aside his newspaper and rising. Her final clue as to dress code had been his own—he picked up his sport coat and shrugged into before guiding her to the garage door in the kitchen.

"How long a drive is it?"

"On a Saturday, maybe three hours."

"Let me get a bottle of water. Want one?"

"Sure."

She took two bottles from the refrigerator and stepped into the garage while Terry set the burglar alarm. The garage door rose as they climbed into Terry's sleek BMW. He backed out onto the sidewalk and waited for a minute for a break in traffic on the street. The garage door slid down as they finally entered traffic.

Terry's parents and his sister and her husband all lived in the part of southeastern Virginia called Hampton Roads. Far enough, Terry had said more than once, to make frequent visits unlikely, but close enough to get there for a day trip. His parents had urged them to stay the night this trip, but he had business on Sunday, so they would be making the three-hour drive back after dinner. Beth was glad: she didn't want to get into the question of sleeping arrangements again so soon after their California stay.

She manned the stereo while he drove, absently noting the route he took out of the city. The in-dash GPS showed her the map and her innate sense of direction helped her to remember the streets and highways. She selected lively Spanish guitar music from his iPod and settled back to work on relaxing before the coming meeting. Something told her Terry's parents were nothing like hers, although he had not said anything to suggest it.

Three hours and one phone call with Jeff later Terry slowed the car and turned into the driveway of an enormous house set well back from the quiet street. All the houses were situated on multi-acre lots with enormous old growth trees that concealed the size of the buildings. Hardly McMansions crammed cheek by jowl, these were well established homes, their spacious yards showing evidence of family life. Terry and his sister Ginny had been raised here.

"Nice," Beth said as Terry parked in the driveway behind an enormous black Escalade.

"The truck?"

"No." Beth chuckled. "The house. Is the truck your parents'?"

"Hell no. It's Ginny's." He opened the door and got out of the car before she could question his apparent disgust. He came around the car and opened her door—an old-fashioned habit that reminded her of her father. She had already become used to it, though.

She got out and stretched her arms high above her head, feeling her thighs and calves ache with the movement after sitting for three hours.

"Do they need such a big SUV?" she asked as they walked to the front door.

"Nobody needs such a big SUV. Ginny likes the way it makes her feel powerful, and Andrew indulges her." Terry explained so tersely she didn't dare ask any more questions. In a moment she would meet the targets of his ire.

Both sides of the double front door swung open as they approached and two women—obviously mother and daughter—stepped out onto the semicircular front porch.

"Welcome!"

"You're here!"

They said in unison. Terry's mother stepped forward with open arms and Terry stepped into them—obviously a typical greeting.

"Beth?" Ginny—for it must be—bypassed her mother and brother and extended open arms to Beth. "It's so wonderful to meet you!"

Beth exchanged a polite embrace with the other woman, who was two years older than Terry, but looked considerably younger. She wore her blonde and precisely highlighted hair in a perfect bob. Sculpted eyebrows over eyes the same blue as Terry's and artificially puffy lips gave her a slightly surprised look.

Beth quickly pushed aside her impulse to judge based on appearance and allowed herself to be pulled into a second embrace by Terry's mother. She was exactly what Beth had expected: tall and slender, with close-cropped grey hair suggesting an active lifestyle. She too wore carefully applied makeup, but unlike her daughter's it served to highlight her attractive features, not turn back the clock.

"Come in, everyone is waiting," she said, taking Beth's hand and leaving Terry to follow with his sister.

They trooped through a wide, marble floored front hall, beige and white striped wallpaper above chair-rail height wainscoting. Two glistening crystal chandeliers marched along over their heads. Beth caught glimpses of a formal looking sitting room through an opening on the right and a dining room, the table set, across from it on the left. They kept going past another opening on the left where stairs swept upward without obstructing the hallway, and finally passed through open double doors into a large living room.

Unlike the formal rooms, this one had a comfortable, lived-in feel. Two seating areas of couches and armchairs were defined by thick area rugs on the wood floor. A third area consisted of armchairs and hassocks facing a brick hearth. A large cabinet against one wall probably concealed a large television and associated electronics. Beth noticed speakers subtly placed around the room, doubtlessly an acoustically designed array. The rear wall of the room was lined with large windows looking out at a seemingly endless backyard. In the late afternoon light Beth could see trees, shrubs, what looked like a fenced vegetable garden, and, off to the left a swimming pool surrounded by a cement deck.

She took all this in before focusing her attention on the people in the room: a boy lay on the hearth rug with a golden retriever, the dog's eyes half shut, her tongue hanging out as she panted lightly. She didn't appear to mind the child's arms around her neck.

A man her age stood up from an armchair as they entered, and a second, older man remained seated. And in the fraction of a second while Beth tried to decide which to greet first, he began to move, rolling forward and turning slowly, driving a motorized wheelchair with light touches of a joystick under his right hand.

Beth instinctively sought Terry's face, and quickly concealed the flash of betrayal she felt at this revelation. All these months of her talking about her father's illness, and he never mentioned his own father's disability. Did he mean it as a trick? A tease?

Terry stepped close to her and rested his left hand on the small of her back. Despite her doubts, his presence was comforting, and she moved with him toward the man in the wheelchair.

"Dad, this is Beth," Terry was saying. "Beth, my father, Terrence Faughnan."

"Mr. Faughnan," she said as he extended his right hand toward her. She reached out and took it, automatically adjusting her grip to his gentle one.

He greeted her with half a smile and a slurred, "Hello Beth. It's a pleasure to meet you."

She recognized the effects of a stroke that had paralyzed the left side of his body.

"And you."

Terry's hand on her back moved slightly upward, a subtle stroke of encouragement.

"And this is my brother-in-law Andrew."

Beth extended her hand to the other man. He was tall, slender, and nearly bald. His bright eyes sparkled with intelligence and his toothy smile was very warm.

"Hello."

"Their son Jake is the young man on the floor. The furry one is Izzy—Isabelle when she misbehaves."

"That dog never misbehaves," Terry's mother stepped into the group, motioning them to take seats.

"Hi Jake, I'm Beth," Beth delayed sitting for a moment to go greet the boy and dog.

"Hi," he said, smiling up at her. "This is Izzy."

"So I just learned," Beth crouched and offered Izzy her hand to sniff. The dog did so, rolled her eyes up at Beth, and resumed panting, mouth opening with a wet pop. Beth stroked the top of her head. "She's a good dog."

"Yeah."

"Would you like a drink Beth?" Mrs. Faughnan asked, signaling that her side trip should come to an end. Terry's mother was not a woman to be crossed, Beth realized. She winked at Jake and stood up, crossing back to the adults to find a seat open next to Terry on a sofa.

A middle-aged woman in grey skirt and blouse covered with a white apron had appeared with a tray full of gasses and a bottle of champagne in an ice bucket. Andrew drew the bottle out of the ice and went about opening it while the maid waited, holding the tray. The cork came loose with a satisfying pop and Andrew poured. The maid offered the tray of bubbling glasses to each of them. As the maid crossed to the hearth Beth noticed a pre-poured glass of slightly darker liquid on the tray. She offered it to Jake.

"Apple?" he asked, taking it.

"Yes sir."

He sighed heavily and climbed to his feet, coming to join the adults as if to a tiresome tradition he hoped to quickly dispose of.

"To our new friend Beth," Mr. Faughnan slurred. He raised his glass, eyes locked with Beth's as he put it to his lips. The others echoed the simple toast and drank. The fizzy, dry champagne tickled Beth's throat. She took a second sip to soothe it.

Another bottle was soon opened, and a few more lighthearted toasts proposed—to a successful business matter for Andrew, a corporate lawyer, and to the three pumpkins growing in the garden. When Jake chimed in with a toast to his new goldfish Beth noticed the maid bring Mr. Faughnan a highball glass filled with ice and amber liquid.

At first the levity of the gathering eased Beth's nerves, but as the party moved from the living room into the dining room, she began to sense underlying tensions between the family members. Despite the champagne she had not forgotten Terry's seemingly offhand comment about his sister. She could see his disapproval as she told their mother about her morning appointment at the salon. She sounded to Beth like the customer from hell as she justified her high-handed attitude toward the salon staff, who didn't work quickly or efficiently enough to satisfy her.

Beth wondered how two siblings could be so different, for she could not imagine Terry exhibiting such impatience and ego. She thought Mrs. Faughnan had probably raised her children with a strict but loving, hand. One had come out well-formed, the other with too-high expectations. Or perhaps Terry's high expectations were of himself, while Ginny's were of other people.

She set her champagne flute on the table, but before she knew it the maid filled the goblet next to it with a ruby red wine. A plate of tossed green salad graced each place, and a basket of warm rolls was passed. She felt lucky that she did not immediately pick up her salad fork when, at a nod from his grandmother, Jake recited a traditional grace to which everyone responded "amen."

Blessings observed, the entire Faughnan family tucked into their supper with abandon. Mr. Fauthnan had rolled up to the head of the table and his wife sat at the opposite end. Beth and Terry faced Andrew and Ginny, with Jake at the end nearest his grandmother. Beth watched him moving his salad around the plate with his fork, left elbow on the table and his head resting on his hand. When his grandmother silently tapped his forearm, he straightened in his chair and speared a cherry tomato with his fork. Beth suspected that visits to his grandparents were a mixed blessing. Obviously, he liked the dog, who had been put outside for the meal, but the formal table could not be much fun. Not that Beth thought he should be excused. If the result of such discipline was a courteous man like Terry, Jake would benefit later from the boredom now. Besides, this dinner must be more formal than usual.

The red wine was excellent—she knew because living with Terry the last few months she'd come to appreciate high quality wine. She hardly noticed when her glass was refilled with the main course: two thick slabs of prime rib with broccoli and mashed potatoes and a pile of tiny onions off to the side. It occurred to her that there must be a cook producing and plating the food for the maid to deliver.

The conversation turned to their months at sea and Beth was surprised to discover how few details Terry's family knew. She conscientiously avoided eavesdropping on his telephone conversations with them, but she assumed that, like her, he told his family about their adventures. When she mentioned the treasure hunt they had participated in, his sister's blank expression surprised her. His parents' encouraging nods suggested they recalled it, but she should explain.

Unsurprisingly, Jake asking the same kinds of questions the children of a cruising couple she knew had asked at the start of the venture: Were there pirates? Did they find gold? Terry's mother smiled indulgently, but as Beth answered Jake's questions seriously, she got the impression she might make a better impression if she put them off as silly.

All the while she skirted the elephant in the story: Terry's kidnapping, the explosion, and his resulting injuries. She had not contacted his family when he was hospitalized, but she assumed he had. When none of them mentioned it, she deftly avoided mentioning it herself. Somewhere at the back of her mind, concern that he hadn't told her exactly what they knew—and what they did not—grew.

Relieved when the conversation started veering off toward Terry's business, she took another sip of wine and found the glass full once more. Was that the third? Could it be the fourth? While Terry described his current deal, she tried to recall how many times the maid had reached over her with the bottle. Bottles. She was, she realized, drunk. She wanted to giggle.

Oh dear.

Half listening to Terry she inhaled a long breath through her nose and released it slowly, imagining the molecules of alcohol streaming out of her system, cleansing it of the demon liquor. She smiled to herself, realized she was doing it, tried to straighten her features—

"Are you all right dear?" Mrs. Faughnan asked.

Beth started, which at least wiped the odd half smile off her face.

"Yes, fine Mrs. Faughnan. Dinner was delicious, I may have over indulged."

"We all have our moments," the woman said mysteriously, or at least it was mysterious to Beth in her current state.

"Why don't we move back to the other room for dessert?" Mr. Faughnan asked. The suggestion came as a huge relief to Beth.

"Oh yes!" she said and began scooting her chair back. She was half way out of it when she realized nobody else had moved. They all sat perfectly still, staring at her. Except for Terry, who belatedly imitated her. She finished rising, realizing as she did that she couldn't quite focus on Andrew's face across from her.

"May I freshen up?" she asked, hoping she didn't slur the "sh."

"Certainly," Mrs. Faughnan said. Beside her Terry put one hand under her elbow and moved her chair out of the way with the other.

"I'll show you where it is," he said, guiding her away from the table. She placed one foot in front of the other, praying she didn't look as drunk as she felt, certain that she must.

"Theresa has a heavy hand with the wine," Terry murmured near her ear.

"Oh God Terry I'm so embarrassed. I'm so sorry! Can we just go?"

He chuckled, slipping his hand from her elbow on around her waist. "Not a chance," he said. But don't worry. Dad's not far behind you. He started on the bourbon before dinner."

"I noticed." She started to say something about the wheelchair, but stopped herself. He had brought her along a hall leading off the living room—not the grand entry corridor, but a narrower, carpeted one—and stopped at a door.

"Here you are. I expect they'll have gotten themselves into the living room by the time you come out."

"What was that, anyway? Why were they all staring at me?"

"Oh, because nobody gets up from the table before Mom says so."

"You might have warned me!"

He chuckled again, then saw the genuine distress on her face. "If I tried to tell you about all this family's idiosyncrasies, it would take all night and you couldn't remember them all. But you're right. I guess I should have briefed you better. I'm sorry love."

His admission lifted her like a cool breeze, dispelling the crazy notion that he wanted to put her into this awkward situation. She found the bathroom doorknob and turned it.

"You okay?"

"Yeah. I just need to wash my face."

"Take your time. By the time you come out they'll have forgotten all about our exit."

After closing and locking the door Beth leaned both hands on the counter around the basin and peered into the mirror. Terry's intended reassurance had the opposite effect. Getting up from the table was a huge faux pas, huge enough for him to want to reassure her.

Ugh.

Her hope to make a positive impression was reduced to desperation to salvage the situation. Given her blood alcohol level, that was probably impossible. When she shut her eyes, her head started to spin. She opened them to stare at the faucet and ward off nausea. With deliberate care she adjusted her clothing to sit on the toilet. Despite her caution, the costume jewelry ring on her left index finger caught on her panty hose, starting a run in the thicker panty part that zoomed downward, but stopped at the top of the sheerer material.

She sat for a few minutes—longer than was appropriate as a dinner guest. When she finally stood up her head didn't spin quite as much, and after splashing her cheeks and neck with cool water, managing to avoid smearing her eye makeup, she felt considerably better. As a final insurance, she bent to the faucet and cupped her hand, slurping up several long gulps of water.

She pulled off the damaging ring before working her hose back up her leg, succeeding in preventing the run from expanding. Smoothing her skirt over her thighs she thanked heaven that she didn't tend toward short hems. If she was lucky—Lord knew she deserved some luck at this point—it wouldn't extend down her leg before they could get out of there.

But getting out seemed to be the last thing on Terry's mind. Beth rejoined the family evening already in progress, slipping into the same seat on the sofa next to Terry where she sat before supper. Her arrival went unremarked, easing her nerves a little. Andrew described in great detail an interaction with an unnamed but difficult client. Mr. Faughnan occasionally interjected a comment or asked a question, and Terry and his mother both listened politely. But Beth suspected from her stiff posture and glassy eyed stare at the dark windows that Ginny was supremely bored. Jake was back by the hearth constructing something out of plastic building blocks. Beth wished she could join him.

As Andrew wound down his story the maid entered with plates of key lime pie on a large tray. She set this down on a side table and disappeared, returning a moment later with a second tray laden with coffee cups, a carafe, a rectangular dish filled with multicolor packets of sweetener, and a sweating pitcher of milk. Although she didn't usually drink coffee in the evening, Beth accepted a cup and overdosed it with what turned out to be cream. It was a long drive back, and she hoped the caffeine would help banish the alcohol molecules dancing around her system.

She loved key lime pie, but this one was a lurid shade of green, always a sign of poor quality. One taste confirmed her fear: it was tart with a gelatinous texture. Choking down enough bites to be polite occupied her next few minutes, so she paid no attention to whatever Ginny was saying.

Until she realized they were once again all staring at her.

She pulled her fork from her mouth and tried to speak around the pie, "pardon?"

To her horror a greenish glob shot out and landed on the coffee table. She shut her mouth and swallowed.

"I said, do you have plans for your boat now—" Ginny paused to stare at the green pie sludge on the table, "— now that you're living with—in D.C.?"

Beth could hear it in her tone, and her little stumble—Ginny didn't want to think about this disgusting creature living with her brother.

"We, um, we're thinking of going down there for a sail at some point this winter, if Terry can take the time," she floundered, eyes on Terry as he leaned in front of her and used his napkin to scoop up the offending ort.

"Oh really? Do you think you'll be able to do that, Terry?" his mother asked, sounding astounded.

Beth tried to shrink into the sofa.

"Never know," he said. To Beth's utter relief he reached for her hand. His gentle squeeze boosted her flagging morale and spoke volumes to his family members, who, to Beth, wore the aspect of an unconvinced jury in a particularly gruesome murder trial.

"We're playing it by ear. I know that by the end of January, or February, I'll be desperate for a break and some time with Beth. Even if it's just a long weekend. We can go sit on the boat in St. Thomas." This last he directed at Beth, the corners of his eyes scrunching up as he smiled at her.

"Seems a bit frivolous," his father muttered, raising his highball glass to his mouth.

"They're young, Terrence. They should be frivolous," Mrs. Faughnan said, to Beth's utter surprise.

"Not that young," he grumbled back. Beth realized this was a private argument. She looked back at Terry, who ignored the interchange and was gazing at her with a delicious smile. She wanted to wrap her arms around him for being her hero. In fact, she couldn't resist. She had to hold him, let him know how much she appreciated him …

"But Terry—" He held her off gently, his smile now more contrived than warm. Across the room Andrew stood up, clearing his throat as he extended a hand to Ginny.

"It's getting late. Jake?"

"I just want you to know how much I lo—"

"I know Bethy. I think Andrew's right. It's a long drive," Terry hauled her up by both arms, making it impossible for her to complete her intended hug. She gave up and instead turned toward his mother, who managed to pull off looking down her nose while seated.

"Thank for you for a lovely evening," she said, appropriate words coming out of sheer habit. She turned toward Terry's father and added, "I'm so glad to finally meet you," she turned toward Ginny and Andrew, "All of you."

"You too dear," Mrs. Faughnan said, leaving no doubt she didn't mean a word of it.

"Jake?" Andrew said again. Beth saw that the boy had constructed an impressive impressionist tower. "Take it apart. It's time to go," his father went on.

"Aww, too bad. It's really cool Jake," Beth said, feeling sorry for the way they squelched the boy's creativity. She started to take a step toward the hearth, but Terry's hands on her shoulders restrained her.

"Leave it," he whispered in her ear.

He turned her toward the front hall and they started walking. She could hear the whine of his father's wheelchair behind them, and the peculiar squelching sound of its rubber wheels on the marble.

And then the cool evening air hit her in the face as they stepped out onto the front porch.

"Drive safely," she heard someone say. She kept walking toward the passenger side of Terry's BMW. She didn't know how he managed to step ahead of her enough to open the door, but he did. She slumped down onto the seat, looked down at her legs, and burst into tears. The run had laddered its way all the way down to her ankle.

She felt the driver's door shut and covered her face with both hands as if that would conceal her weeping.

Eight

Virginia Beach, Virginia

"*I*t's not that bad love," Terry said as the engine roared to life. "Believe me."

Beth watched the house—the ghastly, awful house of her horrors—recede and thought he was in quite a hurry to get away if it was not that bad.

"We were blocking Ginny and Andrew," he said, and she realized she had spoken her thought aloud. "Are you going to cry all the way home?"

"Maybe," she mumbled, taking a deep breath to quel the despair. It didn't.

"Is there anything I can do to prevent that?"

She winced at his sympathetic tone. He had every right to be livid with her.

"Rewind time and keep me from touching the wine?" She wanted to say, "have nicer parents," but even intoxicated she knew better.

Unbelievably, he laughed. She turned red eyes on him and he glanced over, his humor genuine.

"I thought you might ask if I could get different parents," he said. For a moment she thought she had spoken her thought aloud again, but finally realized it was just that he had thought it too. She smiled, giggled, and then as relief flooded through her heart and mind, laughed out loud.

"Well, if that's an offer …"

"Remember last year when I said I trained them not to expect me to be able to join them for holidays? You thought I was evading my family responsibility?"

"I never said that—"

"You thought it. Do you understand now?"

"You mean it's always like that?"

"My father drinks too much and my mother's a control freak. Everyone lives in fear of her. They can't keep the same maid or cook for more than a year. If I could have taken Izzy when I bought the townhouse I would have, but at least Dad's loves her. Ginny, God love her, is wrapped up in superficiality. Andrew should have gotten a job far away a long time ago."

"Would Ginny let him?" Beth knew Terry could easily slip into a "I can criticize my sister, but no one else can" mode. But he barked a dry, sarcastic laugh instead.

"If it's someplace like New York, or Beverly Hills. But maybe he appreciates when she spends time with Mom and runs to her every time they have a fight."

"Jake seems like a nice kid."

"And you're wondering how that can be?"

"Well, yeah. I mean, he built a cool tower—couldn't they have taken a second to appreciate it?"

"I know. I know you wanted to, but we had to get out of there. I'm sorry love."

"You're sorry!" Beth pressed her head back into the headrest and shut her eyes and thought about it. "And you should be."

He glanced over and found her staring at him. "All these months of me moaning about my father, and you never, not once, mentioned your father's handicap. How could you?" The anger she thought she had suppressed broke through with a vengeance, enhanced by the alcohol.

His expression as he turned to watch the road was stony. *I pushed too hard, but I don't care. I want an answer.*

"I didn't want to detract from your situation. What happened to my Dad is long past and I—all of us—worked through it. I know how hard it is. Telling you about it while you're dealing with accepting your father's situation would seem like one-ups man ship."

"It might seem like credentials. You've been through it, you understand."

"What I went through is nothing like your family's situation. I could see that from almost the day we met, and meeting them confirmed it. Your family is entirely different from mine."

They rode in silence for a while, Beth contemplating his motive in not telling her, Terry considering whether he made a poor choice. Both of them wondering how to recover.

Eventually Beth said, "Tell me about your father. How long ago did he have the stroke?"

Terry did not answer right way. Beth turned her face toward the window, staring at the reflection of the dashboard lights. She tried to read the reversed numbers on the speedometer. They almost spelled out a word, but in a foreign language.

"I was sixteen when he had the first one. It was right before Ginny's first junior beauty pageant. Typical spoiled teenager, she acted like he intentionally sabotaged her pageant career. I had recently gotten my driver's license, and Mom made me drive Ginny to all her meetings and rehearsals while Dad was in the hospital."

"You wanted to be with him."

"At first. But I was sixteen and I had the car. I had freedom, other than having to play chauffeur to the beauty queen—that never would have happened otherwise."

"So you didn't visit him?"

Terry shook his head, and Beth recognized a memory of the same guilt she harbored. He understood her far better than she suspected, but his understanding was from the perspective of her future emotional state.

"You said the first stroke."

"He had another one seven years later. That one put him in the chair."

"Jesus," Beth tried to imagine the enormity of having two such massive health events. "He's lucky to be alive."

"So the doctors said. About the time they told him to stop drinking. They told him he had a couple years at most."

"Eight years ago." Beth had managed to do the math despite the alcohol.

Rather than reply he gave her time to think about her own situation. Her expectation that her father would pass on in the six-month timeframe sounded about as selfish as Terry' sister and her junior pageant. She could think of nothing more to say. She appreciated that he honored her silence for the rest of the drive. Unlike the earlier tense quiet, the atmosphere was not charged with anger and accusations, but with contemplation. After a while Terry reached out and switched on the stereo, filling the car with the soulful flamenco guitar that had entertained them on the ride down. The sound reminded both of them of their earlier sense of anticipation over the visit, subsuming some of the horror of the past couple hours. The rhythm beat it into nothing as the melody intensified, punctuated by the musicians' occasional recorded grunts and slaps on his guitar's resonant body.

Terry pulled onto the sidewalk outside the town house, waited for the garage door to finish opening, and drove the rest of the way in. He shut off the engine and turned to Beth.

"We're home," he said softly. She looked out through the windshield at the familiar garage interior: shelves on the rear wall packed with boxes, a shovel and rake leaning against the wall in the corner. The tennis ball hanging from a string resting right on the blue and white emblem on the hood of the car. He never misses, she thought with a smile.

"Yes we are," she said, turning to look at him. "Say, how did Ginny do in the pageant, anyway?"

Georgetown, Washington D.C.

"By the time they see you again they'll have forgotten all about it," Terry assured her the next morning. She had awakened with a headache and a sense of doom that his freshly ground and brewed coffee did not dispel.

"I don't see how. I could tell your mother and sister think I'm a complete disaster."

"My mother and sister had only slightly less to drink than you. They'll forget."

"About my spitting the pie out?"

"Well, you didn't do it because it was bad."

"It was bad, though," she grinned, trying to change the focus from her to the meal. He probably guessed as much, but went along.

"Awful. I don't know why, I told Mom over and over that key lime pie should be yellow, not green."

"She does the shopping?"

"Of course not, but she specifies everything, right down to the brand."

"That poor maid. Do they always serve so much wine?"

"Unfortunately, yes."

"But you like good wine. And it was good."

"All things in moderation," he said, topping off her cup with a grin. "Including morning after cures. Unless you want 'hair of the dog'?"

She shuddered and shook her head, the pain almost unbearable. "Ohhhh," she groaned, putting her head in her hands.

"We should go to the gym. You should sit in the sauna and sweat it out."

"As long as I don't have to move."

*

Beth stopped resenting the cost of the household gym membership when she emerged early in the afternoon after paddling around in the pool—not a serious swim, but a stretch and wade affair—and cycling between the sauna and a cool shower several times. By then she realized it was Sunday afternoon and Terry was busy with Jeff. Disappointed, she wandered around the neighborhood for a while and finally drifted into the multiplex. She realized it had been almost a year since she saw a movie in a theater.

Two hours and a bucket of popcorn later she re-emerged into autumn's early dusk and felt refreshed. The film had been complete escapism, and it had taken her mind off of yesterday's disaster. As she returned home, she thought about Terry's response to it all and felt even more secure. He showed no signs of dumping her based on his relatives' behavior, or hers.

*

Westlake, Texas

Watching the rest of the members of the wedding party squinting into the morning sunshine, flexing stiff limbs, and staring into their cups of coffee Hunter could almost be glad about giving up alcohol. But he was not the only guest at the wedding brunch without a hangover—his brother's new mother-in-law was a sober-headed morning person. She moved from one group to another, apparently trying to have pleasant conversations, but inevitably the objects of her attention were nearly non-responsive, or dissolved into innuendo-fueled giggling that left the older woman looking more annoyed than bemused. Eventually she recognized a fellow teetotaler: she made her way over to Hunter where he stood near a wall holding his black coffee wondering how long it would take for the revelers to settle down to being served.

"Good morning Hunter. How are you?"

He smiled, recognizing her unspoken question. He had not interacted with her during the wedding preparations over the last few days, but he knew his brother had a high opinion of her. "She's a kind woman, but she's got a strong core. I'll be lucky if her daughter ages like her," Parker had said.

"I'm well Mrs. Johnson. How about you? I hope you've recovered from the reception."

"Oh yes, I was up at seven to take a turn around the grounds. I normally take a ride on my Buddy—he's a dear old quarter horse—on Sunday morning. He's probably wondering where I am." She turned her eyes from the groups of guests toward Hunter as she finished her sentence to gauge his reaction.

"Our pets do become dependent on us, don't they?"

"Indeed. Buddy is a fine animal. I hate to disappoint him."

"You'll make it up to him when you get back."

"Indeed. Do you have any animals in your life, Hunter?"

"Other than Parker? No."

She looked appropriately startled, and they both laughed.

"I certainly hope he's not!" She said out of duty.

"The truth is, he's been my rock for a while now." Hunter felt a need to be honest with the woman, for Parker's sake. "I had a bit of a breakdown a year or so ago. Parker rescued me and stuck with me when I probably didn't deserve it."

"You'll miss him."

"Yes. But it's time. I'm ready—I need to move on. He deserves to be happy, and free of me."

"Well, I heard your story, of course. But the way you put it gives me hope for my Becca. She can be very giving. Too giving. But perhaps your brother won't be doing too much taking."

"No, I don't imagine he will. I think they are well matched, Mrs. Johnson. I mean it. It looks like they're finally here. Shall we?"

"I guess this is it. I'm sure you're going to have a blast on your honeymoon."

"Hell yeah we are. Waikiki here we come!"

Hunter was disappointed with himself for not finding a time when his brother was sober to have this conversation. But he kept putting it off until they were down to the end. In a few minutes the limo would arrive to take Parker and Becca to the airport. In fact, Hunter knew he was lucky to have these few minutes waiting with his brother in the hotel lobby, so he needed to make the best of them.

"Listen, I'm heading out myself in a couple days."

"Oh yeah? Where are you going? Did you find a better job somewhere?"

Hunter shot his brother the obligatory grin. Parker had been needling him about his blue-collar job at a hardware store for weeks. He didn't understand that it was stable and structured, and it allowed Hunter to rebuild his self-confidence.

"No, I did not. I had some news a while back and I'm going to check it out."

"There's this amazing thing called the internet, bro. Also, even older, are telephones. Are you quitting your job?"

"I already did. The internet is how I got the information. A friend in the islands sent me a link to a news article about a woman I knew in Jamaica. She had a baby."

"A baby is newsworthy?"

"The baby was kidnapped from the hospital, and then recovered—an unusual enough event to be newsworthy. Thing is, I knew her in Jamaica. Really 'knew' her."

"In the Biblical sense, I get it. You think the baby is yours?"

Hunter nodded. "I think it's possible."

"Why didn't she contact you?"

"I don't know. I think the reason she took off from Jamaica was that she found out she was pregnant. The timing is about right. She isn't one to cling to relationships. Maybe being pregnant scared her. Maybe she doesn't want to see me. But I have to know. I have to know if I have a son."

"Email her."

"I tried. No answer."

"So what? You're going to go find her in the islands? Do you have any idea where she is?"

"No."

"Jesus, Hunter—"

"I'm not going to go find her. I'm going to go find her friend. There's this other woman who was there at the hospital—according to the news article. I'm going to find her and ask her to contact Ori on my behalf."

"Dude, that's convoluted. Do you know where the friend is? Just find Ori. Wait a second, this is the woman who left you a friggin' wreck, isn't it?"

"She did not. It was coincidence that I got mugged right after she left."

"Uh huh. Fine. If you say so."

Hunter knew his brother didn't believe him. He couldn't remember what he told Parker last year about why he was so strung out a pair of Jamaican thugs were able to jump him, beat him more than half to death, and steal his wallet and his stash. Had he talked about Ori when he was in the hospital? He was sure he talked about her in rehab, but Parker hadn't been part of that.

"But so help me," Parker went on, "if you have another breakdown don't call me."

"I'm not going to have another breakdown." Parker couldn't stand the term "overdose" so Hunter didn't use it. "I'm going to find out if I'm a father, and if I am, I'm going to step up. Take responsibility."

Parker, who seemed to have sobered a little, eyed his brother for a long moment.

"You do what you have to do. But keep in touch. Becca and I will be back in a couple weeks."

"I'll keep you updated. Heck, maybe you're an uncle!"

"Right. Look, take care of yourself Hunter. I worry about you," Parker looked across the lobby toward the elevators where a group of mostly women had emerged. "Here comes Becca and her posse. I have to go."

"Safe travels brother," Hunter extended his hand for a shake, but Parker took it and pulled him into an embrace.

"You too, brother."

Nine

Georgetown, Washington, D.C.

As the new pattern of their lives evolved Beth saw hints of what Carole had been talking about. Terry spent long hours closeted with Jeff and their lawyers reviewing endless details of the impending business purchase. When he did come home, he spent more hours reading business news and researching his soon-to-be competitors in the realm of executive training.

New patterns were developing for Beth, too, as she was continually surprised at how much she had forgotten about living on land. She enjoyed waking up to fresh brewed coffee without having to light a propane stove with a match, but she found herself missing the sound of her battered stainless-steel percolator. Laundry magically moved from the hamper back to the closet and dresser, handled by Carrie the housekeeper. When she opened the her underwear drawer, she felt a sense of loss rather than pleasure: she missed the ritual of gathering the laundry and hauling it ashore by dinghy, visiting with locals and other cruisers, and sitting in an internet café waiting for it to be done. Laundry day in the islands was more fun than working on her resume.

Trish's phone call reminded her of her commitment to document their father's stories. When she couldn't take any more job hunting and resume refining, she replayed the recordings using a player Terry produced from somewhere. Although she was a decent typist, and Dad's speech was slowed by his illness, she had a hard time keeping up as she transcribed them. She could not stand doing it for more than a half hour at a time, so she made slow progress.

After doing research herself on the types of employers Tom Biffle recommended and further revising her resume, she met with him again. He tore it apart again, and together they rebuilt it in the image of the job descriptions she liked. He provided a great deal of insight into the meaning behind the words in those descriptions—

subtleties that made Beth apprehensive. She barely understood the Washington employment landscape. But Tom shared salary data showing her the much higher potential of technical and professional writing over advertising and marketing writing. She was convinced. And anxious.

She bought him a real lunch this time since he refused to take payment for his help. When they exhausted her resume, he asked about Terry and Jeff's deal. She realized she didn't know how much she could say: was it confidential? Terry had never said so, and he had talked about it with her parents. She told Tom about the business and of Terry's plans—plans she was sure he mentioned in his conversations with her father. Tom encouraged her stories of the difficulties Terry and Jeff discussed and before long she realized she didn't know whether she was restricting herself to information Terry told others or talking about things she'd overheard in his private conversations with Jeff. As she rode home on the metro, she tried to imagine how Tom might use the information to sabotage Terry and Jeff—or if he even wanted to. She couldn't imagine how, but she decided to confess her possible indiscretion to Terry.

But Terry didn't get home until she was asleep that night, and he took a phone call first thing in the morning, talking on the speaker while he got dressed. He was still talking when he kissed her on the cheek and left, Blackberry held to his ear. Things were much the same the next day.

By Thursday she was fully engaged in her own new business pursuit—job hunting—and Tom's probing questions slipped her mind.

She painstakingly filled out the lengthy forms on job hunting websites. To her surprise, she received several inquiry emails within a few hours. But she quickly realized they were junk with subject lines like "a work-at-home job perfect for you" and "earn thousands in a week." Discouraged, she clicked on the fifth new email with minimal enthusiasm and found herself reading a genuine request for her to contact a recruiter.

Her first instinct was to close the email and do something else. A real job opportunity coming so quickly on the heels of posting her resume scared her. She gave herself a mental slap and re-opened the message, skimming it again to be sure she understood the job on offer. Hand shaking, she picked up her phone and dialed the recruiter's number.

The background noise when the call was answered put her off immediately—it sounded like she was speaking to someone on the trading floor of a stock exchange. Many voices, ringing phones, and other indeterminate sounds were almost louder than the speaker. But the person who answered identified herself as Monica Brushy, the name of the person who sent the email, so Beth introduced herself and explained the reason for her call.

"Oh yes. Thank you for calling." Beth half expected a "so quickly," since the email had only come a few minutes earlier, but Ms Brushy went right on.

"The position is in Pentagon City. Would that be a problem for you?"

"Uh, no," Beth stuck the phone between her shoulder and her ear and pointed her browser at a mapping website. She didn't know where Pentagon City was. Presumably near the Pentagon, but she didn't know where that was, either.

"They're looking for someone who can get a clearance—I don't see any mention of that in your posting ..."

"You mean a security clearance? No, I have never had one."

"I see. Well, your experience roughly matches what they're after—"

Beth couldn't see how, if a clearance was required. Tom must have inserted coded messages into her resume without telling her.

"—so I'm going to give it a try, if you agree."

"Can you tell me anything about the position?"

The answer was a string of acronyms and phrases Beth couldn't make heads or tails out of. All she could glean from it was that they wanted someone who could write for a non-military, non-technical audience made up of vendors. No mention of what they vended, at least in plain English. Beth was more intrigued than interested in the position.

"I see. I'm definitely interested in speaking with them, if they are willing."

"Fine. I'll send it over and we'll see what happens. This security clearance thing can be meaningless—it's on all their requisitions. Let me see if I have your correct contact information. They may want to do a phone interview first."

Beth verified her address, telephone, and email information and the call ended. She glanced at the time on the phone and saw it had taken all of four minutes, including the jargon-filled job description.

The following morning, she received eight more spam emails and calls from two more recruiters. Both of these lacked the background noise, but they were also fast talkers. Their questions were direct and inelegant, and within three minutes both of them determined she was not a fit for the positions they were filling and ended the call. She breathed a sigh of relief that she didn't work on commission.

The fourth call had a very different tone. The recruiter introduced himself as Donald "call me Don" McCarthy and briefly described his firm. Beth felt like he was providing credentials so she would work with him. It was absurdly flattering, given that the employer would pay his commission. In any case, his approach relaxed her, and she listened calmly to his description of the position he had available. It was with a political consulting firm based in D.C. He took a moment to describe their offices and location—quality-of-life concerns she could not imagine the other recruiters taking time over. He had her salivating for the job by the time he finished. She readily agreed he should submit her resume and crossed her fingers that they would call for an interview.

◡

Port de Galisbay, St. Martin

Virgine touched her scented handkerchief to her upper lip and inhaled to mask the stench wafting in from the warehouse. A guard pushed a young woman into the office. Two more women followed him with another guard behind them.

They were so filthy and poorly dressed Virgine had to use a great deal of imagination to see them as anything but refuse, barely human, and not worth any effort. She resisted the impulse to order the guards to return them and find better candidates. There were no others. These were the woman she needed to see. According to the manifest, the rest of the most recent delivery were children, boys, and women past their value as anything other than drudges. While there the market for the children was good, her current need was for young adult females.

They stood in a line before the folding table. Virgine sat on an uncomfortable folding chair: the seat was hard, and the side rails cut into her curvaceous hips. One of the women watched her with an unabashed stare. The other two stared down at the table, although Virgine suspected they were doing it to avoid looking at her. The one with the attitude would need work. The other two should be suitably malleable.

Virgine turned her attention to appearance. All three wore their hair in dark tangles. No, she corrected herself, they didn't "wear" their hair at all. It simply was: rats' nests on top of and straggling down from their heads. Still, it could be washed and styled, the tangles and split ends removed. She signaled to the guards to lift the two women's chins, forcing them to look at her so she could study their faces. The third one continued to return her stare.

Oh yes, you're going to need discipline.

That one and one of the other two were moderately attractive, other than the rather livid bruise and scabbed over cut on the one with the attitude. They had clear skin and eyes a warm cocoa brown. The third one's facial features were pushed together, her wide, straight mouth close below her short nose, her eyes also wide and set low so her forehead seemed to be enormous.

Perhaps with the right makeup.

Virgine sighed, dissatisfied, but with no alternative. She focused on the papers in front of her on the table, scrawling information into a form she had devised. After a moment she looked up at the one that stared at her.

"Your name is Sarah." She said in English.

"No ma'am. My name is Anaishe."

One of Virgine's precisely shaped brows rose. "Your name here is Sarah. Do you understand?"

"I am Anaishe."

At a flick of Virgine's eyes the guard nearest Sarah stepped forward, turned, and slapped her across the face. Virgine was impressed with the young woman, who stood her ground, recovered from the slap, and returned her gaze to Virgine in an angry glare.

"Sarah, you will learn." Virgine made another note on the paper and slid it aside to begin the next one.

When all three women had been assigned proper names Virgine gestured to the guards and stood up. The guards ushered the women toward the exterior door. Last in line, Sarah stopped, glaring at Virgine.

"My son comes with me."

"Your what?" Virgine asked. At the same time the guard behind Sarah pushed her in the small of the back with the butt of his weapon. She bent around the pressure, shoulders leaning back, and stared defiantly at Virgine, who pursed her lips in annoyance.

"My son is inside. He comes with me."

Virgine chuckled, looking at the guard's sloppy grin.

"Bring her son," Virgine said, looking forward to crushing the look of triumph passing across the other woman's face. The guard left through the door into the warehouse, leaving it standing open. Virgine coughed, raising the handkerchief to her nose. The outside door stood open. The guards were loading the other two women into the van. Sarah stood her ground in front of Virgine.

An ungodly racket coming from the warehouse grew louder and louder. A boy of about six was screaming and cursing at the guard who gripped his upper arm. When he reached the doorway, the guard's push sent him sprawling on the floor beside the folding table. Sarah crouched, cooing, reaching for him. Virgine picked up her foot in its designer heel and shoved Sarah's shoulder. The young woman fell sideways, catching herself on her elbows. She uttered a word that Virgine took to be a curse and made to rise. Meanwhile the guard pulled the boy to his feet, holding him against his legs.

Virgine interposed herself between Sarah and the boy as one of the other guards returned and reached down to drag Sarah to her feet.

"Disgusting creature," Virgine said of the boy. He was filthy—much dirtier than the women—covered in dried dirt and dust. His fingernails were black, his teeth brown. His upper lip was covered in the slime running from his nose. Tears had drawn lines down his cheeks in the dirt. He wore rags: filthy underpants and a shredded t-shirt of indeterminate color. Stains down his inner thighs told her he had pissed himself more than once.

Sarah was wailing now, restrained by the guard but reaching toward her son, although Virgine stood between them.

"Stop this noise now," Virgine snapped. Both guards freed one hand to wrap around the mouth of their charge. The woman's head shook violently back and forth, eyes frantic now. The boy froze, the man's hand covering his mouth and nose. Virgine stepped away and watched as Sarah stopped shaking and looked down at her son. She could see it in his eyes—fear, then panic. He started to struggle, but he was already weak. Sarah screamed behind her guard's hand. Tears welled up in her eyes, locked on her son's. She wept as she watched him cease his struggle and go limp in the guard's grip. Virgine nodded at the guard and he lifted the child, carrying it back into the warehouse. Sarah went limp now, weeping, her gaze following the retreating guard.

Virgine let her satisfaction show as the other guard forced the young woman from the room and into the back of the waiting van. She was a little disappointed that was all it had taken to cow Sarah, but it was just as well not to destroy the merchandise. There was a market for the boy, after all.

♪

St. Hillaire, Guadeloupe

Hunter slung his pack over one shoulder and attempted to saunter down the boarding ramp of the inter-island mail boat. He knew his saunter was more like a stagger as the ramp shifted on a swell that lifted and lowered the ship. As soon as his feet hit a stable surface—St. Hillaire's short, ragged wharf—he reached in his pocket for his smokes and the Bic lighter he paid a fortune for at the airport on Guadeloupe.

The sun felt brutal, as hot as a Texas gulf coast summer day. Stepping out into it at the airport yesterday he realized how accustomed he'd become to suburban Dallas's air conditioning. He spent most of the long ride on the mail boat in the crew "lounge" with its wheezing AC unit keeping the humidity at bay. Looking at the quaint, island waterfront of St. Hilaire's one town he suspected an air-conditioned hotel room would come at a premium, if one even existed here.

It's time to acclimate to island climate he told himself, smiling at his own lame wordplay.

As his feet touched the cement seawall, he took a long drag on his cigarette and looked again at the buildings and streets before him. According to the news article, Ori's friend took her, in labor, on a boat from here to Pointe-à-Pitre. The article was unclear about what boat, but described the friend as a sailor, so presumably it was hers. Ori had been staying here at the home of an elderly woman, or rather, with the members of a local band who had taken over the woman's home. Hunter read in a follow up article that the band leader was convicted on several charges and jailed with a six year sentence. Hunter had not been able to find out anything about the other band members in the online local newspapers. The elderly woman reclaimed her home immediately after the incident. Hunter hoped he would not traumatize her by asking questions about her uninvited guests. But first he had to find her house.

The town appeared to have more bars than any other type of business, each of them with a calendar of performances posted on chalk boards or hand-lettered poster board signs. He scanned them as he passed by, looking for the name of the band Ori stayed with. Not that he expected to find it with their leader in jail. More likely the band members had dispersed at the first sign of law enforcement. He paused at a real estate office and studied the listings. The properties seemed to contrast sharply with the rough feeling of the village with its multitude of shabby bars. Almost all of the properties posted in the office window were multi-million Euro places with swimming pools, private beaches, or dramatic views from high atop St. Hillaire's mountains. This wasn't the place to find a room for the night. Or maybe it was.

Hunter dropped his nearly finished cigarette on the paving stones and stepped on it, then opened the door and entered, immediately noticing the cool, dry air.

"*Bonjour Monsieur. Comment puis-je vous aider?*"

The woman seated behind a tidy desk wore her hair pulled into a tight chignon. Her lips perfectly matched her bubblegum pink fingernails, a striking contrast with her dark skin. She wore a pale blue linen blouse. She made Hunter feel grubby.

"*Bonjour Madame. Je cherche une chambre pour ce soir. Je pensais que tu pouvais m'aider.*" His prep school French did not increase his self confidence in her presence. To his relief, though, she smiled pleasantly and nodded.

"I can suggest the Alamanda Guest House. Madame Favre is the proprietress," she said in English, opening the lid on an old-fashioned rotary address card holder as she spoke. "It is on the edge of the village, up the hill. It is quieter than some of the other houses offering rooms in town."

He smiled appreciatively. "That sounds perfect."

She nodded once more as if confirming a newly formed opinion of him, and then picked up a pen and wrote something on the top sheet of a note pad. She set the pen down, tore off the paper, and extended it to him.

"Here is the address. Walk up the hill to the church and turn left. Go two blocks. You will find it on the right. It is a wooden house, painted white, with blue shutters."

"You are most very kind. Thank you, Madame."

"Enjoy your visit on St. Hilaire, Monsieur."

St. Hilaire's reputation as a music hot spot grew more apparent as the afternoon came to a close. Hunter located the Alamanda Guest House and met Madame Favre, whose welcome suggested the realtor *had* telephoned. She guided him to a tiny room with a narrow bed, a white painted dresser, and a sink with a round mirror mounted above it on the wall. The bulb in the light on the ceiling was not more than forty watts. The shared toilet and bath were two separate rooms off of the hall. He'd stayed in worse places for much more than the forty Euro she requested.

He left his pack and walked back down the hill to find a bite to eat. The closer he got to the waterfront the more he understood St. Hilaire's place in the Guadeloupe nightlife culture. In the forty minutes since he came ashore, dozens of boats had crowded into the harbor and more were arriving. Most of them dropped their anchors and offloaded passengers and crew into dinghies to come ashore. A few larger craft drew up beside the wharf where their passengers climbed one of the rusty steel ladders. How ever they got to the village, the visitors, most of them in their twenties, dispersed to the various bars and restaurants. Hunter had not expected to have such competition here finding a table for dinner.

In the end he found an outdoor table at a cafe at the very end of the waterfront. By the time his plate of conch curry arrived all of the other tables were occupied too. He couldn't keep up with the rapid French conversations all around him, so he enjoyed his supper and the view of the darkened harbor where hundreds of white lights marked each of the anchored vessels. A few had underwater lights creating eerie blue pools around them, and a couple had decorative strings of lights around their deckhouses. St. Hillaire might be a lot livelier than he expected.

Later he wandered the streets again, covering the entire village in a half hour, listening to the huge variety of musical styles coming from the bars. There was a lot of reggae, but also country music, trop rock, disco, house music, hip hop, and rap in both French and English. And there were aromas—enticing smells that triggered desires he thought his months in rehab had destroyed. He hurried past the crowds standing outside of the bars smoking, holding his breath as long as he could. He was glad the smells dissipated, and the sounds began to blend and soften as he approached the Alamanda Guest House. Jet lag and two days of travel, even with the short night in a Pointe-à-Pitre airport hotel, were catching up with him. He was asleep on the hard, narrow bed with its faint odor of mildew in minutes.

Ten

Georgetown, Washington, D.C.

Monica Brushy called back about the Pentagon City job the following afternoon. She asked Beth more questions about her experience and her background—had she lived abroad? Really? Where? No set address? The call ended with the recruiter telling her she should not have been deceptive in her application.

On her resume, Tom had described her months at sea as a freelance writing stint and urged her to have copies of her article on Alzheimer's ready as evidence. She did not feel that her resume was deceptive, just omissive: it didn't specify where she was during that time. If it mattered—if they suspected her of espionage or criminal activity or something—she didn't want to work for them. But the thought of espionage reminded her of her friend Burt, a charter captain who described himself as retired from a government position. She didn't doubt his connection to a government intelligence agency, only the "former" aspect of it—and only because Terry insisted nobody retires from the CIA.

Burt had helped her out more than once during her months in the islands, and she could admit to herself that any job requiring a security clearance intrigued her. But not enough to put up with Monica Brushy's attitude.

She was delighted an hour later when Don McCarthy called back with good news: his client would like to do a telephone interview. She agreed to take the call at 8:30 Friday morning. She squelched a momentary hesitancy—giving herself another mental slap—because she had started going to the gym early in the morning and the call would conflict with it.

That afternoon Terry came home before nightfall—unusual enough in itself—and held up two tickets while his face split into a grin.

"What are they?" She moved closer to see. They were the size and shape of concert tickets. He held them out to her.

"Strictly Sail Annapolis," she read out loud. "Oh, the big boat show! When is it?" She looked again at the tickets and saw that it opened on Friday.

"Oh no—I have an interview!"

"Really? That was quick."

"It's just a phone interview, first thing in the morning. It doesn't interfere with this. This is great! I so need to get back on a boat."

"Yeah, me too," he took the tickets back and put them in his wallet for safe keeping. "You didn't say anything, so I wondered if you were missing *Trouble*, and the water."

Beth smiled into his eyes, wondering at his return from the depths of business, but grateful for it. She wandered into the living room and sat down, pulling her feet up onto the sofa. He sat down in his favorite armchair, ready for a talk.

"I'm surprised I don't miss it more," she admitted. "I thought I would. I mean, some things are strange, like all the appliances to do things we do by hand on the boat, and the huge refrigerator that I don't have to dive into headfirst to find anything. And I don't have to buy ice to keep it cold. But I have been pretty busy. I think if I weren't here with you, I'd be miserable, though."

He smirked, "Like I'm here much."

"I wake up when you come in late and it feels wonderful to know you're here, I mean we're together. I'm sorry we don't have more time when we're awake, but it's better than nothing. Better than being alone."

He shook his head slowly, "I would prefer to be more than just better than nothing."

"I didn't mean it that way—"

"I know what you meant love. Carole probably told you how angry she gets at Jeff for being a workaholic. I've been told I do it too, and I don't want it to ruin us."

"Carole's said that to you?" Beth asked, knowing very well it wasn't what he meant and regretting the manipulative nature of her question. He pursed his lips, recognizing her underlying question, which made her wince.

"Someone I dated for a while. We broke up about four months before I met you. She said I was a selfish workaholic."

"Did she talk to Carole?" Beth smiled, disturbed by the seriousness of his tone. She had long sensed that a woman had hurt him, and this confirmed it. Her joke broke the tension evident on his face. He smiled, eyes crinkling merrily.

"Probably. They're of a type, in some ways."

Beth considered it. "I can't see you with Carole—a Carole clone."

He grinned. "Linda is a model."

"Oh great," Beth sighed, shrinking at the comparison she thought must be coming. Terry stopped and stared at her for a moment.

"Don't' tell me: Tall, skinny, gorgeous hair, perfect cheekbones—"

"Yes. And a ridiculous wardrobe, terrible appetite, and a cache of uppers and downers and I don't know what else in her purse."

Beth stopped short and stared at him, taken completely by surprise. He nodded as if to reinforce his statement.

"Did you know?"

"You mean when I met her? No. By the time I found out I was hooked—on her, not her stash. She runs in fascinating social circles. Party every weekend, and during the week when I had time. She went without me if I didn't."

"You loved her though."

"I did."

They both fell silent. This was hardly a revelation, in theory. Neither of them was young enough to be untouched by prior relationships. Beth had long been curious about his past ones. There was little evidence of them in the house—a few photos in the albums on the shelf, a bottle of feminine shampoo under the guest bathroom sink. The evidence of her past relationships was about as scarce— perhaps more so since her belongings were stripped down so much to live on *Trouble*.

"How did it end?" she finally asked. She needed to know he had closure.

"One binge too many. She threw a fit over something stupid. Or maybe I deserved it, I don't know. But she was strung out and started breaking things. I lost it. I put her in a taxi home. She was flying to Milan that evening. While she was gone, I put everything of hers I could find around here in a box and took it to her place— she shares an apartment with a bunch of models. I called her and told her not to come back."

"Did she?"

"No. I guess it was cowardly, doing it on the phone. But I couldn't wait until she got back from Italy. I needed it over. We were starting a contract and I was having a hard time focusing because of her."

"Work pushed the decision for you."

He grimaced as he nodded agreement. Beth appreciated the honesty in his admission. She didn't judge him for what he'd done. She wondered if Linda had.

"But I don't see how she hurt you, I mean, you dumped her…"

He smirked again, looking contrite. "I guess you have a point. But I was hurt. I wanted a balanced relationship, where I could have my business, and she could have her work, and we could have each other. It worked for a while, but she kept pulling me into her world and I couldn't be there. Our clients were conservative. She walked too close to the tabloids with me on her arm, and too often she was glassy eyed. I'm not into the all-night drinking and drugging parties. Eventually I realized I was dating my fantasy of her, but we didn't have anything like the relationship I wanted it to be. It was a horrible realization, but after that I started seeing her in a different way and it felt like she changed. I was heartbroken. All my fault, I know," he raised one hand, palm out, to prevent her from saying what she would not have.

"It's hard when you realize something isn't right. There's no way to avoid being hurt, especially if you're committed when it happens."

"You've been there?"

"I had a similar experience with Peter."

"Your turn, since we're doing this. Come on," his smile came back as he tweaked her to share as he had.

"We learned to sail together. I loved it. He enjoyed it. I was better at it."

"That can't have killed a relationship. You're a better sailor than me."

She stared at him for a moment in surprise, but he was serious.

"Not entirely," she went on. "But it helped me realize he was an experience seeker—from sailing he moved on to rock climbing, which I didn't love—"

"So that's why you said you had done it before, when we were on the treasure hunt."

"Yes. At the gym a couple times. I would hardly have been ready for it if we had to do it on the hunt. The thing is, he was into marking things off on an imaginary experience list. I thought once we found something we both liked we could stick with it. Or maybe he didn't like sailing as much as he said. For a long time, I wondered whether I should have been more patient. But I wanted to be on boats. I found my passion. I didn't want to keep trying other things."

"I thought I was your passion."

Beth could not help smiling at the boldness of his remark, given the context. He may have made a cowardly exit from his previous relationship, but he had never been that way with her.

"You are."

"After *Trouble*."

"You may have scootched ahead of her these last few months."

"No kidding?" his smile turned languorous, as if getting this conversation out of the way was a relief. She didn't bother to reply.

"What time do you want to go to the boat show?"

"Jeff and Carole are going too. We paid extra for the Friday admission because it's a lot less crowded."

"My interview is at 8:30 in the morning."

"Oh right—where do you need to be?"

"It's a phone interview."

"Oh, good. Depending on how it goes, we can head out late morning."

Beth nodded. "This is going to be fun. Thank you so much for thinking of it. Hey, Annapolis. I just realized—"

"Where we met. I know." His smile was more than just happy—there was a hint of something else, something secretive. It made Beth tingle deep inside.

St. Hillaire, Guadeloupe

Over breakfast of buttery croissants and rich coffee, Hunter wracked his brain trying to think of ways to locate one elderly woman with a fancy house on St. Hillaire. The woman had to get her groceries in the village, and she had to receive mail. But he knew the officials at the post office—a desk in the police constable's office—could not tell him her address. A grocer might, if convinced it was worth his while.

Just then Madame Favre re-entered the dining room bearing a tray laden with two more baskets of croissants for two other guests.

"Madame? A word?"

She set the tray on the sideboard next to the half-full French press and picked up the baskets before turning back to the table.

"Certainly, Monsieur. One moment."

Hunter felt rudely impatient as he watched her serve her other guests, exchanging small talk with them and ensuring they had all they needed. Finally, she stepped around the table to stand at Hunter's side.

"Monsieur?"

"I am looking for someone. A woman named Madame Gardien. She has a home on the island. I need to speak with her." He added the last to reassure her, in case she did not trust his motives.

Madame Favre pursed her lips, her narrow face pinching comically. She held her hands clasped over the belly of her cotton print dress as she thought. Finally, she shook her head. "No, monsieur. I do not know her." But she tilted her head to one side and smiled impishly. "Wait!" she said, raising one finger in the air as if to emphasize her idea, and left the dining room. The other guests had watched the exchange and turned curious eyes on Hunter when their hostess vanished.

She came back in an instant carrying the thick telephone directory from the table in the hall. It was the Guadeloupe directory, Hunter knew because he had glanced at it last night. But Madame Favre set it on the table by his place and began to page through it, murmuring "Gardien, Gardien," as she went. Hunter watched the thin paper pages turn until she stopped and ran her index finger down a page dense with individual listings.

"*Viola!*"

He looked at the page where her finger had stopped at a listing for Gardien, Madame. It included a telephone number and an address here on the island. Hunter felt the fool. St. Hillaire was part of Guadeloupe. The directory included it.

"May I use the telephone?"

*

But Madame Guardien did not answer the telephone, and apparently did not employ an answering machine. Hunter considered and discarded the notion of hiring a taxi to take him to her address. It might be quite remote, and he risked frightening the elderly woman showing up unannounced.

Instead he used the guest house's ancient, beige desktop computer, which came complete with internet access via a wire to a dusty router on a shelf above it. He didn't know enough about computer networks to figure out how it reached the internet; what mattered was that it worked. The computer's hulking cathode ray tube monitor slowly painted a map of St. Hilliare: a cluster of roads in the northeast around the bay thinning out to follow the island's coastline, with two or three winding around the interior, climbing and circling the island's mountainous terrain. Hunter typed Madame Gardien's address in the search box, the old mechanical keyboard clacking loudly with each keystroke, and pressed the filthy Enter key.

A red pin appeared next to one of the roads near the southwest corner of the island. It was one of the coastal roads that turned inward to the north of the address. He switched to satellite view. There were other houses along the road, but they were separated by stretches of jungle. Since there was no road between the house and the cove to its southwest, he suspected the house had access to the water there, making it all the more valuable. He reminded himself that he didn't want to buy real estate. What mattered was that it was too far to walk. His best option was to get in touch by phone before taking a taxi there.

He tried calling once more—with no success—before making arrangements with Madame Favre to stay another night. With nothing to do until it was worth calling again, he set out on a walk. He was accosted the moment he reached the main street by a pre-teen boy asking if he was headed for the distillery. He had seen a sign for it the day before, but he had no interest in it since he couldn't consume its product. He declined the boy's advances and strolled on toward the waterfront. The boy followed him at a distance. Two blocks down an older boy made him the same offer, glancing back behind Hunter as he spoke. Hunter declined again and walked on. A block later he turned the corner so he could glance back up the street. Sure enough, both boys were following him, each one avoiding the other. This could get ugly. He stopped and turned. They both stopped, glancing surreptitiously at each other. Hunter grinned and gestured at them, making eye contact with each of them one at a time.

"Come here," he said loudly enough for them both to hear. Continuing to eye one another with what appeared to be hostility they came down the hill to stand before him. He suspected that they understood his English well enough, so he went on.

"I'm not going to the distillery. I don't drink. I don't want to buy any rum. I'm not looking for someone else to show me where it is. Understand?"

The boys openly looked at one another.

"You sure mon? De rum good," the older one said, accent more creole than pure French.

"I'm sure. I don't drink, don't want any rum. I'll tell you what, if you'll tell me where I can get a baguette and ham and some sliced cheese, there's a Euro in it."

The boys exchanged a glance, competition sparking again.

"A Euro for each of you."

The younger boy grinned and Hunter realized he'd been had. *Hell, they're probably brothers.*

The two boys cheerfully guided him down another block and to the right, ending up at a bakery that was emitting delicious smells. He handed each boy a Euro and went inside.

This had to be where Madame Favre got her croissants. But the boys had cheated him after all: the bakery had no sliced meats or cheeses, only breads. Annoyed, he bought a baguette and stepped outside. The boys were nowhere to be seen, although he half expected them to demand two more Euros to show him to a shop with meats and cheeses. Carrying the baguette in its paper wrapper that didn't cover the ends, he walked on, trying to recall where he'd seen a grocery.

He found it and purchased sliced ham and Swiss cheese and a bottle of Coke that cost more than the food. He used his pocket knife to cut the bread in half and fit it into his daypack, then shouldered the bag and set out with his picnic to find a quiet beach. It wasn't difficult. A road at the north end of the harbor took him along the coast past a couple rocky points to a sandy northeast facing beach where a few other people were enjoying the sun and sea breeze. He found a secluded spot where he could read, and made a delicious sandwich from the bread, meat, and cheese. Mid-afternoon he awakened abruptly from an unplanned nap, his paperback novel spread open on his chest.

"Damn, I'm more tired than I thought," he said out loud as he looked around the beach. As when he arrived, a few groups of people and loners were enjoying the sun, but nobody was near him, nor so much as looking his way. He stuffed his book and empty Coke bottle into his bag and strode up the beach to the road.

Back at the guest house he assumed Madame's earlier permission was still in effect and telephoned Madame Gardien once more.

This time there was a mechanical click followed by a steady, female voice. "*Bonjour.*"

"*Bonjour*, Madame Gardien *S'il vous plaît.*"

"This is she," the voice switched to English. Hunter cringed at how bad his accent must be.

"Madame, my name is Hunter Green. I am seeking information about a friend who I believe once stayed at your home. I wonder if I might visit you to speak about her?" He had not considered until this very moment how to ask her about someone who stayed with the gang who had taken over her home.

"A mutual friend?" Hesitancy was clear in her tone.

"I do not believe so, no. She was, I think, an unwilling companion to the leader of the group that occupied your home some months ago."

"The young woman. Yes."

"Oregon Chapman is her name," he said, not sure whether her "yes" meant she would speak to him, or simply that she knew who he meant. "May I come see you, perhaps tomorrow? I will not take very much of your time."

"I know very little."

"Please, Madame. It is very important to me. I came from the US looking for her and for her friend, the woman who took her to the hospital."

"Beth. Very well. You may come tomorrow afternoon."

⏜

"Her situation was very dangerous. I am sorry that I was, at first, reluctant to help. As it happened, the episode restored my property to me. What is it you want to know?"

Hunter had arrived by taxi at Madame Gardien's home at exactly two o'clock, as she had instructed. A young black woman in an un-ironic, unrelated to porn, French maid uniform admitted him and brought him to meet Madame in a great room with a breathtaking view of the Caribbean. Madame had asked him to sit on a settee across from her and ordered cold Perrier for them both.

Unsettled by her abrupt introduction of the subject at hand, Hunter mentally stammered before opening his mouth to speak. Madame's raised eyebrows conveyed impatience.

"There is a chance I am the father of her baby."

Coral pink lips pursed as her head tilted slightly to the right. She watched him for a long moment before speaking.

"Why was she with that creature?"

"I didn't know she was pregnant when she left. I knew her in Jamaica. If I'd known about the baby, I would have begged her to stay with me."

Madame nodded slightly, still watching him. The maid reappeared with a tray of green bottles and glasses, distracting Madame and giving him a moment to form his thoughts.

"You said helping her helped restore your property to you. I hope the positive outcome of that act will encourage you to tell me anything you can." He spoke after the drinks were poured and they each held a glass of bubbling water in their hand.

"He was a monster and she was trapped. I knew that even though I never left my room while they were here. They had moved in on me before she joined them. I don't know why they didn't kill me, but perhaps they knew better than to commit that level of crime. I had retreated to my room where they brought me enough food to sustain me, awful as it was. That night her friend came to my door and begged me to help get her out of the house. I realized if I did not act, I might never dislodge them, and she and the child might not survive."

"Do you know what happened to her after that? I've read the newspaper article about how the musician tried to kidnap the baby from the hospital, over on Guadeloupe. I know her friend, Beth, is the one who got her to the hospital. I'm trying to find Ori, but I think I might have a better chance of finding this Beth Anderson first."

"Ori returned with her parents to Connecticut. That is what Beth and her friends told me when they returned here, afterwards."

"Connecticut!"

"Yes. I'm afraid you're a long way from finding your child, Monsieur Green."

"What about Beth Anderson? You see, I have tried to reach Ori by email, and she has not replied. I think Beth will know how to reach her."

Madame Garden studied him once again. She seemed to be trying to decide whether he was a fool.

"Beth is a sailor. She might be still in the islands. She has her own boat. I don't recall the name."

"She wasn't here on vacation, or to find Ori?"

"She came here to find her friend, but she was not on a 'vacation.' She is one of these cruisers, who go from island to island. I don't know how they cover their expenses."

"A cruising sailor. I see. That does make sense."

"Does it?"

"I mean it explains why she was looking for her friend by sailboat instead of flying here."

"Yes. I have one other thought," Madame said, as if she believed Beth Anderson to be a dead end and she was about to offer his one real hope. "St. Hilaire has been without professional medical care since the incident. Our island nurse practitioner was involved in the scheme to kidnap the infant, so he is in jail. His wife remains at his clinic. She might be willing to speak to you."

"She might know where Beth Anderson went?"

Madame shot him an impatient look. "I have no idea. But she was among the last to see Ori on this island. Perhaps she has contact information."

Realizing this was tantamount to a dismissal, Hunter drained his glass of Perrier and excused himself. As it turned out, his prediction of a half hour visit with Madame Gardien had been perfect. The taxi appeared around a bend in the road as he reached the parking area above the house.

Eleven

Georgetown, Washington, D.C.

*B*eth had just ended the call with the interviewer on Friday morning when her phone rang, the caller ID announcing Tom Biffle. Her last conversation with him rushed back and she realized she never mentioned it to Terry. With considerable apprehension she answered the call.

"Hi Beth, it's Tom Biffle."

Beth found it interesting to see who assumed you had caller ID and who pretended you did not. She didn't know what it said about people, but she was sure it said something.

"Hi Tom, good to hear from you."

"I thought I'd call and see how the hunt is going. Any luck?"

"Maybe. I put myself on a couple of the websites and now I'm getting flooded with junk email from fly-by-night companies."

"Oh dear. Sorry about that."

"Cost of doing business, I guess. But I do have a couple real leads. Well, one, I guess. I get these calls from headhunters who grill me and hang up."

"Yeah, it's a pretty competitive business—they need to qualify you or move on as fast as possible. Don't let it get to you."

"It doesn't—I can tell the jobs are not up my alley. There was one with something in Pentagon City that needed a security clearance. She accused me of lying on my resume, about the last few months."

"Well we know your time sailing is going to be questioned. And the clearance could be a problem. I take it that went nowhere?"

"I think she forwarded my resume to them and they shot it back, that's why she was so hostile."

"Probably—she should have read it more carefully and screened you out. Now her client is annoyed. Not your problem. Any others?"

"I just got off the phone from an interview."

Beth went on to describe the job and firm and Tom coached her should she be called for an in-person second interview. She had no sense of whether it had gone well or not, she was so out of touch with the working world. Tom was kind and encouraging. And then he asked about Terry.

"He must be too busy to do much else. Deal about done?"

"Just about signed, sealed, and delivered. But he's found a little time. We're going to the boat show in Annapolis in a couple hours. I'm so looking forward to it. Which reminds me, I need to call the headhunter and tell him how the interview went."

"Right, they like that. I'll let you go. Have fun in Annapolis."

Beth called the recruiter and described the interview in her best terms. He said he had not heard from the client yet but would call late morning if he hadn't heard yet. She made sure he had her cell phone number and told him she would be out for the rest of the day but would be waiting for him to call.

As she shut down her computer and prepared for the day in Annapolis she reflected on her talk with Tom and decided she was silly. He was just being friendly inquiring about his former bosses.

*)

Annapolis, Maryland

Traffic on Route 50 slowed to a crawl as they neared the exit for Annapolis.

"We could try to park in Eastport and walk over," Jeff said, looking into the rear-view mirror to catch Terry's eye. Jeff was, Beth had realized moments after getting into the back seat of his Jeep with Terry, an impatient driver.

"Sure, if you can get there. And if we can find a spot." Terry loaded his response with unstated messages: the traffic would be just as bad getting to Eastport and parking would be limited. Beth didn't know where Eastport was, so she couldn't express an opinion, but she trusted Terry's judgment. Apparently, Jeff had heard Terry's silent concerns.

"Yeah, let's go with the crowd."

Beth pondered the nuances of this exchange as they inched forward and made it through the traffic light at the end of the off ramp. These two men had a very complex, close relationship. Linda, Terry's former girlfriend, had threatened it. Carole did not. But Beth already knew she was not willing to play the same role to Terry that Carole served for Jeff. Could she possibly make this work? The idea of giving up was too depressing to contemplate.

Jeff followed parking attendants' directions to a large field where he parked the Jeep among rows of other vehicles. When they got out, Jeff slung an empty duffle bag over his shoulder. During the ride he had listed the items he wanted to purchase for his racing boat, *Grace*. Despite owning her own boat, Beth couldn't guess at what some of things he mentioned were for and she gave up asking after his first three technical explanations. His boat competed for his limited attention with his work, his kids, and Carole, and Beth knew it often won out over the family. From her seat behind Jeff she had occasionally seen Carole's face in profile. It remained composed as she gazed out the window, apparently ignoring the conversation. Beth didn't know her well enough to know whether she was lost in thought, angry, or brooding.

Beth had her daypack with enough room for anything she might purchase. Not that she could afford much. She had a list as long as her arm of stuff *Trouble* needed, but even if she shortened the list to what she could carry in the daypack she still couldn't afford ninety percent of it. She knew she would be tempted by all kinds of things she didn't know she wanted. As they walked to the show shuttle bus, she reminded herself that she was not here to shop. She was here to spend a day with Terry. Her hand reached for his of its own accord and he glanced over and smiled, giving her hand a squeeze.

Beth had augmented her recollection of Annapolis from her short visit last year by studying an on-line map last night. Leaning over her shoulder, Terry had pointed out the town dock and explained that the show would be centered there with pavilions in the parking area and temporary docks filling the rectangular inner harbor. The show's website listed hundreds of vendors, including all of the major cruising boat manufacturers. Beth looked forward to climbing all over a lot of beautiful new boats with features that were unheard of when *Trouble* was built.

The bus disgorged them amid a crowd of other sailors at one of the several entrance gates into the show. Beyond the guardians at the gate a row of white vinyl pavilions sheltered vendor booths from the morning sun. It was a perfect Indian Summer day and seeing Terry in shorts that morning, Beth had switched to them too. Now she was glad. Carole, she noted, wore slacks that Beth would reserve for work—a rich woven fabric in beige—and an ivory cotton cardigan over a navy-blue t-shirt. The outfit was vaguely nautical and professional, and somehow made Carole appear much older than the rest of them in their shorts and polo shirts. As they walked along an aisle between booths Beth decided Carole looked like she should be stationed behind one of the insurance companies' tables.

They agreed to go first to the boats amid the network of temporary docks in the harbor. When Beth was there last, this had been an inlet of open water with a promenade, parking, and restaurants lining either side and floating docks along the seawall. She had anchored *Trouble* out in the river with hundreds of other boats. Now the river was so clogged with anchored boats she could almost imagine walking from deck to deck, and the harbor was a maze of temporary floating docks penning the multitude of new and classic boats on display.

In one area the temporary floating docks formed a pond where show attendees were allowed to try out a variety of small boats. Elsewhere huge crewed charter yachts flew flocks of brightly colored flags from their tall rigging while herds of uniformed crew extolled their virtues as a vacation option to visitors on deck. Banners with manufacturers' logos fluttered on the masts of the ranks of boats, most of them sharing advertising space with the biggest charter companies whose logos were all too familiar to Beth from their huge fleets in the Caribbean.

Beth felt her excitement building as she spotted *Trouble*'s brand and other brands she and Terry had discussed, sharing vague dreams about the perfect boat. Now those dreams were potentially real: somewhere among all these hulls might be a boat to capture both their hearts. Beth felt a pang of guilt for considering a boat other than her dear *Trouble*. But she had to admit that as they finished their months in the islands, she had started to see how *Trouble* was her starter boat, like an elementary teacher who would, when the time came, push her onward to her next mentor, and that mentor would be bigger and more modern. But she could not contemplate purchasing this as yet unidentified new boat on her own. The new boat would have to be a joint venture with Terry. The idea both thrilled and scared her: it played to all her phobias about finances and added to her concerns about their relationship. But the possibilities it opened up were tempting enough to overpower her fear.

Be optimistic for once, at least while you're here, she told herself as they stepped down the ramp and onto the floating docks.

All but Carole—who wore cute, strappy sandals—had on deck shoes. But as it turned out they were all required to go barefoot on every one of the boats on display. Leaving their shoes on the dock they stepped on pristine white fiberglass or deeply oiled teak, automatically adjusting their balance against the slight sway of each boat.

Rather than pick a particular boat make or size, they simply started at one side of the makeshift marina and worked their way along the docks. Jeff observed that the extra money for Friday tickets was worth it, because tomorrow there would be long lines to get on every boat. Today they could see them all. Carole wondered why he cared, since he had no intention of buying one. She muttered so softly only Beth heard it, and it made her realize that Carole would not enjoy herself at the boat show. Beth couldn't imagine not wanting to spend a day looking at boats, so she chalked it up to the differences in their interests. But she couldn't help wondering if Carole and Linda had found something else to do together when Jeff and Terry came to the show in the past. No. From what Terry had said of Linda, she had as little in common with Carole as she would have with Beth.

The first three boats were from a manufacturer for which Beth had little respect. Throughout her cruising when a fellow cruiser's boat had structural defects or a shabby interior more often than not it turned out to be one of these. Their designs were targeted at inexperienced and non-sailors—wives whose husbands desperately wanted a boat but needed their spouse to agree. Their galleys, saloons, and master suites were spacious with plenty of headroom. Their cockpits were uncluttered. But Beth's sailor's eye had long ago spotted the flaws: open spaces provided few handholds in heavy seas. They built the boat like an empty eggshell: easy to crush. Beyond the design, the hardware on these boats was second rate, the winches undersized, the cleats insufficient in number and size, the railing and lines lacking in the few extra fasteners that would make them truly seaworthy. In a short time, Beth, Terry, and Jeff trooped off all three vessels. Carole trailed them commenting on the lovely woodwork below.

Next came *Trouble*'s manufacturer. These boats were built sturdily, if not for speed. Looking at the newer, bigger models Beth felt a sense of familiarity—the design of the cabinet latches, the placement of hand holds, the shape of the portals, and the unusual ivory color of the deck and hull were all the same as *Trouble*. Catching Terry's eye as they stood in the forward cabin of one of them, she saw he was having the same reaction.

"You can see the genes, can't you? Like *Trouble* is this boat's little old grandmother," she said, running a hand over the top of a cabinet where, on *Trouble*, she stored her clothes.

"Feels like home." He reached out with his left hand to stroke a lock of hair away from her face. "Miss it?"

"A little."

"*Trouble*'s a good boat. But I want a more agile keel design. All of these have full keels like her."

It was his first concrete reference to this being a shopping expedition. It made her head whirl to realize he had been thinking along those lines too. Suddenly her thoughts about what kind of boat to graduate to transitioned from daydream to realistic and she realized she agreed with him.

"Something this seaworthy, but with a fin keel." She nodded, smiling into his eyes.

"Great minds think alike."

"You have a wish list?"

"Don't you?" He grinned, then his expression turned to concern. "I mean, we're just talking about it …"

"Well, I didn't bring my checkbook!" She chuckled tensely, uncertain again.

He shrugged, looking around the staged cabin with its decorator sheets and throw pillows. "Boat show specials are usually pretty decent." His eyes turned back to hers, his secretive smile from the previous afternoon returning. *He is thinking of buying this weekend.*

"I think we should keep an open mind," Beth concealed her absurd disappointment. Somehow down in her girlish emotional depths she had hoped his secret was a planned proposal. Not that she was ready to deal with one, but on a deep level she wanted to be asked.

"Good. But not one of these. Let's see what else we can see."

Jeff was already waiting on the dock when they climbed out of the boat and moved on to the next.

"Where's Carole?" Beth asked, looking back at the boat they'd been on, although Jeff's wife had not been in the cabin when they left it.

"She went to find a bathroom." Jeff shrugged dismissively. "She'll catch up with us."

"Eventually," Terry said quietly. Not quietly enough that Jeff couldn't hear, but low enough that he could ignore it.

The next set of boats were sleek racers with stripped down living space. This time Jeff kept them waiting while he questioned the sales rep—a portly guy in shirt and tie who Beth thought had been selling cars last week—about technical details. After a few minutes the salesman took advantage of the arrival of more guests and proffered a technical specification sheet for Jeff to take away.

"Thinking of trading up?" Terry asked as they ambled along the dock to the next boats.

"Not sure it would be." Jeff studied the sheet. "They price them as if they are, but their record doesn't support it."

It didn't surprise Beth that Jeff knew the performance records of various types of racing sailboats. He was a serious competitor.

The next boats were hybrids of race boats and cruising boats, a design concept that the manufacturer hoped would attract both the Jeffs and the Caroles of the sailing world. They were designed in France and built in the US, and to Beth's mind they were for coastal cruising and hopping between Caribbean islands. There were three sizes on display: the smallest at thirty-six feet was the same size as *Trouble*; the next was ten feet longer; and the biggest seemed huge at fifty-two feet. They toured the smallest, but both Beth and Terry knew without saying it that they were looking for something larger. The brand new, un-lived in boat did look bigger, but they knew that would change once it was packed with gear.

"I feel like Goldilocks," Beth said as they boarded the medium sized boat, making Terry laugh.

"That would mean this boat is just right," Jeff said.

"I think we have to see the big one too, before deciding," Terry said, testing the flexibility of the steering console by grabbing the wheel and trying to move it back and forth. An attendant shot him an annoyed look. "I read these have quality issues—inferior fasteners, lightweight cables and belts, that sort of thing."

"I heard they're underpowered for cruisers, but overpowered for racers," Jeff put in, smiling winningly at the now irritated attendant.

Beth shot the woman a smile and climbed down into the cabin to distance herself from them. She already knew that, perfect size aside, she didn't want a racer/cruiser. But she did admit that these boats were beautiful, with hundreds of design details missing from the first few boats. Every space was efficiently used, the latches on cabinets and drawers were easy to use but strong, the refrigerator had two openings, top and side. Up on deck the winches were in the right places to be easily used, and the deck hardware was of high quality.

But Jeff was right, the engine in the forty-six-foot boat was about the same horsepower as *Trouble's* at thirty-six feet. It was a light engine for racing, but with insufficient power to maneuver the boat in heavy seas and winds. Beth knew enough about those conditions to know she was not interested in a boat without power attached to the propeller. If she could spend all her time on the water sailing and anchoring it wouldn't matter, but marinas required the ability to make tight turns contrary to wind and current.

As they approached the next set of boats Terry leaned close, one hand on her shoulder, "let's take a look at these. They're designed for blue water sailing."

Beth could see that before they stepped aboard. The deck hardware was serious stuff. There were extra fittings for safety lines and heavy-duty hand holds in appropriate places. The smallest boat was forty feet and felt cozy below with a smaller saloon and larger cabins fore and aft. It had two heads with wet lockers for hanging bathing suits and foul weather gear.

Beth found herself nodding in recognition of a multitude of details to would make long passages easier: storage under the floor boards, a drawer and hooks in the companionway to be reachable from out in the cockpit, plenty of cup holders in the cockpit, and a large swim platform that folded up to form a closed stern when underway. Her excitement grew with each new discovery. This boat could replace *Trouble*.

But Terry tore her away to tour the next one, which was six feet longer. It had twin wheels to allow the helmsman to sit far out to either side while steering. He went to the helm on the starboard side and pointed to a joystick control mounted above the engine gauges.

"What's that?" Beth asked, noting his excited grin.

"Bow thrusters!" He gave the joystick a flick.

"Ooooh," Beth stroked the leather-covered wheel.

"Very handy."

"No kidding. I can think of a few times I could have used them."

Her eyes met his and she knew it—this was the boat he wanted.

"It's big." She looked forward across the seemingly endless deck. "Almost ten feet longer than *Trouble*, and half again as wide at least."

"Don't you dare start thinking about slip fees right now," he said, teasing. "Dream for a few minutes while we look. Promise?"

"Promise," she agreed, and stepped around the cockpit table to climb up onto the deck. On the other boats she'd gone below to explore but made cursory examinations of the decks. This time she led Terry all the way forward to the bow, looking at placement of fittings on deck and the mast. There was nothing she didn't like. They made their way back and inside where they found Jeff sitting at the saloon table talking with the sales woman.

"Here they are," he said. "I was explaining to Gerry here that I'm a racer through and through, but you guys want to head offshore."

"Well, I don't know about—" Beth started, but Gerry jumped right in.

"This would be the boat to do it in. Solid design and craftsmanship, well powered, great fuel and water capacity, and did you see the bow thrusters?"

Beth considered pointing out that thrusters were hardly useful in open water but held her tongue. The woman was just doing her job. Instead she toured at the beautifully appointed galley. By the time she finished Terry had taken Jeff's place at the table.

He's serious, she thought, her heart skipping a beat.

What are we getting into? What am I getting into? I'll have to sell Trouble to pay my share. Hell, I couldn't sell her for anywhere near enough. This is crazy.

Jeff gestured her to follow him into the forward berth. She complied, not surprised when he leaned close and murmured, "let him negotiate. He'll get her to give him a price guarantee for a few months."

"So we can think about it?"

"Charter one somewhere and try it out."

"Oh!"

Beth became distracted by the row of enclosed cabinets along the bulkhead of the cabin. On most boats there were open shelves. She thought the woodwork was walnut and the hardware was definitely bronze. She opened the door to the adjacent head and admired stainless steel fittings and a head that wasn't crammed into a narrow slot as so many were.

She and Jeff worked their way through the entire boat while Terry talked with Gerry. As they passed by the two were in deep conversation, each pointing at information on a printed sheet on the table.

The galley was perfect, there was no other way to describe it: it had room for two people to cook at once and brace themselves in rough seas. The designer had somehow crammed in a freezer as well as refrigerator, and a microwave oven.

"I think it's on an inverter," Jeff said, nodding at the appliance, meaning it could be used when the engine or auxiliary generator was running, not just when the boat was plugged in at a dock. Beth considered that an unnecessary luxury.

But if you have it …

"What do you think?" Terry asked when they were back on the dock. He folded an envelope into his back pocket as he spoke.

"Gorgeous. And priced to match," Beth sighed. She'd seen the sticker price prominently displayed on a specification sheet by the helm.

"About the same as *Grace*," Jeff put in, as if it would help. In a way it did. *Grace* was five feet shorter and hardly live-able. If the same money could buy all this boat's amenities maybe it was a good deal.

Terry shook his head at his partner. "Apples to oranges," he said. "You overfitted *Grace* with racing toys. You're right Beth, this boat is not cheap. But do you want to risk your life crossing an ocean on a cheap boat?"

"Am I crossing an ocean?"

His slight frown cautioned her. Her question had been flippant, and wrong. They had discussed it—day dreamed about it anyway—and she shouldn't pretend they had not. She nodded acquiescence.

"I would love to sail that boat," she said, looking back at it. "Jeff said you might try to negotiate something."

"We could do a charter," Terry said. "Thing is, when? It can't be very soon, and I'm not sure they'll honor the base price I just negotiated for long enough."

"What did you negotiate?"

Terry told her the number. It was less than the one on the specification sheet, but still astronomical. "That's base. We'll want to add about a hundred grand of extras."

She gasped, although she was hardly as innocent of the way this worked than she felt. She knew what the base price would include and what more they needed—the inverter and microwave, for example—but for a moment she wanted to remain the innocent window shopper.

"Come on, let's find lunch," Jeff said, seeing her turmoil. Terry stared at her for another long moment before turning to his partner and agreeing.

"Better call Carole," he said, bringing home the fact that his wife had not returned from the bathroom. Neither man seemed surprised.

Twelve

St. Hillaire, Gaudeloupe

*H*unter just missed the mail boat's departure when he got back to town after his visit with Madame Gardien. He got out of the taxi and stood at the foot of the commercial wharf watching the ship as it's smoke stack spewed a westward pointing trail of dark diesel exhaust. Just like the last two evenings, the pleasure boats were beginning to arrive in the harbor. He was unlikely to find anyone heading to Pointe-à-Pitre now, and he didn't want to catch a ride with someone after they'd been partying at the bars. He hoped Madame Favre would welcome him for another night.

On his way up the main street he thought about Madame Gardien's suggestion. He stepped into a shop whose display of household goods and cleaning products seemed oddly desperate, much of it covered in a thick layer of dust. A middle-aged woman with startlingly enormous breasts looked up from behind an old mechanical cash register. He got the impression she was counting the day's income.

"Nous sommes fermés," she said. Hunter was surprised by her curt tone. Not every creole was friendly, apparently.

"Pouvez-vous me diriger vers la clinique?" he asked, deciding her tone didn't warrant the usual pleasantries.

Scowling, she told him it was two blocks up and along to the right. He thanked her and fled.

He found Madame Lalande, the wife of the jailed nurse practitioner, to be even less friendly than the shop keeper. She held domain over what must have once been a two-room clinic but now appeared to do dual service as a clinic in one room and her living space in the other. She answered the door when he knocked and stood in the doorway listening to his request. Her expression went from passive to angry when he mentioned the two women who had come for help, one of them in labor. He avoided mentioning the aftermath and her husband's arrest, but obviously that was the only part of the episode that mattered to her. She leaned against the edge of her door, one hand wrapped around it near her face. Her glare was almost painful to withstand. When he asked if either woman had left contact information, she straightened, shook her head, and shut the door without another word.

"Yeah," he muttered to himself as he walked back toward the main street. "Bad idea."

Back in the guest house Madame Favre was tidying the common sitting room when he entered. As he hoped, she welcomed him back and asked him about his day. He was disinterested in providing her with a full recounting that would no doubt spread through town in a matter of hours, and he was feeling stung by Madame Lalande's response.

"Madame Favre, do you know Madame Lalande?"

Madame Favre paused, her dust cloth resting on a side table. "Yes. Abigail Lalande. Poor woman."

"Why poor?"

"Her husband is in jail. She lost their home, and I hear she may be forced out of where she lives now. Do you know her?" She gave him a puzzled look and he realized that this tidbit was going to spread.

"I just spoke to her. I thought she might be able to give me information, but she was unwilling to help."

"She was—how to put it?—very proud of her social position because of her husband. Now she has almost nothing. The people do go to her for bandaging and aspirins, but it is out of pity, not necessity. Many to whom she was cruel in the past do not do even that to help the poor woman."

"I see. We reap what we sew."

"A curious expression, but yes, just so."

"Will she be put out on the street?"

"No monsieur, this is France." Hunter could not miss the hint of condemnation of his native nation. "But she may need to move to Pointe-à-Pitre, to inexpensive housing."

"I see. I'm sorry for her misfortune."

"What was it you thought she could help you with? Perhaps there is someone else…"

"No, thank you Madame. It was only a possibility, and not important."

He excused himself and went to his room to drop his backpack before going to find dinner.

I have to get off this island before I start hearing stories about myself.

)

Annapolis, Maryland

Carole met them on the dockside terrace of a restaurant that was part of a chain boasting six or seven members, most in the British Virgin Islands. Beth had been to two of them. This one was populated with sailors enjoying a reminder of a favorite cruising area and tourists who thought they were experience a real Caribbean dining experience. It felt to Beth like an Americanized version of the ones in the islands, closer to Red Lobster than a local island place. She knew, for example, that the items marked "hot" on the menu would not be, and there was no chance of sand on floor in the ladies' room.

Still, it was fun to pretend to be on a tropical vacation for a few minutes. She could see Jeff thought so too.

"Who's up for a pain killer?" he asked, rubbing both hands together eagerly.

"I'll have a glass of white wine," Carole said in a compromising tone, as if she didn't quite approve of drinking at lunch.

"I could do it," Beth decided, imagining the heady feel of the first, cool, fruity sip.

"Let's go for it," Terry concurred, smiling at her.

"Up for the strong one?" Jeff coaxed, referring to the one with three shots of rum.

Beth shook her head but let Terry speak for her, "Not a chance. I want to browse the vendors. A number two will do."

"Three number two pain killers and a glass of chardonnay," Jeff told the hovering waiter, who nodded and disappeared.

"Did you see all the boats?" Carole sounded hopeful.

"No, but I think I've seen enough," Terry said, looking at Beth.

"Terry's started negotiations for a boat," Jeff said.

Carole's eyes widened. "You think you'll have time for a boat now?" Her glance at Jeff was almost accusing. Beth thought she could hear the silent message—if Terry has time to buy a boat, why don't you have time for your family?

"Not immediately, no," Terry said. "But it would give Beth a project."

"I need a job, not a project," Beth reminded him, surprised at herself for not resenting his suggestion that she needed to be amused. Perhaps because she knew he didn't mean it that way. "Especially if we're going to buy a boat."

Carole looked from Terry to Beth and back, her expression enigmatic.

"Always practical," Jeff said to Beth, "I knew I liked you from the start."

"Just always broke," Beth quipped back. "But I suppose there are very few ways I'd rather spend my meager income than on an amazingly beautiful boat."

Terry turned a delighted smile on her.

"You're going in together on a boat?" Carole asked, revealing that her enigmatic expression was surprise.

"Maybe," Terry said cautiously. "We haven't discussed it in any detail yet."

"Yeah, there's a lot to figure out. I'll have to sell *Trouble* to begin to afford my share." She saw Terry watching her and realized he had not been sure she was willing to think about it. "Well how on earth did you think I could consider it?" she asked him, too impatient to wait for him to express what she knew he was thinking.

"Hey, I didn't say anything!"

For a moment she wondered if this entire thing had been a game, with him thinking she would ultimately veto it because she was too attached to *Trouble*. Now he had to put his money where his mouth was or admit he didn't want to do it. His expression was as enigmatic as Carole's a moment before. He looked across at their companions and back at Beth, coming to a decision.

"I thought you would have to be convinced. I wasn't looking forward to it. You'd think I don't love *Trouble*."

"Love her? I guess I don't expect you to love her. She's a boat. My boat."

"Bethy, she's more than just a boat. She's our place. Here I am suggesting we replace her, but maybe neither of us are ready to give her up. I don't know."

Beth was relieved that both Carole and Jeff kept their mouths shut, and she understood Terry's reluctance to discuss it right now. She felt a flash of guilt at forcing the issue but got over it. If she waited until they were alone, he would repeat it all to Jeff anyway.

"It's about moving on," she said softly. "Just like my father."

She heard a sound like a sympathetic groan from across the table but couldn't tell which of them had made it. Terry nodded slowly, eyes locked with hers. Her father's condition may not change for many more months, even years. She could not postpone her life waiting for it. The realization felt like a weight removed. She found Terry's hand and took it, feeling him squeeze back. His sweet, blue eyes were brighter than she could ever remember, and she wanted never to stop looking into them.

The piercing blast of an air horn broke their gaze. Most of the diners turned toward the source of the annoying sound, a guy on one of the luxury crewed charter yachts tied along this stretch of dock.

"Sorry," he shouted to the crowds all around, looking sheepish. They saw him replacing the offending horn in a cup holder on the steering column. One of the boat's crew immediately removed it and disappeared below.

Just then their waiter appeared with their drinks and the awkward, emotional moment passed. Jeff proposed a toast to new boats and old and they refocused their attentions on the menus to make their lunch selections.

They spent the rest of the afternoon perusing the stalls looking at gadgets, tools, clothes, shoes, and toys. Beth lingered over the water purifiers, something she wanted to install on *Trouble*. Even the hand-pumped ones intrigued her.

"I think we should have one installed," Terry said, looking with her at a model that could desalinate sixteen gallons an hour and weighed one hundred sixty pounds.

Beth smiled, slipping back into the shopping game. "Put it on the list."

They admired the high-tech sail materials that Jeff stopped to drool over and waited while he filled out a form requesting a quote.

"*Grace*'s number one has about had it," he explained as they moved on. Beth recalled his largest jib—it had seemed brand new last year when she sailed with him.

Carole stopped at a clothing and accessories booth to admire a line of bags made of old sails. Beth liked them too: they were lightweight, well made, and had interesting graphics because of the numbers and logos from the sails incorporated into the designs.

"Do you want a bag for work? This isn't exactly a Coach briefcase, but it is more you." Terry held up a messenger bag with part of a blue number three on the flap. The lining was a blue and white tropical print and the dark blue webbing shoulder strap was wide and well attached to the bag.

"It would hold my laptop," she said, taking it from him.

"You should get it. It's you," Carole put in. That made Beth bristle. Who was Carole to tell her how to spend money, and to know her style?

But she slung the bag over her shoulder and stepped over to a full-length mirror. She did like it. And now she felt petty for resenting Carole's input. It would be a better shore bag than the open topped canvas tote she used. *Stop it, you're not shopping for cruising right now. Will you carry this around Washington?* She looked at it on her shoulder again. *Yes. It's attractive, and it keeps me connected to being a sailor.*

The price was steep for a retired sail, but she used her debit card to avoid building up credit card debt. While she paid, Carole roped Jeff into trying on new deck shoes—heavily marked down for the show—then Terry got into it too, and before they were done the three of them had all bought shoes. Carole's were an absurdity, at least in Beth's estimation, called "sailing sandals." Not the secure strapped kind, but flip flops—what she called zorries growing up in California—with a razor-cut boat sole. Jeff's expression as his wife modeled the shoes said, "not on my boat." But, Beth reflected, Carole said she never set foot aboard *Grace* anyway.

As they wandered Jeff managed to find several of the items on his list, so by show closing time his duffel bag looked quite heavy.

"Shall we get dinner at the brewery?" he asked as the passed through the show gate out onto the street. Beth first met Terry and Jeff at the brewery. She'd been crashing a racer's party and they'd been celebrating after a day of racing. Jeff had invited her to join his crew the next day because one of his regulars had hurt himself. Accepting his invite had turned out to be a life-changing decision. She recalled her earlier wish that Terry had something more romantic than boat shopping in mind for this day. *The brewery would be the place for it*, she thought. But not with Jeff and Carole there. She agreed to Jeff's suggestion realizing once again that there was no ulterior motive in it.

And yet, as the meal progressed and concluded with no surprises from Terry she felt unaccountably let down. As they found a taxi to take them back to the car—the show busses had stopped running an hour and a half earlier—she decided she was overtired and shoved her disappointment back into the emotional depths from whence it came.

Once they were back in the car it occurred to her to check her cell phone. Sure enough, the recruiter had called and left a message.

"They want to see me!" she cried out, phone pressed to ear, eyes shifting to meet Terry's. He reached for her with both arms, pulling her into a hug. "Monday or Tuesday," she went on, still listening. "Oh damn, I should have called him back this afternoon. Damn damn damn."

"Call now, leave a message. Apologize. These things happen," Jeff said, looking at her in the rear-view mirror. His reassurance was encouraging. She took a deep breath and pressed the call back button. Terry let her go and she straightened up as if proper posture would make her message more professional. When she finished the other three peppered her with questions about the job and the phone interview. The discussion led to their own various experiences with interviews and new jobs—although for Terry and Jeff these were limited to high school and college stories since they had been running their own businesses ever since. Carole, it turned out, had been through a succession of jobs and a few career changes before getting a license to sell high-end real estate. Beth had gotten the impression during previous conversations that she worked at it part time. She realized now she had allowed herself to stereotype Carole as a rich woman with an imagined career that was little more than a hobby. Hearing her describe her work now Beth realized she did take it seriously, and the part time status was in deference to her children. Far from a dilettante, she was a caring mom juggling a career.

Overwhelmed with the long day's twists and turns, Beth couldn't help nodding off in the dark back seat. Before she knew it, Terry was nudging her awake as the came to a stop outside the townhouse. They said their good nights and thanks to Jeff and Carole and trudged up the front steps.

)

Georgetown, Washington, D.C.

Saturday afternoon after a long swim at the gym Beth found a message from headhunter Donald "call me Don" McCarthy confirming her interview for Monday afternoon. This threw her into a frenzy over her appearance, dashing around the bedroom trying on each of her new outfits. She hated all of them. Then she realized where she was in her monthly cycle and railed at the unfairness of the timing. She made herself take a deep breath and try on all the clothes again. She could possibly accept the dark brown suit. No matter that her near rejection was hormonal, it was her current reality. If she had a better blouse to go under it, she could just bear it. The fact that she did have the matching blouse was irrelevant.

Terry would be golfing with Jeff for another couple hours. Beth didn't mind his decision to spend the afternoon with his partner because they had a plan just for themselves for tomorrow: they were doing the sight-seeing Beth had promised her sister she would do weeks ago. They would picnic on the Mall and end up having a romantic dinner somewhere—Beth suspected Terry had made reservations. She trotted out of the townhouse on light feet in search of a blouse to make her feel wonderful for her interview on Monday.

Three hours later she returned satisfied, a shopping bag on her arm. She heard Terry's voice as soon as she stepped into the entry and knew he was on the telephone in the den. The tension in his voice stopped her at the foot of the stairs and she paused to listen.

"Well tell them we want to talk. Get them around a table so we can work it out. Yes, tomorrow if they're willing. Hell, tonight would be better. This is crazy."

Beth gulped, thinking of their now disrupted plans for Sunday. She felt awful for being selfish—something was terribly wrong and all she could think about was her plans.

"I'm not going much higher, that's for sure. I don't think they're worth it. These guys have got to be bluffing."

Beth set her bag on the stairs and walked over to the doorway into the den. The movement caught Terry's eye where he stood looking out the front window. He turned toward her but did not appear to see her. His face was contorted in anger, his eyes colder than she had ever seen them. Beth couldn't suppress a shudder of apprehension at such negative emotion, even if it was not directed at her.

"I don't care what they put in writing. Have you seen the offer letter? Right. Let's demand to see it. We can pick it apart. I know, I know. Yes. Right. I'll be here."

He ended the call and raised both hands to his face, scrubbing at it and running his fingers back through his hair. He took a long breath, then looked up at Beth standing in the doorway. She was relieved when he forced a smile before moving in behind his desk.

"What happened?" Beth made her tone as light as she could. She came into the room and paused, uncertain, then boldly sat down on the plaid upholstered love seat where Terry liked to sit to read. Without realizing it she pulled her legs up under herself.

"You won't believe it. They received a counter offer from someone else."

"Better than your deal?"

"Ridiculous, from what they're saying. But we don't believe it."

"You think they invented it?"

"No, I think they got it, but they're inflating it."

"To drive you up."

He nodded, then grimaced and shook his head. "We'll come back with a higher offer, and later find out their counter was lower. But I don't know. It could be real. There are things about this firm that aren't obvious that make it very attractive. But the buyer would need to be prepared to exploit them."

"Which you are."

"Yes. But not many would be. There are risks, but it's the kind of stuff Jeff and I have done before. Mainly internationally. We know what we're doing."

"Could someone else have seen the potential and think they can do what you do?" A wave of concern washed over Beth, almost like nausea. She thought once again of Tom Biffle and his probing questions.

"Sure. But if they're wrong, they'll drive the place into the ground. It would be a disaster for them. Both of them."

"Are you keeping the management on?" She was scrambling for other possibilities.

I can't have ruined this deal for them by talking to Tom.

"Yes, for a while. They have a stake in making a profitable deal." Terry nodded, understanding the intent of her question. "And the other offer, if they're telling us the truth, is crazy high. We've spent hours—weeks—analyzing this and coming to the numbers we put down—"

"I know you have," Beth said, acknowledging that the hours he spent with Jeff instead of her had real value. Value that she may have undermined in a single lunch. He nodded, his hard features softening a tiny bit as he recognized her acceptance of his commitment to his work. She felt guiltier at causing him to calm down when in fact he should be raging even more—at her.

"We made the right offer. This counter offer is way too high. Either this other buyer has way too much money to spend, or they're seeing something we're not. Or they're just crazy. We have got to convince them of it or we'll lose the deal."

"What happens if you lose it?" She held her breath, dreading the answer. When it came, it was an anticlimax.

He shrugged, eyes falling to his desk and the laptop open on it. "We start over. We've wasted months." He looked up, "we don't lose any money, *per se*—other than ongoing expenses with no income. The money for the deal is safe in escrow. But it's beyond frustrating, and it won't look good to the market. Not that our little deal is well known, but there are analysts who pay attention."

"It could affect whatever you try to do next."

"It could." He sighed, eyes dropping to the laptop on his desk. He wanted to do something productive—Beth knew the feeling. Although she didn't know whether he could do anything, she decided to leave him to it. She stood and up headed for the door.

"It looks like you'll be busy tomorrow...," she said, stopping in the doorway.

He was puzzled for a moment, then realization shifted his expression to one of contrition. "I'm so sorry Bethy. I don't want this stuff to interfere with our plans. But I am going to have to deal with it tomorrow—even if they won't meet, Jeff and I will need to."

"I know. It's all right. I understand."

His eyes warmed as he looked at her for a long moment. "Thank you. It's very important—"

"I understand," she repeated firmly, needing to make her escape.

She ran up the stairs in turmoil, stopping half way to go back for her shopping bag before plunging upward again.

If Terry noticed her preoccupation as they made a big, hearty salad for dinner, ate, watched television, and went to bed, he did not mention it. He was preoccupied too.

The house phone rang at 8:30 Sunday morning while Terry was in the shower. Beth answered saying, "Good morning Jeff."

"Hi Beth. Is he there?"

"In the shower."

"Tell him we're on for ten at their office. We should meet at the café as soon as possible."

Beth knew by café he meant one down the block from the offices of the company they were trying to buy. They often met there before meeting with the sellers.

"I'll tell him as soon as he comes out."

"Okay. Thanks. Take care."

Beth had the impression that Jeff wanted to ask her to go interrupt Terry's shower. *Jerk*, she thought, not unkindly.

She brought a mug of coffee to Terry while he dressed, noting he had on the suit she thought made him look totally sexy. She waited until he swallowed a gulp before saying, "You look like something out of GQ in that."

"Please, don't even think it." he put the mug on the dresser and reached for his favorite tie tack.

"But you do—it's cut perfectly for you."

"I know, I had it made. It's just that Linda used to say things like that. Made me feel like an object."

Despite her fears about her role in his business, she couldn't help laughing, which appeared to annoy him.

"When we first started dating, she wouldn't stop asking me to meet with her agent. She was sure he could get me modeling work. As if I wanted it. We finally had to have a fight about it before she stopped. Please, don't go there Beth."

Sufficiently warned, and pleased that he had not been interested in a modeling career and all the superficiality she believed it entailed, she forced herself to return to the role of supporter. But it also pleased her that his model ex-girlfriend had thought he had potential. He was ruggedly handsome, like the men in Ralph Lauren ads, and she found it hard to believe she, with her extra pounds and hopeless hair, had captured his attention, let alone his heart.

Apparently responding to her quiet, he shot his cuffs as he turned to her and said, "Sorry love. I guess I'm over anxious."

"S'okay. I'd rather know the sensitive spots to avoid. I just hope you feel as confident as you look."

He grinned at her, knowing she'd adjusted her compliment to avoid another outburst.

"I'm confident, all right," he said, taking another gulp from the mug before holding it out to her. He had a thing about food in the bedroom, so she recognized his request that she return it to the kitchen. Which meant he was skipping breakfast, which did not surprise her. "I'm confident that we're going to find out who these guys are and take them apart."

He strode out of the bedroom, Beth following at a much less enthusiastic pace with his mug clutched in both hands.

)

I wonder if I should pack my things now, she thought a few minutes later, sitting in his kitchen nursing her own mug of coffee.

I should have said something before he left. But he was right on the edge of blowing up. It would have pushed him over and he needed to be at least a little bit collected. Besides, maybe Tom had nothing to do with this.

But she couldn't believe that. Nor could she shake the anxiety it caused. She decided to rescue the rest of the day's plans by going to the National Mall, where she visited the Lincoln Memorial and the Vietnam War Memorial. She watched other visitors seeking names of friends and relatives, hands caressing the wall's surface as they ran them along the list until they stopped, settled, followed the etched lettering with a finger, or laid paper over it and rubbed it with a crayon. Beth felt like an outsider, but that made the memorial's impact on her all the more powerful. Walking away from it she felt cleansed, and rebuked. Compared to the tragedies that wall represented the failure of Terry's deal was nothing. An inconvenience.

Thirteen

Pointe-à-Pitre, Guadeloupe

*H*unter stood by the rail on the starboard side of the mail boat smoking a succession of cigarettes and contemplating what Madame Gardien had told him. Like Ori, Beth Anderson was a cruising sailor, a vagabond wandering from island to island on a private sailboat. He knew Jamaica was not a common port for the cruiser fleet, which was why Ori stood out among the honeymooners and reggae fans. But it meant he had not met many other cruisers during his months on the island. He didn't know where they gathered, or how to approach them if he found them. Would they welcome a stranger asking about one of their number? Did they know one another well enough to be able to tell him where to find Beth Anderson?

As the mail boat entered the waters between the southern ends of Guadeloupe's two islands the marine traffic increased. Hunter watched dozens of sailboats heading in all directions, white sails flashing as they changed direction. He knew next to nothing about sailing. He hoped it would not be an obstacle to talking to the cruisers. Maybe Beth Anderson was out there on one of those boats. Maybe he would find her in Pointe-à-Pitre.

A boat heading on a course across the bow of the mail boat caught his eye. As he watched it turned, sails snapping into perfect form on the opposite side of the boat after the bow crossed through the wind. Nicely done, he thought, although he didn't really know.

)

Ori felt *Dream Catcher* find her groove on the new tack and smiled to herself.

"I need to head south anyway to clear the end of the island," she told herself, warding off annoyance at having to tack away from the rusty blue ship in her path. Off to her starboard the ship pressed northward toward Pointe-à-Pitre. She was glad to be free of Guadeloupe, and the whole French thing. Sure, the food was great, but the arrogant attitudes they brought on vacation—at least to the casino—had started to rub her the wrong way. That was no way to feel if she wanted to make decent tips.

When Monique told her about an opening at the Casino Paradise in Philipsburg, the capital of Dutch Sint Maarten, she grabbed the lifeline. So what if the reason Monique threw it was because the French authorities had visited twice in the last week and were threatening to shut the casino down if they found any illegal workers. She could have let Ori go without a reference. Instead she made a call to a friend in Philipsburg, and the job was Ori's if she could get there in three days.

That had been around noon today. Ori had not wasted a moment, trusting her half full water tanks and slightly less full fuel tank to get her to Sint Maarten. *Dream Catcher* was a sailboat, after all. She could get to Deshais at the northern end of Guadeloupe today, although she might get in after sunset. She would bypass Montserrat, Antigua, St. Kitts, and a few other islands along the way. She would have plenty of time to find an anchorage on Sint Maarten, clear customs and immigration, and get cleaned up before going to work at the Casino Paradise.

)

Georgetown, Washington, D.C.

"This is what they gave me," Jack Weintraub, Esquire, Terry and Jeff's business attorney, set a file folder on the café table. He went on as Jeff opened the folder, "you were right, they did exaggerate the dollars in their message to you. But not by all that much."

Jeff paged through the sheets in the file, laying each of them on the table so Terry could see them too. The documents included the counteroffer in the form of a letter from a corporation registered in Delaware. It was signed by the company president, a name neither of them recognized.

"I did a quick search. They incorporated three weeks ago," Jack said. "Can't get much more information on the weekend."

"I take it they don't have a webpage," Jeff said sarcastically. Jack didn't bother to answer. The partners finished looking through the file and Jeff flipped the pages back to the beginning. He shrugged.

"There's nothing much here. We don't know who they are and what their focus is. Only that they're willing to spend more than we think the company's worth."

"Makes it hard to argue that we're the better suitor. I'm sure they've made a sales pitch beyond the dollars. Mack and Ed are interested in their company's future almost as much as the money. They want to be courted."

"Then how could they consider another offer after all the time we've put in with them?" Both Terry and Jack knew Jeff's question was rhetorical.

They examined the documents again, but found little to strategize about before it was time for their meeting with Mack and Ed.

/)

"Thank you for seeing us today, gentlemen," Jeff began once the customary handshakes and greetings were dispensed with. "After all these weeks we feel rather like we're all family."

Terry winced at the accusatory nature of his partner's observation. But across the table he caught a hint of contrition on Mack's always expressive face. He would not have tried for a guilt trip on these guys, but Jeff's instincts were dead on as usual.

"Which is why we agreed to meet, Jeff. We owe you the courtesy of an explanation," Ed replied. He relaxed in his chair, both elbows on the conference table, hands clasped. His casual demeanor suggested they were here for Sunday brunch. In fact, he and Mack appeared to be dressed for golf. Their corporate attorney, Isaac Goldstein, was wearing a suit, but as an orthodox Jew he always wore a black suit, white shirt, and yarmulke.

"As you know, Ed, Mack, our plans for your firm revolve around the potential for international training and consulting inherent in your current organization and staffing. In short, your team is key to our strategy, and I think you agree our offer reinforces that." Jeff reiterated their original sales pitch made long ago. "No financially based takeover could possibly take care of your people the way we intend to." Jeff stopped because Ed was shaking his head, his cordial smile not reaching his eyes.

"In fact, Jeff, this counter offer covers much of the same ground as yours. It's as if they read your minds," he said, glancing at Mack for confirmation. The other man nodded. Deep concern shivered up Terry's spine. *Had they?*

"Are you willing to share the details of their offer? Allow us to consider a new offer ourselves?" Jeff asked. "The information provided to Jack was strictly financial."

Mack and Ed both swiveled their heads toward Isaac, who had appeared to be dozing. But he snapped open a briefcase sitting on the table and reached inside, removing a thick, comb-bound document with a glossy, colorful front cover. With a final look at his employers for confirmation he slid it across the table. Terry reached out and stopped it, then lifted his hand to look at the image on the front.

An abstract stock photograph conveyed intelligence and diversity in an international setting. He remembered looking at the same image when he and Jeff were preparing their presentation. Jeff reached out and opened the document to the first page, and then flipped past it to find an executive summary. The mood in the room was restraint bordering on hostility, and Terry had a growing sense as Jeff turned the page in the proposal that it would read almost exactly the same as theirs. He didn't know how, or when, but someone had gotten enough information about their plans to duplicate them, and enough financial backing to outbid them.

Jeff glanced at him and he nodded, acknowledging he was finished reading the executive summary. Jeff turned the page to a list crediting the proposal team. Hungry for the first hint at the true source of this offer, Terry's eyes skimmed down the list of about twenty names, bounced at the bottom and ran back up to confirm what he couldn't believe he saw. Next to him Jeff stiffened, a quiet intake of breath the only clue that he'd seen it too: Tom Biffle.

Terry was deeply annoyed with himself an hour later as the three of them left the building. Through the rest of the meeting he'd been unable to get past the realization that a trusted former employee, someone who he and Jeff had ensured continued employment when they sold their last business, had betrayed them. Based on his behavior, Jeff was floored from the shock of it too. They stuck to their argument about valuing the firm's people and resources because it was all they had, knowing as they talked that the proposal in front of them made all the same guarantees and included all the same glowing projections. But continuing to flip through it while they talked, Jack had come to the crux of the difference in their plans. He'd slid the open book in front of them and deftly taken over the discussion so they could focus on it.

The counter offer included ridiculously generous compensation for Mack and Ed; the numbers were far beyond the men's worth to the firm, indeed, more than the salaries Jeff and Terry had planned to take for themselves. Mack and Ed had, quite simply, been bought. Neither Jeff nor Terry would consider countering an offer like that. It was time to move on.

"I hope they have Isaac read the contract very carefully," Jeff's tone was caustic, "because I'm sure there's a loophole in there. A tiny little clause that will cost those two their high salaries."

Terry nodded, but did not respond.

Tom Biffle. We asked him to help Beth with her resume. And he agreed! What an unethical turd.

"Have you seen Tom since we sold the business?" he asked after they had walked in silence for a few yards.

"No. The only time I spoke to him was when I called about Beth's resume. Oh no, Terry—"

"No way Jeff. They met for an hour a couple weeks ago. This isn't the result of their meeting. Besides, she doesn't know anything about our offer."

"She knows more than you think, through osmosis. Don't discount the possibility that someone put this together in the last week—it arrived on Friday."

"Come on, Jeff, be rational. Someone put a lot of thought into the numbers, and Beth could not possibly have told Tom enough detail for them to complete it that quickly. Besides which, she wouldn't. She wouldn't discuss our business with him!"

"Then how did they get it? How did they know our angle?"

Terry shook his head, staring at the grey cement of the sidewalk ahead, absently noticing dark ovoids of smashed chewing gum. As convinced as he was that Beth could not have been the source of this, he did want to know what she had told Tom Biffle, and that shred of distrust disturbed him.

"Perhaps Tom knows you better than you realize," Jack said. "Could you have discussed your plans—the type of firm you were interested in and your intentions with it—in his presence?"

Jeff started to shake his head, then stopped and looked Jack in the eye. "There were a couple dinners, right at the end when when we were helping with the transition. Do you remember Terry?"

"No. I went sailing right after we signed the paperwork. You stayed on to transition."

Jeff shot him a sharp look, hearing an unwarranted, and unintended, accusation.

"What do you think you said?" Terry tried not to accuse.

"I sure as hell didn't tell Tom Biffle our plans."

"Of course you didn't," Jack said, accustomed to playing peacemaker, although Jeff was usually the aggressor. "Tom's a smart guy, and he was listening more closely than you realized."

"Could be." Jeff nodded, still eying Terry.

"You need to decide what you want to do. Are you considering a counter-counteroffer?"

"No." Both men said, exchanging a more friendly look.

"Is it your instruction that I notify them that your offer has been withdrawn?"

Jeff and Terry both shrugged. "It's done. Just like that," Jeff said.

"Yeah, I think so. Let's cut our losses and find something else." Terry turned to Jack. "Yes. Notify them that we're withdrawing. I wish them well with their new owners. I'm going home. We had plans for today that I may be able to salvage."

Jeff nodded agreement and Terry turned away toward a metro stop at the end of the block. Jeff could have given him a ride, but he wanted a few minutes to himself.

*)

Pointe-à-Pitre, Guadeloupe

As the mail boat approached its dock Hunter studied the hundreds of anchored boats with a new perspective. Beth Anderson could be aboard any one of them. The hundreds of masts in the sprawling marina complex were more possibilities. The enormity of his task came into sharp focus. As the mail boat clanked and thunked against the commercial wharf he tried to convince himself that he was over-reacting. Most of the boats in the marina were not cruisers like Beth Anderson, they were owned by locals. The ones anchored out, though, they were probably transients. They were who he needed to talk to. He was at a loss as to how to do that short of renting a boat himself to go from one to the next.

Thinking in terms of low-hanging fruit, even if it was less likely to be ripe, he shouldered his pack and set off toward the nearest marina. There had to be a few members of the cruising community berthed there. If he kept his ears open, maybe he could figure out how to find them.

Georgetown, Washington, D.C.

The vibration of Beth's phone during the coming attractions made her cringe. She did not take it out of her bag to look at the caller ID. As the trumpets and drum roll heralding the feature thrummed through the uncrowded auditorium her phone buzzed again, indicating that she had voicemail. She focused on the movie—a frivolous romantic comedy. The comic hero was drinking himself into a heartbreak-healing stupor when it buzzed again, the repeated vibration frustratingly insistent. She ignored it, and the subsequent bzzzt, stuffing her face with the last of her popcorn to help ignore it.

But the movie did eventually end, and although she was tempted to sneak into a different auditorium—something she had never done as a kid—she forced herself to walk, blinking, out into the afternoon sun glaring off the Georgetown sidewalks. She had given up on sightseeing after standing at the base of the Washington

Monument looking straight up made her dizzy. She missed sharing the experience with Terry. Being uncertain whether the chance would ever come to do it with him made her miserable.

When her eyes had adjusted, she stepped out of the stream of people exiting the theater and dug out her phone. The two messages were not both from Terry, as she had assumed. The first was from him, but the second was from her sister. Feeling like a coward she listened to the second one first.

"Hi Sis," Trish's voice sounded strained, "Don't want you to worry, but Mom fell yesterday. She's in the hospital. She broke her hip. I guess that sounds bad, but the doctor says it's a clean break and she's in fair health otherwise, so don't panic. They're looking in on Dad every couple hours—which is why we moved them to Orange Grove, isn't it? Anyway, give me a call when you get this, and I'll update you more."

Beth leaned against the brick exterior wall of the multiplex inhaling slow, unsteady breaths. Pedestrians swirled past her as she tried to manage the chaotic images in her mind: her mother sprawled on the kitchen floor while her father watched recorded golf in the living room; her mother trying to coerce her father into doing something and falling, and him standing over her unsure what to do; her father alone in the apartment for hours, temporarily forgotten while her mother was removed to the hospital. She clamped her eyes shut as if it would banish the visions. When she opened them the crowd of people exiting the theater had thinned out. She looked down at the phone in her hand and wondered whether she dared listen to the other potentially loaded message.

Better get it over with, she thought as she accessed voicemail again.

"Hi love. I'm back and it's all over. I'll tell you all about it when I see you. I thought we might be able to salvage some of our plans, but I can't blame you for going out on your own. I'll come meet you if you want. Unless you're getting a manicure," he ended with a strained chuckle that made her smile despite her apprehension. Did he mean the deal was all over, or the meeting? He sounded tired, but not angry. Could he and Jeff have worked it out after all?

Since she was a few blocks away she didn't bother to call Terry back. A few minutes later she climbed the front steps and used her key to enter the townhouse. She glanced at the alarm panel to confirm it wasn't about to go off—Terry was home.

She found him seated behind his desk in the den. The curtains were drawn and no lights were on. His face was eerily washed out by the glow from his laptop screen.

"Terry?"

His head snapped up as if rising out of deep contemplation of whatever he was working on. He looked around as if surprised at his surroundings.

"Sorry, I got sucked in," he said, rising and going to the window to draw back the curtains. As afternoon light filled the room, she saw he was still wearing his "GQ" suit. He came across the room to her, raising both arms. "I could use a hug," he said.

She stepped into his embrace and wrapped her arms around him, laying her head on his shoulder. She squeezed him, savoring the vitality in his body and its warmth. He smelled of aftershave and coffee, and she wondered if he'd eaten anything. Probably not.

"So tell me," she finally said, turning her head and pulling away a little to look into his eyes. She could see now that they were troubled. He released her and took her hand to guide her to the love seat.

"We were so sure this other offer would be way off the mark," he said. Apprehension crept up Beth's spine. There was a "but" coming, and he was so solemn, she feared it had something to do with her. "We've had very good luck with these transactions so far. Maybe it was our time. I mean, deals do go south for any number of reasons."

"Terry—"

"Their offer is practically the same as ours—the same employment guarantees for their people, the same projections for international training leading to consulting, reducing the smaller stuff and going for the localization training, international executive searching. You know what we were planning." His pause was timed too perfectly, his expression open, inviting her to speak now.

"Tom Biffle asked me a lot of questions. I answered them the same way you answered my parents. I didn't tell him any more than you told them—not even that much since I don't know. I meant to tell you, but we were both so busy. And I felt like I was being silly— he was being friendly. Curious."

Terry's mouth tightened and he glanced down at their clasped hands.

"Tom is named as one of their team members, to be brought on and well paid if the deal goes through."

"I didn't tell him anything! I didn't know how much you were offering, and he didn't ask!" She wanted to pull her hands out of his but he held them tight. "He called here Friday morning. I didn't tell you about that, either," she shook her head, tears flowing now, making her voice heavy.

"And you told him we were going to be out all day, I'll bet." He was serious, but not angry. It made her heart ache, even though she wasn't sure she had caused any of this.

"I mentioned we were about to leave for the boat show—meaning I needed to hang up. It's not like I said, 'hey, Terry and Jeff will be out so you can slip your counter offer in when they aren't looking'."

His lips curled in the hint of a smile. "This isn't your fault Beth. I'm sorry for sounding so—I don't know—severe. I guess on some level I did want to be sure. But there's no way he could have pulled this off in the few days since you first met with him. I told Jeff as much, and I'm certain of it now."

"Jeff doesn't think I intentionally—"

"Of course not. If it were true, we would realize it was an accident. Hell, Jeff put you together with Tom in the first place."

"But you had no idea Tom was going to steal your plan."

"No, not at all. But as Jeff thought about it he remembered talking about it to Tom. When he was helping transition the old company and I was sailing with you."

"You mean this could all be Jeff's fault?"

Terry's eyes widened at her reinterpretation, his tiny smile widening. "I wouldn't go that far, at least not to his face."

Beth found herself smiling back. "I still feel awful that I may have had anything to do with it."

He shook his head, sliding his hands from hers up her arms to pull her back into an embrace. "It's just coincidence, love. I'm sure Tom was pumping you, but I'm also sure that by the time you met with him their offer was almost ready. All you did was confirm we would be out of the way on the day they intended to deliver it."

"What happens now?"

"Our lawyer is rescinding our offer as we speak. Tomorrow we start over."

"Oh geez, that's months of work!"

"I'm sort of looking at it as months of unstructured time commitments."

"What does that mean?" Beth frowned.

"Come here," he stood up and guided her around the desk. He swiped a finger over the laptop track pad to wake up the screen. She saw a web page topped by a photo of a sailboat under sail making way through crystal blue seas. It was the web site of the manufacturer of the boat from the show.

"We can charter one out of Antigua. A test drive. I was thinking Thanksgiving. At your interview tomorrow, tell them you already paid for a two-week vacation—non-negotiable, you have to have the time off, unpaid of course."

The image on the screen called to Beth. She could smell the sea and hear the wind in the rigging. Life was so much simpler there.

"We better book it. Don't make a liar of me."

)

The boat dealer wasn't available to book a charter on a Sunday, so they sent an inquiry and researched flights to get an idea of the overall price. Mid-way through the process Jeff called and, when Terry told him their plan, he invited himself and Carole along. Terry had Jeff on the speaker, and when Beth grimaced at the notion of spending days in close quarters with the other couple, he returned her expression with an exaggerated frown. He reminded Jeff he'd have a hard time arranging child care for two weeks. Beth realized what Terry had known all along—Carole would never spend two weeks on a boat.

But Jeff surprised them both by consulting with Carole immediately. Perhaps because he put her on the spot, she agreed to try to arrange for her parents to take the kids for one week. As this plan gelled Terry looked guiltily up at Beth, but she had accepted it, and as she thought about it, she liked the idea of getting to know Jeff and Carole better. A week on a boat would do that. At least it was only one week of the two.

In an attempt to salvage their plans for the day, Terry took her gallery hopping. Beth's hope of a romantic dinner came true when they found a hole-in-the-wall Italian place with candles in Chianti bottles and chunks of garlic on the garlic bread. Sated and tired, they strolled home hand-in-hand and Terry led her up the stairs to the bedroom.

Consequently, near midnight when Beth dragged on a t-shirt and sweat pants to pad down to the kitchen for something to drink she remembered the other phone message.

Nine o'clock on a California Sunday night meant Trish would have put the kids to bed and was probably getting ready to go herself. Out of duty more than willingness Beth dug her phone out of her bag, dropped to her butt at the bottom of the stairs, and pressed the buttons to dial Trish's number.

"Beth! I've been waiting for your call," Trish sounded weary.

"I'm sorry Trish, we've had stuff going on here too. I'm so sorry about Mom. How is she?"

"About what you'd expect—frustrated with being stuck in bed, worried about Dad, and worried about herself, although she doesn't say it."

"I think when she starts saying it is when we start to worry about her."

"Well, I worry about her now, Beth. She's been taking medication for osteoporosis for a while. Her doctor said she needs to do more or this will happen more often."

"Do more what? More medication?"

"No, more activity. Exercise. After she gets over this."

"Wow, I always thought she was pretty active."

"He says she needs to walk a lot more. The problem is Dad won't and she doesn't want to leave him alone."

"But they're in that facility so that the staff can look after him while she takes care of herself."

"I wish you'd say that to her too. She doesn't want to hear it from me anymore."

"I will when I talk to her. Does she have a phone in the hospital?"

Trish started to recite the number and Beth stopped her as she hurried back into the kitchen where a note pad and pen hung by magnets on the refrigerator. She wrote down the number and sat down at the table. They discussed their mother's treatment and the physical therapy to follow her hospital stay, which sounded to Beth like torture. Finally, Trish came back to Beth's initial apology for not calling sooner.

"So you were busy today?"

"Oh, God, don't ask."

"What's up?" Trish asked, knowing Beth was inviting her to do the opposite of what she said.

"Let's see. Terry and Jeff's deal has fallen through and I thought it was my fault, or I was afraid they would think it was. I was getting ready to start packing—"

A sharp grunting sound drew her eyes to the doorway. Terry stood in a threadbare terrycloth bathrobe over boxers and a t-shirt. His day's growth of beard made him look like a derelict and Beth found it surprisingly sexy. Her smile faded as she saw the concerned expression on his face.

"Beth?" Trish's voice came across the silent phone line.

"Sorry, um, yeah, so their deal fell apart and we decided to do a sailing charter next month in the Caribbean—oh, I didn't mention this gorgeous boat we saw the boat show on Friday. We're thinking it's time to trade up, so we're chartering one to see how it sails."

"Wait a second, go back. You were afraid Terry would blame you for his deal not going through?"

Damnit.

While she chattered Terry dispensed a glass of water from the spigot on the refrigerator door and pulled out a chair at the table. He was watching her, not willing to let it slide by either, apparently.

Beth took a deep, calming breath, avoiding looking at Terry. "A couple weeks ago I met with a former employee of theirs—Jeff set it up—who is great with resumes. He helped me redo mine. He also asked me a lot of questions about Terry's business. I tried to tell him what Terry told you guys, you know? But I don't know, I've been hearing so much about it just being here, I don't know if I said anything I shouldn't."

"Then you should have said nothing at all," Trish said. Beth winced at the rebuke and forced herself to look at Terry. His eyes were calm, his expression supportive. He reached out and put a hand on her shoulder. Relieved, she turned her attention back to the phone.

"I know. But it was hard not to without being rude. Anyway, it turns out he was working with someone on a counteroffer they made on Friday while we were all at the boat show. The company has accepted it and Terry and Jeff are out."

"Just like that?"

"I guess so. I'm not sure what made them switch—I didn't ask Terry."

"Because you think it's your fault."

"Yeah, sort of. But Terry said it's not possible—my talk with Tom was a week or so ago, no way he could have put it all together since then. Jeff remembers talking about it to him months ago."

"So they don't blame you."

"No," Beth looked back into Terry's eyes. "They don't blame me."

He nodded, squeezing her shoulder again, then got up from the table with his water and wandered over to a cabinet where he kept snacks.

"So Terry wants to buy a boat instead of a company?"

"Not instead of," Beth said, ignoring her sister's joking tone to be sure Trish didn't develop any notion that Terry was frivolous with his money. "We were discussing that before this all happened. We did decide to go sail one after the deal died—because now Terry can take the time."

At the other end of the line Trish yawned loud enough for Beth to hear it. "You have the life," she said.

"Well, tomorrow I have a job interview, so that I can maybe afford the life."

"Geez, a lot is going on there. I want to hear about it, but I'm falling asleep here. Call me afterwards to tell me how it goes?"

"Yeah, I will. I need to get to bed too. I want to be rested."

"You'll knock 'em dead Sis."

"Thanks. I need all the encouragement I can get."

As Beth ended the call Terry placed an open package of Oreos on the table in front of her. She watched him separate the two halves of one and scrape off the filling with his top teeth.

"You were going to start packing?" he asked, then tucked one of the chocolate wafers into his mouth.

"I don't know," Beth shrugged, "Yeah, I thought about it. "If anything, I said caused the deal to go down, you wouldn't have wanted anything to do with me."

"Say's who?" He sat back down.

She studied his face, looking for signs of deception. It was easy for him to say now that he would not have been angry.

When she didn't answer, he went on, "I'll be honest. For a little while I wondered if you might have had something to do with it."

Beth felt stunned. She reached out and took a cookie. One of the wafers snapped in half when she tried to lift it off the filling.

"But Jeff said the same thing and I had to think about it. I realized it's absurd. Not that you're stupid, but you didn't know enough about our proposal to articulate it to Tom so that he could steal it."

She nodded agreement, scraping the cookie filling off as he had.

"But listen, it didn't matter. I would have been angry, but I'd have gotten over it. I would never have wanted you to leave over this. Hell, if Mack and Ed could switch horses so abruptly for personal gain, Jeff and I may be well free of them."

"Do you really think that?"

"No, not yet." His wry smile made his eyes twinkle. "But go with it for now and I'll catch up."

"So Tom's offer gives them more money?"

"Yes, a lot more. Jack—our lawyer—would bet on there being loopholes in the contracts so they don't end up getting the full compensation. That's the bulk of the additional money they're offering."

"Do you think their decision is personal greed?"

"We do. Look Bethy, we're walking away and it's fine. But like I said, even if something you said to Tom gave them an advantage, it's not worth breaking up over. Seriously."

His hand was back on her shoulder, then slipping around her back as he leaned closer to pull her into an awkward, seated hug. She swallowed the last of her cookie and brought her face near his, delighted when his lips found hers. Earlier they had satisfied desire that had built through the stressful day. This was a warm, loving kiss that in many ways Beth enjoyed more than those shared in the heat of passion. It made her feel loved, and welcome, and secure. And that was exactly what she needed the night before a job interview.

Fourteen

Georgetown, Washington, D.C.

"*I* have one word. Disaster." Beth flopped onto the living room sofa, her knees sprawled, and arms spread across the back cushion.

"Oh no!" Terry joined her, lifting her left arm up and around his shoulders, then wrapping his around her to pull her close. "Tell me."

"Oh God, I don't know where to start. First, I couldn't find the building. I mapped it, but it was wrong." Beth's innate sense of direction rarely failed her, so this galled her more than it would most.

"Were you late?"

She shrugged, grimacing, "Not totally. I got there ten minutes early instead of twenty. I had to rush through their form, and I was panting when I went in because I ran the last block after getting directions from someone. My heart was pounding."

"So how was the actual interview?"

Beth pulled herself straighter on the sofa, half turning in his arms and putting space between them so she could face him. "I talked to someone from human resources first. Pretty typical conversation. She took me to the real interview. There were five of them. I wish the headhunter had warned me. I should have expected it. They grilled me about politics. All these questions about political events in the last year."

"Uh oh."

"Yeah. I was friggin' clueless."

"And the headhunter didn't warn you about that, either?"

"Not really," Beth shook her head slowly, for the fourth or fifth time trying to recall whether he'd said anything about it. "Maybe I was supposed to expect it from a political consulting firm."

"Well …"

"You think I'm an idiot too!" she smiled wanly. He chuckled.

"No. But, well, yeah, maybe you should have expected it. Maybe when you told me about the company, I should have thought of it too. I'm sorry I didn't."

"Oh no, this is in no way your fault so don't try that. I appreciate it, but I blew this one all on my own."

"You can have it. Say what I always say."

"Which is?"

"Never turn down an interview and learn something at every one."

Beth's eyes narrowed at him, "Have you ever been to an actual job interview? I mean since, like, high school?"

"Well, not really…" He sounded sheepish. "But I still say that."

She laughed outright and pulled him back into a hug. "Thank you, Terry."

"For?"

"For being here. For being honest."

"My pleasure."

They sat in silence for a moment.

"I doubt I'll hear from that headhunter again. I guess I'll get back on the web. I read they don't go further than the newest postings. Mine's already old so I have to make changes to my profile to get it bumped to the front."

"That's ridiculous."

"Yes. But it's reality. Aren't you a master of playing the game by the other guy's rules?"

"Why do you say that?"

"Teaching executives about dealing with foreign cultures?" she said.

"I guess you're right. I don't think of it quite that way."

She shrugged, pulling out of his grasp and reaching for her dropped bag before standing.

"Just a matter of interpretation." She smiled down at him. "I'm going to change."

"Want a drink?"

"Silly question."

)

Caribbean Sea

"Oh shit oh dear," Ori grumbled. Standing next to *Dream Catcher*'s mast she looked ahead into blackness. This was not the familiar darkness of the sea at night—that darkness was not so complete; starlight highlighted the swells and almost spotlighted whitecaps on the sea's surface. The sea ahead was utter blackness. If it was a squall, it was a strong one. If it was a front, it had not been in the forecast a few hours ago. She unclipped her harness from the bale on the mast, climbed down to the side deck and hurried back into the cockpit where she clipped herself to a fitting there.

"Let's make this easier," she said out loud, looking at the instruments on the binnacle. The auto-pilot was steering, holding a course that threaded between the islands of Antigua and Nevis. She touched the button to adjust the course twenty degrees to starboard, turning *Dream Catcher*'s bow more into the wind. Both sails immediately fluttered, no longer trimmed efficiently for the point of sail. Ori touched the button again and the sails began to slat noisily as *Dream Catcher* slowed to nearly a stop.

As the boat stood shuddering Ori worked the three lines to roll up the forward sail. It was a two-person job, so she had to stop and readjust her grip on one or another of the lines several times. As she worked the shrinking jib slapped madly. With no forward motion, the autopilot started making constant adjustments to the rudder trying to keep the boat on course. Its motor whined as if annoyed and the wheel jerked back and forth erratically. Ori kept up her rhythmic heaving, each one easier than the last. Finally, only a small part of the sail still thrashed, and then it was all tightly wound around the forestay. She half turned and pressed the ten-degree button twice to put *Dream Catcher* back on course. The autopilot made more adjustments and the bow turned so the main sail caught the wind once more. As the boat settled back onto the previous course Ori worked her way around the cockpit securing the furling line and jib sheets.

She was standing in the cockpit looking ahead at the darkness through the open plexiglass panel in the dodger when a drop of water hit her cheek.

"Shit!" She shook her head at her stupidity. "I can't believe I'm this rusty!" She had a lot more to do, starting with the dodger. She stepped onto the top companionway step to reach up and unroll the middle panel and drag the stiff plastic zippers down to secure it. *Dream Catcher*'s bow rode up and sharply down on a steep swell and Ori slammed sideways against the companionway opening. "God damnit!" she growled at the pain in her side. But the shock reminded her that she had to get off the top of the companionway ladder before she fell off it. She slid the companionway hatch shut but did not retrieve the hatch boards to seal up the vertical opening below it. She was sure she would need to get down there quickly for something before the bad weather passed.

Knowing the tropical warmth would vanish quickly in the rain she dragged on the rain pants she had tucked up under the dodger before sunset. They were not her durable foul weather pants. Those had been too bulky to fit into her duffel. These were cheap, elastic-waisted plastic pants from the drug store.

Working quickly, she stripped off her harness and put on her rain jacket—her rugged one that she would never be without—and replaced the harness over the top. The harness was tethered to the boat, so she was as secure as she could be out here alone in the Caribbean Sea.

Ori had never been afraid of being alone on a boat in the middle of the night. Champion racing sailors at the Riverside Yacht Club in Connecticut had taught her to sail. By the time she was a teenager they were recruiting her for long distance races, standing watches at all hours. Those sailors had taught her that boat speed was all that mattered and must be maintained and continually increased in even the worst conditions.

She could race through squalls, sitting on the rail with her sea boots almost touching the water while trimming the jib sheet to keep it flying at peak efficiency. She knew how to hunt a breath of air in a dead calm, planning every movement of her body to avoid unbalancing the boat.

The first time she set out alone on her boat was with a flotilla of others for a weekend in Long Island Sound. They'd been a fleet of teenagers using their parents' boats, oblivious to how privileged they were compared to most kids their age. Six boats rafted up in Oyster Bay and the alcohol and drugs circulated from cockpit to cockpit. Clothes were shed, and fondling turned into intimacy that energized Ori in new ways. Later she lay alone on *Dream Catcher*'s foredeck staring at the stars and dreaming of similar nights under different constellations.

After that first trip, she'd craved more solo experiences, and her parents had indulged her. When her father decided he wanted to trade up to a larger boat so they could cruise as a family, she convinced him to keep *Dream Catcher* for her to sail. She had no interest in going for days at a time with her parents, although she knew better than to say so outright. He'd grumbled at the expense of housing and insuring two boats, but given in.

The day after she graduated from high school Ori took off for two months—right when her father had planned to do the family cruise. She made her way east from port to port along Connecticut's coast, passing into Rhode Island. At Block Island she experienced more nights like that first raft up, having hooked up with a group of locals who had little else to do all summer than smoke dope and screw. Moving on to Martha's Vineyard, she found another crowd, and yet another on Nantucket. The ports in Buzzards' Bay were also full of friendly guys and girls who would bring a bottle or a baggie of something in exchange for a night on the water away from their families.

Dream Catcher had glided under her jib back to her mooring at Riverside in the doldrums of August, her fuel tank dry and her main sail torn half way up the mast. The lack of fuel was irrelevant because the alternator was failing and the spark plugs were all bad. Ori's father had come out to the boat and, seeing the filthy saloon, the deck spattered with bird droppings, and the failing engine, issued an ultimatum to his daughter. She would take a diesel mechanics course, and she would repair *Dream Catcher*'s engine, before she would be allowed to take the boat out again. Not, he had also raged, that she'd had permission to go this time.

Ori had chafed at his orders, but she know she needed to learn how to take care of her boat if she was going to escape in it. So she took the diesel course, and, also at her father's expense, took more courses on boat maintenance, sail repair, tuning the rig, and almost as a joke, cooking on a boat. She earned a HAM radio operators license and got her father to buy one that she installed. She deferred her admission to Connecticut College, which did not please her parents. But she assured them she just needed a gap year to get ready for the long haul of advanced studies.

Since her trust fund wouldn't be available to her for years, she got a job at the yacht club running the launches. She loved being on the water all day but hated being subservient to her parents' peers as well as their children. Fellow graduates of the junior sailing program thought nothing of being total shits to her because she was working while they were there to go sailing. She began to see them as the smug elite that she hadn't recognized when she was one of them and longed for the company of the directionless youth in the less wealthy ports along the coast.

When the boating season ended in October her father signed her on as an assistant in his insurance firm, thinking it would be good practice for an eventual career. She thought otherwise, but the paychecks were enough to keep her going every day. On weekends she worked on *Dream Catcher* until late November when the weather made it too cold to be in the boatyard. In the spring she was the first one in the yard. She had finished the engine repair months ago and during the process she had developed pride in her boat. She refinished the woodwork that she'd neglected and damaged last summer. She scrubbed and painted and when the temperature warmed up enough, she varnished. She replaced old hoses in the fresh water system and ran a new bilge pump hose. She touched up *Dream Catcher*'s name on the stern and added an image of a native American *Dream Catcher*. *Dream Catcher* went in the water in late April. Ori set sail in the first week of May.

That summer she sailed north to Maine and in to Nova Scotia, once again reveling in the freedom and enjoying the people she met in harbor towns. The constellations were the same, but the adventures were great. One day she got too close to a rocky shore and scraped *Dream Catcher*'s keel with a resounding thud. She found a boat yard that could haul her for a hundred bucks. It took a compensation of a different type to get the yard manager, a man in his thirties who was missing a front tooth and smelled of diesel, to show her how to repair the chunk she'd knocked out of the boat's keel. She didn't like that type of transaction, but her winter earnings would not extend to expensive repair work.

As the summer turned to fall, she realized she'd already made the decision not to go home or go to college. She found a marina in Rhode Island where she could leave *Dream Catcher* in the water and live aboard for the winter. Then she found a local bar that could use a waitress. She was set for the winter. She caught the train back to Riverside and visited her parents' house at mid-day when her father was at work and her mother was out doing something charitable. The housekeeper gave her a warm welcome, clueless that she should stop the prodigal daughter from collecting her cold weather clothes from her room.

Ori had not returned to the house in Connecticut again, right up until she brought her newborn son there seven months ago. As she worked the lines to reef the mainsail she thought about Tiberius and her plans for him. She did not regret leaving him for her mother to raise, at least for these first few years. No way she was up to the task, and her mother could afford the best nannies if she wasn't up to it either. In a few years Ori would swoop back in and rescue him. Maybe after he'd done the children's programs at the club, so at least he would know how to swim. That would be best. It would the two of them sailing the world. Her trust fund, which she now had access to, would cover both of their expenses.

The squall, for that's all it was—not a weather front—hit *Dream Catcher* hard. But Ori was ready, with both hands on the wheel and her feet braced. She worked the boat into the wind, letting the reduced mainsail luff in the strongest gusts and refill as the wind eased. The boat shot through the turbulent water, heeling, but not dangerously so. Lightning flashes revealed angry greenish black clouds. Ori saw all around her clenched fists and the faces of Orcs right out of the *Lord of the Rings* movies, with gaping, jagged mouths and pitch-black eyes. She held *Dream Catcher* on course as best she could, knowing she had plenty of miles to leeward and energy enough to keep it up for as many hours as it took.

Fifteen

Georgetown, Washington, D.C.

*B*eth recovered from her embarrassing failure by diving into research about political consulting firms, and she further honed her resume and profiles on the job websites based on her experience. She received three more calls over the next two days and did two more phone interviews. The truth of Terry's advice hit home as, during the second of these calls she used the research. Sure enough, that employer requested a face-to-face interview.

She found the offices of The Broadhead Group off of the Mall and entered feeling confident and professional. She breezed through the employment form and even calmly asked to use the restroom before her interview.

The offices were buzzing with young men in shirts and ties and women in skirt suits gathered in a cubicle here and leaning together over a laptop there. Accompanying Clark from human resources, a towering, long limbed fellow who no doubt endured endless questions about whether he played basketball, she walked passed a heated argument over an image projected on a white board in a glass-walled conference room, voices muffled to a musical hum accompanied by white-sleeved gesticulations.

"Three of our congressmen are up for re-election," Clark, explained as he ushered Beth into an office. It was neutral to the point of dullness, equipped with a computer and telephone and a filing cabinet next to the desk, but no personal items. Beth realized with a flash of intuition that it was a shared office. She knew about "hoteling," where employees took whatever space they wanted each day. "Two of our campaigns are up against challenges."

"With the election a couple weeks away, I would expect it to be very tense."

"Yes, but a lot of our people thrive on it." He laid her resume on the desk, ready to get down to business. "I need to review your work history with you. I have a few questions, and I'm here to answer your questions about Broadhead."

Beth could see, even upside down, that her careful formatting of the Microsoft Word document had been lost. She hoped it wouldn't be a strike against her.

She disposed of the man's employment questions, including her months at sea. To her surprise, in response to her explanation of doing freelance writing while exploring the islands, he said, "Yes, your extensive knowledge of the West Indies caught our eye. Raj Gupta will explain more about it."

Curiosity piqued, Beth asked her standard company policy questions—how much vacation time? Did they allow flex time? She told him she had a two-week trip already booked next month and she sincerely hoped they could work out a schedule to accommodate it. To her relief, this did not draw much of a reaction, just "That will be up to Raj, but I can say we've accommodated such requests in the past."

Contrary to his exotic sounding name and swarthy appearance, Raj Gupta acted like a middle-class, mid-western American. He punctuated his description of Broadhead's consulting work with politicians, lobbyists, and corporations with "you know?" and "sure thing!" He explained they had just launched consulting projects with two elected officials in Caribbean nations. Beth had no trouble discussing the islands in question, although she lacked much knowledge of their governments. She got the sense from him that she might know more than a lot of his people, other than the specialist on Central America who he mentioned as the project lead.

She took it as a positive sign that when they were done, he escorted her to his manager's office. Adrian McKeen was a more typical mid-western American, with a diploma from Washington University in St. Louis on one wall and a handful of photos of himself shaking hands with various politicians surrounding it. Beth could see him aging in the images from a rather gawky young man in the oldest to the obese fiftyish man behind the desk in front of her in the most recent. In that one he stood smiling next to a politician Beth recognized, but could not name. Was it the Vice President? The speaker of the house? She squelched the impulse to fret about this knowledge gap.

Mr. McKeen, like Raj Gupta, wore presentable business attire, but hardly of the same quality as Terry's "GQ" suit. Beth had noticed that about the men on the streets of D.C. It seemed like the ones involved behind the scenes in the political world had a frumpy dress code. For the government employees it made a certain sense— whether they could afford finer clothes or not, they should not appear to be too well paid on their government salaries. Perhaps these consultants, who must earn better money than the bureaucrats, did it to fit in with their clients. Beth had learned in her months cruising to never make superficial judgments. But she did observe and make use of the information conveyed by appearances.

As a vice president in the firm, Mr. McKeen explained, he was responsible for the creative staff, which included the technical writers as well as the team that booked advertising and planned public relations events. It struck Beth that this must be the bulk of the firm's activity, based on Raj Gupta's description. But when she asked for a view of the firm's overall business, the answer was far more complicated than she had been led to believe. Broadhead offered research, strategic services, logistics, and several other consulting services Beth did not immediately grasp, in addition to campaign management.

While she was scribbling notes about it all, he asked her more questions about her cruising experiences than her past work, eventually admitting he had a secret desire to charter a sailboat in the tropics. But his wife was afraid, he said wistfully. It was clear he felt constrained. Beth thought he might be one of those people who knew he could profess this deep desire because his wife would never let him.

As they concluded the interview Mr. McKeen thanked her with a firm handshake. She thanked him for his time and assured him she looked forward to chatting again in the future. She tried for a hint at more sailing discussion, wrapped in a desire for business engagement. She thought she achieved it.

Clark, the human resources "redwood"—her impromptu nickname for him—beamed down at her as he escorted her toward the elevators.

"Raj was very happy with you," he said in a conspiratorial tone. "I'll be in touch with your recruiter later today."

Beth floated on air as she swirled through the revolving door and out onto the street a few minutes later. For the first time in this process she felt inspired. She wanted this job.

Using her mobile phone while sitting at a table in a convenient Starbucks, she reported her positive feeling to the headhunter. He congratulated her and said

he would get back to her as soon as he knew something. She bought herself a premature victory coffee, and took the metro home, timing the trip in anticipation of a commute.

She could not help being let down by his call a few hours later: They were seeing another candidate early next week. His "but you're high on their list" was intended to reassure her, but left her feeling down. She had wanted to be the perfect fit. How could anyone else come close to her intimate knowledge of the islands?

)

Caribbean Sea

"Those squall lines between Antigua and St. Barts kind of came out of nowhere last night folks. Anyone get caught? Need assistance?"

Ori keyed the microphone and jumped in "This is sailing vessel *Dream Catcher*. It was a long night. I'm underway from Deshais to Phillipsburg. Over."

Identifying the boat's name over the open radio frequency was a risk. But since she'd easily cleared customs and immigration in Deshais she knew the yacht broker must not have reported the boat stolen. She refused to ponder whether her father was responsible for the free pass.

"Hello *Dream Catcher*. I think I recall you coming through here last year. Everything all right? Over." Captain Howard—nobody knew if that was his first name or his last—hosted the morning cruisers radio network out of St. Kitts. Ori had indeed been in contact with him on her way south a year or so ago.

"Yes, that's me. Everything's fine if you don't count being soaked, hungry, and tired. I'm heading for an anchorage in Simpson Bay. Should get there mid-day. Over."

"How grand. I'm sure you'll be welcomed by our regulars there. Anyone else?"

Ori continued to listen as three other boats described various minor overnight adventures. Captain Howard moved on to announcements, describing events of interest on various nearby islands: a music festival, a regatta, filming of a movie on St. Barts. Some were events that the sailors might want to attend, others they would want to avoid. He ran down the list of markets for the day— fresh food interested everyone. Then he read messages for specific boats. Ori half tuned him out as she spread peanut butter on bread and carried it up to the cockpit to check on the autopilot's progress.

The squalls had blown her further to the west than she liked, although not that close to the string of islands that ran from the northwest to the southeast. She was off the east coast of St. Eustacia when she wanted to be much closer to St. Barts to the east. But the breeze was coming from a hair south of east and Simpson Bay on St. Martin was to the northeast. *Dream Catcher*'s sails were fully deployed again, the boat reaching across the waves like a frisky colt. The morning sunshine had dried the deck and it glittered with the remaining salt crystals. The auto pilot held course, pointing right at their destination and she had enough coffee for a small pot, even though the fresh water pump was starting to suck air.

Life is good.

)

Pointe-à-Pitre, Guadeloupe

Burt Adams settled onto a stool at the end of the patio bar in one of his preferred Pointe-à-Pitre waterfront restaurants. It was bit of a dive, which discouraged the tourists and encouraged the cruisers and locals. He'd sent his most recent charter party to the airport and he didn't have another one scheduled until after Thanksgiving. For many charter captains that might signal financial disaster, but Burt wasn't as dependent on his charter guests as most. He had retired with a comfortable pension, and mostly used the charter fees for upgrades to his motor yacht, *Sandcastle*. He looked forward a few weeks of solitude, doing maintenance on the boat, and a few good meals. The first question was where to spend the holidays. No, before that, the first question was what to have for lunch.

He had ordered a fish sandwich, roasted plantain, and a cold bottle of Carib beer when a group of four cruisers ambled in and took a table. He knew they were cruisers for two reasons: they were dressed in well worn, comfortable clothes and each carried a daypack and several canvas tote bags used to carry supplies and groceries. And he'd seen them on their sailboats at anchor yesterday. One of the men acknowledged him with a nod and smile that he returned. He knew a lot of the cruising community, although not this group.

Kit, the bartender, placed an open bottle of beer in front of Burt, then made for the table where the group had seated themselves. As he went, two more cruisers, young men Burt knew were on a barebones twenty-eight-footer that he wouldn't take for a daysail himself, stepped in out of the sun and took seats at the middle of the bar. Kit soon returned, his note pad covered in scribbles, and took their orders. While he entered the orders into his terminal, another man entered. The lunch rush was starting.

The newcomer looked around the patio, paused to study the four at the table for a moment, and then moved to a seat at the bar in between the two young men and Burt. This one wasn't a cruiser, but he might be an islander. Not a local, for sure. Not French, he didn't carry himself like one, and not creole—wrong skin color. He was, like Burt, an American émigré to the islands—Burt would put money on it. The man's accent supported Burt's opinion when Kit took his order for a Coke. Texas, but with a hint of something tropical. Maybe Jamaica.

As usual, Burt could not stretch one beer through lunch. The dregs of it were getting warm in the bottle before his sandwich arrived. With a sigh of feigned inconvenience, he signaled Kit for a replacement and settled in to study the Texan. He wasn't here for the Coke, he could have gotten it cheaper at a dozen shops. Why come sit in a patio bar at lunchtime to drink it? Not for the view, his back was to the water. What else did the place offer? Obviously the clientele. Six out of the seven patrons were cruising sailors. As he reached this conclusion, two more came in, waving at the four at the table as they moved toward them. Burt watched the Texan half turn to watch the two women, laden with canvas bags like the others, as they greeted the group of four and took the table for two next to them.

Oh yeah, he's here for the cruisers. Why?

♪

Georgetown, Washington, D.C.

If Terry sensed the tension Beth was feeling he didn't mention it as they set out on Saturday for a drive into the country west of Washington. She had been craving scenery other than buildings, and the day provided it. They browsed several antique shops and picked up sandwiches at a small town general store he knew of by reputation.

Coming back late in the afternoon they stopped at the boathouse on the C&O Canal and rented a canoe for an hour from a tall, lean man with a friendly smile. Paddling along the canal a short distance they soon found solitude on the still water. High overhead a bird of prey circled in silhouette against the pale blue sky. Occasional ripples on the water told of fish and turtles all around them. They shipped their oars and drifted, talking softly about trivial things. There had been many such moments of quiet companionship while they were sailing. Beth realized how much she'd missed them over the last few weeks.

"What would it take to set sail permanently?" she asked, half turning to look back over her shoulder at him. The question seemed to come out of the blue, but Terry took it in stride, as if he'd been thinking along the same lines.

"One more solid business turnover, for me," he said, tilting his head to one side as he wore a merry smile. "Would give me enough of a portfolio to walk away. I'd buy interest in something, to generate income, and have a plan B."

"Would you consider it?"

He lifted his oar and took a couple strokes, directing the canoe back out into the canal and away from the shore they'd been drifting near. "Yes. This last episode hasn't soured me, but still… maybe it's a combination of that and our months cruising. Given the choice,

I'd rather face the kinds of problems we had on the water. It's within my power to give myself that choice."

"Even problems like Maggie Hartford?"

"Yes, even those. But she was an outlier. A once in a lifetime situation."

"We hope."

"We learned—I learned—to trust your instincts."

"Really?"

"You were right about her all along."

Beth smiled to herself, happy to hear him admit it and not about to tell him her suspicions about Maggie had been far from convictions at the time. She could let him view them favorably in hindsight.

"But what about you? I thought that was your plan all along."

"Sort of. I didn't really have a long-term plan when I left the dock in New York—geez, I can't believe it was only a year ago. So much has changed, and I've learned so much."

"What have you learned?"

Beth laughed. "I'm in no position to support myself as a permanent cruiser, and I won't be for a long time. I also need to know more about my boat. The mechanics."

"And your plan to sail alone?"

She smiled again, remembering her early determination to prove her abilities. Well, she'd done it. She'd sailed her boat from New York to North Carolina, and from the Virgin Islands to Guadeloupe. She had never intended to try to beat some solo sailing record, just to get away on her own and fend for herself. Having done it, and having cruised for months with Terry, the choice was easy.

"It was just a plan to get to the islands. It wasn't very well thought out. I'm ready to make new plans."

There was silence behind her for a while, and then he said, "Regardless of your father's condition?"

She nodded, not looking back. "Regardless. I realize now that neither of my parents are going to age on my planned schedule. I have to be prepared for their changes when they come, but if I wait, I'll stagnate. I guess you learned that when you were a kid." She thought of a sixteen-year-old Terry coping emotionally with his father's stroke.

"Perhaps," he said. "Or perhaps I've never been as close to my parents as you are. In any case, I can't tell you how happy I am to hear that you're ready."

"Ready?"

"To make serious plans."

She craned her neck around again to see his mischievous smile. But before she could ask him to explain he raised his oar and nodded at her. Their hour was almost up.

♪

Pointe-à-Pitre, Guadeloupe

Burt was halfway through his sandwich when the two guys at the bar finished their beers and walked over to the cruisers at the tables. The Texan drained his Coke and swiveled around on his stool to watch as the young men greeted the others, who ranged from older than them to a couple who could be their grandparents. They introduced themselves and mentioned their boat. Burt saw one man's expression shift from congenial to concerned and quickly back.

That one's seen their boat, he thought. Cruisers were rarely judgmental about others' boats, they all understood the challenges of maintaining a vessel. But an unsafe boat was a concern for everyone in an anchorage.

The two groups chatted for a few minutes. Burt picked up a few words: the names of nearby islands, the weather, typical topics among this crowd. He chewed his grouper and watched the Texan out of the corner of his eye. As the conversation seemed to be winding down, the Texan stood up and approached the diners, stopping next to the two younger men. Unable to squelch his curiosity, Burt strained to hear. The Texan's voice carried more than the younger mens'.

"Hey folks, sorry to interrupt, but I guess you're all sailors?"

This got him a couple curious nods and a couple frowns.

"I'm sorry, let me explain. My name is Hunter. Hunter Green. I'm hoping if you're cruisers you can help me."

One of Burt's brows rose. The Texan wasn't a sailor looking for a crew position. If he was, he would know that cruisers like these rarely wanted or needed a stranger on board.

"What do you need, Hunter?" the man who was concerned about the younger men's boat asked. Burt was starting to like that guy.

"I'm looking for a cruiser. We have a mutual friend who I'm trying to get in touch with. I'm hoping the cruiser can help me out."

"What's his name, or his boat?" the man asked.

"Her," Hunter said. "Her name is Beth Anderson. Her boat is called *Double Trouble*."

Sixteen

Georgetown, Washington, D.C.

*T*he following Tuesday the headhunter called Beth to schedule a follow-up interview at The Broadhead Group. He explained that they had seen the other candidate and wanted her to meet a few more team members before making their decision.

So the other guy is still in the picture, she sighed as she hung up the phone. But I'm worth one more visit.

She focused herself by reading up on the islands Raj Gupta had mentioned and on Broadhead's overall business. She scheduled a haircut prior to the interview.

She walked into their offices feeling confident and it showed. She was introduced to two technical writers who peppered her with more questions about writing—what style guides she used, what dictionary. They showed her a photograph of a shaved-head, red-faced speaker at a lectern in front of a swastika on a banner. How would she describe this situation so the speaker is represented positively? She stared at the image. The speaker's arm was raised in a point at his invisible audience.

Beth gulped. "I'm not sure I'd want to," she said tentatively. "But I would concentrate on his obvious enthusiasm and—" One of her interviewers snatched the picture from her hand and glared at his associate.

"It's okay, it's a trick question. You answered correctly," she said.

Beth smiled, concealing her surprise at the tactic. They couldn't ask about religion or politics, so they resorted to this? If she wanted to, she could probably sue.

That incident aside, the interviews went smoothly and although she spent the ride home picking apart every moment and wincing at a few blunders, she felt positive about it. Even if she didn't get the job, she knew she'd done her best.

But it turned out her best was enough. Early that evening the headhunter called, very happy, to tell her they would be making an offer. She reminded him of her vacation plan, and he confirmed he'd told them, as she had herself, and it was acceptable. They hung up with the biggest question still hanging—what salary would they offer?

Terry took her out to dinner to celebrate and while they were eating, he distracted her with his and Jeff's efforts so far to find a new takeover target. They had both immersed themselves in research since the discovery of Tom's double cross. Such resilience, Beth thought, reinforced Terry's assertions that it was not the enormous setback she had imagined.

Pointe-à-Pitre, Guadeloupe

Hunter Green studied the groups of people on the beach. A group of men were tending a barbecue, while men and women were laying dishes of food out on a picnic table. Kids were playing Frisbee and getting yelled at by adults. Dogs barked and chased each other, the kids, and the Frisbees in and out of the gentle surf. Hunter ambled down the beach toward the table carrying a six pack of beer.

"Hello, welcome," a man said, extending his hand to Hunter.

"Hello. May I join in? I brought this," Hunter held up the beer.

"Sure, it's an open party, and there's plenty of food. Are you anchored in the bay?" one of the women setting up the table asked.

"I'm between boats and I miss it."

"Well, this crowd will either make it worse or bring back fond memories. I'm Laurie. My husband Joe is over by the grill, and our two boys are running around here somewhere."

"It's a pleasure to meet you Laurie. My name is Hunter."

"Want to put those in the cooler? We've got ice in here," the man bent to open a cooler by his feet. Hunter extended the six pack to him. "Want one now?" The man asked as he took the bottles from the cardboard carrier and nestled them in the ice.

"No, thanks. They're for the group. I'm good."

"Mind if I do?"

Hunter smiled and nodded, gesturing at the bottles in the cooler. "Please!"

The rest of the cruisers were just as welcoming. Hunter followed the man, who belatedly introduced himself as Alan, over to the group at the grill. Soon after he met several of the older children when the chef called them over to get hot dogs. Eventually he found himself sitting in the sand among the cruisers with a plate of food on his lap. Finally, he was able to fit his questions into the conversation.

"Beth Anderson? Sure, we know her," Laurie said. "Joe, when did we last see Beth?"

"It had to be at the *Gunkholking* treasure hunt party. When was that?"

"August, Dad," one of the teenage boys replied.

"Right, late August on Antigua," Laurie said.

"Where were they headed? Did they say?" Joe asked his wife.

Laurie shook her head. "No. Remember Terry had a concussion, so they were taking it slow. Maybe they're still wandering around Antigua. Or Barbuda."

"Right, I can see sitting on the hook off of Eleven Mile Beach for a while." Joe's grin suggested a fond memory.

"You remember why he had a concussion?" one of the other cruisers asked, ready to tell them if they didn't. Hunter listened to a story of kidnapping and an exploding boat and drug dealers. The others added details. Hunter was more interested in this man Terry, who he now realized must be sailing with Beth Anderson. He had been envisioning a woman traveling alone. Now he had to readjust his mental picture to include the man. Hunter finished his food as the conversation moved on to other gatherings and people. Nobody seemed to notice when he got up to dispose of this plate and slip away.

After days of hanging around the marinas and approaching strangers, he'd hit pay dirt, as his dad used to say. *Antigua. What's the best way to get there?*

City Island, The Bronx

"So this is where it all began, huh?" Terry asked, scuffing his shoe in the gravel of the marina parking lot. They had driven to New York on Friday night, checking into a hotel on Long Island near the house where Beth had stashed several boxes right before she left New York. Beth's friend Eva would meet them at her mother's house this afternoon. But first Beth had directed Terry over the Throgs Neck Bridge and on to City Island, the nautical enclave in the Bronx where she lived aboard *Trouble* before setting out for the islands.

"Yup, this is it. I lived here for about six months. Almost exactly one year ago I set sail from these docks." Beth stood by Terry's car looking around. There were four other parked cars and twice as many boats with steel stanchions supporting their hulls. Several were already sheathed in white plastic. The marina building housed an office, laundry, and workshop. It was tidy and well-maintained, if not fancy. After visiting so many marine facilities down the east coast and in the islands, Beth now had a much better perspective on this, her first one. She knew what it lacked in luxury and glamor it made up in heart. "Come on," she said, taking Terry's hand.

The office door still creaked, the window in it rattling, when she opened it.

"Sid?" she called. A barrel-chested man well past middle age, wearing a plaid flannel shirt and worn blue jeans stepped into the doorway of an inner room. "Hi Sid, remember me?"

"Beth Anderson! Welcome back!" he said, coming across the room to them.

"Thanks. This is my boyfriend Terry. Terry, Sid manages the marina."

Terry shook Sid's extended hand.

"So you're the fellow who helped Beth get to the Islands," Sid looked Terry up and down.

"So you're the fellow who made sure she had a dinghy and motor before she left," Terry said with a smile. "It's wonderful to meet you."

"I'll tell you now, Beth," Sid said, "we were all a little worried about you when you took off after that transient. Susan shared the news when she got your email saying you'd brought on crew." He gave Terry another pointed look.

"That wasn't Terry—I hired a guy from North Carolina to Florida. Terry joined me there. So Susan spreads my news to you?"

Sid laughed, a throaty sound that made Terry and Beth smile. "You do remember Susan Goldberg, right? Did you ever catch up to that woman? I can't remember her name."

"Ori," Terry said before Beth could, drawing Sid's gaze again. Beth pursed her lips, waiting for Terry to elaborate. But he didn't.

"Yes and no," she finally said. "It's a long story."

"Well start thinking about how to tell it, because they're going to want to hear it."

"Who are?"

"The Goldbergs are down on *Third Million* with a few of the regulars."

"I did email Susan that we were going to stop by," Beth said, glancing at Terry. Sid was chuckling.

"Yes, and she alerted the marina. I'm glad you stopped in so I could warn you. You go on down. I'll be along in a minute."

Beth led Terry out of the office and toward the head of the docks.

"I didn't realize you had such a community here," Terry said as they walked.

"Before I left, when I decided to go, they all gave me a lot of support. The dinghy and motor, the life raft, the auto pilot, even galley gear. But I didn't realize they were worried about me."

They walked down the sloping ramp from shore onto the floating docks and Beth guided Terry unerringly down one of them. Several of the slips on either side were empty. The bright autumn sun and mid-seventies temperature belied the fact that it was the end of the sailing season. One-by-one the boats were being moved up to the parking lot for the winter. About two thirds of the way down she stopped at one of the empty slips.

"This is where *Trouble* lived," she said.

"Lovely piece of water."

"Yeah." Beth sighed and looked around. "This is probably the last time I'll visit this dock."

"Never say never."

"I said probably. Anyway, *Third Million* must be at the end. That was *Second Million*'s berth. She was too big for the slips."

"I'm hearing a boat name pattern."

"Yeah, when I was leaving and Herb had the autopilot installed I protested at the expense. He said not to tell Susan, but he was buying a new boat, and the cost of my autopilot was a drop in the bucket. So I guess he christened it *Third Million*."

"And is it true?"

"The millions? I never asked—seemed rude. But I think so. Probably by a factor of ten."

They had reached the end of the dock where a glistening white trawler was secured. It reminded Beth of her friend Burt's boat, *Sandcastle*, but bigger. It was at least ten feet longer than *Second Million* had been. Several people were sitting on director's chairs on the aft deck.

"Hey, there she is! The woman of the hour!" a man stood up and waved them over. "Get over here Beth. Introduce us to your friend!"

Stepping aboard the trawler Beth was engulfed in a series of hugs and Terry shook many hands as he was introduced to each of Beth's old friends. Beth wasn't surprised that Susan had organized this impromptu gathering. She was a benign busy-body, a mother hen to the marina community who had made Beth feel welcome from her first day there. Susan had been behind Beth's joining Tom's racing crew, which had been her sole credential when Jeff had invited her to race on *Grace* the evening that she met Terry.

As the group settled down with plates of food that issued forth from *Third Million*'s luxurious galley, Beth thanked Susan and Tom for the opportunity to race, explaining that it had led to so much more—indicating Terry. Sid had been right: they pressed for an update on Ori. Beth told them about her solo sail from St. Thomas to Guadeloupe to find her friend. She glossed over the situation Ori had been in, downplaying the drug using reggae band and the attempted abduction of Ori's newborn baby. Her audience was captivated enough by her descriptions of weathering squalls and visiting new ports. She knew the Goldbergs had taken cruises in the islands, but she found out now that Doug had done bareboat charters around the islands that she now thought of as home.

When Tom excused himself, giving Beth another tight hug and patting Terry's shoulder when he shook his hand, Beth checked the time and caught Terry's eye.

"We need to be going too," she said to Susan. "I have to collect my stuff from my friend Eva's mother's garage."

This sparked a round of well wishes, hugs, and promises to continue to write, so it was another fifteen minutes before they finally stepped off onto the dock, waving as they walked away.

"That wasn't too stressful," Beth said when they were out of earshot at the top of the ramp.

"It wasn't stressful at all!"

"Oh good. I was afraid you'd be bored, or feel targeted, or something."

"Good grief! They're sailors. Nice people. And they obviously care about you. I didn't mind them asking me questions, if that's what you mean."

"It is. It's not like they have any right to, they're not family."

"No? I think they are. In any case, it was nice to meet them. Now, how do we get back to Long Island?"

)

Phillipsburg, Sint Maarten

The Casino Paradise in Phillipsburg was far more extravagant than the place on Guadeloupe. Ori paid and got out of the taxi she'd taken from the marina where she'd left her dinghy. She paused in the driveway to peer up at the flashing lights on the facade for a moment, wondering if the bling attracted wealthier customers. She was optimistic given that Phillipsburg was a major cruise ship port: people on cruises seemed eager to spend their money on islands. As she approached the door, it was opened for her by a doorman who peered at her from beneath the shiny black brim of a uniform cap and a thick black unibrow. His eyes as much as his wide mouth smiled.

"Good afternoon Madame. Welcome."

Despite his smile it was an automatic greeting. And it was refreshing not to have to think in French. English was common on the Dutch half of St. Martin.

"Thank you. I have an appointment with Victor Mardenbrough. Can you tell me where I will find him?"

"Very good Madame. Do you see the double doors just there?" The man nodded toward a set of dark brown doors designed to not stand out.

"Yes."

"Go through and down the hallway to the end, to the management offices. The young lady there will direct you."

"Thank you."

Ori anticipated being stopped when she reached for the handle on one of the nondescript doors, but she was not. She did note at least four security cameras within the radius of her short walk. Someone was watching her, and most likely the doorman had already called ahead. This place was much more sophisticated than Guadeloupe. That could be good, or bad, for the employees.

The doorman's "young lady" had been either flattering or just respectful, Ori realized, when a decidedly middle-aged woman with the sagging skin and pointed features of a turtle, guided her to one of the offices in the administrative suite. She knocked twice on the door before opening it without waiting for a response.

"Mr. Mardenborough, Miss Oregon Chapman is here."

Victor Mardenborough stood in front of a bookcase holding an open binder—one of several on the shelves. He turned toward the door, smiling, and set the binder on the desk before stepping across the room to offer Ori his hand. She shook it, noting how warm and dry his skin felt. Glancing down at their clasped hands she noted his skin had the powdery surface of dark skin in need of lotion.

"Welcome to Casino Paradise, Miss Chapman," he said. Looking at the receptionist he added, "Thank you Elaine."

"Thank you for seeing me, Mr. Mardenborough." Ori brought his attention back to her.

"Please, sit down," Mardenborough gestured at the utilitarian chair in front of the desk as he moved around behind it to sit in the slightly more comfortable looking desk chair. Ori sat down, setting her tote bag on the floor by her feet.

"My friend Monique told me you are reliable and skilled at serving guests. I trust her judgment. However, I am not in need of a waitress or bartender just now."

Ori's pulse shot up with her anger. She pushed through hell to get here for a job Monique had practically promised was hers. She opened her mouth, then stopped herself, realizing that if she had any hope of salvaging the situation, she'd better not get mad at this guy.

"However," Mardenborough went on, lips curling in a strange little smile, "I do need black jack dealers. I don't suppose you ever worked as a dealer?"

"A black jack dealer?" Ori asked to stall while she got her anger under control.

"Yes Miss Chapman. We have a training program—it is not very elaborate, but you can learn the house rules and get some practice. You will have a tryout on a slow night."

"How long is the training? I assume it is unpaid."

Mardenborough's smile widened. Ori thought he might appreciate her directness—or he expected the question.

"Yes, it is unpaid. You will attend four sessions of two hours each, over four days."

Four days was nothing. Ori had enough money from her last trust fund transfer to last four months. But it was the principle of it— bringing her across a hundred miles of ocean for a non-existent job. She swallowed down the remains of her annoyance and nodded. It might be fun to deal black jack. It would be more interesting than serving drinks to drunks.

"All right. I'll give it a try."

"Good! Let's go over the schedule." He dragged the binder across the desk. "You'll need a uniform. You can get fitted while you're in training. You'll train mornings when we're slow and I can spare a dealer to work with you. There is one other trainee."

"Am I competing for the job?" Ori's anger started to flare again.

"Not at all Miss Chapman. I have several openings, so I hope to hire you both."

"Okay. Good."

"Tomorrow you'll work with Maurice. Be here at nine o'clock in the morning. The next day it will be," he turned a page in the binder, "Hillary. Same time. We make the schedule tomorrow, so I'll tell you about the rest of the sessions after that. All right?"

"I'll be here at nine tomorrow. Thank you, Mr. Mardenborough."

"Call me Victor."

"Victor."

Long Island, New York

An hour later the navigation system in Terry's car said, "You have reached your destination on the right," and they parked in front of a white suburban ranch-style house. The Long Island community reminded Beth of her childhood neighborhood, except for the variety of trees and plants. She knew it was the house where she'd left her boxes more than a year ago because of Eva's silver-grey Honda with the roof rack parked in the driveway. She chalked the recollection of cars better than houses up to her California upbringing.

"There's Eva's car, so this has to be it," she said, hearing the tentative tone in her voice. As she spoke, the front door opened and a woman Beth's age stepped out onto the square of cement that served as a front porch.

"There's Eva," Beth added, opening her door.

Seeing them getting out of the car, Eva charged across the lawn, arms open wide. She grabbed Beth in a bear hug, then moved her hands to Beth's shoulders and held her so she could look at her.

"Damn, are you still tanned? You look fantastic. It is so good to see you!"

"It's almost gone," Beth said, meaning her tan. It was a truth that bothered her. She hated her natural, pale skin so much she'd started perusing the bronzers at the makeup counters when she went shopping. "Eva, this is Terry Faughnan. Terry, Eva Hamilton. Eva kept me sane when I first moved aboard *Trouble*."

Eva released Beth and turned her attention to Terry, shaking his offered hand. "I am so happy to meet you Terry," she said. "Beth has been talking about you for all these months—she sent a couple pictures. I was so happy when she said you were sailing with her. I know she can do it alone—I knew it from the first time she took me sailing—but she needed someone to keep her from—I don't know—spending too much time in her own head? Does that make sense?"

Terry studied Beth's reaction. She nodded thoughtfully rather than brushing off her friend's concern. "I know what you mean. I enjoy being alone and doing things on my own. But I can carry it too far," Beth said.

"You have to come in and have a cup of tea with my mom. She insists. She went out in the garage and got your boxes down. I told her not to, but…"

"She shouldn't have!" Beth said, setting out with Eva across the lawn. She glanced back at Terry, who shut the car door and followed them.

They spent a pleasant half hour sipping tea, eating cookies, and talking with Eva's mother, who turned out to be a well-traveled widow with a quick wit. She seemed more tolerant of Beth's adventurous lifestyle than her daughter, who still thought Beth was nuts to want to live on a boat.

Teacups drained, they went through the kitchen and into the two-car garage where six boxes marked "Beth" were stacked in the empty space next to Mrs. Hamilton's car. Beth knew it was too much to fit in Terry's BMW, so she had researched the closest second-hand store accepting donations on Saturday afternoon. She urged the others to go ahead and open the boxes and help her sort.

"Put warm clothes and anything you think is from my family here," she said, indicating a patch of cement floor. "Put everything else over there," she pointed to the far side of the stack of boxes. I'll go over both piles."

She barely remembered packing these boxes, so the unpacking was as much a treasure hunt for her as the others. The pile of warm clothes grew quickly. The family pile was limited to a couple photo albums, framed pictures, and a box of papers, including expired leases for previous apartments and cancelled checks. The "other" pile contained kitchen equipment, decorative items, summer clothes, linens, and an vaguely familiar old shirt box. Beth picked it up. It was heavier than shirts would be.

"I wasn't sure what pile that belonged in," Eva said, shrugging.

Beth supported the bottom of the box with her left forearm and lifted the lid off. A row of four dolls smiled up at her, faces so immediately familiar and beloved she shivered, a wave of melancholy for her distant childhood sweeping over her.

"You know them?" Terry was looking over her shoulder into the box.

"I sure do." Beth sighed, smiling back at Meg, Jo, Beth, and Amy. "They're Little Women."

"They're Madam Alexander dolls, aren't they?" Mrs. Hamilton asked.

"Yes. I wasn't big on dolls as a child, but I loved these."

"Then they belong in the other pile," Terry said, reaching for the box.

Beth pulled it to her chest and stared at him. He dropped his hand to his side.

"I don't have room on the boat for dolls."

He shook his head, frowning. Beth stared at him for a moment longer before lowering the box from her chest to look at the dolls again. Suddenly unbidden tears were flooding her eyes. Terry took the box and lid, covered the dolls, and set it on the pile of warm clothes.

Eva's arm slid around Beth's shoulders, pulling her into a hug.

"It's hard to sort through your stuff, and memories," she said.

"You don't have to take it all Beth. You can leave it here," Mrs. Hamilton added.

Terry was regarding Beth with a thoughtful expression. She forced a smile and raised one shoulder in a partial shrug, praying he'd take it as she meant it—part apology, part request to talk about it later. He nodded, returning her smile.

"I've imposed on you long enough, Mrs. Hamilton. I'm sure I can whittle this down to what we can fit in the car to bring back to Washington. Whittling down for the boat can come later."

"I'll leave you to your whittling, then," Mrs. Hamilton replied. "I'll bring out iced tea in a little while."

"I think you need to go through these summer clothes, Beth. You may want them, even if you do think you kept the best when you left," Eva said, trying to suggest a constructive next step. Beth nodded, and crouched next to the pile. In a few moments she was sitting cross legged on the cold cement floor picking through it. She would hold up an item of clothing and both Eva and Terry would give it a thumbs up or down. Before long she had a much smaller pile of items to keep. Terry shoved the discards into one of the empty boxes and carried it out to the car while Beth turned her attention to the kitchen pile.

"If there's anything you want, take it," she said to Eva, "Otherwise it's all going."

Eva did claim a colander, but put the rest of the pans, utensils, and kitchen gadgets in another donation box for Terry to take to the car. Beth made quick work of the pile of decorative items, vaguely recognizing much of it. Clunky wooden candle holders, a wire mesh pencil cup, ceramic balloons with one flat side for hanging on the wall all went into the donation box. Beth picked up a wooden plaque with a piece of bleached coral glued to it and stared at it long enough for Eva to notice.

"Mean something?"

Beth chuckled. "Not really. It was a gift from someone—from my ex-boyfriend," Beth glanced over her shoulder to confirm that Terry was out of earshot, on his way back from the car, although she wasn't sure why it mattered.

"Toss it," Eva commanded.

"No kidding," Beth said, dropping it into the donation box. "I was smiling because I've seen miles of coral in the last year. Once I thought of that as the only piece of a tropical sea I would ever know."

Eva smiled at the notion, but Beth knew her unadventurous friend was thinking it might be more than enough for her. As Beth moved on to the pile of winter clothes, she had an idea.

"You should come sailing with us in the islands."

"Are you speaking to me?" Eva pointed at herself.

"Yes, you. It would be so fun to spend time together in the islands. We don't have to sail a lot. Just relaxing on the boat, swimming, sunning. You'd understand the appeal."

Beth was sure the assurance about not too much sailing brightened Eva's reaction. "Maybe so. It sounds like a great vacation."

With that tentative agreement Beth decided not to push further. She focused on the pile of sweaters and jackets and heavy jeans, thinking she wasn't sure what would fit her now. She had lost a few pounds, and her body had become more muscular. She didn't want to bother Mrs. Hamilton for a makeshift fitting room, so she kept all of the items she liked. As long as it would fit in the car, she could try them on at home.

Home. She smiled inwardly at her acceptance of Terry's place as home. It felt right.

Seventeen

Pointe-à-Pitre, Guadeloupe

"*H*ello Mr. Burt. Good to see you again," Kit said, swiping the bar in front of Burt with his cloth. "Carib?"

"Exactly what I want, Kit." Burt waved the bartender closer, "And information, if you have it."

"Yes sir?" Kit looked open to helping.

"There was a man in here the other day talking to a group of cruisers. Before that he sat at the bar and drank a Coke. Remember him?"

"Yes sir."

"Has he been back?"

Kit's gaze shifted to the rafters for a moment, and then back to Burt. "He tried to leave without paying—you saw him, right?"

Burt nodded. He'd seen the Texan, Hunter, start to leave without paying for his Coke. Kit had summoned him back to the bar and collected the two Euro. Hunter sure was terrible at keeping a low profile.

"He came back for happy hour. Ordered another Coke and paid for it. Then moved in with the cruising crowd. Seemed to be fitting right in."

"No alcohol? Did he have dinner?"

Kit shook his head. "Just the Coke."

"Thanks Kit."

"You want me to keep an eye out?"

"Don't go out of your way. It's just that he was asking for a friend of mine, a woman sailor who sails by herself sometimes. A strange man looking for her is worth keeping an eye on."

"Your friend is the woman he was asking after? I remember her, and her man."

Burt smiled, not sure why it surprised him that a bartender would remember friends he'd dined with months ago.

"That's her."

"I'll let you know if he comes back. He was asking about her again last night."

"And did any of them tell him anything?"

Kit pursed his lips, his head moving back and forth slowly. "I don't think so."

"Thanks Kit. I'm going to sit over by the railing and enjoy the view for a while."

"Yes sir. I'll bring you your beer."

After an hour and a half and two beers, Burt was chastising himself for not following the Texan to find out where he was staying. The notion of confronting him crossed his mind, but that simply was not Burt's style. He also considered emailing, or calling, Beth. He wasn't sure where she was, but suspected she was state side with Terry. He preferred to know more about the Texan before possibly alarming his friend. After all, she had a history of taking drastic, ill-planned action.

)

English Harbour, Antigua

"Thank you so much for the ride. I couldn't have handled the airfare," Hunter stood on the dinghy dock with his backpack over his shoulder. He extended his hand down toward Hank Markham, who was crouching, uncleating the small boat's line. He finished and rose, line in hand, only then seeing Hunter's gesture.

"Sorry. Yes, no problem." He started to take Hunter's hand, paused to move the dinghy line to his left hand, and finally completed the handshake. "Thank you for helping. I'm afraid our Daisy can't get used to inter-island passages. This is the fourth or fifth time we've had to take on someone to make one."

"Maybe next time. I didn't help much, so maybe she'll see that you two can do it."

Hank smiled shyly, as if being complimented. "Very kind of you. Perhaps she will. You've got your passport, yes?"

Hunter patted the pocket of his cargo shorts where he'd put the document when Hank handed it back to him outside of the immigrations office. "Yes."

"Well, thanks again."

Understanding the dismissal, Hunter took a step up the dock. "I'll see you around, Hank. Safe sailing."

"If we meet Beth Anderson we'll let her know you're looking for her. Good luck in your hunt, Hunter."

Hunter smirked and gave him a final wave as he got out of earshot. he'd heard so many plays on his name they went in one ear and out the other. He was pretty sure Hank hadn't realized he was doing it.

Finding a ride from Pointe-à-Pitre, Guadeloupe to Antigua had seemed daunting at first. It wasn't true that he couldn't afford the LIAT flight, but he preferred not to. He'd regretted not asking for a ride at the beach barbecue. Instead he'd put notices on several boards in and around the marina the next morning, and Hank Markham had called him a few hours later. He didn't think he could have tolerated Hank and his wife Daisy for much longer than the two days he'd spent aboard their ketch. When Hank joked in the customs office that Hunter had arrived in English Harbor with an Englishman, Hunter about lost it with the dumb jokes. But he bit his tongue and walked back to the dinghy dock with the man to be polite.

Looking around the harbor facilities, he saw dozens of boats—any one of which could be Beth Anderson's—and hundreds of sailors. He was going to have to do what he did in Pointe-à-Pitre—find out where the cruisers gathered. And he needed a place to stay. The harbor did not appear to offer anything he wanted to afford. The hotel adjacent to the docks used by a charter boat fleet looked too luxurious, and those weren't the kind of sailors he wanted to talk to. The next town over had more prospects—both for a place to stay and for the more frugal long-term cruisers. With a decisive nod he settled his pack on his shoulders and started along the narrow, cobbled road leading out of the harbor complex.

⁋

Georgetown, Washington, D.C.

Thanksgiving and their two-week sailing trip seemed both ages away and right on top of them during the following days. Beth accepted The Broadhead Group's offer at a salary that bested her last one in New York by four thousand dollars and meant she'd have more money coming in every two weeks than she'd spent in the entire three months cruising. In anticipation, she dipped into her tiny bit of available savings to further enhance her work wardrobe. The bulk of her savings could cover *Trouble's* insurance and storage fees for about six months. But soon, she reflected as she paid for a blazer, a skirt, and two blouses, she'd be augmenting the account.

Soon you'll be blowing it all on a new boat.

She squelched those thoughts immediately. The notion of buying a boat like they'd seen at the show, and like they were about to sail on, felt like a dream. There was no need to wrestle with the impact of it on her finances right now.

She spent half of her first day at Broadhead being oriented by a sequence of people from human resources and her new department, then joined Raj for lunch—his treat—at a local deli. Over sandwiches, soda, and chips he told her more about the firm—the less formal information that could now be shared about its history and management—and about himself. He was an Indian immigrant, brought to the US as a young child and raised in Ohio. His parents were westernized, but throughout his childhood and youth the family had been regularly thrown into turmoil by the month-long visits of their two families from India. Beth shared a bit of her family story, including her father's condition and mother's recent fall. They commiserated about the challenges of aging parents.

As was often the case, Beth's first few days were a rollercoaster of tension and boredom. She participated in meetings where she didn't have the slightest idea what they were discussing half the time, and she sat at her desk in a maroon-upholstered cubicle exploring her computer and the firm's networked file system.

At the end of the first week the Equatorial Team, which handled Caribbean clients, invited her to a meeting. Raj attended the meeting, although he told her he usually did not. To her embarrassment he introduced her as their new Caribbean expert. For the first time that week she found herself understanding most of what was discussed and thinking of possible solutions to the problems they raised. It seemed the team was having trouble booking radio airtime. She suspected her colleagues' "Washington consultants" attitude rubbed the local radio station management the wrong way. She kept her own council, however, until, after the meeting when Raj asked her to join him in his office.

"Well, what do you think?"

"About the project? Very interesting—"

"What are they doing wrong?"

"Well, they're doing plenty right—"

"Come on."

Beth hesitated.

"Door's closed. You know the area better than these beltway kids. What do I need to do to get them working with the locals down there?"

Beth resisted the urge to suggest he hire Terry and Jeff to train them. Then she realized he was casting her in that role. She warmed to it instantly.

"The locals want to be respected. They know we're coming from the biggest economy in the world and we're a super power. But they don't want to be treated like a third-world, backward nation. In fact, we need to treat every local businessman and authority as if he's the key to our success there. Which he is."

"That's it?" Raj's eyes widened.

"It's not simple."

He nodded, accepting her assertion at face value for the moment.

"Be more specific—you must have seen something in the meeting."

"Jerry's tone when he described his conversation with the radio station manager. I don't care what he thinks of the guy, his language and tone need to be professional even when he's reporting to the team. If anyone regards this as, I don't know, planting a flag in the soil of a banana republic, it's going to come through to the locals and they're going to kick us out. And the guy who hired us, too, maybe."

"Good advice for dealing with anyone. What about specific strategies for getting through the door on Antigua?"

Beth spent the next hour brainstorming with Raj, articulating subtleties of island culture she didn't realize she knew. As a result, he asked her to compile the recommendations he'd guided her to into a computerized slide deck. He wanted her to do a presentation to the team next week.

She shared her fear of offending them with Terry and he agreed with her concern. He suggested she needed to apply her own advice to the situation—find out about their culture. Feeling chagrined, the first thing Monday Beth made an effort to speak to everyone she met in the Equatorial Team meeting. In previous jobs she'd never been inclined to socialize at the office, so she dreaded making this effort at first. But she discovered it came easily now. She attributed her new openness to her experience in the loosely connected cruising community.

She started in her safety zone by approaching the two women on the team, Claudia and Seetha, and asking if they had a favorite lunch spot they could show her. This generated a heated discussion between the two women. Seetha, petit and initially soft spoken, turned out to be extremely opinionated about many of the local restaurants. Tall, blonde Claudia, who Beth identified with as a basic American woman, turned out to be addicted to sushi and Korean barbecue. Beth regretted asking the question by the time they finally settled on a particular deli with the best beverage selection. Beth couldn't care less about the lunch menu, but she was all enthusiasm as she surveyed the truly ridiculous selection of boutique sodas, juices, teas, and esoteric drinks in the deli's refrigerated case. They each ordered a sandwich along with their liquid find and chatted about food, work, and men while they ate. Beth explained, yet again, about chartering a sailboat and probed them about their hobbies: Claudia was into tennis while Seetha was focused on dating and little else that Beth could glean from their talk.

Beth learned from the women that Howard had grown up in Puerto Rico and used it as an excuse to engage with him in the break room. She learned that his personal perceptions of the Caribbean were those of an active fifteen-year-old boy. He had a treasure trove of stories about snorkeling in luminescent lagoons, riding horses bareback in the foothills, and diving off of cliffs into the sea. But he did recognize his childhood experience wasn't very useful to his current work, other than helping him socialize with their clients. It made Beth sad to think he placed so little value on the rich experiences that formed him.

From Howard she found out Marcus and Claudia enjoyed a rivalry ranging from friendly to aggressive, and when they were feuding the rest of the team stayed out of their way. When she asked Marcus to get together and review a draft document with her, she avoided any mention of Claudia. She took the opportunity to ask him more about his role on the team, and soon realized he felt a strong commitment to the team and its mission and believed Claudia felt the same. He regarded his conflicts with his colleague as healthy—both were trying to do what best served their clients. He was oblivious to the impact it had on the others.

On Wednesday morning at the Equatorial Team meeting there was a stranger in the room. Claudia introduced her to Brendan, the team member who most often met with clients in the islands. He had been on an extended trip since shortly after Beth started with the company, as his deep tan attested. As the meeting broke up it was Brendan who singled Beth out, walking with her toward her desk as he asked her how she liked Broadhead and other typical new coworker questions before switching gears to ask about her experience in the islands. She quickly realized he might be assessing her as competition. She thought that was laughable, but she decided not to sabotage her potential at Broadhead by saying she wasn't qualified to do what he did.

By Friday's Equatorial Team meeting she had subtly positioned herself with most of her audience as an expert on island culture. Her presentation, reviewed by both Terry and Raj, sparked creative discussion about their approach. Beth was thrilled to see Raj's quiet smile as the team rallied around ideas she thought had a decent chance of success.

Her participation on the team was established, although they did not specifically need a technical writer. She was glad to see that the firm was small and agile enough to allow her to participate without an elaborate approval process.

Her other work presented its own challenges: she had to learn how to research all over again, and how to read the language of senate and house bills, rulings, and motions. Terry took to grumbling playfully that she was a workaholic while each of them sat in bed with their laptops.

The hardest part of starting the job was showing up every morning. By the third morning she understood how out of the daily work habit she had fallen. It didn't help that Terry wasn't working. But he made a point of getting up with her and making the coffee while she showered and dressed. He started packing a lunch for her after the first few days when her co-workers stopped inviting her out. But even with all of Terry's support, by Thursday evening of her first week she was exhausted. She resented having to go to bed before eleven. The metro was not a pleasant convenience at rush hour. Her company-issued laptop was heavier than her MacBook, and she hated feeling like her time was not her own.

How did I do this for so many years?

They booked their flights to the Caribbean for early Saturday morning the weekend before Thanksgiving and included a stopover on St. Thomas to check on *Trouble* in storage. Jeff and Carole were to fly from Norfolk on Sunday to meet them on Antigua and would depart the following Saturday. As a treat and a diversion from dwelling on being a corporate slave, Beth pored over possible itineraries within Jeff and Carole's time constraints. Carole would not make an inter-island passage, so they would stay around Antigua. At the end of the week they had to be in a location where a taxi could reach them. But that included many beautiful anchorages around the island. Once Jeff and Carole left, Beth wanted to sail north to Antigua's national partner, Barbuda. They could spend a couple days exploring the flat, undeveloped island before sailing back to Antigua's popular beaches. Beth secretly looked forward to that part of the trip the most.

J

Pointe-à-Pitre, Guadeloupe

"Hello Burt!"

"Joe, good to see you again."

Burt was taking a stroll through the marina—for the exercise—looking for familiar faces, although he knew long term cruisers were more likely to be out on moorings or anchored. He'd spotted *Kelpie*, Joe and Laurie's boat, and Joe in the cockpit.

"What have you been up to since Antigua? No good, I hope," Joe said, stepping onto *Kelpie*'s stern swim platform to extend his hand to the other man. Burt leaned out to shake it.

"You know, the life of the charter captain. Taking groups from island to island. Some diving. Lots of bars."

"You with a group now? Hiding from them?"

Burt chuckled. "No, I'm off duty for a few weeks."

"No holiday charters?" That can't be good for business."

"It's fine with me. Say Joe, have you run into anyone asking about Beth Anderson, on *Double Trouble*?"

Joe's surprised expression answered the question. "As a matter of fact, yes. At a beach barbecue last week. Guy said he was between boats and missed the life."

"Was he about six feet, muscular, dark blond hair in a tail, Texas accent?"

Joe nodded. "Yeah, that's him. He said his name is Hunter something. He told a story about looking for someone, and Beth is a mutual friend."

"Story?" Burt latched onto what sounded like suspicion about the Texan.

Joe shrugged, "I don't know. It seemed like he's doing a lot of leg work to find a person who isn't even the person he's looking for."

"Did he say why he was looking for the 'mutual friend'?"

"Nope, and we didn't ask. Why? Do you know what he's doing?"

Burt shook his head slowly. "No. I saw him asking about Beth at *le Poisson*. I suppose I should have asked him what he's after, but I got the feeling I wouldn't get a straight answer. That worries me, for Beth."

"I know. She's can sail her boat alone, but Laurie and I have talked about the risk she takes being alone in the islands. I don't want to sound sexist, but it's the reality here."

"I don't think you're being sexist, Joe. I share your concern. I was very glad when Terry joined her last spring. But I'd never suggest she shouldn't sail alone. I'd rather keep her as a friend." His smile garnered a knowing smile and nod from the other man. "Say, did you get this Hunter's last name?" Burt had searched the internet for men named Hunter from Texas. The results were far more numerous than he'd expected.

"Yeah, it was—shoot—I think it's a color. Black? Brown? I'm not sure. hang on," Joe stepped back into *Kelpie*'s cockpit and went forward to lean into the open companionway. "Hey Laurie, Burt's here. Do you remember the last name of the guy who was asking about Beth last week?"

Burt heard a voice from below decks, and Joe straightened as his wife Laurie ascended the companionway ladder.

"Hi Burt. That guy's name was Hunter Green. I remember thinking 'poor kid, every time he opened a box of Crayons...' and Aiden said something about it too."

Both men chuckled. "Hunter Green," Burt repeated, trying to remember whether he'd seen that last name in the results of his search. "Thanks Laurie, Joe. I'll leave you to it."

"See ya Burt."

Burt started down the dock, then stopped and turned back.

"I forgot to ask, what did you tell this guy Hunter about Beth?"

"We told the truth—we last saw her on Antigua at the *Gunkholing* party—along with you and a thousand other cruisers."

"Antigua, right. Thanks."

"Do you know where she is now?"

"Not for sure, but I think she might have gone with Terry to Washington, D.C. She would have left *Trouble* on the hard somewhere."

"Has she given up cruising?" Laurie asked, surprise evident in her tone.

"Not likely. But I know she wanted to try to rebuild her bankroll. I suspect we'll see her back in the islands soon."

"I hope so."

Burt nodded and continued along the dock toward *Sandcastle*. Back on board he plugged in his cell phone and noticed the message light was blinking. He listened to his US booking agent describe a Thanksgiving week charter. Burt was solvent, but not immune to the lure of extra income for minimal work, which is what this charter with three women sounded like. As he returned the call, he speculated that they'd be avid deep sea fisher women or something and he'd be working his ass off. But he accepted the charter anyway and settled down after the call to make a to-do list.

Eighteen

Dickinson Bay, Antigua

*H*unter lifted another plastic crate of liquor from the hand truck to the counter and began placing the partially used bottles on the shelves. Gin before vodka, then rum, he reminded himself. He'd received a painful tongue lasting after getting it wrong a couple times. Both of the bartenders at Cecil's were ridiculous about it. Like they couldn't read the labels, so they always needed the bottles in the same place. After six months in rehab, Hunter's interest in liquor was academic. Since his problem was drugs and he never much mixed the two, he didn't mind being around liquor. The rehab counselors drilled into him that he had "an addictive personality," and they didn't mean he was charming. So he thought returning to the job he'd held in Jamaica—tending bar—might be pushing it. But beach bars were the best place to encounter cruising sailors, and on any given beach you could find one in need of reliable help. Hunter could haul the liquor and glassware and bus the tables. The boss who'd hired him observed that his looks were "exotic," which seemed to be a positive. In any case, he was earning a few bucks, and every day he was among drinking sailors.

He'd lost count of how many times he'd dropped the name "Beth Anderson" into a conversation. He'd believed before he started this search that cruisers all knew each other. Even before leaving Guadeloupe he'd realized that was bullshit. At least the time he'd spent there had set his expectations here, prompting him to find a place to stay and a job. But even so, after two weeks and no Beth, he was beginning to believe she had moved on from Antigua. What made him hesitate was Thanksgiving. Maybe she'd settled in some anchorage for the duration. He hoped she hadn't left the islands to spend the holiday with someone in the US.

After being dropped off in English Harbour by the British couple, Hunter had wandered around Falmouth and decided the mega yacht population was too high. So he'd caught a bus to Jolly

Harbour on the west coast of the island. It was better, but still not the kind of place the cruisers he thought he needed to speak to would visit. He needed an anchorage. As evening descended, he'd caught another bus to Dickinson Bay on the North West corner of the island. The long curve of beach was dominated by resorts, but there were a few independent bars tucked in on property of questionable ownership. They were the kind of palm frond and bamboo pole places that frugal sailors liked. Generators hummed out back, overland access was limited to rutted alleys and jungle paths, and the food menus, if they offered more than bags of chips, were limited to grilled items.

At the third one, the man in charge made the "exotic looks" comment and hired him on, cash only, through New Year's. He'd gotten a room in a motel that was dirt cheap by island standards but far too expensive for an extended stay. When his new co-workers learned of his need for a room, one of them put him in touch with a guy with a poorly made-over garage about a half hour walk from the beach.

He returned the grey plastic milk crates to the store room, locked it back up, and handed the key to the boss. He returned to the bar and began arranging the stools, benches, and tables in to some semblance of order. They'd be all over the place again by the end of the night, but he didn't mind. It gave him something to do. He was placing fresh ashtrays on each table when the first of the lunch drinkers turned up.

He listened to them greet the bartender on duty and order rum drinks—starting strong. The two men and a woman were American and proud of it, given the stars and stripes pattern of her t-shirt. They were all in their forties, tanned, self-assured, sunglasses pushed up onto their heads or tucked into the necklines of their shirts. By the time the bartender had lined up three drinks, another woman joined them from the beach. She complained in a whining voice that reminded Hunter of some of his mother's socialite friends about her companions not ordering a drink for her. They bartender waited patiently until she finally wound down and told him what she wanted. Meanwhile the men moved to one of the tables while the women stuck together at the bar. Hunter decided they were charterers, not long-term cruisers, and not likely to know Beth

Anderson. He finished with the ashtrays and moved on to the sand buckets.

The bar was a decrepit wooden structure with no floor, covered in dried palm fronds, with a propane fired grill in back. They kept buckets of sand around the building for dousing fires. Hunter rather enjoyed combing through the top layer of sand to remove debris. If it had rained—and when hadn't it?—he dumped the buckets and refilled them with lighter dry sand.

By the time he dumped and refilled the last bucket there were eight or nine more guests and the first group had finished a round. He went by their end of the picnic table and collected their empty cups.

"Another round?"

"Yes please!" whiney voiced woman replied.

"Sure," one of the men added.

Hunter wasn't paid to wait tables, but it gave him an in with the customers who otherwise ignored him. Cecil liked that it kept the customers drinking and the bartenders didn't begrudge him the tips, too much anyway. he went up to the bar and placed the order for the same drinks he'd heard the group order the first time.

"Excuse me, can you take our lunch order?" a woman with an unfamiliar accent asked him as he turned to look for his next chore. He felt a touch on his upper left arm and turned to find Cecil tapping him with a note pad and pen. Cecil nodded at the woman, so Hunter took the pad and pen and headed for her table.

It was a group of six who had placed wet snorkeling gear in the sand under the table. That was disappointing, usually only short-term charterers snorkeled here. There wasn't much to see, but the charterers didn't have time to be picky. Hunter took their orders for beers and sandwiches and brought it back to the kitchen where Cecil was doing the cooking, then to the bar for the beers.

The next group he served were escapees from one of the resorts on a courageous adventure beyond the false security of the compound. He felt sorry for them and their ilk. They would go home thinking they had been to the Caribbean, when they'd not experienced one bit of the real place.

Washington, D.C.

Beth worked hard to resist the urge to replace her sea bag—she sewed several patches on the faded blue duffel she'd brought from *Trouble*, but there was no removing the musty odor embedded in the fabric. The anticipation of funds in her bank account was having a surprising effect on her sales resistance. Washington D.C. in the late autumn was gearing up for the holidays and every storefront she passed shilled the kinds of products and services she had not been able to consider for almost two years. The notion that she deserved to buy a few things, now that she could, sometimes pervaded her thoughts as she made her way home from work, and she fell prey to it more than once. Later looking at a pair of lovely wine glasses or a fuzzy scarf in jolly pinks and yellows she experienced deep regret at her failure. Finally she found a photograph of the boat they were chartering on-line and printed it to fit into her wallet in front of the credit and debit cards. Knowing it was there, ready to rebuke her at the cash register, gave her the courage to resist the shopping urge.

The weekend before their trip she packed her sailing wardrobe—the stained shorts and worn t-shirts she'd brought north—back into the faded blue bag. Soon Terry's familiar green bag joined it on the floor in the bedroom and the sight of them nestled together made Beth smile.

On the Monday of the week before the trip Beth reminded Raj and a few others at the office of her impending departure. She discovered that Raj was not the type to monitor his staff's work very closely. Indeed, although he was aware of her coming absence, it was obvious to her when she mentioned it that he had forgotten the exact dates. By Friday Beth was entering vacation mode already, checking flight status, reviewing her packing list, and confirming via email with the yard in St. Thomas that someone would be in the office tomorrow for them to check in with when they visited *Trouble*.

She had her to-do list in her notebook when she attended the weekly Equatorial Team meeting and was reviewing it when Marcus's tense tone drew her attention.

"This meeting is critical. Brendan has to be there."

"It's impossible." Claudia shook her head. "The Natural Resources Congress on St. Lucia is the same day, and we committed to that months ago."

Marcus was leading the effort to get their client on Antigua appointed to a powerful land use committee. The meeting was an appointment hearing for the committee. Their client, a capable administrator and creator of intelligent policy, was unskilled under the pressure of questions from his peers. He'd hired the firm to help him advance his career. To hear Marcus talk, he would outright fire them if they failed to be at his side during the hearing. If he got onto the committee, his re-election by constituents whose interests were affected by the committees' recommendations would be nearly guaranteed.

"We can't lose this client over one meeting," Marcus said. "A couple hours is all it will be!"

Claudia was still shaking her head, her expression one of bafflement over what to suggest. Beth disliked her uncooperative attitude. But Claudia was primarily on the St. Lucia project and defending her own client's interests.

"Isn't Beth going to Antigua?" Howard broke in. All eyes turned to Beth and she froze for a moment, processing what he'd said.

"You are, aren't you Beth?" Marcus said, leaning toward her across the table. Beth flipped her notebook shut so nobody would notice her list.

"Yes. We're leaving tomorrow."

"So you'll be there next week. Beth, this is perfect!" Marcus stood up, his mood changing instantly. Beth craned her head up at him, unwilling to believe what she knew he was thinking.

"Can you take the meeting?" Claudia asked, also leaning toward her hopefully.

"I—well, what day is it?" Beth heard herself saying, and regretted it. Of course she could take the meeting, whenever it was. She would love to be the savior. But could she advise Mr. Codrington? Or would she be setting herself up for failure?

"It's not until the end of the week—you have plenty of time to prepare," Marcus said.

Howard rolled his eyes upward, "That's not the point. She'll be on vacation."

"This is critical!" Marcus's voice went shrill again.

"I don't mind spending time preparing." Beth was speaking before thinking again. "But I don't know if I'm qualified—"

"You'll be fine. This guy is socially awkward. All you have to do is whisper names in his ear when he forgets them and prompt him with the prepared answers when he hesitates."

"Really Beth, you'd be good at it. You have a calming influence."

"I do?" Beth wondered why Howard had gone from eye-rolling objection to encouragement so quickly.

"Definitely," most of the team chorused. Beth knew the compliment wasn't sincere but intended to convince her to solve the problem.

"Will your ship be there on Friday?" Claudia asked. Beth smiled. So many people simply didn't get the difference between sailing and taking a cruise she usually gave up explaining after the second try.

"I can be wherever I need to be on Friday," she lied. Terry and the others had a say in the matter. But she was the skipper in the eyes of the boat broker—a role Terry had insisted she assume. She thought he and the rest would want her do this—it would play up to Jeff's work ethic.

"Beth's not taking a cruise," Howard told Claudia. "She's sailing her own boat."

Beth didn't bother to correct him—close enough.

Claudia looked confused, but she didn't respond.

"So you'll do it?" Marcus half pleaded.

"Yes, of course. I'll do it," she said, quaking inside.

)

Dickinson Bay, Antigua

After the third pickup truck rumbled down the road past him splashing filthy water onto his bare lower legs Hunter emitted a mild curse and stepped further off of the road onto the bank covered in long grass and thorny shrubs. Squalls had blown across the island all night, leaving deep, unavoidable puddles. The thunder and waves of pounding rain had interrupted his sleep over and over again and he'd finally awakened to the bright morning sunshine feeling grouchier than he could recall being during his rehab days.

Ordinarily he made do in the morning with a glass of water and a piece of fruit, which he bought from a woman with a garden down the road and kept in a bowl in his rented room. But today he needed help being civil to people. Today he needed coffee. Every morning he walked past the coffee shop across the road from where he stood now. Two people came out there were three cars parked out front; it must be open. Hand-printed signs in the front windows advertised "hot coffee" and "muffins and breads." He dug his hands into the pockets of his cargo shorts and calculated how much money he had in his wallet. Enough, he decided without pulling it out to check. Looking both ways and remembering they drove on the wrong side here, he trotted across the road, taking a final leap over a spreading puddle on the far edge. The gravel and dirt of the area that served as a parking lot crunched under his shoes.

The coffee shop was cool and filled with the aroma of baking muffins. He couldn't overcome the urge to indulge—his mouth watered at the sight of muffins with glistening blueberries baked. They reminded him of the bakery back home. He ordered a muffin and a cup of coffee and took them to a table. Maybe if he sat and absorbed calories his mood would improve. He had time. Cecil didn't watch the clock.

Sipping the coffee, he became aware of a voice chattering somewhere behind the counter. It wasn't a person, though. Or rather, the speaker wasn't in the cafe. The voice sounded like it was coming from a radio. For a moment he thought it was just a talk radio show, but as he tuned in on the voice, he realized he was hearing conversations: people talking on a two-way radio.

The woman who had poured his coffee paused as she reached into the pastry case for a croissant for another customer, head tilted as she listened to the voice for a moment, and then she laughed. Hunter focused on listening to the voice too, curious about what was funny.

It took him a few more minutes to realize that what he was hearing was sailors—cruisers—talking to one another. Except the most prominent voice, a man with an Australian accent—was running things. Hunter heard others identify themselves by name and boat, say where they were, and report interesting information like the weather conditions or anything special going on. The man would stop the roll call every now and then to make announcements about local market days, missing pets, and local events. He interspersed the notices with bad jokes, which is what the waitress had paused to laugh at.

"Refill?"

The woman from behind the counter was standing by his table with the coffee pot in hand. Hunter realized he had sat listening long enough to finish his breakfast. The sailors were still talking.

"Yes. Sure."

She nodded as she poured warm coffee into his paper cup.

"You never heard Papi before?"

"Papi?"

"On the radio. I see you listening."

"No, I never have. It's entertaining."

"He is that. He's my sister's man. Used to sail every race around here, until the accident. Now he looks out for the rest of the sailors."

"I see. Where is he broadcasting from?"

"House up on the hill. Nothing fancy, but he's got a tall antenna."

"And the sailors know about him?"

"Oh sure. News travels. Every island has a Papi."

"I see. Thanks for the info."

"No problem. Enjoy."

He'd taken a few sips of the fresh coffee when he heard Papi signing off, promising to be back tomorrow morning. Hunter rose, cup in hand, promising himself he'd be having coffee every morning from now on.

⟩

Phillipsburg, Sint Maarten

"She is a regular, an islander. He is from a cruise ship, see the lanyard around his neck? The next one is local. You will do well," Rupert, the pit boss, whispered.

Ori listened to him as she took her position at the blackjack table. Her eyes flicked from one player to the next as Rupert identified them. The first woman was statuesque and dressed to enhance her curves. Her hair was perfectly styled, straightened and swept up and around her head. Her rich, dark complexion showed the benefit of regular care. It was hard to pin her age, but she had to be close to forty. The man from the cruise ship had a thick head of salt and pepper hair and wore a buttery yellow polo shirt. He was in his fifties at least, but his arms were muscular, and he sported a deep suntan. The other local was much younger than the other two, underdressed by most standards in a velour hoodie over a black t-shirt with something printed on it that she couldn't see. A heavy gold chain hung around his neck and when he opened his mouth, she caught a flash of gold inside. Drugs. Dealing, maybe using.

She introduced herself and focused on instructing the players to place their bets, wondering at the same time what Rupert meant. Were these players easy going?

Rupert stood behind her and to one side, indicating to the players that she was a new dealer. Ori didn't mind. His presence felt supportive, even though she knew he was watching her every move and listening to her every word. Any misstep and she'd be off the floor.

But she didn't misstep, at least not too badly. The house won the first two hands, and she hadn't had to try very hard. The woman player had lost three hundred Euros and the young guy was in for five hundred. The cruiser stuck with the table minimum.

The woman won the next hand, recouping her loss and gaining a hundred. But Ori won it back for the house on the next hand. The young man won two hands and Ori half expected Rupert to take her off the table, but instead he moved away.

Ori's confidence rose, but plummeted as the cruiser managed to win a hand, followed by the woman, and then the young man. And so it went, with the house winning more than the players, but losing enough to keep them engaged. Finally, the cruiser collected his remaining chips and stood up. He tossed a ten Euro chip to Ori with a "thanks" and walked away. As Ori picked up the chip Rupert reappeared, signaling her to step aside. He'd brought another dealer.

"Good work," he murmured as they walked away from the table.

"Really? I couldn't keep that guy there."

"You weren't going to. He's on a budget."

"How do you know?"

"You'll learn. Take your break. You're back on in fifteen."

)

Virgine accepted the thin stack of euros from the cashier, counted them herself, and folded them into her satin evening bag. Stepping away from the cashier's cage she looked around the gaming floor, barely concealing her disgust at the tourists in shorts and lurid shirts and the underdressed locals. She'd ended the evening up a couple hundred euros. Not where she needed to be, but that new dealer had put a crimp in her game. Her eyes wandered to a banner suspended from the ceiling. It promoted an upcoming black jack tournament. That was how she would make the money she needed.

She strode out of the casino with stiffening resolve.

)

Washington, D.C.

Upon hearing of the plan for Beth to take the meeting in Antigua, Raj asked her to see him before she left. She entered his office expecting to be told he'd found someone else—someone more qualified—to fly to Antigua next week. In the ninety minutes since the meeting Marcus had sent her a pile of background information and the meeting specifics. She'd started reading and growing more excited about the opportunity.

"Marcus tells me you are the perfect person to handle the hearing with Mr. Codrington," Raj said as she sat down. Her head snapped up to meet his gaze. She struggled to hide her surprise. "I think he's desperate," Raj went on. "But he's not necessarily wrong. Beth, it's an important meeting, but not a terribly difficult one for someone with your personality and skills."

Beth breathed, her confidence soaring.

"I checked. You haven't accrued time for this vacation. We agreed you'd take it unpaid, right?"

"Yes, I booked it before this job opportunity arose." *Not long before, but no need to say that.* Beth wasn't sure what was coming.

"Well, I think we have to compensate you for saving the day on this one. Please report your time next week as work. I can't stretch it to the following week, I'm sorry."

Beth was dumbfounded. She hadn't given a thought to compensation for inserting a business meeting into her holiday. "Thank you, Raj. I appreciate that."

"My pleasure. Taking a day out of your vacation is above and beyond, Beth, let alone the preparation time you'll spend before the meeting. It says a lot about your commitment to us. Marcus has given you the background information?"

"Yes. I've been reading it."

"Well don't hesitate to call if there's anything else you need before the hearing. We'll overnight it if we need to."

"Or email."

"Right. I do ask that you call after the hearing. Marcus will die of anxiety if you don't let him know how it went before the weekend." Raj's smile was infectious, and Beth shared it. Marcus was nothing if not excitable.

Terry was almost as excited about the meeting as she was, and Jeff observed that having the boat near Antigua's capital on Friday would be convenient for getting a taxi to the airport on Saturday.

The trip had taken on a new cadence: the week before the hearing and the week after. Beth was glad the meeting nearly coincided with Jeff and Carole's departure. Until now, their friends' departure had been the chief event on the itinerary. Now the meeting loomed larger. The week leading up to it was shadowed with her need to be prepared for it. The week after, sailing alone with Terry, would be her real vacation.

♪

Pointe-à-Pitre, Guadeloupe

Sandcastle's systems were humming perfectly, her fuel and water tanks were full, she was spotless inside and out, and provisions and fresh laundry for the charter party were due any minute. Burt relaxed in a deck chair, a mild rum and tonic at hand and his laptop on his lap. He double checked his pre-charter list even though he knew he was ready, then scrolled through his email to make sure they hadn't cancelled, although his agent would have telephoned if they did so this late.

Conscience clear with regard to his charter duties, he opened a new email and typed Beth Anderson's address. Over the last week and a half while he was working on *Sandcastle*, he had thought several times about contacting Beth. He believed he shouldn't tell her about the man from Texas who was looking for her—she could be unpredictable, and she didn't always put her own safety first. She might go off in search of Hunter to confront him. Burt wanted to know where Beth was and what her short-term plans were. With that information he could decide whether he should step in on her behalf and track down the Texan himself, or let the guy keep roaming the islands. With that goal in mind, he wrote Beth a short note telling her of his upcoming charter and a few other bits of news about mutual friends. He didn't mention meeting Joe and Laurie, or that he thought she was in Washington. He wanted her to tell him her plans and she might not if she realized he already knew some of them. Instead he asked what she was up to and where she was keeping herself. Satisfied there was nothing alarming about his message, he hit send.

Nineteen

St. Thomas, USVI

"She looks lonely," Beth said as she and Terry approached *Double Trouble*'s ivory hull standing on stanchions in the St. Thomas boat yard. Terry laid a companionable arm across her shoulders. A ladder propped against *Trouble*'s hull at the gate in the lifeline invited them to board. The flap cut in the white shrink-wrap deck cover was clipped open above it. The clerk in the yard office had told them Mr. Henderson, the yard manager, was already aboard.

They had left *Trouble*'s deck, cockpit, and cabin neat, but Beth was shocked when she climbed down the companionway ladder at how empty it felt. The familiar surroundings brought back myriad memories—the gashed galley counter from the slip of a knife blade, the annoyingly short VHF radio microphone cord with its permanent kinks from being overstretched, the water stain on the dining table that she wanted to sand and refinish.

It was home, and yet it was not. *Trouble* was stripped of their personal items—some jettisoned, the rest carried to Washington.

Mr. Henderson greeted them in the saloon and started talking about the boat's condition—the weather had been fair, so there was no damage. The yard crew regularly checked her battery levels and reported that the solar panels were doing their job.

"You want to sell it?" he asked, startling Beth.

"Maybe," Terry answered for her. It came as a shock, as a betrayal of *Trouble*'s loyalty. But he was right, and he knew she wasn't ready to say it, so he did it for her.

Mr. Henderson studied *Trouble* as if appraising her. "A couple people have asked. You want me to let you know next time someone does?" Now he turned to Beth, knowing the storage payments came from her.

"Yes. Please do. We're not sure we want to sell, but we'd like to know." Beth's gaze took in *Trouble* and ended up on Terry's patient face. "I guess this is all we needed to do."

"Yes ma'am. We take good care of it. You don't worry."

"No, I don't. Thank you, Mr. Henderson." Beth put a hand on the ladder handle and paused to take one more look around. It wasn't the last time she'd see *Trouble*, she was sure, but it felt that way.

)

English Harbour, Antigua

The thrill of arriving at a tropical marina by taxi was new to Beth and she enjoyed the ride along busy main roads from the airport to English Harbour on Antigua's south coast. The silly grin didn't leave her face as they offloaded their minimal luggage—dwarfed by the bags of the charterers with whom they'd shared the taxi—outside of the marina office. The taxi did a three point turn in the open area between the wooden office building, an adjacent stone structure, and a huge stone and cement paved slab covered by a roof on thick wooden supports. By the time the taxi was facing out another vehicle was coming along the one-lane road from the gate. They watched with interest as the Taxi reversed along the lane between buildings until it reached a wider stretch, where it let the oncoming vehicle pass it before making for the exit.

Nelson's dockyard and English Harbour had been built in a past century of ballast stone and timbers from the English ships that sheltered in this natural harbor. Thick stone walls protected the former military garrison from the interior of the island, and batteries of cannon, several still in place, defended the seaway. The streets were as wide as the carts and wagons of their time had required, and few vehicles were admitted through the guarded gate. The stone wharves that had once provided secure mooring for English naval vessels and probably a few privateers now held the lines of a variety of modern vessels, mostly sail.

The yacht broker who had arranged their charter was meeting them on board the boat, which was two years old but of the same design of as the one they'd toured in Annapolis. They crossed a patio to the seawall where they could see a row of modern sailboats, but when they got closer, they realized they were all part of a charter company fleet.

"Can I help you?" A British man in cargo shorts and a polo shirt with the charter company logo stopped in front of them. He was holding a deflated fender in one hand and a wrench in the other. His mirrored sunglasses were perched on his head amid sun-bleached brown waves.

"Hi. We're looking for a Bavaria named *Mana*. She's not one of yours, though," Beth said.

"You know it's on the seawall?" He asked and Beth realized he wondered if it was anchored out.

"Pretty sure."

"You'll have to go around, or though, the sail loft to the other part of the seawall, it has to be over there. This section is our boats." he pointed across the water. Beth recognized a café she and Terry visited when they were here last August. Several sailboats of about the right size were secured stern-to the sea wall in front of it.

"I'll bet it's one of those," Terry said, following her gaze.

"Thanks," Beth said to the Brit, who responded with a nod as he went on his way.

Beth and Terry returned to the patio and found their way from it across the ruins of Nelson's boat house and sail loft, an impressive double row of columns with paving stones in between leading away from a shallow slipway. Once across the historic site they stepped back onto the modern paved seawall walkway and followed it around between the boats and the cafe. They found the one named *Mana*, registered in Jacksonville, Florida. They knew the owner was a lawyer who was reconsidering his need for her. He allowed the broker to charter her out to partially cover his expenses, no doubt with the hope a charterer would decide to buy her.

As they set their bags down on the seawall several feet back from the edge, a man climbed up the companionway from below and stepped into the cockpit. He moved past the cockpit table to stand in between the twin steering wheels.

"Terry and Beth?" His smile was a toothy affair, his round face giving the faint impression of a yellow smiley face emoticon.

"Hello. Yes, this is Beth and I'm Terry."

"I'm glad to meet you in person. I'm Frank Rivera."

Terry had exchanged several emails with Frank the yacht broker over the last couple weeks.

"Frank. Yes. Nice to meet you too. So this is *Mana*."

"This is she. Come aboard," the broker took a step back and waved them forward. Terry jumped down from the seawall to *Mana*'s broad stern swim platform, then turned and offered Beth his hand. She took it as she hopped down. There was no handhold within reach of the back of the platform, a design feature that hadn't been apparent at the boat show, where railings had been extended from the dock.

"Have a seat in the shade," Frank nodded at the lazarette opposite him. "And a cold drink." He lifted a hatch embedded in the cockpit table to reveal a compartment full of ice and frosty bottles of beer and soda. "What would you like, Beth?"

"An ice-cold beer would be great," Beth answered, eying the ice skeptically. It would melt within the hour in the tropical heat, even if the compartment was insulated.

"Same for me," Terry added.

Frank pulled three green bottles from the ice and replaced the lid, then used an opener cleverly welded into the table support to pop the caps off. Beth caught Terry's eye and they both smiled approval at this simple convenience. Frank did not appear to notice, but Beth sensed the entire ritual was choreographed.

"We have paperwork to do—not too much," Frank raised a hand, palm out, as if to forestall an expected complaint that Beth had not considered making. "And I'd like to show you the boat. I'll answer any questions. If we find anything amiss, I'll take care of it."

"Thanks. We're ready to see the boat," Terry said after taking a swig of beer. "Shall we start up here?"

If Frank objected to Terry's suggestion, he showed no sign of it. But as Beth and Terry methodically opened each storage compartment and examined the gear inside he offered un-necessary explanations of almost everything they found. Beth wished he'd go away and let them do it themselves. After reviewing the standing and running rigging and the anchor they went below to repeat the review in the ship's accommodations. Their beers were quickly depleted, and Frank left them for a moment to get another round from the cockpit.

"When I first inspected *Trouble*, I didn't know what to look for. I just now realized how much I've learned."

Terry nodded with a smile, snapping shut the first aid kit they'd been examining. "And no matter how careful you are to check everything, there will be something you missed, and it's the thing that will break."

"Nice attitude."

"Someone said it to me once, a guy who's done a lot of charters. He backed it up with stories."

"Great, now I feel like I have to spend more time inspecting."

"It's not necessary, Beth," Frank said, overhearing as he returned with the beer. He handed her a cold bottle. "*Mana* is in immaculate condition."

Beth resisted the urge to point out a half dozen minor flaws she'd noted just to be contrary.

"She's a lovely boat, and I know we're going to have a great time on her," Terry said. Beth thought he knew what she was trying not to say.

They completed their review with tests of the engine, bow thrusters, anchor windlass, and dinghy motor. By then a light, cooling breeze stirred the papers left on the table, so they returned to the cockpit to sign the rental agreement.

Frank spread three multi-page documents out on the table and studied each one as if orienting himself to them. After a moment he tapped his right index finger on a signature line on the document on the right and looked up. Beth had printed, signed, scanned, and emailed it to him several days ago.

"I see that the charter agreement has Miss Anderson as the captain," he said, the question mark apparent in his tone.

"That's right," Beth said.

"Beth's boat is on the hard in St. Thomas while we think about trading up," Terry explained.

"I see," Frank said. He picked up the contract and turned to the second page. It was the sailing resume Beth had put together last week. She stopped breathing. Watching Frank she knew exactly what he was reading. What she did not know was how he would react.

"Well, this resume seems adequate, although your boat is somewhat smaller than *Mana*."

"I have a little more experience than Beth on a boat this size," Terry said. "But Beth has more experience overall."

Frank nodded, but he had already turned his attention to the next document.

"This is your provisioning order. We chose Antigua's best delicacies for your party. You should check that you got everything when it arrives, which will be in about thirty minutes." He handed the list to Beth. She wondered whether he did it because she was the skipper, or because he always gave the grocery list to the woman.

The last document was *Mana*'s owner's papers, cruising permits, and other official paperwork. Frank put this and the charter contract into a folder and handed it to Beth as well, which mollified her.

"My card is clipped to the agreement. Call me if there's anything we missed. At the end of your trip, call me at least an hour before you get here so I can have someone meet you."

"Thank you, Frank. We will," Beth said, extending her hand as they stood up.

Frank shook her hand and Terry's before climbing out between the two wheels, down on to the swim platform, and up onto the seawall.

"I can pass you your bags if you like," he called from the wall.

"Yes, that would be great. Thanks," Terry said, rising to go take the bags from him.

)

"How much time do we have before Jeff and Carole arrive?" Beth asked after Frank had gone.

"About an hour and a half. Their flight lands at 3:45."

"Let's stow our gear before the provisions get here."

They stowed everything they'd brought into the forward cabin's spacious drawers, and folded up their duffle bags so they could stash them in the bottom of the cedar-lined hanging locker.

Beth carried her sailing gear back out to the saloon, placing her hand-held VHF radio, hand-held GPS receiver, and sailing gloves on the chart table. Terry followed carrying a net bag that held sunscreen in three different strengths.

"I'll put these in the cockpit," he said, climbing the companionway ladder. Beth followed him and watched him open the top of the table to put the bag inside, remembering the ice and beer. He stared into the compartment for a moment, one hand holding the table top, the other holding the net bag.

"Melted?" Beth asked.

"Completely." He flashed her his knowing smile and dropped the bag into the compartment. The melted ice, Beth saw, had drained through a hole in the bottom of the table onto the cockpit floor. The beer bottles rattled against the plastic bottles in the mesh bag.

"Might as well pass those to me. I'll put them in the refrigerator," she said.

A friendly shout from the seawall signaled the food delivery. Leaving the beers on the galley counter Beth climbed back into the cockpit beside Terry and was thrilled to see a man with a hand truck loaded with crates of beer, soda, and water.

"Are any of those remotely cold?" she asked, smiling. The delivery man's flashing grin was contagious.

Terry stepped from the aft platform to the wharf and reached out to touch a beer bottle.

"It isn't cold, but it's cooler than the ones I took out of the table."

"Your food is coming next," the man said, angling the hand truck to slide the three cases of drinks onto the ground.

"Thanks." Terry lifted a couple beer bottles out and handed them to Beth, who carried them to the table with its built-in opener. The man disappeared with his cart, one wheel squeaking rhythmically.

Leaving the stack of crates for the moment, Terry climbed back into the cockpit and sat down in the shade of the blue canvas Bimini. Beth sat across from him.

"I feels good to be here," he said.

"Sure does." Beth took a long sip of her beer, a locally brewed sour lager, and took another look at their surroundings. It was one of the most interesting harbors she'd ever been in. A few months ago, the party for the treasure hunt they'd participated in had been in Falmouth Harbour, the next bay over. They had anchored *Trouble* there and walked to English Harbour to pick up their mail at the customs office. Beth was glad to be here this time rather than in that much larger bay next door.

But something prevented her from complete relaxation: *Mana* was squeezed by the boats on either side, each one anchored with stern lines to the sea wall. Undoing this arrangement was not difficult. What she was worried about was when they came back: She would have to squeeze *Mana* backwards in between two boats while Terry deployed the anchor and got stern lines ashore. All without damaging anything. The only other time she'd done it was with the much smaller *Trouble* and a crew of four. Sipping her beer, she debated with herself whether to talk to Terry about it. But he was so relaxed and happy she didn't want to worry him. Not this early in the trip, anyway.

After a while the man with the hand truck returned, unloaded boxes of food, and left to make another trip. The food sitting on the seawall in the hot sun demanded their attention. They formed a daisy chain to move it aboard and stow it. The boat's commodious galley swallowed up their provisions; on *Trouble* they'd have crammed food into drawers with their clothes if they loaded so much at once. They rewarded themselves with bottles of water.

Soon a taxi pulled up and discharged Jeff, Carole, and a huge pile of luggage. Beth shot a look at Terry, who smiled back in silent understanding of her reaction. They each had at least twice the amount of gear as he and Beth combined. *Mana* had two aft cabins for Jeff and Carole to choose from—or they could each have their own if they wanted. After greetings and more beers—now further chilled by the refrigerator—Beth made up an errand for herself and Terry to give the other couple a chance to get settled.

"What on earth did they bring?" she said once she and Terry were out of earshot. He chuckled, shrugging.

"Who knows? Carole doesn't surprise me, but I'm not sure what's up with Jeff. He barely allows his crew to bring anything aboard *Grace*."

"It's compensation—this isn't a race, so he brought everything including the kitchen sink—that he misses when he races."

Terry laughed again, "Could be."

⌡

Whatever the had in their multiple bags, they stowed it in the aft cabins by the time Beth and Terry returned a half hour later. It was late afternoon, so they set out on foot for a walk to Falmouth Harbour, where there were more restaurants and shops than English Harbour's limited choices.

"Those women near the gate told us not to go outside the compound," Carole said when she realized what her companions meant by walking to Falmouth.

"Why not?' Beth asked.

"They said some tourists were robbed." Carole's concern appeared to be genuine. "They said not to use any ATMs. There's a virus."

Beth frowned, first trying to decide whether it was possible, and then wondering whether it was true.

"Oh that," Terry said, "I saw a notice at the airport. Someone's been putting skimmers on them and stealing access numbers and pins. There's no virus. You need to look carefully at the machine before you use it to be sure you're not putting your card through an extra reader."

"Like they do in the states sometimes," Beth added, remembering such scams several years ago in New York.

"Yeah. I guess the American banks have driven them off," Jeff said. "It's okay, I have enough cash for the time being. As for walking to Falmouth, what are you afraid of honey? You've got me and Terry to protect you."

Beth thought Carole stiffened as Jeff wrapped his arm around her waist, but it may have been her imagination.

Twenty

Antigua

"*W*hy don't we pull out the main now before we get out into the swells?" Beth said from behind the starboard wheel. They were motoring out the sinuous channel through Freedom Bay, the anchorage outside of English Harbour. In a moment they'd poke the bow out into the Caribbean Sea where swells that had started their lives in Africa met this tiny lump of rock. Even on a calm day they could be twenty feet high. Her words were pitched as a question but intended as a command. This was her style, and Terry had accepted it from the first day they'd sailed together. He appreciated that she left room for discussion, which she accepted when he occasionally offered it. In urgent situations her tone changed, and her orders were just that, brooking no argument. Terry had not been trying to flatter her when he'd handed her the skipper's resume form from the broker weeks ago. By virtue of living aboard for a year and because of innate talent she was the better sailor. He knew he contributed a great deal to their progress and safety at sea, but he trusted her judgment implicitly when the pressure was on. So he was shocked when his partner and friend took Beth's command as an actual question.

"Well yeah, we should. It'll be a lot harder out there." Jeff shot Beth a concerned look, before turning to the lines that controlled the mainsail. "Put her into the wind please."

Beth's eyebrows rose as she stared at Jeff's back and alarms went off in Terry's head. When he'd first joined Beth on *Trouble*, she had been threatened by her incorrect assumption that he wanted to take charge. They had been through several very rough days while she resorted to passive-aggressive anger before he'd forced a discussion and convinced her that he respected her authority. Fortunately, at the time they'd been waiting out the weather in a marina in Miami, not at sea where the situation could have become dangerous very quickly.

Beth had grown over the last year into a self-assured skipper. But Terry had been her lone crew and they sailed together with little need for orders or discussion. Jeff skippered his own boat, and on those rare occasions when he sailed under someone else's command, that someone was always another man. It had never occurred to Terry that this might be a problem. Judging from her expression, it hadn't occurred to Beth, either.

He caught her eye and sent her calming thoughts, praying she'd let the moment pass, wanting to tell her he'd have a word with his partner once they were under sail. Perhaps she understood, for without another word to Jeff she slowed their forward motion and turned into the breeze. With a grunted "good" Jeff began to grind the winch that drew the main sail out of the mast and along the boom.

In the forward port corner of the cockpit Carole was oblivious to the tense dynamic between captain and crew as she watched Jeff. She had the familiar look of the complete novice trying to understand what she was watching and completely baffled by it. Terry felt apprehension about this first week of cruising.

For the next hour Beth, Terry, and Jeff each took a turn steering the sailboat through the huge, well-spaced swells keeping as close to the wind as they could. But unfortunately, the wind was blowing from exactly the direction they needed to go to reach Nonsuch Bay to the northeast. The wind forced them to sail either southeast away from the island or north directly toward it. After going away from shore for an hour the island had diminished enough that Carole was looking back at it with concern.

Beth emerged from the cabin where a trip to the head had included a stop at the navigation station to consult the electronic chart plotter that showed their position as well as the proper heading to their destination.

"Let's tack," she said. This time absolutely not a question.

"Nah, let's get to the lay line," Jeff replied from the helm, looking down at a duplicate chart plotter display.

Shit, Terry thought, for Beth's angry expression scared him. He looked at Carole. "Carole, what do you think? We can turn back toward the island now, but we'll probably end up motoring for a while when we're closer, to get to our anchorage."

Carole's answer came so quickly it was almost comic. "Let's go back. Would it be faster to turn on the engine now?"

To Terry's relief, both Beth and Jeff laughed. "Okay, we'll tack back," Jeff said with altogether too much authority. Beth stepped the rest of the way into the cockpit and moved toward the working jib sheet, but Terry was sitting in her way. She stopped, looking down at him and he refused to move, staring pointedly up into her eyes for a long moment, once again trying to convey calm and patience and a promise to help sort Jeff out. Her mouth was tight, her eyes hard. He reached out and stroked her thigh where it pressed his leg. Then a particularly heavy swell rocked the boat and she lost her balance. He caught her, strong arms and shoulders holding her not insubstantial weight firmly above him for a moment before giving in to the urge to bring her close. He used the opportunity to give her a reassuring hug and whisper, "be patient and we'll talk it out later."

She got a knee onto the bench and lifted her weight off of him, meeting his eyes with a softened expression and a smile. She was, he thought, also thinking of their own early troubles sorting out authority.

"Thanks," she mouthed. Then, louder, "Will you handle the sheet?"

"You got it skipper," he said with a wink. She pushed away from him and made her way around the cockpit to the other sheet that needed to be hauled in when they turned.

"Ready helmsman," she said, her arch tone and use of the less-than-skipper title clear to Terry but probably lost on Jeff.

As they glided past Green Island into Nonsuch Bay Beth stunned Terry by saying, "You guys anchor her while Carole and I get the appetizers ready for cocktails."

"We're almost there?" Carole asked, which was so obtuse Jeff groaned out load.

"See the land all around, and the boats anchored up ahead?"

"I'm new to this! I don't know we were stopping here," Carole protested. Beth obviously had to hide a grin.

"I'm sorry Carole, Terry and I are so used to sailing together we hardly talk about what we're doing. I'll make a point of telling you more about what's going on."

With that Beth descended the companionway ladder.

Carole got up and followed her, leaving the men to select a spot and anchor the boat.

"How about between the cat and the one with the blue hull? Drop it there and drop back to the open spot behind them?" Terry asked.

"Looks good."

Jeff throttled down to reduce their speed as they moved in among the handful of anchored boats.

"Jeff, it didn't occur to me to bring it up before we got here, but you know, Beth's the skipper on this trip."

"Oh, sure," Jeff put him off.

"No, really. She's the most qualified of all of us."

Jeff's expression was genuine puzzlement. "I know you love her, buddy, but you gotta see it: she doesn't act like it."

"You mean, because she asks instead of orders?"

"Yeah. She wants me to do something, she should tell me."

Terry sighed and looked again at their surroundings as much out of habit to check their progress as to collect his thoughts. Jeff's course to their selected spot was true.

"It's her style. This isn't a race boat. Maybe it's a girl thing, but she's not going to bark orders when we're having a pleasant sail. Believe me, if we run into trouble, she'll be barking."

Jeff studied him for another moment before returning his focus to the boats ahead.

"You going to drop the hook?"

"Yeah, I'll go. Will you back off? If you think she's wrong about something, speak up and make your case. Don't just challenge her."

"Fine. I'll try to squelch my racer's instincts."

"Thanks. We can have a great time if we all relax."

Hoping he was right, Terry climbed out of the cockpit and went forward to handle the anchor.

It took four tries to get the anchor to hold, which embarrassed Terry. Jeff shrugged it off saying "racers don't anchor." Beth and Carole prudently stayed in the galley until the process was complete. By the third attempt they had laid out cheese and crackers and Beth had made a pitcher of rum punch, so they were sipping their first round when Beth felt the anchor finally take hold.

"There we go," she said, picking up the pitcher and putting her full cup into the top of a stack of two more for the men.

"They're done? How do you know?" Carole asked.

"You can feel when the anchor sets. Jeff was reversing the engine on it and we were dragging backwards, and then we stopped because the anchor dug into the bottom."

Carole shook her head, bewildered, "I don't know how you could tell that from all the other movement. Amazing," she said, picking up the tray of cheese and crackers.

"Will you plug in an anchor waypoint, Jeff?" Beth asked, setting the pitcher and cups on the cockpit table.

"Use a man overboard mark?" he asked, looking at the navigation controls.

"That'll do," Beth agreed, watching him. Without further comment she picked up her hand-held GPS, kept handy as a familiar backup to the ship's system, and entered a waypoint at their current position. A quick glance at either display would tell them if they'd moved significantly away from the recorded position, which would mean the anchor wasn't holding.

Terry returned from the bow pulling his gloves off as he climbed down into the cockpit. He tossed them in under the dodger, the canvas and plexiglass screen that created a windbreak at the front of the cockpit as well as a protected area of deck to either side of the companionway. By the end of a day of sailing it sheltered delicate items like books, binoculars, sweaters, and cameras.

"We're not going anywhere," he said, reaching for a cup. Beth caught his eye, sharing a moment of delight at being back at anchor in paradise.

♪

Nonesuch Bay, Antigua

They had selected Nonesuch Bay as their first stop both because it was a short sail on their first day, and because it was a beautiful, mostly uninhabited spot. The next morning they took their dinghy to nearby Green Island to look for shells and beach glass. A local company had set up shop on the beach offering parasurfing lessons for a high fee. Jeff eagerly handed over his credit card and got suited up, urging Terry to join him. Terry declined with an indulgent grin. The other three laughed watching Jeff repeatedly splash into the water and come up snorting until he finally got the hang of controlling the parachute from the surfboard. Once he was zooming across the water Carole snapped dozens of photos of him, although Beth had noticed she kept the lens covered during his initial floundering.

Back aboard *Mana*, Beth got out her bottles of shampoo and body wash and sat down in her swimsuit on the edge of the swim platform. While sailing, the platform was raised beyond vertical to close the back of the cockpit. Once lowered, its surface was about a foot above water level. They had installed the swim ladder, which doubled as the ladder for the sail locker up on the bow. It hung deep into the water. For the first time in months Beth slipped into the warm embrace of the Caribbean Sea.

She swam a lap around the boat, and then another. Then she used her fingers to clear sand from the beach out of her swimsuit. If Jeff and Carole weren't there, she would have stripped it off, and maybe in another couple of days she would do it anyway, but not quite yet. Standing on the bottom step of the ladder she picked up her shampoo and lathered her hair with one hand while hanging on with the other. Carole had changed and was sitting in the cockpit watching her.

"The water's great," Beth said. Yesterday she had made a point of showing Carole the handheld shower on a hose tucked into a compartment at the back of the cockpit, saying, "we never use the showers in the heads, it gets too damp down there."

"Are you washing your hair?" Carole asked as if they'd never had the conversation yesterday.

"Yup, I love washing in salt water." With that Beth pushed off of the ladder and felt the sea start to rinse away the shampoo. She dove a couple more times to get it all out, and then returned to the ladder. Terry had appeared on the swim platform in his swimsuit, a beer in hand.

"Your turn," she said to him as she climbed the ladder. On the third step she paused to reach for a higher handhold and realized there was none. The ladder hung out there off the back of the boat with the nearest railing well beyond arm's reach. The ladder handles extended up about a foot from the platform, too short for Beth to use to pull her body up higher. Worse, the ladder was less than a foot wide, so she couldn't use a wider stance for more stability. She looked up at Terry, who was watching her curiously.

"This ladder sucks," she said. Terry extended his hand to her. She took it, although she would have preferred a fixed handle. She hated letting him heave her weight up. She quickly climbed the last two steps and stood on the platform, staring down at the offending ladder. Terry handed her the beer.

"Thanks, on both counts," she mumbled. "I'm going to get a line." She was already studying the configuration of wheels, cockpit table, backstays, stern railing, and the levers that raised and lowered the platform.

Terry dove into the water. A moment later Jeff joined him. By the time the men were done swimming Beth had tied a spare line to the base of the stainless-steel stanchions on either side of the back of the cockpit and left it laying on the swim platform within reach of someone standing on the ladder. Jeff climbed up the ladder and out without so much as a glance at it, or any difficulty, which irritated Beth. Terry followed, pausing on the ladder to pick up the line. But when he pulled on it to leverage himself up, it had too much slack. He tumbled back into the water with a laugh.

"It's too long," Beth said, and retied one of the knots to shorten it. Terry climbed back up, but now he could not reach the tighter line running across the forward edge of the platform.

"I'm fine," he assured Beth, climbing the rest of the way out by placing one foot on the platform outside of the ladder's narrow width. Beth frowned at her line. She knew Carole would need it—if she ever decided to go swimming.

◡

Late in the afternoon they set out in the dinghy for dinner in a restaurant at the other end of the bay. Although Beth knew it would be a long ride and she was sure Terry did too, she didn't say anything for fear Carole would want to back out. She wanted to try this restaurant when they were here last summer, but they had never found time.

Designed for six adults, with four passengers the dinghy felt palatial. Beth got a thrill out of revving the outboard engine and feeling the bow pick up, almost planing over the small chop in the protected bay. She took the driver's seat without consultation, knowing that given the chance Jeff would do it. But playing gentleman—holding the boat steady for the ladies to board—made him last to get in. Sometimes it was fun to be both a girl and the skipper.

She drove them along the southern shore of the bay, which ran roughly east to west, looking for the restaurant's dock described in their advertisement and the cruising guide described. After they'd been going for almost a half an hour and seemed to be approaching the western end of the bay she started to worry. She regretted relying on a glance at the chart before departure—she hadn't thought to bring it or the GPS.

They passed a marina tucked into an inlet and the shore ahead curved to the north, suggesting the end of the bay.

Lowering the throttle Beth said, "I don't know, guys, I thought it would be obvious, but I don't see it."

"It's not that?" Carole pointed at the marina. It was a collection of docks and buildings with a shutdown look, although there were a few boats in the slips.

"I don't think so—the photo in the cruising guide shows a short dock and stairs up a hill to the restaurant. It's an old mill."

"Let's go over and ask," Jeff said.

Beth could hardly argue since she hadn't seen any other docks during their trip so far. She turned the bow toward the marina and throttled up.

She bumped the inflatable up against the dock with its dark rubber bumpers and Jeff hopped out with the painter in hand. He secured it to a cleat and walked off toward the nearest building. It looked like a concession stand, its vending window covered with a wooden shutter. Rows of kayaks were leaning against the side of the building. Beth suspected this was the marina outpost for a fancy resort up in the hills. She had lost sight of Jeff when they heard voices carrying clearly on the light breeze. Jeff reappeared, walking with another man and talking animatedly. The stranger was carrying a glass they realized must contain something highly alcoholic.

By the time they got to the dinghy he was already giving slightly slurred directions to Jeff. Beth listened carefully while Jeff crouched to uncleat the painter and the man rambled on about going around the island and looking for a fleet of dragons.

"Have a good dinner," he concluded, raising his half-full glass to them as Jeff climbed back into the dinghy. "I'd come along, but this is my fourth one."

They thanked him and Beth turned the dinghy away allowing a quiet laugh under the roar of the engine. The others were grinning too.

"Where did you find him?" Terry asked.

"On one of the boats. He said to go past this island and around the next point. I think."

"And look for a fleet of dragons," Beth added, picturing rows of ornately carved Chinese rowing boats. It seemed unlikely. But the chunk of land to the west had resolved itself into an island, or perhaps she could see it as such now because she knew it must be. She steered them north around it and the next headland came into sight. Within minutes they were abeam of the island and saw a fleet of small white sailboats on moorings.

"Oh, it's a class," she said, meaning a class of racing sailboats that were all the same due to specific rules.

"Yeah, they're hot," Jeff said, and Beth realized he hadn't been nearly as puzzled by the directions as she had.

Beyond the boats she could see the end of a dock at the base of a long flight of stairs. The old stone mill was silhouetted against the darkening sky on top of the hill.

They enjoyed a delicious if pricey dinner. Jeff grabbed the check before Terry could and slipped a credit card into the portfolio after a quick glance at the amount. On the way out, they spent a few minutes in the restaurant's gallery and shop featuring the work of local artists. Eyes fixed on a framed watercolor of boats racing across an azure sea, Carole asked if they'd be back here before the end of the week. That drew Jeff into a heated consultation with her, and Beth and Terry moved away.

Ten minutes later they emerged from the shop, Carole carrying a thickly wrapped rectangular package and Jeff looking gloomy.

Twenty-one

Marigot Bay, St. Martin

*V*irgine's gaze took in the table on the warehouse floor. Ten men and women stood around it, endlessly peeling the stickers from the bottom of the wooden figures and replacing them with new ones from sheets laying on the table. Every now and then small hands placed coconut fiber into the boxes of figures on the floor between the adults. Virgine was proud of the seemingly local touch. Nobody needed to know she ordered it from a Chinese company that sourced it in Sri Lanka. It gave the children something to do until she could find suitable homes for them.

"There will be a visitor to the village in a few weeks. I need more women working there," she said, half turning her head toward Morten. He nodded once, his attentive gaze fixed on the workers as if to show her that nothing got past him. Unlike his men, he did not wear a semiautomatic rifle slung across his chest, but rather a holstered handgun on his belt. As if weapons were required to subdue these people.

"Three, I think," she went on.

"Do you wish to review them?"

"You chose. Use the older ones in case I have a request from a client."

"We get too many old ones."

Virgine stared at him. He wasn't wrong, but it was not his place to comment on the quality of the inventory.

"They all have a use," she said, hoping she sounded convincing. She wanted to berate him, but he was, after all, wearing a gun. No matter that she employed him, she did not trust him.

"Three," he said with another curt nod.

"Take them to the village. They need to be trained and productive by the new year."

"Not the stupid one, then," he said, his eyes landing on a middle-aged woman wearing a dopey grin as she scraped at a sticker with a broken thumbnail. Virgine's insides twisted. Something about his comment felt threatening. She tightened her core muscles, competing with the unwanted tension. She was in charge of her operation. He was an employee.

"No. Not her. She can continue with the figurines. Pick three others and get them to Columbia tomorrow."

"As you wish, madame."

)

Carlisle Bay, Antigua

They got an early start in the morning for the run west along the south coast of Antigua. Their goal—a notch of a bay about two thirds of the way along the coast—was reported to have decent snorkeling and good holding ground for the anchor. If conditions weren't favorable there, they would have time to backtrack to Falmouth Harbour for the night.

With a strong breeze and the swells behind her, the boat surged forward under full sail. Beth, Terry, and Jeff took turns at the helm, each of them energized by the perfect sailing conditions. Beth and Terry exchanged occasional observations about the way the boat handled and the placement of controls. They were favorably impressed with the boat's design and construction, other than the swim ladder.

But while three of the crew were having a great time, the fourth was struggling to maintain a happy front. Carole's stomach lurched when the first big swell picked up the port quarter and hurled the boat forward. The thundering bang of the jib collapsing when a large swell sheltered the boat from the wind and refilling an instant later as they rose on the next one, brought her heart as well as the contents of her stomach to her throat.

None of the others noticed her grimace as she swallowed down fear and nausea. She faced forward, legs curled under herself on the cockpit bench and tried to be feel better through force of will. A half hour later, once they were away from the southeast corner of the island, the swells flattened and the jib's massive shudders stopped. But the damage was done to Carole's internal balance and the nausea finally overcame her control. Remembering what she'd been told every time she'd sailed with Jeff—which was not very often—she leaned her shoulders across the side deck outside the cockpit and ducked her head under the lifeline before her insides erupted.

"Carole!" Beth, from behind the wheel, was the first to notice.

"Uh oh," Terry said, moving around the table to put a steadying hand on Carole's back. Jeff, who was lounging on the seat behind the wheel Beth wasn't using watched for a moment, immobile. Then he dropped his feet to the deck and stood up, wordlessly making his way around Terry and his wife to go below. When he returned a moment later with a fist full of paper towels and a damp washcloth his expression was one of duty, completely lacking in compassion. He took over from Terry, offering Carole the washcloth and holding the paper towels ready to mop up anything that hadn't gone over the side.

"Carole, will you drink some ginger ale?" Terry asked. She was kneeling on the lazarette resting on her forearms with her head hanging out over the side.

"No, nothing," she croaked. Beth felt for her. She had avoided mentioning seasickness and remedies for it, believing if it hadn't occurred to the potential victim there was no reason to scare her. She had an assortment of remedies in her bag, but they needed to be administered before the sickness happened. There was nothing they could do now but wait and hope it passed. Experience told Beth that Carole would be out of it for the rest of the day. Once they anchored, she might recover, although it might require taking her ashore to solid ground.

Carole continued to suffer during the rest of the four-hour sail. Despite their urgings to sit up and stare at the island, she curled up on the forward end of the lazarette, her face hidden in her arms. Three or four more times she unfolded and leaned out, quickly reduced to dry heaves that made Beth and Terry feel terrible for her discomfort. Each time Jeff pumped a pitcher of salt water from the galley sink and slopped it across the side deck and hull, although there was nothing to clean up. He was solicitous at first, but after she refused to take his advice about watching the horizon he stopped offering sympathy.

They rounded Carlisle point into Carlisle bay in the middle of the afternoon. The medium sized swells that had carried them so far swung around the point and at first Beth feared it would be an uncomfortably rolly anchorage. But as they got further in, they crossed over an invisible line where the sea flattened out and the headland cut the wind to a pleasant breeze. Even though it was no more than a right angle with the headland pointing due south, Carlisle was a well-protected in the current easterly wind and seas.

The anchor bit hard on the first try, which Beth took as another good sign. When they were secure Carole climbed up onto the deck to sit with her back against the mast, her head leaning against it.

"Feeling any better?" Beth asked.

"A little."

"A swim might help."

No answer. Beth looked at Terry.

"We'll put the motor on the dinghy and take you ashore," he said, gesturing to Jeff to help him.

"Once you set foot on solid ground you'll be amazed at how quickly you'll feel better," Beth said.

"Okay."

Once he and Terry had maneuvered the heavy outboard motor from its traveling position on *Mana*'s stern rail down onto the dinghy, Jeff helped Carole get in. Beth was already sorting out her snorkel gear, having looked forward to this stop since she'd started planning the itinerary.

"Not coming?" Jeff asked.

"Nah, you go ahead."

Beth got the impression as she watched the dinghy motor away that Jeff wanted additional company. But her train of thought was lost at the sound of a splash: Terry leaping from the side of the boat. He came up shouting with pleasure. Grinning, Beth grabbed her mask and snorkel and jumped off the swim platform.

)

Carole's skin was a healthier color and her smile seemed genuine when they returned an hour later. She told them about the beach resort and the town they'd walked to. Beth and Terry described the local aquatic life at the bay's rocky headland in return.

Beth felt assured that Carole was fully recovered when she asked if she'd have time for a swim in the morning.

While the others prepared dinner, Beth spent an hour reading more of the material she'd been given for her meeting on Friday. Reading the background information her colleagues had compiled made her fear that her self-confidence was misplaced. Her knowledge of the island nation's politics was based on the various cruising guides she'd read and her limited dealings with the local immigration and customs authorities. Later that night when she stretched out with Terry in their bunk, she shared her growing concern. To his credit he did not dismiss it, but countered it.

"They're sending you to hand-hold your client, to keep him on topic during the hearing. You have sharp instincts about people, and you understand Caribbean cultures. You keep him from speaking out of turn and get him to respond when he should. He's the one who understands the politics."

)

Jolly Harbour, Antigua

Beth's concerns were to be answered the next afternoon. They left Carlisle Bay after everyone had a swim. Then Beth took a quick vote between sailing and motoring, and they set the sails. She pointed the boat south of west to go outside the double reef that shadowed the next stretch of southern coast.

Beth pressed ginger tablets on Carole and watched her take several throughout the morning, but whether it was the ginger or luck, the other woman professed to feel fine all day. They rounded the southwest corner of the island and turned north, staying in deep water off shore until they could line up their landmarks to turn east toward the entrance to the biggest marina on the island. Here they could refill the water tanks, although they hadn't used much so far, and visit the island's largest supermarket, although they didn't need much. There were also boutiques and restaurants to explore. The stop was more a concession to Carole's desire to see the island than a necessity.

"Guess we're back in cell phone range," Beth said at the sound of hers ringing. Service had been spotty since they'd left English Harbour, but she could see a cell tower up on the hill behind the marina. She picked up the phone and flipped it open.

"This is Beth."

"Finally—we've left you three messages."

"Hello Marcus. I got back into cell phone range a few minutes ago." Beth held the phone away from her face to look at the display then put it back to her ear. "Yes, now it says I have messages. What's up?"

The others were moving around the cabin doing post-sail tidying. At a signal from outside Terry flipped a switch on the panel and the boat started to hum. A vent next to Beth wheezed out a breath of cool air. She smiled at Terry. Leave it to him to make air conditioning a priority. What an amazing thing to have on a boat!

"Mr. Codrington wants to meet with you before the hearing."

"Oh. Okay," Beth hesitated long enough to make a quick decision, "I think that's a good idea. Has he mentioned a time?"

"We explained to him that you're sailing and may not be able to."

"No, no, tell him I'll work it out. In fact, I'm in a position now to contact his office myself if you want."

She could hear voices speaking to Marcus. "Hang on Beth." The silent line gave Beth a wave of discomfort—they'd put her on hold. What were her co-workers saying that they didn't want her to hear? But she squelched it. That was Marcus's style, not the others'. He returned a minute later.

"Here's his number—"

"Hang on," Beth opened a drawer in the navigation desk and found a pen. She pulled the Antigua cruising guide to her and flipped it open to a page with room in the margins. "Go ahead."

"His secretary is Mrs. Stafford," Marcus added after reciting the phone number. Beth wrote that down too.

"Do they know my name? If I call and say who I am will they know?" Beth rode another rush of uncertainty.

"Say you're with Broadhead and you're scheduled to be at the hearing." Marcus sounded as uncertain about her as she suddenly felt.

"Right, of course. Okay. I'll see what we can set up and let you know."

"Please. Thanks for being flexible Beth. How's the trip going, other than this?"

Beth was surprised at his uncharacteristic friendliness. She imagined the others in the office pressuring him to ask.

"Great. The weather's perfect and the boat's wonderful. We just got into a marina. We have to go check out the shops. But I'll make this call first."

"Sounds awesome. I wish I were there."

Beth wished there were an excuse to put off calling Mr. Codrington. But she knew her case of nerves would not get any better. In fact, if she delayed, she'd add guilt to her arsenal of self-destructive emotions. She took a deep breath, sat down, and punched his number into her phone.

And then it was ringing and she felt better. Terry shooed the others out of the cabin, explaining what was going on, then returned, watching her face as she listened to the clicks of the call being answered. His smile was all encouragement.

Beth introduced herself and the woman who answered instantly transferred her to Mr. Codrington.

He greeted her in warm tenor tones, his lilting accent adding spice to the mix. He thanked her for calling with a mix of graciousness and enthusiasm and explained that in his anxiousness about the upcoming hearing he may be behaving foolishly, but he must meet her before in advance so he'd be completely at ease.

Beth assured him that she agreed with his impulse, which was not foolish at all, and inquired about his schedule.

"Am I to understand that you are sailing around our island?"

"Yes. I'm trying out a boat we're considering buying."

"Delightful. We are so pleased with the numbers of sailors who visit us each year. What is your itinerary?"

"We've just come in to Jolly Harbour. We plan to go Bird Island tomorrow—"

"But you're in Jolly Harbour now? This is short notice, but I will be there later this afternoon."

"Really? What a convenient coincidence—if you'll have time to meet while you're here."

She saw Terry's brows rise.

"I shall make time, Miss Anderson. Do you know the sports club? It's to the south of the marina."

"No, but we just arrived. I'm sure I can find it."

"Yes, ask anyone, or follow the dock to the south. It will take you to a bar—a sports bar. Beyond it is a swimming pool and tennis courts."

Beth flipped the cruising guide open to the page for Jolly Harbour and studied a sketch map of the area.

"I see it on the map. It couldn't be more convenient."

"Excellent. Would five p.m. be acceptable? I will meet you at the bar. If you can't immediately identify me, ask the bartender to point me out."

"Five o'clock. I look forward to it Mr. Codrington."

She closed her phone and took a deep, relieved breath, grinning at Terry.

"I'm meeting him at five in a bar down the dock."

"Then you'd better get cleaned up—it's nearly four now."

⏀

Beth left the others constructing a comprehensive, if unnecessary, grocery list for the next few days—she could tell Carole felt she could contribute in this area, so she had no compunction about leaving it to her. Teaching the other woman about the peculiarities of cooking in a boat galley would come later. Exploring while Beth was showering in the marina's facilities, Terry found the sports club and bar. It was so close he was able to point it out to her from the boat when she got back.

She had brought along one outfit of appropriate tropical business garb—all of her recent purchases were for the mid-Atlantic fall and winter, so she'd returned to her sail bag for her reliable blue and white skirt combined with a white cotton collared, long sleeve shirt. She would add a navy blue scarf on Friday and wear her work pumps, but this afternoon she wore deck shoes and skipped the scarf. She thought it unlikely that Mr. Codrington would notice she was wearing the same basic outfit twice, and if he did, he could guess why. Terry assured her that she was silly to give it a thought.

With her new sailcloth bag slung over her shoulder, laptop, notepad, and background documents inside, she opened the unlocked gate in a low fence separating the marina from the sports club and climbed four steps onto the shaded, wooden deck that housed the bar. The actual bar was in the center of the space with stools on three sides. Tables and chairs around it were less than half occupied by a mix of locals and tourists. Besides the bartender, another man behind the bar fiddled with the settings on a computer projector sending an image against the back wall. He seemed to be trying to project the feed from a satellite television service.

A waitress in short skirt and cropped shirt leaned on the bar watching the bartender assemble a tray full of drinks. In addition, an American-looking couple and a local man in a suit occupied three of the stools. Beth decided to take a shot at the man.

"Mr. Codrington?" she asked, approaching from behind and to his left. He half turned, then stood up.

"Miss Anderson?" He extended his hand. Beth shook it, nodding.

"Yes. It's a pleasure to meet you. Thank you again for making time this afternoon."

"I think the thanks should be from me. Your team may think I'm demanding, and perhaps I am. I do understand you are taking time away from your holiday for these meetings. I appreciate your dedication."

"It's not a problem, Mr. Codrington. The scheduling did not require any changes to our plans, and I am happy to be able to meet you in person."

"Well I'm very glad I did not inconvenience your skipper or the rest of your party. Please, won't you sit down?"

Beth hiked herself onto the stool next to him, considering suggesting that they moved to a table. She decided to go with his direction, but she could not let his assumption go unanswered.

"I'm the skipper, so it's strictly a matter of my crew having to accept my itinerary needs."

"You are! Well, that is impressive. She noticed red veins in the whites of his eyes as he studied her more carefully than he had at first. "Is it a women's sailing program?"

"Not at all. I'm sailing with my boyfriend, his business partner, and his partner's wife."

"Excellent. I feel that I must be in very good hands, if your crew is reliant upon you."

"Well, sailing is not the same as your political world, Mr. Codrington. Perhaps we can discuss a bit about what you expect to be asked on Friday?"

They talked for nearly ninety minutes, each of them beating the other to purchase rounds of plain iced tea. Their discussion was winding down when a boy of about twelve came into the bar and walked up to them. The bartender waived a hello and the boy returned it. He was carrying a cricket bat.

"Grandad, are you coming?" he asked Mr. Codrington.

"Is it time already? Beth and I have been enjoying our discussion so much I lost track," Mr. Codrington said, slipping his arm around the boy's shoulders to pull him into their conversation. "Beth, this is my grandson Isaiah. He is a budding cricket star."

"Pleased to meet you Isaiah. Do you have a game—a match is it?—today?"

"Yes ma'am. A test match."

"The boys play a modified version with very short matches," Mr. Codrington explained.

"Yes, don't the matches go on for days?" she asked.

"Ours are too short," Isaiah said. "Only three hours."

"That sounds pretty long to me."

"You are right, Miss Anderson—regular matches do last several days. But the local league wants the boys to have an opportunity to finish several during their playing season. I have no doubt you will be playing full matches soon enough," this last was delivered to his grandson. The boy grinned. "Miss Anderson, it would seem that I must go. I will see you house on Friday—we agreed you will come to my office a few minutes early?"

"Yes, good plan," Beth got off her bar stool and extended her hand once more. Mr. Codrington shook it, then turned with his grandson and walked away, already in conversation with the boy.

Judging by the selection of produce, cookies, liquor, and fresh meats in the galley, the grocery store was very well supplied indeed—a true rarity in the islands. Carole was finishing stowing it and Jeff had researched and made dinner reservations at a restaurant up on one of the surrounding hills. Although Beth desperately wanted a drink, she could see the others were champing at the bit to be off to dinner. She stowed her bag and followed them up the dock, taking Terry's hand as they walked.

"It went well?"

"I think so. He's a pleasant man. I met his grandson. He was impressed that I'm skippering."

Terry chuckled. "He has no idea what you're capable of, love."

Twenty-two

Dickinson Bay, Antigua

The next day they motored North from Jolly Harbour and dropped the anchor in Dickinson Bay mid-afternoon. Beth had planned to make the much longer voyage across Antigua's north coast to a beautiful, remote anchorage at Bird Island. But her crew resisted her attempts to get them going early enough—first Carole disappeared to the shower and then Jeff followed her, both of them returning after ten o'clock bearing the packages Carole acquired in her unannounced shopping expedition. While they were gone, Terry dashed back to the supermarket on a mysterious errand, returning on their heels. Although disappointed, Beth bit her tongue and announced their destination as if it didn't represent a change in plans.

"I thought we were going someplace else—bird something?" Carole said.

"That's tomorrow," Jeff said.

"It's too far to get there today," Terry added, glancing at Beth's strained expression. She rather hoped he attributed it to concentration on the very narrow, shallow channel out of Jolly Harbour that she was negotiating. She didn't want to discuss her frustration with them. But he added, "We're not leaving early enough," and shot her an apologetic smile.

Once the anchor was set Jeff was anxious to go ashore and explore. Still feeling out of sorts about the itinerary change, Beth knew the best way to get over it was time alone. So she begged off from the shore party while urging the others to go. When Carole begged off too Beth had mixed feelings—she didn't much want another girls' social hour—but there was little she could do.

"You good?" Terry murmured when they were alone in the saloon for a moment.

"I am. But I need a few minutes alone to remind myself not to be selfish."

Terry stared at her, startled. "Selfish?"

"I'm too used to going when and where I want and not having to adjust to other people."

Terry inhaled a breath and let it out slowly, clearly thinking about her interpretation of the situation.

"You could have issued firm orders this morning, set shower deadlines, laid down the law."

"I know. I hate to do that when we're on vacation. Then I hate that everyone isn't inside my head doing what I want without being told. I know it's my own problem."

"Stop beating yourself up."

"I'm not. Not exactly. I'm retraining myself."

Terry's wan smile told her he understood but was still concerned.

"Go, get Jeff out of here before he explodes!"

Beth felt relief as she watched the men climb into the dinghy and motor away with a wave.

She wanted everyone to have fun. Terry was right, if she had a real schedule for them, she had to communicate it, even if issuing orders was contrary to her nature.

So here they were anchored amid the crowd of other charter boats with jet skis, windsurfers, Hobie Cats, and day sailors weaving around them. Some of these were expertly handled, others were not, providing entertainment for the two women. Beth went for a swim, washing her hair in the sea and dousing it with conditioner in the hope of taming the split ends. While it dried she opened a beer and strung her lightweight woven hammock on the bow of the boat. It swayed back and forth as the boat rocked on the low wakes of passing craft.

Carole finally tried Beth's bathing technique after driving her nuts for three days asking about how the salt water affected her hair. Washing in salt water was one of the things Beth missed the most living in Washington. It wasn't so much the salt, but the freedom of diving into a whole ocean to rinse away biodegradable soap and the delicious sensation of sunshine on her freshly washed hair and skin.

"May I join you up here?" Carole stood by the mast, drink in one hand, book in the other, the strap of a white flotation cushion in the crook of one arm. Beth shaded her eyes from the afternoon sun and smiled.

"Of course."

Carole dropped her cushion and sat down, leaning her back against the mast so that she faced the beach while Beth had consciously elected to lay in the hammock with her head at the bow so her view was of the sea to the west.

"Think they'll be long?" Carole asked.

"I bet they'll stop for a drink. There are a lot of bars on that beach."

"And a lot of bodies to look at."

Beth tilted her head to study Carole. She had not noticed Jeff's eyes roaming, but perhaps Carole was more sensitive to what Beth considered male human nature.

"I guess. I'm sure they'll have a drink and come back to report."

Carole was quiet for a minute. Beth was about to raise her book again when she finally spoke.

"Beth, I hope Jeff and my problems aren't ruining your vacation."

"Ruining it? I'm not sure what you mean, Carole."

"I'm about done and he knows it. We've been going at each other for weeks now. I couldn't believe he suggested we come."

"You mean you've been fighting a lot? I haven't noticed it on this trip." Beth lied. Although she wouldn't exactly call it fighting, just a noticeable lack of caring. Carole and Jeff's relationship was devoid of lovers' touches—they did not hold hands or give one another affectionate pecks. Beth had chalked it up to years of marriage. But she'd seen Jeff's coldness toward Carole when she was seasick. That had seemed genuinely unkind. He'd seen to her needs out of duty—duty toward his other shipmates to shield them from his wife's unpleasant condition.

"I've been trying to be patient, so we don't screw up your trip. But the truth is, I've made my decision. I'm leaving him."

"What?" Beth stared at the other woman, questioning what she'd heard, but internally feeling the signs come into alignment.

"I told you how he is when they're working—we become the support network. You haven't seen it yet, and I hope it's better for you and Terry. I was ready to accept it again for a while with that last deal. I lined up two classes I've been wanting to take and committed to helping more with the shelter. When it fell through Jeff expected me to cancel everything in order to spend time with him, since he'd be more available. That was the last straw. Or no, this trip was."

"You don't want to be here? I'm so sorry Carole, it was Terry's idea to invite—"

"No, Beth, don't think that. I've always wanted to come to the islands. Hell, Jeff's been here three times racing—did you know that?" she paused to watch Beth nod, "He's never invited me on one of those trips. But this time he waits until the eleventh hour and pops this on me. As if it's going to save our marriage. He's selfish and inconsiderate and I've had enough."

Her words rushed out in such an angry flow Beth slipped into rumination as they washed over her, wondering how Carole planned to support herself to do the classes and volunteering she'd been so upset about having to drop. It seemed to Beth that Carole was dependent on Jeff's financial support to live the independent life she wanted. She expected substantial alimony.

Realizing Carole had stopped speaking Beth turned her head and saw tears streaking down her cheeks.

"Well, I have to say I did think he was not very nice to you when you were seasick. I thought it was strange."

"He was embarrassed."

"That's silly."

"That's Jeff. I embarrassed him by getting sick."

"Ridiculous. I'm so sorry, Carole. I didn't realize how unhappy you were, or I would have tried to stop Terry from inviting you— you didn't need to spend a week down here right now."

Carole was shaking her head slowly as if to pardon Beth from any responsibility, "I could have put my foot down, told him I was leaving. But I had this absurd idea that maybe this would help—get him away from the business stuff completely for a few days. The trouble is, I forgot he treats sailing the same way he treats work. It's serious business. You saw how he was the first day, until Terry told him off."

"Terry did?"

"Oh yeah, he was grumbling about it later. Beth, I want you to know that I appreciate how you skipper the boat. You really pay attention to how everyone is doing. You don't yell," Carole shrugged.

"Thanks Carole. I try. I'm not used to it being more than Terry and me, and with just us I hardly feel like I'm in charge—I mean, we make mostly joint decisions. That was a shocker, when Jeff countermanded what I thought was an order. But I didn't know Terry spoke to him about it."

"Yeah, when we got to that first place. Jeff said Terry's blinded right now, following his dick."

"He said that?"

"Yeah, my husband's a charmer in private."

They both fell silent for a while, Beth replaying in her mind her interactions with Jeff over the last few days. Carole sipped her drink and stared off into the distance where the little boats stirred up the water with their wakes.

"Do you want to get off the boat?" Beth finally asked.

Carole did not respond immediately. Beth saw her mouth tighten, then she inhaled a deep breath. "You mean, leave him here, now?"

That had not been what Beth meant, but Carole's question made her realize that's what it would amount to. "I guess that would be pretty extreme," she said, reconsidering.

To her surprise, Carole chuckled. "It would get his attention!"

Beth smiled.

"He doesn't believe I'd leave him. I mean, even with all the fights I haven't ever said it to him."

"You mean it's possible he doesn't know how upset you are?" Beth couldn't imagine Terry not sensing anger in her. But if he did, he would bring it up, not ignore it. It was possible Jeff was oblivious, or thought Carole's unhappiness was normal.

Carole shrugged and gulped her drink, then said, "You know how people treat their pets like they have human emotions?"

"Anthropomorphism."

Carole frowned and Beth realized she didn't know the word. "I know what you mean."

"Sometimes I think I do that with Jeff. I think he's tuned in to my mood. I think I know what he must be thinking to do and say the things he does. But what if the whole time he's just, like, 'I'm hungry,' and 'I want sex,'…" Carole did a deep-voiced imitation of her husband. "… and 'Terry better call,' and 'fuck, we would have won that last race if Joe didn't blow the tack'?" By the time she finished they were both giggling, and Beth was imagining a goofy dog with Jeff's eyes, tail wagging, tongue lolling.

"It could be," Beth finally said. It was difficult to imagine someone so obtuse, but, Beth considered, that could be a primary difference between men and women. Maybe she was wrong about Terry, too. There were times when he had no idea she was angry or upset. But that was in the beginning of their relationship, when he didn't know her well. She couldn't imagine applying Carole's imitated internal monologue to Terry.

"I have to lay it out for him. I think I need to stick this out and do it when we get back. If I walk away from this boat, he'll use it against me."

"Wow," Beth heard herself draw the word out as she thought about how bad Carole and Jeff's relationship had to be. "I guess you know him better than anyone."

*

Philipsburg, St. Martin

"Place your bets, please." Ori paused to give her clients time to select and move their chips, her eyes scanning the four players' hands as they moved across the table. When everyone had anted at least the minimum she began to deal cards from the shoe. The patter was second nature to her now, a running verbalization of her and the players' actions. One player got an ace, another a three, the other two had mid-value cards. The house got a jack.

She had learned not to think of the dealer hand as hers. It was the house. She was detached, a human automaton facilitating the house's success at taking in more money than it paid out. She had no personal stake in the hand. She had thought dealing would be hard, that she'd lose and be fired. But she hadn't understood how a casino worked. The odds were never in the players' favor. The dealer had strict rules about how to play the house's hand. As long as she stuck with them the house would come out ahead. Once she had realized that, the challenge became keeping engaged with the game and the players at her table. It was easy to become bored. But a bored dealer was not fun for the players, and bored players didn't tip.

She entertained herself by constructing backstories for the players. The cruise ship guests were the easiest because they could be from anywhere—well, anywhere in the US, for the most part. She imagined were retired auto industry workers, or on a stressful family reunion. If their ship was from one of the pricier cruise lines she imagined business executives and their trophy wives.

The local regulars presented a more interesting challenge, because over time she got to know more about them—real information gleaned by chatting with them at the table, or from her fellow dealers. The more she knew, the less she could invent, but it made constructing her own fictions around the known facts quite interesting.

There, for example, was Madame Guesnon. Ori observed the curvaceous black woman as she dealt another hand, identifying the cards as she tracked the woman in her peripheral vision. Ori knew she was a local business woman, a low-worth heiress, who had split an inheritance from her banker father with a brother. The brother got the bank, and Madame Guesnon aspired to outdo him. Ori had learned that mostly from the other dealers. From observation at her table she knew Madame had a gambling problem. She played well, but too much, and over time Ori had seen her lose thousands of Euros. Ori imagined a shopping habit, perhaps a fetish for couture or diamonds. Madame would be much more interesting if she was into slutty boots.

Past the roulette wheels and, surprisingly, on past the blackjack tables as well, Madame proceeded through the susurrus of cards and dealer patter toward the short staircase to the high stakes room. That was a new development in Ori's invented story. Madame had lost four thousand Euro last night, and now she apparently intended to lose even faster.

)

Dickinson Bay, Antigua

Jeff and Terry realized that most of the restaurants in Dickinson Bay had been absorbed by the chain resorts that dominated the beach. They beached and secured the dinghy near the northern end of the bay and walked south along the shoreline past guarded stretches of sand. They could tell when they passed out of each resort's beach area because of the concentration of local vendors who followed them offering trinkets and tours until they entered the next resort's domain. It was like they passed through an invisible barrier.

"I like to think I don't look like a resort guest," Terry said after waving off the third dreadlocked, tied-dyed guy promoting jet ski rentals in their last one hundred steps.

"It's a numbers game. They approach everyone," Jeff said, looking at another Rasta-styled man holding up a pink and cream colored conch shell. He brought the side of the shell to his lips and blew. The shell resonated with a deep, loud tone. "I wonder if the kids would like those?"

Terry shook his head. "I've been on beaches lined with them."

"But he cut a hole in it to make a horn."

"The restaurant cut the hole in it to get the conch out."

"Really?"

"Yes."

"So where are these beaches lined with shells?"

"Petit St. Vincent, for one."

"We're not going to Petit St. Vincent."

Terry shrugged in defeat. "Good point. Go ahead, spend your money."

Jeff laughed as he headed for the conch man. Terry ambled further along the beach while his partner selected two shells and tried ineffectively to make the same sound as the vendor. Terry spotted an independent bar amid the trees between resorts and aimed for it by the time Jeff caught up.

"Time for a rum drink," Terry said, nodding at the palm frond-roofed shack.

"I'm in!"

"So how do you like this boat so far?" Jeff asked after the American waiter had taken their order for pain killers.

"Other than the stern ladder being hard to use, I like it a lot. It handled well sailing. Those were good sized swells on the south coast."

Jeff nodded. "That was fun sailing. It felt like a lot more boat under me than I'm used to with *Grace*."

"*Mana* is heavier than *Grace*—by design. I feel a lot more confident in a boat like it making blue water passages."

"For sure. And you have more room for the gear you'd need, like extra fuel."

"I want to do as much more sailing as we can this week, though. I wish we had a full inventory of sails so we could change the jib. Maybe fly a spinnaker."

"That would be fun, huh? Did you ask the dealer for one?"

"I didn't think of it until we were out there running down wind the other day. Maybe we ought to call and ask him."

They continued to discuss the possibility as the waiter brought their drinks and Jeff put a handful of eastern Caribbean dollars on the table. The waiter picked them up and walked away.

)

More charterers, Hunter thought as he handed the money for the two pain killers over to the bartender. It seemed like charterers and resort guests were all he'd met for days, but until he could think of a new strategy, he would have to keep hoping and hanging around the bar and listening to Papi and the cruisers every morning.

Later that night Hunter stretched out on the lumpy box springs that passed for his bed and pressed his cell phone to his ear. The repetitious "burr-burr" was quickly interrupted by his brother's voice.

"Hunter! Good to hear from you."

"Happy Thanksgiving bro. How's it going?"

"Great. Everything's great. Are you coming home?"

"What, for Thanksgiving? Tomorrow?"

"Hell yeah. Family holiday, right?"

"No. I'm on Antigua. You guys should come here." They were empty words. He knew his brother would be spending tomorrow with his new wife's family. He'd gleaned that much from their occasional conversations over the past few months. He resisted the urge to accuse his brother of being whipped because he would be opening himself up for more criticism of his current quest.

"Maybe next year. Or maybe you'll have come to your senses and be back in the great state of Texas."

"Could be."

"Have you made progress?"

"I'm still on the trail. I've met people who know her, and they've pointed me in various directions. The last information I got put her here on Antigua, but that was back in August. I don't know which direction to go until I find someone who's seen her more recently."

"What if you never do, Hunt? I mean, she could have left the islands, and you'll be there forever."

"Of course I won't. I mean, I won't wait here forever."

"So when do you stop? What's the signal to give up?"

"I'm not sure. But I'll know it when I see it. Or feel it."

He heard Parker sigh. "Look, dad's willing to bring you back on, but he's not going to wait forever. You need to figure it out soon."

"Figure out if I want to sell drilling equipment to filthy rich oil men instead of drinks to sailors?"

"You're selling drinks? You're in a bar? Jesus Hunter! After what you went through. What we went through——"

Hunter groaned. He'd managed to conceal his job from Parker until that stupid slip.

"Stop it! Stop, Parker. I'm on the wagon. No drinking. No drugs. I'm not a bartender. I clear the tables and take orders and listen to the gossip in case someone mentions Beth Anderson or her boat. I'm fine."

There was a disgusted sound on the line. "Fine. Wasting your time in a beach bar when you could be productive."

"You mean, 'could be making money in Texas'."

"Well, yes. What's so wrong with earning a living and contributing to the economy?"

"Nothing's wrong with it. It's just not what I want right now. Right now I want to find my son."

There was silence for a moment, and then Parker responded. "I get that. I guess all I can do is wish you a happy Thanksgiving. They don't have it there, do they?"

"No, Parker, the Antiguans didn't participate in the first feast in New England." Hunter smiled. "I'll bet I could find a turkey dinner, though, in one of the resorts. But I think I'll skip it. I'll be thinking of you guys. Give my love to everyone."

"Okay. I'll tell them you called. What about Christmas?"

"I don't know yet. I'll let you know."

"Right." Parker sounded unconvinced. Hunter decided to leave it at that.

"Good night bro."

"Night Hunter."

Twenty-three

Dickinson Bay, Antigua

After their talk, Carole's mood seemed lighter, as if she'd offloaded some of the stress she'd been carrying onto Beth. Beth refused to accept the burden: she had enough to worry about with Mr. Codrington's meeting tomorrow. When Carole decided she would go for a swim, Beth moved back to the cockpit where she could keep an eye on her, hoping it wasn't obvious. She tied a dock line to the stern rail with a bright orange lifejacket on the other end. She tossed this out into the water.

"Try not to go further away from the boat than that," She told Carole. "Hopefully the jet skiers will see it, too."

"Okay," Carole replied agreeably before jumping in the water. Beth stretched out on the port side lazarette and opened her book. Carole's splashes near the boat were slightly louder than the ever-present drone of outboard and jet ski motors in the middle distance. Every now and then a few strains of music or raucous laughter carried over the water as well. Beth reveled in the symphony of Caribbean beach life, allowing her eyes to shut as she drifted with it. After a while she realized she was getting hot. Opening her eyes, she saw that the sun had crossed the sky and was shining into the cockpit from the west. There was nothing for it but to cool off in the water. As she stood up and took off the shirt she'd pulled on over her swimsuit, she realized she'd completely lost track of Carole.

She dropped the shirt and stepped through the cockpit and out onto the swim platform. No Carole. Beth stepped back into the cockpit and up onto a lazarette to look forward. After a moment she realized there was a body in her hammock on the bow. Just to be sure, she climbed out of the cockpit and walked forward as far as the mast. She caught a glimpse of blonde hair as the hammock swung. Carole. Relieved, Beth took hold of the shroud, stepped over the lifeline with both feet, balanced on the edge of the boat, then let go and dove into the water.

There was nothing better, in Beth's opinion than, diving into the warm ocean. She swam a few strokes underwater then surfaced. She wiped the water from her eyes and took leisurely strokes toward mana's stern. After paddling around for a while, she swam to the ladder and got up to the third step. Her current configuration of the line had it tied taught across the stern with a bight of line in the middle that stretched back toward the ladder. She grabbed the looped line and hauled on it to help herself climb the last three steps. Pleased with herself for successfully jury-rigging a solution, she wrapped herself in her sarong and sat down to think about how she wanted the ladder designed on her boat.

"So what's the dinner plan?" she asked a while later when Jeff and Terry had returned in the dinghy and climbed aboard, clearly having had a few drinks on shore. After all, they had, ostensibly, been going to find a restaurant.

"Coconut Grove," Jeff said. "My treat."

"You don't need to do that," Terry protested. Beth thought it sounded like habit more than commitment.

"But I want to," Jeff said firmly. Turning to Beth he said, "It's on the formal side."

"Okay with me," she said, although a beach bar with a sand floor would have been fine, or cooking dinner on board. She wondered if Jeff knew Carole would like something fancier, then she wondered with a private smile if she was anthropomorphizing.

While the men took a sobering swim, Beth fetched Carole and they both got dressed. They sat in the cockpit with cold beers while Jeff and Terry rinsed off, happily making a show of it, and got dressed themselves. Finally, they climbed into the dinghy and Jeff, who had moved into the driving position before Beth could, pointed it to the southern end of the beach.

Dinner was delicious seafood combined with local vegetables and sauces. The restaurant was positioned to draw the island's more affluent visitors, with its massive veranda, ocean view, and, when the sun set, strings of twinkling lights. Afterwards they strolled back across the beach to the dinghy, drunk on good food and two bottles of wine.

"Can we just walk back?" Carole asked. This brought the others to a quiet pause. She looked around at them. "I mean, along the beach. I know we have to get to the boat eventually."

"Oh," Beth said, drawing the word out. "I can bring the dinghy along the beach and pick you up closer to the boat if you want."

"I'll go with you, Beth. You guys walk and we'll pick you up near the dock. Where we beached it earlier, Jeff." Terry said.

Beth watched Jeff. A tight mouthed nod was his silent response. He offered Carole his arm to guide her along the beach.

Beth caught Terry's quick frown before he bent to unearth the dinghy's anchor where they'd buried it in the sand.

They launched the small boat through the light surf and Terry pushed it off using a paddle while Beth got the motor going. She steered them into deeper water and motored slowly along. The outboard was quiet enough to allow them to speak over it.

"Dinner was delicious," she said. "Jeff didn't have to treat us."

"His prerogative, though. I've learned not to argue about that kind of thing with him. He gets it into his head he owes, and you go with it."

"I'm not sure he wanted to walk."

"I know."

Beth considered saying more. She wanted to share what Carole had told her. But she felt like it was a confidence that she shouldn't betray. At least not so quickly, and not while their guests were still with them. She kept her mouth shut and enjoyed the starlight and the hollow sound of the rippling waves hitting the inflated hull of the dinghy.

Back aboard *Mana* Beth laid out their options for the following day, Thanksgiving. The massive amounts of food they'd brought aboard included the makings for a turkey dinner. Is she and Terry were alone she would have suggested grilled grouper, but back in Washington Carole had started talking about the wonderful Thanksgiving turkey they would have. So now they were committed to cooking a traditional American Thanksgiving dinner.

Beth needed to be at Mr. Codrington's office in St. John, Antigua's capital, at 1:00 p.m. on Friday. She could get a taxi from any of the resorts along the beach here, if they stayed. Or they could and sail to Deep Bay south of St. John's Harbor. She could get a taxi the following day from there.

Looking over Jeff's shoulder at the chart, Carole said, "Why don't we sail in to St. Johns? We can practically sail you to your meeting."

"It's a commercial port." Jeff's tone was preemptory.

"They aren't set up for sailboats our size." Beth explained. "We could anchor in one of the bays along the south side of St. Johns harbor, like Ballast Bay," she touched the chart, "but they're fairly exposed, and I'm not sure I could get a taxi from the beach there. Deep Bay has a road and some facilities. I think I can get a taxi from there."

"I see," Carole said.

"Or we can just stay here and chill," Jeff said.

"Get up late, have a leisurely breakfast," Terry said. "Cook Thanksgiving dinner."

"Go ashore, rent a jet ski," Jeff said. Then added, "I thought you wanted to get in more sailing, Terry," Beth watched Terry, curious about his answer.

"Beth and I have another week to do all the sailing I want." Was Terry's reply.

"So if we stay here, I could go for a walk on the beach? Could I go to the resorts?"

Beth smiled at Carole. "I think you could wander in. If someone stopped you, you'd go back out to the beach."

"She wants to shop," Jeff said. "Aren't you going to help make Thanksgiving dinner?"

"Of course. But that won't take all day!" Carole said.

"On Friday We could take a taxi into St. John with Beth, or earlier, and see the town," Jeff said.

Carole lit up. "I'd like that! Let's do it!"

Beth looked to Terry. "You okay with staying here?"

"I'm in favor of whatever will get you to your meeting on time and confident. If we stay here tomorrow, I'll skip the jet ski, but I'll try windsurfing, and come back and help with dinner. On Friday you can all go to St. John, and I'll stay aboard and guard *Mana*."

If Jeff noticed Terry's offer to cook, he didn't react.

"Are you sure it's okay?" Beth asked Terry.

"Have I ever been bored on a boat?"

"Not that I know of."

"It's a plan. Late breakfast, relaxing day, great dinner. Friday I run you three ashore and you find a taxi to town."

"You guys should taxi back whenever you want," Beth said, looking first at Jeff, then Carole. "I'll get one when I'm done. I don't know when it will be and I don't want you wasting time waiting for me."

"Are you sure? We can—" Carole protested.

"I'm sure. It's a plan."

)

Staying in one place for days was the pace Beth and Terry had grown used to during their months of sailing. The two-week timeframe of this charter felt over-urgent. Beth knew without further discussion that Terry was happy to stay put, especially since they had a forty-mile passage to Barbuda to look forward to. She was surprised Jeff hadn't found a reason to complain about not sailing for most of the last half of his trip. She wanted to take it as a sign he knew Carole was happier not sailing, but she suspected it was more that he respected her business requirements.

Whatever, she told herself as she brushed her teeth over the head sink. Carole's problems with Jeff weren't hers, and she knew without doubt that Terry was happy. She'd seen evidence of that when he was undressing a few minutes ago.

)

Beth was awakened by the aroma of coffee and the sounds of cooking coming from the galley. Terry was absent from their bunk, so Beth could relax in the knowledge that he was the one cooking, not Carole. In Carlisle Bay Carole had insisted on cooking a pot of spaghetti and meat sauce. Somehow, she'd used almost every pan in the galley.

Beth pulled on her swimsuit and stood in the cabin doorway watching Terry for a moment. He glanced at her as he was salting the pan of scrambled eggs, then put down the salt shaker and picked up the full percolator, which had been banished to a trivet so he could use all three burners on the stove. He sloshed coffee into her travel mug and extended it toward Beth.

"Morning! Milk and sugar are on the table."

"I love you," Beth said, sticking the mug under her nose to inhale the coffee steam. Terry grinned back, then picked up his wooden spoon and focused on the eggs.

Beth slid in to the settee at the table and reached for the carton of long-life milk. She smiled at the sight of the smaller carton of Trader Joe's long-life whipping cream she'd brought. She dosed her coffee with part milk and part cream to obtain her favorite: half and half.

"Jeff or Carole up?" She asked after taking her first few sips.

"In fact, Jeff took the dinghy ashore to see about renting a jet ski. I asked him to ask about a wind surfer for me."

"Good. Support the locals and have fun."

"Your client would approve."

"No sign of Carole?"

"She's in the cockpit, last I looked."

Beth got up and crossed to the companionway ladder and on up, carrying her coffee to the cockpit. Carole was indeed sitting there with a mug and a book.

"Good morning. Lovely day!" She said.

"It sure is," Beth said, scanning the horizon to the west, then pivoting to look east at the island. White, fluffy clouds dotted the sky, but there was no sign of anything more threatening. That could change in an instant, but she took it for the time being.

"Still want to visit the resorts?" Beth sat down across from Carole.

"Jeff said he'd take me after breakfast. Do you want to join me?"

Beth thought about it again, for she'd already convinced herself she had no business shopping in resort shops. Nor did she have an obligation to entertain Carole.

"My budget says no. The more time I spend on this boat, the more I like it, so the more I will need every penny to help pay for it."

"This boat? I thought you were buying a new one."

"One like this one. Although," Beth looked around at *Mana*'s configuration and equipment.

"Although what?"

"*Mana* is for sale." She leaned forward to project her voice down into the saloon. "Hey Terry?"

"Yah?" He appeared at the bottom of the companionway ladder, wooden spoon in one hand.

"Do we really need a brand-new boat?"

He squinted up at her, mouth curling in a smile.

"You mean, buy this one instead?"

"Maybe."

"Not a bad idea. We could take delivery a lot sooner."

)

Terry had served the eggs, toast, fruit salad, and more coffee by the time Jeff returned.

"I've got a ski for three hours starting at noon. You have a windsurfer for the same. Carole, we'll take you in with us. What do you want to do, Beth?"

"Since Terry will be here guarding the boat tomorrow, I thought I'd do that today."

"All by yourself all day?"

"It's hardly all day. I need to speak to my office and review material for tomorrow. I'll get dinner started, too. You should know by now that hanging out in my hammock is one of my favorite things. I do expect Jeff and Terry to both come by and buzz me."

Jeff chuckled and nodded.

"I'll probably tire out long before my three hours is up," Terry said. "Carole, you should take a hand-held radio with you so that if the dinghy is back here at the boat when you're done you can call us."

"What about me?" Jeff asked.

"If the dinghy is here when you're on your last circuit of the bay, come by and give a shout and one of us will come meet you," Beth said.

"I wouldn't know how to use a radio," Carole said, eyes darting from Beth to Jeff.

"It's easy," Jeff said, almost a scoff.

"I'll walk you through it," Beth assured her.

"If you're sure it's okay. Don't you need a license?"

"Technically yes, but it's not a problem. Let's do the dishes, then I'll show you."

)

Beth was not confident that Carole would use the VHF radio even after showing her how to press the key to talk and let go to listen and running several times through what she should say. She called *Mana*'s primary radio with the hand-held radio so Carole could hear how it would sound. To keep it simple she tuned both radios to a less-used non-commercial channel and left the hand-held radio turned on.

Standing on the swim platform she tossed the dinghy painter to Jeff and waved as Terry reversed the small boat away from the big one. The guys' schedule would have them off playing until mid-afternoon. She suspected Carole could easily use all of that time exploring the resorts, assuming she could bluff her way in. The wicker tote bag with dyed seashells sewn on it that she thought made a good boat bag would at least be a prop for her imitation of a resort guest. Not having the "all inclusive" wrist band might exclude her, but Beth suspected that if she told whoever stopped her that she wanted to spend money she'd get beyond the beach easily.

Not having internet access was inconvenient if she was to work while on board. She had arranged to be reimbursed for her cellular phone usage, but it hadn't occurred to her that she'd want access to her email. She might have to break down and get a Blackberry like Terry's that could receive email directly. For the time being, she could have joined the others in the dinghy and taken her laptop ashore to hunt for wifi, but the prospect of sitting in a noisy bar, if she even found one that had it, sounded unpleasant. Instead she settled in a shady corner of the cockpit with her cell phone and called the team.

As she expected, about an hour later a yellow and white jet ski came roaring up to *Mana* and circled several times. Jeff waved and grinned. Beth reluctantly waved back, hating to encourage the annoying personal watercraft even when driven by a friend.

Friend? As the annoying vehicle zoomed off, she contemplated her relationship with Terry's partner. That was how she thought of him most of the time. Not her friend, but Terry's. Carole's description of his treatment of her couldn't help but color Beth's perception of him. A concern that she'd only heard one side of it nagged at her. She had never been a "female unity" kind of woman. She didn't want to stick up for Carole out of gender loyalty. But she had seen Jeff being unkind to his wife, including when she'd been afraid to use the radio.

On the other hand, seriously? Afraid to talk on a radio? Something about Carole's hesitancy felt manipulative. It reminded Beth of herself as a child, when for reasons she'd never been able to articulate she'd pretended not to know things. Her parents would become frustrated when she "played dumb" over math problems. She didn't remember now, but she suspected she had known how to solve the problems and had refused for some subconscious reason. What she did remember now was the sense of failure her parents' reaction had caused in her. As she grew up, she had overcome whatever had caused her hesitancy and become a problem solver and learner, but just like the underlying cause of the "playing dumb," she didn't know what the motivator had been, and had never seen the point in investing time and money in therapy to help her figure it out. All she knew was that Carole had to find confidence within herself.

A half hour or so after Jeff's noisy visit Beth heard her name called across the water. Terry was on a windsurfer reaching across the water toward *Mana*. She exchanged the laptop for her camera and started snapping photos as he approached, passed across *Mana*'s stern, and fell into the water trying to tack the windsurfer.

Beth laughed and clicked away as he climbed back onto the board and knelt there wiping water from his face.

"If you give up here I can't help you. No dinghy," Beth called.

He shook his head. "Remember I said I'd tire out before Jeff?"

"I do."

"I think it took everything I have to get out here."

"Come on, you're in better shape than that. You can get back to the beach. Haul up that sail."

He did look weary as he climbed to his feet, the board wobbling. He pulled the line that brought the sail vertical and grabbed the wishbone, leaving the sail angled downwind until he got his balance.

"You can do it!" Beth cheered.

"I know I can. I know!" He called back. He was building up his courage. After a few seconds he grabbed the wishbone with both hands and pulled the sail toward him, angling the board toward the beach. He picked up speed quickly and Beth heard a receding "woohoo!" As he sailed off. She kept an eye on him until he because lost among the other surfers, jet skis, dinghies, anchored boats, and party catamarans plying the waters of the bay.

By the time Terry returned with Jeff Beth had lunched on mango, papaya, and lime salad and slices of ham and cheese rolled together. She had put the turkey breast in the galley sink to defrost and boiled three potatoes in salted water. She'd found the bag of fresh green beans in the refrigerator and unearthed from a cabinet the cans of mushroom soup and crispy onions that had cost an arm and a leg.

As she expected, the men had found lunch on shore and now were mostly interested in cold beers and salty snacks. She went for a swim, then joined them.

She almost missed Carole's voice coming from the VHF radio below, even though she'd turned the volume up high.

"*Mana, Mana*, this is, um, Carole calling?"

"Was that—?" Terry angled his ear toward the companionway.

"I think it was," Beth said, standing up. Terry leaned back so she could squeeze past his legs and go below.

"… do you hear me? Read me?"

Beth picked up the radio microphone. "Hello Carole, this is *Mana*. Over."

"Oh, right. Over."

"Carole, are you ready for pickup? Over."

"Hi Beth. Yes. Please." Pause. "Over."

"Please walk to the dock. I'll meet you there. Over."

"The dock?"

Beth waited, but no "over" was forthcoming.

"Where we picked you and Jeff up last night. Over." She emphasized the "over" that time and felt bad for it.

"I remember. Okay. I'll go there. Um, over."

"Be there in a few minutes. *Mana* standing by on six eight."

"Okay. Over and out."

Beth cringed at the meaningless phrase, but let it go.

"I'm going to go get Carole," Beth said as she returned to the cockpit. Terry shifted his legs to let her get past him.

"Alone?" Jeff asked. Terry shook his head, eyes closing for a moment, then stared at his partner.

"Yup," came Beth's reply as she stood on the swim platform and reached for the dinghy painter where it was cleated on *Mana*'s stern.

"Is there anything we should do about dinner?" Terry asked.

"You could mash the potatoes. They're boiled, in the colander in the sink. Then zest a lemon and an orange, for the butter for the turkey. If you can find a zester."

"We can do that. See you in a bit," Terry said, noting that she had wrapped the line around the base of a stern stanchion and was climbing into the dinghy holding the end of it. A moment later the outboard engine started, and then the sound of it receding told him Beth had pulled the line aboard and motored away. Jeff's gaze turned toward the bowl of pretzels on the cockpit table.

"You realize she's sailed by herself for months, right?" Terry said.

Jeff glanced up, frowning.

"Yeah, why?"

"She's gotten in and out of a dinghy thousands of times. More than you or me."

"Terry, seriously, you've got to stop protecting her."

Terry shut his eyes and shook his head again.

"What? You think the sun rises and sets on her!"

"I do not, Jeff. But I do respect her and what she can do. You don't realize that Beth isn't Carole."

"Of course she isn't Carole."

Terry took a sip of his beer to stop himself from responding too quickly to what sounded like a criticism. Jeff did the same, eyes drifting out across the crowded bay.

"Okay. I get your point. She does know how to manage a boat. And Carole, which might be harder. I apologize."

"Thank you. Can you try to show her that too? I'd rather my wife and my partner be friends."

"Yeah. You're—your wife? When did that happen? Why didn't you say something?" Jeff slapped the table top, grinning.

"I just did, and it hasn't yet. I'm going to ask her after you guys leave."

"You sneak! You have a ring?"

"Yes. I'm waiting until we're anchored off the beach in Barbuda."

"Let's see it then. I thought you were saving money for the boat!"

"I didn't spend that much. Beth wouldn't want anything too flashy," Terry said, rising to go below.

"Don't fool yourself, buddy. She may be a competent sailor, but she's still a girl!"

Terry retrieved the ring box from where he'd hidden in his laundry bag.

"She's a girl with a fear of going into debt," he said as he climbed back into the cockpit and handed Jeff the box.

Jeff made appropriate admiring noises as he examined the discrete diamond offset by a row of three bright blue stones in graduated sizes.

"Are these aquamarines?" He asked, holding the ring up in the late afternoon sun.

"They're Paraiba tourmaline."

"Never heard of it."

"Neither had I. They're from Brazil and, apparently, pretty rare. I think Beth will love the color."

"I'm sure she will. Nice job."

"Thanks. I hope she likes it."

Jeff handed back the ring box and Terry returned it to his laundry bag. He could hear the approaching dinghy motor as he came back to the cockpit.

"Not a word! Not even to Carole," he said to Jeff.

Jeff shook his head, grinning, "Not a word. I promise."

Realizing he'd asked what to do to help with dinner, then not done any of it, Terry stayed below in the galley while Jeff met the dinghy. Carole came down the companionway ladder a couple minutes later. When Terry glanced up at her happy "hello" he got the impression of more shopping bags than woman. She disappeared into one of the aft cabins.

When Beth turned up a moment later she didn't seem too surprised to see him mashing the potatoes.

"No zester?" She asked innocently. He glanced at her and saw an amused smile. She knew full well that he and Jeff had sat and drank most of the time she was gone.

"I, um, didn't check yet."

"Uh huh." She was smiling as she nudged him a foot to the right so she could open the drawer of galley tools and search through it.

"I asked Jeff to put charcoal on one side of the grill and light it," she said as she searched. "The turkey should not be directly over the coals."

"Did you explain why?"

"No, should I have?"

"Probably. He'll think you were just telling him how to get them to light."

"Oh," she drew out the word. "Like I think he's dumb. Geesh men are sensitive." She set a bent, but serviceable looking zester on the counter and shut the drawer, then turned to climb part way up the ladder.

"Hey Jeff, I don't know if I was clear. We want the coals on one side of the grill so the turkey can sit on the other side, not over them. Indirect heat. Don't spread them after they're going."

"Got it!" Jeff called from the back of the cockpit. Wondering, but not caring, whether he had understood in the first place, Beth stepped back into the galley. She put her hands on Terry's hips to shift him a couple feet to the left so she could get to the turkey where it was sitting on the counter on the other side of the sink. He was cleaning mashed potato off of a fork with is index finger. He held it out to her so she could taste a lump of the potatoes.

"Good?"

"Ummm. Yummy."

"What next?"

"No, no, let me in there Terry. You go relax," Carole said, stepping empty-handed out of the aft cabin. Beth groaned. She loved cooking with Terry. His half smile at her as he moved away told her he didn't want to go either.

"Carole, can you zest these?" Beth asked, holding out a lemon and an orange she'd taken from the hanging net hammock full of produce. She nodded at the zester on the counter.

"Sure. I can try," Carole looked askance at the battered tool.

"Just do what you can. It's to season the butter, for the turkey."

While Carole wrestled with the citrus rinds Beth got butter and a bag of assorted herbs from the refrigerator. She sorted through the greens to find rosemary and thyme. She didn't think cilantro belonged on turkey. She chopped the herbs fine and took a head of garlic from the hammock, extracted a clove, and chopped that up too. By then Carole had two piles of zest on a paper towel.

"That should be enough," Beth said, taking the paper towel. "Can you find the casserole pan in the compartment under the oven?"

While Carole went diving for the pan, Beth mixed the herbs and zest with a chunk of soft butter. Out of habit she added salt and pepper. She carefully rubbed herb butter on the turkey's flesh under the skin, patting the skin back down on top of it. Carole came up with the pan and stood watching until Beth realized she was waiting for her.

"The pan's not for the turkey. It's for the green beans." Beth said, gesturing with her chin at the beans and cans of soup and dried onions on the counter.

"Oh! I thought—okay. I'll put it together."

"Great, thanks."

Beth put the turkey on a plate and squeezed past Carole to the companionway ladder. She called to Terry and he came and took it.

"Put it on when the coals are hot. Put the lid on. Keep an eye on it, make sure it doesn't go out. I'll hand up the basting stuff in a few minutes."

"You got it."

While she melted the rest of the butter Beth monitored Carole's assembly of the green bean casserole. It came together without mishap.

"The turkey's going to take about ninety minutes. The beans will take about a half hour. Put foil over it and leave it. Let's have appetizers!"

"Goody! Appetizers means cocktails!"

"Yes it does."

The grilled turkey came out better than Beth had expected, probably because Jeff had been very attentive at brushing on the melted butter repeatedly while it cooked. The one thing missing from the meal, Carole declared when they were seated around the cockpit table, was stuffing. Beth glanced down into the saloon, picturing the dried out half loaf of French bread from Jolly Harbour sitting on a shelf. She'd forgotten about stuffing.

"Never mind," Jeff said. "We don't need more carbs anyway. This is great."

Beth didn't care whether he was sincere or not. She appreciated his compliment.

Taking a cue from him, Terry raised his plastic wine goblet. "To Beth and Carole," he said.

"To Beth," Carole said. "She organized it—that was the hard part. It's delicious."

Beth smiled and thanked them, then urged them to dig in. She had organized it—including researching the turkey recipe and making sure they had everything they needed—except stuffing. It *had* taken a bit of effort on top of everything else. She liked being appreciated.

Twenty-four

Dickinson Bay, Antigua

"You'll do great Beth. We're all sure of it," Marcus said.

"You couldn't be more prepared. And Mr. Codrington told Marcus he liked you," Howard said. Beth was on speaker phone with the team. She was sitting in the cockpit, dressed in her work output, laptop in her sailcloth bag by her side. Jeff and Carole were below getting ready to go to town. Terry was in the dinghy, bailing out rain water, fiddling with the fuel line—occupying himself while he waited.

"I feel prepared. I've read everything you guys found about the committee, as well as what Mr. Codrington gave me. I have my notes organized. I think I've memorized the names of everyone who we expect to be there."

"Then it's time to focus on success," Marcus said. He was like that, coming up with new-agey silliness that, when Beth squelched her automatic eye roll, did make sense.

Jeff emerged from the saloon.

"I need to get going guys," Beth said into the phone. "It might take time to get a taxi, and I don't want to be late."

"Absolutely not!" Marcus said, tone shifting instantly from focused calm to urgency. Beth smiled.

"I'll call when it's over."

"You better! Bye."

"Ready?" Jeff asked, moving past the table to make room for Carole, who was coming up the ladder behind him.

"As I'll ever be." Beth rose and shouldered her bag.

It was early enough in the day that the water was calm, so their landing was smooth. Jeff held the bow of the boat while Carole and Beth climbed out into ankle deep water. Beth held her bag high as she waded to dry land.

"Knock 'em dead, Beth!" Terry called out as Jeff pushed the boat back into deeper water.

They walked up the beach to the shade of the trees and picked their way between them on sandy ground until they reached a path.

"This goes to the road," Carole said. "I came this way yesterday."

Sure enough, they stepped over a drainage ditch onto tarmac a few minutes later. To the right the front wall of the nearest resort protected its ornamental garden from the road. They walked along the road to the driveway and turned in.

"I came this way," Carole repeated.

Sure enough, when they got to the front entrance, a doorman smiled at her. "Welcome back, Madame. More shopping?"

"No, Oscar. My friends and I do need a taxi, though. Can you help with that?"

"No problem. Where are you headed?"

"St. Johns, Independence Avenue."

Jeff insisted that they go to Beth's destination first, he and Carole would find their way to the shopping district from there.

A few minutes later a dusty white sedan came up the drive and stopped. Oscar walked over and spoke to the driver, and gestured to them. Beth saw Jeff slip Oscar a few coins before getting into the car and was grateful. She hadn't thought of a tip.

Some island expert I am!

)

St. Johns, Antigua

"Miss Anderson, thank you for coming early," Mr. Codrington said, coming around from behind his desk to extend his hand as Beth entered his office.

"Good morning Mr. Codrington. It is my pleasure to be here. Everyone at Broadhead knows how important this hearing is. Do you feel ready?"

"Please, sit down," Mr. Codrington gestured at an armed, unpadded wooden chair in front of his desk. Beth sat down and noticed that despite the hard surface it was very comfortable. Mr. Codrington returned to his more traditional desk chair before going on. "I feel ready, Miss Anderson. I have a few concerns that I want you to watch for during the meeting and be prepared to help me address them."

"Absolutely. Let's go over them," Beth said, ignoring a sense of panic.

What concerns? Why didn't he mention them before?

"Names, Miss Anderson. I am forgetful of names. I know it appears disrespectful, as if I don't care who people are. I assure you it is not. When I meet someone, my mind is usually pre-occupied with the social niceties—can I think of an appropriate compliment on their appearance? What topics can I bring up that will be interesting or amusing? Then I realize I do not remember the name I was just given, and I grow more nervous. I start listening for other introductions rather than listening to the person. It's a terrible situation, and entirely my own fault."

"Not at all, Mr. Codrington. It's quite common. There are dozens of people offering training in memory retention. I'm sure you've heard of the techniques—let whatever image comes to mind when you're introduced become associated with their name, for instance."

"Yes, but that requires remembering to listen to the name! Remembering to remember it, so to speak."

Beth chuckled. "I know. I've experienced what you describe. It is stressful. How do you think I can help?"

"Very simple. If you see me not addressing one of them by name, find a moment to whisper it to me. Or write it down and put it in front of me."

"How about this. When we get inside, I'll make a seating chart with their names. You'll have it on the desk in front of you the whole time."

Mr. Codrington's eyes widened, his thick, grey brows arching. "And that is why I hired Broadhead. Brilliant, Miss Anderson."

"What else can I help you with during the hearing?" Beth felt buoyed by the success of her easy answer.

"The other item is harder, and it really is why I contracted with your organization. I become quite nervous sometimes. Even with their names in front of me, if the questioning becomes heated, I can lose my train of thought, stammer, and get angry."

"I see. Do you have a suggestion for how I can help you prevent it?"

"I don't hear it in myself, but friends have told me they can tell when I'm starting to go astray. My voice rises. I start skipping words."

"So I should be able to hear your discomfort."

"Discomfort. Yes. An apt term. If you hear these signs, touch me—on the arm, or on the thigh if it would be better to be discrete—I won't take it as anything inappropriate."

"Just a touch?"

"Yes. That should be enough to make me realize what I'm doing. If you can place information related to the question in front of me, that would be supremely helpful. It would allow me to focus."

"All right. I can distract you. I think my notes are fairly well organized. Throughout the hearing I will try to have my notes on the current topic in hand and be able to set them in front of you. Hopefully they won't raise any subjects we didn't go over."

"Indeed, Miss Anderson. I hope not!" Mr. Codrington seemed to have relaxed, apparently re-assured by Beth's structured plan. "I think we are ready to proceed to the hearing."

)

The conference room was tastefully decorated and furnished, with pale peach walls and white trim, subdued tropical print curtains. A portrait of Queen Elizabeth II hung on the wall above an arrangement of tropical flowers on a side table, reminding Beth that Antigua and Barbuda were part of the British Empire. The flowers were flanked by a coffee urn on one side and an urn of hot water with a wooden box of tea bags on the other. Ranks of ceramic cups sat upside down on their saucers beside each vessel. The conference table could seat thirty, and there were additional, matching chairs against the walls all around the room. Beth realized that the only island government buildings she'd been in before were customs and immigrations offices. Clearly those departments had smaller decorating budgets than the island leadership.

Mr. Codrington paused to greet first one group gathered in the room and then another, introducing Beth as his consultant to each one. Beth found herself struggling to remember their names, completely failing at assigning clever symbols to them as she heard them. By the time they got to the third group she felt sweat threatening to stain her shirt. Yet Mr. Codrington easily greeted person after person by name. Baffled by this apparent contradiction between his stated weakness and his behavior, Beth kept smiling and nodding and shaking hands, channeling her growing fear into her left hand where it clutched the strap of her bag with pale white knuckles.

"Would you like to set that down? It looks heavy."

Beth's head snapped to the speaker, Theo—was it Theo?—Jones—yes, Jones. She'd met him in the second group they'd greeted. There was no chance she could remember his job title although she'd heard it moments before. He wasn't on the list of committee members her team had provided.

"Oh, no, it's just my laptop. Thanks."

Mr. Jones leaned closer and said quietly, "You can release the death grip on it. Nobody here bites."

Terror crept up Beth's spine at the notion that her nerves were so obvious. His smile was warm and seemed sincere, the corners of his eyes crinkling slightly. He was her age, his complexion flawless, his suit, tie, and shirt impeccable in both color coordination and tailoring. He reminded her of Terry in his "GQ" suit. Amazingly, that thought calmed her. But even so, she recognized Theo's supposed concern as intimidation disguised as kindness. She'd encountered it throughout her career—the superior male taking pity on the flustered, out-of-her-depth female by offering a few words of encouragement. Which he could safely do because she was no threat to him. Not that Beth wanted to be threatening, but it irritated her to be seen as of no consequence. She focused on the suit and thought of Terry who had never once treated her as inconsequential.

She smiled back and said, "Thanks. I didn't notice I was doing it." She forced her left hand open. The fingers ached.

"Good luck today."

"Thank you."

At the far end of the room, a woman in a bright yellow skirt suit raised her voice to be heard over the drone of voices.

"All right, everyone, let's take our seats. We have a time constraint, and we want to be sure everyone has their fair time."

She was, Beth knew from her preparation, Mrs. Erika Cooper, chairwoman of the land use committee. Mrs. Cooper was an imposing figure even beyond the flamboyance of her yellow suit. She wore her straightened hair in a chignon with the texture of sculpted of mahogany. She carried close to a hundred extra pounds, and carried it well, with curves but not unattractive bulges. Her calves were shapely, enhanced by three-inch heels that Beth could never have worn for more than a few minutes.

She strode behind the chairs on one side of the long table and stopped in the middle, hands on the chair back. To her right and left the rest of the committee lined up as well, a mix of five men and two more women. Others in the room, including Theo Jones, moved to chairs against the wall behind the committee members.

Mr. Codrington touched Beth's elbow and nodded toward the other side of the table. They walked together to the middle chairs and Mr. Codrington took the seat across from Mrs. Cooper.

Beth hesitated behind the chair next to him and he looked up.

"Sit at the table," he murmured. "I need you beside me, not behind me."

Appreciating his clear instruction, Beth pulled out the chair and sat down.

Mrs. Cooper called the hearing to order and delivered opening comments about the importance of the land use committee and its significant work toward improving the quality of life on Antigua and Barbuda. When she finished she asked the members to introduce themselves. Relieved to have the information handed to her, Beth printed their names in order of seating on a blank sheet of paper as they spoke. She wished she had studied the islands' geopolitical landscape more as each person mentioned their parish or whatever segment of the population they represented. Not all of them, she knew, were members of parliament. There were local business people and representatives of special interest groups. Knowing so little, she couldn't use this information to advise Mr. Codrington, although she did note it under each name in case he found it valuable.

When the members finished, Mrs. Cooper asked Mr. Codrington to introduce himself and make his opening statement. He stood up to address the committee.

Nice move, Beth thought.

Mr. Codrington made his case succinctly while projecting an emotional commitment to the citizens of St. Mary Parish, who had elected him to the house of representatives. He invoked a humble tone when he said this, bowing his head for a moment. Beth thought he might be laying it on a little thick, but she saw two of the men and all three of the women nod.

Mr. Codrington was concerned about the construction of resorts and rental properties without sufficient infrastructure, and their construction and growth to the exclusion of other traditional uses for the land.

"Tourism is critical to our economy. But someone must stand up for Antiguan tradition! We farm our land. We fish our seas. If every beach is allowed to be dominated by resorts, where will our fisher people go? I am here to speak for Antiguans. I am here to speak for our island's heritage."

Whispers behind hands, common across the room while he spoke, stopped abruptly. Mrs. Cooper gazed around the room, eyes stopping on various people in the seats against the walls. Beth wondered what silent messages she was sending or receiving.

"Thank you, Mr. Codrington, for your inspiring comments. We will begin the questions with Mr. Howe from St. John Parish. Mr. Howe?"

Beth wasn't convinced that Mrs. Cooper was inspired. Her gut told her that this imposing chairwoman was against adding Mr. Codrington to her committee. Research told Beth the chairwoman was a staunch supporter of tourism growth, representing the nation's capital and resort-heavy Dickinson Bay. It was probably why she'd started the questioning with her associate, the senator from her parish.

Mr. Codrington did well enough responding to Mr. Howe's questions. He made it clear that he was not against all resorts and tourism, and he appreciated the revenue these businesses brought to their island. He did not become flustered or angry, allowing Beth to focus on the discussion rather than having to bring him back on point.

The next questioner was from the eastern side of the island, which was far less developed. His questions were designed to allow Mr. Codrington to make his favorite points. No question this man was in favor of adding an ally to the committee. Two more committee members were neutral in their questioning. Then Mrs. Cooper called upon one of the other women, who was a member of the island's trade commission. As Mr. Codrington began to answer her very first question, about the construction of rental properties, his voice began to rise. Beth snapped into focus, letting him speak another sentence to be sure. Anger was becoming clear in his voice as he searched for his words. Beth discretely tapped his thigh and, lacking any notes on the topic, slid a blank piece of paper along the table in front of him.

He stopped speaking, staring down at it for a long moment. Without acknowledging Beth, he raised his head, smiling.

"I have just been reminded of the amazing success of the Frangipani development near Carlisle Point. Clearly there is room on our islands for rentals to attract vacationers from our wealthy northern neighbor."

Beth pulled the paper back and heaved an internal sigh of relief.

The hearing went on in the same vein for another forty-five minutes. Beth intercepted anger twice more, on one occasion actually managing to put relevant information in front of her client. At last Mrs. Cooper called the proceedings to a close. She asked Mr. Codrington for a closing statement, which he made as eloquently as his opening had been. When he finished the chairwoman thanked everyone and dismissed the committee.

Mr. Codrington gathered his papers between two hands.

"Thank you, Miss Anderson. You were extremely helpful."

"I'm very glad, Mr. Codrington. But I expected a conclusion. Do we just leave?"

Mr. Codrington chuckled. "The wheels of government turn slowly, Miss Anderson. The committee will meet again in a few weeks and decide my fate."

"A few weeks?"

"Never fear, Miss Anderson, I will be using the time wisely."

"You mean you will lobby the members. Do you need any help?"

He met her eyes, his smile pleasant, but his gaze calculating. "Perhaps. But I will begin on my own. I am quite comfortable one-on-one with my peers."

Feeling slightly chastised, Beth nodded. "I'm sure you are sir."

"My dear Miss Anderson, do not worry. This was the moment to shine. Whether I did or did not, you helped me achieve the best presentation I could."

"Thank you, sir. I wish you the best of luck over the next few weeks. You'll inform Broadhead of the outcome I hope."

"Certainly."

And that's it, Beth thought as she stepped onto the sidewalk. The committee members, press, and other observers had dissipated quickly, including her client, who had excused himself to return to his office.

Suddenly feeling as insecure as Theo Jones had thought she was before the hearing, Beth walked for a couple blocks until she realized she had no idea where she was in relation to the port, or the shopping district where she might find Jeff and Carole. She started scanning the traffic and spotted a dark blue sedan with a taxi sign on top. She waved, stepping off the sidewalk to get the driver's attention. When he pulled to a stop beside her, she realized there was someone in the back seat.

"Where you goin' miss?" the driver asked.

"Dickinson Bay. The Sunshine resort would be great."

"Got it. You'll be second, though."

"Okay with me."

Beth opened the back door and looked in before getting in. The smiling face on the other side of the seat took her by surprise.

"Theo Jones, wasn't it?"

"Exactly right, Miss Anderson. Come, get in. When I saw you there, I asked the driver to stop for you."

"Very kind of you. Thank you." Bristling once again at having given him another chance to "save" her, Beth got into the taxi and shut the door. The driver drove on.

"So you are staying at the resort?" he asked. Alarms went off in Beth's mind. She could see the headline: Anti-tourist Representative's Consultant a Resort Guest.

"No, I'm on a sailboat anchored in the bay. Sunshine is the closest resort. Easier to explain to a cab driver."

"Indeed. I see. You're a sailor?"

"Yes. We've chartered a boat for a couple weeks."

"We?"

"My boyfriend and I, and another couple. What's your interest in the hearing, Mr. Jones?"

His radiant smile broadened. "I represent a trade alliance."

"Of resorts?" Beth asked with a smile.

"No. Of island tradespeople. My clients' businesses are not nearly as glamorous as resorts. They assemble electronics and automobile parts, that sort of thing."

"I see. Part of the island's diverse industries. Mr. Codrington believes it's important for these businesses to be supported."

"No need to campaign for him," Mr. Jones said, his voice full of amusement. "I have no vote in the matter. But I do hope he is successful. We need more minds like his on the committee."

"My client will be glad to know you think so."

"Your client is well aware, Miss Anderson. My association contributed generously to his campaign."

"Of course. How silly of me not to realize."

"No, no, not at all. Island politics are convoluted and dull. Well, this is my destination. One of my members."

Out the window Beth saw they had stopped in front of a one-story industrial building badly in need of paint and landscaping. Theo Jones got out and handed the taxi driver several EC. Watching him walk away, Beth wasn't sure if she imagined the enticing wiggle of his hips.

◡

Dickinson Bay, Antigua

Standing in the shade of one of the resort's pool umbrellas, Beth called Terry's cell phone and asked if he could come get her. He seemed to recognize her urgency to get back to the boat, for he did not ask her any questions about the hearing. He simply said he'd be there in a few minutes and hung up. When she saw *Mana*'s dinghy depart the boat she took off her shoes and set out across the beach to meet him at the water's edge.

"So?" Terry asked from his seat next to the raised dinghy motor. Beth was standing in calf-deep water holding the bow of the little boat with one hand as she set her bag, shoes crammed inside, on top of the raised compartment in the bow. The surf was moderate now, whipped up by the wakes of the jet skis and other boats. A wave lifted the dinghy and threatened to knock her down.

"Can I get in first?" She immediately regretted the caustic tone in her voice. "Sorry. Hang on." She added, moving around to the side of the boat, and simultaneously pushing it away from the beach while swinging her left leg over the side. She wound up laying on the inflated side, hands slipping on the slick rubber. Her left knee landed and skidded painfully on the floor of the boat where sand, seawater, and spilled fuel sloshed around.

"Shit."

Even with the pain of her scuffed knee and her embarrassment, she was more concerned about her bag and the laptop inside. But it was sitting safely up on top of the bow compartment. Unwilling to give up her clothes to the muck in the bottom of the boat, she got her weight onto her stinging left knee and raised her torso. By straddling the inflated side, she was able to swing her right leg on board. She saw that Terry was using one of the oars to push the boat off the beach.

"Here, let me," she reached for it. As she plunged the blade of the paddle into the shallow surf, hit bottom, and pushed off, Terry peered over the stern, hands on the motor tilt release.

"One more heave," he said. Beth complied. This time she almost lost the paddle as the boat accelerated—she'd pushed during a lull in the surf. She heard the motor splash and felt Terry's body jerk the boat as he pulled the starter cord. She plunged the paddle into the water to keep the boat from turning as the next wave rolled under the stern. "Okay, we're away," Terry said over the sound of the running motor.

Beth stowed the paddle on the floor and checked her bag again. Still safe.

"That was embarrassing," she said.

Terry grinned and shrugged. "We've seen worse."

His grin was infections. She smiled back. "I think I've done worse, but that doesn't make it less embarrassing."

He did not respond. Instead he focused on identifying *Mana* in the crowd of anchored boats before speaking again.

"Can I ask now?"

"Yes. It went well, I think. But there was no decision. Turns out, he didn't expect one today. It felt like a letdown."

"Frustrating. Did he tell you how he thought it went?"

"He's not an exuberant man. But he thanked me, said I was very helpful. He did start to get angry a couple times and I managed to refocus him. He had specifically said he needed me to do that."

"You did good, then."

"The thing is, I realized once it started, I didn't know anywhere near as much as I should to advise him properly. All I could do was push information in front of him when I realized I knew what they were asking about. I couldn't connect dots that weren't already connected in my notes."

"You didn't know how much you didn't know?"

"Something like that. I feel like a fraud, at least with Broadhead. Some Caribbean expert I am."

"Well, they're probably right in that you know more than some of them. Don't forget your mission here was to be present. You did that."

"Feels like a minor accomplishment."

"But it takes a lot of small steps to lay the groundwork to take a big one."

"Who said that?"

Terry frowned. "I just did."

"Oh. I thought you were quoting someone."

"Nope. It's my own wisdom. Like it?"

"It's deep."

"Uh huh." He smiled at her sarcasm, slowing the engine as they approached *Mana*.

"Did Jeff and Carole come back?"

"Not yet. They're not due until five."

"What time is it?" Beth asked, realizing she hadn't thought of the time since leaving the hearing.

"A little after four."

"I have to call the office. I'm sure Mr. Codrington has already talked to them."

"While you do that, I'll make you a special celebratory cocktail."

"With rum?"

"If you like."

"And what else?"

"It's a surprise. Get the painter."

Beth felt silly to be excited by the prospect of a surprise cocktail, even though she knew exactly what ingredients were available in the galley. But she knew better. She knew it had nothing to do with mixers, and everything to do with being with a man who she loved, who loved her enough to do silly favors to make her happy. She climbed onto *Mana*'s swim platform with the dinghy painter and held it while Terry shut off the engine and handed up her bag. He got out and took the line, shooing her forward through the cockpit to make her call while he took care of the boat. And her drink.

)

"Beth, finally! Mr. Codrington called more than an hour ago," Marcus said by way of answering the phone.

"I'm sorry, I had to get back to the boat." as Beth spoke she realized she could have stayed on shore and found a Wi-Fi connection to check her email. She could have called from the resort.

"Does it leave soon?" That was Claudia. Marcus had put Beth on speaker phone, as usual.

"No, we're staying here tonight." Beth once again ignored Claudia's incorrect assumption. It was a lost cause. "What did Mr. Codrington say?"

"That you were great! He said you saved him from some serious blunders."

"Thank heavens."

"What, you didn't think so?"

"No, no, I just—I think I should have been able to be of more help to him. I didn't know enough detail about his situation."

"Seriously?" Claudia said. "You had every shred of intel we could get."

"There's a man, Theo Jones, who works for an association of industrial businesses. Did we know about him?"

"Checking," Claudia said. Beth could imagine fingers on a keyboard.

"What about him, Beth?" Marcus asked.

"He said his organization contributed a lot to Mr. Codrington's campaign. I didn't know going in whether he was friend or foe. I might have treated him differently."

"Were you rude to him?"

"No, but—"

"No 'but.' You did fine."

"I could have done better."

"Found him!" Claudia said. "He's addressed the committee in the past. But I don't see him as a donor to Mr. Codrington. We do have that info from his last campaign."

"He lied to me?"

"Probably not," Marcus said. "Claudia, check for the name of a trade association. The donation would have come from it, not him personally."

"Of course," Beth said, relieved.

"It's here," Claudia confirmed.

"If we're to continue working with Mr. Codrington, I think we need to know about every donor," Beth said.

"Beth's right," Marcus said, speaking to the others in Washington. "Thanks Beth. When you get back, I owe you dinner. You are officially on vacation starting now."

"Thanks Marcus. But you can call me if something comes up."

"Not a chance. Have a great week." The connection ended. Beth took her phone from her ear and started at it for a moment, then turned it off and dropped it into her bag.

She changed into a swimsuit and stopped in the head to clean off her scraped knee before stepping into the saloon. Terry wasn't there, but there were juice containers, the rum bottle, and parts of various pieces of fruit on the counter. Beth eagerly climbed out into the cockpit.

"As promised!" Terry, sitting at the table, held up a large plastic cup filled with a colorful liquid. Beth could see chunks of the various fruits inside and grains of ground nutmeg floating on top. She took it and sat down beside him.

"The call went well?"

"They're very happy. So I'm happy. Marcus said I was officially on vacation and not to call them again."

Terry tipped his matching cup toward hers and the plastic thunked together.

Twenty-five

Dickinson Bay, Antigua

*W*hile Beth paddled around in the water Terry took the dinghy back to the beach to meet Jeff and Carole. They came puttering back a while later—long enough that Beth knew Terry had to wait for them. When she saw them coming Beth climbed out, rinsed off, and stood waiting to take the line. When they got close enough, she saw with dismay that Carole was not happy. They unloaded several packages and climbed out of the dinghy.

Terry took over preparing steaks for the grill while Beth monitored Carole in the galley preparing rice and a salad. Sitting at the table cutting up vegetables, Beth took the opportunity to ask Carole how the day had gone.

"It was fun." Carole's reply was so preemptive Beth hesitated to probe deeper. She selected another carrot to slice. "Jeff didn't want to be there. Nothing unusual in that."

"Didn't he suggest it?" Beth asked, sure she remembered correctly.

"He did. But that doesn't mean he wanted to do it. He knew I would like it."

"I see. Have you given more thought to what you told me the other day?"

"You mean—?" Carole looked over her shoulder, wooden spoon poised over the steaming pot where she'd just poured the rice into boiling water.

"Yeah." Beth said before Carole said more.

"I haven't changed my mind. Today didn't matter. I mean, it's not a contributing factor. Hell, if he'd been enthused and into it today, that wouldn't matter either."

"What about your children?"

"I'll get custody. He'll have visitation."

"I guess that seems likely. You don't think he'd push for custody?"

Carole's eyes shot toward the companionway, but Beth was sure the men were out of earshot of their quiet conversation. And for some reason she wanted Carole to have to talk about this. She wanted the other woman to realize that it wasn't a subject to bring up casually and then drop. If she was serious, she had to begin to own the decision. And then Beth wondered if she was being as manipulative as men like Theo Jones. She squelched that thought as too much to deal with right now.

"I'm pretty sure he won't."

Both women fell quiet for a few minutes, and before either could think of more to say Jeff was leaning down through the companionway asking for a plate. Carole got one from the cabinet and handed it to him.

"Are the steaks already done?" Beth was alarmed because the rice had minutes to go.

"No. One might be. We need to check it."

"Oh. Phew. You worried me there."

"How much time do you need?"

"Carole? How much time on the rice?"

"Time?"

"Did you set a timer?"

"I don't have a timer."

"Let me," Jeff said, setting the plate down and pulling his phone from his pocket. "How long should I do it for?"

"The box says twenty minutes," Carole said, reading the empty box.

"Eighteen," Jeff repeated, intent on his phone.

"But it's already been about five," Beth put in. "Make it fifteen."

"Okay, fifteen," Jeff said, sounding slightly annoyed. "Done." He pocketed his phone, picked up the plate, and withdrew from the companionway.

Carole opened the cabinet with the trash can inside, crammed the empty box in, and shut the cabinet with extreme force. Beth focused on cutting up the last fresh tomato.

By the time they sat down to their steak dinner Beth had resolved to ignore Carole's mood, which Jeff and Terry didn't notice anyway. Terry produced a couple bottles of sparkling wine—the surprise he'd gone to the store for back in Jolly Harbour, Beth realized, and raised a toast to Beth's successful client meeting. The rest of the bottle, and the second one, helped to put everyone in a warm and fuzzy frame of mind. The dishes were done in a sink banging, dish-rack rattling frenzy and the two couples settled back in the cockpit with jazz playing just loud enough to be heard and refreshed wine cups in hand.

"This has been a lot of fun guys," Jeff said. "Thank you for inviting us."

"Yes, thank you so much," Carole sounded remarkably sincere. "I hope I didn't put too much of a damper on the sailing."

"Not at all," Beth said. "I thought I was the one doing that, having to be in certain places to get to my meetings."

"Everything was perfect," Jeff insisted. "I got to play on a jet ski. The sailing to get here was awesome. Terry and I did a beach pub crawl—oh, I wasn't supposed to mention that," he looked guiltily at Terry, who shook his head, smiling.

"It's been great having you," he said. "Beth and I love to share our fun."

Beth nodded, thinking that was a total invention of Terry's—they'd never discussed wishing they could have family and friends on board. But it sounded like the right thing to say at the moment, and as she thought about it, she realized she'd suggested the same thing to her friend Eva a few weeks ago. Maybe they needed to discuss it. It had not come up when they were sailing *Trouble* because the boat was too small. But then she remembered that one of Terry's arguments for looking at a bigger boat was room for guests. They had discussed it, at least in the abstract. Beth filed it away for later. She was starting to fade now. The others' words were becoming a pleasant buzz in her ears. She realized sleepily that her head was on Terry's shoulder and her eyes wouldn't stay open.

♪

The delicious aroma of coffee woke Beth up. She opened her eyes and saw Terry on knees and elbows on the bunk holding her mug, blowing across it to send the scent her way.

"Thought you'd never wake up." He smiled, glancing at the mug.

She rolled onto her back and sat up, then took it from him. As soon as she did, he leaned in and kissed her.

"Good morning."

"Thanks for the coffee, and good morning. Am I that late?" She took a careful sip of the steaming beverage.

"It's almost eight."

"Late for me." She nodded, taking another sip. She already felt more awake. "I guess I conked out last night."

"You did. You let it all go."

Terry's eyes shown with sincerity, amusement, and the deeper spark she had come to recognize as love.

"Are Jeff and Carole getting ready to go?"

"Yes. It's going to take two dinghy trips."

"Really?"

"Yes. Jeff said he'd make a run with Carole and leave her to guard the first round of luggage."

Beth started to object—Jeff and Carole and a dinghy full of luggage sounded like a bad idea—but Terry went on before she could speak.

"I told him I'd go too—we'd need another set of hands to haul the dinghy up far enough to unload the luggage."

"Good plan."

"And they're almost ready, so you'd better get out there to say good bye."

"Seriously? I'm so sorry! I'll be right out."

Beth was secretly glad she'd slept through a lot of the packing and hauling of luggage up the ladder. It shortened the possible time for good byes and well wishes, so Carole's farewell was simple—a quick hug and peck on the cheek before she climbed into the loaded dinghy. Beth tossed the line into the boat where Jeff caught it, and Terry drove them away.

Beth was working on her second cup of coffee and a stale croissant when Terry and Jeff returned. She left her breakfast on the cockpit table to help them load the rest of the luggage. Standing on the swim platform, Jeff extended his hand to her.

"Well skipper, this was great. I hope we can do it again." Beth took his hand and he pulled her in to a friendly hug.

"Thanks Jeff, it was great having you. See you back in Washington. Safe flight."

"I hope so!" He replied as he climbed back into the dinghy. Beth freed the line and tossed it to him, her eyes meeting Terry's as he put the engine in reverse.

I'll be right back, and then it's just us, his expression said. Or maybe she was anthropomorphizing.

Beth had half the contents of the freezer out on the counter when Terry got back.

"Yikes, this looks like work!" he said as he climbed down the ladder.

Beth straightened holding another package of frozen chicken retrieved from the bottom of the freezer.

"I don't want to have to find provisions in Barbuda—town is nowhere near Eleven-Mile Beach where we want to be."

"It seemed like we loaded an entire market aboard."

"I know. But we did put a dent in it feeding four people. More than I expected. I'm used to provisioning for myself and you."

"Do we need to make a run?"

"If we make a menu for the next few days, we can see if there are any holes."

"Okay." Terry went to the navigation desk and got out a notebook and pencil. "Breakfasts, lunches, dinners," he said as he drew a grid on a blank page. "Today, tomorrow, Monday. How long do you want to stay at Barbuda?"

Beth set the chicken on the counter and plunged her arms back into the depths. She emerged holding a plastic bag with the remains of a block of ice in it.

"As long as I can," she said with a grin. She tore the plastic bag open and let the chunk of ice drop back into the bottom of the freezer. "I was thinking we'd hang out there through Monday, then come back and go to Bird Island. If we can get away at dawn on Tuesday. We can stay there a day or go somewhere else on Thursday. Then go around the Eastern shore of Antigua and back into English Harbour on Friday."

"I'm not hearing civilization anywhere in your plan. I like it. But it means we need to stock up for the rest of the trip."

Beth nodded, scanning the defrosting food on the counter. "Better inventory it and put it away," she said, glancing at Terry. He held his pencil poised to write.

"I'm ready. Start dictating."

)

It took an hour to make a menu and shopping list. They rooted out unsavory looking leftovers brought back from restaurants and spoiled produce from the net hammock. With shopping bags, garbage, and wallets in hand they secured *Mana* and took the dinghy to the beach.

"I guess it's too early to stop for a drink," Beth said as they walked past a bar made mostly of palm fronds. A tall, shirtless man was wiping down the tables, a cigarette hanging from between his lips. His long brown hair was pulled back in a tail.

"Jeff and I stopped there the other day. They had strong rum drinks. Maybe later on?"

"Sure."

But by the time they got a taxi to the nearest market, loaded their bags with fresh produce and bread, fish, steak, and all the other items they'd decided they needed, and taxied back, all they wanted to do was get their purchases back to *Mana*. So they strode right on by the palm-frond bar, which was busy with a post-lunch crowd.

)

Pointe-à-Pitre, Guadeloupe

Burt made a final wave at the three women dragging roller bags along the dock away from *Sandcastle*. They'd turned out to be middle aged former high school classmates who got together without their spouses every year for a few days of reminiscing. Burt had enjoyed their camaraderie as well as their failure to regard him as a perk of the charter. Some men might be hurt not to be hit on, he supposed, and each of the three women had been attractive in her own way. But he was glad to have enjoyed the week without the sexual tension that sometimes came with female—and sometimes with male—charterers.

He stepped back into *Sandcastle*'s saloon and fished his notepad and pen out of a drawer. They'd been fun guests, but they'd had an impact on his boat. He went back outside and settled in a deck chair to make a list. Unclogging the aft head was at the top.

By the time he'd finished the list he knew it would take about a week to complete. He needed to find the right size hose and replacement cockpit shower head, which one of them had been holding onto when she fell overboard. The aging hose had split, but the plastic shower attachment had already been cracked. The anchor windlass needed lubrication and some of his fishing gear needed maintenance. He wanted to head for Antigua to look for Hunter Green, but he could not in good conscious plan the trip before seeing to his boat and checking in with his booking agent.

He got up and returned to the saloon, taking his laptop out of a cabinet. He checked his email, scanning the list of incoming messages looking for two senders: his agent, and Beth Anderson. The message from his agent was an inquiry about how the charter had gone. He replied, advising the agency of his plan to go to Antigua. Then he scanned his inbox again for a reply from Beth, but there was none.

"That settles it. We'll get you ship shape, then go after the mysterious Mr. Green," he said out loud, looking around the saloon as he spoke as if *Sandcastle* could hear him.

Twenty-six

Caribbean Sea

*B*y 8:00 the following morning Diamond Bank, the reef along Antigua's north coast, was abeam to starboard and Beth was pointing *Mana* due north toward the south west corner of Barbuda. The bow sliced through low swells, throwing handfuls of sparkling diamonds across the foredeck. Beth grinned with delight when an occasional wild wave splashed the plexiglass windows of the dodger protecting the cockpit. The spray wasn't strong enough to reach her at the back of the cockpit behind the leeward wheel, and Terry was comfortably ensconced at the front of the cockpit where the dodger protected him.

The sails were perfectly trimmed for the steady trade wind and the boat was so balanced Beth could take her hands off of the wheel for several seconds at a time to drink her coffee. On every level she was content. Or so she thought until she heard a distinctive snort. She glanced over her shoulder at *Mana*'s wake.

"Terry, look! Dolphins!"

As she spoke, she turned on *Mana*'s auto pilot and stepped around the wheel to the table for her camera. Terry stood up.

"Where?"

"Behind us. Heading for the bow, I'll bet. We're not going fast enough to entertain them for long." She climbed out of the cockpit with the camera and headed for the bow. She scanned the waters all around the boat as she went, checking not for the aquatic visitors, but for anything else that might require her to be at the helm. The only other boats in sight were miles away, and there was no land for the next twenty-five miles. Terry came up behind her with his own camera, crowding in beside her on the narrow bow.

Five or six sleek dark grey bodies were competing for space next to *Mana*'s bow where it sliced through the sea throwing up a small wake. One would get into position in the wave for a few seconds, until another nudged it from behind or the side. The first one would shoot forward across *Mana*'s bow and disappear while the next one took its place. Sometimes the displaced one would leap from the water or cross back and forth below the surface for a while before moving into position to for another turn in the bow wave. There was no doubt in Beth's mind that this was a game. *Or maybe I'm anthropomorphizing*, she thought with a private grin.

"See how still they are. They barely have to move their fins to go this fast," Terry said.

"And look at how fast they go when they get knocked out of position. We're going slow from their perspective."

"And you can't see them working at it. They are so hydrodynamic."

"Wow!" A dolphin erupted from the water a few feet in front of the bow.

"Show off," Terry said, laughing.

"Mom is going to love hearing about this."

They took dozens of photos, many of empty water as they missed the dolphins' leaps. Beth switched to video mode and captured half a minute of the creatures competing for the bow wave, their snorts audible over the sound of the wave.

And then they were gone, zooming ahead of *Mana* and out of sight until two leapt from the sea ahead and off to port, and then another repeated the acrobatics further away.

"Magnificent!" Terry said, turning his camera on Beth and snapping a shot of her delighted expression.

"What a treat. I hope they come back."

"Maybe they'll bring friends."

The dolphins did come back a couple times throughout the six hours it took to reach Barbuda. *Mana*'s crew didn't tire of hurrying forward to watch them play and take more photos.

Mid-afternoon Terry was steering as they came abeam of Palmetto Point at the southwestern tip of Barbuda. Beth studied the island's contours and compared them to the paper chart as well as the electronic one. The GPS plotter showed *Mana*'s position in relation to the island, shoals, reefs, channel markers, and known shipwrecks. It also showed the depth of the water at low tide. It was easy to fall into the habit of relying on the nearly magical device, one that *Double Trouble* didn't have. But it was not perfect—atmospheric and geologic anomalies could make it show them in the wrong place.

So Beth kept the paper chart on hand and double checked their position using her eyes.

"We should be able to keep sailing along the beach inside the shoal. We want to be up at the northern end, right? To be closer to the Frigate Bird sanctuary?" As she spoke, Beth heard the tentative tone Jeff had reacted to a week ago. "That's what I want to do."

"Me too. When we get settled, I'll try to contact someone to set up a tour tomorrow."

"Okay, great. We're going to make dog-leg here to get safely inside the shoal that parallels the beach. The water is going to get thin in a few spots, but we should be all right."

"I'll keep an eye on the depth gauge. Unless you want to take it?"

"Only if you're tired."

"Nope, I'm having fun. Sail trim is on you. The island may blanket the wind."

Beth groaned. She hadn't considered that. She appreciated that he hadn't blatantly said she might be wrong. Sure enough, as they passed into the island's wind shadow the breeze lightened and fluctuated. Terry kept *Mana* moving, but their speed dropped to two knots and every few seconds the sails collapsed and refilled with an annoying crack. After fifteen minutes Beth stood up and studied the island to their starboard, bent down to look at the electronic chart, and then at the wind speed indicator.

"It's been fluctuating between three and nine," Terry said when he saw what she was checking. "Direction changes with the speed."

"Yeah," Beth sighed. "I think if we want to get settled and have time for a swim we need to give in and motor."

"It's been a great sail. I say we get there and have time to relax before dark."

"Okay," Beth looked at the chart again. "Start the engine, then go about twenty degrees to port for a few minutes to give us room to starboard to turn into the wind. I'll get the jib in, then we'll head up to pull in the main."

"Yes ma'am."

Beth was pleased that she had little trouble rolling in the huge main sail, a job that Jeff and or Terry had done so far on the trip. "It's not too bad," she observed when the sails were stowed and Terry was back on their previous course.

"I know. Not as fast as freeing a halyard in an emergency, though."

"No. But if the wind is screaming, you can't drop the halyard anyway, you have to go up and pull the sail down." She'd done that more times than she liked to think about. "That's slow too. Rolling it in from here is safer."

"Sounds like you're a convert."

"I could be. Let's give it a few more tries."

The final few miles of their voyage took another hour, but at last they selected a spot and anchored in ten feet of water over an endless sandy bottom. They passed a couple large motor yachts anchored in deeper water and one sailboat with all the accoutrements of a long-term cruiser, but all of them were a couple miles to the south. It felt like they had the entire length of Eleven Mile Beach—which was actually about five miles long—to themselves. The sole sign of other humans was four permanently placed wooden umbrellas on the beach, one pink, one green, one blue, and one unpainted. There was no sign of activity at the half-built resort tucked into the trees at the very northern end of the beach. The beach itself was an uninterrupted stretch of white sand with a strip of trees and underbrush behind it. Beyond the growth they knew there was a large salt pond. Across the pond and to the south was a town. The mangrove forest housing the frigate bird sanctuary formed the pond's northern border.

"Welcome to our little piece of paradise," Beth said, returning from below where she'd shut off the engine battery to prevent running it down by accident. She handed Terry an open bottle of beer and clinked her own against his. "Anchoring beer."

Terry took a gulp, then set his down and stepped behind the starboard wheel where he pressed the button that lowered the swim platform. "I'll get the ladder in a few minutes," he said.

"If we buy this boat, we have to come up with a better swim ladder," Beth said, sitting in the cockpit watching the stern go down.

"The ladder itself, or the fact that it lives all the way up on the bow?" Terry asked, stepping back into the shade under the bimini to retrieve his beer.

"Both."

He nodded, sipping his beer.

"If we buy this boat, are we changing the name?"

"Why?"

"I don't know. I've gotten used to sailing *Double Trouble*. The '*Trouble*' part of it fits."

"*Triple Trouble?*" Beth suggested, not sure she wanted to play this game, but still intrigued by it.

He shook his head. "That would be for three people."

"Humm." Beth's sound was somewhere between agreement and puzzlement. *Is he hinting at what I think he is? Probably not. Think of something else, quick.* "Double Trouble Too—t-o-o, not number two."

"*Double Trouble Too.* I kind of like that," he said, taking another sip of beer and turning his gaze aft toward the western horizon. "Might be a good night for a green flash."

Beth dragged her gaze from him to the horizon, thoughts abuzz over the notion of three people on the boat. The sky to the west was cloudless. "You're right," she said. The green flash, an elusive optical effect at sunset, was most likely to happen when there were no clouds on the horizon. She took another refreshing sip of beer. "I need a swim."

"I'll get the ladder."

He was up and out of the cockpit before she could tell him she'd go, but then, she hadn't reacted very quickly. Feeling slightly guilty for being lazy, she slotted her beer into a cup holder and went below to get their towels.

)

Eleven Mile Beach, Barbuda

"I'm making dinner," Terry said when he had finished rinsing off and Beth was reaching for the cockpit shower. They'd spent a blissful hour splashing around in the gin-clear water, diving to check that the anchor was well buried in the sand, and looking for sand dollars, rays, and lost treasure on the bottom. Although they'd only been anchored for an hour, a pair of long, muscular barracuda were already hanging out in the shadow of *Mana*'s hull. They watched the human intruders swim around the boat, and the human intruders watched them. But neither party made any aggressive moves. Beth, and, to a lesser degree, Terry, was accustomed to the toothy predators that tended to watch for prey near coral reefs. It had taken her time to believe they'd only attack her if she threatened them or wore something shiny. Like ravens, they were attracted to sparkly things.

"I can make—"

"Nope. Leave it to me. I have a plan." He threw his towel over his head and rubbed at his hair.

"A plan? That sounds ominous."

Terry drew the towel down around his neck to reveal a mischievous grin. "I hope not! I know what I want to make, and it's not complicated. You get dried off and comfortable." He started for the companionway ladder, then stopped. "I take it back. You can set the table out here when you're ready."

"I'm on it." Beth said, rubbing her fingers on her scalp to get the conditioner out of her hair.

A few minutes later while she was changing into shorts and a t-shirt, no bra, she realized she had completely forgotten to tell Terry what Carole had told her. She felt guilty. Terry should know what was going on with his business partner.

Out in the galley Terry was presiding over a couple of steaming pots. All kinds of ingredients were arrayed on the counters. It didn't look simple. However, her attention was drawn away from the food preparation to a bottle of wine standing open on the dining table, two plastic wine cups next to it. *He thinks of everything.*

He glanced at her as she slid onto the bench at the table so she could reach the bottle.

"Stuff for the table is there," he said. Beth noted the two plates with flatware wrapped in paper towel napkins on top and realized the wine and cups were part of the table setting. She poured wine into one for herself anyway.

"I have been meaning to tell you something Carole told me the other day," she started, following up with a sip of wine. It was a dense, dry French red that made her mouth pucker.

"What's that?" Terry asked, focus remaining on the sauté pan where he appeared to be frying bacon.

"Carole says she's very unhappy. She's going to leave Jeff."

Terry paused, fork poised above the sizzling pan, and half turned toward her. "Pour me some of that," he said.

Beth complied, handing him the cup. He took a gulp and set it down, flipped the bacon in the pan, then picked the cup back up again.

"He's a jerk about relationships," he finally said.

"So you're not surprised?"

"No, I am. I thought Carole had figured it out and was satisfied with the deal."

"You mean, like, she gets a renovated kitchen in exchange for being unhappy with her marriage?" Beth did everything in her power not to sound sarcastic. She didn't mean to be, but it was hard not to.

Terry took another gulp of wine and nodded. "I know, put it that way and it sounds terrible. But some marriages are like that. More like a business arrangement."

"Is your parents'?" She couldn't believe she'd asked that. She couldn't even blame the wine after only a couple sips.

The fork banged the pan and she craned her neck to see if the sound was a reaction to her words. He was shaking bacon grease off, tapping the rim of the pan. He lowered the heat and scraped chopped garlic from a cutting board into the pan.

"My sister's is pretty close to it," he said. "Andrew has gotten a huge amount of business from my dad over the years."

"Do they not love each other? Did they ever?"

"My sister loves herself enough for everyone."

"Woah, harsh!"

"It's the harsh reality. She's still my sister. I accept her faults and love her, even though she will always come first. Andrew accepts her faults and loves the business his marriage has brought to him. I have no idea whether he loves Ginny. He said he did when they got married, of course."

"Wow. I can't imagine being in a relationship for those reasons. It feels like such a waste."

"You're not any of them. You have a completely different set of values. Which is one reason why I love you."

"I'm glad there are more reasons!"

"So many more," he said, turning a brilliant smile on her, eyebrows waggling in an exaggerated flirt.

"Very nice. How did you escape the 'marry for money' gene?"

He was stirring the pot now, peering into it through the steam rising from it. Beth waited, wondering if she'd pissed him off. He straightened and lifted the pot, which was obviously heavy. Beth realized the colander must be in the sink as he poured water and spaghetti from the pot.

"I don't know," he finally said, setting the pot back on the burner. He lifted the colander and shook it up and down a few times, then dumped the pasta back into the pot. "To answer your earlier question, no, my parents' marriage isn't like Ginny's, or Jeff and Carole's. My parents did—do—love each other. I guess I learned more from them than Ginny did. Or maybe it was the soap operas."

"The soap operas?"

"When I was home sick from school, and in the summer, I'd watch the soaps with our maid. All those people manipulating each other, betraying each other, and all so unhappy. At least that was my take-away. Who wants to live like that?"

"Not me."

"Nor me."

"I think Carole loves Jeff. But she needs more from him."

"Yeah, I think you're right. He does love her, in his own limited way."

"Do you think she's wrong? Should she keep trying?"

"Not my business—our business."

"I know. I'm just wondering what you think."

"I think marriage is a binding contract, and they both should have given it more thought before they signed up. I knew at the time that I wasn't ready, and I didn't think he was either. But he wanted what he saw as the whole 'young entrepreneur' picture. This is sad. I feel bad for the kids."

"I know. She expects to get custody and a lot of alimony."

"And she's probably right."

"How does that effect your business plans?"

Terry shrugged, his back to her as he added ingredients to the pot. Beth got the impression he was thinking of something else.

"This will be ready in a couple minutes."

Beth understood his meaning, although she didn't understand why he didn't want to answer her question. "I'll get the table ready."

She scooted along the bench, rose and picked up the stack of plates, and headed for the companionway. She didn't see Terry's concerned expression as he watched her climb the ladder.

*

This is it, and she's in a terrible frame of mind about relationships. How can I ask her after that conversation?

Terry poured the bacon, garlic, and bacon grease into the pot and stirred it, coating the pasta with the aromatic bacon grease. He turned off the heat and gave it another stir, then added drained canned peas. Finally, he picked up a bowl he'd mixed up earlier and poured the egg and parmigiana cheese into the pot.

Beth came back down the ladder and collected the wine bottle and her cup.

"I'll be right up," he said. "Can you take my cup too?" He picked up his wine cup and extended it to her. She took it, holding the bottle and her cup in one hand and his in the other. He continued to stir the pot as he watched her stand on the lowest step and reach out to set the cups and bottle on the cockpit floor before climbing the rest of the way.

How can I not do it? It's everything I want. She can't say I'm doing it for money! No, she'll say she'd be doing it for money. I'll point out that she's got a great job now.

She was out of sight. He shut off his internal monologue, wiped his hands on a dish towel and slipped forward into their cabin. A moment later he returned, the bulge of the little box not noticeable in the pocket of his cargo shorts.

He dumped the carbonara into a serving bowl and plunged a serving spoon and fork into it. He stepped over to the companionway and held the bowl up.

"Delivery."

Beth stepped into view and took the bowl from him.

"Anything else?" She asked.

"One sec."

Terry returned to the galley and swept the remainder of ingredients off of the top of the refrigerator so that he could raise the lid. He took out a bottle of champagne and two chilled crystal flutes, then double checked the stove and shut off the overhead lights. At the navigation station he inserted a CD into the stereo. Smooth jazz filled the saloon and cockpit at a volume high enough to be heard but quiet enough to talk over—he knew because he'd selected the best fader and volume settings on Friday when he was alone on the boat. Everything was ready. He climbed up the ladder to the cockpit where Beth was waiting.

"This smells amaz—I thought we finished that!" Beth was looking the bottle he was carrying. "And where did those come from?"

"I know, I know, glass on the boat. We'll be careful."

"But where did you find them?"

"I, uh, didn't. I brought them."

)

Beth felt herself freeze. She literally could not move. She couldn't even ask him why he'd carried delicate glasses from Washington, because she thought she knew, and she hoped she was right but feared she was wrong, and this would be the worst night ever. She couldn't look at his face. She focused on his hands as he removed the foil from the bottle and twisted the wire cage. She realized it wasn't the same sparkling wine they'd had the other night. It was French champagne.

"I thought we'd have a romantic dinner. We're just in time for sunset," he said. She tore her eyes away from his hands to look toward the western horizon. He was right. The sun was creeping toward the sea and his earlier prediction looked like it might come true. The horizon was a sharp line where sea met sky.

Beth forced herself to breathe. *Just a romantic dinner. And it makes perfect sense.*

She heard the familiar "pop" of the cork and watched him hold one glass and then the other at an angle to the bottle as he poured. He set the glasses on the table and the bottle on the floor, then sat down across from her.

"Here's to the green flash," he said, picking up his glass. Beth picked hers up and touched the rim to his, the crystal making a different tone from the plastic they were used to. "Here's to old Sol's daily show."

They sipped and watched the sun. After a moment Beth realized he was serving the pasta. The delicious aroma of garlic and cheese grew stronger.

"I'm torn between eating and watching."

"Take a bite. You can watch while you chew. It will take longer than you think, and the food will get cold."

She rolled spaghetti onto her fork and ate it, and then rolled another bite. The cheesy, rich flavor was decadent, but she felt she'd earned it with a long, active day. The sun continued its slow fall. Terry ate and watched as well. Finally, the bottom edge of the orange orb touched the horizon.

"Here we go," Terry said. Beth set down her fork and focused on the horizon. The sun began to disappear. It was half gone, three quarters … and flash—for a fraction of a second the last of the orb turned bright green before it disappeared.

"Amazing! Did we really see it? Did you see it?" All of the tension Beth had been feeling vanished, replaced by elation. Sailors bragged about seeing it, now she had a perfect example to talk about.

"I did. It was fantastic. We really saw it. Together. Beth?"

His tone went serious on her name. Startled, she looked across at him, wondering what could be wrong. And then he was rising and she felt her pulse quicken. *He really is mad, he's not going to eat dinner.*

But he did not get up, he lowered himself to his knees in the space between the table and the companionway and reached for her hands.

Holy shit.

"Beth? After the discussion earlier, I'm not sure what you'll say. But I'm hoping you'll agree to be my wife."

Beth realized he was pressing a velvety box into her hands, but she couldn't bring herself to look away from his amazing, deep blue eyes. She felt like she was falling into them as he stared unblinking at her.

"Beth? Please don't leave me hanging here." His smile crinkled the sides of his eyes. She felt like she was going to burst. She didn't know what to say, how to answer this question that she had hoped for and feared for months. She had moments ago tried to convince herself he was not about to ask. Now he had and she was as terrified as before. Her fingers pried at the box halves, rotating it until it opened on its hinge. She dragged her gaze away from his eyes to stare at the ring. A diamond sparkled in the light reflected from the cockpit lamp hanging above the table. There were blue stones around it. They seemed to glow with all the tranquility of the sea.

"It's beautiful. It's perfect. You're perfect," she whispered, unable to find full breath to put behind her words.

"So is that a—"

"Yes. Yes Terry. It's an absolute yes. Forget everything we talked about earlier. Forget about bad relationships and unhappy people. I am the happiest woman on the face of the earth right now. Maybe further than that, are there any women astronauts in space right now? Because I have them beat. I'm happier. I mean, I saw the green flash tonight!"

Terry dragged her into an embrace there beside the cockpit table. She let him pull her from her seat, landing half on him, half on her knees, her mouth finding his to seal her happy fate.

After a few minutes she drew back, awkwardly pushing herself off of him with her left hand, the right clutching the box. Terry struggled to his knees and helped her back onto the lazarette at the corner of the table.

"Let me see that," he said, holding his hand out for the ring box. She gave it to him. He removed the ring and took her left hand, sliding it onto her ring finger, wiggling it to get it over the knuckle.

"It fits," she said with a sniff. Quite suddenly tears were streaming down her cheeks.

"I borrowed your class ring to have it sized—remember you found it with your stuff in New York and were surprised that it fit so well?"

Beth nodded, sniffing again, staring at the sparkling jewels on her finger. "I remember." But this ring was nothing like her clunky gold class ring with its aquamarine stone. This ring was pure magic. It had to be, because it had cast a spell on her, and she couldn't stop looking at it.

Terry had returned to his seat across from her. He was watching her.

"You okay?"

Beth forced herself to look away from the ring and up at him. His eyes glimmered in the twilight. His teeth shone. He was grinning despite the concern in his voice.

"I am more than all right. I'm—amazing. I'm so happy I can hardly think. I—"

"You thought I was never going to do it. I'll bet you were thinking of asking me."

"What? No, I didn't—"

Terry laughed, reaching across to take her hand. "Remember once I said I was going to marry you?"

"How could I forget? You terrified me!"

"A minute ago, you looked terrified. Are you sure you're good with this?"

Beth took a deep breath to squelch the tears streaming down her cheeks. It didn't work.

"A minute ago? I was terrified—that you were upset about our conversation and were changing your mind."

"Changing it? You knew?"

"No! I mean, the glasses, the champagne, making dinner—for a moment I thought so. Then I thought I was an idiot for thinking it. Then I thought I was right, but you weren't going to do it. I can't keep up with my emotions. Maybe I should eat and calm down."

"I knew the glasses would give it away. They're my parents'."

Beth picked up her champagne flute and took a sip that tickled her sensitive sinuses. She held the glass up and studied the crystal pattern. She knew very little about fine glassware.

"They're lovely."

Terry picked the sweating bottle from the floor and refilled her glass.

"I told Jeff the other day I was going to do it. Makes what you said about Carole all the more ironic."

"What did he say?"

"He was supportive. But I knew he would be. Carole might find that he's very surprised when she tells him what she wants."

"She said that too." Beth stopped herself from telling him that Carole sometimes thought of Jeff as a big, not too bright dog.

"Forget them," Terry said. "Sorry I mentioned him. When do you want to get married?"

Twenty-seven

Washington, D.C.

Raj Gupta's desk phone was ringing when he entered his office on Monday morning at 8:47 a.m. He stifled a grumble and set his take-out coffee on the desk before picking up the receiver. The caller ID said "McKeen."

"Adrian. Good morning."

"Good morning Raj. Good weekend?"

"Restful." Raj shrugged off his nylon backpack and settled into his chair, dropping the bag on the floor. He cradled the phone on his shoulder so that he could take the lid off his coffee.

"Sometimes that's best."

"Yes. I enjoyed it."

"Good. I understand our Antiguan client's hearing was on Friday. How did it go?"

Raj swallowed a sip of coffee and reached for his backpack, then grabbed the phone as it slipped from his shoulder.

"Mr. Codrington called shortly after the hearing. He was very pleased."

"And Beth Anderson?"

"She told the team she was frustrated that she didn't know more about the client's history." Raj wedged the phone back between his shoulder and ear so he could unzip his bag and take out a brown paper sack.

"She felt unprepared?"

"Not by the team, if that's what you mean. She's not the type to blame others." He removed a paper-wrapped egg and cheese sandwich from the sack, setting the crinkly paper aside carefully so it didn't make noise.

"Do you think she was underprepared?"

"Not for the specific assignment. From Mr. Codrington's perspective she performed as required. What Beth was frustrated about was that she couldn't provide contextual information on the fly. She wanted to exceed her charge and couldn't."

"I like people who exceed their charge."

"Yes. I think Beth has a lot of potential. I'll be better able to asses it when I speak to her in person next week."

"The reason I ask is that I'm thinking about the best resource for an upcoming assignment."

"I assumed so. Can you tell me anything about it?"

"Not yet. Touch base with me after you've debriefed her."

"I'll do that. Thanks Adrian."

Raj hung up the receiver and picked up his breakfast. He examined the distribution of the layers of bread, egg, and cheese before taking a bite. Adrian's mysterious assignments always made him nervous because they were usually for governmental clients, not political, and that could mean higher degrees of security and risk. Nothing in Beth Anderson's background qualified her for a high-risk assignment.

)

Eleven Mile Beach, Barbuda

If the sea water beneath *Mana* was the clarity and color of gin, Codrington Lagoon could best be compared to strong tea. The water lapping on the narrow beach was clear at the surface, but within a few inches the suspended algae and whatever else was washed from the nearby mangroves made it opaque.

Beth and Terry had dragged the dinghy up onto the beach on the ocean side and secured it to a tree, then picked their way through about two hundred feet of trees and undergrowth, avoiding thorns and stickers by trying to walk on patches of sandy ground crossed with shoots and runners. Now they stopped on the foot-wide beach on the other side, peering out across the dark water of the nearly land-locked lagoon looking for their guide.

Frank Rivera, the yacht broker, had recommended the Barbudan local and Terry had contacted him by radio the previous afternoon. He was due to pick them up "in the lagoon across from your boat" in a few minutes. Right on schedule they saw the white froth of a bow wake moving toward them from across the water. The wake resolved into a deep red local wooden boat driven by a man in his fifties with a broad chest under a short sleeved, collared shirt worn unbuttoned. His shorts had come from somebody's basketball court, and his shoes, she saw when he placed his foot on the gunwale to climb out of the boat, were men's locker room shower sandals. None of this phased Beth—he looked perfectly normal to her.

"Hello! Good mornin'!" He said as he stepped from his boat into the ankle-deep water. He'd run the bow right up onto the narrow beach. Terry reached out to put a hand on it, expecting to be tossed a line, but the guide simply let the boat sit. Beth supposed there might be a current here, but the water was so calm she doubted the boat would move on its own.

"I am Mr. George Geoffrey. Welcome to Barbuda!"

"Hello Mr. Geoffrey. I'm Terry, and this is Beth. I called yesterday."

"Yes you did sir, and that is why I am here. Today we are going to see our birds!"

Beth couldn't help but smile at his enthusiasm.

"First I will take you to the office in Codrington where you must pay the park fee. I cannot collect it from you, you must pay it to the office. But that will not take long. If you need anything, you can go to the store there are well." He paused. Beth knew that a shopping stop meant an additional fee to him. But she squelched the thought—they could afford to pay him a few more dollars.

"We could use ice," she said.

"Ah, but ice," Mr. Geoffrey said, his tone artificially mournful, "we cannot buy ice now, you see. It will melt. We will have to go back later." Beth could practically hear the Eastern Caribbean dollars adding up in his head.

"So we'll do that," Terry said firmly. "We can talk about the cost later. I understand the tour is fifteen EC each?"

"Yes Mr. Terry. Plus the park fee to the office."

"I understand. We can't wait!"

Mr. Geoffrey appeared to brighten. He patted the gunwale of his boat next to the large open cockpit that contained several benches.

"Climb aboard! Let's go."

Mr. Geoffrey moved further back and climbed onto the boat near his steering console. Beth hauled herself up and got her right leg over the side to straddle the gunwale, then swung her left leg in. Terry got his foot on the deck and took one giant step up and in. They sat down on the bench in the middle of the cockpit.

"Did you need me to push us off?" Terry asked.

The other man grinned and turned the key on his console. The boat's massive outboard motor roared to life. He moved a control and the boat pulled back off the beach. They found out how powerful the outboard was when he pointed the bow across the lagoon and began to accelerate. Even on the relatively flat water, the stiff, wooden boat bashed and rattled as it rose up on plane. Beth clutched at the wooden bench, eyes drawn to the ring on her left hand as they had been over and over since Terry slipped it onto her finger. It still took her breath away.

A few minutes later the boat sank down into the water as Mr. Jeffrey slowed it to approach a dock complex adjacent to a building on shore. Additional buildings formed a main street that stretched back from the waterfront.

"This is Codrington, the capital of Barbuda," Mr. Geoffrey said proudly. "You pay for the park entrance inside." He nodded at the building at the head of the dock. They could see a government sign on it, but they weren't yet close enough to read it. Beth had asked her client, Mr. Codrington, about his apparent connection to Barbuda during her first meeting with him. He'd explained that his branch of the family had moved to Antigua two generations before, but he did enjoy visiting his cousins on the island.

Mr. Geoffrey came alongside the dock behind another local boat and secured a stern line to a cleat while a man on the dock grabbed the bow line and cleated it.

"Thank you, Angel," Mr. Geoffrey said before turning to his passengers and offering a hand. Beth stepped onto the bench and took his hand mostly out of courtesy as she stepped from there up onto the gunwale and then the dock. Terry followed. They walked up the dock and entered the building. A petit woman in a khaki uniform sat behind a desk, a three-tiered file organizer to one side, various office tools on the other, and a blotter covered in doodles in front of her. She was talking to a skinny man in a white t-shirt so thin it was almost transparent, tattered cargo shorts, and very old looking sports sandals. They both turned toward Beth and Terry with expectant looks.

"Good morning," Beth said. "We're going to visit the bird sanctuary, if we may."

The woman nodded and waved them toward her desk. The man watched for a moment, and then turned to study a rack of forms against a wall.

"The fee is two EC per person," the woman told them. Terry already had the coins in his hand. He set them on her desk. "Thank you, sir."

She picked up the coins and opened a drawer where she placed them in a coin tray. She drew a pad of forms to her and filled out the top one, signed it with a flourish, and stamped the date on after vigorously inking the stamper. The second permit was soon signed and stamped as well.

"Keep these on your person while in the park," she instructed as she handed each of them one.

"Thank you, we will," Beth replied, pocketing hers.

Outside Terry leaned close to her ear, "Who do you think someone will be checking for them up there?"

Beth chuckled. "The birds, of course. If we don't have a permit, they hide."

They both giggled, Terry wrapping his arm around her shoulders as they walked back along the dock.

Mr. Geoffrey's boat carried them at speed to the north end of the lagoon. He slowed down as they approached a red navigational buoy that was leaning at an awkward angle—it was sitting on a shoal.

"This buoy washed into the lagoon during a storm last year," he explained. "We towed it here. This buoy," he paused for dramatic effect as they drew closer, "is from Nova Scotia."

"Nova Scotia?"

"One of the men researched the number," he nodded at the N6 in reflective paint on each side. "It was lost from a channel there four years ago. We believe it was carried by the gulf stream. This buoy went to Europe and came back across the sea to enter our pond."

Beth was skeptical, but stuck with an impressed "wow" rather than challenging him.

Having started the tour with this oddity, Mr. Geoffrey continued into the channel between mangroves at a sedate pace. He explained the lifecycle of the frigate birds, their eating and mating habits, and their habitat. He pointed out males and females in the trees and pointed out the many other species of birds in the sanctuary. The large black birds soaring above their heads were the females. The ones in the trees calling to them were the males.

"There, you see his neck pouch?" Mr. Geoffrey asked, pointing into the trees off the starboard bow. Beth caught a flash of red between the leaves and focused on it. As the boat inched along their angle changed and she had a full view of the huge black bird with his bright red pouch.

"That would attract me," she said.

"I'm making a note of that," Terry said. Beth elbowed him.

"He's a handsome one. He'll have a mate in no time," Mr. Geoffrey said.

"I guess the islanders like the sanctuary?" Beth asked.

"We like to show it to visitors," Mr. Geoffrey confirmed. "Nobody on this island would hurt these birds."

"Because they bring visitors?" Terry asked.

Mr. Geoffrey grinned and shook his head. "No, because all they eat is fish, so they taste terrible!"

"How do you know?" Beth asked. He seemed taken aback by that. His eyes narrowed for a moment as he gazed at her, then he answered.

"A few years ago, I come upon some men who were cooking one. It was already dead, you know? So I tasted it. Yuck!"

"Ah." Beth nodded. It seemed just as likely that he'd been among the hunting party all along. She hoped his income from giving tours was sufficient to convince him not to hunt.

Eventually they'd wound their way back to the salt pond.

"You want to buy ice?" he asked them as they idled past the lost red buoy.

"Yes, that would be great," Beth replied.

"I'll take you back to Codrington first, then across."

"What can we pay you for the extra ride?" Terry asked.

Mr. Geoffrey hesitated for a second, probably calculating how much he could reasonably ask for, then said, "The tour was fifteen

EC each. You give me twenty, okay?" In the past Beth would have negotiated, but she just nodded as Terry agreed to the amount.

Back in Codrington Mr. Geoffrey directed them to a market on the main street. They brought four bags of ice for eight EC each up to the cashier's counter where Terry started examining a rack of assorted candies, mostly from the United Kingdom. A rack of batik pareos caught Beth's eye and since Terry was distracted, she felt justified in having a look. She was holding out an aqua pareo with a pair of birds, one with a distinctive red neck pouch, soaring. There were dark green leaves across the bottom.

"Buy that," Terry said from right behind her. She looked over her shoulder at him. "I mean it. It's a perfect souvenir. I don't want to forget this trip. You can wear it, or we can have it framed."

His blue eyes were sparkling in a way that conveyed affection, excitement, and sincerity. Beth felt her lips curling into a smile, but at the same time she felt her cheeks reddening with emotion.

"I don't either," she said, her voice husky. Hearing her emotion, he leaned close to place a kiss on her cheek.

"Buy it. But hurry, the ice is melting, and Mr. Geoffrey is waiting."

Back on *Mana* Beth draped the frigate bird pareo over the back of one of the seats in the saloon while Terry unpacked the freezer in order to stow the new ice at the bottom where it would do the most good.

"It's lovely. Thank you for urging me to get it," she said. He turned, letting the freezer lid shut.

"You're welcome. Sometimes you're too frugal for your own good. Glad I could help."

Beth chuckled, wrapping her arms around him to enjoy his body against hers for a moment. He happily obliged her with a kiss. She realized he was damp with perspiration, his skin warm through his clothes. She realized that she was too.

"We have one more afternoon of swimming in this water," she said. "I intend to make the most of it."

"I'm right behind you."

≀)

Caribbean Sea

Beth studied Barbuda as it retreated into the distance. Turning her gaze forward, the ring on her hand resting on the wheel caught her eye. Barbuda would forever be the island where her life changed. On the one hand, her dream of sailing alone to distant shores had come to an end—but the truth was it had ended months ago when she'd first taken on crew, and after that she'd more than proven her ability to sail alone. On the other hand, she was ready now to take on all of the challenges of marriage—whatever they turned out to be. In a way, her new adventure was just as frightening and filled with unknowns as the one she'd undertaken over a year ago.

"Is it my turn yet?" Terry had climbed into the cockpit from below and stood idly scratching his chest at the far end of the cockpit. Beth stood up.

"All yours. Which wheel do you want?"

Terry came to back of the cockpit and stepped behind the other wheel, placing both hands on it. "I'll start with this one and if I don't like it, I'll switch," he said.

Beth stepped between the wheels to the cockpit and arranged a couple cushions on the low side lazarette. She settled in to watch her fiancé steer. It was a lovely show.

They'd pulled up the anchor as the sun rose over the low island. The coffee hadn't yet started to perk when Terry put them on their southerly course between the beach and the shoals. They'd breakfasted gazing at the beautiful, empty beach as it went by. A frigate bird soared above them and they waved at it. It didn't notice. Terry stowed the breakfast things while Beth took the helm and steered them around the final shoals and on out into the open sea. Terry set the sails so they could turn off the engine.

Their goal was Great Bird Island on the east side of Antigua. They would have to return the way they'd come, passing Diamond Shoal on their port side, then navigate between Antigua and the string of reefs running east from Diamond Shoal. If they couldn't make it, they could always anchor at Dickinson Bay again, or go south to one of the other bays along the west coast. Looking off to the east, Beth wondered if they would have to resort to that contingency: the wind was picking up early, which meant that by mid-afternoon it might be very strong and blowing from exactly where they were heading. She forced herself not to dwell on it. They might have a great time tacking up the channel between a rock— the island—and a hard place—the reefs. Smiling at her private joke Beth picked up her e-reader and turned it on.

When the electronic chart plotter told them they were passing Diamond Shoal Beth took compass bearings on several landmarks on the island and did a rough position plot on the paper chart. She decided that she agreed with the electronics.

"We need to harden up and head as much into the wind as we can now," she told Terry.

"What's my new course?"

"Let's see what you can do. We pretty much need to head exactly where the wind is coming from."

"Of course," he sighed, smiling at the sailor's standard complaint.

Beth put the winch handle into the sheet winch for the jib and began to grind it in, flattening the sail by drawing its lower corner further aft.

"Want me to head up?" Terry asked, offering to take pressure off of the sail and make it easier for Beth to pull in.

"No. I'll do what I can this way, then I'll do the main. If the jib needs more after that you can head up."

When she couldn't turn the winch any more, and the sail was in tight, she removed the handle and took it to the winch holding the main sheet. This winch was electric, an unfamiliar luxury.

"Actually, maybe you should head up now to take some load off this winch as I turn it," she said. Terry laughed.

"You don't mind grinding yourself, but you want to give the electric winch a break?" he said as he turned the wheel.

"I don't know how much it can take and I don't want to break it. I know when I can't take any more," she replied, pressing the button to activate the winch. She held it down and used her other hand to make sure the line fell to the cockpit floor without tangling. The boom gradually moved toward the center of the boat, making the main sail parallel with the adjusted jib.

"This is good," Terry said after a couple minutes. "She feels balanced."

Beth stepped to the back of the cockpit to check the gauges mounted by the starboard wheel. The apparent wind speed was hovering in the high teens. Their course was taking them toward the north end of Antigua. They would have to tack before too long and she wasn't sure whether they'd be able to make progress up the narrow channel into the wind. As she thought about it, watching the gauges, the wind shot up to twenty-five knots and *Mana* heeled over precipitously. Terry handled the gust with confidence, angling *Mana* slightly more into it to take full advantage of the speed gain, then adjusting again when the gust subsided.

"If it's going to hold like this we need to reef, at least a little."

"I can handle the gusts," Terry said.

"I know you can. But if it starts to be steady at that velocity we'll be heeling too much. You know what they say about reefing."

"Do it before you have to."

Beth nodded, moving toward the front of the cockpit. "We can always undo it if the wind subsides."

"Tell me when you need me to head up," was Terry's reply.

Beth took a moment to review the lines that controlled the mainsail. She uncleared two of them and wrapped one of them that was labeled "in" around the other electric winch.

"Head up. It's going to be noisy when I release the sheet."

Terry nodded and turned the wheel slowly to port. *Mana*'s bow turned and the jib collapsed with a snap. The mainsail fluttered and the boom bounced and rattled above their heads. Beth pressed the button on the winch to begin hauling in the main sail. At the same time, she took the main sheet out of the self-tailing cleat at the top of its winch and let it out a little. Immediately the other winch sounded like it was not working as hard. She let go of the button and secured the main sheet for a moment so she could lean out around the bimini and peer up at the sail. She'd rolled up about a foot—not nearly enough.

"Done?"

"Hardly. Hold tight." She returned to her lines. It was another tooth-rattling three minutes before she had the sail rolled up to the foot-high red stripe that indicated the first reef point. She cleated the "in" and "out" lines and pressed the button on the other winch to tighten up the main sheet. It hauled the sail in fast and they both felt the wind begin to fill it, but the jib was still flogging around on the foredeck and *Mana* was barely moving through the water.

"Can you handle the jib sheet while I roll it in some?" Beth asked. Terry stepped to the starboard wheel and held out his hand as Beth went to the winch, uncleated the sheet, and handed it to him. Then she crossed the cockpit to the other side where the jib's reefing line was coiled and hanging on the lifeline. She freed it and wrapped it around the other sheet winch.

"Okay, here I go," she said as she hauled in on the line. It didn't move. She groaned and tried again. The line jerked against the winch as the sail flogged.

"Grind it," Terry said. Beth realized he was right. She had to go back across the cockpit to get the handle, but once she had it slotted into the winch and put her weight into it, the line began to come in, rolling the jib up around the forestay.

"How does it look?" she asked after a couple minutes of grinding.

"Another foot," he said, left hand on the wheel, right holding the sheet.

Beth ground the winch ten more turns and paused, panting.

"Looks good," Terry said, making Beth wonder if it really did, or he knew she was out of breath and wanted to give her a break. She cleated the line and crossed the cockpit to take the sheet from him. She cleated it and studied the shape of the sail as Terry turned *Mana*'s bow away from the wind. The jib filled, the flogging stopped, and *Mana* began to glide forward through the water.

"How does it feel?" Beth asked, itching to take the helm and feel for herself, but determined not to take it from Terry. She glanced at him and saw concentration on his face as he made minute adjustments to his course, then he studied the instruments.

"Apparent wind is holding at twenty-two now. You were right. She feels balanced. Better than before."

Beth smiled and nodded. "I had a feeling it wasn't going to get lighter. Now we've got to sail as close hauled as possible or we're going to get nowhere making tacks back and forth.

"I can see that. I'll go as high as I can, you trim. Let me know when you need me to take a turn on the winches."

For the next two hours they worked together to keep *Mana* sailing as close to the wind as they could. They made twenty tacks, sometimes with as little as ten-minutes in between. They switched off several times between steering and handling the sails. During each tack the jib had to be brought in quickly at first—a series of elbow-tossing hand-over-hand yanks on the sheet as the winch spun—and finished with precision grinding of the winch handle to find exactly the position where the tell-tales—ribbons glued to the sail—streamed back and not up or down. It was a challenge to make sure each turn was not a one-hundred-eighty-degree reversal of their course, taking them back the way they'd come. *Mana* had to be steered with precision and intuition to take best advantage of the minor fluctuations in the wind.

When a shift forced them to steer a few degrees further away from East for more than a few minutes they tacked because on the other angle they could point closer to East. But sometimes tacking on such a shift was impractical—they'd just tacked away from the island or the reef, or the new course would intersect the path of a ship.

Beth fretted during these times, continually checking their position and heading based on landmarks and the electronic chart plotter. When they didn't make progress, she struggled to resist the urge to turn on the motor. Each time it paid off as the wind finally shifted enough to allow Terry to point the bow more to the east.

Beth was at the helm when they finished the twentieth tack and she saw they were finally lined up on the channel running southeast between Antigua and its small neighbor Long Island. She exhaled a relieved sigh and fought off a wave of doubt as a gust pushed the bow further west, aiming them out of the channel. Gritting her teeth, she carefully worked it back up into the wind without loss of drive from a collapsing sail.

"We can hold this for a while, but I think we're going to have to resort to the iron jenny for the last couple miles, it's dead up wind again, and there are a lot of barely submerged rocks. I'm sure the locals sail it, but it's been a long day."

"It's been a long, beautiful day and my arms are tired. I'll go turn on the battery," Terry said. Beth was grateful to him for admitting being tired. Her arms and shoulders were starting to ache too, and she'd broken a fingernail down to the quick on her right hand. It throbbed painfully, but she refused to voice a complaint.

)

Great Bird Island, Antigua

"Here's to doing what we came here to do," Beth said, clinking her beer bottle against Terry's. The anchor was set and they had a magnificent view of Great Bird Island to the east and Antigua to the west across several miles of water. There were two other boats in the anchorage, both of them with the distinctive markings of charter boats from two of the well-known companies.

"I don't know about you, but I did what I came to do a couple days ago. The great sailing is icing on the cake." Terry said. Beth glanced at her ring with a foolish grin. "And don't think I don't see you doing that," Terry added. "I hope you like it."

"I adore it. Don't be a meathead."

Terry took a sip of beer, swallowed and said, "A what?" He laughed "That's a pretty dated expression."

Beth shrugged, chuckling. "I don't even know where it came from."

"All in the Family."

"What?"

"TV series from the seventies. Archie Bunker? Rob Reiner, the meathead son-in-law?" he raised his eyebrows in inquiry. Beth frowned, then understood.

"Oh yeah. My mom thought it was funny. I was too young to get it. But I meant I don't know why I said that instead of 'idiot' or something."

"Gee, yeah, I wish you would be more selective in your derogatory terms for me." Terry took a gulp of beer and leered at her. She snorted, adjusting her grip on her bottle to place the tip of her injured finger against the cool glass. It was still throbbing.

"Tomorrow I want to walk to the top of the Island and check out the conditions on the east side. And do some snorkeling. There will be day boats and locals coming in, I think. It will get more crowded."

"It's not the deserted island it looks like."

"We can pretend, for now."

"What do you have in mind?"

Twenty-eight

Bird Island, Antigua

*T*heir early morning hike up to the top of Bird Island highlighted the strenuous upper body workout of the previous day's sail. Beth's legs were fine, but her core muscles along with her shoulders and arms made their weariness known as she heaved herself up over rocks on the trail. At least her finger didn't hurt any more.

Terry didn't mention any pain, so she assumed his better conditioned body had recovered overnight. Forty minutes after setting out from the beach in the pre-dawn gloom they stood looking east at the open sea dotted with white caps gleaming in the morning sun. A lot of them. Much closer there were spots of rough surf where rolling waves collided with reefs. Occasional spectacular plumes of white spray that the sunlight refracted into rainbows indicated large swells and shallow rocks.

"Yikes," Beth said, studying the waters to the north of the island. "There's supposed to be a channel out there. I can't see obvious clear water."

"Look at the waves hitting that tiny island," Terry said, pointing to what was basically a rock. "Is the channel between us and it, or north of it?"

Beth shook her head. "I'm not sure. North of it, I think."

"The water does look calmer further north."

"The reefs there are not shallow enough to break the swells. But they are too shallow to sail over."

"Hidden hazards."

"Exactly." Beth checked her watch. "The cruiser's net is on in a half hour. Let's get back and see if we can listen in, ask about the channel."

"We better hurry."

"I'm much faster downhill."

Dickinson Bay, Antigua

Hunter was half way through his muffin and coffee, listening as usual to the tinny voices on the VHF radio behind the counter at the coffee shop. He hadn't missed a morning yet, but by now the ritual was as much about the caffeine and muffin as the broadcast. He frequently caught himself tuning it out as he let his mind wander.

"This is Beth Anderson. We're at Great Bird Island considering going out Great Bird Channel tomorrow. Wondered if anyone has been through there recently. Over."

Hunter's hair stood up on end. He rose from his table and crossed to the counter, listening intently. The waitress watched him from the other end of the shop.

"You need something?" she asked. Hunter raised his right hand, palm toward her.

"No! Shhhh. I need to hear this."

The waitress's eyes widened, and she turned back to the man sitting in front of her whose coffee she was about to refill. He shrugged in commiseration with her insult.

"Good morning Beth—*Double Trouble*, isn't it? You've been on before. Over."

"Yes, Papi, it's good to join in again. Over."

"Let me check my notes about Bird Channel. Anyone out there have any advice for Beth? Over."

"This is Isabel aboard *Windover*. We started that way two days ago and abandoned. We couldn't tell reef from deep water. The seas were enormous rolling in there. Too easy to get knocked out of the channel, even if you are in it to start with. Over."

"That doesn't sound good," Papi's voice returned. "The forecast is for very high seas coming in off the Atlantic for the next few days, Beth. The channel is not advised. I'd say wait, or go around the other way. Over."

"Understood, Papi. We'll go to the west side. Too bad. I wanted to see the other coast. Over."

"Safety of ship and crew is number one," Papi said. "Anything else you want to ask, Beth? Over."

"That was it Papi. Thank you Isabel, too. I've got to go plot a new course. Standing by."

Hunter eased down onto a stool at the counter, ignoring Papi's continued broadcast as he thought through what he'd heard. Beth Anderson was at Great Bird Island and would be coming to the west side of Antigua. She had wanted to see the eastern coast, which meant she planned to go south, since Bird Island was in the north east. Coming west, she would have to stop at Dickinson Bay or one of the other bays further south along the west coast.

"Excuse me," he called to the waitress, who was talking with the other customer. She looked toward him, annoyed at his rude behavior. "I'm terribly sorry. But I've been waiting to hear news of that woman who was speaking."

"All these mornings, that's what you were here for?" the waitress asked, walking toward him.

"Well, no, I came in for coffee," he protested, then shrugged. "But yeah, I came back every day to hear the radio."

"Imagine that," she said, looking back at the other customer. He grinned at her, playing along with whatever trouble she was planning for Hunter.

"Yes, I know, it was a long shot. But it paid off. Now I know where I can find her. But I wonder, do you know anyone who can rent me a boat?"

)

Great Bird Island, Antigua

After the conversation with Papi and Isabel, Beth and Terry put it all aside, packed lunch, and went on a snorkeling expedition. Hours later they returned in time for afternoon cocktails. Beth spent a few minutes plotting a new route back the way they'd come and south along Antigua's west coast. She stood at the navigation desk, pencil in hand, marking the route on the chart, while Terry mixed up a pitcher of rum punch.

"We have time to make one stop before we need to get back to English Harbor," Beth said.

"Not Dickinson Bay."

"No. I agree. I'm thinking Five Islands. It's north of Jolly Harbour. Large anchorage, plenty of room. Potential for green flash viewing…"

"Sounds good to me."

"Then back on around to English Harbour the day after."

"And we return dear *Mana* to her caretaker, Mr. Riviera."

"Right."

Terry stirred the pitcher with a wooden spoon, looking across the saloon at Beth's hunched shoulders.

"We don't have to make any decisions while we're here, it's not like a boat show special," he said.

Beth's head rose and she turned to him. "You read my mind."

"No, I read my own and guessed at yours."

Beth ran her hand over the varnished wood bulkhead enclosing the aft head. It was silky smooth to the touch. "I've already gotten fond of her," she said.

"Me too. It's not quite the boat we saw at the boat show, but the price is lower, so we could make the changes we want."

"Like the swim ladder."

Terry nodded.

"How about we start a list. Pros and cons, what we'd change?"

"Okay. You bring paper and pen, I'll bring the drinks. Meet you in the cockpit."

)

St. Johns Harbour, Antigua

Hunter had to settle for hiring a local guy with a boat. He couldn't prove proficiency with anything bigger, or better powered, than a rowboat, so nobody was willing to rent anything to him. Cecil wasn't thrilled when he said he was going to miss work the next day, but Hunter pointed out his lack of absence since he'd started working at the beach bar and Cecil conceded to his reliability and good health—unlike both of his regular bartenders.

He climbed aboard and sat in front of the steering console of the brightly painted wooden local boat driven by Hector. When he explained his mission—to find a sailboat named *Double Trouble*, which was sailing from Great Bird Island to one of the bays along the west coast today Hector laughed at him, his tongue shining pink through the gap where he was missing a top incisor.

"We heading for Bird Island, then? Try to intercept them?"

"No, we can look for them at anchor in the bays on the west coast. I need to talk to her, so she shouldn't be trying to sail the boat."

"Well man, we might as well get lunch, have a few rums, because they won't be there until this afternoon."

Hunter looked at his wristwatch. In his eagerness to find Beth Anderson, he had not thought about the woman's travel time. It was eleven o'clock in the morning.

"Shit."

"Yah, Mon. I can take you on a tour of St. Johns if you want, then we'll swing up to Dickinson and look at the boats there. What time they leaving Bird Island?"

Hunter shrugged, disgusted with himself. "I don't know. I guess she'll want to get over here while it's still light out."

"Earlier than that, to anchor in a good spot."

Hunter was reminded again of how little he knew about sailing, despite all the time he'd spent talking to sailors.

"Let's putter around St. Johns for a while, then we can start looking for her. I guess if we spot the boat, we can follow it and wait until it's anchored."

Hector shook his head, grinning, as he nodded at a boy on the dock to cast off the bow line. He stepped to the side of the cockpit to free the stern.

)

Five Island Harbour, Antigua

From the comfort of her hammock on *Mana*'s bow Beth watched a bright green and yellow local boat enter the anchorage from around Fullerton Point on the north. For the next half hour while she lay reading and sipping a beer she was aware of it making a zig zag course around the bay, passing behind most of the anchored sailboats. When it passed near *Mana* she saw a black man driving and a white man on board looking at the sailboat.

"Guess he didn't find whoever he was looking for," Terry said a few minutes later, startling her. He was standing beside her holding out a fresh cold beer.

"Thank you!" She took the sweating bottle. "Yeah, he looked at every anchored boat."

"And then headed out to the south. He wasn't official, just a local looking for someone, I guess. What are we doing for dinner?"

"Everything must go."

"I was afraid you'd say that. Any creative ideas?"

"A few. But now I have this cold beer to drink," she took a sip from the bottle. "When I finish it I'll come back. Unless you're starving."

"I'll survive. But I think I will get into any cheese and crackers I can find."

"There's a can of mussels that Jeff insisted we get still in there somewhere. Get into those, too."

"Yes ma'am."

)

Falmouth Harbour, Antigua

Hunter leaned on the inflated gunwale of yet another local's small boat scanning the rows of luxury sail and power yachts secured stern-to the docks in Falmouth Harbour. This is what he remembered when he'd arrived on the island—these docks were populated by the rich and famous, not cruisers. He suspected that Beth Anderson's *Double Trouble* was not a mega yacht like these. But there were a few smaller boats in among the behemoths. The problem was most boat owners had the name painted on the stern, so he could not see them from the water. He was going to have to walk the docks after all. He turned to his driver and shook his head.

"That's it. I'll check the docks myself."

He had hired Donald to take him on a tour of the anchored boats in Falmouth. They'd cruised around the large anchorage for an hour looking at every sailboat. No *Double Trouble*. Donald turned toward the dock near the dive shop where they'd started.

Hunter chastised himself for not listening to Papi's radio broadcast yesterday morning, and again this morning after not finding her yesterday. Beth might have called in again.

Donald brought the boat up against the dock and Hunter handed him a fistful of Eastern Caribbean Dollars.

"Thanks."

"Good luck finding your girlfriend."

Frustrated and weary from the fruitless hunt he walked through the parking lot to Dockyard Drive and turned right, heading for the larger marinas.

An hour later he had toured every finger of the mega yacht docks and seen truly sumptuous ocean-going vessels. The trim, tidy crew members in their white or tan shorts and nautical striped polo shirts eyed him with everything from curiosity to suspicion as he walked by looking at boat names. That dismissiveness from jumped-up boat bums irritated him.

Stuck-up jerks.

He stopped in a convenience store and bought a bottle of cold water, then set off down Dockyard Drive toward the last place he was going to look: Nelson's Dockyard in English Harbour.

⁂

English Harbour, Antigua

"Remember Frank said to call him when we got close so he could have someone meet us," Terry said.

Mana was off of Windward Bay in between the entrances to Falmouth and English Harbours. They had tacked south, and Beth hoped they could put *Mana* on a perfect heading into English Harbour on the next tack north. She did not remember Frank saying anything about calling him. She'd been fretting for the last hour and a half about backing the boat into the crowded dock.

"He did?"

"Yeah. Want me to call?"

"Yes please!"

Beth knew being met by someone would not make docking any easier, but it made her feel better. At least it would be another pair of hands. She focused on enjoying this final leg of the trip, splitting her attention between *Mana* rising up and over the rolling swells and the chart plotter showing their position in relation to the mouth of English Harbour. Terry had been steering for most of the trip along the south coast of the island, she didn't feel any guilt for taking the last turn at the helm.

Terry came back from below and said he'd reached Frank and the yacht broker was sending someone to meet them in Freeman's Bay.

"In the bay? On a boat?"

"I assume so. He didn't say to watch for a swimmer."

Beth smirked at him, mostly to hide the wave of relief that his news caused. The next wave was of disgust with herself for being a coward about the docking. She didn't want to go into any of this with Terry, so she kept her mouth shut.

A while later they tacked, putting *Mana* on a heading straight into Freeman's Bay.

"Nice," Terry said, leaning out of the cockpit to look ahead.

"I guess get the dock lines and fenders out. Did Frank say anything about them?"

"No. We had fenders on both sides when we left. We'll need to anchor, and we'll need stern lines."

"Right. Set them up. But leave the fenders on deck."

Terry shot her a puzzled smile as he moved to execute her orders. She knew why: she didn't have to tell him not to hang the fenders overboard. It was her nerves showing.

Because they could, they sailed right on in to Freeman's Bay before Beth turned into the wind and Terry rolled up first the jib and then the mainsail. While he worked Beth started the engine and kept *Mana* into the wind. She spotted a dinghy motoring toward them as Terry was securing the lines from the now rolled up main.

"I think that's him," she said. Terry followed her gaze. Beth put *Mana* on course to meet the dinghy with the throttle at forward idle. Within moments the white inflatable boat was abeam and then astern making a u-turn. Beth put *Mana* in neutral while Terry stepped to the stern to greet the small boat's crew.

"Welcome back." A woman's voice carried easily over the grumble of engines. Beth glanced over her shoulder in surprise to see a tall, slender woman, suntanned with glorious blonde hair loosely contained in a pony tail, standing in the dinghy with one foot on the gunwale. A burly man sitting in the stern was driving.

"Thank you. We're not necessarily glad to be here," Terry said. She grinned, eyes traveling over *Mana*'s stern. "Coming aboard?" Terry asked.

"I'm going to scramble up the side I think," she replied. Beth realized she had an accent—either English or Australian, or maybe New Zealand. The woman gestured at the dinghy driver and he revved the motor, pushing the boat's bow up along *Mana*'s port side. The woman took hold of the stanchions supporting the lifeline and pushed off the dinghy's soft gunwale, bringing her other foot up to *Mana*'s toe rail and swinging over the lifeline in a powerful, graceful move. She waved at the dinghy driver and he turned his boat away.

"I'm Lucy. Frank asked me to come help you bring her in. Not that you couldn't—"

Beth shook her head, stepping to the side of the wheel while still holding it. "Please, be my guest. I haven't Med moored at a crowded seawall."

Lucy smiled, her expression understanding. "Why end your vacation on a stressful note, hum? I'll take her. I do it all the time."

As Beth handed over the helm to Lucy she felt a pang of regret. Mana *isn't mine anymore.* The sense of loss was surprisingly strong. She saw something like it in Terry's eyes.

Does he feel it too?

She had no time to think about it. Lucy had powered *Mana* forward while surveying the cockpit. Quick glances took in the ready fenders and the coiled lines in the stern.

"You've got her ready then. Right, so let's get these lines secured to the stern cleats and kick those fenders overboard."

Beth and Terry moved to follow her orders, glancing up as they worked to see the many boats secured to the seawalls of Nelson's Dockyard come into view.

Lucy slowed *Mana* as they came around the final bend into the protected harbor.

"Right, now one of you is going to drop the anchor when I give the signal. Let's have the other back here to hand off a line to the dock. Ready?"

"I'll anchor, Terry's better at tossing lines," Beth said, climbing out of the cockpit. She went up to the bow and got the anchor ready to drop, then stood looking aft for Lucy's signal. She held her breath as she watched Lucy back *Mana* toward the row of boats already tied up. there didn't appear to be any room between them, but Lucy kept going. As if by magic, space opened up. When *Mana*'s stern was in between two bows Lucy lifted her arm and dropped it, a clear signal. Beth pressed the button for the windlass to let the anchor go. It rattled and splashed. She kept paying out the chain, watching their progress backwards and listening to the chain rattling over the bowsprit. *Mana* was shouldering her way in between the other boats without seeming to make any physical contact. It was like magic.

Beth felt the engine rev and knew that Lucy had shifted into forward to slow down. She saw Terry toss a stern line to a man on the dock who caught it first try. Terry climbed around behind Lucy to get the other stern line and toss it to a second man.

"That's enough!" Beth heard Lucy shout and realized the other woman had made a stopping motion before resorting to yelling. Beth took her toe off the deck-mounted button, feeling foolish. She covered the button and started back toward the cockpit.

"Wait!" Lucy's hand was up facing her. Beth stopped. Lucy kept her hand in the air as she looked over her shoulder at the seawall and the activity there. Finally, she turned, lowering her hand.

"Take up about two meters and wait for my instruction," she called. Beth walked back to the anchor well and uncovered the buttons. She pressed the up button, watching the chain clank in over the bowsprit, trying to estimate two meters. The chain had been hanging straight down off the bow, but by the time she stopped it was at a broad angle to the surface of the water. *How did she know exactly how much to take in?*

"That's it!" Lucy called.

Beth wasn't prevented from returning to the cockpit this time. She found Lucy lowering the swim platform. The stern lines were secured and Terry was coiling the ends on the boat.

"That was impressive," Beth said.

Lucy smiled again. "Not if you do it every day."

"The problem is doing it the first time."

"Yeah, I hear that. Frank should be here any minute, so I'll clear off."

"Bye. Thanks," Beth said as the woman stepped onto the swim platform.

"Thanks a lot." Terry watched her step nimbly from the platform up to the seawall. She thumped one of the dock men on the back and they all walked off together.

"That was something," Beth said. Terry stepped up behind her and wrapped his arms around her waist.

"I have no doubt you would have done it if you had to."

His kiss on the side of her neck was cool, but it sent a jolt of electricity through her.

"And that's why I'm going to marry you," she said, grinning.

By the time Frank Riviera arrived they were enjoying a late lunch of assorted leftovers and cold beers at the cockpit table. They welcomed him aboard, got him a beer, and went over his return checklist with him. He noted the half a dozen minor issues that they'd found—a loose hinge, a portlight that dripped during a squall—nothing significant, and nothing that they had broken or lost. After Beth signed the list he put it in his leather portfolio and sat back holding his beer.

"So, to the more important part. Still thinking of buying a boat like this?"

Terry was watching Beth from across the table, waiting for her to speak first.

"Nothing about this trip has caused me to change my mind."

Terry laughed out loud. "Pretty cagey. I'll be more direct. I like it even more after two weeks aboard. It sails wonderfully. I got used to the in-mast mainsail. The living space is good for us with company. I do have one concern, though."

Beth was surprised. She and Frank both said "What?" At the same time.

"I'm not sure Beth could single-hand her."

"You single-hand a lot?" Frank asked Beth, with a hint of skepticism.

Beth shrugged, then mentally chastised herself for minimize her experience and sat up straighter. "I single-handed my boat from New York to North Carolina and from St. Thomas to Guadeloupe."

"Well," Frank said, apparently at a loss for something more meaningful. "That's impressive. I had no idea. Do you plan to sail your new boat alone too?"

Beth felt her lips curling into a secretive smile as she looked across the table at her fiancé. He tilted his head, curiosity written all over his face.

"I don't plan to, but you never know when the need will arise."

Frank looked from Beth to Terry, clearly realizing there was subtext in her statement that he could not follow.

"Let's discuss what you would need to make this boat manageable for a single-hander. Have you thought about it?"

It was an intriguing question and it sucked Beth right in as she imagined how she would move around the cockpit and what tools and controls she would want immediately on hand.

)

As Beth and Frank talked, Terry's mind and gaze wandered. He had every intention of making their new boat one that Beth could sail alone "if the need arose," but he wasn't in the mood to think about the details of it this afternoon. The nearby restaurant with its open dining area had a view of the Harbour. He was full from their late lunch, but he couldn't help but think of dinner. A man walked through his field of view. His long hair was tied at the nape of his neck, he had a deep tan and wore nondescript shorts and shirt. And yet Terry knew he'd seen him somewhere before. The man glanced at *Mana*'s stern, and at Terry. His eyes darted away, almost as if he didn't want to be seen looking. Terry remembered where he'd seen him: the bar in Dickinson Bay.

No reason why he can't come here on his day off. Doesn't seem like the kind of thing a local waiter would do, but to each his own.

Still, the guy seemed shifty. Terry kept an eye on him as he made a circuit of the seawall, looking at all the boats. He was relieved when, a while later, he saw the man headed toward the dockyard entrance.

)

The hostess seated Beth and Terry at a table for four near the edge of the covered dining area within sight of *Mana* and the other boats along the seawall. Beth supposed that for a non-sailing tourist it was an exotic sight, but she felt like she was looking at her living room.

After they ordered cocktails—a dark and stormy for Terry and a gin and tonic for Beth, who needed a break from the rum—she slid her laptop out of her bag and set it on the table.

"Really?" Terry smiled.

"I haven't checked email in a week. I wanted to come up here earlier, but I got busy on the boat."

Terry sighed expansively and pulled his Blackberry out of his pocket. Beth swatted at his arm, laughing.

The wifi password they'd used in this restaurant a few months ago still worked. Beth watched her email inbox fill up with unread messages, scrolling through the subject lines as they piled up. She quickly eliminated the junk, then went back to the earliest unread messages and worked her way forward.

Her sister had sent a couple messages, unable to stop herself despite knowing Beth was out of service. Beth skimmed them and made sure they were downloaded to read more carefully later. She didn't see any surprises or disasters.

There was a message from Eva and a few from the folks back on City Island that she and Terry had visited. Beth skimmed and downloaded these, too. She took a few minutes to reply to the message from her mom, who was still uncomfortable using the computer that Trish and Mike had set up for her. After a couple sentences about her success with work and their relaxing vacation she paused. She'd been about to tell her mother that she was engaged. *I have to call her, I can't put it in an email.* She signed off and sent the message without her most exciting news.

Then she read a message from her friend Burt. Their drinks arrived and she started to put the computer away but stopped.

"I just want to reply to Burt, I'll leave the rest for later," she told Terry, picking up her drink to take a sip. Terry, staring at his own email, didn't reply.

Beth wrote to Burt about how strange it had been returning to the north east, and about landing a fascinating new job. She mentioned checking in on *Double Trouble* on St. Thomas on the way to Antigua to charter a boat they were considering buying. She apologized for not seeing his message earlier, but she'd been detached from the Internet. She said she hoped his charter was going well and clicked "send."

"Shoot!"

"What?" Terry looked up at her as she closed her email application and shut down the laptop.

"I forgot the biggest news," she waved her left hand over the laptop. "But I'm going to send a note to more people when we get home, so I'll include him in that."

"I guess we should coordinate informing our families, even though they don't talk to one another."

"I know. I just emailed my mom, but I didn't mention it. Have you told yours?"

"Are you kidding? In an email? That would not go over well."

Beth snorted a laugh at the notion of his mother being indignant at receiving such news via email. "Yeah, I thought an email wouldn't be popular with my family either. Mom probably wouldn't read it right away, and then Trish would be talking about it and she wouldn't know what she was talking about."

"I think we're going to have to go tell my family in person. I hope you don't mind."

Beth cleared her throat as a delaying tactic. "Of course I don't mind. They're family, and close. If we were that close to mine, I'd want to tell them in person, too."

Terry nodded, sliding his Blackberry back into his pocket and picking up his drink.

"Can we wait until we're back in the States? I'll call yours with you, and I'll set up a visit with mine."

"It's a plan," Beth agreed. She picked up her own drink and took a large swallow, trying not to think about seeing his family again.

The final hours of their trip passed in a rush of off-loading leftover provisions and stuffing their salt-saturated clothes back into their bags. Making a final tour of the boat, Terry came from the starboard aft cabin—the one Jeff and Carole had stowed their luggage in, holding a pair of conch shells.

"What's that?" Beth asked from across the saloon where she was struggling to zip her duffel bag full of salt-saturated clothing and gear, and wondering if it was going to survive the airline baggage handlers.

Terry looked down at the heavy objects in his hands. "The conch shells Jeff bought for the kids in Dickinson Bay. He forgot them."

"Maybe Carole said 'no way' and made him leave them."

Terry nodded. "Could be. What should I do with them?"

"Throw them overboard? Back where they came from."

"Jeff paid for them. I feel like he should have a second chance to decide what to do. Why does Carole get to say the kids can't have them?"

Beth studied Terry for a moment, wondering if he heard himself already taking a side. But she agreed with him.

"Beth?"

"Sorry. Let's see if we can fit them into something," she looked down at her duffel. "I can probably get one into my daypack."

Terry's grateful smile was the reward for her openminded reaction, but the whole thing left her feeling uneasy. Terry's loyalty was clear and understandable. Beth had no such connection to his partner, and she felt more resonance with Carole's position than Jeff's. Yet as the newest member of the social group she felt that it was up to her to minimize the impact of the other couple's problems on her own relationship. She hoped her open mind would rub off on Terry.

Part II

Twenty-nine

Washington, D.C.

Sitting down in her cubicle on the fifteenth floor of Broadhead's office tower on Monday morning Beth felt like the past two weeks were a dream. The trip from Nelson's Dockyard to the airport, the flight, another airport, another car ride, and then collapsing in bed in Georgetown she'd grown gradually more tired until none of it seemed real. She'd gone through the motions of getting herself dressed and off to work, but she was still tired. As she picked up her coffee mug to fill it in the break room her ring caught her eye.

Very real. All of it.

After the Equatorial team's morning update Claudia and Seetha pulled her aside as the men filed out of the conference room.

"Let us see your hand!" Claudia said, reaching toward Beth's left hand then pulling back as if realizing she didn't know Beth well enough to touch her.

"I saw it flash during the meeting. I think Marcus noticed too," Seetha said.

Beth lifted her left hand to show them her ring.

"Wow!"

"Beautiful!"

"Were you surprised? Did you guys talked about it?" Claudia asked, emboldened to tilt Beth's hand side to side to see the diamond sparkle.

"We've talked a few times about the future. I don't think the 'm' word came up, but we talked around it." Beth said, avoiding mentioning Terry's declaration nearly a year ago of wanting to marry her as too complicated to explain. She retrieved her hand from Claudia's grasp and held it up, looking at the ring.

"When are we going to meet him?" Seetha asked in her sing-song intonation.

"I'm sure if we go for drinks or something I can get him to join us," Beth said.

"How did he do it? Tell all!" Claudia demanded.

"No, wait, she can't right now. I have another meeting. She can tell us over lunch," Seetha said.

"Sure, let's do that," Beth said before Claudia could protest any further. "I have a meeting with Raj anyway."

"Okay," Claudia said, disappointment in her tone. But Claudia was perfectly capable of being disappointed over the most trivial things.

"Great. Twelve thirty work for you guys?"

"Good for me," Seetha said, moving toward the conference room door.

"Yes, that's fine. See you then," Claudia added.

Beth followed Seetha out and made for Raj Gupta's office.

)

"Welcome back Beth. How was the second half of your vacation?" Raj asked when she was seated in his office in front of his desk.

"It was wonderful. Thank you again for allowing me to take it after starting here so recently."

"I heard you might have special news to share."

"Really?"

"Howard is quite observant," Raj said. "He said you are wearing a very lovely ring that he doesn't remember seeing before."

Taken aback, Beth put her left hand on Raj's desk. As usual, the sight of the ring made her smile. Raj leaned forward to look at it but made no move to touch her hand.

"My boyfriend Terry proposed to me last week, after Mr. Codrington's hearing."

"Congratulations! What wonderful news. I hope our assignment for you didn't disrupt his plans."

"No, not at all. I understand Mr. Codrington called the team and was satisfied with how the hearing went."

Raj sat back and gave Beth an appraising look that confused her. A wave of apprehension washed over her.

"Mr. Codrington is quite happy with the service that Broadhead has provided him—that you provided him. How do you feel about the assignment?"

"I was glad to do it. Nervous, but glad to have the opportunity. I realized that for all I know about the islands, there is a great deal more that I should learn before a meeting like that."

"On the contrary, Beth, you provided exactly the service Broadhead was contracted for. This is important advice, so please pay attention: never downplay your own success. Your client is happy, we're happy, you scored a win for Broadhead."

"But if I'd known more—"

Raj held up his right hand, index finger pointing up. "You won. Never say otherwise. Do you understand?"

Beth nodded. She did understand what he meant. Accept the praise. Use your desire to do better for next time but keep it to yourself now.

"Good. Now, please document the type of information you felt was lacking in your preparation. What could the team have done better?"

"The team was great. They provided—" Raj was shaking his head, so she stopped.

"What is the expression I'm thinking of? It's very apt. It has to do with the tide coming in and lifting all boats equally."

"A rising tide raises all boats?"

"Exactly!" He slapped his desktop with an open hand, smiling. "Your feedback to the team strengthens it. It does not diminish their contribution to your success, but it strengthens the entire team for the next challenge. Does that make sense?"

"It really does. But does everyone on the team feel that way?"

"You should assume that they do because it's expected. You will present your thoughts on what more you could have used, and you will all discuss it."

"I'll prepare something. When do I need to present it?"

"Try for the end of the week, while it's fresh. What else do you have on your plate?"

Beth felt herself relax as she went over her work assignments with him. He re-prioritized them based on changes that had happened while she was away. She left his office feeling positive about the week ahead and realizing he was the first manager she'd known who was able to do that. She was, she decided, pretty lucky.

)

"Hi Mom, it's Beth."

"Bethy! When did you get back?"

"Last night. I had to work today."

"I remember a day when you would call the moment you got home from a trip."

"So do I, Mom. But I was too exhausted last night to talk to anyone. I'm sorry." Beth felt Terry squeeze her with the arm he had draped around her shoulders. She had settled on the sofa in the living room to make her call and Terry had joined her, wanting, she supposed, to speak to his future in-laws. She didn't have the call on speaker, but he could probably hear both sides of the conversation.

"Well I'm glad you're safe and home. Did you have a good time? I hope you have new stories."

Beth laughed. "We had an amazing time, and I do have at least one story. But first tell me how you're doing. How is your hip?"

Her mother groaned, a familiar sound of disgust. "I'm allowed out of bed now—into a wheelchair to go rolling around the gardens with an attendant. I feel like I'm never alone."

"That's good, Mom. Imagine if you were still living in the house?"

"Stop it. I know. But I wish they'd leave me alone for a while. I'm constantly being taken to physical therapy. I hate it."

"You want to walk again?"

"Just stop. Can't I bitch a little? Enough about me if you're not going to be sympathetic. You only have one story? I'm sure there are more." Beth was relieved by her mother's attitude and bad language—it meant she was in good spirits despite what she was saying.

"There are. But let me tell you the big news first."

"Big news? Okay." Mom sounded apprehensive. Beth smiled, knowing her concern was about to change.

"Terry and I are getting married."

"Oh Beth! Oh! Sam, come here!" Mom called out to Beth's father, then returned to the phone. "Beth, I'm so happy for you. You're right—this is big news! Does Trish know?"

"Not yet. I called you first, Mom."

"Well you need to call her! She's going to be so excited. You're going to have her be your matron of honor, right?"

"Mom, I haven't thought about it yet. But yes, of course."

"Here's your father. Tell him what you told me."

Beth heard a rustling and imagined her mother holding the telephone receiver up to her father's ear and him slowly taking it.

"Hi Daddy, it's Beth. How are you?" She heard the tentative tone of her voice and winced. Surely Mom wouldn't have put him on if he wasn't lucid.

"Beth? How are you sweetheart?"

"I'm great Dad. I called to ask you if you'll walk me down the aisle. I'm getting married."

"You are? Isn't that something? Our Bethy is getting married. How old are you now, sweetie?"

"Old enough to get married, Dad. You remember Terry? He came with me when I visited last time."

"Terry?" Dad paused and Beth cringed, fearing she'd pushed too far. But he went on, "that young man who asked me about sales. Nice guy. Good to you."

"Yes he is Dad. I'm glad you remember. He's here if you want to speak to him."

"Here's your mother."

Tears welled in Beth's eyes and she blinked, avoiding looking at Terry despite his comforting squeeze. On the other end of the line there was rustling, and Beth heard her mother telling her father to go sit down.

"Beth? That was good. He's happy for you."

"I asked him if he wanted to talk to Terry, and he gave you the phone," Beth's tears flowed despite her efforts to stop them.

"Well ask me instead," her mother said, obviously hearing the pain in her daughter's voice. Beth handed Terry the phone and shrugged out of his embrace, rising to go get a tissue.

She heard Terry greet her mother and exchange pleasantries about the engagement while she went to the powder room and got a couple tissues from the box there. Terry was listening when she returned and sat down. He was smiling, nodding, and then saying "yes, of course. I know. I know. Thanks Mrs. Anderson—Mom. Here's Beth."

She couldn't figure out what he was thinking as he handed the phone to her. His expression was enigmatic.

"That man is a find, Beth. I'm so happy for you. Now I want you to hang up and call Trish right now. I don't think I can stand having to wait to talk to her about this."

"Okay mom. I'll call her now. Love you. Both of you."

"I know dear. We'll talk to you again soon."

Beth ended the call and dropped the phone into her lap. She leaned her head back against Terry's arm and heaved a deep sigh.

"You okay?" Terry asked.

"That was draining. It shouldn't have been, but it was."

"Your mom told me she's happy you have me to take care of you. It was sweet."

"She thinks I need someone to take care of me?"

"She's a mother. You're her rebel daughter. She worries."

"Does your mother worry about you?" Beth wondered if that had something to do with his enigmatic expression.

Terry laughed, then stopped as if deciding that wasn't answer enough. "She does, in her own way."

"Well now I think you've got another mom to worry about you. Hope you don't mind." Beth picked up her phone and hunted for her sister's phone number. "Better call Trish, or Mom will beat me to it."

"I think I'll leave you to that one." He rose, leaving her to settle in on the sofa.

She listened to the distant ringing until her sister answered.

"Hey Trish, I'm back."

"Beth? I'm so glad to hear it! How was it? Amazing?"

"It was great. My work meetings went well—I told you about them, right?"

"Yes. It sounded like you were worried about it. It was okay?"

"Very okay. My team is happy with how it went."

"Great. You know I like it when you're gainfully employed."

Beth chuckled, thinking back on the several times she'd called Trish to tell her she'd been laid off from a job. "I have more news, too. Terry and I are engaged."

Beth heard a thunk followed by rustling on the other end of the line. Trish's voice came back.

"No shit? He did it? He asked? Or did you ask him?"

"He asked me. I don't think I would have the courage to ask him. He asked me, on a beautiful evening while we were sitting on the boat anchored off a pristine beach on Barbuda. It couldn't have been more romantic, Trish."

"I am so happy for you Beth. He's the best. Absolutely the best. Did he have a ring?"

"Of course. I'll email you a photo. It's beautiful. He even got the size right, he borrowed another ring of mine and I never noticed." Beth caught herself admiring the glittering diamond on her left hand as she spoke and forced herself to switch the phone to that hand.

"Yes, send me a picture. Have you told Mom yet?"

"I just got off with her. Now you have to tell me how she's doing. She put on a happy front on the phone, but I know her. The next thing she will think about, after the happy part, is logistics. Where will the wedding be? How will she get there? Is there any chance of Dad participating?" With the last question Beth felt tears fill her eyes. Her voice cracked and she stifled a sob.

"Oh Beth, I'm so sorry you have to think of that. It's not fair that Dad's sick, that you may not have him to walk you down the aisle. But you know I'll do whatever I can to help both of them be part of it, right?"

Beth sniffed back her tears and used her sleeve to wipe her eyes. "I know you will Trish. The truth is we haven't made a single plan yet. We haven't talked about location. I got back to work today and I'm going to be busy catching up."

"You're going to have to figure out how to fit wedding planning into your schedule, Beth. It's more work than you realize."

"I know, I know. I hope we can have a lot of conversations about it. That reminds me, you'll be my matron of honor, won't you?"

"I thought you'd never ask. Now, depending on when you pick, I might be enormous. But I would never say no."

"Oh geez, I didn't think of that. How are you doing?"

"You forgot I'm pregnant? I wish I could. I'm doing fine, thanks. The morning sickness is mostly over."

"I did not forget. I just didn't put it together with my wedding timing. I'll talk with Terry about it. I think we won't be ready before you're due. When is that, anyway?"

)

Caribbean Sea

Standing on *Sandcastle*'s bridge Burt studied the chart of Antigua, then looked out at the island itself on the horizon ahead. *Sandcastle* was making a comfortable fifteen knots, her engines humming after the tune-ups he'd done before leaving Guadeloupe. He'd spent one night anchored in lovely Deshais at the north end of Guadeloupe watching a British film company shooting a police drama under bright lights. He'd pointed the bow north early this morning. He'd be drinking sundowners tonight at a bar. The question was, which one?

He didn't expect to find Beth still on the island. Her email had come Saturday evening, and she hadn't exactly said it, but he was pretty sure she was heading back to the US on Sunday. He'd been a day short of getting here in time to catch her. But much as he enjoyed her company, she wasn't the one he had come here to find.

)

Dickinson Bay, Antigua

Hunter lit a cigarette, waving the match to put it out before dropping it into one of the sand buckets. Chirping frogs and the surf's soft hiss were the predominant sounds on the beach now that the bar was closed. Underlying these, strains of music drifted on the light breeze from one of the resort restaurants. Hunter inhaled a restorative drag, blew the smoke out, and dug in a pocket for his phone.

"Hey Hunter, good to hear from you. How's it going?" his brother Parker's voice belied an evening buzz. Hunter resisted commenting on it.

"Okay. Long day, no cruisers in the bar."

"Seems like that's every day, bro."

Hunter had to admit that Parker was right. He felt like he'd searched the entire island for Beth Anderson and *Double Trouble* over the weekend. There wasn't a sign of her anywhere, although he knew she can't have gotten away from Antigua that fast. She had been at Great Bird Island, and then she had not been in any of the west or south coast anchorages or marinas. There were not a lot of other places she could have gone, as far as he knew.

"She's here somewhere, but I can't figure out where else to look," Hunter said, shaking his head as he started walking along the sandy path through the trees toward the road.

"Do you know what I think?"

"I can guess."

"Come home. At least for Christmas. You can start fresh after the new year. Try to reach Ori directly again."

"I can't give up now."

"I didn't say that. Take a break. Spend time with your family. We miss you. We're worried about you."

"Who's we?"

"Fine, you got me, I'm worried about you. I think dad is too, even if he doesn't say anything. You know him."

"Oh, that I do," Hunter said, exhaling smoke.

"Are you smoking?"

"You want me to come home?"

"Forget I asked. Hey, you're considering it!"

"Yes, I'm considering it. I've got to come up with a better strategy. Paradise is starting to get to me."

"Speaking of paradise, did I tell you about the volcano tour on Hawai'i?"

"Not now bro." Hunter had reached the road and turned toward home, trudging along the edge of the pavement trying to listen for oncoming traffic while he listened to his brother.

"So you'll come? I can tell mom and dad?"

"You're relentless. All right. I'll look into flights and let you know. I'll have to tell Cecil."

"Who?"

"My boss. The guy who owns the bar."

"Seriously? You know a Cecil?" Parker broke down into giggles, and Hunter wondered whether the buzz was more of a high. That worried him.

"I'll call and let you know when I'm coming," he said with much more conviction. His brother might need him.

Thirty

Marigot, St. Marten

*T*he guard swiped a rag across the seat of the folding chair and stepped back. Virgine sat down, crossing her ankles and folding her hands on top of a file on the table in front of her. She nodded at the guard standing by the warehouse door, his hand on the doorknob. He opened it. Virgine shut her eyes and wrinkled her nose, unclasping her hands to reach into the pocket of her tailored silk jacket for her handkerchief.

Guards herded a row of five children into the space in front of her table. Virgine tucked the handkerchief away and opened the file. She scanned the top sheet of paper in the file, and then the row of bedraggled children. There appeared to be two girls and three boys. It was impossible to know their ages, but the smallest could not be more than four. The tallest was a boy whose eyes kept darting around the dim room, from a guard to her, to the door behind her, back to a guard—he was far too alert for her tastes—he must be approaching puberty.

Too old.

"Return him," she said, pointing at him. One of the guards took him by the upper arm and dragged him back through the inner door. The other four watched him go. She could see panic growing in their faces.

He must be their leader. Unsupervised children always form a tribe.

She turned her attention to the next one. It appeared to be a girl, although with its young age and disgusting state of hygiene it was hard to tell.

"Show me," she said to the guard, nodding at the child. The guard bent and stuck his fingers into the waistband of the child's filthy underpants. It screamed as he dragged them down to reveal soiled flesh and female genitalia. Virgine nodded and wrote a name—Babette—on the paper. There was no point in telling the child her name, she would not remember. Virgine reserved the right to name each person she provided to her clients. The guard stepped back, leaving the child's filthy underpants around her ankles. Virgine glanced up and saw the girl silently weeping.

"Pull them up," she said, making an upward gesture with her right hand. The little girl gulped, glanced at the guard, and bent to drag her underwear back up and cover herself.

Virgine was already looking at the next child. *Another girl*, she thought. Its hair was a wild mess of spikes that, had anyone bothered to pay attention, could have been trained into dreadlocks. There was a market for that. As it was, they would have to be cut off. But Virgine had no choice, she needed girls.

"Amber," she said out loud, writing the name on the paper.

The next child's face was half covered with a port wine stain. Virgine started at him, trying to remember why he was familiar to her. He was trembling, his eyes wide as he stared at her.

Whatever, it doesn't matter. He's not acceptable for this client. Too bad.

She couldn't tell what the last, smallest child was, but it didn't matter either, as it was too small, or young, to meet this client's requirements. No matter, there were other clients with different tastes. She looked back at the two girls.

"Deliver them to the village for preparation. The others go back."

One guard moved in and took the arms of the two girls, another ushered the rejected children back through the warehouse door. Virgine made a few more notes in her file while the guard took the two girls out to a waiting van.

Virgine stepped outside into the night and inhaled to clear the stench of the warehouse from her sinuses. When the van had driven away, she went to her car where her driver was waiting.

)

Phillipsburg, Sint Maarten

Strolling through the lobby and entering the gaming room at Casino Paradiso was Virgine's favorite way to relax. The male casino staff acknowledged her with darling subservient head nods while the women's eyes always showed their envy as they bobbed their heads. Virgine ignored all of them, which was her right. The other guests, as the casino liked to call them, also acknowledged her. The men showed uniform admiration, and a few displayed overt lust. As with the female employees, most female guests could not conceal their envy of Virgine's perfect curves, perfectly styled hair, exquisite makeup, and inimitable fashion sense.

Let them envy. I work hard at it.

She stopped at the cashier to convert five thousand euros into chips. After her losses in the high stakes room she'd felt chastised for trying it and resolved to stick to what she knew: the black jack tables in the main room. She still had half of Elvis Rink's money. She just needed a run of good luck. As she approached her favorite blackjack table, the pit boss was changing the dealer from the one she preferred to a woman Virgine vaguely recognized. Virgine paused to see if Kevin went to another table, but instead he headed for the door marked "Staff." Virgine moved on to the table he had left: if she couldn't have Kevin, at least she would have her lucky table. She took a seat to the dealer's right, her preferred position. There were two other players, both men that Virgine had shared the table with many times before.

The dealer welcomed Virgine with a thin smile and nod of recognition as she shuffled the cards and introduced herself to the players.

"Good evening. I am Ori, and I will be your dealer. Please place your bets."

As the dealer loaded the cards into the shoe Virgine and the two men pushed stacks of chips into place on the table in front of them. Virgine had not formed an opinion of this dealer yet. Maybe this time.

"No more bets please," the dealer said as she checked that her clients had met the table minimum of one hundred Euro. She peeled the first card from the shoe and set it on the discard rack, "One discard. Player one is a ten," she drew the second card from the shoe and placed it in front of the man to her far left. Player two received a seven, and Virgine's card was a four. Not a great start. The house drew a nine. One by one the players each took another card, bringing the two men both up to sixteen. Virgine's card was a ten. The dealer dealt the house another nine. Both men folded. Virgine saw no reason to: either she'd lose with the fourteen, or she'd go over, but at least by taking a card she had a chance of beating the house's eighteen. The dealer cheerfully pulled another card from the shoe and placed it in front of Virgine. A seven. Virgine's pulse shot up. She wanted fireworks and a brass band. She wanted to crow. But women of her stature in business and society did not engage in such public displays. So she smiled and nodded and wondered if the dealer swung. She was attractive in a white girl way. Virgine imagined all the dark, curly hair freed from the tight knot at the back of her head. What a lovely contrast her white skin would make against Mathieu's delicious dark.

"Player three wins with twenty-one. Congratulations," the dealer said, pushing her winnings toward Virgine and sweeping up all the cards with practiced motions. Virgine brought her imagination back into check and placed her next wager: double the first one.

Virgine went out on the next three hands, although the other two players had better luck: each received payouts for two of the three. On the fourth hand, though, when Virgine forced herself back down to the table minimum, she won with a twenty. Frustrated now instead of happy about the win, she wagered five hundred on the next hand and grimaced as the dealer collected her four cards totaling twenty-two points and all of her chips.

)

Ori was relieved when she felt Rupert, the pit boss, tap her shoulder. She had collected another hundred Euro in chips from the black woman—making her loss an even thousand. The woman wasn't happy. Ori raised her hands and clapped once. "Thank you all. Good luck," she said as she stepped away from the table and watched the next dealer step in. It was Jaime, the dealer they brought in when a customer was in trouble. He was six four and two fifty pounds. No gambler would cross him. Little did they know he had the sweetest disposition of anyone Ori had ever met. But he knew how to play the heavy and they paid him to do it. Ori wondered if Miss Thing was about to be yanked. The gossip among the dealers was that she had lost a lot in the high stakes room, and probably turned to ill-advised sources for credit. The casino might suspect someone would be coming around to collect tonight.

Unfortunately, or maybe fortunately, Rupert didn't direct Ori to another table, but told her to take a break, which meant she had to leave the floor. When she was called back a half hour later Miss Thing was gone.

)

Washington, D.C.

Beth sat down at her desk after the team update meeting. Her eyes went to the diamond ring on her left ring finger, but what she noticed was that her tan was fading. She'd been living in a self-created bubble of happiness. It had not quite faded, but it was beginning to wear thin. This morning's divisional meeting had contributed to its degradation. The aggressive results expected by the Broadhead leadership were starting to feel more and more like unobtainable stretch goals. Clients were not quite as wealthy nor abundant as originally projected. As a newer member of the team, Beth worried about being annexed away to another team, or worse. She felt most at risk since she had not been hired to do what she was now doing—consulting with her colleagues on Caribbean culture and joining in conference calls with clients. She knew her team mates valued her insight, but she alone wasn't going to make the team successful.

The open side of her cubicle faced the team common space, where most of her teammates were standing around the table to debrief on the messages they'd received from division management. Beth logged into her computer as she listened to them. Having been hired just six weeks ago, she was too new, both on the team and at Broadhead, to interpret the subtext in their management's words, so in this arena she needed them to translate the body language and facial expressions. What she heard as warnings, the others heard as a pep talk. Revenue is not meeting projections? Let's find more clients, let's sell more services to the ones we have. Beth had never been interested in, nor talented at, selling anything. A headhunter in New York City once told her she couldn't begin to sell herself. When she was in school her dad had always been the guy selling stuff on her behalf to his co-workers. But then, he *was* a salesman.

Beth dragged her mind away from her father and focused on listening to her colleagues. Marcus picked up a red marker and began making a list on the standing whiteboard adjacent to the team table. He vigorously erased part of a diagram someone had left to make more room. Their engagement in the discussion soon drew Beth in, and she joined them at the table and in the discussion of their clients and prospects. Her previous concerns dissipated as she realized her team had a plan, and the skills to execute on it.

Thirty-one

Washington, D.C.

"*W*e haven't talked since your feedback to the team after the Codrington project. I thought that went well—did you?" Raj Gupta asked. When he'd called and asked Beth to stop by his office, she'd felt an all too familiar surge of dread not completely overridden by the team's collaborative enthusiasm. She'd gone ahead and gotten the cup of coffee she'd been about to fetch, then carried it with her into his office. Her mug with its drawing of a sailboat and the word "Captain" on it sat steaming on the edge of his desk, and she couldn't help feeling like bringing it was a mistake.

Bringing coffee to your boss's office is unprofessional. To further complicate her inner turmoil, she wanted to slap herself for slipping back into office stresses after her year of freedom at sea. She was certain all of her inner conflict showed on her face as she met Raj's eyes.

"Yes. I guess you knew I was a little concerned they would feel I was criticizing them. But you were right, they took the feedback positively."

"Good. Are you settled in since your vacation?"

"Yes. We were strategizing on client development before lunch."

"Good. It's a strong team. Diverse, complimentary skills."

"Yes. I'm glad to be part of it."

Raj nodded, glancing at her steaming coffee. "Don't let that get cold on my account."

"Oh, no, it's still hot," Beth said, feeling utterly stupid. *What the hell is wrong with me?*

Raj smiled, trying, she thought, to ease her nerves. He was probably baffled by her behavior.

"I think you know we were very happy with your success on Antigua. Marcus is about to close on more business with Mr. Codrington. He may request you, I don't know."

"That's great, I didn't realize. It was a great opportunity for me." *And everything is just great. Great.*

"We have another project for your special touch. I know you just got home from the islands, but can we send you back? To St. Martin this time."

Beth felt herself simultaneously relax—he wasn't laying her off—and tense with excitement—St. Martin!

"Yes, of course. I'd be glad to go to St. Martin." She reached forward and wrapped her hand around the warm mug.

"This is going to be a longer assignment. Perhaps a couple weeks. I wanted to be sure you would not mind being away." His eyes flicked to her engagement ring. A flush of warmth suffused her face and she couldn't help but smile. The bubble was reinforced. She took a sip of her coffee as he went on, "Have you set a date yet?"

"Not yet. We both have to wrangle families, please everyone. Probably not until next fall."

He nodded, and she wondered if he had any idea of the challenges she was going to have to overcome—starting with her ailing father. No, he didn't, and it wasn't his problem. She took another sip of coffee.

"Well, the client we'd like you to work with on St. Martin needs Broadhead's services to make trade connections in the US. She's got a line of hand-crafted goods that would be a fit for certain major retailers and grocery chains. Your team can get the contacts here. You would funnel their information to her."

Several questions crowded for Beth's attention. She uttered the one that came first, "Grocery chains?"

"My daughter is always making me buy the bracelets and earrings and scarves at Whole Foods. All that fair trade, organic, locally sourced stuff with astronomical price tags?"

"I try to avoid that section."

"Well it's the kind of product our client is sourcing from local crafters in the islands."

"And she's a business woman?"

"Yes. From one of St. Martin's more prominent families. Her father was a banker. Her brother inherited the business, but she inherited a stake in it and a personal fortune that she's used to start her business. She's well known for supporting causes related to women's rights in the islands."

"She has a goal I can admire," Beth said. "Much of island culture is centered around male leadership."

"Virgine Guesnon seems to be making headway, but she *is* based in a department of France. Not a small, independent island with a fledgling government."

"Right. Someone like that is in a good position to push ripples of change outward, though."

Raj smiled, leaning back in his chair to regard her for a moment. "So you're on board."

"Yes, it—"

"Don't lose sight of Broadhead's objectives."

Beth sat up straight, realizing she'd leaned into the conversation as she contemplated a strong woman leading change in the islands.

"Understood."

"I understand that for your recent trip you chartered a sailboat. But your boat is somewhere in the islands, isn't it?"

)

Georgetown, Washington, D.C.

"... and he said if I wanted to move *Trouble* to St. Martin over Christmas, I could have a few days to do it." Beth set her bag of groceries on the kitchen island and turned toward Terry, who set two more bags next to it. He'd met Beth on her way home at the local Whole Foods, where Beth had made a point of examining the merchandise in the personal care aisles. Charming bracelets, earrings, and pendants that held a few drops of essential oil, all priced beyond what she was willing to pay, and allowing for a comfortable profit margin. On the walk to Terry's Georgetown brownstone she'd told him about her next assignment.

"Are you proposing Christmas in the islands?" Terry asked, eyes sparkling as he turned toward her.

"I guess I am," she said, stepping to him, arms slipping around his waist under his coat. His arms settled around her and, as always happened, everything in her world fell into place. She placed a demure kiss on his mouth, then laid her head on his shoulder and enjoyed his hug. "Are you on board?"

"Silly question. I'll talk to Jeff," he paused, pressed his lips to her forehead, and amended, "I'll tell Jeff."

Smiling, Beth wriggled out of his arms and shrugged off her coat, then reached for his. While she hung them in the mudroom off of the kitchen, he started unpacking the reusable bags he'd brought to the store. While Beth talked more about the assignment, he put the prepared food they'd bought into the microwave and got out plates and flatware.

"Want a beer, or wine?"

"I'd love a beer."

They discussed the logistics of returning to *Double Trouble* on St. Thomas, launching her, fixing anything that needed it, provisioning, and sailing from St. Thomas to St. Martin. Half way through the discussion Beth got a pad of paper and pen from a drawer and started making notes.

"It sounded simple when Raj suggested it," she sighed as she flipped to a new sheet of paper.

"Why don't they have you stay in a hotel?"

"It is an option if we don't want to do this. Raj said Mr. Codrington was impressed that I was a sailor—it lent credibility to me."

"Makes you closer to being a local. Less of an outsider in any case."

"I guess so. I'm not sure how true that is on all islands. So, honestly, is this," she tapped the pad with the pen to indicate her notes, "too much trouble, so to speak?"

Terry shook his head. "To spend a week or so sailing with you, over Christmas? Hardly. Besides, it would be better for *Trouble* to get her back in the water for a while, check her systems, make sure she's in working order. If we get there and find something is wrong, you can abandon and go get a hotel room on St. Martin. It's a good island to get repairs done—a lot of options."

"True. That would be plan B. Okay, I'll call the marina tomorrow and talk about them launching, maybe we should pay them to check her over. That way if they find something wrong, we'll know about it before we go."

"Who are you and what have you done with my girl fr—fiancé?" Terry laughed. "I think that is the first time I have heard you suggest paying someone to do something you can do yourself."

Beth chuckled. "I know. Having a salary is making me a spendthrift. I'm thinking like an office drone too, schedules and deadlines. Ugh."

"There's balance in there somewhere. We'll find it. In this case, you've got an appointment right after New Year's, and we need to do what we have to for you to be there."

"Right. Okay, so my first to-do is calling St. Thomas. What else can you think of?"

)

Washington, D.C.

Beth blew across the top of her container of hot soup, then dipped in her spoon and touched it to her lips.

"Ouch."

Still too hot. She dropped the plastic spoon into the container. It descended until half the handle was submerged. Beth rolled her eyes at her clumsiness and reached for the telephone receiver.

She should use her cell phone to call her sister in California. But it was expected that people made personal calls on the business line, right? As she dialed, she remembered her first job in New York, where most people's phones were blocked from dialing outside of the 212 and 718 New York City area codes. Not a chance that would work today, with so many people using cell phones with random area codes.

As she listened to distant ringing, she checked the time display on the phone and did the mental calculation. It was nine fifteen in California. Trish would be at work with her second cup of coffee— it had better be decaf—and her work email open in front of her. Unless she had a morning meeting, which Beth knew she hated.

"Bethy? Good to hear from you again so soon!"

"Hi Trish. Is it a good time?"

"I'm at work. It's never a good time. But you mean to talk. Sure, I'm just entering my timesheet early. I'll take any distraction."

"Weren't you complaining about having to get those done before the end of the day on Fridays?"

"You remember that? Geesh. I'm sure I did complain, yes."

"So you're doing it early."

"Who are you, my boss?"

"I don't want you to get in trouble talking to me when you should be doing something else." Beth was wearing an evil grin. Trish was usually the one nagging her, and it was fun to turn the tables.

"You know, I could hang up now."

"But you won't because you would rather talk to me than do that timesheet. And because I have news."

"Why didn't you say so? What is it?"

"Because it was fun teasing you. What is it? They're sending me to St. Martin to work with a client for about half of January." She drew her spoon out of the soup and leaned in to lick the handle, glancing around to be sure nobody saw her.

"Oh no, I can hear it coming. You're going to elope to St. Martin."

"What? No!" The notion sent an unexpected wave of panic over Beth. *I'm not ready to get married!*

Realizing that was something she needed to explore later, Beth pushed the fear away and focused on her sister. "We're not eloping, or getting married on St. Martin next month. But Terry is going with me, to move *Trouble* from St. Thomas so I can live aboard her while I'm there."

"Beth, why can't you be like normal people on a business trip and stay in a hotel?"

"Because I'm not normal. You've said it often enough."

Trish laughed, which made Beth do the same.

"How are Mike and the kids?"

Trish willingly launched into recent news of her branch of the family, including the kids' soccer games and the small raise Mike had received after more than five years in his job. It wasn't a lot, Trish said, but it would help with the expense of the baby. They ended the call with Trish extracting a promise that Beth would call their mother and tell her about Christmas. But by then Beth had finished her soup and the team was gathering for a one o'clock meeting. Mom would have to wait until later.

Washington, D.C.

Raj Gupta looked up at the figure standing in his office's open doorway.

"Adrian! What brings you to our floor? Come in." He gestured at one of the chairs in front of his desk.

Adrian McKeen stepped into the office and shut the door. He rested one hand heavily on the back of the proffered chair as he maneuvered his bulk around it and lowered down onto the seat. It seemed to Raj that his boss was less healthy than usual—pallid and heavier, and out of breath after what had to have been a short walk and elevator ride. Raj was not concerned about the closed door. That was typical Adrian.

"I understand that you have made the assignment. The Anderson woman," Adrian said. His gravely tone made everything he said sound slightly sinister.

"Yes. She is very willing. She will need a couple days off to move her boat to St. Martin, but she'll take them around Christmas, so it won't be noticeable. And the overall expense will be reduced—well below the billed per diem."

"You know very well that is not my concern, Raj. You are confident she can handle the assignment?"

"I have confidence in Beth. She performed well in Antigua. Perhaps more importantly, the team has confidence in her, for the most part."

"This is not the same as the Antigua assignment. Virgine Guesnon is nothing like Mr. Codrington. Certain parts of our organization have a special interest in Ms Guesnon."

"I understand that to be the case. I believe Beth will work with Ms Guesnon as instructed, and as the instructions change—if they do."

Adrian's mouth puckered as he stared at Raj for a long moment. "If she is successful, it will be good for you. But she might become more attractive to other parts of the organization."

"As would be the case with any of the Equatorial Team who went on this assignment, it seems to me," Raj said. "I would be unhappy about losing any of them. But of course I will accede to the Broadhead's greater interests should that be the case."

Adrian nodded. "As we must. However, I believe she needs more experience. Also, unlike some of my peers, I believe she should be aware of the situation and the risks. But that is in conflict with Broadhead's greater interests at this time."

"Do you have any specific instructions for me?"

"No specific instructions. I trust you to do what is right to protect our valuable asset. No need to bother me with the details, like her use of per diem."

"I understand," Raj nodded very deliberately and watched Adrian nod back, eyes lock with his.

Thirty-two

Georgetown, Washington, D.C.

"*H*ello Mother, it's Terry."

"Terry sweetheart, do you think I don't recognize your voice?" Bebe Faughnan replied. "Although given how infrequently we speak, one would not be surprised if I didn't."

Terry resolved to ignore that, and in the same instant changed his mind about how to deliver the news of his engagement. He unconsciously leaned forward in his armchair, resting his elbows on his knees as he held the phone to his ear.

"I know Mother. It's been weeks. You know Beth and I went with Jeff and Carole to the Caribbean for Thanksgiving?"

"I am not senile, if that is what you are suggesting. I am aware of your typical excuse for missing the holiday with us."

Typical? He had never gone sailing over Thanksgiving before. But then, to his mother any trip was every trip, and he supposed he had used Jeff as an excuse often enough. He rubbed at his eyes with his free hand.

"Well, I have news."

"About the Caribbean? Or about Jeff and his wife?"

"Try again Mother. About Beth and me."

"Oh?"

"We're engaged."

"I see."

"Mother, stop speaking in single letters. You sound like a text message. Congratulate me on making the perfect decision."

"What are you talking about? A text message?"

"Never mind. Are you at least excited to help plan another wedding?"

"Well, Terry, I don't know. That is usually the bride's responsibility. Shouldn't you be asking her mother?"

"Maybe so. Maybe I should have just called her instead. She's very excited about her daughter's engagement."

"Now Terry, sweetie, you know I'm pleased you're happy. Don't be like that. When are you and Beth coming to visit? You know your father will want to congratulate you in person. Why don't you come Christmas Eve?"

"Well actually, that's the other news I have. Beth has an assignment in St. Martin starting on January third. We're going to the islands before Christmas to move *Double Trouble* from St. Thomas to St. Martin. We'll be spending Christmas and New Year's there. Together."

"Well. You expect me to be surprised? When was the last time you were here for a holiday? How many years has it been?"

"I don't know Mother. I'm sorry about this, but I'm not going to have Beth go move *Trouble* alone over Christmas."

"You can pay people to move boats, you know."

"You're forcing me to be blunt, Mother. I'm sorry. But I'd rather spend the holidays sailing with Beth. We won't have an opportunity like this very often."

"Really? Seems to me you spent last Christmas sailing with Beth, too, or had you forgotten?"

"I have not. But who knows where we'll be next year, and after that? This year we have this opportunity and we're taking it. It doesn't mean I don't love you all." He stopped short of saying, *I just love Beth more.*

"Well. If it has to be that way, so be it. But you must bring Beth down before you go. I simply will not take 'we're too busy' as an excuse."

Terry smiled to himself, because he had been about to say exactly that.

"Sure. How's next Saturday? We're leaving the following week."

"Next Saturday, the seventeenth?"

"Yes."

"I have added it to the calendar. Your father will be glad to see you."

"And you?"

"And me. Honestly Terry, I am your mother."

Terry gritted his teeth to refrain from saying something very out of line. Instead he asked how his Dad was doing, which led to a less tense discussion of what everyone was up to in southern Virginia. By the time the call ended Terry was awash in suburban news that simply didn't interest him. He stood up, shedding it as he walked through the house to the kitchen to find something to drink. Beth would be home in an hour or so, and he had to tell her of their weekend plans.

)

Washington, D.C.

"You had repair done on the hull," Victor Henderson told Beth, his voice thin over the island cellular connection.

"Yes, we had a bad leak, and the bilge pump went. A lot of hand pumping." As she said it, Beth knew the marina manager in St. Thomas did not care.

"The shop that did it marked their work, did you know?"

"Marked it? What do you mean?"

"There is a stamp in the patch. Quite readable. I will email you a photo now."

"Yes please. I never noticed, but we were in a hurry to get her back in the water."

"Yes, I can imagine. The photo is on its way. I recommend you have us sand it out. We can fare it out with an additional patch. Here in the islands it does not matter, but if you bring the boat back into the US …"

Beth wondered whether that was true. Would a US customs inspector notice and have a problem with a repair done in Cuba? Or did Victor sense an easy target? She opened a browser tab on her computer and navigated to her personal email. Victor's message was there. Sure enough, his photo showed an oval near the propeller shaft with the name of the shop that had done the repair and "Mariel, Cuba" below it.

"It's a small job. Fifty dollars will cover it."

Beth stared at the coffee she'd picked up on the way in to work, a stupid habit since Broadhead supplied coffee. Fifteen or twenty of those would pay for the work. Maybe he wasn't trying to take her.

"Yes, do it. Did your crew find anything else?"

"*Double Trouble* is in good shape for her age. We'll service and tune the engine and I'll have the rigger tune the rig. She could use a coat of bottom paint if you're keeping her in the water for the season."

"I'm not sure how long it will be. But you're right, she needs it. Okay, what is it all going to cost?"

The amount was both painfully high and manageable since she'd started working. It would have been impossible before.

What had she been thinking when she'd set out from New York over a year ago with a few thousand dollars in her bank account and no income? On the other hand, so far, things had turned out all right. Except, she was in debt to Terry. She did not believe he kept an account, but she did. She made a note of every part, repair, load of laundry, and slip fee that he paid for because he wanted the safety, convenience, or a clean shirt. It wasn't fair to include the set of chart books he had called a gift, but if she made that exception, he could call everything a gift.

Unfortunately, her imagined debt to him was escalating at a much faster rate now that they were living in his house, because although she did not know what his monthly housing expense was, she felt responsible for half of it as long as she was living there. Never mind that he paid the same before she moved in. That's what he'd said about it when she suggested contributing.

She did not feel that their engagement excused her debt. She had not accepted him for his money, and she didn't want anyone to think so. Something at the back of her mind kept intruding into her thoughts, telling her to discuss this this with him and either make a plan to pay him back, or throw away her accounting. But she kept pushing the thought away.

)

Dickinson Bay, Antigua

Hunter grudgingly undertook his last day at the beach bar. It wasn't Cecil's fault, nor anyone's else's, that he hadn't found any cruisers who knew where Beth Anderson was, but he felt as if he'd wasted months here and he resented it. Tomorrow he would fly back to Texas. After that, well, he wasn't sure what he was going to do next, but he knew he wouldn't come back here.

The fourth table he served that afternoon changed everything. They were already tipsy when they wandered into the shade of the bar. He heard the word "pub crawl" a couple times as the eight of them crowded up to the bar and ordered beers. They took over one of the tables and continued their boisterous conversation. Hunter's ears perked up when he heard one of them mention a night crossing and the Anegada Passage and two of them comparing laundry facilities in different places. These were cruisers, not short-term charterers. He approached the table and asked if any of them wanted lunch. That garnered a laugh from several of them and one asked if they looked like they were drinking too much.

"You look like you're having a great day," he replied with a return chuckle.

"We are!" one of the women said. "Aren't we?"

"Yes, Dottie. Let's get some fries or something," a man, possibly her husband, put in. That opened the door and a few minutes later Hunter was putting in their order for food and drinks. When he brought their second round of beers, he took a chance on engaging them.

"Where are you folks coming from?"

"Most recently? St. Kitts. Ever been there?"

"No sir. I'd like to see it. Have you been to Jamaica?"

"Can't say that I have. Any of you guys ever stop in Jamaica?" the man asked his companions.

One of the men had, on someone else's boat years ago. Hunter explained that he'd lived there for a while. As usual when he shared this history with cruisers, they got into an analysis of the best route from the States and whether Jamaica was a safe stop. Hunter left them discussing it to go get their lunch. When he came back, he lingered again, learning that they were from several sailboats and had travelled in company from the east coast. *Perfect*.

"Any of you know a woman sailor named Beth Anderson?"

"*Double Trouble!*" one of the women said.

"Yes. Do you know her?"

"Yes, we've run into Beth and Terry several times."

"I'd like to catch up with her," he added. "Do you think she's heading this way?"

"Do you know Beth?" one of the men asked Hunter. He provided his well-practiced "friend of a friend" story and saw from their faces that they mostly believed him.

"Last I heard, she was taking *Trouble* to St. Thomas," the man told him.

"Right. I expect she's got *Trouble* there now," one of the women said.

"St. Thomas," Hunter repeated. His spirits had first soared at the concrete information, then plunged at the notion of moving to another island and starting over. At least St. Thomas was an American island.

"Thanks for the info. I appreciate it."

"Good luck finding your friend," the woman said.

"I'd better let you eat your lunch. Need another round?"

⫯

Georgetown, Washington, D.C.

"Are you looking forward to this even a little bit?" Terry asked.

He was driving his black BMW across the Key Bridge with Beth buckled in next to him for the three-hour journey to his parents' home in Virginia Beach. Buckled in as much to keep herself in the car as for protection, she liked to think. Her first dinner with his parents had been an utter disaster due to over-served wine. She barely remembered Terry dragging her from the house on wobbly legs clad in ruined panty hose. Fortunately for her, Terry's parents were both guilty of the same sin—which was why a glass was never left empty at their table.

"A little bit. Sure," She replied, reaching over to wrap her hand over his on the stick shift.

"Well, I'm thrilled to be spending the holidays with you in the islands. I hope you are too, and see this as a small price to pay."

"I'm totally on board with that thinking. It won't make your mom any nicer to me, though."

He sighed, then turned his hand over to clasp hers. "Have I told you how she treated Andrew when Ginny got engaged to him?"

"No, I don't believe you have. Spill."

He pursed his lips and glanced over at her. "Maybe this isn't the time, right before you see her."

"Maybe you better tell me or it's going to be a very long night. What with me not talking."

"Come on—"

"All right. I'm bluffing, that would be even worse. But *you* come on. Tell me. Just a little bit? Please?"

"She had been dating him for about a year, and everything was fine. He's an attorney—suitable for her daughter in mom's world— and he golfs, so even though Dad can't anymore, he could talk about it."

"And what happened when they got engaged?"

"Mom wanted to hire a detective to investigate him. Ginny was livid."

"Wait, your mom told your sister she wanted to do that?"

"Oh yeah. When Dad didn't let her—at least as far as I know, she might have done it anyway—she started criticizing everything about him. Poor guy couldn't dress, worked for the wrong firm, was in the wrong specialty. She invented some family medical history, I don't know what she said to justify it, but she said he would produce autistic children."

Beth shivered and wrapped her arms around herself. *Family medical history.*

"Cold? Need more heat?"

"No. I'm fine."

Terry glanced at her, eyes narrowing. "What's wrong?"

Beth made herself unwrap her arms. "Is she going to throw my father's Alzheimer's in my face?"

"If she does, we leave."

"What did Ginny do when she attacked Andrew?"

"Ginny kept trying to placate her, and when it got too hard, she would go to Andrew's place. But she kept coming back and mom would start over. My relationship with her, with all of them, is different. I have no problem with walking away and letting them come to me when they're ready to be human beings."

"I don't know Terry, I don't want to be the cause of that."

"Beth, you wouldn't be. Mom would be the cause."

Beth thought for a few minutes. She knew he was right, but she didn't want to be the center of such a rift.

"My mom could complain that your family is prone to stroke," she finally said.

"That would not be well received." His tone was not amused. She'd struck a chord she hadn't meant to. Nothing for it but to get through it.

"Exactly," she said.

Terry nodded slowly, apparently processing this harsh side of his fiancé.

"Look, I don't want to do that. I won't do it. Did your mother make these accusations in Andrew's presence?"

"No. She was cordial to him."

"So for all I know, she's already ripped into me. You'd tell me, wouldn't you?"

"She has not, at least not to me. I'm not sure if I would tell you."

"Seriously?"

"I wouldn't want to repeat the vile stuff that she's capable of spouting. What good would that do? You'd feel awful, you'd hate her forever. That's a terrible way to start a marriage."

"How does she treat Andrew now?"

"You've seen them together."

"Right. Wrong question. Does she still say those things about him behind his back?"

"No. At least not that I have heard. Since the wedding she's been fine with him."

"Wow. That's, like, psychopathic. Try to destroy your daughter's relationship and when you fail, just stop. Not even an apology?"

"Not that I know of, but if she did apologize, it would be to Ginny, not me."

"Right."

They rode in silence for another quarter hour, Beth contemplating how she was going to deal with her future mother-in-law, Terry wondering whether he was going to be able to hang on to the love of his life. The truth was, he knew his mother was compiling a list of Beth's faults, and she'd unleash them on him the first chance she got. He hoped she'd show the same restraint that she had with Andrew, and not do it in Beth's presence.

"All right. If she tears in to me behind my back, you can keep it to yourself. Like you said, what good would it do me to know? But promise me that after we're married—it can be a year later, or five years, whatever you need it to be—you'll tell me what she said about me. So I know what I'm dealing with for the rest of my life."

"Deal," Terry said, perhaps too quickly. He was glad she'd said, "for the rest of my life."

)

Virginia Beach, Virginia

They were greeted at his parents' house with warm embraces, cries of "congratulations" and "welcome to the family Beth," and glasses of champagne. Terry's nephew Jake stepped forward and handed Beth an envelope that he urged her to open. Inside was a handmade card everyone had signed, including Izzy the dog. Beth was so touched she had to press her hands to her eyes to stop rising tears. Her honest emotion borne of relief at not being immediately criticized went over well, and Terry's mother ushered her into the living room to sit on a loveseat beside Terry and tell everyone about their engagement. Somewhere in the telling she realized that they had not heard the story before: Terry hadn't told them how he'd waited until they were in one of the most beautiful places in the world and the setting sun turned the sky shades of pink and red. She wondered if he'd left it for her on purpose, so that in her telling she could convey the depth of her love for him.

She did her best, and she thought at least Terry's sister Ginny was touched. His mother wore a cordial smile but was otherwise unreadable. Ginny's husband Andrew's smile was alarmingly similar to his mother-in-law's, but he had little to say. Beth supposed he was preoccupied with work or something. Terry's father had obviously started drinking before their arrival, so Beth included him as she looked from one to the other during her telling but didn't bother to try to figure out what he was thinking.

After the friendly start, dinner proceeded without incident. Beth made sure that three out of four of her sips of beverage were water so the maid refilled her wine glass only once, not several times like on her last visit. She was glad that questions for Terry about the deal he and Jeff were looking for lasted through the salad and well into entrée. When that topic petered out Andrew was quizzed and provided an amusing narrative about a recent case. As dessert was served Ginny asked Beth about her new job. She tried hard to downplay the St Martin assignment and focus on the steep learning curve. Either it worked, or nobody cared, because by the time they had finished their spice cake they had also run out of questions.

Thirty-three

Dickinson Bay, Antigua

"*I*t's the best lead I've had in weeks. I have to follow up on it. I'll be there one day later, that's all," Hunter said before pausing to take a breath. Parker was already starting in again, though.

"—incredibly irresponsible. You know mom has a luncheon planned in your honor? We have tickets to the Nutcracker—they're are almost impossible to get! I cannot believe you're doing this last minute."

"I know bro. I'm sorry. I'll call mom and apologize. Maybe she can postpone the luncheon—"

"Seriously? On Christmas Eve? Are you crazy?"

"Probably. Look, I have to do this. I have to take a day to search for her on St. Thomas, since I have to stop there anyway. I was lucky to change my flight, by the way, it might have been sold out."

The sound that came through the phone was unintelligible, and Hunter realized he should not have expected his brother to sympathize with his luck in a change that Parker disagreed with vehemently.

)

Virginia Beach, Virginia

Back in Terry's car Beth eased her feet out of her shoes and let her head loll back.

"I didn't think it went that badly," Terry said as he craned his neck to see behind them and back the car out of the driveway. He paused before facing forward, giving her shoulder a playful shove. "Okay?"

She raised her head and smiled at him. "I'm okay. Relieved it's over, and a little tired."

"Ah," he said, refocusing on the road and accelerating.

"Just 'ah'?"

"For now." Was his enigmatic reply. Beth let her head drop back into the space between headrest and window and shut her eyes. The car's humming engine and gentle motion lulled her into something close to a doze for a few minutes. When the car turned she felt a twinge in her neck. She raised her head and looked around.

"Where are we?"

"This is the Chesapeake Bay Bridge Tunnel. Ever crossed over it? Or under it?"

"No. To both. I didn't go out in the ocean on the way south, remember?"

"Sorry I wasn't there. But yes, I do remember. You weren't too far from here when you called me that first time."

"I wondered if that was going to come up on one of these trips. It was further south, in North Carolina. Anyway, why are we on the Chesapeake Bay Bridge Tunnel? What is a bridge tunnel anyway?"

"Really?" He glanced at her.

"The why or the what?" She asked, sincerely not knowing what he was skeptical about

"You don't know what it is?"

"I know what it is. Two bridges and a tunnel?"

"Nope. Three causeways, one bridge, and two tunnels."

"Right."

They rode in silence over the first of the causeways. The two-lane road narrowed down to one as they plunged down an incline into the first tunnel.

"So you're not going to tell me why?"

"Not quite yet, no." He glanced at her, his grin mischievous.

"Okay then."

The car rose back up to the next causeway and hummed along it in light traffic. Brake lights shone ahead as they approached the next tunnel, but it was nothing more than the natural reaction to the lanes merging. A few minutes later they were leaving the bridge—which did rise higher above the water than the causeways.

They crossed Fisherman Island, according to a sign that flashed by, and exited the Bridge Tunnel, passing the tollbooth for the lanes on the other side. Terry drove a couple miles up the highway and slid into a left turn lane. Beth waited patiently, certain that an explanation was coming soon, and also certain that it would be a nice one.

They proceeded along a dark road between agricultural fields for a few more minutes before entering the outskirts of a town. Beth soon realized it wasn't the outskirts—it was the entirety of a very small town. At last Terry parked in front of a large Victorian house with a porch light on. He got out of the car and came around to open her door. She was struck by the scent of the ocean and inhaled a deep breath as she stood up.

"We are in Cape Charles. This is the Sea Breeze Inn. It's a long drive home, so I thought we'd spend the night here, have Sunday brunch, and drive home up the Eastern Shore. It'll take a little longer, but we have all day."

"This is why I agreed to marry you. I can't begin to thank you for this."

"I don't know. Let's see if you can't get creative." Terry chuckled as he wrapped his arm around her shoulders and guided her up the walk.

)

Cape Charles, Virginia

Beth's gratitude extended right up until she stretched out on the bed in their quaint upstairs room. She was wearing the oversized t-shirt that Terry had secretly packed for her. By the time Terry came out of the bathroom she was asleep.

The rising sun warmed their room and dappled light shining through the lacy curtains onto their faces woke them. Beth recalled her deferred and made up for it with very tender attention to her lover. It was late morning when they descended to the wrap-around porch where other guests were enjoying the inn's brunch.

Traffic was light when they got back in the car and Terry pointed it north along narrow lanes that had been unpaved farm roads not long ago. Views of the Chesapeake Bay came and went as they passed through un-named seaside settlements in between modern housing developments with marinas.

"This feels like an area undergoing change," Beth said. They were at a stoplight and she was looking out at a development of enormous modern houses with no mature trees and bright green lawns. It was out of place, as if it was inhabited by robot people, or eternally happy zombies. On the other side of the road a lovely old wood frame, singled house was gradually settling into rubble and kindling, the porch supports had collapsed, the vibrant colors faded to uniform grey. "Why couldn't someone restore that one instead of building all those?"

Terry glanced over at the derelict, then refocused on the red light. "It's too far gone. Sad."

Beth sighed, studying the old house. Sometimes while watching weekend **PBS** do-it-yourself shows she imagined restoring an old place—not like that one, but something with a straight roofline. Then she reminded herself she had an old boat and chastised herself for forgetting her life choices.

"I know you passed through the bay very quickly last year. You didn't have time to experience sailing here."

"Yeah. I was running out of time to get south."

"*Trouble* would be a good Bay boat. The draft's not too deep, she's easy to anchor—most of the time."

"We've talked about this. I need to sell *Trouble* to help pay for the new boat." Beth sounded more adamant than she needed to because she wasn't ready to have this conversation, to settle her debt to Terry before marrying him.

"Stay with me for a minute. What's wrong with having two boats for a while? *Double Trouble* here in the Chesapeake Bay and the new one in the islands. I'm afraid you'll be unhappy in Georgetown if you can't go sailing without having to fly to the islands. We have this huge body of water right here. We should use it." His words couldn't have been timed better; as he finished speaking the road took a turn and they had a view of a peaceful, secluded creek with enough room for a boat to anchor. Even though it was winter, and the water was empty, Beth easily imagined waking up on a boat anchored there, listening to the birds greeting the sunrise, diving into the water for a swim …

"It's a summer place. We'd have to store her all winter."

"The season is pretty long around here—longer than New York. We could start sailing in April and keep on through

November. Long weekends exploring all the little creeks and inlets—look at the chart, there are hundreds. Maybe thousands."

Beth smiled at his enthusiastic argument.

"I looked into the cost. We can get a slip in a marina south of Annapolis for a lot less than the ones there. It's a great jumping off point for going north or south in the bay. You could take your colleagues sailing, too."

"You're devious. Making it an asset for my job is not fair."

"Think about it though: how many on your team? Five? You can take them all on a team building daysail."

Beth pictured her co-workers aboard *Trouble* taking orders from her to trim the sails. It was an appealing notion, not because she wanted to boss them around, but for the chance to show them what she excelled at.

"What about the new boat expenses? It would defer my being able to pay my share for years."

"There is no 'your share.' It's our boat. They're both our boats."

Terry fell silent and focused on driving while Beth continued to think. He had always said *Trouble* was her boat. This was the first time he'd laid any claim on her. But rather than feeling threatened by this change, Beth felt an overwhelming sense of comfort in the state of unity he described. She wanted him to feel he had a stake in *Trouble*, and to make joint decisions about her as well as the new boat.

"Let's think about the logistics. We can consider bringing *Trouble* back from the islands in the spring."

Terry glanced over, his expression converting from surprise to delight as he took her hand in his and squeezed it.

"Okay. Let's see how to work it into the rest of the plans."

Thirty-four

St. Thomas, US Virgin Islands

*O*ver the next week Beth spent all of her spare time planning their sail from St. Thomas to St. Martin, making a list of supplies for *Trouble*, and researching where they could shop when they got to St. Thomas. She simply couldn't bring herself to buy basic non-perishables at island rates, so she started to buy things like coffee and soap with the intention of carrying them in a checked bag. She added a couple strings of battery powered twinkle lights and a fake pine garland with red bows tucked in with her clothing so Terry would be surprised.

She gathered the valuable sailing gear that had somehow dispersed itself all over the house since their return from Antigua. The pile of food, electronics, charts, safety gear, and other supplies she started in the corner of the den grew and grew until she knew they would have to take two checked bags each. It was more luggage than she'd ever used, but Terry just dug out two more duffel bags from somewhere in the basement.

As the days flew by Beth became very glad she'd told the marina to prepare *Trouble* rather than planning to do it when they got there. Raj agreed to enough days off to move *Trouble*, but not enough to do all the necessary preparation. The sail would, at minimum, take three days. With of the Christmas holiday they would have five days from their arrival on St. Thomas to when she wanted to reach St. Martin. That would have her in place well ahead of her meeting on the second of January—a buffer in case bad weather delayed their departure.

Terry took care of travel arrangements, including a rental car for their two days on St. Thomas. By the time they walked out of the airport terminal into oppressive, humid heat, she was glad to pile all their luggage into the trunk and settle into the passenger seat with the air conditioning blasting at her face.

Terry took the wheel and navigated along the island roads to the marina. They'd made the same trip by taxi a month ago when they stopped to check on *Trouble* on their way to Antigua. This trip felt different because they were going to use *Trouble*, not just look at her sitting forlornly on the hard. The closer they got, the more Beth's mind buzzed with anticipation. She was looking forward to all the chores they faced, like flushing and refiling the water tanks, scrubbing months of accumulated dirt off the decks, and putting on the sails.

There she was, *Double Trouble*, floating again. The mast was stepped, the standing rigging all in place. The heavy yellow power cord was connected to an outlet on the dock and to the fitting on *Trouble*'s stern. Before beginning to load their luggage, Beth opened up the cabin, climbed down the ladder, and went to the power control panel at the navigation station. Terry climbed down behind her and started opening hatches and port lights.

"How's it look?" he asked, coming out of the forward berth.

"Battery charger is working, batteries are topped up. Cuban bilge pump," she flipped a switch and they heard a familiar ca-thunk, ca-thunk, ca-thunk, "works. I'll flip on all the lights, instruments, stove, and stuff and we'll check them as we go. I don't remember how much propane we had."

"Me either. Another item for the list."

They took one of the marina-supplied dock carts to the rental car and Terry unloaded all of their luggage while Beth went to the marina office to check in with Mr. Henderson. They met on the dock and returned to *Trouble*, Beth walking next to the cart with a hand on top to keep the luggage from shifting.

By the time they had stowed their personal gear and the supplies and spare parts from their luggage *Trouble*'s cabin was still bare—at least compared to when they were living aboard for months on end.

"I don't want to deal with shopping today. Can we put on the sails and stuff, and go to dinner? We can get out there shopping first thing."

"That makes sense to me—we'll think of more things we need anyway."

They spent the rest of the afternoon checking over all of the boat systems beyond what the marina crew had done. Beth hauled the entire anchor rode out of the anchor locker and inspected the connection to the boat and to the anchor. Terry made his way around the entire boat with a screwdriver, tightening every hose clamp he could find. Beth lit the oven and each of the stove burners to make sure they worked. She checked the propane tank and added it to her shopping list.

"One thing we should have picked up," Terry said, emerging from the cabin with his screwdriver to see Beth hosing the decks.

"What's that?"

"Cold beer."

"Damn. You're so right." Beth looked toward shore and Terry followed her gaze to the market that was part of the marina complex. He set the screwdriver on the cockpit table, took his wallet out of the pocket of his shorts, and checked the cash compartment.

"I'm on it," he said.

Beth grinned and watched him stride up the dock before resuming her hosing.

)

The next morning they set out with their lists. They bypassed the gourmet market in the marina in favor of a larger grocery store in Charlotte Amalie and several smaller specialty shops for bread, produce, and other local specialties. They stopped at a ship's chandlery for the last few spare parts and other boat items that Beth hadn't gotten into their luggage. By early afternoon everything was on board and they were ravenous, so they adjourned to the restaurant in the marina.

"What else do we need to do?" Terry asked after the waitress took their order.

"Sail to the BVI?" Beth replied.

"Are we ready to go?"

Beth nodded, lifting her sandwich with both hands. "It's not like we're heading into the outback. If we realize we forgot something, or something goes wrong with *Trouble*, we're not going to be far from services. At least not until we head across the Anegada passage to St. Martin.

Terry spooled pasta onto his fork as he thought about it. "I've realized over the last few weeks that I've never had to think about getting a boat ready. Jeff takes care of *Grace* for races, and with you I've always had the luxury of walking aboard and asking where to stow my gear."

"Come on, that's not true. You've done a hundred maintenance projects on *Trouble*. Yes, while we were traveling, but that counts. You know as well as I do what the boat needs, and how to do it. What do you think we have left to do?"

"I just thought of something!" He said, putting down his sandwich. He was genuinely pleased with himself, which made Beth wrack her brains for what she could have missed. His mouth twisted into a very self-satisfied grin. "You can't think of it, can you?"

"Just tell me."

"We need to inflate the dinghy and check for holes."

Beth's brows rose, and she looked out across the docks toward where *Trouble* floated. The dinghy was deflated, rolled up, and secured on the foredeck in front of the mast. They'd had to work around it when they'd put on the jib yesterday.

"Well damn, you're right. We checked the outboard, but I never thought about the dinghy. Assuming it's not leaking air, we can knock that out this afternoon. Tomorrow we can clear out with customs and immigration, return the car, and sail over to the West End of Tortola. If we can, we'll check in and out there at the same time. We'll go around to one of the anchorages on the eastern end of the BVIs before crossing over to St. Martin. The weather seems to be holding for us, but we'll want to get a positive report before we head out. It's about ninety miles, at least eighteen hours."

"Christmas at sea." Terry said, then took a bite of his pasta.

"We can delay, spend it in the BVI, then go."

"Or," Terry paused, waiting until Beth set down her sandwich. "Or we could clear out, return the car, and go anchor out tonight."

"A very appealing option, but what about the dinghy?"

Terry shrugged, "We'll pump it up once we get anchored. If it's leaking, we have a patch kit—didn't I see a fresh one in your giant pile?"

Beth grinned. "You did. Okay. Let's finish up and get *Trouble*'s paperwork."

)

Customs and immigration went smoothly. If anything, Terry got the impression that the customs officer was glad to see *Trouble* move on after her extended stay on his island.

After returning the rental car, they took a taxi the short distance from the airport to the marina. As the taxi drove away, Beth stopped on the hot asphalt parking lot and took a deep breath, earning her a puzzled look from Terry.

"We're back," she said. "Just us and *Trouble* and the wide ocean. Let's go!"

Terry repressed his thought that their freedom was temporary, and she'd be working hard come January. But as they strode down the dock, Beth's step quicker than usual, he realized that maybe this is what "back" was going to be in the future. Them and a boat and the wide ocean, working when and where they needed or wanted to, including while on board. That had been Beth's plan when she first set out and she'd acted on it with some success. But he'd never, until this moment, thought about making the same kind of arrangement for his work with Jeff. Was it remotely possible? He was going to spend time over the next few days thinking it through. Suddenly as energized as Beth, he grabbed her hand and matched her pace down the dock toward *Trouble*.

)

St. Thomas, US Virgin Islands

The ancient school bus rattled to a halt at the side of the road and the door opened with a rust-induced shriek. As if fleeing from a disaster, passengers gushed out, parcels, chicken cages, small children, and goats in their arms. Three school boys in pressed uniforms preceded the white man with the rucksack and stained canvas hat. He stopped when he stepped off, earning himself a tap on the shoulder from the woman behind him on the bottom step. Glancing over his shoulder with a muttered "sorry," he moved away from the bus.

Despite the shabbiness of the public transport, the street before him was lined with prosperous looking shops, small office buildings, and a few cafés where wait staff were opening umbrellas to shade the outdoor tables. With a slight smile of anticipation, Hunter started down the street, which curved and sloped slightly toward the waterfront. This was his fourth marina in Charlotte Amalie, the capital of St. Thomas. He had once again under estimated the enormity of his task. There were thousands of sailboats around this island and its neighbors, and he only had the one day to search. He'd decided to concentrate on the marinas because of something the cruisers had said—Beth was taking her boat here. It had sounded like she intended to leave it. The irony of finding the boat, but not the woman, was not lost on him as he strode down the street past the shops and cafes, headed for the entrance to the next marina.

After receiving suspicious looks from people while he wandered the docks in other marinas, he had resorted to openly asking about *Double Trouble* rather than searching. He stepped into the marina office, which served as a mail drop for sailors and a workspace since it had wifi. Two boaters sitting at bare desks with laptops glanced up and immediately returned to their computers. Another man sat at a cluttered desk with papers spread on it.

"Can I help you?" he asked.

Hunter introduced himself and explained that he was looking for Beth Anderson and *Double Trouble*. When the man nodded, he didn't realize what it meant. When he spoke, Hunter's awful luck became clear.

"She left yesterday. Sailing to St. Martin, she said. We got the boat into shape for the passage."

"Yesterday?"

"Yes. Changed her mind and decided to leave a day early. Were they expecting you?"

Hunter swallowed down growing anger. *One day late? One fucking day?*

"No, no. I just hoped to catch her. St. Martin, huh?"

"Yes. She didn't say whether she'd be coming back to us, or when."

"Well, that's it then. Thank you for your help. Merry Christmas to you."

"You too. Have a pleasant day."

Standing outside in the shade of the building's eaves Hunter dropped his backpack to the ground, his shoulders slumping.

One day. She'd planned to be here and changed her mind. Now she's out there on the water again, somewhere between here and St. Martin. *Another damn island to search.*

Inhaling a deep breath, Hunter straightened himself and took out his phone to check the time. He had a flight to Texas to catch. The notion of changing his flight to St. Martin flickered through his mind but he squelched it. He needed to see Parker and his family.

Thirty-five

St. Thomas, US Virgin Islands

"*W*oohoo!" Beth shouted, one fist raised in the air, as she steered the heavy, black rubber dinghy in a tight circle. Standing on *Trouble*'s stern, Terry grinned and shook his head.

"Dinghy donuts? Really?" he shouted back.

Beth opened her fist to wave, although the outboard motor's roar drowned out whatever he'd said, then straightened her course and steered across the anchorage to enjoy the wind in her hair. She laughed out loud, reveling in the feeling of freedom as the resilient boat bounced over low waves.

After a few minutes she slowed the engine to an idle and turned the dinghy around, pausing to take a look at the other boats in the anchorage. Beth had lived here aboard *Trouble* for a few months last year. She recognized a few boats as belonging to people who were permanent live-aboards. She also recognized a couple boats from other harbors where she alone, or with Terry, had spent time over the last year. The cruising community was a vagabond one, but not large, so it wasn't unusual to meet the same people over and over. At this time of year, the anchorage held a number of boats on their way further south, having come from the east coast of the US or the Bahamas over the last few weeks. That had been Beth about a year ago.

Engine on forward idle, she puttered from one familiar boat to another. She stopped to exchange a few words—a quick catchup and then move on—when she found sailors aboard. Several mentioned a Christmas Eve beach party. She thanked them and said she and Terry would be heading on tomorrow to get to St. Martin in a few days. By the time she returned to *Trouble* and secured the dinghy to the stern cleat, Terry was lounging in the cockpit with a beer, wearing one of the faded sets of swim trunks that he'd worn for most of their months cruising. Both of their towels were sitting on a lazarette.

"I'll be with you in a sec," Beth told him, climbing below to get ready for a swim.

)

She was about to dive overboard a few minutes later when her phone, tucked into a drink holder near the cockpit table, rang. She stepped back into the cockpit and picked it up. Seeing the caller ID on the front, she flipped it open.

"Merry Christmas Burt! It's wonderful to hear from you."

"Merry Christmas to you Beth. I hope I'm not interrupting a family gathering?"

"Not at all. You're delaying my swim, but it's okay. Terry and I are aboard *Trouble* anchored in St. Thomas. We're on our way to St. Martin."

Sitting on *Sandcastle*'s aft deck looking out at the boats anchored in Dickinson Bay, Burt's eyes widened in surprise. He'd found Hunter here working in a beach bar and felt comfortable knowing Beth was far away in Washington. But she was much closer than that, and vulnerable.

"Last I recall you were heading back to DC to restock your treasury. Are you already back to the cruising life? Did you hit the lottery?"

"Wouldn't that be nice? No, I'm going to be working from St. Martin after the holidays."

"You've been employed with these people for how long? A few weeks? And they're letting you telecommute from the islands?"

"They're sending me to work with a client. The Antigua job went well, so they sent me back to work with another one. I'm feeling my way, this is not what I was trained for. But the people on my team at Broadhead say they have confidence in me, so I'm doing my best."

"Wow, Beth, this is tremendous. But I'm not surprised. You don't realize how much you know. How long will you be on St. Martin?"

"Why? Thinking of dropping over for a drink?" Beth teased. He could make the trip in a matter of hours on *Sandcastle*.

"Maybe. I'm not doing anything else and I'm getting bored."

"Terry's aboard through New Year's. We're sailing *Trouble* from St. Thomas together. My first meeting with the client is on January second. I expect to be working with her for at least two weeks, so I'll be there through mid-January."

"Oh, I get it now, you're cheaper to send because you don't need a hotel."

"Very funny. I'm going to move into a marina while I'm working with the client. Broadhead will pay for it. I guess it's cheaper than a hotel, though."

"Most likely, at least a hotel that you'd be comfortable in. Although I know you're more comfortable aboard *Trouble* no matter what. Well, I'll let you know if I'm coming your way. Give Terry my regards, will you?"

"I sure will Burt. I hope you do, it would be good to see you. Merry Christmas."

Burt ended the call and set down his phone, a satisfied smile curling the corners of his mouth. The Texan was here on Antigua, and Beth would soon be on St. Martin. It would be better if she was in D.C., but this was okay. He could go keep Beth company on St. Martin and be there if the Texan happened to show up.

Beth folded her phone and stuck it back in the cup holder, then snatched it back up and flipped it open. She had once again forgotten to tell Burt she and Terry were engaged. Although she'd had a couple more conversations with her parents and Trish about it, preparation for this trip had pushed her plan to email all of her friends right out of her head. She resolved to do that once she got to St. Martin, where she was sure she could find plenty of wifi hot spots.

"Are you coming or what?" Terry's voice called from the water behind *Trouble*.

Beth closed the phone and put it in the cup holder. She climbed up on the gunwale and spotted Terry treading water below her.

"Burt called. He says Merry Christmas."

"Merry Christmas to him."

"He's gone now, and I forgot to tell him our big news again. I'll call him back later." As she spoke, she climbed over the lifeline and let her toes hang over the toe-rail. Then she jumped into the air and executed a dive into the crystalline water.

⁂

"That was yummy," Beth said, patting her stomach as she leaned back to see the stars beyond the edge of the canvas bimini that shaded the cockpit from the sun, but was inconvenient at night. Terry had grilled steaks to a perfect medium rare and served them with canned potatoes sautéed with garlic and a spinach salad. He'd opened one of the few bottles of wine that he'd bought on their shopping trip—he planned to do a real wine run when they got to St. Martin. Watching him pick the bottles Beth had begged him not to go overboard, so to speak, or they'd end up having to carry, or ship, it back to Washington like they had the last time. He'd conceded her point and exercised great restraint.

"Thank you. I was afraid my grilling skills might be rusty."

"Sharp as ever," Beth sighed.

"Here's an idea," Terry said. Beth raised her head to look across the cockpit at him. "It's what, about a hundred miles to St. Martin?"

"Something like that."

"So, between twenty-four and thirty-six hours?"

"Depending on conditions and how skillful we are at sailing," Beth smiled. He could see she had guessed where he was going with his idea.

"And if we stop in the British Virgin Islands, we have to do customs and immigration."

"We should."

That caught him off guard. He had never known Beth to willingly cheat the authorities. Except for Petit St. Vincent a few months ago, but everyone did that. No, he decided, she wasn't suggesting they stop over in the BVI without following the government formalities.

"Let's sail straight through. It's hardly a long trip in the grand scheme of things—people cross oceans on boats like *Trouble*. Is there anything we haven't done to prepare her for it? I mean it's forty or fifty miles more than our original plan, right?"

"Something like that. I'd have to plot a course. But yes, it's not crazy. We have to be prepared for two days—and at least one night—of watches. If the weather holds and we set out tomorrow, we'd arrive on St. Martin late on Christmas Eve. We might have to anchor out under quarantine all the next day, if none of their offices are open."

"And that's a problem why?"

)

Anegada Passage

Terry was fighting off sleep when the squall blew in from the east, coming so fast he couldn't have spotted it in the dark early enough to prepare even if he had been watching. *Trouble*'s bow slewed to the left to point into the first gust of wind and the sails shuddered and flapped like wash rags. As boat speed dropped to nothing, the needle on the wind speed indicator gauge swung from fifteen to thirty, then inched up to thirty-five. But Terry was too startled to pay attention to the instruments.

The boat lurched on confused waves. He grabbed the binnacle and swung in behind the wheel to switch off the auto pilot that had been holding *Trouble* on course. He put his hands on the wheel, gently and then more firmly turning it to the right. As the gust passed, the bow responded to the rudder and the sails refilled. *Trouble* surged forward again as another gust howled through the rigging.

This one carried the inevitable rain, and Terry was not wearing his foul weather gear. Within seconds his light fleece was drenched, but his discomfort was irrelevant. He fought the helm, trying to keep *Trouble* sailing under too much sail for the velocity of the gusts. He managed to keep her from rounding up into the wind again, but instead the pressure on the mainsail caused her to heel so much water lapped up over the toe rail on the leeward side. Terry braced his right foot on the side of the lazarette, which was closer to horizontal than vertical, and fought the wheel to the left, surrendering the bow to the wind. But it was for naught. Another gust, as strong as the first one, thundered through and with an ear-splitting ripping sound *Trouble* straightened right up, sails once again flapping like snapped wash cloths.

The first gust did not so much wake Beth as roll her over on the double forward berth into the lower corner. She rolled back as the boat straightened and shuddered under the flapping sails. When the motion returned to normal, with a normal amount of heel, her sleeping brain settled as well—a momentary round-up was not worth her concern. But as *Trouble* heeled over again, rolling Beth onto the side bulkhead, Terry's book—fortunately a paperback—fell from the shelf on the opposite side and hit her in the chest.

"Ouch!"

Discomfort dragged her toward wakefulness and the boat straightening once again, the irritating sound of flapping sails truly ending her rest. With a sigh, she heaved her legs around to the edge of the bunk and inched off of it. Her feet landed half on her shoes, half on the bare floor. She wriggled her shoes around to get the toes aligned. Standing, she reached for a fleece hanging on the back of the door, pulled it on over her t-shirt, and took a couple steps while working her feet into her shoes. Rain falling through the companionway formed a puddle on the floor. She picked up her foul weather jacket from where she'd left it on the navigation desk seat and peered out into the cockpit as she shrugged into it.

Terry was trimming the jib, grinding a winch with one hand and tailing the line from it with the other. In the glow of the instruments Beth could see that the rain had already turned his light blue fleece dark and plastered his hair to his forehead. She zipped her jacket and raised the hood, then layered her safety harness with the built-in auto-inflating life jacket over it. She climbed the ladder. Terry saw her and paused in his grinding.

"The main's ripped. Trying to get the jib in."

Beth stared up into the rain at the boom, which was bobbing and swinging, fittings rattling, loops of line cutting arcs through the air. The sail was flapping so hard she could not tell where or how bad the tear was.

"I can't see it. Where did it rip?"

"About a third of the way up, belly of the sail. Did you have the yard check the sails?"

Beth's eyes snapped from the sail back to her fiancé, surprised at the anger in his voice. He was grinding again, and now she saw that his expression was somewhere between anger and fear. She couldn't take time to think about it now, but this could be the first time he'd experienced something like this at night, and being alone on watch magnified the impact. The shaking boat and wildly flapping sails played upon her nerves too, but her reaction was to plan her next steps and then take them carefully, one by one. No more than a second had passed when she reached for the end of the lazy jib sheet and hauled on it, taking up the slack. That reduced the sail's flapping some. With that line in hand she moved across the cockpit and grabbed the other sheet to haul it in too. A fair amount of the banging had been coming from these heavy lines slapping against the mast, the deck, and the shrouds. Beth peered forward in the darkness and realized she couldn't see the forward sail because Terry had already gotten most of it rolled up on the forestay.

"You're almost there. I'll secure these," she said. He responded with a grunt. She left him to finish and moved to the main sheet mounted on the top of the cabin at the front of the cockpit. The sail had been trimmed in close already, so there wasn't much slack to pull in, but she did it anyway. The boom and sail kept rattling and banging, but now Beth could make out the tear. Her spirits fell. It was huge, a horizontal rip spanning almost the entire width. Terry was right: she should have had the yard look at the sails. Or she should have done it herself. As Terry coiled the cleated jib furling line, she prepared the main halyard to lower the sail. Her mind darted from one option to another: *we have a full tank of diesel; the jib might be in good enough shape to keep using; is the tear in the main sail above the reef points?*

"We might be able to reef it," she said to Terry. "I can't quite tell if the third reef is above or below it. I'm going to go up and look. You handle the halyard. We'll either lower it all the way or reef it." As she spoke, she prepared the line for the third reef point—the one that would reduce the sail to the smallest possible size without taking it down completely. She reached inside the companionway and grabbed from their hook the four lengths of nylon webbing they used to tie the sail down when it wasn't in use. "Okay?" she asked, looking over her shoulder since he hadn't responded.

"I'm sorry," he said. Now he looked guilty. "I shouldn't have said that."

Beth swallowed down the caustic response that came to mind. "We'll talk it through later. Let's get back underway first."

Terry nodded, lips pursing with concern for a moment before widening into a smile. "That's why you're the captain. I'm on the halyard."

Relief at his recovered equanimity washed over her as she climbed out of the cockpit and clipped her safety tether to the jackline that ran along the side deck from the aft cleat up to the bow. She climbed up next to the boom and grabbed a fitting on the underside, then reached for the back edge of the flapping sail.

"Okay, start lowering. I'll try to pull it down from back here."

She felt the sail's wild flapping change as the tension on it released, but it did not lower and no amount of pulling at the back edge helped.

"I've got to pull at the mast. Hang on," she shouted, carefully making her way back to the mast. Her tether moved along the jackline with her. She reached as high as she could and grabbed the forward edge of the sail, shoving her hand in between the sail and the mast. "I'm pulling. Give me some."

She nearly raised her feet off the deck, using most of her weight to drag the sail down a couple feet before repositioning her grip and doing it again. Her hood blew off, her hair became soaked, and she felt water drip down the back of her neck. The sail lay in flapping folds over the boom, the wind catching it and dragging it this way and that.

What a mess.

But at last she could see that the tear was right below the three grommets in the sail that formed the third reef point. That was both good and bad—it meant they could use the top part of the sail but setting up the reef was going to be difficult in these conditions.

"Stop!" she yelled. "Start hauling on the reef line."

Rarely used pulleys and line squealed, telling her he had heard her command. It would take a few minutes to haul the line, which brought the back edge of the sail down to the boom at a point in line with the grommets. While Terry did that, Beth grabbed the larger grommet sewn into the forward edge of the sail in line with the reef points and dragged it down. She needed to get it under the stainless steel hook mounted on the mast above the boom. She couldn't pull it down far enough.

"Terry, stop for a second. I need more slack on the halyard."

"On it," she heard faintly through the wind. Suddenly the sail lowered several more feet, folds of it collapsing onto her head. But she was able to get the fitting onto the hook.

"Stop! Take it back up some!" She yelled, pushing the folds of sail out of her way. The fitting would slip off the hook if the sail was too loose. She heard the halyard rattle in the mast as he raised it again, and the sail inched back up. "We're good, it's all you now. Get that reef line tight!"

As Terry ground the reef line in, Beth inched along the boom to the first of the three grommets and took one of the sail ties from around her neck. She wrapped her arms around the folds of sail and the boom, finding the grommet on the other side with her left hand and pushing the wedge-cut end of the sail tie through the tiny hole. She worked the sodden tie through the grommet, pulling on it with her left hand until it was more than half way through. Then she bundled up the mass of sail fabric and felt around with her right hand, still holding that end of the tie, until she found the top of the boom. She passed the left side of the sail tie through the space between sail and boom, then tied the two ends together to create an ugly mass of restrained sailcloth hanging beside the boom.

One down.

By the time she had repeated the process with the second and third sail ties Terry had the reef line tight. The remaining sail flapped above her head, in, she realized, a much lighter breeze. The squall had passed. *Figures.*

"What time is it anyway?" she asked as she climbed back into the cockpit. The reefed main sail was an ugly bundle, but at least they still had use of about two-thirds of it. Terry was already preparing to redeploy the jib. He glanced at his watch.

"Three twenty."

Beth moved to the jib sheet that she had secured earlier and released it.

"Bring out about half to balance the main."

"Right."

She watched him manage both the working jib sheet that pulled the sail out, and the furling line that he used to keep it from pulling out all the way. When half the sail was flying, he stopped hauling and cleated the furling line so that no more could unroll.

"Auto pilot is on," he said. "Do you want the helm?"

Beth chuckled, hoping to soften his stressed expression and tone. She recognized his response: he'd had a fright and he wanted her to take over. But there was no way he was going to abandon his responsibility for the watch just because of a squall. When she'd sailed alone she'd had to suck it up and carry on. She wasn't letting him off the hook just because he wasn't alone.

"You kidding? It's still your watch. You take it, put her on course and I'll trim the sails for you."

The tension visible in his eyes did soften. Although her command was not what he wanted to do, it did show that she still trusted him—and that had been as much a part of her intent as making him see things through. He cleated the jib sheet before moving behind the helm, then turned off the auto pilot and rotated the wheel to starboard, watching the compass.

"I doubt that we've drifted too far off course, but I'll check it once we're back underway," Beth said as she eased the main sheet, trimming the sail for the close reach they'd been on before. She moved to the jib and did the same.

"Hey," Terry said when she had cleated the sheet and was trying to see the sails in the darkness.

Where's the flashlight?

"Yeah?"

"So, that was scary, and you were pretty awesome. Just sayin'."

"Just sayin', huh?"

"Yeah. I feel foolish. I know, logically, we weren't in terrible danger as long as we took care of it quickly. But my emotional response overrode logic. I couldn't think of the next step, other than holding her into the wind and getting rid of the jib."

"We have been very lucky with weather, so you haven't been through very many squalls. We haven't done that many night passages. I guess I've been through this kind of thing—well, not the sail tearing, but the squall—in daylight often enough to go on automatic and deal with it, day or night."

"Yeah. I guess I never thought about it—what I'd do all by myself. So as I said, I was out of line. It was a moment of 'this isn't my fault! Who do I blame!' It was totally unacceptable."

"Assigning blame is never useful," Beth agreed, "especially not in the heat of the moment, before dealing with it. But in fact, I'm the captain and it's my boat, and I should have a better sense of the condition of the sails. I've been using them since I got the boat and I don't know how old they were then. I've gotten used to just sailing and not thinking about them. Shame on me. Okay?"

"Okay. There are plenty of sail lofts in St. Martin."

"Don't get me started on the expense. It's fuckin' three-thirty in the morning."

"Sorry."

"Love you."

Thirty-six

Marigot Bay, St. Martin

*T*he sun was low in on the western horizon when Beth steered *Trouble* around Pointe Falaise into Marigot Bay on the northwest shore of St. Martin. The sight of land a couple hours before had been at once a relief and a disappointment for Beth: she was tired of living life divided into four-hour watches, but land meant dealing with strangers and life ashore, and she loved the simplicity of two people and a boat.

They were both tired after more than forty hours of sailing. In fact, even *Trouble* felt sluggish, but Beth knew that was because she labored under reduced sails. As they glided along past the larger boats anchored in deeper water further from shore Beth was sure they were getting curious looks. The breeze in the mid-teens was perfect for *Trouble*'s full mainsail and jib, so her reefed sails had to be a puzzle to every sailor who noticed.

Seeing an open space, Beth signaled to Terry, who was crouched over the jib winch, furling line in hand. Beth turned *Trouble*'s bow into the wind, and while Terry rolled the jib the rest of the way up she started the engine. She had yet to try sailing all the way into an anchorage and anchoring under sail. This was not the time.

When the jib was rolled up Terry moved to the front of the cockpit and took up the main sail halyard. He looked back over his shoulder at her expectantly. Beth corrected *Trouble*'s angle to the wind so the bow was pointing into it, then nodded at Terry. He released the halyard and climbed out of the cockpit and up to the mast where he hauled down on the sail. Once the rest of the cloth was laying over the boom on top of the already secured folds, Beth revved the engine to slow cruising speed and steered toward the area where other boats about the same size as *Trouble* were anchored.

Terry went forward to the anchor well on the bow. Beth watched him lift and secure the lid open against the bow pulpit, then lean down into the space to do something. She refocused her attention on the boats around her, looking for a good spot to anchor. Presently Terry stood up and leaned over the bow.

"Patches of sand," he called back to her. She nodded. They wanted to drop the anchor in sand where it would dig in. Finding a good spot with room on all sides between her and other boats, Beth let *Trouble* glide upwind to the spot where the anchor should go.

"How's this?" Beth yelled. He stared down into the water and raised his left hand, gesturing for her to go that way. She did, giving the engine a tiny bit of power to force the turn, then easing off to let *Trouble* drift that way. Terry gradually raised his arm, indicating that the bow was coming over the spot he wanted. In a flash he bent down, lifted the shaft of the anchor, and let it run over the roller on the bow, dragging clanking links of chain with it. He drew more chain out of the anchor well and fed it out. Beth waited, felt the boat begin to move backward, and watched Terry. A minute later, when all of the chain was overboard and he was holding onto rope, he wrapped the rope around a cleat and held onto it, putting another wrap around the cleat as the line grew taut. Beth felt *Trouble* stop, her bow swinging to starboard. Terry looked back at Beth and she nodded and made a figure eight motion with one finger. He bent and properly secured the line on the cleat. Beth shifted the engine into reverse idle and *Trouble* immediately backed, then stopped. Smiling, Beth increased the engine power, at the same time staring off to starboard at one particular palm tree aligned with of the stanchions that held up *Trouble*'s lifelines. She knew that up on the bow Terry was staring at something on shore too. After thirty seconds their relative bearing to their chosen objects had not changed. The anchor was holding.

Beth checked the depth gauge and signaled with her fingers that it was fifteen feet. Terry nodded and bent down to uncleat the line and let out more rope. Beth shut off the engine and locked the wheel. She had finished coiling up all the lines when Terry came back from the bow.

"Nice job," he said, patting her on the butt.

"You too." She snaked her arm around behind him to return the pat.

"You know what I want most right now?" Terry plopped down on the lazarette and peeled off his gloves.

"A nap?" Beth asked, turning around to back down the companionway ladder.

"Exactly!" Terry replied with a laugh followed by a deep sigh.

"How about a beer first?"

"Yes, I'll amend my wish list."

"And I'll fulfill it."

A couple minutes later Beth returned from the galley with two cold beers. "Merry Christmas."

Terry took his as Beth settled on the lazarette opposite him. "This is probably the best Christmas present I've ever received."

"Yeah, I know what you mean. But speaking of Christmas presents, was that a way of admitting you don't have any with you?"

"Why? Do you?"

"Well …" Beth winced. She'd spent far too much time over the last couple weeks trying to decide on a present for him that would represent everything he meant to her. Finally, she'd given up. It wasn't possible. She couldn't afford it if she could figure out what it was. So she'd bought him new swim trunks, which were hardly romantic, but which he did need after living in his two old ones for months.

"Well, I have something for you," Terry said when she didn't go on. "You have to accept it even if you don't have my gift on board."

"Oh thank heavens! I do have something for you, I didn't want to embarrass you if you didn't."

Terry chuckled and took a sip of his beer. "Open them tomorrow?"

"Yes. Does your family open gifts on Christmas Eve?"

"No. No matter how good we thought our arguments were to our parents about opening just one."

"Pretty strict!"

"Yep. Builds character. What about your family?"

"Nope, nothing until Christmas morning. In fact, we couldn't open any wrapped gifts until everyone was up. But we could go through our stockings. I think Trish lets her kids open one gift the night before—I have no idea why she's indulging them." Beth chuckled and Terry smiled.

"So what island do you want to do for Christmas next year?" Beth asked.

"Good question. Let's sleep on it." He swung his legs up on to the settee to sit facing aft, his back against the cabin bulkhead with a view of anchored boats and the water. Beth did the same. They watched the sun slip behind distant clouds, then peek out, then paint more clouds in shades of red and coral as it set behind them.

"We need to get the mainsail off." Beth said between sips of beer.

"Not right now."

"No. But we have to check in with customs and immigration."

"They're closed. It's Christmas Eve. This half of St. Martin is French and mostly Catholic so they'll be closed tomorrow. Put up the quarantine flag and we'll go on Boxing Day."

Beth took another long sip of beer and let her head thump against the winch mounted on the cabin top behind her. The prospect of spending tomorrow on board in customs quarantine, swimming, sleeping, reading, and cooking Christmas dinner sounded amazing. "Deal. What's for dinner?"

)

Marigot, St. Martin

A catalog-perfect silver Christmas three decorated in blue and while glittered in front of floor-to-ceiling windows in a starkly modern great room. A handful of presents wrapped in matching colorful paper were tastefully arranged beneath it.

Virgine had dressed casually for Christmas morning in a deep green micro velour track suit with a gold zipper and piping on the pockets. Every hair, styled yesterday, was still in place thanks to the cotton cap she'd worn to bed. The tiny chip in the glossy polish of her left ring fingernail irritated her even though she knew nobody would notice. She would have Mathieu redo it later.

She crossed the room to her accustomed armchair—a Jean Prouve upholstered in light tan leather—and seated herself. Within seconds a young woman in a classic French maid's uniform appeared at her side, offering a cup and saucer on a silver tray.

"Thank you, Elise," she said as she took the cup and saucer.

"Madame," the maid muttered. She straightened and took a step backward before turning to walk back toward the kitchen.

Virgine took a sip of the coffee, already adjusted to her taste with cream and sugar, and sighed, eyes closed, as the aroma suffused her with energy. After a moment she opened her eyes and set the cup and saucer on the glass side table next to her chair. She raised both hands and clapped twice.

The maid returned along with Mathieu, two older men, and a much older woman. They stood in a row, arranged by age and rank, to one side so they did not block Virgine's view of the Christmas tree. She rose and stepped closer to the row to examine them. She took her time to give each one her attention for a full minute so they would not feel slighted.

Elise's uniform still had that stain on the apron despite Virgine's slap yesterday. As Virgine's left eyebrow arched, the maid's eyes dropped to the floor. It was Christmas morning. Discipline could be deferred for now. She examined Mathieu. At sixteen he was over six feet tall and seemed to be determined to continue growing. The woman smiled, her eyes fondling him, her lips parting in a lascivious smile that made Elise shiver. *Jealous? Perhaps.*

Virgine's gaze moved on to the man on Mathieu's right. He was shorter than Mathieu, a trait that did not inhibit his masculinity, the woman knew well. He returned her lascivious look with a frank, almost angry, stare. She ignored his expression as she examined his taupe cotton shirt and canvas trousers and found no fault. She moved on to the next man, a rugged outdoorsman with pocked skin, a close-cropped beard, and large hands accustomed to holding tools. She disliked the beard, but granted it because the skin beneath was worse. Finally, she turned her attention to the old woman. Her salt and pepper hair was properly brushed and controlled in a rudimentary bun this morning. *Good. A well-timed slap always works.* Her simple black dress had been pressed and her cook's apron was clean.

"Mathieu, please play Santa," she finally said, looking toward the base of the tree as she returned to her chair.

Mathieu stepped out of line and went to the Christmas tree. Crouching, he picked up one of the wrapped presents and read the tag on it. He rose and carried it back to the row of servants, handing it to the rugged looking man.

"Albert," he said as he handed it over. The man took it, eyes meeting Mathieu's for a moment before the boy turned away. The man carefully unfastened the wrapping paper and eased it from the box inside. Mathieu returned to the tree and stood waiting. Albert handed the wrapping paper to the man next to him and opened the unmarked brown cardboard box. Inside was a blade sharpening kit with whet stone and oil and soft rags. Albert half bowed at Virgine in her seat.

"Thank you, Madame."

She nodded. "Thank you for your service, Albert."

Mathieu bent to pick up another gift, checked the name, and brought it to the old woman. She repeated the ritual, opening her box to find a set of electric hair curlers.

One by one each member of staff opened their gift, passing the wrapping paper to one another so that in the end Elise was holding it all and each of them held their item in its bare box. In unison they concluded the annual ritual:

"Thank you, Madame. Merry Christmas."

"Thank you all. Merry Christmas," she replied, basking in the glow of their gratitude.

Thirty-seven

Marigot Bay, St. Martin

*T*he yellow quarantine flag flapped in *Trouble*'s rigging all Christmas day. They slept as late as the tropical heat allowed and enjoyed a breakfast of bacon and eggs with buttered toast in the cockpit. When she climbed down the companionway ladder to clean up, Beth found a wrapped gift on the dining table. She set down the plates she'd brought from the cockpit and hurried to the forward cabin to find Terry's present. He was in the galley when she got back.

"Want to open them now?"

"Let's do it!" Beth said, feeling like a little kid. Terry wiped his hands on a dish towel and joined her at the table. She'd wrapped the swim trunks without a box to make them easier to pack, but the wrapping paper had not travelled well. Terry took the limp package, eying it with mock suspicion.

"I had to fit it in with everything," Beth said, looking at the pristine wrapping on the box on the table. "I guess I could have done better."

"Stop it! It's fine. Easier to unwrap!" Terry suited action to words. The bright floral print tumbled out into his hands. He held the trunks up to admire them. "I love them!"

"Not too wild?"

"Not at all. They're great. Thank you." He wrapped his arms around her and found her lips, his kiss reinforcing his happiness with her gift. "Open yours." He said, releasing her.

Beth picked up the box. It was heavier than she expected, so she set it back down and found an edge of wrapping paper to tear at. The logo of a reputable optics company was revealed.

"New binoculars! Perfect!" Beth opened the box.

"*Trouble*'s are shot, and a skipper needs good binoculars. They have—"

"The built-in compass! I have always wanted these!" Beth finished for him. She wrapped her arms back around him for another kiss. "They're perfect. Thank you so much."

As this was a French island, and they had reasonable distance from the neighboring boats, they tumbled naked into the water to cool off, and stretched out in the cockpit slathered in sunscreen. Boat traffic was very light, although they did watch launches from the large yachts carrying parties of Christmas revelers ashore.

"I'll bet there's not a reservation to be had for lunch or dinner," Terry observed after watching one particularly overcrowded launch go by.

"We should make one for tomorrow night."

"Great idea. There's a restaurant I've been wanting to try for a long time."

"Here?"

"Yes, right here in Marigot Bay. I'll find it." He got up and stretched, smirking at her as she leered at his naked body. "Dinner for two at seven sound good?"

"Sounds great," she purred. He rolled his eyes and climbed down the companionway ladder. Beth's e-reader had fallen to her lap as she drifted off to sleep when he came back wearing a t-shirt and his new swim trunks. As he resumed his seat, she roused enough to look over at him.

"Cold?" she asked.

"Burning the delicate spots," he replied. "I made us reservations. It's supposed to be an excellent French restaurant. I hope it is."

After another round of paddling around in the water and drying in the sun, Beth brought her files up into the cockpit and settled in to read more of the background her team had prepared.

"Is that work?" Terry asked from his spot across from her.

"Yes. I know. But I'm anxious and this helps."

Terry smiled and returned to his own reading. The day drifted by, the shore boats going back and forth, the water refreshing when either of them decided to jump in, and the breeze gentle, but cooling. The only excitement was when two fast launches with colorful spinning lights departed the government dock and ran at speed to the northeast corner of the bay.

"I wonder what that's about," Beth said, then she put down her notes and went below to turn up the VHF radio, which was monitoring the hailing channel.

"Hear anything?" Terry called out a few minutes later when she didn't return. He'd heard a couple bursts of talk, but couldn't make out what was said.

"Nothing that I can understand—no boat putting out a distress call," Beth replied, standing at the base of the companionway ladder so he could hear her. "I don't know what channel the police use, probably not VHF 16."

In a few minutes she emerged from the cabin carrying both of their water bottles. She pressed his to his upper arm and he reached over with his other hand to grasp it.

"Thanks."

She stood for a few minutes looking over toward the northeast corner of the bay. She could see the bright lights on the two boats. They were standing off shore beyond the commercial port in that part of the bay. It was an uninviting stretch of shore with several tiny, rocky inlets between rocky outcropping. She raised her new binoculars and focused on the boats.

"See anything?"

"No. I mean, I can see the boats and there are people on them. They bear zero three seven degrees," she paused to turn her head and smile at Terry, "But nothing else." She lowered the glasses and sat back down to resume preparation for meeting her client.

*)

Marigot Bay, St. Marten

"I'm glad we got a bigger dinghy," Beth said as she used her foot to cram the bagged mainsail into the foot well in front of the dinghy's seat. Terry stepped off of the ladder hanging over *Trouble*'s side and planted his feet carefully on the seat. While Beth held the dinghy against *Trouble*'s hull, he detached the ladder and lifted it up onto the side deck, then fastened the lifelines. It was a cosmetic protection against the occasional thief that they'd been told came through the anchorage. The locked companionway and closed hatches were *Trouble*'s only real defense. But thefts generally occurred at night and it was now broad daylight on the day after Christmas.

Terry untied the dinghy's line, dropped it down on top of the bagged sail, and sat down on the seat facing Beth in the stern. Beth shifted the outboard motor into gear and Terry pushed off of *Trouble*'s hull. Beth headed for the channel into the lagoon where they would find the boatyard and sail loft.

The eight-person black rubber boat was arguably too large for *Trouble*, and more than one or two people needed. But it had quite possibly saved Terry's life last summer when the boat he'd been on had blown up. He'd regained consciousness floating in the water amid flaming debris. Despite a concussion and other injuries, he'd managed to climb into and paddle the dinghy, which had come loose undamaged as the larger boat blew apart. Their friend Burt had arrived on the scene and taken Terry and the dinghy aboard *Sandcastle*. Since he could claim it as salvage, he had been within his rights to give the rubber boat to Beth and Terry to replace the smaller, aging dinghy she'd gotten for practically nothing back in New York.

As she worked it in between the many other boats secured to the dinghy dock Beth once again reconsidered the decision to take it. The smaller dinghy had been a lot easier to maneuver in tight quarters. Eventually, with much shoving aside of other boats, they got next to the dock where Terry could get out and, more importantly, heave the sail out. He secured the dinghy's line and Beth scrambled on hands and knees from the dinghy's gunwale to the dock.

"I'll be back as soon as I can. They should be available to clear *Trouble* in," Beth said.

Terry sat down on the bagged sail and leaned back against a convenient piling. He looked quite comfortable as he opened his water bottle and took a swig.

"See you soon," he said with a grin. Beth turned and strode up the dock, half wishing she could lounge around too. But then, he'd be carrying the heavy sail in a few minutes, so he deserved a preparatory rest.

She found the marina office and was directed to a side office where a marina employee handled her check in and collected the fees. Beth was used to dealing with government officers, but the cruising guide had been clear about this being the way it was done in Marigot Bay. She did like that the process was completed in twenty minutes instead of the usual forty-five.

Terry was helping another boater secure his dinghy to the dock when she got back. When she got close, he double checked his cleat of the man's line and stepped over to the sail still sitting on the dock.

"Are we all legal?"

"Stamped and paid."

"I'll carry this," Terry said, and heaved the awkward Dacron bag onto his right shoulder.

"I won't argue. Let me know when you need me to help." Beth started up the dock. He followed without comment. The sail loft was part of the marina and boatyard complex, so they didn't have far to go. They found the building after asking directions of a worker wearing coveralls and a filter mask. Beth heaved open the heavy wooden door and held it for Terry.

"Good morning."

The office they'd entered was dim compared to the exterior sunshine. Beth blinked several times and followed the sound of the voice to a counter across the room. A man in his thirties, neat haircut, friendly smile, pencil behind his ear, was standing behind it.

"Good morning. I'm Beth Anderson. I called earlier about my mainsail."

"Yes Miss Anderson. I'm Brian. You said it's torn below the third reef, right?"

"Yes. I hope it can be patched. A new main isn't in my budget right now."

"I understand. Let's lay it out and see."

He came around the end of the counter and picked up the sail bag before Terry could, bundling it into his arms as he pushed through a pair of double doors into a much larger space—the entire ground floor of the building, save the corner walled off for the office.

He walked out to the middle of the floor and dropped the bag, then bent to loosen the drawstring. With one end of the bag open, he grabbed the other end and heaved. The sail slithered out, partially unfolding onto the wooden floor.

"If you can grab the corners, we'll spread it out," he instructed. Beth grabbed the empty bag and tucked it under her arm, then picked up an edge of the sail and worked her way along it to find the clew—the fitting at the bottom corner of the sail. Brian picked up the narrow head of the sail and Terry soon found the tack—the other bottom corner.

"Okay, let's go," Brian said. He started walking away from Beth and Terry. Beth in turn walked away from both men. Gradually the sail unfolded on the floor, revealing the torn, frayed edges of the rip in all its glory. Beth felt her pulse quicken at the sight. Yes, she had a job now and the paychecks deposited into her account every two weeks was more than she'd earned before in her life. But there hadn't been that many of them yet, and she had a very long list of deferred expenses.

Brian walked along the leach of the sail—the edge that went up the mast, studying all of it, not just the obvious damage. He crouched to examine it more closely a few times, each time raising Beth's pulse higher. Terry came over and put his hand on the middle of her back. She leaned into him and felt her heart calm. Sure, if she couldn't cover it he would pay for the repair. But she didn't want that, didn't want her fiancé to have to support her lifestyle.

Brian completed his inspection and came to stand with them looking out across the expanse of worn fabric.

"The sail is in decent shape for its age," he said. "It's at least eight years old, based on the logo." He pointed at the sail maker's logo sewn onto the sail near the tack. "They changed the design of it about eight years ago. I don't think the sail can be much older than that, though. It needs reinforcement in a few places. If you don't, you'll have more tears like this."

He crouched again and indicated an area on the sail. Beth bent and saw what he did—the fabric was thin, the fibers frayed.

How have I never noticed?

"The tear is clean. Any closer to the reef points and you'd have to replace them, but I think we can patch it straight across without having to. That will be patches on both sides..." he went on to describe the patch fabric and stitching, and then he described his recommendation for the other reinforcements. Beth found herself nodding and agreeing to his proposal as the Euros piled up.

"Still cheaper than a new sail," she said to Terry as they walked back through the boatyard toward the dinghy dock.

"It's like car repairs. At some point you start doing the replacement vs repair cost comparison."

"You don't think it's worth fixing?"

"No, I do. I think he would have said so if it wasn't. After all, he sells new sails. I'm just saying that next time might be the time to replace it. I'll bet *Trouble* would be easier to trim."

"You think she's hard to trim?"

"I think it was easier to balance her a year ago than it is now, and the one thing that has changed is the age of the sails. It's inevitable. They're like tires on the car. They wear out."

Beth sighed, knowing he was right but hating to have to face yet another expense that she had never considered before setting out from New York. But if she had understood all the expenses, she never would have left, never would have met Terry, and never would have visited a French sail loft on St. Martin on a sunny December morning. She smiled despite herself and took Terry's hand. He glanced at her, saw the smile, and smiled back.

"How about finding a place with a view for lunch?" she asked

"*Trouble* has a great view."

"I'd like a change of view."

They took the dinghy back out into Marigot Bay and over to a dock in the more touristy part of town, where they stopped in the tourist information office to look for a restaurant with a view. They settled on one overlooking Oyster Pond on the east side of the island. The tourist office clerk happily made reservations and called a taxi for them.

As they neared their destination Terry noticed a sign advertising horseback riding on the beach and pointed it out to Beth.

"You want to do it, don't you?" she asked. She had gone through her teenaged horse phase, including riding lessons at a dusty, run down barn on the outskirts of her home town in Southern California. While her father's income was comfortable, there had never been a chance of having a horse of her own and although she'd loved visiting the stable and working with the horses, in high school she had allowed other pursuits to take over. She hadn't ridden a horse in years.

"It's been on my list for a long time."

"I'm willing to try it. It does sound fun."

When she'd agreed, she hadn't meant that day. But Terry took out his phone and started punching in numbers. He had, she realized, read and remembered the phone number on the sign. By the time they reached the restaurant he had made a reservation for that afternoon.

Thirty-eight

Orient Bay, St. Martin

*T*he prospect of riding made Beth apprehensive through lunch. She ordered a salad and iced tea and thought about the sports sandals she was wearing, not to mention the shorts. But Terry had asked about attire and been told they would be fine. She tried to enjoy the spectacular view of busy Oyster Pond, a deep indent into the eastern coast with a rock-infested entrance so tricky the charter company based there guided their clients in and out and sometimes went aboard to drive the boats. They watched these operations from high above and chuckled at near misses by charterers getting used to their rental boats.

They taxied from the restaurant to the stable, which turned out to be not unlike the ramshackle barn where Beth rode as a girl. That made her more comfortable with the entire undertaking. They were greeted as they approached the barn by a slender woman in cutoff jeans and a red plaid shirt, with wind-styled wavy brown hair. Claire, who was the owner, stable hand, and guide, asked if they had ridden before.

"When I was a young teenager," Beth said. "Western saddle. I took lessons for a few years."

The woman nodded approvingly and turned to Terry.

"My experience is similar, although I've ridden a couple times a year since the lessons. Mostly English tack."

Beth looked at Terry in surprise. How had they never talked about horseback riding?

"*Bon.* We use western tack, and my horses are as calm as the sea on a day with no wind." For some reason that made Beth smile. Perhaps because it was the first time in a long time the notion of a day without wind sounded promising.

Claire guided them through the dimly lit barn with its stalls, stacks of straw bales, and equipment hanging on hooks, to a fenced paddock where six horses stood. Some had one rear hoof cocked up, others were trying to reach a fringe of grass outside the fence. It had been cropped out of reach long ago. Two of them raised their heads to watch Beth, Terry, and Claire approach.

"We will be six all together. Beth, I think you and Sugar will get along quite well," Claire patted a grey horse with a darker grey mane. The horse, one of the ones trying to get to the grass, raised her head and looked at the humans. Beth stepped closer, looking into Sugar's large, brown eyes.

"Hello Sugar. It's nice to meet you." Sugar snorted and pushed her nose at Beth's chest. "Hey!"

Claire laughed. "You see, she appreciates your courtesy. Now, Terry, Sam is for you, I think." Claire left Beth with Sugar and walked across the paddock to a tall brown horse who watched them coming with what Beth thought was a skeptical expression. Terry patted his shoulder, then placed his left hand on Sam's nose. They could hear the bit in his mouth rattling as he played with it with his tongue. Claire nodded. "He is comfortable with you."

"That's good," Terry agreed.

The sound of car tires on the gravel out front came through the barn.

"That will be the other party. Please, get to know them, but do not mount yet. I will be back in a moment."

Beth was content to stroke Sugar's withers and her velvety muzzle until Claire returned through the barn leading a man and two women, all about Beth and Terry's age.

"So here we are. This is Beth and Terry, and now we have Pearl, Estella, and Jack. Let me introduce you to your horses and I will assist each of you in mounting. Please wait until I can help you."

Claire's repeated insistence that nobody try to mount their horse without her made Beth's nerves build as she waited. It didn't help that Terry was completely calm, standing with Sam's head pressed against his chest as he scratched the horse's ears. Claire led each of the other three with their horses to a ragged tree stump, much worn on the top from people stepping on it. Each rider climbed on the stump, put their left foot in the stirrup, and swung into the saddle. It looked simple enough. Next Claire gestured to Beth to lead Sugar over. Sugar's reins were looped around the top rail of the paddock fence, so Beth unwound them and held them near Sugar's chin, tugging gently as she stepped toward Claire.

Sugar stood firm, causing Beth to stop short, her arm extended behind her.

"Come on!" She urged, giving a little tug. Sugar leaned back, her forelegs straight and unyielding.

"Sugar!" Claire barked. The horse's ears rotated toward the woman. Claire crossed the paddock, eyes locked with the recalcitrant horse's. "This is how she got her name. I prefer not to use bad language, but this one brings me close to the edge. Sugar!"

Despite herself Beth laughed at that. Sugar relaxed her rearward lean as Claire got close and Beth felt the reins go slack.

"She only does this. Otherwise she's a good girl," Claire assured Beth, taking Sugar's reins from her. Sugar stepped after Claire without complaint.

"How did you do that?" Beth asked, following Claire. The other woman shook her head and laughed.

"The first sixty or so times she did this she got a swat on the derriere from me. Horses are not the smartest creatures, but they do learn eventually. Climb up on the block."

Beth put one foot on the stump and realized it was very high. She planted her hands on her lower thigh and pushed herself up as she straightened her knee. Claire had positioned Sugar, so Beth grabbed the saddle horn, put her foot in the stirrup, and swung her right leg over Sugar's back. Her left foot rose up out of the stirrup and she couldn't reach the right one.

"Swing your leg forward," Clair commanded, tapping Beth's left calf. Claire adjusted the left stirrup and told Beth to put her foot in it, then she went around to adjust the right one and told Beth to stand up while she stood in front of Sugar to study her.

"*Bon.* Now make her walk over there." She pointed toward a stretch of fence to the left of Pearl on her horse. Beth took up the reins in her left hand and took up the slack. Sugar's head rose immediately, and Beth pressed her heels into the horse's sides, loosening the reins a little. Sugar took ambling steps across the paddock: a confidence boost for Beth.

Claire got Terry mounted and his stirrups adjusted, and then collected her horse, a short, muscular, buckskin quarter horse she called Gypsy. She swung herself into the saddle from the ground and guided Gypsy over to the paddock gate where she paused to study the assembled riders.

"Jack first, and then Pearl. Estella, you follow, and Beth and Terry, you are last. *Bon?*"

"Got it," Beth said amid the others' positive responses. Claire nodded curtly, then leaned over and lifted a wire loop from around the fence post that held the paddock gate shut. She pushed it all the way open and guided Gypsy through it. Jack followed, and then the rest.

The first part of the ride was slightly down hill on a rocky, rutted trail through bushes and spindly trees. Cacti grew on open patches of ground, and overall the terrain gave the impression of being parched, although Beth knew very well that it experienced frequent showers. The trail leveled out and widened, and Estella moved up beside Pearl. Terry came up alongside Beth.

"Doing okay?" he asked. Beth noticed the way his pelvis rocked with Sam's stride and wondered how she looked. Not ridiculous, she hoped.

"So far."

"Try to relax."

"I am relaxed."

"Okay. Try to enjoy it."

"I am enjoying it!"

Terry smiled, but didn't offer any other suggestions.

And she hadn't lied. She was enjoying the sensation of being carried along the trail, and of seeing a part of an island that was new to her. She couldn't help that her enjoyment was tinged with her fear of falling off. She'd done that as a kid, and she knew it would hurt more now.

After a quarter of an hour of winding through the lowland scrub, the trail led out onto an eastward facing beach with a condominium complex.

"We must walk in the water, below the high tide line," Claire called out to her group. "Do not worry, there is another beach where you can canter if you wish."

"Great!" Terry said, although not loudly enough for anyone but Beth to hear.

"Are you going to?" she asked him.

"If Sam will. Are you?"

Beth wanted to, very much. But she wasn't sure if she'd have the courage when the time came. Also, there was Sugar's opinion in the matter.

"I want to. I'll try."

The beach was not crowded, but there were a number of individuals and families settled in, and a few playing in the choppy water. None paid much attention to the passing riders. At the end of the beach they climbed a short rise to a path along the top of a short cliff—about fifteen feet above another stretch of beach. There were bathers there too. A glance told them that this slightly more isolated beach was clothing optional.

The trail turned away from the edge of the cliff and in a few minutes, Claire had stopped to let them catch up at the side of a road. A black sedan went by, and then a van going the other way. They were not going fast, but they were fast enough to be dangerous to the riders and horses.

"We will cross here. All at once, when I command. Yes?"

"Yes," they chorused back. Claire watched the traffic for another minute and when no vehicles were visible in either direction, she signaled them to follower her. On the other side she indicated to Jack that he should follow the trail as she brought Gypsy to the rear of the group, moving in between Beth and Terry.

"Everything is all right?"

"Yes, fine. Sugar is being a very good girl."

"She will be, if you are kind to her. Would you like to canter on the beach?"

"I would like to. Can I?"

Claire chuckled. "Whether you can is up to you. You may, if you wish." She turned to Terry. "And you?"

"Definitely!"

"Very good. Now I must ask the others." With that she urged Gypsy forward to come along side Estella.

Beth was starting to grow weary of the palm trees, cacti, and rocks along this stretch of trail when they bunched up again at another road.

"We have cut off the loop," Claire said, "and now we cross once more." Beth assumed that meant this was the same road and the trail had cut across a bend. Once again, they waited for Claire's signal and then urged their horses across the pavement and back onto sandy ground on the other side.

"And now for some fun," Claire said, leading them onto a trail much like the previous stretch. But this one was short. Soon they stepped out on to a narrow beach looking across an inlet at a matching one on the other side. "Hold onto your saddles. Keep your feet in your stirrups. You're going to get wet!"

Before anyone could react, or refuse, Claire and Gypsy plunged forward, and the rest of the horses followed them into the water. Beth looked down at it, first on one side of Sugar's withers, and then the other, seeing her legs churn it frothy as she waded confidently in.

"Let them swim, they love it!" Claire said.

Soon the water was dragging at Beth's legs and despite Claire's earlier instruction, her feet slipped out of her stirrups. She held onto the saddle horn as the water rose further, dragging her legs behind her. Sugar's motion changed, the saddle wiggled side to side. She was swimming! Beth held on, dragged through the warm, salty water for twenty feet or so. When she felt Sugar get her footing again Beth realized she was in a dangerous position. She pulled hard on the saddle, dragging her legs forward and tilting her pelvis to get herself seated. Just in time, she felt her toes bang against the stirrups, dangling now above the water as Sugar climbed up the opposite shore.

"That was amazing!" Beth cried, grinning broadly. Terry was dripping wet and grinning from ear to ear.

After the swim, urging Sugar to join the other horses in a canter up the beach a short while later seemed like nothing. Beth tried not to hold onto the saddle and managed to ride the canter properly for a while, but when Sugar shifted sideways slightly to avoid one of the other horses Beth grabbed the horn and clung to it for the last few strides.

"Very good!" Claire called as they walked the horses onto a narrow trail showing evidence of bicycles, walkers, and dogs. By the time Claire led them into a clearing the seawater had dried on their skins, but their clothes hung damp and heavy. Two water troughs, several large tree stumps, and the hoof prints of many horses indicated this was a regular stop. Claire swung her right leg over Gypsy's back and jumped to the ground.

"Dismount. If you walk through there," she pointed at a path between the trees, "you will find refreshments and a few shops. You have thirty minutes."

Beth took her feet out of her stirrups and held onto the saddle horn as she swung her right leg behind her. Her heel dragged across Sugar's rump, causing the horse to raise her head sharply and take a step.

"Sorry girl!" Beth gasped as she slid down the horse's side, her grip on the saddle all that kept her from collapsing onto the ground as her knees threatened to buckle. "Oh my!" The pain in her legs and behind was completely unexpected. She clung to Sugar for another minute, tensing each leg and flexing her knees one at a time.

"What's wrong?" Terry asked, standing at Sam's head holding the reins about to lead him to a rail with the other horses.

"My legs are stiff!" Beth said and gasped, releasing the saddle as she spoke to force herself to stand normally. Her legs held her, but as she stepped to Sugar's head, lifting the reins over it, her knees hurt.

"I will take her. You walk now." Claire was there, smiling but not to be crossed. Beth handed her Sugar's reins and stood there as the horse followed her mistress away. Terry came over, having left Sam tied to the rail, and wrapped his arm around Beth's shoulders.

"I'm stiff too. But I expected it. Come on, slow steps at first. We'll walk it out."

They followed the trail through the trees and discovered that it came out on another beach. As Claire had promised, there were vendors in colorfully painted booths. Terry produced a few soggy Euros from a pocket and bought them ice cold Cokes. The sugary goodness tasted like ambrosia to Beth, who rarely drank soda.

They spent their thirty minutes walking along the beach trying not to stare at the people who exercised the option to not wear clothes.

They had a look at the trinkets and jewelry on offer in the booths. Beth wondered if any of the inventory was supplied by her new client's business. She stopped at a booth where a woman of indeterminate age, who did not appear to have any teeth, sat on a stool. Her display included jewelry made of string with shells and beads woven in, painted tin jewelry and decorative items, beeswax candles, and other small items. Beth examined a beaded bracelet and asked if the vendor worked with or knew Virgine Guesnon. The woman's expression darkened, and she shook her head.

"Bad," she said.

"Her items are not good quality?" Beth asked, hoping the woman hadn't been speaking French or creole and said something entirely different. The dark, hooded eyes locked with Beth's. The woman shook her head again without releasing Beth's gaze.

"Bad business."

"I see. Thank you. I'll take this one," Beth extended the bracelet with one hand, reaching for the daypack that she wasn't wearing with the other. "Oh, wait." She turned, looking for Terry. "Terry?"

He came over from the next booth.

"Can I borrow—" she examined the little paper tag on the bracelet, "Two Euro?"

Wordlessly Terry pulled a handful of damp coins from his pocket and handed it to her to sort through. She found two Euro coins and handed them to the woman, who took them without comment.

"Want me to tie it?" Terry asked. Beth was grateful that he didn't question her purchase. He tied the bracelet in a perfect square knot, and then grasped the string with the tag between his thumb and index finger and tugged at it sharply. It broke. He pocketed the tiny tag rather than let it fall to the sand.

"Thanks," Beth said, guiding him away from the woman's booth. "I bought it because I started to grill her about Virgine Guesnon and I felt obliged."

"Makes sense. Do you at least like it?"

"Sure, it's cute. And it wasn't a big price to pay to see her reaction to my question."

"Which was?"

"All she said was 'Bad Business'."

"Well that's not encouraging. Maybe Broadhead should invest in research about her local reputation."

"I was thinking the same thing. I might be making the rounds of the tourist gift shops."

When they returned to the clearing Claire was helping Pearl mount. They went to their horses and in turn guided them to one of the stumps so Claire could help them. This time Sugar stepped along with Beth with no complaint. In fact, all of the horses seemed more cooperative, even eager.

Claire led them back along the same route. When they came to the beach, they all cantered. Sugar was more energetic now. Beth caught herself holding onto the saddle as her horse accelerated toward the end of the beach and took the slight incline onto the path with leap. Beth was very glad she had a good grip on the saddle as she felt her behind lift off of it. She used her legs to keep herself from slamming back down hard.

On the swim back across the inlet Beth worked to keep her feet in her stirrups and enjoy the strange sensation of Sugar swimming under her. Being wet and salty on the last leg of the journey wasn't as charming as it had been on the outbound. When they got back to the paddock, Claire pointed out a fresh water hose they could use to rinse off as much as they wanted. Beth splashed water over her arms and legs, letting it soak her shirt and shorts and sandals while Terry retrieved his daypack from the barn and called for a taxi. They had both dried enough to not soak the taxi's seat when it arrived for them twenty minutes later.

They got back to *Trouble* with a couple of hours to spare before their dinner reservations. Despite the freshwater rinse at the stable, Beth peeled off her clothes and dove into the bay. Terry was right behind her. They swam around the boat, stretching and flexing muscles that Beth knew were going to be very sore later. Each of them shampooed and washed, rinsed with another dunk in the sea, and had a final fresh water rinse with the shower hose installed in *Trouble's* aft lazarette. They both felt refreshed and hungry by the time they got into the dinghy and headed for shore, leaving *Trouble* once again locked up tight.

Thirty-nine

Marigot Bay, St. Marten

*T*he next day, after researching her options by touring the waterfront on foot, Beth visited the office at Marina Fort Louis to arrange berthing for *Trouble*. Most of the berths were like those in English Harbor—Mediterranean mooring, with the boat backed up to the dock and a mooring securing the bow instead of the anchor. This configuration was fine for most catamarans, power boats, and monohulls with a stern swim platform. You could step from the dock to the swim platform and into the cockpit. But *Trouble's* stern was steep and high. While it was possible to climb to and from the dock, it was difficult to move gear on and off the boat, and Beth would have to bring the main sail back aboard by herself and carry her laptop on and off many times. In her months in the islands, she had learned to ask for what would make her life easier: in this case, a side tie berth. Most of the marina's resident boats were much larger than *Trouble*; some of the yachts had tenders were almost as big. It stood to reason that the marina might have a stretch of dock too short for its typical clientele. Indeed, they did. Beth reserved it for two weeks with the understanding that she might stay longer.

After breakfast the following morning Terry hauled *Trouble's* anchor while Beth used the motor to maneuver her over it as he worked. When the anchor was up and secure Terry returned to the cockpit and hauled out the jib while Beth kept *Trouble* pointed into the light breeze. When the sail was set she turned the wheel until it caught and *Trouble* moved off across the water. They took turns steering and trimming, tacking back and forth across the bay and north toward neighboring Anguilla, then back, for several hours. Beth went below and made sandwiches while Terry steered. They switched off so he could eat his. They talked about how *Trouble* handled under the jib alone and noted that they never achieved the speed they would with both sails. Finally, mid-afternoon, they headed back to the anchorage. They rolled up the sail and drifted for a while taking turns going for a final open water swim. Cocktail hour was approaching when they finally started the engine and headed for the marina entrance at the open end of a nearly circular seawall. Having already seen the stretch of dock that they'd be using made a huge difference in Beth's confidence as she navigated the marina's internal channel and angled toward it. She was used to finding her way into tight spaces based on verbal instructions received over the radio and without knowing what they looked like. This was like coming home.

She brought *Trouble* alongside the dock close enough for Terry to hop off with the spring line—the line attached to the cleat at *Trouble*'s middle. Before he could do much else two men in matching polo shirts materialized on the dock. One took the line he was holding while the other came to *Trouble*'s stern and took the stern line that Terry had left within reach from the dock. In no time *Trouble* was neatly secured. It was a mixed sensation for Beth and Terry: the convenience of stepping off the boat to a dock rather than a dinghy ride was appealing, but *Trouble* would be subjected to the attention of anyone walking by on the dock. There would be no diving overboard for a swim here.

"Nicely done," Terry murmured as he stepped back into the cockpit. The two dock boys were making neat coils of the excess dock line on the dock next to the cleats.

"Thanks. I need to get them a tip," Beth started to move out from behind the wheel.

"I'll get it," Terry said, holding up one hand, palm toward her while he reached into the pocket of his shorts with the other one. Beth conceded by leaning down to shut off the engine.

With the dock boys tipped, Terry climbed down below and retrieved two bottles of beer.

"So here we are cooped up in a marina," Beth said as she took a beer from him. She had slid into her favorite seat with her back to the cabin bulkhead and her legs stretched out on the lazarette. She was looking at the massive powerboats Med moored to the dock off *Trouble*'s stern.

"You going to feel like a caged animal while you work with your client?" Terry asked, taking a seat across the cockpit from where she'd settled. He followed her gaze to the huge boat.

"I don't think so, most of the time. I'll be busy. But I will miss being able to dive in for a swim. I might have to go to the beach to get my fix."

"And it's such a long trip," Terry observed, looking across Beth in the direction of the beach outside of the marina. Beth followed his gaze and shrugged.

"I guess I do have to admit it's closer than the gym at home."

"Home?" Terry grinned. Beth's gaze snapped over to him and she took a covering gulp of beer.

"You know, I will always think of *Trouble* as home. But I guess I do think of your place as home now too."

"Our place."

"Our place."

"Say it again. I like to hear it."

"Our place."

"Okay." Terry took a swig from his bottle and sighed contentedly.

"Burt never called back, after Christmas Eve."

"Ummm."

"He said he might come here. Maybe he got a last-minute New Year's charter."

"Probably." Terry sounded half asleep. Whether he was or not, it was clear he didn't want to talk about Burt. Upon further reflection, Beth realized she didn't want to either. She sipped her beer and watched seagulls circling above. In the islands, even a marina was paradise.

Beth had not expected there to be any long-term cruisers staying in the marina because it was on the pricey side. Many—maybe most—of the cruisers she'd met in her months in the Caribbean had been as frugal as she was. They anchored for free whenever they could, avoided paying anchorage fees when they could, and when they could not anchor, they paid for a mooring before a marina berth. Marigot Bay offered plenty of space for anchoring. Beth was sure a lot of captains didn't pay the daily five Euro fee and maybe the harbor patrol asked them to leave when they were caught. She might have done the same before starting with Broadhead.

She was taken completely by surprise when, about the time she and Terry were finishing their beers in companionable, drowsy silence, a vaguely familiar voice from the dock reached them in the cockpit.

"*Double Trouble*, where did you come from?"

Beth opened her eyes and looked over the lifelines at the dock to see Evan, a cruiser she and Terry had met last summer, and last seen in August at the *Gunkholing* magazine party on Antigua.

"Hey, Evan! Good to see you." Beth got up and went around the cockpit table to lean out over Terry and the lifelines and extend her hand. They shook as Terry got up to do the same.

"This is a surprise," he put in.

"Yeah, well, I guess I kinda got stuck here in the Islands. Still planning to head for the canal eventually."

Beth suspected there was more to the story. Evan's boat, *Petrel*, was a beautiful Italian made sloop that he and his son had brought from Europe last spring. He had told them his wife was joining them to take her through the Panama Canal and sail to the south pacific.

"Still have Connor and Marney with you?" she asked. Connor was paid crew and Marney was his girlfriend. Beth had never found out whether she was paid or a plus-one.

"Actually, we're here on St. Marten for re-rigging, to make *Petrel* easier to sail with two people. Connor and Marney moved on to a mega yacht that needed a hand and a cook. Good move for them. Actually," he half turned to look down the dock, "It's the one beyond this one." He pointed at the huge yacht that Beth had been contemplating earlier. "You might see them. Is this a permanent spot for you?"

"Well, not permanent, you know how that is. But I'll be here for at least a couple weeks."

"A couple weeks? Still convalescing, Terry?" Evan knew they had spent more time in marinas while Terry recovered from a concussion and other injuries after the exploding boat.

"No, but I'm heading back to Washington after New Year's and Beth will be here working."

"Oh no! Not the 'W' word," Evan said with a laugh. "I thought you were a free spirit, Beth."

"Only as free as my bank account could tolerate. I wanted to work for a while to build it back up, but I ended up with a job that has me working in the islands some. It's kind of a dream job. Except it is actual work."

"Not another travel or food blogger I hope," Evan said, shaking his head to express his opinion of such pursuits. Beth smiled. There had been a period when she'd thought she could do something like that while sailing. People did. But she had come to realize that for all the people who tried to make a living that way, the ones who succeeded—who earned enough to cover all their expenses without relying on savings—were a small percentage. Beth was too pragmatic to play the would-be starlet serving lunches in a Hollywood diner hoping to be discovered.

"No. Consulting."

"Hah, the great catchall."

Beth caught herself bristling and squelched it. He was smiling, and his reaction was to the generic term, not to her.

"Yeah, I know. I'll be working with a business woman here who wants to get distribution in the states. I'm on a team that does all the work while I'm the front woman because I'm the only one whose spent real time here, not just vacations."

"You're the only one on the team who has experienced the Caribbean bureaucratic mindset," Evan said, nodding. "That makes sense. Do you two have plans for New Year's Eve?"

"Not yet," Terry said. Beth glanced at him and wondered how much time he'd been spending contemplating it. She would love to do something special that night, but the usual glittering parties in formal attire had not appealed to her since she'd stopped watching Guy Lombardo with her parents.

"Join us. I've got a section of the deck reserved at Le Spinnaker starting at nine o'clock. Ordered a lot of champagne and food. Otherwise it's cash bar. I've tried to invite all the cruisers I can find. In fact, please let any who you run into know. Doesn't matter so much if I've met them, as long as they're cruisers."

"Thank you, Evan. We'd love to," Beth said, glancing at Terry again. He nodded. "What's the dress code?"

"Island formal. It would be good if you wore shoes and a shirt," Evan replied with a laugh.

"Got it. No swimsuits, and preferably with combed hair."

"You get the idea."

"Hey this is interesting," Terry said. He and Beth were both peering at their laptop screens. They were sitting across from one another at the saloon table, dinner dishes shoved aside.

"What?" Beth asked, looking up and noticing the mess between them.

Terry read from his screen, "'Authorities removed the corpse of a young girl from the beach below Pointe Arago on the afternoon of Christmas Day. The unidentified girl is thought to be approximately four years old. The cause of death is yet to be determined, but preliminary examination of the body revealed signs of malnutrition and sexual assault.' Jesus. I'll bet the minister of tourism is having a cow. This is gruesome: 'the body had been in the water for several days, making determination of cause of death harder. It's being sent to the medical examiner on Guadeloupe'."

"That's got to be what those police boats were doing." Beth said.

Terry nodded. "Must be. What an awful way to spend Christmas."

"The police, or the girl?"

"I meant the police," Terry shrugged, mouth tight. "I mean, she was already dead. Not that I don't feel for her as well."

"I know, I didn't mean to be critical. It doesn't say anything about why she was there?"

Terry skimmed the article for a moment, shaking his head. "They don't know, or they aren't saying. It does say they aren't even sure whether she's a local—nobody has reported a four-year-old girl missing."

"Strange."

"Oh, wait this is an interesting conclusion, 'human trafficking has been on the rise in other Caribbean nations. Investigation is underway to determine whether this is an indicator of such activity on our own island'."

"Wow. I think of St. Martin as a safe, westernized place."

"Human trafficking happens in westernized places. There's a sidebar about it here. Haiti is a big focus."

"Haiti is in the west, yes, but certainly a third world nation. I guess I meant first world."

"Ummm. Fair enough." Terry was reading the sidebar. "According to this, it's a bit more widespread than I—we—thought." He went on to read parts of the article.

"Send me that link, will you. I need to get more familiar with it."

"Pleasant reading," Terry said, clicking keys on his keyboard. "You have it."

Forty

Marigot Bay, St. Marten

The boy with the port wine stained face cowered under the work table. His hands automatically picked coconut fiber off the bale under the table and dropped it into the boxes in between the adult workers. His eyes were focused beyond their pairs of legs, watching the guards prowl the perimeter of the work space.

The stacks of boxes forming the walls of the space grew and shrank as the days passed. Shipments came, shipments went. Tonight they were in the most depleted state he'd seen since he'd been brought here. Only the back wall that curtained the work space from the sleeping space was as high as ever.

Suddenly the new girl—she was as nameless as him—gave out a pained yelp. His head snapped around and he watched her dragged out from under the table, coconut fiber falling from both hands. The guard holding her by the arm said something sharp to one of the others as he shook the girl. She wailed, and from somewhere over in the sleeping area a woman cried out.

She had a mother over there, or a sister, or aunt. Someone who cared for her. The boy was glad he did not have a mother anymore. When they hurt him nobody else got hurt too.

The guard dragged the girl by one arm around one of the walls of boxes and off into the darkness under a staircase up to the catwalk above. Two of the other guards shared a joke, their disgusting laughs momentarily covering up the girl's cries.

The boy kept dropping coconut fiber in the boxes, desperate not to draw attention to himself. A while later the guard came back alone. When one of the others asked him something he responded with a sharp denial. The other guard slipped away into the darkness. The boy held his breath, waiting for more cries from the girl. But they did not come. The other guard came back. The boy couldn't see his face, not without getting too close to the edge of the table. The girl was not being hurt anymore. The boy was grateful.

Presently it was time for the sleepers to take over and the workers to sleep. The guards pushed the adults from around the table, and the one who'd taken the girl reached in under and grabbed for the boy. He darted away, coming out from under it on the other side to stumble after the adults. The guard made a gurgling, laughing sound, but didn't chase him. He walked after the last guard behind the adults, giving every impression to the laughing guard of following them to bed. Meanwhile, other guards were bringing a new group around the other end of the box wall, sending them to the table to pick up where the departed had left off. The boy knew this would occupy them for a few minutes. As the adults and their one guard entered the dim sleeping area, the boy angled off to the right into the darkness near the wall. He crouched in the shadow of a pair of casks, part of a wide variety of rubble scattered around the warehouse. The guard, who hadn't been aware of the boy following him, left the area without noticing him.

The boy sat, knees drawn up to his chest, arms wrapped around them, and gazed across the dusty floor listening to the guards haranguing the new batch of workers. Across from him, a man sat on a burlap bag stuffed with coconut fiber. The boy could see the whites of his eyes as he stared into the shadows. He knew the boy was there. The boy stared back, certain he was invisible.

The man raised his right hand and made a sweeping away gesture.

Go. Get out.

The boy knew that every now and then one or two of the guards opened the great front door enough to step out and smoke a cigarette. There was no smoking inside: the chief guard enforced that one rule. He did not know how far from the building they went to have their tobacco, and whether they watched the door while they stood out there in the free air. He did know it was his best option.

When the new workers had settled into a pattern and the retired ones were beginning to snore, wheeze, and moan, the boy unfolded his arms and legs and began to crawl along the base of the wall. As he passed by the opening in the wall of boxes leading in to the work area, light from the work table briefly illuminated his rags and spindly limbs. He darted through it and back into the shadows, listening for an alert from the guards. But none came. They had not seen him. He moved on until his hand landed in dampness. He lifted it and sniffed. Blood. Grimacing, he reached forward until his fingers brushed flesh. It was warm and soft. He inched forward, his knee landing in the blood, and felt the girl's thigh. He crawled further, coming alongside her, pressing his mouth to her ear when he found it.

"Can you walk?" he whispered.

Her head shook and she started to whimper. Realizing the danger and hating himself for doing it, he slapped his bloodied hand over her mouth.

"Shhhhh. Don't attract them. I'll send help, but I have to get out first." He felt the pressure against his hand subside. She had stopped trying to wail. "Help will come."

He moved quickly into the cover of the steel staircase, looking up through the steps, wondering if he should try it instead. But the catwalk was visible from almost everywhere in the warehouse, and everyone would see the door up there opening. He knew this from when the woman visited. No, he couldn't escape that way.

After a long while listening to the workers hands brushing the table and dropping the figures, he eased out from under the stairs and went around them, returning to the wall to crawl to the front corner of the warehouse. The sliding front doors were pulled shut. He could feel the track that the door ran in under his hand as he inched along the front wall. There were no convenient casks or boxes, and the wall of boxes concealing the work area stood twenty feet further into the warehouse. All he had as cover was the shadows at the base of the wall. He waited.

He waited so long he drifted off, losing focus, when two guards came around the boxes at the far end and went to the doors. They slid the right-hand door a few feet and stepped outside. The boy inched toward the opening, soon feeling a fresh, oddly scented draft. It invigorated him, bringing memories of bright sun and swaying trees, of things and people who had been trying to forget. He realized the strange smell was the sea, one of the aromas of his home. He'd been breathing the stench of filthy bodies and sewage in the warehouse so long he didn't recognize the sweet scent of the sea. Coming to the very edge of the left hand door, he flattened himself onto the ground and peered around it.

The night was bright. Stars, the moon, and orange lights on poles created sharp shadows of the cars and trucks outside. He blinked back tears as he tried to focus on the guards, to see where they were looking. Obviously not at the base of the open door, for they did not react as he poked his head further out, looking for cover nearby.

A rumbling sound grew loud enough for him to notice, and then louder. He pulled his head back, rose to his feet and plastered his back to the door. The rumble became a low roar as a vehicle—large, engine running rough—rolled up to the front of the warehouse and stopped. The boy frowned, ready to dart back to the corner if the door behind him moved, or any more guards came from the work area. He heard a truck door creak open. Heard voices outside. Holding his breath, he dared to turn his head, cheek against the door, and peer out.

Both guards were standing on the far side of the truck's cab along with the driver. The boy didn't hesitate. This was his chance. He rolled around the edge of the left door and half ran, half stumbled along the outside of the warehouse, not daring to look back until he was around the far corner. He flattened himself against the wall there, a few feet from the base of the external stairs and peeked back around the corner.

The guards were hidden by the huge trailer talking to the truck driver. Back along the alley between the warehouses, orange lights mounted high on the walls cast a strange shadow of the openwork staircase. Out across the paved parking and loading area there were orange lights on poles. He was weak, deprived of adequate food, water, and sleep for weeks. Once he could have sprinted across the parking area in seconds. Now he knew he could not run that far. He turned into the alley past the staircase, heading for the rear of the warehouses. When he got there, he found a paved walkway lit by lights on the rear walls of the warehouses. He turned right, toward the road the truck had come from, and kept walking.

Barefoot, his clothes a filthy undershirt that had been white and basketball shorts that might have once been red, the boy plodded along the side of the road toward the glow of lights from a large city. An enormous building to his right was four times larger than the warehouse he'd left behind. He could hear and smell the sea somewhere beyond it. That encouraged him to keep walking. The sea was his friend. The sea touching this shore touched the shore of his home.

He faltered as his right foot dropped into a rut and wound up on his knees, the one that had been clean now stained with his own blood, the abraded skin stinging. He didn't notice. The sound of a motor coming from behind presaged a flash of headlights on the wall of the building above his head. He flattened in the sharp grass growing in the narrow space between the road and the building.

They had to see him, he was certain. The vehicle rumbled toward him, headlights brighter than the sun illuminating everything. Then it was upon him, its right-side wheels crunching on the gravel road inches from him. He raised his head and peered after it, watching the red lights on its back end recede. He swallowed, dry and dusty, and pushed himself up, one hand leaving dirty prints on the building beside him. He pressed on, dragging his dry tongue over his drier lips.

The corner of the building was near, and at its base he made out the profile of a spiky-leaved plant and a palm tree above it. He stumbled the last few steps, grabbing the corner of the building to stop himself from falling onto the spiky plant. Hands shaking, he reached down near its base and grabbed an outer leaf, twisting and tearing it loose. Leaf in hand he pressed himself against the building, inching in between it and the plant, ignoring the sharp leaves scraping his bare legs. He pressed the broken end to his lips. Cool and gelatinous, the aloe soothed them more than he could remember it doing before. He licked at the leaf, then sank his teeth into its flesh and bit off a chunk.

Chewing was harder than he remembered, the long unused muscles reluctant to cooperate. The skin of the leaf shredded and caught between his teeth. The flesh disintegrated and oozed down his throat. He leaned his head back against the wall and imagined it trickling into his stomach, leaving a path of moisture that revived him. A few bites of the leaf felt like a heavy meal. He dropped the remains and looked beyond the planter where he stood. He could see the water now, beyond the building and across a stretch of land where vehicles were parked. He could hear it more clearly now, too, and the salty odor was almost intoxicating. He wanted to go to it, to feel it against his skin and scrub away the stink of the work place and the sleeping place.

Then he remembered the girl. He looked at his hand. In the moonlight he could see it was stained with blood. Twisting around he saw he had left dirty, bloody marks on the side of the building.

He had to get to the city and find help. He had to stop touching things and leaving a trail.

He pushed back through the bush to the roadside and resumed his trek.

The road went on forever. The lights never got closer. He trudged onward, off of the road in the spiky grass and rocky dirt, ready at any moment to dive to the ground. Always looking for cover. He passed hedges and more buildings, but none as large as the first one. He came to a circular road, skirted its edge and continued on the next road which seemed to head back toward the sea. More vehicles passed him from both directions. He plastered himself against buildings, dove under bushes, or crouched and ducked his head, hoping whoever was in the car or truck would not notice him. He needed to find help, but he could not know whether someone in a truck or car wasn't one of the guards sent to find him. He wasn't sure who he would ask, when he found people who were not driving. He would look for a uniform. He thought the police would help him.

Eventually the sound of gentle waves on a beach became louder and he realized his road had brought him right up to the edge of the sea. He stepped off of it into soft, warm sand and his feet carried him across a strip of beach to the water itself. He splashed into it feeling the dry beach transition into a sandy bottom. He crouched, then sat down in waist deep water. He scrubbed his hands together and rubbed at the stinging scrapes on his legs. He pulled the undershirt off over his head and balled it up, soaking it in the sea and squeezing it out. After three or four times he shook it out it and put it back on. He flopped back to lie in the water and feel its cooling touch.

A loud truck passed by on the nearby road. He sat up, half turned to watch its red lights disappear. He had to move on.

He was still damp when he came to the first sign of life other than cars and trucks. He studied the building as he approached it, watched people coming from inside and going to parked cars. There was a quiet about them, as if they were tired after a long evening. Music played inside the building.

As if an invisible barrier stood between him and their world of fine clothes and cars and music, he could not approach them. They were other. They would turn away from his stink and stains of the dying girl's blood. He had to find people like himself. He kept walking along the road. It curved, following the edge of the sea. It comforted him to walk just above the lapping water.

Gradually he realized he was in the city. The other side of the road was lined with buildings. People were walking, talking, laughing. They held on to each other, and to bottles and cups they were drinking from. They were happy and friendly. Their clothes were more ordinary. Not disgusting and filthy like his, but not sparkling and shimmering either. He crossed the street into the open plaza where the happy, ordinary people were.

At first, he tried to approach a woman who reminded him of his mother. She wrinkled her nose and turned from him the moment she saw him. So he turned toward a man because the man on the boat had been kind to him. This was not the man from the boat. He glanced down at the boy, pointed at him, and said something to his companions. They all laughed. The boy stared at them dumbfounded. He did not understand the sounds that they made. How could he ask for help?

Somewhere nearby the sound of shattering glass punctuated angry voices he'd heard getting louder for the last few minutes. A woman screamed and a man bellowed something threatening. The boy turned to find the source of the disturbance so that he could run from it.

All of a sudden, the reveling people cleared and he found himself standing a meter, hardly more, from four men who were facing off, two against two. One gripped a broken bottle in his right hand. The boy looked at his own right hand from which he'd washed most of the girl's blood, and then back at the men. Around them the revelers had taken up a chant. To the boy it sounded like "Weee-goooo, Weee-goooo."

Suddenly one of the men lunged at the one facing him and instantly all four were a kicking, hitting, slashing mass bowling right into the boy. He was trampled, stepped on, kicked. An elbow slammed down into his ribs and he cried out. He tried to roll aside but his chest was on fire. He heard the high-pitched sound of whistles before a sharp-toed boot slammed into his temple and he heard nothing more.

*)

Marigot Bay, St. Martin

Beth reached for Terry's hand as they stepped out of Le Spinnaker restaurant.

"That was fun," she said, listening to herself for slurred words. Evan's champagne had flowed freely all night.

Terry squeezed her hand. "One of my best New Year's Eves."

As they strolled along the sidewalk it became obvious something was going on at the market square, which lay between them and the marina.

"It looks like the party got out of hand. Shall we go over a block?" Terry asked.

"Maybe cross the street," Beth said. That would put them across the street from the open square where they could see a lot of people gathered and police vehicles with flashing lights. The square had been full of revelers when they'd walked by earlier on their way to Evan's party.

As they came abreast of the open square, they saw an ambulance emerge from the crowd, switching on its two-tone siren as it sped away.

"What a lousy way to start the new year," Terry said.

*)

Westlake, Texas

Hunter's eyes drifted from the middle-aged woman listening to Parker's story—one of their drivers delivering a drill to the wrong well ran afoul of a very defensive oilman—to the mid-century modern wall clock over the fireplace. An hour left in the old year and so far he'd managed to avoid being cornered by his father at the party by sticking close to Parker. His brother was adept at working the room at these Green family business gatherings, as Lyle, their father, liked to call them. Hunter could not remember a major holiday with just family. Employees and clients were always invited, and always got the lion's share of Lyle and their mother Faith's attention. As a boy Hunter had complained after one particularly dull Christmas party where all of the guests received presents except Parker and himself. His father had lectured him for a full thirty minutes over Christmas morning breakfast on the importance of the employees and clients to their family's success. Parker had been angry at him the whole day since he'd also had to sit and listen. That was an especially lousy Christmas.

Hunter refocused on his brother's story. Parker always seemed to know who to make a point of talking to at these things and what to say to them. It was one reason why he was so successful in the family business, and he'd been good at it since they were kids. Hunter always lingered around the edges of any group observing while his brother stood in the thick of it, telling jokes, spurring hijinks, and always managing to evade any blame.

Hunter saw the look in Lyle Green's eye the moment he got to Dallas before Christmas. His father had something to say to him, and he wasn't going to wait much longer.

Sure enough, here he came, highball glass sloshing amber liquid and ice in his hand as he swaggered across the room. The middle-aged woman and her two friends, all of them Green Equipment Leasing employees, wore bemused smiles suggesting they'd heard Parker's story before, although not as embellished by the boss's son. Lyle stepped into the group and grinned at Parker, nodding encouragement as his son came to the rifle-toting well owner. As Parker launched into his imitation of the man's dense drawl, Lyle touched Hunter's shoulder and jerked his head to the side.

"A word, son," he said.

Hunter swallowed and nodded, unable to think of an excuse this time. As they walked away from the party, he struggled to come up with another reason not to join Green Equipment Leasing. In the past he'd used a gap year before college, and then college itself, and then another gap year after graduation—that stretched into five years in Jamaica. After that there was rehab. When he decided to search for Ori—for his son—he avoided having this conversation by simply leaving, using the frenzy around Parker's wedding to keep his father from pinning him down.

He knew what was to come all too well. His father's arguments for him to join the firm had not changed. *It's a family business and you're my oldest son. We're growing, we need you. It's your* legacy.

Hunter could not justify not joining the company. His father guaranteed him a high-level position and good salary. He'd have interesting work and great benefits. He'd put his degree in engineering to use at last. It was a better way to spend his life than tending bar on tropical islands.

They settled in armchairs in his father's study, a wood paneled, leather furnished cave that represented disciplinary visits with dad to Hunter and Parker. As children and teenagers, they had been allowed in by invitation only, issued almost exclusively when one of them committed an infraction of household rules. As Hunter heard the leather chair creak beneath him, he wondered how his father could think this room was comfortable. Then he realized his comfort was irrelevant to his father. Absurdly, that made him feel better about it.

"Parker tells me you're going back to the islands on Tuesday."

"Yes sir."

"Can I ask why?"

That was how he talked—couching demands as requests. It infuriated Hunter. He fought the urge to tell his father he could ask, but that didn't mean he would answer. Flippancy would irritate Lyle, and that wasn't to Hunter's advantage.

Lyle took a sip of his bourbon, blue eyes watching his son over the rim of the glass, oblivious to the fact that Hunter could not drink. No, courtesy around other people's addictions and failings was not part of Lyle's playbook.

"I have a solid lead on finding the woman who knows how I can find my son."

Lyle sighed and Hunter braced himself. He knew what was coming, but when it did, it was more vitriolic than usual.

"It's a wild goose chase. You don't know whether the woman's child is your son. He's probably the get of some filthy Jamaican. For all you know she was raped by them every night. Why do you insist on bringing this bastard child into our family?"

"If I fathered a child—I said if," Hunter raised a finger to silence his father's imminent interruption. "I want to take responsibility. I will not have a son out there in the world who does not know I exist."

"He'll know you exist—he's livin' and breathin', isn't he? He'll know someone fathered him. Leave it at that."

"I can't. I'm responsible for him."

"You're a fool. If the woman isn't demanding anything of you, leave it be. Find a woman to marry and have legitimate children. Forget the by-blow. She had her chance to lay this on you and she didn't."

"You don't understand her. Or me. I am not letting this go."

"Fool." Lyle repeated, gulping more bourbon. He lowered his glass and his gaze wandered around the room, landing on a photograph of his father in front of a green oil drill rig, the name Green painted across it in blocky black letters. "He wore himself out founding this company, and you're kicking him in the balls."

"I am not kicking anybody in the balls. I'm taking care of my personal business."

"It's the family business you need to be thinking about, son. The family business needs the family to run it. I've got new contracts coming in. Parker's a newlywed, he can't handle it all. Your duty is to him, and me, and your granddad. Not some non-existent baby son."

"I guess I see it differently, Dad. I can't commit to serving Green until I've settled this."

Lyle's eyes narrowed and he held Hunter's gaze for a long moment. Finally he spoke, "Are you saying you can commit after you've settled it?"

Hunter shut out his father's stare and inhaled through his nose. The tang of leather cream, pine, and his father's bourbon filled his mind with dozens of fragments of memory.

They aren't all bad.

"What aren't all bad?" Lyle asked. His voice had taken on the softness of inebriation, but his hearing was sharp. Hunter had spoken his thought out loud.

"Nothing." Hunter exhaled, trying to squelch a sense of impending doom. "Yes. That's what I'm saying. Once I find my son and settle my relationship with him, I'll come home and join Green Equipment."

Forty-one

Marigot, St. Martin

"*M*a'am, there is an urgent call for you," Mathieu stood inside the doorway to his mistress's bedroom holding the cordless telephone handset. "Ma'am?"

Across the room in a luxuriously dressed king sized bed, the covers stirred. Her head rolled on a pillow, causing a pink silk sleep mask to come askew. She snaked one hand out from under the sheet to push it up on to her forehead as she focused on Mathieu.

"Who is it?" she growled, voice rough from not enough sleep and too much champagne.

"Morton. He says it's urgent."

"It's New Year's Day. How is it possible Morton has anything to say that demands my attention?"

"Shall I ask him ma'am?" Mathieu asked, serious. The woman shut her eyes and exhaled an exasperated huff. Opening her eyes, she reached out to him.

"Give me the phone."

If she noticed Mathieu's reluctance as he crossed to the bed she didn't react to it. She dragged herself up to sit against the pillows, tearing off the sleep mask and giving it a mighty hurl. It flopped onto her lap. She snatched the telephone from Mathieu's hand, shooting him a scowl that pushed him back two steps as she put the device to her ear. She turned to look toward the floor to ceiling window from which she could see the vast turquoise sea. Mathieu took the opportunity to back further away and slip out, shutting the door.

"Morton." She said.

"Ma'am. We had an incident in the night. One of the guards— one of the girls—is dead, and—"

"Which is it? One of the guards or one of the girls?"

"Forgive me, ma'am. One of the girls."

"And was one of the guards responsible?"

"Maybe, ma'am. Or it was the boy. One of the boys escaped. We—we think he killed her before he left."

Virgine's face was as stony as her voice. No doubt a guard was responsible for the rape he was avoiding admitting. But perhaps Morton's lie was the better choice, even if he was telling it to cover for his man. She didn't like the staff spoiling the merchandise, but it was an unavoidable cost of doing business. "How did the boy escape your men? Nevermind. What have you done to recapture him?"

"At sunrise I detailed two men to search the port. They found nothing. I sent them out in the van to search further. He can't have gone far."

"But he can have gone far enough to find someone who will ask questions."

"He will have to find someone who speaks English, and can understand him, ma'am."

Virgine huffed again. *Idiot.* There were plenty of English speakers in Marigot.

"Find him Morton," she finally said. "Find him and find out how he escaped. Report to me this afternoon."

"Yes ma'am."

The woman lowered the telephone handset and peered at it for a moment before finding and pressing the button to end the call. She reached over and placed it on the bedside table.

A light tap on the door was followed by its opening and Mathieu's head poking around it.

"Come in."

"Coffee, ma'am." The young man pushed the door open, revealing a tray. The woman's eyes narrowed as she watched him approach the bed, his steps slowing the closer he got.

"Put it over there and come here." She instructed, pointing at her dressing table. Mathieu stopped, looked across the room at the dressing table, and then turned slowly toward it. He slid the tray onto the glass covered table top, shoving bottles of scent, jars of creams, and assorted makeup containers out of the way. He straightened and turned back to the bed. The woman had folded down the layers of covers beside herself. She patted the bare bottom sheet and smiled at him. "Right here."

Head down, he paced the floor to the side of the bed and sat down to remove his shoes.

"That's my boy. Come see what I have for you …"

)

Fort Louis Marina, Marigot Bay, St. Martin

"This has been one of the best holidays I've ever had," Terry murmured into Beth's ear as he embraced her. They were standing in the driveway of the marina. Terry's duffle bag and day pack lay on the ground at his feet.

They had watched the sun rise from *Trouble*'s cockpit a little while ago, and now they were waiting for the taxi to take him to Princess Juliana airport where he'd board a plane for Washington D.C.

"Me too. Maybe better than last year."

"That's a close second." Terry loosened the embrace to look into her eyes. "This year I like having an idea of where we're going."

Beth smiled into his sparkling eyes, her happiness over their engagement was still a touch overwhelming. The rumble of car tires interrupted their gaze. Terry saw the approaching taxi over Beth's shoulder. He impulsively pulled her into one more tight hug and let go.

"I'm going to be lonely at home without you."

"And I'm going to be lonely on *Trouble*. But we both have plenty to do."

"There's my practical Beth." He smiled ruefully.

"You got sentiment a second ago, now I need coping mechanisms."

"True that!" Terry lifted his two bags and stepped toward the back of the van where the driver stood by the open the doors. They loaded his luggage and he got into the rear seat. Before closing the door he leaned out, "You'll do great with your client. I'll call you tonight."

Beth waved at the retreating taxi until it turned out of the marina parking lot, then made her way back through the marina complex to the docks and on to *Trouble*.

This is it. She had two hours until she met the taxi that would take her to her first meeting with her client.

"Shower first," she said to herself and went to collect her shower bag with her toiletries and towel already packed. Thirty minutes later she was back on board, clean and feeling energized. She fired up her laptop and connected to the marina's wifi to check her work email, not that she expected anything new since it was eight-thirty in the morning, Washington was an hour earlier, and yesterday was a holiday after a weekend. In fact, her last communication from the team had come on Thursday, and she'd spent several hours, off and on, reviewing everything they had provided about the client, her business, and possible trade connections they could help with. She felt like she could not be more ready, which in itself felt like a risk because she was sure there would be surprises. Her best bet now was to review everything one more time.

Trouble had no air conditioning, and within the hour the growing heat of the day made it uncomfortable below. Dressed for the meeting, Beth didn't want to sit and sweat through her blouse. She gathered everything she'd need, locked *Trouble*, and went to the marina's air-conditioned lounge. In no time the alarm she'd set on her laptop buzzed. Time to meet the taxi.

Marigot, St. Martin

Although the client had an office in Marigot, she had asked Beth to meet with her at her home in the hills above the seaside town. The team had assured her this wasn't unusual for the kinds of people they worked with. Beth calmly watched the scenery go by as the taxi carried her up winding roads. The turquoise sea sparkled below, with the colored roofs on buildings on the waterfront and flatlands lending a lovely contrast. It was nice, she reminded herself, to get this bird's eye perspective now and then.

The taxi turned in at a steep drive and labored up and around a curve to stop in front of an enormous house, part of which must be suspended out over the hillside.

"Thank you," Beth said as she paid the driver. "You'll return in ninety minutes?"

"Yes ma'am. I'll be here."

Beth studied at the house. Drapes masked the windows. The front door was two solid panels. "Um, can you wait to be sure someone's home?"

The driver half turned to look at her over his shoulder. "I will ma'am. Don't you worry."

Beth smiled, embarrassed. "Thanks." She checked that everything was in her sailcloth messenger bag and got out of the taxi.

The door was opened by an older teenaged boy with medium brown loose curls and darker brown skin with an almost reddish tinge that was both unusual and attractive. His eyes were blue.

"Good morning," she said. "I'm Beth Anderson from Broadhead Consulting, I'm here to see—"

"Beth Anderson! You are here to see me," a voice came from a woman coming up behind the boy. "I'm Virgine Guesnon."

The boy slipped away as she took his place, but before he could get far she turned and called sharply, "Mathieu, coffee for two on the patio."

"Yes ma'am," he replied before vanishing around a corner. Virgine turned back to Beth.

"Come in. I am pleased to meet you."

"And I you Ms Guesnon." Beth extended her hand and the woman took it in a strong grip and then released it. Terry had told Beth about a theory of handshakes: the pressure and duration were clues to all kinds of things about the person's personality and objectives. Virgine Guesnon's handshake felt like determination and professionalism. Beth could appreciate that.

She followed her hostess through a cool, marble floored lobby and into a cooler, much larger great room. Clerestory windows above grand sliding glass doors let in so much light the white walls, furniture, and floor nearly glowed. Beyond the sheets of glass an infinity pool shimmered almost electric blue against the dark grey flagstone patio.

"Your home is lovely," Beth said with genuine sincerity. She appreciated the clean modern lines, even though she knew she could never keep it tidy. Maybe if should could afford staff to pick up after her all day …

"Thank you. I'm quite pleased with it, but it has taken several years and more designers. We'll sit out here, if you'll be comfortable?" She walked through an open door from the great room to the patio and indicated a table under a broad canvas umbrella. A sea breeze ruffled the edges of the blue canvas.

"This will be fine," Beth said with a slight hesitation over possibly needing to plug in her laptop.

You'll deal with it, if it happens.

Virgine gestured at one of the chairs and took the one adjacent to it so they both had a view of the pool and ocean. Beth also noted that Virginie was also positioned so that she could see the laptop screen.

"To begin, perhaps you can tell me more about your business. That is, the aspects of it you would like Broadhead to assist with. I have read the agreement, and your correspondence with our team, but hearing it from you will help me and the team shape our efforts. You don't mind if I make notes while we talk, do you?"

"Yes, of course. Something is always lost in emails," Virgine said, her expression suggesting slight impatience with being asked to repeat herself. Beth's first impulse was to cringe over a miss step, but no, this impatience was another useful piece of information. She wanted to hear what Virgine had to say.

The boy came through the open glass doorway carrying a tray laden with a coffee service. Beth watched Virgine, who watched Mathieu's every move with a deeply critical expression. The boy watched his own hands as he placed cups and saucers, creamer and sugar bowl, spoons, and a china carafe on the table.

"That will be all Mathieu," Virgine said as if he'd shown signs of sticking around, which Beth thought he had not. Virgine poured for both of them and left it to Beth to add cream to her cup. Virgine took hers black.

As the business woman described her products and the distribution agreements she hoped to make, Beth listened to her tone and observed her body language. The words were familiar, aligning well with the written descriptions Beth had read over and over. What Beth saw was a composed professional who understood her own business. She was self-confident and carefully groomed, a factor she believed to be important in her dealings with men. Beth wondered what the local women she contracted to produce the goods she distributed thought of her styled hair, which had been straightened and treated until it shined, and her precise makeup. Were they impressed with the quality of her clothes, or intimidated, or resentful? Was Virgine Guesnon seen by her workers as the savior and protector of poor women that she claimed to be, or did they see an oppressive boss adding to her wealth on their backs? Beth couldn't know unless she could meet the women who made the craft items Virgine distributed.

When Virgine wound down her description of her company's virtuous mission and her hopes for the distribution deals Broadhead would make for her, Beth switched from her notes to a list of questions she and the team had compiled. Virgine had already identified retailers she wanted to do business with, but the team wanted to test whether they were a good fit. The questions about annual production goals, materials costs, and the ability to deliver on time, were challenging. Virgine lost the soporific tone that colored her vision of lofty goals. Her facial expression hardened, and for a moment Beth feared she would end the meeting. But instead, she began providing what sounded like honest answers: yes, deadlines were hard to meet. Deliveries to the airport shops were sometimes late and quantities were inconsistent. She'd had to pay fees to the hotel shops for shelf space.

After more than an hour, Beth knew she had to refocus their immediate goal on building up Virgine's supply chain. This is what the team had suspected from the start, so she was well prepared to address the concerns Virgine herself raised. The American chains would not accept under-supply and late delivery. If they were to place her products, she had to increase her production. Virgine listened to the team's proposals, nodding, her face impassive until Beth had finished.

"Tomorrow I would like to take you to visit our local craft guild. Seeing the women will answer your questions. You will understand the challenges."

"I think that would be an excellent next step, Ms. Guesnon," Beth said, although she had an idea of what she would see, and it would not change the team's recommendation.

They agreed Beth would meet Virgine at her office tomorrow at nine o'clock in the morning. Then Virgine asked Beth where she was staying.

"Aboard my boat, in Fort marina."

"Aboard your boat?" Virgine's tone conveyed incredulity.

"Yes. I've been cruising the islands on and off for about a year."

"So you are not based in Washington?"

"I am now. My year of sailing was before that, and my boat remains in the islands so I can easily resume life here. I will make St. Martin my base for as long as you need me here."

"The best of both worlds," Virgine said rather archly. Beth chose to take her words at face value and ignore whatever the tone intended to convey.

"Yes. Broadhead has found it quite useful. We're about at the end of our meeting window, unless you'd like to continue?" All Beth wanted to think about now was getting into the taxi.

Virgine raised her wrist to consult a bejeweled wristwatch. "So it is. In fact, I have another appointment shortly." She paused and looked toward the open door. Beth followed her glance and saw Mathieu standing inside. "Mathieu will show you out. Thank you for your time today. I look forward to tomorrow's tour."

Beth had already shut her laptop. She crammed it into her bag and stood up, her chair scraping on the flagstone.

Virgine rose as well. "Good day."

Forty-two

Fort Louis Marina, Marigot Bay, St. Martin

"*H*ow did it go?" Terry asked almost immediately after answering the phone and greeting Beth.

"It was so tiring! But it went the way I wanted it to. Tomorrow she's taking me to see the women who make her products here on St. Martin."

"That will be interesting. Did she agree with your team's assessment, that she needs better production and delivery?"

"She did. After I managed to get her to come to that conclusion."

"Nice job. How was her handshake?"

"Firm, strong. She's no-nonsense, but touchy. Easily offended, but I think she gets over it. Or at least she sets it aside. I might have accumulated a couple black marks that will come back to haunt me."

"Unavoidable. You can't please everyone all the time. It sounds like you're off to a good start. Which doesn't make me any less lonely."

"Awe, so sad. How was your flight?"

"Not even an 'I miss you too'?"

"I miss you too. *Trouble* misses you. The marina cat misses you."

"I fed that cat a lot. Anyway, the flight was uneventful. At least you're on an island with direct service from Dulles. Jeff and I went over the numbers again on code name Harvest. They're still looking good."

Harvest was the code name they'd given to a company they were considering purchasing majority interest in. It was the first time they'd considered investing in a publicly traded company.

"What's the possible timeframe?"

"You mean, when will I be available to sail again?" He asked, then he added, "Or do you mean, when can we get married?"

"If I confess to the first one will you be disappointed in me?" Beth could remember a time when she would have denied thinking of anything but their wedding. She was relieved he'd mentioned sailing time before wedding planning. Sailing together represented their life together. The wedding was a single event.

"Far from it. I didn't want you to think I wasn't thinking about wedding planning too. I'm relieved you're not already upset it's not the first thing on my mind."

"How could it be? It feels abstract. Your next deal is very real, as is my job. I guess we both need to make weddings planning more real too, but I'm glad you're not there yet either. Let's set ourselves a deadline to get started."

"Set a deadline for picking a date?"

"It's a start."

"Okay. How about February first?"

"We decide on the date by February first?" Beth felt her voice squeak. "Oh God, even doing that feels scary!" She admitted, fearful of what he'd say, but determined to be honest. Her heart had started to race.

The line was quiet for a few seconds that felt like an eternity. Finally, he said, "It does, doesn't it? This is nuts. How about this. We talk about the wedding, at least a little bit, every time we speak. We need to get used to the idea."

Beth felt her heart slowing. She inhaled a long breath and decided to do as he suggested. "I wish we could find a way to have the wedding in the islands, but I suspect it's not possible. How far would your parents travel?"

"You want to talk now? Okay. Um, they would travel if we picked a destination. Dad does fly—I mean, travel on airplanes. Mom kind of likes it because they order a wheelchair and get special attention. What about your Dad?"

"Yeah, he's the reason I'm hesitant. Also the expense, for Trish and Mike more than Mom and Dad. Would they bring the kids? She'll have a new baby. It might be too much."

"Do you want to get married in California?"

"Oh, I hadn't thought of that," Beth replied, realizing she wasn't making much sense. That was the only option if she didn't want her family to have to travel. "You got me. I haven't thought it through. And I haven't talked to Trish about it. Maybe I should ask her. I might be limiting us without reason."

"So you know, if you want to get married there, I'm fine with it. We could have a beach wedding."

That caught Beth off guard. An image of standing barefoot in the sand facing Terry flashed in her mind and she felt her heart race again. She drifted with the breeze as it rustled his hair in her imagination.

"Or not," Terry said when she didn't speak.

"What? Oh, sorry. No, I got distracted imagining us on a beach. It's a possibility. Let me talk to Trish."

"Okay. Meanwhile, Harvest is about three months out. Public companies are more complicated. I'm not totally sure we want to get into it."

"I can understand that. Seems like higher risks."

"Some, yeah, and a lot more work for us to get ready, since it's new to us. But that's boring. What else did you do today."

"Debriefed with the team. I wanted to tell you about something that's been bugging me all day."

"What's that?"

"Virgine Guesnon has this young man, a teenager, who's like a houseboy or something. He answered the door, then brought us coffee, and showed me out. But he's too young to be working for her. Legally, I mean."

"Relative? Is she married?"

"No, not married, and as far as we know she has no significant other. If he's related, I doubt he's immediate family. He looks nothing like her."

"Son of a staff member? Does she have a cook or maid or housekeeper? Often their children help out in exchange for lodging."

"Could be. I didn't think of that, never having had a cook or maid or housekeeper. That's your background."

"Yes. We had a maid when I was very young whose teenage daughter babysat us. He's probably the maid's son."

"Yes, I guess so. Anyway, it was odd. Or it felt odd."

"You didn't say, is Virgine Guesnon black?"

"Yes."

"Now I see."

"I'm being racist, aren't I?"

"I didn't say that."

"It's my American upbringing. Slaves are black. A black woman with a black servant is like a slave practicing slavery. I've been trying all afternoon to decide if that's what's going on in my head. Inbred prejudice."

"I don't want to simply agree with you. I know you're not a racist. But I do get what you're saying. If this experience helps you identify an unconscious bias you want to change, be grateful for it."

Beth continued to contemplate her automatic reaction to Mathieu and Virgine as she made herself a salad with canned tuna for dinner and sat in the cockpit enjoying the sunset through the forest of masts in the marina. She felt an unusual tug from the bars on shore—unusual because she rarely hung out in bars alone unless the local cruisers were gathered there. She had lived aboard *Trouble* by herself for long periods of time, so feeling lonely without Terry surprised her.

Instead of going up the dock to find the companionship of strangers, she settled in with her laptop below and wrote an email to her sister. She'd talked with her family on Christmas Day, explaining that she and Terry couldn't leave the boat until they could check into France with customs and immigration. A couple days later Trish had sent her an email with the subject "prisoner of St. Martin." She settled down to answer the message now and introduce the subject of wedding location to her sister.

⧏

Marigot Bay, St. Martin

Beth wasn't sure why she thought Virgine's office must be as classy as her home, perhaps in one of the modern two-story buildings in the blocks up from the waterfront in Marigot. When she pulled up an online map, expecting to plan her walking route, she realized the address was at least a mile from the marina, near—or maybe in—the industrial port in the northeast corner of the bay.

Fortunately, the time she'd allowed to walk through town was enough for a taxi to take her to the far less glamorous location. The taxi quickly departed the tourist-friendly waterfront and made its way past gas stations, a fuel storage facility, and an industrial complex that, Beth reflected, took up a considerable stretch of the bay's beautiful beach. Soon they were rolling along a waterfront road with a hillside to the right and a stretch of undeveloped land to the left next to the water. They passed a long row of parked trucks and detached trailers and entered a traffic circle. The first exit went up the hill, the second and third continued into what was obviously the commercial port, with a welcoming sign above an attractive building between the two roads. The taxi driver was craning his neck looking for addresses as he skipped the last exit and continued back around the circle to where they'd entered.

"I did not see it, did you ma'am?" he asked as they swung around again.

"No, but I wasn't looking. Could it be in those buildings?" Beth pointed across the circle at a complex on the side facing the water. The driver glanced over.

"Maybe. That is the turn before the circle." He continued on around the circle and exited it back where they came in, then made an immediate right turn into a driveway ending in a parking lot. They both scanned the area for addresses.

"There!" Beth said, spotting a sign listing several businesses and suite numbers. At the top of the sign was the address.

"Ah yes. Very good. Thank you, ma'am."

Beth handed him the fare and climbed out of the back seat. She heard the car roll away as she strode toward a smaller sign at the base of an outdoor staircase. She climbed up and proceeded along a balcony facing the water past darkened windows and a door for a company called M-Gen. The next set of windows were alight from within, and Virgine Guesons's company was stenciled on one of them as well as on the door. Beth opened it and stepped inside.

The room was a typical office lobby, with four upholstered chairs in a neutral print against pinkish beige walls. A desk with telephone, stack of file trays, and computer was unoccupied. Behind it, facing the door, a print of a group of women crouching around a campfire was the only distinctive thing in the generic room.

"Hello?" she called in the direction of an open doorway to the right of and behind the empty desk. She stepped further in so she could look through it.

"Hello. Beth? Come in," came Virgine's voice. Beth followed the sound of it into a hallway that opened up to the left into a kitchenette. A few steps beyond that was an office, door open and Virgine inside standing next to a desk. More images of women in tribal attire and locations covered the walls, along with a bookcase carrying dozens of craft items and very few books.

"Good morning. Thank you for coming. I need to be sure I have the right files, and the payment for the group we're going to meet. Would you like coffee?" Virgine extended her hand as she spoke and Beth shook it.

"Good morning. No, thank you. Take your time. May I look at your shelves?"

Virgine glanced over her shoulder at the bookcase. "Yes, of course. Some of the items are no longer in our inventory—too difficult to manufacture in bulk."

Beth stepped closer to the bookcase and studied the range of items. Jewelry was the primary product: there were unique, beautiful, designs and ordinary, cute ones like the braided fiber bracelet she'd bought in Orient Bay. Most of the metal items were made from bent wire and colorful beads and crystals rather than cast metals and finer stones. There were ceramic items, mostly thick handled mugs and squat, wide topped vases. Carved wood took up an entire shelf, and sheets of steel bent and cut into shapes and painted in bright colors was another common medium.

"All right, I have everything. My car is waiting downstairs."

Beth wondered about the curious turn of phrase until they were on the stairs to the parking lot. A stately white Cadillac stood near the base of the steps, a driver in black trousers, shirt, and jacket, standing by the rear driver's side door. He looked hot, despite the relatively cool morning air. The driver opened the door of the idling car and cold air issued out. Virgine gestured for Beth to get in. She did, and immediately realized that Virgine was not going around to the other side. Beth scooted awkwardly across the leather covered bench seat, dragging her bag with her. Virgine got in after her, settling her own black leather attaché on her lap over her short hemline and bare thighs.

The driver got in behind the wheel and put the car in gear without putting on a seatbelt. Beth considered searching for her seatbelt, but she could see the buckles for all of the backseat belts were shoved down between the seat and back cushion. It wasn't worth it. She had taken hundreds of rides in the back seats of New

York City taxis and never bothered to wear a seatbelt. She settled in her seat and looked out the window.

"Colombier is in a valley south east of here. It's a very old village that produces a medicinal root. The entire village used to live by selling it. They still hold a festival and produce some. It's used for animal feed and cooking, too. But like so many local agricultural products, the commercial farms have started producing it and squeezed Colombier out. Now the women who used to tend the plants and dig the roots are making and dying fiber from other local plants and creating jewelry with it." Virgine withdrew a photograph of a dozen or so women seated along both sides of a wooden table set under a venerable old tree. Sunlight filtered through the tree's leaves, highlighting a hand here, a smile there. Trays of beads sat in the middle of the table within easy reach as the women, all dressed in colorful ethnic garb, braided lengths of fiber. The photo was so obviously staged and professional it made Beth suspicious.

"So these are the women who make the braided bracelets and things?"

"Yes, some of them. There are three who make jewelry from wire and crystals. Their pieces are on my shelves." Virgine showed Beth a studio shot of familiar earrings made of silver wire clasping lovely blue crystals.

"Yes, I saw them. They seem more upscale than the fiber items."

"Yes. I have better luck with them in the higher end resort shops."

"Can we have more of the women learn to make them?"

"That is a possibility. However, the older women are very attached to the braids and beads. They have deep cultural roots. But I can think of two or three younger women who I think would like to try the wire jewelry."

"I understand. Supporting these crafters' traditions is a part of what your company is selling. We don't want them complaining that they were strong-armed to give up their traditional craft."

Virgine sighed. "Even though they were already strong-armed by the big farms to give up the agricultural work their people have been doing for several centuries." She said. "This is a small shift. But a critical one to them because—and this is important for you to realize—although these people profess to be Catholic, and they are all baptized and attend mass, there are older religions in place here."

"I see."

"The traditional colors of the beads and the fibers are important to them. They see their product as a way to share their real beliefs without offending the parish priest, or the visiting tourist."

"I should think a lot of visiting tourists would be intrigued by the old religion, not offended. Especially the type who would make the trip to Colombier. Do the cruise ships send busses there?"

"Fortunately not. That is who I was thinking of, not the occasional backpacker who hikes to the village. The backpackers don't have much money to spend on trinkets."

Virgine began showing Beth a series of photographs of the village women and their workshop. The tone of these photos was more natural, the composition less perfect. She identified each woman and Beth tried to remember the faces and names. She would have liked to compare them to the first photo, but Virgine had put that one away. The car passed through industrial and suburban zones and onto a road between scrub-covered hillsides. This lasted for less than a mile before there were houses on one side, and then both, and they were driving through a village where people walked along the side of the road, dogs barked at the passing car, and chickens scattered at its approach. Beth noticed people staring at the car. They did not look friendly. The woman selling jewelry in Orient Bay popped into her mind.

Bad. Bad Business. Suddenly she felt like she was riding in Cruella DeVille's car on her way to collect Dalmatian puppies. *Ridiculous. Focus on reality.*

The driver pulled off the road onto a patch of hardened ground in front of a typical Caribbean cinderblock building. A porch defined by several columns of blocks was protected by heavy iron bars in between. A gate in the middle of the porch stood open, leading to the open front door. The windows on either side of the front door were unglazed. Flimsy curtains hung half in, half out, at the sides of each window.

The driver got out and opened Virgine's door. Beth resisted the urge to open the door on her side, and instead scooted back across the seat dragging her bag after her. She tugged down on the back of her skirt as she got out, before turning to bend and pick up her bag.

The driver closed the door and turned to stand with his back to the car, eyes on the building.

"They are expecting us," Virgine said. "This way."

Beth followed her the rest of the way across the hard, uneven ground of the yard, admiring the way Virgine managed to walk with confidence in her two-inch heels. Once up on the porch the going got much easier. Beth noted a hammock strung from heavy hooks at one end of the porch and several mismatched chairs and a table on the other end. Two of the chairs were painted metal a lot like a set her parents had when she was a kid.

How many times did dad spray paint those things before he finally gave up and let the rust win?

The rust had won on these long ago.

"Good morning ladies. How is everyone?" Virgine said as she stepped through the front door. She moved far enough into the room for Beth to step in as well.

They were in a room that spanned the entire front of the house. The room looked like the one in Virgine's photos—in fact, it was definitely the same place. A work table with a row of bead trays down the middle and women on either side braiding dyed fiber were a poor imitation of the first, staged photo. No sun dappled the workers, and their garb was cheap American drab, not colorfully ethnic. A string of bare light bulbs—not more than forty watts each—hung above the table suspended on lengths of twine affixed to hooks in the ceiling. The light string was plugged into an outlet screwed into a light bulb socket in a chandelier stripped of ornamental crystals.

"This is Ms. Beth Anderson. She is here to help us bring your beautiful work to more people in the United States. Beth, meet my favorite team!"

Beth had to hand it to Virgine, she knew her audience. To a woman they all preened under her enthusiastic praise as they welcomed Beth.

"Ms Virgine, do you see I have mastered the double braid?" One woman asked, pointing at her work. "Do you love these colors as much as I do?"

Virgine moved closer to the table to look over the woman's shoulder at her work. "No, Agatha. I believe I love those colors even more than you do."

Beth smiled at the enthusiastic chuckles this garnered.

"Come around Beth, look at how fast they work," Virgine said, gesturing for Beth to follow her in a circuit around the table. Indeed, the women's fingers, when they focused on their work, moved so fast Beth couldn't follow them. The work they were doing was, Beth realized, a much more sophisticated version of the Macramé she'd learned when she was a kid. She'd made a purse from a kit she'd received one Christmas, using unbleached cotton twine and wooden beads. But her handiwork had been nothing compared to the precise knotting and weaving being done here.

The strands of fiber were secured to nails hammered into the table in front of them, allowing the women to tug their knots and braids into place. Beth now saw that the trays down the center also held findings—a term she'd learned last week that meant the rings, clips, and fasteners used to finish the work. As she watched, a woman took a complex bar with several rings welded to it and began tying the strands of her piece through the holes. In moments she completed a simple bracelet with a hook and eye closure. She held it up for Beth to inspect.

"Lovely," Beth said, holding it across her palm. "How many can you make in a day?"

"Well, I don't make just those, you know. Including the other pieces I think about fifteen."

That didn't make sense to Beth given how quickly she'd made the bracelet, but she held her tongue.

"Oh no, Heloise, you make twenty at least," the woman next to her said.

"You think so? Maybe."

"And how do you decide what to make? What will you start on next?"

"I make what the spirit tells me. They telling me to make a necklace now."

While Beth spoke with the crafters Virgine moved with one of the women to the other side of the room. They spoke quietly for a while, and Virgine handed her an unsealed envelope. The woman opened it and looked inside, her smile widening. She thanked Virgine, folding the envelope before putting it in a pocket.

"Beth, come meet the wire jewelers," Virgine said, moving toward a door in the back wall opposite the front door. Beth finished her circuit of the table and followed her.

This room was smaller, with a single window looking out the back of the building. Bare light bulbs dangled above another table about half the size of the one in the other room. The same trays of beads and findings sat among spools of differently colored and sized wire. Three women were working here, and they all paused to look up as Virgine and Beth entered.

Virgine introduced Beth and this time each of the women introduced herself as well. Beth stepped closer to see their work.

"As we've discussed, the wire jewelry sells better in a different market from the braided," Virgine said.

"The designs are very intricate. Is each one unique?"

"No, we use templates, see?" The woman who had introduced herself as Sophie held up a wooden block with channels cut into it. The women were pressing and twisting lengths of wire into the channels in various blocks. More were stacked on the table.

"How many designs do you make?"

"About fifteen at any given time."

"And how do you decide when to add a new one?"

Sophie blushed and dropped her eyes to her work. The woman called Rosette tsked at her before turning to Beth.

"When Sophie comes up with something new. If we like it—I mean, if Ms. Virgine likes it—we have Prosper carve a block for it and add it to the line. Sometimes we stop making something that we don't like."

"So all the decisions about adding and removing are based on what you like to make?"

"Well, Ms Virgine is the one who decides," Sophie hedged. Beth glanced at Virgine and saw a friendly, encouraging expression.

Does she really not control production, or is this all an act?

"I am ready to solder this, want to see?" Rosette held up a template with wire and crystals in all of the channels.

"Yes!"

Beth followed Rosette to a workbench against one wall where a soldering iron stood in a wire rack. She plugged it in and selected a roll of thin solder wire. Beth had done her share of soldering electrical connections aboard *Trouble* and knew it wasn't easy to make them smooth, at least not for her. She watched with growing admiration as Rosette carefully extracted the earring from the template. She slipped a ring over one end of the wire before warming both ends on the iron. Abruptly she touched the solder to the join and moved the piece from the iron into a cup of water where it hissed for a second. When she took it out she held it by the ring, which Beth could see rested right at the soldered join because the piece was perfectly balanced.

"I'm impressed. It's lovely. Now you add a post, or a hook?"

"Yes. We make both types. But no clasp earrings."

"They hardly sell anymore," Virgine put in.

"And how many earrings can you make in a day?"

"I make five, six pairs. I like to do the complex ones."

"The simpler ones take less time, but they don't sell as well," Virgine said, confirming Beth's impression that she recognized her lack of control here.

"Can you think of ways to make it go faster? Do you need different tools?"

"Get more of them," Rosette tilted her head toward the doorway and the women in the other room, "To do it."

"More people, sure," Beth agreed. "But anything else? Better lighting? Another soldering station?"

"The crystals," Sophie said. Virgine's pleasant smile faded for a moment. "A lot of the holes are too small. We spend a lot of time sorting through to find the ones that will work."

"And what happens to the ones that don't?"

"They go out there and get sewn on with thread—if that needle will through the holes. Or they are glued on."

"I see. So they are used, but not for these pieces. But I didn't see a lot of crystals like this out there."

"The braided pieces do not traditionally have crystals," Virgine explained. Only two of the women will use them."

"I understand."

And Beth did. That didn't mean she thought it was acceptable, but she wasn't going to get into it here and now.

"Why don't we go meet Prosper, who makes the templates for the ladies?" Virgine said.

"Yes, I'd like that."

Virgine took Beth back out through the front room and into the yard. The driver was still waiting beside the white Cadillac. They crossed the road to a more affluent looking house across the street and went around it to the back. In a muddy yard chickens clustered around a tall, muscular man who was tossing handfuls of feed among them.

"Prosper, your flock is thriving," Virgine said, striding toward him across the soft earth with one hand extended. He half turned toward her and whipped his right hand on his pants before shaking hers. "This is Beth Anderson. She's working with me on getting our ladies' jewelry to markets in the states."

"It is a pleasure to meet you, Beth." Prosper extended his hand to her after releasing Virgine's.

"You too. I understand that you're the talented man who makes the templates for the wire jewelry."

"Yes I am. I've always been partial to whittling. Some of the designs are a challenge."

"Are you working on any now?"

"Two or three. Let me take care of these birds and I'll show you."

They watched as he tossed the last few handfuls of feed to the gathered chickens, upending the empty bucket over their heads. "You see? All gone. Now shoo."

Beth chuckled as the chickens followed him toward the back door of his house. She and Virgine trailed after them.

"Shoo now," he repeated, making a sweeping gesture toward the birds. "Not you, ladies. Those ladies," he added, nodding at the chickens.

"We understood," Beth replied with a chuckle.

They entered the kitchen, which was much more modern than Beth expected, nothing like the bare cinderblock rooms across the road. He guided them through it and into a bedroom converted into a modest woodworking shop. One wall held shelves covered with carved wooden objects.

"Oh my," Beth said, looking at row upon row of animals, flowers, and other objects. The sails of a miniature sailboat were nearly paper thin. "Is this all one piece of wood?"

"Yes ma'am. It wouldn't be honest otherwise."

"I don't know about honest. But these are marvelous."

"Thank you ma'am. They are not finished."

"No? They look it."

"No ma'am. They—"

"Come see the new templates Beth," Virgine interrupted. Beth reluctantly turned away from the shelves.

"Do you market Prosper's carvings?"

Virgine shot an annoyed look at Prosper. His eyes dropped to the floor as he turned away from her. "Yes," Virgine said, "I've placed them in the local shops."

Virgine directed Beth's attention to the work table. Four wooden blocks were lined up there, each with channels carved in them. Sitting next to each was a piece of wire jewelry, a display set up for her benefit. Beth could see the relationship between the shape of the jewelry and the carved channels in the wood blocks.

"How long does it take you to carve a template?"

"Three, four hours. But some of the designs need two or three, when the wire design isn't flat."

"Right, of course. The ladies join the separate pieces from the different templates?"

"Exactly. I figure out how to divide each piece up. They put them together."

Beth nodded, understanding it wasn't a simple matter of drawing and cutting a channel. He had to dissect the piece and understand how the wires fit into several templates would come together to replicate the piece made freehand by Sophie.

"I have to sand it, make sure it won't cut the ladies. They get mad if my templates cut their fingers."

"Yes, I can imagine," Beth stroked the roughest looking template. It definitely needed sanding.

"This has been instructive," she said, looking from Prosper to Virgine.

"My pleasure," Prosper said.

"I'm glad. I knew you would need to see how it all works in order to move forward," Virgine said. "Thank you Prosper. Modeste has this week's payment."

"Very good. Thank you, Ms. Virgine. Thank you, Miss Beth."

As they walked back around the house to the Cadillac, Beth couldn't shake the sensation that the people here had a very different opinion of Virgine than what they expressed in her presence.

On the drive back to Marigot Virgine peppered Beth with questions about her impressions of the workers. Beth wanted to talk with the Broadhead team before making any grand pronouncements about productivity or inventory control. She knew her complimentary observations were wearing thin by the time the car entered the outskirts of Marigot.

"I know you and your team need to debrief. We are speaking tomorrow afternoon?"

"Yes. Two o'clock at your office, unless you will be home?"

"At the office. Where may I drop you? I know the office is not convenient."

"That's very kind. Rue de la Republique at Marina Fort Louis would be perfect. Anywhere along there is fine."

Virgine nodded and Beth realized the driver was watching for a signal in the rearview mirror. In a few minutes he turned into the marina driveway and rolled to a stop. Before he could get out Beth opened the door on her side. She had never seen a man move so fast, but he was out and around to her door, pulling it the rest of the way open before she could swing her foot out.

"Ma'am," he said as she stepped away from the car and shouldered her bag.

"Thank you," she replied, realizing Virgine had never told her his name.

She fretted about the faux pas for the entire walk through the marina complex and out to *Trouble*. Most likely the driver was going to come around to her side anyway, since Virgine had no reason to get out of the car. She'd come off as an untrained lout opening her own door in a chauffeured car. She stopped next to *Trouble* and forced herself to take a deep breath.

"Let it go. It isn't important," she told herself out loud.

"You sure?"

Beth turned her head to see Evan and his wife Denise strolling toward her. Evan had spoken.

"I just got out of a rich woman's car before her driver could come open my door," she blurted, immediately regretting her description, given that she thought Evan was fairly affluent himself.

"And you're afraid you insulted the driver?"

"No, I looked unprofessional in front of my client."

"I see. Well, if something like that matters to her, you have bigger problems to worry about. Do you have lunch plans?"

"Lunch? I haven't thought about it. It is lunch time, isn't it?" Beth pulled her phone from her pocket to check the time displayed on the front. She had a call with the team in an hour and a half and plenty of food on board.

"We're walking up to the marina restaurant. Want to join us?"

On the other hand, it was close, and she did have time.

"Sure!"

Forty-three

Georgetown, Washington, D.C.

*T*he words on the page blurred yet again and Terry blinked hard before trying to refocus. He could not recall being so bored by a corporate annual report before, but this one, for the company Jeff had identified as a likely prospect, was putting him right to sleep. He'd even printed it, hoping that reading paper instead of pixels would help. But no, the words once again swirled into a watery current flowing over him. He liked the color though, close to a royal blue, but darker, with long, dark green strands of kelp waving in the current. He floated for a while watching, waiting, and then someone was there, taking his hand and leading him through a doorway into a house where he could see a dense forest and a crowded subway platform. So many people! Someone's phone was ringing. One of the passengers on the train. Everyone was looking around, patting their pockets. The train rolled in. The people dissolved. It kept ringing.

Terry gasped and reached for his Blackberry, eyes peeling open just enough to see the caller ID.

"Burt. Is something wrong?"

"I might ask the same thing, are you all right Terry?"

Terry cleared his throat and took a breath to clear the train from his mind. "Yes, I'm fine. I guess I drifted off. Dull reading."

"Sorry to have disturbed you—"

"No, it's okay. I needed to wake up and finish. What's up?"

"No emergency. But I wanted to ask if you know whether Beth knows anyone in Texas. An old friend, perhaps?"

Terry frowned.

Odd question. "No, not that she's mentioned. But she doesn't talk much about childhood friends." *And why don't you ask her?*

"I wasn't thinking childhood, since she grew up in California. But maybe a college roommate, or someone in New York?"

"No. Not that I recall. But that doesn't rule it out. Sorry. Why?"

"There's a man from Texas here in the islands who's looking for Beth. He says he's actually looking for a mutual friend and hopes Beth can help him. It seems to work with the cruisers, it doesn't sound like he's threatening to Beth, so they tell him what they know about her. I have a guess about the mutual friend, if his story is true."

"Ori." Terry said the name with far more venom than he intended. His opinion of Beth's so-called friend had never been high, and when he finally met her last summer it had not gotten better.

"Ori," Burt repeated, his tone not dissimilar from Terry's. He shared Terry's opinion, which could explain why he called him and not Beth herself. "Any idea if she's still in Connecticut?"

"Beth hasn't talked to her, that I know of, but there were a couple emails in the summer. Nothing recently, I don't think. I don't think Beth has told her about moving to D.C. You know about that, right?"

"Yes, I spoke to Beth on Christmas Eve."

"Oh right, she told me. So you know she's in St Martin."

"Yes. The Texan is in Antigua because someone told him they saw her there not long ago. You're back in Washington?"

"Yes. I came back Tuesday morning. But we were in Antigua around Thanksgiving. I don't remember meeting any cruisers."

"No, it was someone who saw you there in August. But it's likely he will eventually find someone who knows where she currently is. He's very good at finding and talking to cruisers. Is she returning to Washington when she finishes her assignment?"

"Yes. Unless they want her to work with another client. We didn't talk much about it, but I think she'll leave *Trouble* in a marina on St. Martin. I guess nobody has given him her phone number."

"Not so far, I don't think. I only know what they say they told him. Someone might have and not mention it to me when I ask."

"Have you confronted him?"

"No. I suppose I should have when I first saw him asking about her in Pointe-à-Pitre. I haven't seen him since, just his trail. It turns out Laurie and Joe are the ones who pointed him to Antigua."

"And they didn't know we would be there in November."

"Right. It was coincidence you were actually there that recently."

"So he followed an old lead that happened to be the right direction a month ago. We're lucky he didn't come across us while we were there."

"Yes. But wasn't Beth job hunting in November? How were you in Antigua?"

"We did a charter to try out a boat we're thinking of buying."

"So you weren't aboard *Double Trouble?*"

"No. But Beth is now."

"I know. But nobody has sent him to St. Martin. I didn't want to tell Beth about this. You know how she can over react."

"No, really?" Terry said, laughing. "Not to mention being over protective of Ori for some reason."

"Yes. Well, I think her behavior demonstrates she's a loyal friend, perhaps to a fault. It's not my place to protect her from someone who might be completely honest and benign. But I can't help think about Ori's baby."

Terry had come to the same conclusion as Burt said it. "And who the father might be," he said.

Why does Ori keep coming back to haunt Beth?

"Right."

"Which does not make this Hunter a bad guy, or a threat to Beth." Terry forced himself to say. *Innocent until proven guilty.*

"But it also doesn't explain why he's looking for Beth and not for Ori herself."

"Why the 'friend of a friend' thing? I don't know. But you're right we have no reason to think he's dangerous. In any case, I'm between charters and I thought I might enjoy a visit to St. Martin. Good food there, you know."

"Knowing you're there would make me a lot happier, Burt," Terry said.

"Tell me where I can find Beth."

Terry gave Burt the marina name and *Trouble's* location in it. Then something else occurred to him.

"Burt, remember Ori's father put her boat up for sale in Pointe-à-Pitre? Find out if it's still there, or it sold."

"You think Ori's come back to the islands? With her infant son?"

"No idea, but maybe somehow this Texan does know she is in the islands. That would explain why he doesn't just go to Connecticut."

"Maybe he doesn't know she left the islands," Burt said, which cooled Terry's excited reasoning.

"Right. Maybe he doesn't know she's from Connecticut in the first place. But it doesn't explain why he's looking for Beth and not for Ori herself."

"Yes. I think that's the reason I'm not comfortable with the situation. It's a good idea, knowing whether Ori's boat is still sitting at the brokerage. I'd better let you get back to your dull reading."

"Right. I think I'll stay awake now, thanks to you. Happy New Year Burt."

"Happy New Year."

After the line went dead Terry realized that, like Beth, he had forgotten to mention their engagement, even though he'd mentioned their Antigua trip. *Beth will tell him when he finds her in Marigot.*

Terry felt lingering doubt about withholding information from Beth about someone stalking her. Burt's rationale was fine for him, as a friend who had in the past gone after Beth when he thought she'd put herself in a dangerous situation. What she didn't know wouldn't cause her to take action dangerous to herself. But as her fiancé, he should be completely honest with her. He should tell her. And yet, as he thought about how he would phrase it, he felt the same caution Burt was exercising. What would she do? Would she go looking for this guy like she had Ori a year or so ago when Ori seemed to call for help?

*)

Princess Julianna Airport, Sint Maarten

Hunter waited patiently while the baggage attendants unloaded the suitcases and other assorted luggage of his fellow travelers from on top of his backpack. When one of them finally heaved it from the cart to the ground Hunter moved in and picked it up, then joined the line at customs.

Since boarding the flight in Dallas he'd been unable to stop brooding on the conversation with his father on New Year's Eve. The following day—January first—he'd received three emails from his father about the work he'd be taking on when he returned. Despite the messages' annoyingly victorious tone he had dutifully skimmed the new client profiles and agreements, the specter of Green Equipment Leasing looming in his future. He'd grown disgusted with himself when he caught himself getting interested in the business and closed all the files on his computer.

The customs officer glanced at his form and waved him on. Released into Dutch Sint Maarten he banished the blocky black letters of the Green logo from his thoughts and smiled into the bright Caribbean sunshine.

Drivers for hotel and resort vans stood inside and out holding signs, some with their company logo and name, others with the names of expected guests listed. Similarly, representatives from the various boat charter companies were gathered over to the right with their signs. Beth Anderson would not be in the same harbor on her private boat that was inhabited by a charter company. Those were not her people. But where would she be?

He went back inside to a map of the island highlighting many of the hotels, guest houses, resorts, and tour operations. Both the Dutch and French halves of this island had a lot of places for a sailor to anchor. He discarded Oyster Pond because it was the home of the sailboat charter companies. He'd learned in his months of searching that the cruisers with their own boats looked down on those who came to the islands to rent one for a week or so. North of it was Orient Beach, with a protected bay, and a famous nude beach. Could be, but the high tourist population might be a deterrent. Moving south along the east coast he considered Guana Bay and others further south, but he knew the eastern shore of many of the islands was rocky, the sea perpetually rough, so very likely the bays along there were not attractive to sailors. He studied the south coast. There was Great Bay and the Dutch capital of Phillipsburg—a cruise ship port. Further west the first bay with potential was Cole Bay followed by Simpson Bay and the sprawling internal salt pond. The west coast didn't appear to have many spots attractive to sailboats, based on the photos on the map of empty turquoise waters. Following around the North West point of the island he found

Marigot Bay. Huge, protected, and well known. It was a good bet, and so was Simpson Bay and the lagoon. Further along the north coast was Anse Marcel, a protected spot that might attract a loaner like this Beth seemed to be.

From the airplane he'd looked down on Simpson Bay and the lagoon and seen thousands of boats. If Beth and *Double Trouble* were there, he'd have a long search. But if they were there, other cruisers were too, and talking to them had been his best strategy so far.

Ignoring the resort drivers, he walked back out to the taxi stand and leaned into the passenger side window of the first car.

"I'm looking for someplace cheap around the lagoon. Price matters more than location. Got any ideas?"

The driver stared straight ahead for a moment, thinking, Hunter hoped, not ignoring him.

"Pool? Beach?" the man asked, still staring out the windshield.

"Don't need 'em. Just need a place to drop my gear while I explore, take a shower, get some sleep."

The driver turned his head to study Hunter, then nodded.

"I know a place. Clean. Honest people. You gonna be walking to get anywhere, though."

"How far?"

The driver shrugged, "kilometer to the waterfront," he estimated.

"I got legs. I'm good with that." Hunter opened the rear door of the car, shoved his pack inside, and got in.

⌡

Dickinson Bay, Antigua

"*Merci. Au revoir.*" Burt ended the call and set his phone down on *Sandcastle*'s galley counter. He picked up the sandwich he'd made while speaking to the yacht broker and carried it out to the aft deck where a cold beer was waiting.

Ori had come to the brokerage back in September and taken her boat—which actually belonged to her father—off the market. She'd left the marina without settling the outstanding marina charges.

He contacted Ori's father and requested final payment. His description of George Chapman's reaction over the phone included very colorful French, some of it so obscure Burt didn't know it. What he did know was that Ori was into the wind, so to speak, on a boat she had technically stolen. She did not, and the broker was very clear on this point, have an infant with her. Burt had mixed feelings about that detail—it was good that the woman had not brought her son along to sail single handed in the islands. The boat and her own safety were enough of a responsibility. But the fact that the new mother would leave her baby—with her parents, he hoped— revealed a great deal about Ori.

Burt was under no illusion that all women were cut out to be mothers. Ori's actions simply confirmed she was one of the non-maternal ones. She hadn't fallen in love with their infant at birth. Or maybe she did love her baby, but she loved herself more. Burt suspected the latter might be closer to the truth. He'd seen a spark of maternal instinct in Ori right after giving birth, when the baby was kidnapped from the hospital. In her post-partum haze Ori had appeared to bond with the little tyke. But very possibly the life with her parents that she'd fled before had simply worn thin again, and her new baby hadn't been enough of a draw to keep her there.

The fact that Ori's personality was nothing like Beth's was what made Burt worry about his friend's affection for the other woman. He knew Beth had followed Ori south from New York, and she never would have come to be sailing on her own in the islands now if she hadn't met Ori back then. But Beth seemed to idolize her friend. Events after the birth of Ori's son had tarnished Beth's admiration, but Burt didn't think it was entirely gone. To Beth, Ori represented the free spirit Beth thought she should be.

On the other hand, Beth's recent, rational decision to get a job and earn enough money to support her lifestyle suggested she was out from under Ori's unintended influence. Ori, Burt had discovered months ago after the whole baby kidnapping incident, had a trust-fund. She could afford to appear to be sailing on a shoestring because she came from New England old money. Her parents had banked a sizeable fund for her when she was born. It was far larger than a typical college fund: she had enough to support her in modest comfort on the interest. She might have started out as broke as Beth, but by the time Beth met her she had reached the required age to use the money. Burt doubted Beth knew. Ori had enticed her to undertake a lifestyle she knew Beth wasn't equipped to afford. But Ori didn't reveal how she herself managed it. She made it look to Beth like she survived on no income and encouraged Beth to do the same. That was what made Burt dislike the woman.

He doubted Ori was looking for Beth in the islands. That wasn't her style. All it would take was an email to Beth—Beth would definitely tell her friend where she was. The fact that Ori had a boat and was somewhere out there now shouldn't matter. Except for Hunter. If Hunter found Beth, Beth would most likely try to reach Ori. That would likely lead to the two of them reuniting, with this Hunter character thrown in for good measure.

It was none of Burt's business who Beth associated with. But something told him Ori would always be a bad influence, and Burt did not want Beth getting into trouble. He thought of her like a daughter, even though it was not his place. He'd be proud to have raised a person like Beth, had his life path been different. Perhaps if he could be around when Ori, Hunter, and Beth converged, he could exert influence in the right direction.

Forty-four

Marigot Bay, St. Martin

On Wednesday morning Beth was up with the sun and off of the boat with her canvas market bags not much later. At the weekly Marigot Bay market, the produce stalls stacked with fresh mangoes, coconuts, tamarinds, and all manner of vegetables drew her attention first. She waged a constant battle with a realistic consumption projection versus the beautiful produce as she selected one of this and a small bunch of that. She kept telling herself she would be back in a few days and the lovely produce would too. With one bag full, she moved into the meat section and purchased a whole chicken and a pork loin. Both appeared to have been raised in the islands—they were not frozen and not in vacuum sealed packaging as all of the imported meat was. Bits of feather on the bird further supported its origins in someone's farm yard. As she stuffed the paper-wrapped packages into another bag a head of dark, curly hair over in the cheese stalls caught her eye. She thanked the butcher and made for the cheeses. She had to be wrong, how could it be Ori?

As Beth approached the stall offering a wide selection of cheeses catering to the French population of the island, the dark-haired woman looking at them glanced over at her.

"Beth?"

"Yes. Ori, what are you doing here?"

"Buying cheese, silly. Wednesday is the best day because Chloe comes," she said, looking across the counter at the cheese vendor, a young woman who smiled warmly. Beth inhaled a quick breath to squelch the annoyed response she wanted to make. Ori had left the islands for Connecticut with her parents and newborn son several months ago. Now here she was buying cheese in Marigot Bay, clearly without her tiny son.

"Good to know. But when did you come back to the islands?" She almost asked why, but managed to change the word in time.

"About four months ago."

"Four months ago? Wow, what have you been up to?"

Ori glanced at Chloe, who was watching them impassively, then back at Beth. "Let's go get a coffee and talk."

"Sure." Beth had a conference call with the team at half past ten, but it wasn't yet nine o'clock. She followed Ori to one of the coffee and pastry stands on the edge of the market. Beth ordered a latte and a *pain au chocolat* while Ori had a *café Americain* and an unappetizing, healthy sounding multigrain muffin. They sat at a tiny café table under an awning beside the booth.

"So, how is Tiberius?" Beth figured it was best to get her biggest question out there: where was Ori's son?

"He's wonderful, growing and learning and slobbering like a champ."

Beth took a sip of her latte to hide her frown.

This is like pulling teeth.

"And where is he? Do you have a nanny or something?"

"He does have a nanny," Ori nodded, chewing a bite of her muffin. It had strings of shredded carrot and other vegetable matter hanging from it. "She's with him in Connecticut."

"You left him with your parents in Connecticut?"

"Don't sound so shocked. You had to know I'm not mom material. I do regret she'll do to him the same things she did to me. But I figure once he's old enough to steer a boat I'll go get him and correct whatever she's done."

Beth took another sip and tore off a tip off her chocolate croissant. Trying to keep the crumb explosion contained gave her a moment to absorb Ori's explanation.

"You have *Dream Catcher*"

"Yeah. I went to Guadeloupe and got her from the broker dad left her with. He hadn't sold her yet, so I told him his time was up."

"You stole your boat back?"

Ori looked hurt. "I have the documentation. She's my boat. He didn't have any choice."

Beth refrained from asking if Ori stole *Dream Catcher*'s registration papers from her father before leaving his home. She recalled him saying he was the documented owner when he asked for advice about what to do with the boat after Ori gave birth.

"So why St. Martin?"

"Oh, you know how it is. I got a job at a casino on Guadeloupe, but they had to let me go. My manager there hooked me up with a job in one of the casinos here. Even got me training. I'm a blackjack dealer."

"No kidding? I can't imagine it."

"I know, right? Not my style. But it pays well and the tips can be outrageous. Some of the customers are pigs, but that's life. And watching of these fat cats lose to the house is very satisfying. I figure it's a portable job skill—people play blackjack all over the world."

"Is that where you're going now? All over the world?"

"Aren't you? Hey, where's they guy?"

"Washington. I'm based there now, too."

"No shit? You gave up? Why are you here alone, then?"

"I didn't give up cruising. But I pretty much ran out of money, and Terry ran out of time. I went back to the states with him and got a job. Which is why I'm here now—I'm working too."

"Well look at you, from lowly copy writer to—what? What do you do in Washington that you can do here, of all places?"

"I work for a consulting firm. They hired me as a lowly technical writer, but it turned out my months in the islands are useful to them. I understand things about the people here. I was put on a team working with clients in the islands."

"Working how?"

"Whatever they hire us for. The first one was a politician who had us help him get appointed to a committee. I attended his hearing. That was on Antigua. Now I'm working with a business woman who wants us to help her make distribution agreements with stores in the US."

"And you know about distribution in the US?"

"Not at all. Well, I do know a bit now. But I'm part of a team. I'm here being the face, but behind me there are a half dozen people doing the leg work and telling me what to say and do."

"You're the tip of the iceberg, huh? Tricky balancing act."

Beth nodded. Ori had always been perceptive. "It's nerve wracking. Yesterday I spent the morning with her visiting with the women who make her products. She's placed their jewelry in shops in Phillipsburg and several of the hotel gift shops."

"Doesn't sound very scalable," Ori said, shaking her head. Beth was not surprised her friend easily identified the flaw in Virgine's plan.

"Exactly. I told her at our first meeting. I half expected to be shown the door, the contract cancelled. But she agreed and is listening to my team's advice."

"Well if they can come up with a way to scale it, I'll applaud them," Ori said. "These islanders are not reliable when it comes to meeting deadlines and filling quotas."

Beth tried not to grimace at Ori's sweeping disparaging of Caribbean islanders. It contradicted her new role as consultant and cheerleader.

Her coffee cup was nearly empty, and all that remained of her croissant was a pile of crumbs.

"I have to finish my shopping and get back to *Trouble* for a conference call. Can we get together again? Are you on your email?"

"Yeah, absolutely. You've got your boat here? I thought you were staying in a hotel."

"Nope, *Trouble* was laid up in St. Thomas for a couple months. Terry and I had her launched and sailed her here over Christmas. I'm in Fort Louis marina."

"Oh ho, the high rent district. *Dream Catcher*'s in the lagoon. We should go sailing on one or the other of them. Hey, we could go to St. Barts for a few days!"

Beth smiled at Ori's enthusiasm, but she suppressed the urge to jump on board the plan. "I could get away with an afternoon sail, but I'm being paid to be here for the duration. Maybe before I leave I can work it out, though."

Ori was nodding, studying her. She crumpled up the paper bag from her muffin as she rose. "Even though you escaped, you haven't changed. Dedicated to the job."

Beth rose too, shouldering her bags. "Just like you, I have to make ends meet, what can I say?" she said, determined not to get angry. Ori's escapist attitude had pushed Beth to cast off her lines in the first place, and for that she would be forever grateful, no matter that she eventually realized she could not imitate Ori's no-money-worries lifestyle. A lifestyle that seemed to have changed for Ori now too, Beth reflected. She wanted to know more about Ori's abandonment of her newborn son. "Why don't you come have dinner aboard *Trouble* tomorrow evening?"

"Evenings are my best shifts for tips. Let's have lunch tomorrow. Email me—it's the same address." Ori was moving away from the table.

"That sounds great. I'll email you later," Beth called. She gathered her own trash and carried it to a nearby can, her thoughts swirling.

A bus drew up to the curb spewing diesel fumes. She moved away: the smell was comforting because it reminded her of boats, but the bus was so smelly she felt the twinge of a headache. As she re-entered the rows of market stalls a man climbed out of the bus and stepped away from it, pausing to swing a daypack onto his shoulders as he studied the milling shoppers and vendors all around him.

♩

Fort Louis Marina, Marigot Bay, St. Martin

"Hey, what's up?" Beth was standing in *Trouble*'s cockpit, her shore bag slung over her shoulder. She'd almost ignored her cell phone ringing, but pulled it out of her pocket and found Terry's name on the caller ID.

"I'm having dinner with Jeff and people from the company tonight, so I'm not sure we'll be able to talk. I thought I'd leave you a message."

"I'm heading out to visit the shops that sell Virgine's products. But you won't believe the morning I've had."

"I won't? Why?"

Beth thought he sounded far more concerned than he ought to.

"I went to the market. I know it's hard to remember when you're in Washington, but today is market day—"

"I remember," Terry interrupted, chuckling in a way that dispelled any concern. "I wish I could have been there."

"I'm sure. But can you guess who I ran into in the cheese section?"

"I don't know. Laurie and Joe? Burt?"

"No. Ori."

"Ori? What the hell?" The concern was back loud and clear. But Beth understood it. Ori was always a troublesome topic.

"I know, right? That's pretty much what I thought. She left her son with her parents and came back to the islands. I'm going to see her again, try to get the whole story."

"And she just happens to be on St. Martin when you are?"

"Yeah. Total coincidence. As usual, she didn't explain why she hasn't answered my emails."

"Beth, I know she's your friend, but—"

"Keep her at arms' length?"

"It's hard, Beth. I know how important she is to you. We would never have met if she hadn't inspired you to head south. That is incredibly important to me. But yeah, keep her at arms' length."

Beth smiled. "I owe Ori for that. But it's not enough for me to buy into whatever she's up to now."

"God, I don't want to ruin your friendship, Beth."

"Stop. It's okay. I can be her friend without being sucked into her drama. Really. I have my own work drama to worry about."

"You're going to check up on your client's products in shops?"

"Yeah. Remember the woman in Orient Bay? I want to see what other shop owners say."

"Be careful."

"How can talking to shop owners be dangerous?"

"I have no idea. You're just so far away, I can't not worry."

"I love that someone is worried about me. Someone who understands where I am and what I'm doing, I mean. Trish and Mom worry about me, but that doesn't count since they're clueless."

"Woah. That's way too much for me to process. I do understand, and I know you can safely visit gift shops on St. Martin. But be careful anyway, okay?"

"Okay. I'll be careful. I've got to get going. I love you."

"I love you too."

Terry ended the call and set down his phone. She was fine. She was working. Ori was an interesting development, but Beth was focused on her own responsibilities. There was no point in telling her about the Texan who was on an entirely different island.

So why did he feel guilty for not being entirely honest with his fiancé? As he refocused on his work, he wished Burt had never called him.

)

Philipsburg, Sint Maarten

Beth grimaced as she got out of her third taxi of the afternoon. Even though Broadhead would reimburse her for the fares, it went against her frugality to hand over so much cash. But the various hotel and tourist area gift shops she wanted to visit were too far apart to walk within a reasonable amount of time. Even a rented bike would make it a two-day expedition instead of an afternoon.

The smile of the doorman as he opened the door of the Sun View Hotel forced her to smile back as she walked into the lobby. She quickly spotted the gift shop opposite the registration desk and headed for it.

So far she had visited four shops located on the property of high-end hotels around Philipsburg, the Dutch capital of Sint Maarten. Two displayed wooden racks draped with Virgine's braided bracelets, anklets, and necklaces. One carried the wire and crystal jewelry on a clear Plexiglas rack. Beth had introduced herself in that shop and asked about the display. No, Virgine did not provide it, they reused it from a previous vendor. Custom displays were a discussion item for Virgine on the team's list.

A little bell rang when she opened the door of the Sun View Hotel shop.

"Hello," a woman's voice called out from somewhere.

"Hello," Beth said, looking around for the source of the greeting. Several tall racks of resort clothing with hats and beach bags on top of them obstructed her view across the space. The clerk materialized from behind one of these: a petit woman dressed in colorful flowing linen. Beth loved the relaxed look that she wasn't able to pull off herself. Such garments just made her look enormous.

"Can I help you find something?" the clerk asked.

Beth decided to be open about her intentions, it had gotten her useful information in the last shop. "My name is Beth Anderson. I'm a consultant working with Virgine Guesnon, and today I'm doing research. Do you know if you carry any of Guesnon's products?"

"Guesnon? Yes, over here," she guided Beth toward a glass display counter.

Beth saw several wire jewelry pieces arrayed on a mirrored shelf inside. In addition, a rack of braided items stood on a shelf behind the case. But something else drew Beth's eye. On the same shelf as the braided jewelry, but set apart from it, were four carved wooden figures. One was a sailboat with paper-thin sails.

"And Guesnon supplies those too, right?"

"The artist, Mr. Hugon, brings us those every few weeks. They are a cut above the trinkets from Guesnon."

"They are beautiful." Beth reached across the counter and picked up a leaping dolphin. The wood was polished to a lustre, the lines of the creature lifelike. Out of habit she turned it over to check the price. Twenty-five Euro. "I must have misunderstood Ms. Guesnon. I'm sure she said she supplies Mr. Hugon's work to the shops."

"Perhaps she does, to some. But I have known Mr. Hugon for many years. We sell two or three a week. Guesnon's jewelry does move—we sell a lot of the braided bracelets. They are the only inexpensive jewelry item we carry so the youngsters buy them."

"I see. And the wire jewelry?" Beth looked down at the mirrored shelf, recognizing the designs from yesterday's tour.

The woman shrugged. "Not as much as the cheaper product. But enough. They are lovely pieces."

"Would you replace them if something else came along for a better price?" Beth was trying to find out whether the shop had any social mission to support local women.

"My rent here is three thousand Euro per month. I have to stock what sells."

"I understand. Thank you for your help."

"I would not carry Guesnon's products if they were not made here on Sint Maarten. Madame Guesnon is not always convenient to deal with."

"Do you care to tell me how?" Beth sensed growing reticence in the woman.

"Late deliveries. Early requests for payment. Sometimes it is as if she is doing me a favor."

"I see. I appreciate your honesty."

"Then I suggest you look closely at your client." With that she nodded curtly and moved away toward a door marked "Private."

Beth accepted the dismissal and left the shop.

She mulled over the woman's suggestion as she walked across the hotel lobby. The slow deliveries were symptomatic of Virgine's supply problems. But the early demands for payment were unwelcome news. Virgine had not said a word about cash flow being a problem. And then there were Mr. Hugon's carvings. Was Virgine's relationship with him troubled? If so, his work on the jewelry templates could be at risk. Beth decided to ask her team's input—maybe she should go back to Colombier and pay another call on Mr. Hugon.

She was lucky to catch a taxi dropping off guests outside, and took it to her next destination, a shop at a resort in Oyster Pond back in the French half of St. Martin. When she got out of the taxi she felt right at home—this resort was the base for one of the charter companies. The docks were crowded with sailboats.

There were several customers in the shop, so Beth was able to look around without immediate attention from the staff. She located a jewelry counter and identified both of Guesnon's jewelry lines. She saw a display of painted steel items familiar from Virgine's office. Above them on a shelf there were dozens of wooden carvings, including several leaping dolphins. Beth picked one up and studied it closely. She was far from expert in wood carvings, but everything about this one seemed like the one in the previous shop, and Mr. Hugon's workshop. Everything except the rough, lackluster finish, the round, "made in China" sticker on the bottom, and the five Euro price tag.

On impulse, she took the carving to the counter and bought it without asking about Guesnon products. She tucked the receipt in with her taxi receipts and left the shop. Now more than before she wanted to return to Colombier. Alone.

Forty-five

Marigot Bay, St. Martin

"*H*e's in the best place for him right now," Ori declared. "Between Mom and the nanny and the doctors he wants for nothing."

She was sitting across from Beth at a picnic table in the sand. They each had containers of food from a nearby stand. Ori had revealed something that Beth had not realized when Tiberius, her son, was born, kidnapped, and rescued by Terry and Burt last summer: he was quite premature. Ori said if he'd been born in a hospital in the states he would have been put into intensive care. Since he had instead been treated like any other newborn, he had residual health issues.

As Ori described the hospital stay followed by constant doctor's appointments and treatments her tiny son had undergone during his first months in Connecticut, Beth saw how the responsibility had worn Ori down, and she understood. She understood because her father's health was failing, and she, like Ori, chose to live far from him and leave the details of his day-to-day care to others in her family.

Even so, she wanted to respond to Ori's declaration by saying, *he wants for nothing but a mother.* Ori leaving her child behind was not the same as Beth not moving back home to be with her ailing father. *It isn't.* But Beth held her tongue rather than challenge her friend's self-delusion. What would be the point? And what if Ori picked apart her own self-delusion out of self-defense?

Beth told Ori more about her work, and how it provided her a much-needed financial infusion. This time Ori didn't react with caustic criticism. Without naming names Beth went on to describe her client's home and office. She mentioned her business challenges that Broadhead was working on.

"She sounds like she is, or wants to be, a power player—this island has a lot of them. Bullish on the local chamber of commerce, trying to create change through business development. I see them in the casino. They bring clients in to show them a good time. It's either them or the cruise ship people."

"I wouldn't have expected the locals to use the casinos that much. I thought they were built for the tourist trade, to attract more of it."

Ori nodded and took a bite of her food.

"But I can see how it might be useful to oil the wheels in business."

Ori swallowed. "Some, yes, but there are locals who have a problem. There's one woman who seems to like my table. She's in at least once a week, always alone so she's not using it to entertain anyone. There's a guy who has lost a lot over the months, but it doesn't seem to matter. He has a great time at the table. I think he considers it his entertainment."

"People do, I know. I wouldn't find it fun, but I get that people do."

"You should come check it out. You couldn't sit at my table, but you could check out the crowd, play some slots. You shouldn't leave St. Martin without at least seeing it."

Beth thought about that, tried to picture herself in a noisy, glittering casino, based entirely on what she'd seen in movies. It might be fun.

"Maybe I will. Once we get my client's company on track."

)

Fort Louis Marina, Marigot Bay, St. Martin

Back aboard *Trouble* Beth opened the file on her laptop with the team's recommendations for Virgine. She had reviewed them twice already, and other than a couple minor questions she knew she understood what they were proposing. She placed the pad with notes from her visit to the shops in front of her on the saloon table and called into the Equatorial Team's conference call. The whole team was on, so greetings and the usual social amenities took longer than usual. Beth felt herself growing impatient with Brendan's golf story and squelched the impulse to interrupt. He finally finished with a boast about an impressive hole-in-one that he'd foreshadowed from the start. Beth begrudgingly added her voice to the polite chuckles and congratulations. Finally, Marcus started the usual around-the-room updates.

Seetha and Brendan were working together on a project for their client on St. Croix. Beth did her best to listen and learn, but when the discussion went on for twenty minutes she caught herself zoning out, doodling on her notes and wondering what cold drinks she had in the cooler. She almost missed it when the topic was brought to a close and Marcus asked her for an update.

"I did some leg work yesterday," she said, frowning at her doodled sailboat on the corner of her pad. "I visited the gift shops at a half dozen resorts across the island."

"Ouch. You must have some taxi receipts to submit," Brendan said. Beth wasn't sure how to take that, so she ignored it.

"The shop managers and owners do not have overwhelmingly positive opinions of Guesnon."

"They don't like the products?" Claudia asked.

"No, their opinions on the product range from neutral to favorable. The criticisms were about delivery schedules, demands for early payment, customer care type stuff."

"Typical small business," Seetha said. "She has no staff, right?"

"Only the locals who make the product. No assistant or anything," Beth's mind flashed to the young man at Virgine's home.

"We should help her fill the gap. She needs someone to manage the books and inventory, take customer calls …" Claudia trailed off as if she was making notes.

"There's something else about what I found in the shops," Beth went on. "In one shop I found a wooden carving made by Prosper, the man in Columbier. The owner of the shop said he supplies her directly."

"And does Virgine distribute his work?" Marcus asked.

"Yes, she said she does. But it gets more complicated. In another shop, I found a figurine a lot like his, but it was much rougher. It was also much cheaper, and there was a 'made in China' sticker on the bottom."

"What's up with that?" Marcus asked. Beth wished she had an answer. The flicker of disappointment she felt made her realize she had been hoping for an explanation, or at least reassurance, from them.

"I bought one. I'm wondering if I should ask Virgine about it when I meet with her tomorrow."

"Isn't it likely Prosper gets ideas from the cheaper items in the shops?" Claudia asked.

"Right," Brendan agreed.

Beth wasn't so sure, Prosper hadn't seemed like the type to wander the resort shops. But she couldn't articulate why she thought they were wrong.

"I think you should hold off on challenging Virgine about this right now," Marcus said. "You'll be presenting her with challenging recommendations as it is. Hang onto the Chinese figurine and we'll see where things go."

"Okay. No problem," Beth said. "I think you're right that Virgine will be challenged enough by the recommendations. I have a couple questions about them."

"Sure, let's go over them," Marcus said, a faint tone of relief in his voice. Beth wondered why he'd been concerned, but she let it go and concentrated on the recommendations.

ↄ

Philipsburg, Sint Maartin

"Ten to you Madam. House is now sixteen." Ori placed the seven on top of the nine she'd previously dealt the house and turned to the player to the left, a thin, balding man in a tropical print shirt who must be from a cruise ship. He had about another hour before he had to scurry back to the launch. Despite Ori's contempt, she had to admit he was good. He stood on his eighteen and Ori looked to his companion, a woman about twenty years his junior who was dressed for clubbing, and not the gambling variety. As she signaled to take a card on her seventeen, he groaned. But to Ori's surprise, the next card was a four. The woman clapped, hopping up and down on her seat. Her companion stared down at her hand, his lips twisting in a forced smile. The next player, a man in his twenties who Ori suspected was trying to count cards, stood on his seventeen, which drew a gloating comment from the woman. Thankfully he ignored it. Finally, Ori turned to Virgine Guesnon, who had a five and a ten.

"Hit me," Virgine said. Ori drew a card from the shoe and turned it over as she placed it on top of the ten.

"Twenty-three Madam." Virgine's expression was dark, but Ori wasn't sure if it was anger, disappointment, or something else.

Ori drew one more card. "House has twenty."

She collected all of the rest of the bets and paid the woman who had drawn the lucky card. She swept up all of the cards with her paddle and placed them in the discard rack.

Virgine's stack of chips was not tall enough to meet the table minimum. The woman was picking up the stack and watching the chips fall one by one like a catholic murmuring her way through her prayer beads.

"Do you wish to exchange for more chips, madam?" Ori asked. If not, Virgine was obliged to leave the table.

Virgine's head snapped up to glare at Ori. Ori felt the presence of the pit boss behind her.

"Madam, I believe you have business to attend to," Rupert said, indicating with his right hand at someone behind her. The rest of the players followed his gesture and saw a tall man standing behind Virgine. He wore an immaculate blue suit and stood with his hands clasped in front of him. He was watching Virgine intently. Virgine turned her glare from Ori to the pit boss, and then slowly rotated to look at the man. He nodded, mouth pursed tightly. Ori felt a flash of pity for the woman. Elvis Rink was a well-known loan shark, and he was not gentle with those who failed to pay him back.

As soon as Virgine vacated her seat, Ori resumed the game for her other customers. As she observed them making their wagers and then dealt the first hand, she caught glances of Virgine being walked out of the casino by Mr. Rink.

⟩

"Get in." Rink twisted Virgine's arm up behind her back so forcefully she yelped and bent over, her head aimed into the car. She reached out with her other hand to prevent herself from falling onto the back seat.

"All right. Let me do it!" she hissed through the pain. The pressure on her arm eased and she was able to straighten enough to lift her left foot into the car. She shot Rink an evil stare as she rotated her behind onto the car seat and lifted her right leg in. Rink's smirk made her angrier.

He stepped away from the car and his driver shut the door. Virgine took the moment alone to adjust her short skirt and compose herself. Before she could become truly calm the far door opened and Rink got in. At the same time the driver opened his door and got in front. In a moment the car was in motion.

"Where are we going?" Virgine asked She was surprised at how calm she sounded. But then, she was a talented performer.

"Just for a drive, Virgine. And a talk."

"We could have talked over a cocktail at the casino."

Rink laughed far more than was necessary and reached over to place his long-fingered hand on her bare thigh. It was warm. "I think you have spent enough time at cards this evening, Virgine. Perhaps forever."

Virgine cringed at his touch. The skin beneath his hand felt like it was covered with squirming insects. She ground her teeth together to hide her disgust. The car moved out of the casino drive and on across the parking lot to the street.

"I have been very patient, Virgine. Don't you agree?"

Virgine stared straight ahead at the back of the headrest on the front passenger seat. "Very well. We will assume you do. Our agreement was that you would pay me the agreed upon amount after Christmas. But now it is after New Year's and here we are having the same conversation again."

"I am making arrangements. I will have the money in a few days." Virgine said. Again, she was surprised at how calm she sounded.

"Virgine, Virgine, tsk, tsk, tsk," Rink shook his head as he spoke. Virgine quivered as his fingers moved to her inner thigh. "We have reached the point where money is not enough."

*

Marigot Bay, St. Martin

There was something different about Virgine Guesnon this morning. Beth couldn't put her finger on it, but the other woman seemed somehow lessened. Previously her strong personality had felt dominant, even threatening. This morning Beth could swear that her client was avoiding her gaze. She sat behind her desk with her hands wrapped around a mug obscuring what looked like seagulls in flight baked into the glaze. It struck Beth as a remarkably commercial product for a woman who distributed local pottery.

"I have reviewed your team's plan, Beth. The opportunities are exciting, and I agree with the need for more control over production," Virgine said, her eyes finally flicking up to look at Beth's face before dropping back to her mug. She lifted it to take a gingerly sip. Beth waited for the other shoe to drop.

"I'm glad you're excited. Should we talk about how to make it happen?"

"Yes, definitely."

Beth couldn't help but notice that the old Virgine seemed to be coming back. Her voice was stronger, and she met Beth's gaze once more. "Everything your team suggests is possible. In fact, most of it is change I have hoped to do myself."

Beth nodded. She had been briefed by Marcus on client behaviors, and the claim "I already thought of that" was a typical requirement of ego. Now Virgine would tell Beth why she had not done those things.

"The obstacle has always been capital. I have invested that part of my family's funds over which I have control in building support systems for my women so they can safely produce the jewelry. My profits today mostly go back to the workers and cover my business expenses. To recruit more workers and provide them with additional tools I need more money."

"I see. I'm not sure we understood your cash position clearly," Beth said. In fact, she'd been briefed on this eventuality. Perhaps she'd been naïve to think it wasn't likely. She'd been taken in by Virgine's persona. But the Virgine who had first greeted her today and refused to meet her eye was a different person—perhaps the real person.

"I have not made it clear," Virgine said, slipping back into her other persona. As she drew herself up and wrapped herself in her strong façade, she looked Beth in the eye. "Broadhead is well known to excel at funding. My business model is strong, and my mission is attractive."

"You want to add investment to your contract." Beth said, not a question.

"I want to prioritize investment. I love your team's plan, but I need funding to execute it. I know Broadhead will want to succeed."

Wow. Just wow. Beth was appalled at Virgine's open attempt at manipulation but couldn't help being impressed. From shrinking victim to turning her poor cash flow into a critical Broadhead objective in a single sentence.

"Can we get more specific? My team will need an idea of what you need in order to make the proposal to our investment team."

"Yes. Let's talk numbers." Virgine turned to her computer and started tapping on the keyboard. Beth waited. After a moment the laser printer behind Virgine hummed to life and began issuing pages. "I think this will help you, and your team, understand the scope of the problem," she said, rotating to pick up the printout.

Forty-six

Fort Louis Marina, Marigot Bay, St. Martin

"So just like that she switched the engagement to investment." Beth was sitting in *Trouble*'s saloon speaking into her cell phone. She was getting the hang of Broadhead's lingo; it wouldn't have been prudent to say the client had started begging.

"Did she have a number in mind?" Marcus asked, to Beth's utter surprise. She had anticipated laughter or annoyance or frustration. Not constructive discussion. She was glad she had worked with Virgine to come up with a number that was supported by the expenses they'd reviewed.

She told the team, who were gathered in a conference room around a speaker phone, about the calculation exercise and the result.

"So what do we do? Cancel the contract?"

"What?" Marcus's voice rose to almost a squeak. Beth's eyes widened in surprise. She held the phone away from her face and stared at it for a moment, until she realized someone was speaking again.

"… pivot at this time is entirely doable. It will extend the contract duration, of course. We may need you to stay with her longer, Beth."

"We'd let her make a demand like this?" Beth blurted, instantly regretting it. She should have saved her reaction for a private conversation with one of them.

"Oh come on," Jerry said, and in his words Beth heard the lack of respect she'd suspected. "Business is business." Jerry was her one teammate who hadn't been supportive of sending her to St. Martin, and hadn't been especially congratulatory after her success on Antigua. Still, he had a point.

"Right, okay. I was just surprised she'd do it," Beth backpedaled. "I can stay here if I need to. But don't we have to revise the contract? Get her to pay more?" Beth had not been involved in pricing their services. In fact, she didn't know how that part of the business worked.

"Yes, we'll have to revise the agreement. But operations will take care of it through backchannels," Claudia explained. "She may want to talk to you about it, but you should refuse. You're not there for that. As for more money, if we're getting her investors, we'll structure it so we get paid—don't worry about that."

"I see," Beth nodded at the empty saloon. Sometimes she felt like a child trying to operate in an adult world.

"Claudia is already preparing the request for the investment team. We'll need a couple days," Marcus told Beth. "Virgine should hear from us by Tuesday. In the meantime, keep her engaged on the changes. She must be able to afford to start on some of them. Needless to say, you're authorized if she wants you to accompany her to any other islands to recruit."

"She said she will be entertaining houseguests over the weekend, so I do not expect to talk to her before Monday. I'll let you know on our Monday call if anything changes."

When Beth ended the call after more logistic discussion and wishes for fun weekends, she felt drained. It was the middle of Friday afternoon and she had planned to spend it researching jewelry making techniques and tools. All of the hand knotting and sorting of beads that she'd seen at Columbier limited productivity. But she couldn't bring herself to open her laptop. She flopped back on the settee and blew upward at a strand of hair that kept falling into her eyes. If she'd been at anchor, she'd have stripped and jumped overboard for a swim. She knew the water would refresh her, maybe enough to come back and do the research. Swimming in the marina was out—the protected water was cloudy with mysterious discharge from the hundred or so boats inside. She shut her eyes and felt a faint vibration coming through *Trouble's* hull. A motor somewhere, the sound converted to waves traveling through the water. After a few minutes during which she nearly dropped off to sleep, Beth heaved herself up and climbed into the cockpit. At least she could get some fresh air.

⋀

Washington, D.C.

Raj Gupta knocked on his boss's door and waited. It was after five o'clock, but Adrian did not keep typical government office hours.

"Come in."

Raj opened the door and offered his best "everything is great" smile as he entered and closed it behind himself.

"Raj. It's Friday evening, I hope this isn't an emergency."

"No, not really. Just an update I thought you would want before the weekend."

"Have a seat. Drink?" Adrian opened a lower desk drawer and lifted out a bottle of Knob Creek. "Sorry. I forgot." He lowered the bottle back into the drawer with a wistful look. Raj didn't drink, but he didn't care if others did around him. His religious convictions were strong, and not threatened by others' behavior. He let the moment pass without urging Adrian to go ahead.

"Virgine Guesnon has requested that we reprioritize and introduce funding as an immediate concern. Beth informed the team this afternoon. She was agitated about the change in direction."

"And what did the rest of the team do?"

"They immediately drafted the request for the investment team, and assured Beth that this was not an unusual event."

Adrian nodded and said, "clients don't realize until we get into the details that our proposal will cost money beyond our fee, blah blah blah."

"Exactly."

"How much does the team think Ms. Guesnon needs?"

Raj named the amount.

"Seems do-able. I will confirm that we have the resources for this operation. It might require further on-site supervision."

"You don't want to pull Beth, do you?"

"I do not. We can add supervision without disturbing her relationship with the client. I will take care of it."

"All right. That's all I had, for now." Raj stood up.

"You have a pleasant weekend Raj."

)

Marigot Bay, St. Martin

The ringing phone brought Beth back below a few minutes after she'd fled the heat of the saloon. Her mainsail was ready. For no rational reason, the news revitalized her. She dropped her wallet into her daypack, wriggled her feet into her shoes, and locked up the boat. Without Terry to help she'd have to take a taxi to and from the sail loft and use a dock cart to bring the sail back to the boat. But the sail loft was not far from the marina, so when she flagged down a taxi and told the driver her destination, he shook his head. Thinking fast, she added that she would pay him to wait a few minutes and bring her back. More than doubling the fare was enough to buy his participation, so Beth got in.

They were there in ten minutes, and that was only because traffic was heavy on a Friday afternoon. In the sail loft, Brian had the sail spread out on the floor for her to inspect. The double patch on the rip was a bright white stripe, emphasizing how discolored the older fabric had become. The smaller reinforcements stood out too.

"At least I can see where they are."

"You'll get another year or two out of it. Come back any time you're ready to order a replacement," Brian said. Beth nodded, but made no promises.

Together they refolded the sail and slid it into its bag, then Brian carried it to the office to collect her payment.

"Do you need a hand getting it to your dinghy?"

"No, I have a taxi outside. I'm in the Fort Louis Marina now."

"Let me carry it out for you." He heaved the bag onto his shoulder and made for the door, Beth following.

Back at the marina Beth left the sail on the curb outside the marina reception office and hurried to the dock to retrieve one of the wheelbarrow-like dock carts. When she came back she found two employees from the office standing over the bag, the young man scratching his head. Both of them turned to look as she rolled the cart up to them.

"It is your sail!" the woman said. She was Beth's age and her professional hair and makeup elevated the marina polo shirt and white shorts that matched the dock staff's. She emanated authority.

"Yes. I brought it back from the sail loft," Beth said. "I needed to get a cart. I didn't think anyone was likely to steal it while I was gone."

"No, certainly not. But this is what our staff does. You should have asked. We will bring the sail to your boat. Would you like us to rig it?"

Taken aback, Beth set the back wheels of the cart on the pavement and considered the offer, which she knew would not be free of charge. She was capable of getting the sail up on *Trouble*'s deck and feeding the plastic cars into the slots on the boom and mast. But it was hard work, and that drained feeling was seeping back into her system.

"Yes, okay. Please do it for me." It came out of her mouth almost before she'd finished thinking it through. Then an idea struck her that felt so decadent she didn't want to keep thinking about it: She wanted to go to the beach.

A dock hand wheeling a cart with the sail in it came toward her when Beth stepped off of *Trouble* a little while later, beach bag over her shoulder. She felt absolutely free as she watched him climb aboard and drop it on the deck. She walked on down the dock to find the best path to the beach.

ⅎ

Simpson Bay, Sint Maarten

Any time his satellite phone rang Burt felt a shot of anticipation—or dread—as he picked it up. As he expected, the caller's identity was displayed as an unknown number. He touched the button to answer the call.

"Burt Adams here."

"Hello Burt. Good to hear your voice. It's been a while."

Not long enough, Burt resisted the urge to say out loud.

"Yes, I suppose things have been quiet in your domain."

"Just focused elsewhere, my friend. But a request crossed my wire that appears to have you written all over it."

"Why? What does it say?"

"We have financial resources going to a high-risk subject on St. Martin. Additional supervision is required."

Burt cocked his head to one side, then looked out of *Sandcastle*'s ports at the other boats anchored in Simpson Bay.

"Additional?"

"Yes. And confidential. There is an asset in place, but I don't believe we can put her in a supervisory role for the kind of funds needed. But that's why this operation has you written all over it. You first requested information on this asset some time ago, before she became one, as I recall. In fact, your previous inquiry influenced our decision to user her."

Burt didn't speak. He knew the name he was going to hear, and it revived the spark of anticipation, this time clearly on the "dread" side of the line.

"Is she in any danger?" Burt finally asked.

"Not if she does her job and stays out of the rest of it. Which is where you come in—doing the rest of it. Now when can you get to St. Martin?"

Burt admitted to already being there but managed to avoid saying why, or admitting that Beth had anything to do with it. By the time they ended the call he was scrolling through a file sent to his laptop via the satellite phone's Wi-Fi hot spot, including transcripts of conference calls between Beth and her team.

Any thought he'd been harboring that this had something to do with Hunter and Ori vanished as he read about Virgine Guesnon. He'd been given free rein to contact Beth or not. It was clear Washington was interested in her safety, which eased his conscience for having brought her to their attention. Months ago, he had requested a background check on her and on her boyfriend Terry. He thought they were both excellent additions to his network of cruisers in the islands—people who he knew were trustworthy and at low risk for corruption. Their background checks confirmed that they fit the profile: both were free of legal concerns and of the kind of social and community indiscretions that were distasteful to his associates in Washington. No college sit-ins, no protest marches, just a couple traffic violations between them. Their families were free of controversy and inappropriate connections. Burt knew it was a matter of time before he would have to be open with Beth about it. He was sure she suspected his "retirement" was not entirely complete. Terry was too smart to deceive much longer, and Burt had come close to revealing more when they spoke about Hunter last week.

Thinking of Hunter brought him back the present: he needed to formulate a plan for approaching Beth and her client Virgine.

Forty-seven

Marigot Bay, St. Martin

"*L*ook at you, driving off the dock like a boss," Ori said, stepping into the cockpit dragging the three fenders she'd removed from the lifelines. Behind *Trouble's* wheel, Beth shrugged one shoulder, her eyes roaming from their surroundings to the instruments and then over to Ori.

"Just toss those below, we're not going to be out that long."

Ori followed orders, dropping the three inflated fenders down the companionway to the cabin sole.

"Can you stand up by the mast and watch for cross traffic? Coming in here we noticed it can get busy."

"On it." Ori climbed back out of the cockpit.

Beth wasn't used to having to ask. Either she made do on her own, or Terry simply did what needed doing without direction. It felt strange and reminded her of the week with Jeff and Carole. She stifled that train of thought.

Ori pointed at a boat leaving its dock in the marina. Then she spotted another one approaching the marina from out in Marigot Bay. By the time *Trouble* was free and clear of the marina's tighter channels she had pointed out five boats crossing them and two oncoming. She returned to the cockpit and plopped down, the too-long sleeves of her grey hoodie dangling over her hands.

"Busier than I expected on a Sunday afternoon," she commented.

"I know." Beth couldn't think of anything to add, so she remained silent, enjoying the fresh air and beautiful colors all around them. She hadn't realized how cooped up the marina made her feel.

In companionable silence they sailed out of Marigot Bay and north toward nearby Anguilla. Beth gave Ori the helm while she raised and set the sails. When they were full *Trouble* surged forward, her bow slicing into the low swells. Beth shut off the engine and studied the patched main sail for signs of impending failure. The patch looked solid.

"What happened there?" Ori was sitting behind the wheel steering with one hand, clearly comfortable and in control.

"Surprise squall in the middle of the night in the Anegada passage. Terry never saw it coming, no time to reef."

Ori nodded, sympathetic. "Those are the worst. Well, I guess much worse can happen on a night passage, but that sucks. What did they charge you to patch it?"

Beth told her and described the last-century feel of the sail loft. After a while Ori handed the helm over to Beth and went below to get the lunch she'd brought: grilled vegetables wrapped in flatbread.

While they ate Ori asked Beth more about her job. Beth got the impression Ori did it to keep her from asking any more questions about her baby. But she let the tactic work. She was struggling to accept her employer's handling of their demanding client and talking it through with an impartial outsider lent another perspective. Well into a rant about Virgine's request for funding she didn't notice herself saying Virgine's name. Ori interrupted her.

"Wait, your client's name is Virgine? What's her last name?"

The wind whooshed out of Beth's rant when she realized what she'd done. It was silly, but identifying her client by name felt like a breach.

"Guesnon," she said. "Why?"

"She's one of my regulars."

"Playing blackjack?"

"Yup. And losing. A lot."

Beth's stomach curdled, and she was not prone to seasickness. Far from alleviating her guilt for mentioning the name, this information made her feel worse. But Pandora's box was open now. She had to unpack it. "How much is a lot?"

"The other night it was almost ten grand."

Beth tried to finish chewing and swallow despite her heaving stomach.

"Her loan shark was there. He cut her off."

"So she's been getting credit from the casino?"

"No. Not any more, I guess. Another dealer told me they cut her off too. She had to pay them back before she could make any more wagers. She came in one night with the full amount, plus another stake that she's run through now. It had to have come from the loan shark."

"Enough to pay the debt and keep gambling. Lovely." Beth's knowledge of loan sharks and gambling debt was entirely derived from movies and television, and in them the debtor never came out on top.

"So did the loan shark threaten to break her knees caps?"

"Hah. No, not in the casino. He and his friends escorted her out, though."

"Jesus, Ori, didn't the casino do anything? They could have killed her!"

Ori shook her head, smiling thinly. "The casino doesn't interfere with independent business men. From their perspective, the customer was out of funds and was welcome to leave."

Beth peered out across the water, both hands gripping the wheel. Virgine had been threatened by her loan shark Thursday night and asked Broadhead for financial investment the next day. Beth fought a strong urge to call someone on her team and tell them, even though it was Sunday afternoon.

"That was Thursday night?" she finally asked.

"Yes. She hasn't been in since. Do you think they hurt her?"

"No. I met with her Friday. But I have to talk to her about this. Broadhead can't find her funding so she can gamble it away."

"Don't you need to talk to Broadhead about it first. Isn't it their decision?"

"Why would they continue?" Beth was surprised anyone could think they might.

"Dunno. But if I were you, I'd get direction from my boss before telling the client anything."

Beth considered Ori's advice. Beth hadn't expected Broadhead to agree to getting the funding in the first place, but they had. Her instincts weren't attuned to their decision making.

"It's time to head back, ready about?"

)

Fort Louis Marina, Marigot Bay, St. Martin

Burt stood staring at an empty stretch of dock in Fort Marina—the stretch of dock where *Trouble* was supposed to be, both according to Terry and according to the woman in the marina office. Burt had brought *Sandcastle* around the island from Simpson Bay and taken a berth in the marina so he could have a reason to be around should things get ugly. He wondered, the hairs on the back of his neck rising, if something already had.

A group of crew disembarked from one of the enormous yachts up the dock and started his way, so he stepped to the edge of the dock to let them pass. As he exchanged "*bonjours*" with them, a man at the back of the group did a double take and stopped, head tilted to one side.

"We've met," he said, his accent pinning him to New Zealand. Burt studied him for a moment. Maybe they had. Suddenly the man started nodding, smile widening.

"You're a friend of that woman, with the boyfriend and the explosion, what's her name?" He snapped his fingers several times. A couple of his companions had paused and were looking back at him.

"Beth. *Double Trouble*." Burt said.

The Kiwi's grin widened as he pointed at Burt. "Yes. That's the woman, and the boat. Yeah. I'm Connor. We met in Le Marin, and at the *Gunkholing* party, right mate?"

"Right. Burt. Burt Adams. How's it going?"

"Burt. Yes. It's going great. I'm on *Legacy*," he tilted his head back along the dock toward the power yachts. "Good crew, good skipper."

"Hey Connor, coming?" one of the others called out.

"Yeah, yeah, just had to say hello to a friend," Connor called back. "I've gotta roll. Nice seeing you mate."

"You too," Burt said to his retreating back, and then, "Hey Connor?"

Connor turned to walk backwards, "Yeah mate?"

"Have you seen her? Beth and *Double Trouble*? She told me she was here."

One of Connor's companions stopped and looked back at Burt. "You looking for *Double Trouble*?"

"Yes. She's a friend of mine."

"Yeah, I saw that boat. Right here," he pointed at the empty water that Burt had been contemplating.

"When?"

The guy shrugged, a very Gaelic gesture with multiple meanings. "This morning. Last night. Yesterday…"

"The boat sitting here was *Double Trouble?*" Connor asked his companion, incredulous.

"Pretty sure, yeah."

"Huh. I never noticed. There you have it mate." This last he called out to Burt.

"Yes, thanks a lot, guys."

The yacht crew moved on as Burt took one more look at the empty stretch of dock. He was about to head back down the dock to *Sandcastle* when something caught his eye: the stern of a black dinghy sticking out from under the dock. He went to it and crouched on the dock, staring at the outboard motor locked onto its transom. He knew that dinghy, and he knew that if Beth had moved *Double Trouble,* she would have taken it with her. But if she had been compelled to take *Double Trouble* somewhere, she might have left it on purpose, as a clue. He reached out and gave the motor housing a shove, pulling the rest of the dinghy out from under the dock. It looked absolutely fine and offered no clue to where its mother ship might be.

He was squatting there, elbows on thighs, considering his options, when he heard a motor getting close. Looking up he saw *Trouble's* ivory hull angling toward him. Fenders were deployed along the near side and a woman with a fuzz of dark curly hair was standing amidships holding a line.

"Hey Burt!" Beth yelled from behind the wheel. "Take a line, will you?"

ʝ

Sitting in *Trouble's* cockpit clutching a cold beer, Burt was impatient for Ori to shove off. Once he'd helped her tie up *Trouble* Beth had insisted that he come aboard and have a beer while she and Ori finished stowing sailing gear and covering the mainsail.

When they finished she got out two more beers and she and Ori joined him, Ori saying she had a few minutes before she had to get going for her evening shift.

He sipped his beer impatiently while asking the expected questions about Ori and her baby. He was neither surprised nor particularly interested that Ori had left her son with her parents, reclaimed her father's boat, and was working at one of the casinos. Naturally her description of this made it sound absolutely justifiable—at least to herself. That she'd run into Beth at the market the other day wasn't terribly surprising, Marigot's market was very good and it was a small island. It did reassure him that she did not mention Hunter, although it wasn't likely she would.

He asked Beth if she'd seen Connor and she said no, but she knew he had been hired on to on one of the motor yachts. She explained that *Petrel* was in the marina and she'd spent time with Evan and his wife. As they compared notes on Evan's former Kiwi crew Ori went below. In a couple minutes she came back carrying a tattered daypack with a foul weather jacket hanging through the straps.

"I've got to get going. Thanks for the sail Beth. You should come by the casino one evening. Let me know and I'll get you some drink comps."

"Okay, I will. See you Ori."

"Nice seeing you again Burt," Ori said before climbing out of the cockpit and onto the dock. Burt took another sip of his beer and turned his attention to *Trouble*'s captain.

"So." She said.

"So you went for a daysail with Ori. You don't find it alarming that she's left her infant in Connecticut?"

"Seriously Burt? I can't imagine it. I can't get from the gushy mommy we last saw in Pointe-à-Pitre to this version of Ori. I know you and Terry both think she's a flake. I'd agree with you, I should agree with you, except every now and then she offers something—" Beth stopped, trying to come up with a word to encompass encouragement, support, insight, and tough love. She gave up, shrugged, and took a sip of beer.

"I think I get it. You're loyal to a fault, and you attribute your decision to start cruising to her."

"I guess so, yeah."

"Let me present an alternate view."

"Go ahead." Beth took another sip of beer and waited.

"In New York, you came to a juncture in your life where you had to make a choice. You were living aboard *Trouble*, but you didn't own her—right?"

"Right. I worked out the purchase when I decided to go."

"So, you lost your job and you had no place of your own."

"And the marina wanted to know my winter storage plans."

"More pressure. So, if Ori had never blown through your marina in New York that summer, would you have paid for winter storage and stayed there? Remember, no steady income." Burt watched her thinking it through, gratified that he'd gotten her to do so.

After a few minutes she responded. "It was Peter's letter—he's my ex-boyfriend. That was the last straw," she said, rising and reaching for Burt's apparently empty beer bottle. "Another?"

"Maybe. What's your plan for dinner?"

"I have none. But I have food. Can I make us dinner?"

"No. But I can."

"Oh ho, really?"

"Yes ma'am. I think I owe you one, you've treated me often enough. I'm going over the *Sandcastle* to see what I've got. You think about your answer and come over when you're ready. Don't be long. I'm going to open a good bottle of wine."

"Let me bring a bottle."

"You're on. See you in a few minutes."

"Actually, I may go take a shower, if you don't mind waiting."

"Say a half hour then?"

"Yes. I'll be there."

)

"This was delicious Burt. Thank you," Beth said, placing her fork across the side of her plate, which she had wiped clean of marinara sauce with a piece of baguette.

"Thank you for the perfect wine pairing," Burt said, draining his wine glass.

"It is good, isn't it? Terry had such fun picking it, I couldn't bring myself to remind him I probably won't be aboard *Trouble* long enough this time to drink it all. Thanks for the help."

"Always happy to help reduce alcohol stores. How long do you think you'll be here?"

"It was supposed to be two weeks. But our client has asked for additional services and they may want me to stay. I don't mind— who would? The alternative is Washington, D.C. in winter."

"The alternative includes your boyfriend."

Beth grinned and nodded, "True. And he's not my boyfriend anymore. I meant to tell you when we spoke on Christmas Eve. We're engaged."

"Congratulations! What wonderful news, although I must say not unexpected. When's the big event?" Burt rose as he spoke, returning to the galley.

"Don't know yet. Probably next fall. It happened when we were in Barbuda after Thanksgiving. Then we got home, and I got this assignment. I haven't had time to stop and think it through, and Terry is balancing a new business deal with being supportive of me and my assignment. We're deferring it until things calm down."

Burt laughed, returning to the table with a new bottle of wine. "When will that be? Easter?"

"Stop it. My sister Trish said something similar. Why the pressure?"

"No pressure from me, Beth. I didn't mean it that way. But I recognize avoidance when I see it. You need time to prepare yourself before you can prepare for the event." Burt tore the foil off the top of the bottle and inserted a corkscrew. "I've been saving this for a special occasion. I do wish Terry could be here too so I could toast you both, but ..." His hands twisted the cork out as he spoke. Beth watched, processing his comment about avoidance. It resonated all to too much with her own realization of a few days ago that she was not ready to get married. She had thought of it as a failure, but when Burt said it, he made it sound like a natural state to be transitioned through in time.

"Were you ever married, Burt?"

The cork slid out of the bottle and he set the corkscrew on the table. "Drink up," he nodded at the quarter inch of wine in her glass. She complied, and he poured a splash of the new bottle into the glass. "Make sure it's okay." He nodded at the glass. "My wife Betty died when she was thirty-eight. We'd been married nearly fifteen years." Beth hid her surprise as she picked up her glass, inhaled the scent of the wine, and took a sip. It bloomed in her mouth, sour and sweet, rich and smoky. It was a hundred times better than the bottle they'd finished. She nodded, setting the glass down. Burt poured for himself and then topped hers up. He set the bottle on the table and sat back down.

"I'm sorry Burt, that must have been awful." The fact that Burt's wife had been only a few years older than she was now when she died did not escape her.

"It was difficult. I focused on my work. For the first time, I was glad we did not have children. But it's old news. Here's to your next adventure. May it be safer, and more enjoyable, than the last one!" He raised his glass, inclining it toward her. She picked hers up and touched it to his and they both took a sip.

"This is delicious. Thank you."

"My pleasure. Literally. I didn't mean to upset you with my comment about delaying."

"You didn't. In fact, you made me feel better. I've been feeling like I'm a coward, not ready to do it yet. I'm not that strange, am I?"

"You are the furthest thing from a coward I can imagine, Beth. You're allowed to need time for such an important commitment. Don't worry about it. So, can you tell me about your project here?"

"I'd love to. Can we sit outside? I'll clear the table."

Burt insisted that they stack the dishes in the sink, he would load the dishwasher later. Beth almost laughed at the notion of a dishwasher in a boat's galley, then she remembered he had a washer and dryer outside the guest cabin below. A few minutes later they were sitting in comfortable deck chairs on *Sandcastle*'s aft deck looking out across the marina at the shore. The sun had set while they were eating and the lights of Marigot twinkled beyond the boats.

)

Burt listened to Beth describe Virgine Guesnon and her business. She explained the original agreement and her surprise at Broadhead's willingness to find investors when Virgine demanded it. Then she told him about Virgine's gambling debt, which she'd learned from Ori.

So the woman has some use, Burt thought.

On a roll, Beth described a puzzle she was wrestling with about carved wooden figures. She wound down describing her discomfort with Virgine's young male houseboy.

"You're perceptive, Beth, and sometimes you overthink things."

Beth shook her head, smiling. "I did not overthink Ori's situation on St. Hillaire."

Burt sighed. She had a point. That didn't help his effort to allay her suspicions about her client, correct as they were. He had been conducting an internal debate since receiving the assignment yesterday: tell Beth the truth, or work to keep her safe while taking care of the situation? To tell her would be a violation of the rules of the agency that he'd retired from. He was expected to work within them, for the most part, even now. But Beth was an employee of a contractor to that agency—an eventuality that both surprised and pleased him. Even so, if her own supervisors weren't telling her what the real assignment was, it wasn't his place to do so.

"Fair enough. So this Prosper is taking credit for carving Chinese made figurines. You have no proof Virgine's company is distributing them, do you?"

"No. Not yet. But Prosper did have carvings that were much better quality than the Chinese ones. I think he carved those, and Virgine did say she distributes them. I have not had a chance to challenge her on the ones I found with the Made in China stickers."

"And your next meetings with her needs to be about investment funding." Burt pointed out, hoping to dissuade her from pursuing the carvings.

"I don't know what my next conversation with her will be. I have to tell Broadhead about her gambling. We can't find her investors so that she can lose their money too."

"You haven't told them about that yet?"

"I just found out, from Ori, this afternoon."

"Right." Burt's nearly empty wine glass told him he'd had enough. Once again Beth's connection to Ori was complicating things and he didn't want a fuzzy head while he talked with her. It would have been so much better if Beth didn't know about the gambling.

"Ori suggested I visit the casino. What if I went there and saw Virgine gambling and losing?"

"She has no idea you know she's in debt to a loan shark. You would have no reason to accuse her of gambling away her investors' money."

Beth was silent for a minute, then said, "You're right. I could go see her doing it and she wouldn't suspect anything."

Burt suppressed a groan.

Forty-eight

Fort Louis Marina, Marigot Bay, St. Martin

"*H*i Beth, it's Marcus. Nobody else is here yet. I'll bet you didn't know we've had four inches of snow this morning and it's still coming down."

"Wow, that much? I knew you were going to get some." Beth worked hard not to sound smug about missing a snow storm.

"Yeah, it stalled on top of us when it was supposed to keep moving northeast. They might send us home if it doesn't stop by noon."

"I haven't yet experienced snow in D.C., but I guess the streets can get pretty bad?"

"This town has no idea how to deal with it. Things grind to a halt. That does not excuse the people who ride the train, but somehow they manage to get stuck, too. Anyway, we got a thumbs up from the investment group, they're working on Virgine's request. Andrea said she could think of a couple possibilities right off the top of her head."

"Well, about that Marcus. I learned something yesterday that might change things."

"What's that?"

"Virgine is in debt to a loan shark. She has a gambling problem."

There was a whistle, and then Marcus said, "No kidding. That's some nerve."

"Yes. So we won't want to fund her?"

"I wouldn't jump to any conclusions about it. There's a bigger picture than just Virgine Guesnon. Maybe her business is worthy of investment, even if she is not. But most likely they'll put restrictions on the funding—they would no matter what, but they might make them stricter."

"Will you tell the investment people about this, or should I?"

"I think you should, in writing. Tell you what, I'll forward the email I got from Andrea," he paused, and Beth imagined him finding and forwarding the message, "and you can reply to her and whoever she included. So how did you find this out about her?"

"Pure coincidence. It turns out a friend of mine is a dealer at one of the casinos. We talked about my assignment—nothing confidential, you know? Just what my job is and all. She told me what it's like at the casino, and about some of her regulars, and somehow we realized that one of them is Virgine."

"The first thing Andrea will ask is why we didn't find this in our background check."

"Well, when did we do it? My friend said the loan shark is fairly recent."

"Good question. I'll look into it. Can you get a better idea of when she started with the loan shark? Maybe your friend can come up with a date?"

"She might be able to narrow down when Virgine was cut off by the casino—when she went to the loan shark."

"She spent through whatever credit they offered, and the loan shark's money?"

"My friend said she paid the casino back and had more money to gamble. After she lost that, the loan shark came to the casino and escorted her out. That was last week. My meeting with her was the next morning—when she asked us to find her funding."

"So she lost the company's liquid assets. Luckily for our team the background checks aren't our responsibility—it's not our team's fault if the check missed a financial liability like this. She may have incurred this debt recently, but it takes a bad gambling habit, and we should have caught it."

"Does Broadhead do background checks on all prospective clients?"

"Prospective, no. Only when we get to the point of a contract."

"But we do them on all clients?"

"Clients, employees, the guy who runs the lunch cart out on the sidewalk ..."

Beth felt as if someone was peeking at her through one of *Trouble*'s windows, but she realized it was the uncomfortable sensation of knowing someone had checked into her background.

"Well, I guess I'll need direction by tomorrow morning. I'm scheduled to meet with her, and she expects news on the funding."

"Gotcha. You send the email to Andrea. I'll look into the background check. We'll have something for you by the morning. Promise."

"Thanks Marcus. Stay warm!"

Beth ended the call feeling dissatisfied. She had a suspicion that someone at Broadhead already knew all about Virgine, even though it made no sense for them to take her on if they did. She composed the email to Andrea, and then she got started on her planned outing for the afternoon.

J

Colombier, St. Martin

Beth opened the glove box and slid the rental agreement in on top of the automobile's manual still sealed in its original plastic bag. Straightening, she scanned the controls of the Kia Sorento. They looked familiar and straightforward, even though Beth had not driven a car regularly for several years. She picked up the paper map of Marigot that the rental agent had given her after marking her best route to Colombier. After orienting herself she set the map back down on the passenger seat and started the car.

She'd paid attention to the route on the ride to Colombier with Virgine, which boosted her confidence. Familiar landmarks told her she was not lost. Soon enough she found the stretch of road between scrub-covered hills, with the outskirts of Marigot behind her. She'd passed quickly through a settlement called Helligard, or maybe it was Rambaud—she saw signs for both—before entering this final stretch. The closer she got, the more nervous she grew about calling on Prosper. What had seemed like a great idea in the abstract was quickly becoming terrifying as she passed into the outskirts of his home town.

"I'm not cut out for this," she muttered as she turned left where Virgine's driver had. She stopped short as a chicken ran across the road in front of her.

Great Beth, take out one of Prosper's birds. With the hen safe on the roadside she drove on. Her memory suffered a momentary lapse as she proceeded along the street and right on past the workshop and Prosper's house across from it. Realizing her error as the road curved, she stopped, did a K-turn, and parked facing back the way she'd come. She could see the workshop with its packed dirt yard. Prosper's house was on her side of the street, the yard shielded from her view by a hedge of oleander and low growing palms. She sat there with her hands on the steering wheel watching the neighborhood while she summoned the courage to get out.

"Okay, pretend you're a detective. You need to talk to this witness. You don't know what he knows. He may not know anything, but you have to find out. Go talk to him. For God's sake you've already met him!"

Disgusted with her own cowardice she snatched up her daypack, pulled the keys out of the ignition, and swung open the door. She pressed the button on the key fob and the car locked with a beep and flash of its lights.

There. Committed.

She walked along the roadside past the hedge and turned up the stone path through Prosper's yard. Virgine had led her around the back the other day, but that seemed inappropriate for this visit. Still running on the determination she'd mustered at the car, she marched right up onto the front porch and knocked on the wooden front door. It was in much better condition than the one across the street: a solid wooden frame and panels, painted a clean white with no dirt around the handle to indicate use. The trim was a pastel green.

Her determination was slipping when she heard footsteps inside, and then the door swung open. Prosper stood inside peering out at her, a curious expression on his face.

"Hello Prosper. It's Beth Anderson. I was here the other day with Virgine Guesnon. I hope I am not disturbing you."

His expression changed to a guarded smile.

"No, you are not. How can I help you Ms Anderson?"

"I would like to ask you a few more questions about your work for Virgine. I won't take much of your time."

He nodded and took a step backward, an invitation for her to enter. She was not proud of the flash of fear she experienced as she entered his dimly lit home. Headlines about missing American woman flittered through her mind, and then, out of nowhere, the news story Terry had read about the body of the child found at Pointe Arago.

"I have the varnish open. Will you come into the workshop?" Prosper gestured across the front room toward a door that probably led to the kitchen.

"Yes, of course. Don't let me slow down your work."

Beth took in the front room as they passed through it. The cinder block construction had been smoothed with something—wallboard perhaps, or wood panels—and painted a tasteful off white. The furniture was low-end contemporary: an arm chair with striped upholstery, a love seat in a contrasting solid color, a coffee table of wood. A television rested on a cabinet. Behind the sofa there was a much older, more substantial sideboard—perhaps a legacy of an earlier generation. A ceramic—maybe bone china—lamp stood on it flanked by two China figurines of dancing ladies.

There has to be a woman in this home. That made Beth feel less concerned for her safety, which she knew was absurd.

Prosper guided her back through the modern kitchen and into the workshop. The familiar aroma of varnish melded with sweet paint thinner. The room's single window was wide open, and Beth could hear the chickens out in the back yard. The sound summoned the memory of his gentle treatment of the birds, which made her feel more comfortable.

"Would you care to sit?" He indicated a stool with a paint-stained seat. It looked dry.

"Thanks," Beth planted one butt cheek on the stool, one foot firmly on the floor the other on a low crossbar. She cradled her daypack in her lap. He went to the workbench and sat down on a similar stool. He picked up a brush that was laying across the top of a varnish can. Beth watched him gently stroke varnish onto a carved wooden bird in flight. The figurine was positioned on a stand at eye level with a bright, focused work light illuminating it. That gave Beth her opening.

"You said the other day the carvings weren't finished."

"Did I?"

"Yes, the ones on the shelf."

There were two figures there now, a hummingbird and a flower. "I guess you've nearly finished them?"

"Yes. I was about to start varnishing when you called the other day. Virgine was perturbed with me because the ladies need another template and I had not yet finished it."

"But Virgine distributes your figures, too. Why did it matter so much?"

"Virgine has her priorities."

Something in his tone made Beth pause to examine his profile. His features were tense, and she thought it was more than the effect of concentrating on the carving he was varnishing.

"I wanted to show you something," she said, unzipping her daypack. "I found this in a shop in Oyster Pond." She drew the dolphin with the "made in China" sticker on the bottom from her bag and set it on the edge of the worktable to his left. The light highlighted its unfinished surface. On an impulse, Beth stood and reached up to the shelf. She picked up the carved hummingbird and set it beside the Chinese dolphin.

Prosper paused in his painting, holding the brush in the air near the soaring seagull. He picked up the dolphin with his left hand and turned it over. Beth suspected he knew he would find the sticker there. He set it back down with a scowl. Beth waited as he refocused on the seagull and gently stroked it with the varnish brush.

"They copy my designs and sell them for nothing," he said, brushing the seagull's head with a very gentle touch. He rotated the stand, studying his work.

"So this figure is a rip-off of your version? It's not as delicate as yours, but it's close."

"They steal my designs." he shook his head, clearly determined to stick to this explanation.

"Very frustrating, I'm sure," Beth conceded. "I visited a shop in Phillipsburg where the owner said you supply her directly. She also had some of Virgine's jewelry, so she does buy from Virgine as well. Is that right?"

He set his brush back down on the can and straightened, looking directly at her.

"Mrs. Abshire is from Colombier. Her family and mine have been friends since arrowroot days."

"Virgine does not mind that you deal with her directly?"

"I did not say that," he shot Beth a wicked smile before turning back to his work. She watched him slide the stand holding the seagull aside and bring another similar stand forward from the back of the table. He reached over and picked up the Chinese dolphin, moved it toward the stand, then stopped, put it back down, and picked up the hummingbird. "Sorry," he said. It sounded like he was trying to conceal one error—picking up her figure—with a different one— picking up a Chinese figure because he'd varnished many of them.

Beth picked up the dolphin and put it back in her bag. She excused herself, thanking him for his time. He walked her to the front door and watched her leave his yard. She allowed herself a glance back as she turned toward her rental car and saw him shut the door. She sat in the driver's seat with her notebook on the steering wheel writing down her impressions of the visit. She was dissatisfied with almost all of his answers, with the possible exception of his reason for supplying Mrs. Abshire's shop directly. In fact, that felt like the only honest information he'd provided. His accidentally picking up the Chinese dolphin had practically screamed the truth. Virgine had him refinishing cheap Chinese figures to resell as his own work. If Beth hadn't seen the women making the jewelry, she would suspect it had the same origin. The rest of the products she carried were suspect now too.

She was staring at her last note, trying to decide how to share her thoughts with her team, when the rumble of a diesel engine drew her attention out through the windshield. A panel van had pulled off the road into the bare yard of the womens' workshop. As Beth watched it backed out, using the yard to turn around and park on the other side of the road faced in the same direction she was. She reached into her daypack and took out her camera. The driver and a passenger got out and opened the rear doors. They each took out a cardboard box. As one of them set his down on the ground and shut the van doors Beth took several photos, focusing on the boxes and the Chinese characters printed on them.

She was reviewing the photos and almost missed the men's return from Prosper's house. The flash of the Van's reverse lights as the driver put it in gear spurred her to set the camera aside and start her car's ignition.

She followed the van at a distance back along the rural roads toward Margot. After passing through Helligard there were more vehicles and she worked her way closer to the van in order to stick with it. It turned right onto a road she didn't know and passed through an industrial neighborhood, and then turned left onto an unpaved road.

"Shit."

She was about to give up, afraid to take her rental car onto an unpaved road that might end in a rutted mess, when another car came from the other direction and turned down the dirt road behind the van. *If they can do it* ... Beth made the turn and followed, trying to spot the van through the rising dust behind it and the intervening car.

The van passed a side road to the right. The intervening car turned there. Beth crept along the rough road, hoping its bad condition was sufficient excuse for her snail's pace, watching the van stop at the next intersection and then turn left.

The van went for a couple hundred yards before turning right. She accelerated to the intersection, made the left turn, and bounced along to the road on the right. The van stirred up more dust on the next stretch of road. She followed at a distance of several hundred yards. The van turned to the right again, and then to the left, following the road. It bypassed several more side roads and finally turned left onto a paved drive where Beth lost sight of it behind a row of large buildings. Emboldened by her success so far, she made the turn when she got to it and searched for the van. The buildings were warehouses, and there were cars, vans, and trucks parked on the pavement outside of them—but not the white van. She proceeded along an open lane in front of the warehouses. The wide doors on the first one were closed. As she passed the second one she saw the van inside through the open doors. Two men dressed in grey and black camouflage patterned trousers and black t-shirts, each with an automatic weapon slung across his chest were flanking the van, watching as the driver opened the back doors.

Gulping down a wave of fear Beth drove to the end of the row of warehouses and turned around, pulling in next to another car to blend into the crowd. Stacks of shipping containers nearly blocked the view, but she could see the glimmer of the sea between them. They were at the water's edge.

Down the row of warehouses, she could see that the doors to the second warehouse were now shut. Her bravery ended there. No way she was going to go knock. But she could try to find out who owned it. Mastering her fear of the men with guns, she eased the car into a lane with a row of cars between it and the warehouses. She proceeded at a sedate pace along this lane until it ended adjacent to the first warehouse. The door of the second one remained steadfastly shut, and she was glad. She turned left and then an immediate right in the driveway and out onto the road, which was paved from this point onward. It passed by the rear facades of two large industrial buildings and then a smaller one and ended at a traffic circle.

And suddenly Beth knew where she was. The building that housed Virgine Guesnon's office was on the other side of the traffic circle, within walking distance of the warehouse—and of the men with automatic weapons and boxes from China.

Forty-nine

Fort Louis Marina, Marigot Bay, St. Martin

*B*urt turned the corner of the dock onto the stretch where *Trouble* was tied up alongside. She was locked up tight. Beth must be out. As he strolled on past Beth's boat, his gaze lifted toward the head of the dock and fell on an all too familiar figure. Hunter Green was standing on the seawall leaning on the railing a few feet to the right of the security gate. Burt stopped and made a show of patting the pockets of his cargo shorts, and then his fishing vest. He shook his head and turned around, heading back out the dock. No way he was going to open the gate and allow that guy to get in.

But someone else would. Individuals who would challenge someone trying to get through the gate were few and far between in marinas. Burt rounded the corner and stopped when the mass of a large power yacht blocked his view of the top of the dock. He carefully stepped back toward the corner until he could see Hunter. He hoped the other man's focus was on *Trouble* and he wouldn't notice the strange guy watching him on the dock further out.

Within less than a minute someone came along from the marina complex and used a keycard to open the gate. Hunter stepped sideways and grabbed the gate before it could shut. The sailor— crew from one of the motor yachts—was oblivious. He sauntered on down the dock with a loose-limbed gait and a vacant grin on his face.

Meanwhile, Hunter slipped through the gate and walked down the ramp to the dock. Burt watched as he approached *Double Trouble*, read the name painted on her stern and smiled. Burt could imagine how he must feel after looking for this particular boat for so long. He was glad Beth wasn't aboard and the boat was locked up. Had Hunter made a move toward boarding the boat, Burt would have been on him faster than his bulk suggested possible. But what Hunter did was unshoulder his daypack and crouch down with it on the dock. He removed a notebook and pulled a pen from the spiral binding. He wrote something on a piece of paper, then tore the paper out of the notebook and held it between his teeth while he returned the notebook to the bag and zipped it up. He stood up, leaving the bag on the dock, and studied *Trouble*'s side deck for a minute, folding the paper as he did. Then he leaned over the lifelines and tucked the folded paper underneath one of the lines running across the deck from the mast to the cockpit.

Burt waited until Hunter had exited through the gate and moved out of sight before rounding the corner of the dock and walking on toward *Trouble*. Still watching that Hunter wasn't lingering up on shore watching, he ambled along until he was next to the note. Seeing no sign of Hunter, he reached over and pulled the note out from under the line. He felt exposed as he unfolded the note and scanned it, and then replaced it.

Satisfied, and already forming a plan, he walked on up the ramp to the gate.

⌒

Fort Louis Marina, Marigot Bay, St. Martin

The slip of paper tucked under the halyard on *Trouble*'s deck was so out of place it was impossible for Beth to miss. She collected it as she stepped aboard and held it between her teeth as she used both hands to open the combination padlock on *Trouble*'s companionway. Down in the cabin she dropped it on the navigation desk and her daypack on the seat before making her way through the stifling boat opening up the hatches. The cool breeze pushed the stuffy air out of the cabin and rustled the folded note, catching her eye as she moved toward the galley. She turned and picked it up.

Hello, my name is Hunter Green. I'm looking for my friend Ori Chapman, and I believe you might be able to help me. If you're willing to hear me out, I'll be at Burger 12 at five o'clock. I hope to see you then.

Beth settled onto the navigation desk seat, shoving her bag to the deck with a clunk that reminded her of her camera inside it. She reread the note three times, but it remained the same matter-of-fact request to meet about Ori.

"Who the hell is Hunter Green?" she muttered, directing the question at an absent Ori. When no answer was forthcoming, she lifted the navigation desk lid and took out her laptop. She followed the cord with her fingers to confirm it was plugged into the outlet under the electrical control panel. With *Trouble* plugged into the dock's electricity Beth could keep the thing's battery charged. She turned on the laptop and bent to retrieve her camera from her bag on the floor. Lifting the desk lid again she fished out the cord to connect it to the computer. By then the computer was ready for her password.

While the pictures downloaded—and there were several days' worth before this morning's—she brought up her browser and searched for Hunter Green. She scrolled past dozens of entries about color, paint, and fabrics, a couple about an apartment complex in Texas, a band, and finally a few individuals with the name.

"Well this isn't going to work," she said, scrolling rapidly through useless search results. Without more information she couldn't possibly narrow it down. The pictures were ready, so she minimized the browser and went through them. The last two of the rear of the van were not bad. The Chinese characters on the boxes were clear, and she had captured the van's license plate clearly enough to read it. She attached the photos to an email and addressed it to everyone on her team, then wrote up a brief narrative of her expedition. She asked if they could get someone to translate the Chinese and they might as well see if someone could run the license plate.

She started to ask if they could get a title search on the warehouse. But before hitting "send" she checked her own files. She skimmed through Virgine's dossier and found nothing about a warehouse. Then she reviewed the file on Virgine's company. There it was: a lease for a warehouse in Port de Galisbay, right after the information on the lease for the office. She backspaced through the request for the title search, added the fact that Virgine owned the warehouse, and sent the email.

⁀⁀

Washington, D.C.

"You're still here too?" Raj Gupta said, not a real question, as he crossed Adrian's office. His boss was sitting at his desk with several files in front of him, the top one open.

"I parked the SUV at the station. As long as the trains are running, I'll be fine."

"Likewise. Although I don't look forward to digging out when I get off the train."

"I hear that."

Knowing that was about all the chit-chat Adrian would tolerate, Raj sat down in the guest chair across from his boss. "Our asset on St. Martin has connected Virgine Guesnon to the Chinese merchandise."

"You told her to?" Adrian asked, incredulity a little too contrived in his tone.

"No, certainly not. She discovered Chinese merchandise in the shops that looks suspiciously like Virgine's locally carved figurines. She took the initiative to look into it further, without Virgine's awareness or consent. She distrusts Virgine."

"Good instinct can be dangerous for someone in her position."

"Yes, well, she doesn't know her position, does she? That is my concern."

"You want to pull her out?"

"No. I want to brief her. I think she's losing faith in us. She thinks Broadhead is crazy to continue to meet Virgine's demands. Her psychological profile suggests she will disengage if her satisfaction drops much lower."

"Her psychological profile? Her satisfaction? How the hell are you measuring her satisfaction?"

"All right. Fine. I'm guessing. But it's true her profile suggests a low tolerance for …"

"For?"

"I was going to say bullshit. Look, Adrian, do we trust her?"

"We do. But this project is need-to-know. And don't try the 'she needs to know' line."

"But she does if she's going to know how to stay out of trouble."

"We've put an experienced man in place. He'll keep her out of trouble."

)

Marigot Bay, St. Martin

Ever since coming home to find the note on *Trouble*'s deck, Beth had been fretting about this man who was looking for Ori. His note gave no clue how he knew Beth knew Ori, nor any reason why he was looking for her. He could have been sent by Ori's father. He could be looking for *Dream Catcher*, which Ori wasn't supposed to have. Beth waffled back and forth between meeting him and skipping it. But she knew if she didn't go, he'd come looking for her again—he'd pretty much said so in his note. She would rather meet him on neutral, public ground than aboard her boat. He knew where she was, and she felt exposed. He'd obviously had no trouble getting into the marina.

With plenty of time to spare she set out on foot to the burger place he had identified. It was across the road from the marina next door to a yoga studio. She'd eaten there before, but she did not intend to order anything this evening—that would prolong the meeting.

As she darted across the road toward the restaurant's open front, she saw Burt sitting at the front counter looking at a menu. The coincidence felt artificial, as if he'd known she'd be here. He looked up as she reached the sidewalk.

"Hey Beth, where you headed?"

"Same place as you." She stepped up into the shaded, open dining room. The counter seat next to Burt was empty, as was the one next to it at the end of the counter. Beth was tempted to take the one at the end, which was conveniently right by the entrance. But that would look strange to Burt, so she sat next to him and left the other seat for her mystery guest.

"I was thinking about a hamburger. It's been a while," Burt said, looking at the menu again.

"They're okay."

"You don't sound enthused about them."

"No, it was good."

"What are you going to have?" He set the menu down in front of her.

"I, um …" She picked it up, looked at it, put it down, looked out at the road.

"Beth?"

"I'm meeting someone. I wasn't going to order anything."

"You're meeting someone not for dinner?" he asked with a smile. Looking at him she knew she should confide in him. She sensed that he knew why she was here, but she didn't know how he could if he did. More importantly, she was glad of his company and wanted him to stay.

"I found a note on *Trouble*'s deck asking me to meet here. It's pretty mysterious, and I'm a little spooked. But I thought I better come here, rather than have him show up at *Trouble* again."

"Is this about your client?"

"No, not at all. It's this guy who says he's looking for Ori, of all things."

"And it's a coincidence that she's actually here on this island?"

"As far as I know, yes. Geesh, Burt, I hadn't thought of that— if she knows this guy's here looking for her, and didn't tell me…"

She stared at Burt, but he was looking outside. She followed his gaze, half turning. A man standing on the sidewalk was peering into the dim restaurant.

"Him?"

"Maybe. But I'm not going to make it easy," Beth said. She was frightened, and she didn't like it. She refocused on the menu, holding it so she could see him in her peripheral vision.

He stepped up into the restaurant.

"Excuse me, ma'am." His voice rang with a southern twang. Beth bristled at the "ma'am" and tried to hide it as she looked up at him. He was tall and tanned, with rugged skin and long brown hair.

"Yes?"

"Are you Beth? Beth Anderson?"

"I am. You must be Hunter Green."

"That I am. Thank you so much for coming. I know it was strange, finding a note on your boat and all."

"Yes, it's more customary to leave a message with the marina office."

Hunter's brows shot up and his cheeks reddened. "I'm sorry ma'am, I didn't think of that. I mean, I wasn't sure it was your boat until I got onto the dock and read the name. Then I was there, and, well—"

"Never mind. Just think about it next time," Beth lectured. She sensed Burt shift in his seat beside her and glanced over her shoulder. He had reclaimed the menu and was studying it far too carefully. "This is my friend Burt. He's here for dinner."

Hunter extended his hand to Burt, who reached around Beth to shake it. They held one another's gaze for longer than was necessary. Beth read recognition on Hunter's face, which was curious. She didn't have the nerve to swivel around and look at the expression Hunter was seeing on Burt's face.

"Have we met?" Hunter asked.

Point for honesty, I guess, Beth thought.

"I don't believe so," Burt said. But there was something in his tone that wasn't right. She glanced around at him again, but saw nothing untoward in his face.

You're imagining things because you're nervous.

"Why don't you sit down. They won't kick us out too fast, unless it gets busy."

Hunter hung his daypack on the back of the stool next to Beth and sat down. "I was planning on buying you dinner," he said.

"Well, let's just discuss whatever it is you want."

"You said Burt is here for dinner."

"And Burt will order when he wants to. You should tell me what you want." Beth couldn't quite believe the words had come out of her mouth. She hated that she was sitting in between the two men so she couldn't watch Burt to gauge his reaction without being obvious.

"Well okay then. It's all friendly. Really."

Beth declined to respond to his continued delay in getting to the point. Hunter sat there watching her for a very long moment. She held his gaze, summoning all of her patience. He broke first.

"Last year I met this great woman. I was working at a bar on Jamaica."

Beth nodded, but said nothing. "We really had something. Or so I thought. But one day she just left. Sailed away. I was pretty raw for a while there, and I made mistakes. I ended up back in Texas for a while. Taking care of me, if you know what I mean."

Beth didn't, but she guessed he meant something like rehabilitation or medical treatment. She did not respond. After another moment Hunter went on.

"Then a friend from the islands sent me a story from one of the Caribbean newspapers' web sites. It was a French paper, based in Guadelopue. He remembered Ori, and that's who the article was about, sort of."

"And my name was in it?"

"Yes. Your name and your boat were both mentioned."

"And so was Ori's name. Why did you track me down? For that matter, how did you track me down?"

Hunter nodded and swallowed hard. Beth sensed he had rehearsed what was coming next. "Ori left me. I don't know if she'll want to see me. But I have to find out. I have to find out if her little boy is mine."

"Again, why don't you ask her?"

"I did. She won't answer my emails. I don't know where she is. I was hoping you would help me."

Beth shook her head, and finally turned to Burt. He offered her a polite, "this is your problem" smile. And again she got the feeling he wasn't surprised by Hunter and his story. She twisted her mouth at him in a fake scowl, then calmed her features before turning back to Hunter.

"I have no idea how Ori would react to you. She never told me anything about you, not in any emails when she was in Jamaica, and not since then. I hope you're ready for rejection."

"I—" Hunter's gaze dropped to his hands and he exhaled a long breath. "I am. She left me, so I don't expect to get her back. But if he's my son, I want a chance to be his father, in some form."

That surprised Beth. She glanced at Burt and knew he was surprised, too.

"I want to do what's right by him," Hunter went on.

Beth couldn't help it. If the guy was acting, he was good. "I will contact Ori and tell her you are looking for her. Do you have contact information I can give her?"

Hunter's head lifted. His eyes were glistening with kept tears.

Good lord he's good, or sincere.

"Thank you so much. You have no idea—my mobile number, and my email address. I'll check it every day." He slung his bag around the chair and unzipped it, digging around in it. Out came a little notepad, the type she used as a school girl to scribble notes to her friends. There was a pen stuffed into the spiral binding.

He scribbled on a sheet of paper and tore it out. Beth read it out loud to confirm she had it right. He nodded.

"How long will you be on St. Martin?" Beth realized the question would sound odd to someone who didn't know Ori was here too.

"As long as it takes to find out if Ori will talk to me. I'll go wherever she is."

"I'll let her know we spoke and what you want. The rest will be up to her. No promises."

"I guess I can't ask for more than that, ma'am. Maybe we'll meet again, and you'll let me buy you dinner then."

"Maybe." Beth stuffed the folded paper into the pocket of her shorts. She wanted to say, "not a chance," but he was earnest enough that she was half convinced of his sincerity. Hunter got to his feet and slung his bag over his shoulder.

"I'll be going then. Nice to meet you, Burt."

"Have a pleasant evening," Burt said.

Hunter stepped out of the restaurant and turned left, walking toward the market square. Beth inhaled and released a deep breath and turned toward Burt.

"Damn, Beth, you were cold to him," he said.

"What the hell? He left a note on my boat. He snuck into the marina and visited my boat when I wasn't there. I'm not going to do anything to encourage him."

"Are you going to relay his message to Ori?"

"I guess so. I think if I don't, he'll be back. If I do, and she doesn't reply, he'll be back. Why am I in the middle of it this time?"

Burt outright laughed at that, which brought back Beth's scowl. Burt's laugh wound down and he placed a large, warm hand on her shoulder.

"I think you were right to be tough on him. You don't really know who he is or what he wants."

"Yeah? I mean, yeah!" Beth found herself chuckling. "I was in full-blown bitch mode, wasn't I?"

"You were. It was impressive. Has Terry seen that?"

"No, I don't think so."

"Well I hope for his sake he's never on the receiving end. Me too."

"I do too. I feel bad now."

"Stop it. You were dead on about him coming to your boat. He seems like soft spoken and friendly ole' Texan. But he's pretty pushy. I'm glad you pushed back. Makes me feel like you can take care of yourself."

"You know I can."

"I know, but you're constantly tested. My confidence in you keeps growing. So, are you going to tell Ori?"

"Yeah, I think I will. I'll make her promise to email him. I might make her do it in front of me. To get me out of the loop. I do not want to play a game of telephone with the two of them."

"Smart. If she does contact him, he is going to be surprised to find her right here on St. Martin."

"You say that like you don't think it's all a bizarre coincidence."

Burt shrugged, his expression all innocence. "Who knows? Now, will you let *me* buy you dinner?"

Fifty

Fort Louis Marina, Marigot Bay, St. Martin

*B*eth realized the next morning that Burt had distracted her from asking him whether he'd known about Hunter with stories of his last charter while they ate their hamburgers. Had he done it on purpose? Or was she imagining because he'd been there that he knew about Hunter, the note, and the meeting?

She resolved to ask him, and to try not to make it sound like a challenge, while firing up the computer to check her email over her morning coffee. Broadhead's financing offer was there, giving her plenty to focus on instead of Burt, Hunter Green, and Ori. She read the proposal twice to absorb all the details and read it several more times until she could get past the dollar amount being offered with a smile rather than a grimace of outrage. She'd struggled in the islands for a year, never gambling, never wasting money. But Broadhead was offering Virgine Guesnon—a losing gambler—more than Beth had earned and spent in the last decade. There was simply no justice in the world, but if she did not present this offer to her client she'd be out of a job and broke once again. By the sixth read through she could maintain her professional smile throughout. She felt dirty.

At ten thirty she had the marina office call her a taxi and she directed it to Virgine's office. Beth felt increasingly nervous as the car approached the port with its warehouses—not about the meeting with Virgine, but about her visit there the previous afternoon. What if one of the guards had seen her, saw her today, and recognized her?

She climbed out of the taxi and shouldered her bag to climb the external stairs of the office building and walk along the balcony to Virgine's office. An hour later when she returned to the warm sunshine of the balcony and paused to look out across Marigot Bay she felt dirty again. The fresh sea air did little to cleanse her soiled conscious. Virgine's eyes had lit with what Beth knew now was greed when she read Broadhead's offer. She had seized a black and white

Monte Blanc fountain pen from the desk blotter and scrawled her signature on the last page. Beth had maintained her smile as she pointed out the clauses requiring her initials. The clause assigning Broadhead majority rights if she did not repay them, the clause saying Broadhead was the legal representative of any investors it obtained on her behalf, the clause about the balloon payment in two years, and the increasing interest rate. None of it deterred Virgine. Her scribbles had grown maniacal by the time she'd finished initialing her company away to Broadhead. Not that Virgine thought of it that way. Beth's professional smile remained plastered on her face throughout the meeting.

To her right was the commercial pier, a small container ship tied alongside. A loading crane lifted steel containers from the ship and stacked them on shore in neat two-high rows. The office building hid the row of warehouses from Beth's view, and she was glad. Feeling relief that the meeting was over, Virgine was pleased, and Beth's visit to the warehouse had not been exposed, she headed down the steps watching the road for the taxi she'd arranged to pick her up.

Back at the marina she stopped in the office to have them scan the agreement. They loaded the file onto a portable memory stick she provided and happily added the charges to her bill. Aboard *Trouble* Beth loaded the file onto her laptop and attached it to an email that she sent to Andrea and Marcus. She described their client's response as very positive and left out any comments about the unfairness of giving Virgine access to so much money. A quick reply from Marcus told her, "good work, stand by for the next steps."

Still aggrieved, Beth resolved to go on strike for the rest of the day. She composed an email to Ori inviting her to meet for breakfast at the Marigot market the following morning. She did not mention Hunter Green. She would do that in person.

She was tempted to call Terry, but in the middle of the day he was bound to be busy with Jeff. Instead she wrote an email that, in re-reading, she realized was totally boring. She'd left out everything about her trip to Columbier because she didn't want to worry him, and she'd left out Hunter Green for the same reason. She'd mentioned that Burt was there in the marina, said the project was moving along, and told Terry she loved him. She added that she'd call him tonight and sent it off with a sigh. Then she packed up her beach bag and headed for some sand and ocean.

The next morning just before dawn she crawled from her berth and into the head compartment. She used the marina toilet most of the time; the marina facilities were more spacious than *Trouble*'s, and waste from *Trouble*'s toilet went into a twenty-gallon tank under the forward berth. The tank had to be emptied periodically—either at a pump-out facility, which were few and far between in the islands, or when the boat was at sea far from land and delicate coral reefs. But first thing in the morning she had to take care of business on board. When she pumped the handle to evacuate the toilet bowl, it didn't move. She pushed harder. Nothing. She knew better than to force it—too much pressure might make a hose clamp give out and she'd have pee all over the floor.

"Son of a—sea biscuit," she said, dropping the lid on the bowl with a hollow thunk. She pulled up on the pump handle and tried once more. The mechanism wheezed ominously. She was scrupulous about not putting anything down the toilet that she hadn't eaten. Paper went into a bag under the sink. Hygiene products too. It wasn't possible that she'd clogged it. But, other than Ori the other day, she was the only one who used it, and it had worked last night.

As she washed her hands and face, she reflected on her last use and decided maybe the pump had been stiff, but she'd been too tired to pay attention.

She gave the bowl a disheartened kick, then left the head and got dressed. She did not have time to get out the tool box and take the toilet apart. She gathered her shopping bags and headed for the weekly food market. Ori had accepted her invitation to meet for breakfast. She had not received any messages from her team at Broadhead, but they knew her next scheduled meeting with Virgine was tomorrow, so she expected she'd hear from them by the time she got back.

Three quarters of an hour later, her bags laden with fresh fruit, bread, cheese, and meat, she got to the cafe and found Ori already seated at a table for two. Once Beth was settled a waiter materialized and took their orders for coffee and croissants. He looked a little disappointed that the two American women hadn't ordered typical American breakfasts as he strode away from their table.

"How's the project?" Ori asked when he was out of earshot.

Beth grimaced, thinking of the money Broadhead had agreed to give Virgine, knowing they were not really giving it to her, even if it felt that way. "My company is investing in Virgine Guesnon's company."

"I wonder if your company's terms are any better than the loan shark's."

Beth frowned. "That's an interesting way to think about it."

"They're both loans," Ori said, shrugging. "I'll bet your company had her sign a long contract that gives them a lot of control over her company. To her, that might be worse than the loan shark roughing her up."

"You think he roughed her up?" Beth was surprised that Ori knew so much about business contracts.

Ori shrugged again, meeting Beth's eye. "They can be pretty physical when they don't get their money. I'm just sayin'."

"Broadhead won't send anyone to beat her up. But you're right about the contract. She signed it though, happily."

"She probably expects to win big. They always do."

Beth nodded, lips pursed. Talking about Virgine made her uncomfortable, and she had to change the subject anyway.

"The other day when I got back to *Trouble*, I found a note on the deck."

"From Virgine Guesnon?"

"What? No, no, different topic. Sorry. The note was from a man named Hunter Green."

Beth waited for a reaction, but Ori was saved by the waiter returning with their breakfast. When cups and plates were arranged and he had left them Ori responded.

"What did he want from you?"

"You haven't responded to his emails."

"He told you?"

"I met with him on Monday. He thinks Tiberius is his son. Is he?"

Ori shrugged, saying, "Probably. Hunt was the only white guy I was with in Jamaica, and Ti doesn't look black, thank God. My mom would have a cow. But that doesn't explain what he wanted with you."

"He found an article on line about what happened at the hospital in Pointe-à-Pitre. My name was in the article. Since you weren't answering him, he decided to look for me."

"That's ridiculous."

"I agree. And yet, it worked. Against all odds, he found me."

"What did you tell him?"

"That I would ask you to contact him. Why are you hiding from him?"

"Hold on. You said you met with him. He's here? On St. Martin?"

"Yes." Beth resisted pointing out that she'd said that. Ori could be forgiven for not listening carefully the first time.

"And you told him I'm here?" Ori's cheeks flushed. Anger, Beth realized. She glanced around at the shopping crowds beyond the cafe's island of calm.

"Of course not. He thinks you're in Connecticut. If you don't talk to him, he might go there looking for you." Beth added the threat out of frustration, even though he'd said nothing of the sort. Still, he was a persistent guy, so maybe it was true.

"Better there than here," Ori muttered, tearing apart her croissant and Beth's intended threat.

"What the hell, Ori. He might be your son's father. He does have some rights in this. He didn't run out on you, if what you've said is true. He wants to be involved in his son's upbringing. You're kinda on the wrong side of this thing."

"Well aren't you miss righteous!" Ori said, making Beth glance around again to see if anyone was listening.

"Are you going to run away forever?" Beth asked, finally fed up with the other woman's immature lifestyle. "Because I need you to take care of this, so he stops bothering me." She stopped short of threatening to call Ori's parents. She had their phone number, but until this moment she hadn't considered telling them where their daughter—with her father's stolen boat—was. She realized that if Ori didn't take care of Hunter, and he kept bothering her, she was willing to betray her friend.

"He's too good." Ori said, voice barely more than a murmur.

"Who is, Hunter?"

"Yeah. Nice guy, nice family, doesn't fit in with my—my immature lifestyle."

"Too bad, because you're kinda tied up with him now. You don't have to marry him. But you do have to let him see his son."

Ori sighed, fingers making crumbs of her pastry. "I know. He deserves to know, to meet him if he wants."

"He said he wants to take responsibility. Be a father."

Ori shook her head. "I don't know how much I can take. How close I can let him get. But I guess as long as Ti is in Connecticut and I'm here, he can go do daddy stuff with him."

Beth covered her outrage by sipping her coffee. Watching Ori, she realized she might be judging too harshly. Ori was sad. She had feelings for Hunter Green that she did not want to admit.

"I need you to email him at least. You don't have to tell him you're here. But you do have to talk to him."

Ori's eyes narrowed, then she smiled her thin, devious smile. "I'll email Hunter if you'll come see your client gambling."

The bargain made little sense to Beth. It was a minuscule price for her to pay to get Hunter taken care of. "Okay. Fine. Deal."

"There's a blackjack tournament on Saturday. Virgine always enters them. She'll be there. You be there too."

"What time?"

"Starts at eight."

"I want you to email Hunter now. Today."

"No Wi-Fi here, no computer."

"Come over to *Trouble*."

Ori sighed, feigning inconvenience. She checked the time on her cell phone. But Beth knew that if she was working today, her shift didn't start until late afternoon.

"You're done with your croissant. Come on."

Beth put several Euro on the table, stood up, and hefted her shopping bags.

"I was going to shop," Ori said, eying the bags.

"You can come shop after."

Ori stood up, shouldered her empty shopping bags, and followed Beth out of the cafe.

*)

Little Bay, Sint Maarten

Hunter stubbed his cigarette in the clogged bar ash tray and picked up the fancy smart phone that his brother had given him for Christmas. Then he deliberately set it back down on the bar and took another gulp of coke. His hand started for the pack of cigarettes and he stopped it, picking up the phone instead. One compulsion or the other had to win, he reflected as he entered the passcode to unlock the device.

How long does it take to send an email? He groused, scrolling through the messages from family and friends. He didn't want to contemplate the likely truth: Beth Anderson had contacted Ori, but Ori refused to contact him. He had been so bent on finding Beth all these months, he had not prepared himself for this outcome, even though Parker expected it and said so. Hell, everyone who knew about his search said so. Ori wasn't interested.

The phone in his hand vibrated and made the annoying chiming sound that he hadn't figured out how to change. He had figured out that it meant he had new email. He watched the list of messages refresh. Parker again. His father copying him on business correspondence. No, blind copying him so if he flaked out and didn't come back the client wouldn't know he'd been in the loop. A few junk messages. Something from a college classmate about donating to their alma mater. He dropped the expensive phone on the bar and reached for the cigarettes.

It had been two whole days. Did they understand that he was sitting around waiting to hear? Had Beth explained to Ori? He inhaled deeply and felt the smoke spread through his lungs. A textbook photo of the lung of a twenty-year smoker Parker had emailed him the other day popped into his head and he coughed several times, drawing looks from the few mid-day drinkers in the bar. He set the cigarette on the ash tray and pounded his chest dramatically a couple times, then took a sip of Coke.

He was sick of the bare room at the motel, sick of the tourists, sick of the humid heat and no air conditioning. Now that he'd achieved his objective, he was sick of waiting. He had not yet told Parker of his success—because it didn't feel like success and would not be if Ori didn't contact him. The bitter realization that he hadn't prepared himself for another rejection overpowered the sweet soda he was drinking. He had to do something. Maybe he should go home to Texas.

Or he could go see Beth Anderson again.

Fifty-one

Marigot Bay, St. Martin

"*I* hope my mysterious invitation isn't alarming, Beth," Burt said as they walked together up the Rue de Concordia.

"I'm not alarmed, I'm curious, and wondering how far we're walking." She was also wondering how long it would take. *Trouble's* head was still clogged. After Ori left, she'd searched through *Trouble's* file of manuals, most of which had come with the boat. There wasn't anything for the head. So she searched the internet and found a maintenance manual that included a diagram of the pump. She'd assembled the necessary tools, a bucket, and an old towel when Burt came by. She hadn't mentioned her problem to him, even though he'd probably offer to help. When he'd asked her to join him on an excursion, she'd felt a rush of relief at the reprieve from plumbing and accepted.

"I guess it is a little far. I make a point of walking when I can," he patted his moderate belly with both hands. "We can get a taxi if you want."

Beth wiped perspiration from her forehead. He was right about getting exercise. With *Trouble* in the marina she wasn't swimming nearly as much as she liked. But he had evaded her question. "No, let's walk."

"It gives us time to talk."

Beth took a few strides in silence before asking, "You have something specific you want to talk about?"

"I do."

"Now I'm starting to feel alarmed," Beth said. He chuckled again. It was a comforting sound, knowing the big man was relaxed usually calmed her. But this time it did not. She watched him for a stride. She could see he was trying to decide what to say next.

Then he spoke.

"*Sandcastle* is my retirement job, you know that."

"Yes."

"But sometimes I accept work from my old line. When it's interesting, or I'm in a position to do some good. I like to think I help out when it matters."

Beth sighed, glancing sideways at her friend. This confirmation of her suspicions—he was connected to an intelligence agency, and he was only partly retired—cast doubt on everything he said and did. It was like he was a different person who she had to get to know all over again. And yet, since she'd suspected this all along, he wasn't different at all. The difference was his admission. She wished Terry were here. They had talked about Burt so many times, she wanted to know what he thought.

"Okay," she finally said, knowing he was waiting for her to react. "Are you working now?"

"Yes. As of three days ago."

Beth stopped. Burt took another step, stopped, and turned to her. His eyes were full of concern, his mouth tight.

"Why are you telling me?"

He nodded, lips curling at the corners. "That is the right question, Beth."

"And the answer is?"

"Because we are working together."

"You work for Broadhead?" She was almost positive he did not.

"No. But Broadhead has a lot of clients."

"And you work for one of them?"

"Correct. Let's keep walking." Burt gestured with his head up the road.

"Why? Are you afraid someone is listening?" She said it as a joke, starting to walk again even as she spoke. But she didn't miss the way he glanced around at the apartment buildings on either side of the street.

"Visiting hours are limited."

"Visiting—we're going to a hospital?"

"Yes. But I'll get to that. I have been engaged to oversee the transfer of a large sum of money to Virgine Guesnon—your client. Ms. Guesnon is a subject of a multi-agency investigation."

"Is it her gambling?" Beth asked, setting aside his careful avoidance of saying who had engaged him, and the multi-agency thing. "Or the fraudulent goods? Selling Chinese stuff as locally made?"

Burt stared at her for a moment, and Beth couldn't tell if he was surprised or, to her horror, amused.

"She's an awful business woman," Beth said.

"You don't know the half of it."

"I don't?"

"Virgine Guesnon is involved in human trafficking. She receives human cargo and holds it for distribution in the islands."

Beth heard the words and focused on them, suppressing any emotional reaction until she could digest the information intellectually.

"Don't you mean 'them'?" she said. "Virgine holds them?"

"Yes. Thank you. It is too easy to fall into official-speak. She holds her human victims somewhere here on the island before selling them on."

Virgine Guesnon is a slaver. She's in the same business that brought her ancestors to this island. Beth let the idea sink in and matched it with her other perceptions about her client. She was sad to realize that it did not contradict them, and it enriched her overall negative opinion.

"She keeps some of them." Beth pictured the young man at Virgine's house. She'd sensed something odd about him, and she'd been right.

"What?"

"She has a boy at her house. He can't be eighteen. I told Terry about him after I met her there. He's not a relative. Terry said he might be the son of a maid or cook. But now I think he's her—merchandise."

Burt nodded. "It's possible."

They walked a few paces. Beth struggled to shut off her disgust and anger and focus on Virgine's crime—her real crime that overshadowed the other petty stuff.

"Why is Broadhead giving her money? Why aren't these multiple agencies arresting her right now? I'll give a statement. I have proof of her merchandise fraud, and I bet Ori could testify about her gambling losses. We could put her away—" She stopped because Burt was shaking his head. "What?"

"She's a link in the chain. Take her out and someone else steps in. They want to follow the chain, get evidence on the bosses. If they can do that, she'll be swept up in it too."

"So, Broadhead has to keep her in business."

"Exactly," Burt actually looked proud of her. "That has been your role all along. Keep her front—the local trade goods—up and running while they put together the pieces in the human trafficking."

"Except she's been dishonest about that business too. Everything she does is a fraud. I've been a pawn all this time?"

He shrugged, then shot her an apologetic look. "It seems so."

"And my entire team knows about this?"

"I doubt it. Your boss might. From what I understand, your department at Broadhead is mostly what it appears to be: consulting for business and political development. But Broadhead is a big company, with lots of interests. Sometimes what your group does overlaps with the interests of the less overt departments. It's not unusual in DC firms like yours."

"Jesus."

"He has very little to do with it."

Beth snorted. "That's for sure."

They walked on in silence for a while, turning left onto Rue du Soliel Levant to walk past more apartments and office buildings.

"What is your role in this," Beth finally asked. "You said to oversee the transfer of money. But won't Broadhead use a wire transfer?"

"Yes. It's not about a pile of cash. It's to monitor the recipient, in case she decides to take the money and run. Your supervisors did not think you were ready to handle that kind of assignment."

"Ready to handle it? Like, maybe next time I will be? Won't I need to know I'm on the assignment first?"

Burt chuckled again and it cooled her flash of anger. "It's not exactly like you're being tested here."

"Except that's exactly what it is, isn't it?"

"Not what they told me."

"What did they tell you? Whoever 'they' is?"

"I can't get into who 'they' is. But they told me to ensure the safety of Broadhead's asset."

"I'm Broadhead's asset." Beth wasn't able to suppress a harumpf.

"Yes, and they value you. If I think you're in danger I'm to pull you out. You want to know what I think?"

"I'd be crazy not to."

"True." He shot her a sharp little grin. "They think you have potential. They want to bring you along. Next time they'll probably let you in on things going in. If this assignment goes well."

"If I don't panic or do something stupid, you mean."

"Pretty much," he nodded grinning at her again. Then his smile faded, and he turned away to watch where they were walking.

"Will I have the option to decline, do you think?"

His little smile encouraged her. It seemed like he had expected the question and approved.

"Probably," he said, not looking at her. She imagined he wanted to add something like, "but you'd be a fool to." She wondered what her value was to Broadhead if she wasn't prepared to handle this kind of work. She could imagine her bright career there taking a sharp downward turn if she didn't cooperate. But why wouldn't she want to help stop a human trafficking ring? They counted on her interest in doing the right thing, even if she felt manipulated. *The end justifies the means.*

"A lot of lives are at stake in this," Burt went on. "Don't think I don't realize that. The agencies involved are dedicated to stopping human trafficking. They're the good guys, no matter how twisted you think their methods are right now."

Beth thought about it for a few minutes. Long enough to notice that her feet were getting tired.

"I understand everyone is trying to do the right thing. Are we at the part where you explain who's in the hospital?" *Because this walk better be worth it.*

"On New Year's, around one o'clock in the morning, police broke up a brawl in the market square."

"Right. Terry and I walked by there."

"You saw it?"

"We saw an ambulance drive away."

"The fight was between drunken tourists. But a little boy got pulled into it. He was hit and someone fell on him. He was taken away in the ambulance."

"Who is he?"

"Exactly the right question to ask." Burt gestured that they should turn right and cross the street. They turned right again at the next corner.

"He did not speak and did not understand the doctors and nurses. He had a couple broken ribs and a head injury, and he was severely malnourished and dehydrated. The next morning someone spoke English near him, and he reacted. He called out to the doctor who had spoken. He begged the doctor to go help someone else, a little girl who was hurt. He was so frantic about it they sedated him, fearing he'd injure himself."

"Did he tell them where the little girl was?"

"He couldn't. He described walking a very long way, stopping at the beach to rinse blood off himself, and walking more until he found the party in the square. They found traces of someone else's blood on him that he had not managed to wash off."

"Did he say what was wrong with the girl?"

"The hospital psychiatrist has talked with him several times. She thinks he saw the girl raped. Possibly that is what drove him to escape."

Beth shuddered. She couldn't imagine what he'd been through. "Why are you taking me to see him?"

"Because I think it will help you to meet him. He is one of the people Virgine Guesnon is trading in."

"How can you be certain he's not a run-away?"

"Because he has described the journey from his home, the other prisoners, the work they're doing. And he's described Virgine Guesnon."

"You mean he's seen her?"

"Yes. She has visited her inventory."

"Jesus. I know. He has nothing to do with this. I'm glad I'm not overly religious, because I'd be struggling with it right now."

"I have long preferred to believe we humans are empowered to be God's agents—if we so chose. Not that I'm all that religious either. But it's helped me through challenging times."

Beth studied the side of Burt's face for a few steps, thinking about what his life had been like so far—as much as she knew of it. When she looked ahead again, she saw a low white building unlike the hospitals she was used to. The hospital in Guadeloupe had been much grander. This was more like a clinic.

They walked through the glass front doors into an airy white-painted lobby. Burt spoke to an attendant at a reception counter and received approval to proceed along a side hallway. Beth followed.

They turned twice more, walking for a while beside an outdoor garden before re-entering a rear wing of the building. Burt stopped outside a wide wooden door that stood open. Inside Beth could see a double row of hospital beds with curtains hung from the ceiling. Several of the beds with curtains pulled back were occupied by children.

"He's in here," Burt said, leading the way down the corridor between the beds and stopping at the foot of one of them.

Beth instinctively smiled at the boy in the bed who was staring back at her with wide eyes. His head was bandaged and one of his arms was in a sling. Between the bandages she could see unusual skin pigmentation on his face—an unfortunate birthmark.

"Hello Kelvin. I brought a friend to meet you," Burt said. His tone had become grandfatherly. Beth glanced at him, wondering whether he'd ever played Santa Clause, because he could pull it off easily, then looked back at the boy who was smiling now, too.

"Hello Kelvin. My name is Beth. It's a pleasure to meet you."

"Hello Beth." The boy's accent was thick, his voice soft.

"I had the pleasure of meeting Kelvin on Sunday," Burt explained. "I think he was pleased to meet someone who speaks English, weren't you Kelvin?"

"Yes, Mr. Burt."

"Kelvin is from South Africa. Right?" Burt said to Beth, turning back to Kelvin as he asked for confirmation.

"Yes."

"And you'd like to go home, wouldn't you?"

The boy's curious expression turned grim. He cast his eyes to the side and shrugged.

"Why don't you want to go home, Kelvin?" Beth moved alongside his bed without thinking. She looked at the top of his downcast head. "Do you miss your family?"

Kelvin slowly raised his head to look at her. His eyes were brimming. "No Miss. Nobody misses me."

Beth glanced at Burt, unsure of her misstep.

"Kelvin and his mother were both taken. He isn't sure about his sister and brother—right?"

"Yes Mr. Burt. They were at school. I was with mama when they came."

"And your mother?" Beth asked, regretting it the moment the words came out.

The tears flowed down his cheeks as he shook his head.

"She die. On the boat."

"I'm so sorry, Kelvin. I am so sorry this happened to you."

The boy met her gaze, tears streaming, but eyes no longer sorrowful. He was angry.

"Nothing happened to me. It was done to me. Done to me by bad men and the evil woman."

Beth couldn't suppress a sharp intake of breath.

"The evil woman?" she asked, throat dry.

"The devil woman," Kelvin nodded. "I will kill her, and I will kill the men."

)

"I know where he came from." Beth told Burt after they left Kelvin and returned to the front of the hospital. Burt stopped at reception and asked the attendant to call for a taxi, much to Beth's relief. That had given her enough time to decide to tell Burt everything she knew.

His brows rose in inquiry, but he said nothing.

"On New Year's Eve. He walked into town from Virgine's warehouse."

"In the port? Why do you think that?"

"You know about it?"

"We know about all of her holdings. I assume you know about it because it's in Broadhead's files, too."

"It is. But that's not why I think he came from there."

"Why do you?"

"On Monday I rented a car and visited one of Virgine's craftsmen on my own. When I was getting back in my car, a truck came to his house and delivered boxes labeled with Chinese characters—the Chinese statues that she's passing off as local. When the truck left, I followed it. It went to her warehouse. There were armed guards. Who needs armed guards at a warehouse full of crafts and knickknacks?"

A dun-colored sedan pulled into the hospital's drive and stopped. Burt stepped toward it and opened the rear passenger door for Beth. She got in while he went around to the other side. He told the driver to take them to the marina, then sat back.

"Kelvin is looking better," he said to Beth, one brow arched slightly.

Catching on to his reticence within the cab driver's hearing, she nodded. "I'm so relieved. I was very worried. How long did they say they were keeping him?"

"At least three days. Until the weekend."

)

Fort Louis Marina, Marigot Bay, St. Martin

Hunter had no trouble slipping through the marina gate behind a group of young, pretty sailors in matching polos and shorts. *Must be a team or something.* He thought as he approached *Double Trouble.* Standing on the dock he could see that the boat was locked up, the padlock hanging on the outside of the hatch.

A wave of guilt for involving Beth again shook him. For so long he'd been too focused on getting her to help him. Now that she had agreed to, the pushiness of his behavior had started to sink in. He'd hunted down a stranger to ask for a favor. He was lucky she'd agreed to do it, but here he was to bug her again. He was glad she wasn't there. He hurried up the dock, afraid now that she'd come back and catch him. He got out the gate and back on his bike, which he'd left unlocked leaning up against the marina building wall, without being caught.

)

Beth begged off when Burt suggested dinner at one of the restaurants in town. He seemed to understand when she said she needed time to think, and she had stocked her galley that morning. But once she was in *Trouble's* saloon, she looked through a port and saw him standing on the dock looking at the boat. His expression was what she'd call pensive.

He's worried I'll do something impulsive now that I know the depth of Virgine's crimes. I don't blame him. But he's wrong. This time.

While she constructed a supper from her market groceries, she tried not to think about the impulsive actions she was tempted to take. Among the ideas she discarded were confronting Virgine and telling the team what she'd learned. The men with guns at the warehouse were enough of a tangible threat to keep her from saying anything to Virgine. Burt had told her in absolute terms that she could not tell the team a thing, even though she'd pointed out that if Virgine was arrested they would have to be told. He assured her that Broadhead would manage things. What he had not said, and she had not asked, was whether she could tell Terry. She was pretty sure Burt knew she would, so he had not put her in a position to violate his instructions. She thought it meant Burt trusted Terry, and that made Beth trust Burt more.

Fifty-two

Fort Louis Marina, Marigot Bay, St. Martin

"*R*emember when we were walking back from Evan's New Year's Eve party, and we saw that disturbance in the market square?" Beth asked Terry later that evening. He'd answered her call with enthusiasm in his voice and she'd started out by asking him how things were going. He'd told her about progress with the deal he and Jeff were working on. The fact that it sounded like it was going to go through made her anxious, and she realized she had been harboring a hope that it wouldn't, and Terry would be freed up to be with her. Even though he'd said he needed another profitable deal before he could afford to stop.

"Vaguely," he replied to her question, adding to her anxiety: their experiences together were fading in his memory.

"We crossed the street to keep away from the crowd?" she prompted.

As if picking up on her unspoken complaint about his memory, he said "Right. There was an ambulance, and police."

Mollified, she said, "Right. Well, today I met the person who was in the ambulance."

"Really? How did that happen?" Now he sounded interested, and Beth felt a sharp sense of victory, as if she'd won him back from Jeff. It was immediately followed by embarrassment at her petty reaction.

"Burt took me to visit him. Are you sitting down? I've got quite a story to tell you."

"I'm in my favorite chair in the den. Go ahead."

Picturing him where he'd described, she told him about Burt's assignment, and Broadhead's involvement, and finished up with Ori's demand that she visit the casino and see Virgine gambling on Saturday. He barely spoke while she talked, making the occasional sound that told her he was listening. When she finally ran out of steam there was silence on the line. It went on far longer than was comfortable.

"Terry?"

"Yeah. I'm thinking." But there was another sound now, clicking. He was typing.

"What are you looking up?" She imagined him at his desk searching the internet for human trafficking.

"Did Burt say anything about the girl's body they found on Christmas Day?"

"He said they have not tied her to Virgine, but they suspect she died either en route to or in Virgine's holding place."

"This is horrifying. I wish I could tell you not to see Virgine Guesnon again."

"Terry, I—"

"But I can't. I know. You have to keep on working with her. It sounds like they all think you're not in danger. But I'll bet you didn't tell Burt you're planning on seeing Virgine gambling on Saturday, did you?"

Beth gulped. "I made a stupid deal with Ori to get Hunter off my back."

"Hunter?"

Oh shit. How had she left out Hunter? Until today he'd been the most threatening thing going on. "This guy who's looking for Ori. He's probably Tiberius's father."

She sensed a strange hesitation in Terry as he said, "So what does it have to do with you?"

"When Ori wouldn't answer his emails, he decided to look for me. He found my name in an article in the Pointe-à-Pitre online newspaper. He's spent months tracking me down. But he doesn't know Ori is here. I didn't tell him."

"I think you should invite them both somewhere and walk away once they meet."

Beth frowned. "Why didn't I think of that?"

"Because you're loyal to your friend. What is this deal with her?"

"She emailed Hunter, and I had to promise to go to the casino on Saturday."

"Why does Ori care whether you witness Virgine gambling?"

"I have no idea. Could be she's bothered by this business woman leading a double life, and being dishonest, and she thinks I'll get Broadhead to take action if I see it in person. She doesn't know about the human trafficking. She thinks Broadhead is what it says it is."

Terry sighed audibly, a sign he was processing information. Beth waited, picking at the worn fabric covering the saloon settee. She heard more typing.

"I'll be there Friday evening." Terry finally said.

"You'll be here?" Beth's heart soared, and she realized how unsettling Burt's news had been. Knowing Terry would be by her side again made all the unknowns more manageable.

"Don't go near the casino without me. Or Virgine's warehouse."

"I was not planning on going to the casino until Saturday. I won't. I can't believe—are you sure you can afford the time to come here?"

"I am positive that I have to. I want to be with you this time when you take off on some mission." The hint of amusement in his voice softened the sexist nature of his declaration. His follow up completely mitigated it. "You don't get to have all the fun by yourself."

)

Beth supposed that the revelations about Virgine and Broadhead softened the impact of Hunter Green putting her in the middle of his hunt for Ori. Since meeting with him, Beth had been fretting about how to tell Terry about it. The fact that it was practically a footnote in their call tonight didn't conceal the fact that Terry's reaction had seemed underwhelming. It was almost as if that part of her story wasn't a surprise.

As she did her evening check of the boat and got ready for bed—avoiding the head—she thought through the sequence of events related to Hunter. She still thought that Burt, too, had not seemed overly surprised at Hunter's appearance, and she had forgotten to ask him about it during their trip to the hospital. Burt had arrived at the marina on Sunday, but he'd said today he'd been asked to assist with Virgine on Monday. Why had he come to St. Martin in the first place?

The pieces slid into place. He'd known about Hunter. He'd come here to protect her, maybe even followed Hunter. At some point he'd told Terry. But neither of them had elected to tell her.

She didn't know how long she lay on her bunk staring up through the hatch that night, both livid at the two men and loving them for caring. As the hatch turned grey with pre-dawn light, she dragged herself up and went to watch the sunrise from the cockpit. She knew who she needed to talk to, but it was the middle of the night in California.

Beth spent a stressful hour with Virgine in her office going over how much of the investment funding Broadhead had promised would go toward an employee to manage the administrative aspects of her business. Had Beth not known about Virgine's financial shenanigans, she would have been baffled by her client's hesitancy at hiring someone to keep an eye on the books, cashflow, and inventory. By the time they parted Virgine had agreed to the job posting Broadhead wanted to list with various local employment services.

Back aboard *Trouble* Beth emailed this news to her team. Then it was finally time to call her sister.

"I need your advice, Sis," Beth told Trish after they'd covered the usual catch-up topics: Their mother's hip was healing, Dad's condition wasn't much changed, the kids and Mike were doing well, and Trish's pregnancy was progressing normally. Beth could tell Trish would stay on the topic of a wedding date if she could, so she hoped her request would distract her.

"On the wedding date?" Trish said. Beth suppressed a groan.

"No, something else. I realized last night that Terry and Burt kept something from me."

"Burt? Oh, that guy you met in the islands?"

"Yes. He's here in Marigot right now. He moves around a lot."

"Shifty."

Beth snorted, thinking, *you don't know the half of it.*

"He's a charter captain. He goes where there's business."

"Okay, whatever. How did he and your fiancé conspire to keep something from you? And what is it?"

"Well, there's this man who has been looking for me for months. He finally found me here and I met with him. But Burt was there when we met, and afterwards, last night, I realized after I told Terry about it that neither of them had acted very surprised about it."

"Woah, back up. What man was looking for you?"

Beth sighed, realizing there was no way to provide an abridged version. Not if she wanted Trish's advice. She explained who Hunter was, and why he had been looking for her, and about the note he left on *Trouble*.

"So your friend Burt found the note before you did, and went to the burger place so he'd be there when you met this Hunter," Trish said.

"Right. He must have. He was already there when I went to meet Hunter. I agreed to ask Ori to email Hunter directly, and Hunter went away."

"But Hunter could come back and bother you again if Ori doesn't contact him."

"I made her email him yesterday morning. I watched her do it. He's got no reason to contact me again."

"Beth, you have no way of stopping him from coming back to you if he doesn't get what he wants from Ori."

"Trish, I have no way of providing what he wants, and I think he's smart enough to know threatening me won't get Ori to cooperate."

"Fair enough. Let's hope you're right. Why do you think Terry knew about Hunter?"

"It was the way he reacted—or didn't react—when I told him. I didn't recognize it at the time, but when I thought back on it, I realized he was not upset enough. I think Burt told him about Hunter before I did. I think Burt found out about Hunter and followed him here because he knew Hunter might find me. I think he called Terry too, maybe thinking Terry was with me."

"Why are you making all these assumptions? Ask one of them. Or both of them."

"Because if I'm right they kept it from me, and I don't want to confront them."

"Why not?"

"Well, I—" Beth couldn't come up with a reason that didn't make her sound like a coward.

"Do you love Terry?"

"Of course I do."

"Do you trust Terry?"

"Of course—well…"

"This isn't good, Beth. You need to talk to him about it, you can't carry around suspicion about deception. You don't have to confront him or accuse him. You can just ask him. Calmly."

"Maybe I should ask Burt first. You know, to warm up."

"Burt is way less important than Terry."

"I know, I can practice on him."

"Why are you being a coward?"

"I'm not being a coward. I'm afraid—I don't want to—" Beth bit back an unwelcome, and surprising, sob.

"Make Terry angry? Do you think he'll break off with you? Is your relationship that fragile?"

Beth swallowed hard and squeezed her eyes shut. "No. It is not. But I'm that insecure."

"Okay. Good. You admit it. It's ridiculous, but you admit it."

"Don't call me ridiculous."

"I didn't. I called your insecurity ridiculous. That man loves you. He's well aware of your faults as well as your strengths. He's not going to dump you for asking him about this. He made a deal with your mutual friend to keep something from you. He's got to have a reason, and you should know what it is."

"I can guess what it is. He didn't want to scare me."

"Are you scared?"

"Not now. But when I first read Hunter's note, yeah. Strange man wants to meet me for an unspecified reason. It scared me. If I'd known he was looking for me, it would have been much less frightening."

"So that's what you need to tell Terry. Tell both of them. Tell them they can't be keeping secrets that affect you."

"But they meant well. Burt came here to watch over me."

"You said he goes where the work is."

"He's not working here, he came for me." She couldn't tell Trish Burt's other reason for being on St. Martin. Besides, he had come here because of Hunter, she was sure of it. He'd been asked to help out with Virgine after that. But the more she thought about the sequence of events, the more she could imagine bringing it up with him. If he would admit to contacting Terry, she'd feel better about talking to Terry about it.

"Okay, whatever. You need to talk to both of them."

"Yeah. You're right Trish. I'm going to do it. Thank you."

Beth walked along the dock to *Sandcastle* that afternoon, but the motor cruiser was empty. Walking back, she ran into Evan, and then Connor, offering brief greetings to both. Back aboard *Trouble* she faced the clogged head. She crammed the old towel under the fitting for the output hose and tried to position the bucket where she could direct the flow from the hose. It wasn't going to work, the head compartment was too cramped to position the bucket correctly. She was going to end up with pee in the bilge, she knew it. At least she'd been scrupulous about going up the dock to the office when she needed to do anything else.

She unscrewed the hose clamp, expecting seepage to begin from the first turn. But when the clamp came loose the hose remained solidly on the fitting. She wrapped both hands around it and wiggled it side to side. It flexed stiffly but didn't loosen its grip on the fitting at the base of the head. She was sure that when it let go, it was going to do it fast and spew all over everything, including her.

She inserted the blade of a flathead screwdriver between the end of the hose and the fitting, twisting it to force the hose off. The seal broke. Liquid oozed between the hose and the fitting. She grabbed the hose and wiggled it back and forth once more, watching the seepage increase, lighten, and increase again. Alternating twisting the screwdriver at different points around the hose with the forceful wiggling, she finally got the hose off. But by then most the liquid in it had already oozed out onto the now sodden towel. The head compartment was filled with an acrid, sour smell. Knowing it was all her own waste didn't make it any less awful.

As the last of the liquid flowed out of the hose it carried grayish gravel onto the towel. Frowning, Beth bent the hose up so she could see into it. She definitely had not thrown gravel down the head. The two-inch diameter heavy black rubber hose was constricted to an opening of about a quarter inch by more of the grayish material. As she bent the hose she heard and felt it crackling inside. She laid the hose back on the towel and tapped it with the screwdriver. More of the grey stuff came out.

"What the hell?"

She backed out of the head and shut the door, then washed her hands in the galley sink and went to her laptop. It didn't take her long to learn that the substance clogging the hose was years of mineral build-up from the seawater that flushed the head and from human waste. It was probably clogging the entire length of the hose, which was several feet long. It was not an unusual size or type of hose—she could probably buy a replacement at the chandlery right here in Marigot. But just then she couldn't take any more. She found a cold beer in the ice box and took it out to the cockpit. The fresh air revived her, which emphasized how bad the smell below had gotten. All of *Trouble*'s hatches were open, all she could do was wait it out.

She sat in the cockpit for the remainder of the afternoon, sipping a succession of beers and reading everything she could find about human trafficking on her laptop. It was not a pleasant afternoon, and it intensified her desire to speak to Burt. After a walk up the dock to use the head she went back to *Sandcastle*, but the boat was still locked up and quiet. She went to *Trouble*'s galley to make a meal of leftovers, looking up through the portholes every time she heard someone on the dock. After dinner she walked to the head and then to *Sandcastle* once again. Thinking Burt had better have a damned good excuse for not being there, she returned to *Trouble* and made a conscious decision to stop looking for him. At least the smell had dissipated so that she could sleep below.

Fifty-three

Fort Louis Marina, Marigot Bay, St. Martin

"*I*'m in a taxi," Terry's voice over her cell phone sent a shiver of anticipation up Beth's spine. She'd wanted to taxi over to the airport and meet him, but he'd begged her not to bother, so she'd stayed aboard *Trouble* preparing for a dinner of seared duck breast, roasted new potatoes, and asparagus. The potatoes were in the oven and the duck and asparagus were ready to be cooked when he called. She slid the pan of asparagus into the oven with the potatoes and went forward to change into clean clothes.

A few minutes later she walked up the dock and saw him get out of the taxi, a bundle of flowers in the crook of one arm and a bottle of wine in the other. He switched the bottle to the other hand and collected his bag from the taxi's trunk, then headed toward the gate where Beth was standing. She pushed it open.

"Welcome back," she said, wrapping her arms around him, letting flowers be crushed between them along with the bottle in his hand.

"It is so good to see you," he dropped his bag to wrap his free arm around her. "I'm so glad to be here."

He turned his head toward hers and their lips met in a long, deep kiss that made her heart race. She actually gasped for breath when they parted, and he grinned.

"You missed me," he drawled.

"You missed me," she said with a smirk. He shrugged it off, grinning.

"Of course I did. These are for you." He offered the flowers and wine, and she realized he wanted her to take them so he could pick up his bag, so she did, pressing her face into the flowers and inhaling.

"They smell wonderful. They'll definitely freshen up the boat," she said, simultaneously thinking of the broken head and unintentionally taking the edge off of the romantic gesture.

"I figured I needed them," he said as they started down the ramp to the dock. "I have to talk to you about something."

"What?" she asked, unnerved.

"Let's get aboard," he said in a "this is serious" tone. Beth hoped she already knew what he wanted to say.

And she did.

"I have to apologize. When you mentioned Hunter Green, I did not tell you I already knew about him. I should have." They were standing in *Trouble*'s saloon. Terry had dropped his bag on the v-berth bunk while Beth crammed the flowers into a plastic pitcher with water from the galley sink tap.

"You already knew?" Beth was peeling the foil from the neck of the wine bottle.

"Let's take that up to the cockpit and I'll explain. I forgot how stuffy it can be in here," he said, wrinkling his nose.

Beth was proud of herself for being grown up about it, knowing full well she would not have been if she hadn't already guessed that he knew. She had not connected with Burt today, and now that Terry was here, she was glad she hadn't. Burt's deception was far less important than her fiancé's, and had she confronted him, it might have colored her reaction to Terry.

She pulled the cork on the wine and grabbed two plastic wine cups and took them up to the cockpit.

"Burt called me right after I got back to D.C. and told me about Hunter Green. I should have told you then, but he said he was thinking of coming here, so I let him convince me you were safe."

Terry's words tumbled out so quickly Beth was left standing holding the bottle and cups, staring down at him where he sat at the cockpit table.

"Here, I'm sorry. Sit down. Let me have that," he added, reaching for the bottle and cups. She let him take them and sat down across from him, her back to the dock. She watched him set the cups down and pour a couple inches of wine into each one. He picked up one and held it out to her.

"Please," he said. She took it. He picked his up and touched the rim to hers.

"To us. If you'll still have me."

Beth took a sip of the delicate wine. He'd gotten it at the airport so it might have been overpriced, but it was a delicious full-bodied French red.

"Of course I'll still have you. But tell me why. Why didn't you tell me?"

"Burt was worried about telling you, after what you did with Ori before."

Beth nodded, sipping more wine. She wasn't surprised at Burt's opinion. He thought she was impulsive, he'd almost said so. But that wasn't the issue. Terry's actions were the problem.

"But that's Burt's opinion. Why didn't you tell me?"

"I just said—oh. Yeah. Fair enough. Why didn't I ignore Burt's choice and make my own?"

"Right."

"Because I'm an idiot?"

"That is a distinct possibility, and we can work on it. But really?"

Terry chuckled, relieved.

"Have I mentioned that I love you?"

"Not tonight, but I'm not sure it's the right answer right now."

He nodded, sipped more wine. "The way it sounded, Burt was going to come here and be around, so if this guy Hunter did find you, he'd be on hand. I trust Burt. Also, the likelihood of Hunter finding you seemed low. Like, not gonna' happen low."

"So you left it to him because if you told me I might—what? Go looking for Hunter?"

"Ouch. But I guess so. It was a lazy, lousy thing to do. Burt was on the job and I could let it go and focus on the deal, and I didn't have to worry about you being afraid about this guy looking for you."

"What I didn't know wouldn't hurt me."

All of a sudden, he was miserable, and Beth felt bad for making him so. She took an overlarge gulp of wine to mask her feelings, then remembered that awful dinner of too much wine at his parents' home and set her cup on the table.

"It was wrong. I should have told you. I should have told Burt to tell you." He set his own cup on the table, watching her. She inhaled and exhaled a long breath.

"I guessed that you knew, after we talked the other night."

He nodded.

"It hurts me that you didn't tell me. I want us to be able to be honest with one another. What else are you not telling me?"

Even as she said it, she knew it was a cheap shot, suggesting there were a lot of secrets he was withholding. He looked stricken, and she felt awful again.

"Forget I said that. It came out wrong. I don't think you're keeping secrets from me. Only the ones you think I might act irrationally on, or that someone else is handling."

And his pained expression made her feel worse. *Shit.*

"I apologize for not telling you when Burt told me. It was thoughtless and yes, part of my reason was that Burt would be handling it. But that's a terrible excuse. In the future, I will share information when I get it, even if it may not matter, or someone else will take care of it, or even if I suspect you might do something crazy."

"Crazy?"

"Ill advised."

Beth nodded, accepting this less severe description.

"I would not want to do anything ill advised," she said, hoping to lighten the mood. Her anger at Terry, and even her anger at Burt, was gone. They had both done what they thought was best. Retraining them to stop protecting her from herself would take time. She wanted the rest of this night with Terry to be as perfect as possible. Even as she thought it, she realized the potatoes and asparagus in the oven were probably done.

"And leaving the vegetables in the oven any longer would be exactly that," she said, standing up. "I'll be right back."

She climbed back down into the galley, picked up a hot pad, and opened the oven. The olive oil on the asparagus was sizzling. She pulled the pan out and put it on the counter, then took out the other pan with the potatoes. She shut off the oven and crouched in front of the stove to work the controls to light the broiler.

"Everything okay down there?" came Terry's voice from the cockpit.

"Yes. It's okay. I'm going to put the duck on. Dinner will be ready in fifteen minutes."

The broiler sparked to life under the two-handed lighting process. She slid the broiler pan with the seasoned duck breasts into the top rack and shut the door.

Back in the cockpit Terry had refilled both their wine cups. He had moved hers over to his side of the table. He scooted along the lazarette to make room for her, so she sat beside him and felt his arm lay comfortably across her shoulders.

"So you'll accept my apology, and my promise to do better?"

"Yes."

"Thank you. I'm so glad to be here."

"Well, you may change your mind. The head is broken."

"*Trouble*'s head?"

"Yeah. The hose is clogged—bad—and the chandlery in Marigot didn't have the right size. I took a taxi to Phillipsburg. Did you know there are three marine supply stores in Phillipsburg? They didn't have it either. After that I got a little smarter and called the one in Oyster Pond. No luck. So I came back here and the marina staff ordered it. They get pissy when I try to do things for myself, by the way. It's coming on Monday. Or Tuesday. How long are you staying?"

Beth was tempted to suggest they take *Trouble* out into the bay and anchor out until the Saturday afternoon, but as dinner progressed Terry's romantic advances intensified, and her own responses were equally amorous. Sipping the last of the wine snuggled together in the cockpit the idea of separating in order to untie lines and drive the boat seemed like a silly waste of time.

Much later as she trudged back from the marina head, the dull reality of *Trouble*'s disabled equipment sank in. Somehow having to use a bucket and dump it overboard took the sparkle off of her vision of making love under the stars.

She awakened to the sounds of Terry banging around in the galley. When she groggily emerged into the saloon a few minutes later she remembered why she had concluded that sailing alone wasn't all it was cracked up to be: He pressed a warm mug of coffee into her hands.

"I love you," she said, then cleared her throat of the frog that made it crack. Terry leaned in and kissed her forehead.

"I was thinking of playing tourist this morning. What do you say? You've been stressing out about Virgine and *Trouble*'s head. I can tell. Let's get away from it all."

"There's something wrong with me if I'm living on St. Martin, but I have to make a point of getting away from it all," Beth said ruefully.

"True. But it goes to show you that work is a state of mind, not geography."

Beth slumped down onto the settee across from the table and took a long sip of coffee. It was just right—strong and lightened with long-life milk warmed in a sauce pan. She let her head tip back against the cabinet behind her and smiled at him. He was standing in the galley sipping from his own mug. Four eggs were lined up on the counter.

"You going to cook those?"

J

Plum Bay, Sint Maarten

They rented a car and drove to the western end of the island and the secluded beach at Plum Bay. Spending half the day laying on the beach and swimming in the light surf was like a vacation. For a few hours Beth did not think about Virgine, Hunter and Ori, or *Trouble*'s clogged head. She couldn't completely stop thinking about the people being held in Virgine's warehouse, and after a while she said so to Terry. They were stretched out on towels on the beach letting the sun dry them after their most recent swim. Terry, stretched out on his stomach with his head cradled on his forearms, turned his face toward her.

"I read everything I could find about human trafficking after we talked," he said. It was almost as if he had been ready for this conversation since he got there, waiting for her to bring it up. "And then I read everything I could find about Broadhead."

Beth turned onto her side to face him, head propped on a hand. "What did you find?"

"About Broadhead?"

"Yes. I've been so focused on Virgine I never thought of looking at them."

"Not much beyond what the publicity department wants the world to know. But I found a few oblique references—a news source within the company commenting on an investigation of a senator. A mention in a news item about an attempted coup in Central America. A couple references in stories about the middle east. Like, an adviser to the military was a contractor from Broadhead. For comparison, I did the same search on a couple of the known military consulting companies—the ones that are in the news. I got similar results."

"So Broadhead is one of them, they just haven't gotten pulled into anything newsworthy?"

"Yet. Yes, I think so. They aren't one of the big players."

Beth flopped onto her back, processing this confirmation of what, at the back of her mind, she'd started suspecting since Burt's revelation on Wednesday.

"I didn't see anything that suggested they're doing nasty stuff."

"But you wouldn't, would you, unless they get caught," she said to the cloudless sky.

"I think what I'm trying to say is, you shouldn't go all self-righteous pacifist liberal and quit because they might be involved in that stuff."

"Self-righteous pacifist liberal?" Beth squeaked, half laughter, half offense. Terry's politics were about as left of center as her own, which was not that far, but far enough to call herself a democrat—except that her voter registration had lapsed while she was cruising, and she hadn't re-registered.

Turning her head toward him, she saw that he was abashed. He rolled onto his side to look her more directly in the eye as he said, "Sorry. I got into it with Jeff the other day. He called me that and it stung."

"You didn't tell him about Broadhead, did you?" Beth was alarmed. This was none of Jeff's business.

"No! It was totally unrelated. And not important. Let me start over. I think you should stick with Broadhead and see where they take you. If you find out they're doing things you have moral objections to, you can quit, or blow the whistle on them."

"You want me to stay employed," she said in a mock pouty voice. The truth was, she wanted to stay employed, probably more than he wanted her to.

"I want you to be happy, and you have been happy for the last few months. I think Broadhead's role in this thing with Virgine is on the side of the good. They're helping shut her down. More than her. You can be proud of what you're helping with."

Beth lay her arm across her eyes and stared into the red darkness of her eyelids. He had a point, and she admitted to herself that she did like the adventurous aspect of it. She'd been on edge, but eager, when she'd trailed that truck on Monday. Plus, it let her think in terms like "trailed."

"I know. Okay. I think you're right."

They lay quietly for a while longer before Beth sat up and put on more sunscreen, then nudged him with the bottle. He needed it more than she did. Somehow they got onto the topic of television, and when he told her the suspense series they'd been watching all through the fall had aired two new episodes she made him catch her up. As the sun tipped past high noon their stomachs started grumbling and they abandoned the beach for a waterside cafe in Phillipsburg.

"Have you heard from Ori? Did she speak to Hunter?" Terry asked between bites of a grouper sandwich.

"No. I'll bet he replied to her on Wednesday though, as soon as he got the message. Maybe she's met with him by now."

"If she admitted being here."

"True. She probably didn't. I hope she'll talk to him, otherwise he might come to me again."

Fifty-four

Marigot Bay, St. Martin

*B*urt patted the pockets of his fishing vest, feeling familiar shapes of multitool and flashlight. Standing in the passage at the base of the stairs on *Sandcastle*'s lower deck he pressed one side of the metal plate covering the space between the stacked washer and dryer. The plate popped open on a hinge and he reached inside, tugging a box secured with Velcro to the underside of the dryer. He opened it and withdrew a Glock 19 and two extra high capacity magazines from foam recesses. He dropped the magazines into a pocket and returned the box to its hiding place. Then he pulled back the slide on the Glock to make sure a round was chambered. Finally, he reached back into the space and withdrew a holster that would secure the weapon at the small of his back.

A few minutes later he steered *Sandcastle* out of the marina and aimed her to the northeast. The sun was descending the sky to the west, making the industrial port a smudge against the line of beaches and brown hills at the north end of the bay.

Twenty minutes later he snugged *Sandcastle* up against the outer side of floating, L-shaped dock to the right of the commercial wharf. The loading crane was at work there, lifting containers from a small cargo ship and stacking them on shore.

There was nobody on the dock, so he tossed a spring line from amidships around a cleat as a temporary hold, then stepped off to secure stern and bow lines. He walked purposefully up the ramp leading to a couple buildings—the shipyard office and an old, small warehouse that served as a repair shop.

He stepped into the office where three men were standing over a desk looking at a diagram of the shipyard. Charles Gibson, a humorless American agent, was the only one of the three who Burt knew. He suspected the other two were French police, possibly connected to Interpol. Gibson looked up as Burt shut the office door.

"Welcome, Mr. Adams. Come, we will brief you."

The human trafficking task force knew of the imminent arrival of a ship carrying more victims. Meeting with them and planning tonight's action had kept Burt occupied for the last few days and prevented him from checking in on Beth.

The agencies making up the task force had been developing sources for years, in some cases decades. They had reliable information that the cargo vessel *Phoenician*, bound for St. Martin, was carrying one container that was not full of sugar, nuts, or fruits. Any suspicion that the information was not correct had been dispelled when the ship's Automatic Identification System signal—which should provide its identity and position to authorities and other vessels—had been shut off two days after it departed Saldanha Bay, South Africa. The captain would claim a malfunction, of course, after ripping out a wire himself.

The task force had been watching for the ship in waters near known human trafficking ports since then. A US Coast Guard cutter on drug patrol spotted it approaching the Caribbean on Wednesday morning.

Gibson outlined the plan and the timeline in typically concise terms. The ship would arrive in an hour, replacing the one at the wharf now. The shipyard crew would begin unloading, but it would be another two hours—after dark—before the container with the victims would be lifted to the shore. It would be placed on the ground with others stacked on top of and around it, but its door would remain accessible. Virgine, Gibson explained, paid several shipyard workers to make it so. The yard crew would go off duty shortly after the container was unloaded. The ship's crew of four would be dismissed and head into town. Once they were all gone, leaving a security guard who Virgine paid, her guards would remove the people from the container.

The task force on site included two US Navy Seals, a Green Beret, and two other highly trained former soldiers from un-named Caribbean nations. Gibson guided Burt and the police officers into the old warehouse and introduced him to the US and Caribbean agents.

J

Fort Louis Marina, Marigot Bay, St. Martin

The brakes on Hunter's bike squealed as he stopped outside the Marina in Margot Bay. He got off the bike and leaned it against the side wall of the building, out of sight of the staff, although hardly hidden from passersby. So far nobody had stolen the rusty, decrepit thing.

It had been five days since he'd talked to Beth Anderson. He'd given her enough time. It was fair to approach her again, to ask her why she hadn't kept her promise. The possibility that she had, but Ori had refused to contact him was hard to contemplate. But he had to know, and Beth was the only one who could help.

He ambled past the marina office, eyes on the locked gate to the docks. He couldn't stand outside of the gate waiting for someone to open it—the office staff would accuse him loitering, and they'd be right. So he wandered past, stopped and lit a cigarette and stood at the fence looking out at the boats. He could see if someone was coming from the boats and get back to the gate before it shut behind them.

He finished the cigarette, dropping it in among the rocks below the fence, and lit another. Movement on the dock caught his eye. It was her, climbing off her boat. She was followed by a man who took her hand as they turned to walk up the ramp to the gate. They were dressed formally—at least formally for the islands. The man must be her boyfriend, Terry. He hadn't been around before, Hunter was sure of it. *Why is he here?*

He didn't want to approach her with the man at her side. He watched them stand by the marina driveway talking, oblivious to him. Shortly a taxi drove up and stopped. The man opened the rear door for Beth and went around to the other side to get in.

Another taxi, probably hoping for a large party, came pulled up as the first one drew away. Hunter felt himself moving before thinking. He tossed his cigarette over the fence and went to the taxi.

"I'm with them," he said pointing at the departing taxi. "Follow them."

"Where to, monsieur?" the driver asked, putting the car in gear.

"Just follow them," Hunter said, catching the man's eye in the rear-view mirror. He withdrew a ten Euro note and held it up next to his face where the man couldn't miss it.

"Yes sir." The driver nodded.

)

Philipsburg, Sint Maarten

"Have you been to one of these island casinos before?" Beth asked Terry as they strolled into the gaming room. She was scanning the people, anticipating finding Virgine and worried about it at the same time.

"My folks like to play baccarat. Mom thinks it's sophisticated. I've been in a couple with them, before I figured out how get out of their island vacations."

"Baccarat sounds sophisticated to me. Very James Bond," Beth said, scanning the crowd as they made their way around the outer perimeter of the floor where there were fewer people.

"Do you see her?"

Realizing her searching was too obvious Beth smiled and shook her head.

"The Black Jack tables are over there." Terry nodded toward an area where the crowed seemed denser. A banner suspended from the ceiling over them announced the Black Jack tournament. It would start in five minutes.

"Wow. A lot of spectators, or a lot of players," Beth said. "How do we get close? Who knew this was so popular?"

"Up there," Terry said, pointing at a mezzanine overlooking the main floor. Slot machines lined the wall, but the railing was open, and a few people were already standing at it looking down.

"Let's go," Beth scanned the room once again, this time looking for stairs.

"Stairs are near the entrance," Terry said, guiding her to turn with a hand on her back. Up on the mezzanine they found an open spot at the railing with a clear view of the black jack tables below.

"There's Ori," Beth said, "Third table in, on the right." The table where Ori was beginning to deal was close below them. They could see the top of her head and her hands as she dealt cards to her players.

"Is that—?"

"Virgine. Yes. At Ori's table."

"Why do you sound surprised?"

"I don't know. I guess I've been wondering whether this is a trick of Ori's. Maybe she wants me to come here for some other reason."

Beth was glad Terry didn't respond, mainly because she knew he didn't trust Ori. He probably agreed with her.

"How many hands will they play, do you know?" Terry asked as Ori's players placed their bets.

"Fifty. That sounds like a lot."

"It goes pretty fast, depending on the dealer. A minute or so for each hand. Wow, look at that!"

Below them, Virgine had wagered three times as many chips as the other players at her table.

"Aggressive play. I read about strategies. I'm not surprised."

"Good way to go out fast, too."

"Yeah. Ori says she's not a bad player, so maybe she has a good hand."

"She did," Terry said a moment later when the cards were revealed and Virgine beat the house. She was the only one at the table who did, and her pile of chips grew much larger than any of theirs.

On the next hand she bet the minimum and watched Ori sweep the chips away. She bet high on the third hand and won again, but so did one of the other players. Still, Virgine had the most chips.

Beth let her eyes wander to the other tables. At one, every player was betting aggressively, and the spectators were flocking over to watch the battle. A chorus of "ahs" indicated that the first of them had lost it all in the twelfth hand.

"That was fast," Terry said.

"Amateur." Beth chuckled at herself—she had absolutely no basis for making such a judgment. Terry grinned at her.

"Expert already after watching twelve hands."

Virgine was doing well by the twentieth hand. One of the players at her table had lost after nineteen hands and a succession of lousy cards.

"This is going to get boring," Beth said.

Port Galisbay, St. Martin

The old warehouse held on to the heat of the day. Even in light weight black trousers and polo shirt under his fishing vest, Burt perspired as he sat with the two Caribbean agents. They took turns watching the cargo holding area and parking lot through the slats of a venetian blind hanging at an angle over a duty window. The rest of the team was located in two other positions—the warehouse next to the one Virgine owned, and the one closest to the stacks of containers in the cargo holding area. Burt had tucked an in-ear transmitter/receiver into his left ear. It was uncomfortable, but worth it, as he was able to hear each check-in as well as updates from the other members of the team.

The yard crew had shut down the crane and one-by-one punched the time clock on the outside of the office building. The security guard had made his rounds of the yard, stopping for a few moments next to the container where the victims were being held. Burt had watched him reach out and touch the sun-warmed steel door as if he wanted to open it. Then he'd glanced over his shoulder in the direction of Virgine's warehouse and hurried away.

Second thoughts about his choice of benefactors? Burt wondered. In his ear one of the Americans said, "That was close."

"Silence," Gibson barked. Burt smirked.

Gibson had elected to take a position with the two Seals, silently signaling who he trusted the most. Burt was happy to be with the two Caribbeans, Michelle and Tobias. He'd drawn them out about their backgrounds and how they had joined this team, and in the process developed a feel for their skills and experience. They were as deadly as the Americans over in the warehouse. He could tell they were suspicious of his ability to contribute to the operation. That was fine with him, and he played to it by urging them to do their job, he'd stay out of the way.

"Here we go," came Gibson's voice in their ears. Tobias was peering through the window. Michelle picked up her weapon and stepped over behind her associate. Burt slid off the table he'd been sitting on and watched them, listening for more information.

"Three guards, semi-automatics ready, crossing the yard. Two more staying by the warehouse door."

Fifty-five

Philipsburg, Sint Maarten

"*U*h oh, look who's here," Beth said as Ori dealt the twenty-fifth hand.

"Who?" Terry glanced at Beth to see where she was looking.

"Tall man, under-dressed in a green polo shirt and jeans. Long brown hair in a tail. See him? He's in the crowd, heading for Ori's table."

"Is that this Hunter guy?"

"In the flesh. How did he find her?"

"Can't have been luck. Any chance he followed us?"

Beth shrugged. It hadn't occurred to her that Hunter would watch her and follow her. Why would he? He didn't know Ori was on St. Martin. But then, searching for Beth for months didn't make much sense, so following her around didn't feel strange for this guy.

"I wouldn't have noticed. He could have," she said.

"Creepy. And he looks familiar. I'm sure I've seen him somewhere."

"Yeah, well, he's been on creepy patrol for months. Enough to make Burt follow him here."

Below them, Ori glanced up past her players and spotted Hunter among the spectators. Her hand slipped on the card shoe revealing the next card. She refocused, discarded the card, and dispensed the next one to deal to the next player. Behind her, a pit boss focused on her. He could not miss the way she kept glancing up at the man in the crowd. Ori finished the deal and asked for wagers. She stared at Hunter as the players moved their chips. Beth and Terry could not hear her or the players at her table over the casino noise, but obviously Virgine said something to her because her eyes darted to the woman, and then she focused on the first player's hand. One by one the players revealed their cards. Virgine had nineteen, another player had twenty. Ori revealed the house's hand with eighteen and paid off the two winners. The pit boss stepped in behind her and tapped her shoulder. She nodded at him, turned to thank the players, and stepped away from the table as a new dealer stepped in.

"I don't think she meant that to happen," Beth said.

"He had to replace her, she was distracted."

"I know. Now she has to deal with Hunter."

"Which is a good thing. Do you think Virgine has the most chips at the table now?"

Beth recognized his attempt to draw her back to their reason for being there, but she couldn't help watching Ori motion to Hunter, then lead him away. She guided him out of their sight under the mezzanine. Beth reluctantly returned her attention to Virgine's table.

)

Port Galisbay, St. Martin

"Everyone hold!" Gibson barked. In front of Burt, Michelle and Tobias both tensed.

"What happened?" Burt asked. Michelle half turned, then moved enough so Burt could see out the window.

"One of them got away from the guards," she said. "He was fast. He ran around the side of the container before any of the guards could get a weapon aimed."

"The guards are complacent," Tobias said. "They expect the prisoners to be passive."

Across the shipyard Burt saw two guards herding a group of about twenty people toward Virgine's warehouse while a third one was stalking along the row of containers, weapon held at ready, peering in between each stack of huge steel boxes.

"He'll kill him if he finds him," Burt said. "Can we collect him?"

"I said hold!" Gibson said.

"We're here to rescue them, not watch them murdered," Burt said. Out of the corner of his eye he saw Tobias's thin smile.

"We're here to get Virgine Guesnon and her superiors. Hold your positions."

"I've got eyes on the one that escaped," one of the navy seals reported to the team. "I can pull him in."

"Hold your position. Don't expose your mission."

Burt suppressed his instinct to challenge Gibson again. A minute passed, then another.

"Too late. The guard sees him," the seal reported, a request to intervene evident in his tone.

A burst of gunfire echoed within the stacks of containers.

"He's down," the seal reported, unable to mask regret in his tone.

One of the guards who was herding the captives to the warehouse turned to look, then shouted.

"What happened?"

The third guard emerged from between two stacks of containers. "Got him. We'll need to get rid of him."

A woman among the captives emitted a soulful wail, raising her arms to wrap them around her head. The second guard stepped through the group to her, butt of his rifle raised.

"Shut up!"

She kept wailing, oblivious. Two other women wrapped their arms around her, both staring at the guard as they quieted her. The guard raised the rifle toward each of them, one at a time, laughing at the way they cowered away from him. Satisfied, he pushed back to the edge of the group.

"Get over here. She'll be here any minute and she's going to be angry," the first guard shouted across the shipyard. Burt knew he didn't mean the wailing woman. The guard reached into his trouser pocket and withdrew a mobile phone.

The third guard trotted toward the first two and their group of captives.

"Keep the objective in sight," was Gibson's belated direction to the team. In the old warehouse Tobias grunted and Michelle turned away from the window. In the dim light Burt could see she was troubled. Burt didn't buy the regret that Gibson's tone projected. He cared less about Virgine's victims than about the credit he'd get for mission success.

*

Philipsburg, Sint Maarten

Virgine was still in the lead at the fortieth hand. Another player at her table had lost, and a third was down to about five chips as they wagered on hand forty-one. He pushed all of his chips forward, glancing at the modest stack Virgine wagered. Even if he won this hand, it was mathematically impossible for him to regain enough chips to beat her.

He did win, but so did Virgine. On the next hand he bet it all again.

"He's trying to go out without just walking away," Terry said. Beth nodded.

The dealer revealed a twenty and everybody lost the hand.

That left Virgine and one other player—an elegantly dressed white woman with a habit of tapping a chip on the edge of the table while she looked at her cards. Beth had noticed Virgine's aggravated glances at the woman several times as they played. But apparently aggravation wasn't upsetting her game, because she won the next two hands, increasing her winnings. The other woman had about half as many chips as Virgine.

"She could take the lead if she gets a solid hand and bets it all."

"Virgine wouldn't like that."

The dealer started placing the cards for the next hand. A man pushed through the spectators behind Virgine. Although dressed in a grey suit over a white button-down shirt, he seemed out of place among the formally-dressed crowd. His dark hand reached out to tap Virgine on the shoulder.

She started, then glanced around, anger clear on her face even from the mezzanine. Beth gasped.

"You know him?"

"It's Mathieu, her houseboy."

"The one you told me about?"

"Yes."

Virgine's head swung between the dealer's hand as he dealt the second card of the hand and Mathieu standing behind her left shoulder. The pit boss had moved in behind the dealer and was obviously about to say something. He raised a hand and nodded at someone beyond the edge of the crowd.

"He's calling security," Terry said. "The pit boss."

Virgine was speaking to Mathieu, her mouth contorting as she spoke. She was livid, it was obvious even without hearing her.

But the boy was equally animated, gesturing toward the door of the casino, waving his hand in agitation, and shaking his head as she tried to shoo him away. Finally, he put his hand on her left arm and tugged at her. Just then a security guard in a plain black suit stepped through the crowd and wrapped his own hand around Mathieu's bicep. Virgine shook her hand free and glared at the boy in a way that made Beth shudder. She snapped something at him, and then at the guard who released his grip on the boy.

She slid off of her stool and turned to the dealer, said something, then said something to the other player. The other woman nodded graciously. Virgine's expression was anything but gracious. She swung back around to Mathieu, grabbed him by the forearm far more roughly than the guard had, and dragged him away. The crowd parted before her.

"Let's go!" Beth said, grabbing for Terry's hand in a gesture a lot like Virgine's.

"Go?" Terry growled, pulling his hand away.

"After her!"

"Beth!"

"Come on, aren't you curious? What could he have said to her to get her to leave the game?"

She stared at Terry, eyes wide with encouragement. *He has to want to know too.*

"Okay. You're right. Let's go. Hurry!"

Once committed he outpaced her quickly, taking the stairs down two at a time and rushing through the lobby ahead of her. Beth didn't mind—he could catch them and see where they went.

"Taxi!" he was calling as she exited the casino. A dark sedan rolled forward from a queue of them in the casino drive. He flung open the rear door and ushered Beth in, then ran around to get in on the other side.

"Do you see the Cadillac up there?" he asked the driver.

"That's her car!" Beth said.

"Yes sir."

"I've always wanted to say this: 'follow that car'."

"Yes sir!" the driver said with surprising enthusiasm as he accelerated away. He simultaneously engaged the meter.

Beth eyed Terry chuckling. "Now who's being all James Bond?"

"I'll leave the espionage to you. I was thinking more Jimmy Cagney, gangster stuff."

"Ah."

♩

Philipsburg, Sint Maarten

Her mind whirling, Ori guided Hunter through the open doors of the casino bar. She spotted a round table for two in a dim corner and sat down. Hunter scraped the flimsy chair on the floor and sat down on it across from her.

"What are you doing here? Did Beth tell you where to find me?"

"No! She refused to tell me anything. She promised to ask you to contact me."

"How did you find me here? This is my work, by the way. You got me in trouble." It wasn't true—dealers were switched in and out all the time. Her momentary distraction would be forgotten.

"I'm sorry. I didn't mean to, but when I saw you, I couldn't believe it."

"But why are you here? In the casino? Don't tell me you decided to come play slots."

She was surprised at the way he ducked his head. Embarrassed? All the gentleness, the sweet quirks that had drawn her to him back in Jamaica resurfaced. She hadn't lied to Beth about that. He was a good guy.

"That's exactly what I decided to do," he said, nearly a mumble. Then he raised his head. "Look, it's been days and I haven't heard from you, so I figured either she didn't contact you like she said she would, or you weren't going to contact me. I decided to go see her again."

"So you were going to harass my friend. How did you end up here?"

He visibly cringed and Ori felt a sharp pang of guilt. That was why she'd left Jamaica—he made her feel like a bitch.

"When I got to the marina she was leaving, dressed up, with a guy. They took a taxi. I took another one and followed them. When they came in here I figured what the heck? I've never seen the inside of this place."

"Beth's here?" Ori asked, looking toward the entrance to the bar. Then she realized why: their deal. She'd email Hunter if Beth would come tonight and see her client gambling away the money Beth's company gave her. So, Beth had kept her side of the deal. That made Ori feel like an even bigger bitch. Sure, she'd sat with Beth's laptop, logged into her email account, and written an email to Hunter, but she'd sent it to an email address that was one character different from his. She'd closed the browser as soon as the message was sent, before the distant servers across the Internet could determine that the email address was invalid. When she checked her email later and found the automated message that her email was undeliverable, she'd felt tremendous relief. She was off the hook and Beth would never be the wiser, or so she'd thought. "Never mind. What do you want?"

"Ori, you know what I want. I want to see our son."

"You don't know he's yours."

"I don't know he isn't, yet."

"Oh no! No. No testing!" Her voice grew louder with each declaration.

"Okay, Ori, okay." He made a lowering gesture with his hands that made her want to yell louder. "Let's take this one step at a time. Where is he? Do you have a sitter or something?"

"What? Oh. No, he's not here. Not on St Martin."

"He's—"

"He's with my parents in Connecticut."

"Connecticut? You left him in Connecticut and came here? For what? Are you with someone?"

Ori snorted derisively at his immediate assumption. "What, I have to be with a man?" she hissed. He visibly paled.

"No. I know that's not you," he answered without conviction.

He did not know. He did not understand her at all. She'd known that from the beginning when she'd sailed into his bay for a drink and found him behind the bar. Hanging out with the Jamaicans wouldn't have changed his chauvinistic Texas attitude toward women.

"I was suffocating there. But he needs to be there. He was premature. He needs a lot of care, and he's getting it from the best."

"What's wrong with him?"

Ori hated the tone of his question, as if her son was a reject. As if Hunter wanted nothing to do with a defective child.

"There is nothing wrong with him. He's small. His system needs time to finish developing."

Hunter was shaking his head, eyes locked on her accusingly.

"I couldn't stay, Hunt. I couldn't handle it," Ori said, her voice betraying the fear for her son that his questioning had brought back to the surface. Fear she had spent weeks suppressing, locking it away and bricking it over with casual disregard.

"No surprise." The sharpness in his tone was out of character. She stared at him, seeing anger and, more hurtful, disappointment. She felt herself shrivel under his glare. His expression accused her of cowardice. She had been a coward to leave Jamaica when she found out she was pregnant. She had been a coward to leave Tiberius with her parents in Connecticut.

"No," she said, then realized she'd spoken aloud."

"No what?"

She gulped a breath, shaking her head to emphasize, or was it to convince herself, "I did what's best for him. I was like a bystander there. My mother is handling everything, my dad is paying the bills. The nanny is filling in when they aren't. He didn't need me there too."

"A child always needs its mother."

Ori flinched. "I didn't need mine," she said. But it wasn't true and the way he shook his head told her he knew it. "He didn't know I was there when I was. In a few years, maybe ..."

"In a few years he'll know your mother as his, or the nanny. It's a lousy way to grow up. Trust me."

So that was it. He knew what it was like to be raised with money, just like she did. She knew that, but she hadn't thought it could shape him so differently from how it had shaped her. Her gaze wandered over to the bar where the bartender was carefully drawing off a pint of beer for a man. Few of the gamblers came into the bar, it was largely the domain of the waitresses who circulated on the floor taking and filling orders. As she watched, one of them came in carrying a tray laden with dirty glassware. She glanced at Ori and Hunter, did a double take, and then nodded a silent greeting. Ori nodded back, offering a thin smile before looking back at Hunter.

He was watching her, but he did not look across the bar to see who she had nodded at.

"You want to go see him, I'll give you the address and phone number."

"Let's call them together."

"No way."

"Ori—"

"No. I can't call them, and you have to promise not to tell them where I am."

"What the hell, Ori. You're hiding from them? Why are you acting like a wayward teenager?"

"A what?"

"You heard me. Grow up. Take responsibility for your damn life."

"I am responsible. I came here, got a job, learned a trade."

"You abandoned our son."

"I told you, he's fine!"

"He's—" Hunter stopped himself, shutting his eyes and shaking his head. "No, let's not go around again. Let me ask you this, do you hate me?"

Ori had already started to make an immediate denial before hearing his question. She stopped, mouth open. Hate him? Far from it. He was the nicest guy she'd ever met. Crazy to have hunted her down like this, but that just proved his sincerity. *Damn him.*

"No. I do not hate you Hunter. But I'm not sure I can be with you."

"Woah, easy there. Let's not get ahead of ourselves."

"Get ahead—"

"No, I didn't mean that. Can we try to be civil? Try to be parents to our son?" He had changed his meaning, but she knew better. All along this was what he'd been hoping—to pick up where they'd left off when she left Jamaica. But she was sure now that where he thought they'd been was not what she thought. He'd been building a relationship. She'd been having an island fling. Or had she?

Fifty-six

Port de Galisbay

*T*hrough the dirty warehouse window Burt watched a white Cadillac drive into the shipyard and coast to a standstill near Virgine Guesnon's warehouse.

"Subject has arrived," came Gibson's voice in his ear. "Stand by."

The driver got out and walked around the car to open the rear passenger door. A woman got out, followed by a tall, slender man.

"Can anyone ID the man with her?" Gibson asked.

"Negative," a couple of the team members replied.

"It might be her house boy. Possibly a trafficking victim who she took in," Burt said. Behind him he heard a rustle of paper and then Michelle spoke.

"Boy is named Mathieu, according to the file. If that's him."

"Right, Mathieu," Burt agreed, adding again, "most likely one of her victims."

"We want both of them alive to testify," Gibson said.

Whatever it takes to protect the boy, Burt thought as Virgine strode toward where the three guards had the group of victims standing. The Cadillac's headlights illuminated their bare legs and feet but left their faces in shadow.

"What are you doing out here?" Virgine growled. "Get them out of sight!"

The guards snapped into action, each one shoving the nearest captive toward the warehouse. Two of them stumbled and one went to his—or her, it was hard to tell—knees. A guard grabbed the person's right arm and hauled them up and forward. Another captive reached out and caught the stumbling person and they moved forward together.

Virgine stood rigidly erect watching them go past like a general inspecting the troops. Burt's stomach turned. He had witnessed plenty of inhumanity over the years, but something about this woman touched part of him that he tried to turn off while working.

The ragged group vanished into the warehouse followed by the last guard. Virgine raised her mobile phone to her ear and stood outside the warehouse talking, the tall young man beside her gazing through the open warehouse doors.

"Who's that? Coming up the drive near the first warehouse?" Tobias asked. He was looking out the window at an angle toward the driveway and traffic circle outside of the shipyard. Burt followed his gaze.

"B team, intercept the two people outside your position," he said, not caring whether Gibson would be pissed at his issuing orders.

"Identify them, Adams," Gibson said.

Yup, he's pissed, Burt thought.

"Our Broadhead asset and associate," Burt said quickly.

"Intercepting," one of the Interpol officers replied. Burt saw the first warehouse's door slide open half a foot and a hand wave outside of it to attract Beth and Terry's attention.

"What is she doing here?" Gibson asked as Burt watched Terry see the hand and steer Beth toward it. To his relief, she didn't resist or hesitate. His eyes went back to Virgine, but she was staring toward the containers and the ship. Mathieu, however, had glanced toward the first warehouse.

"Mathieu might have seen," Burt said. "Let's see what he does."

What he did was stare at the slightly open door for a long time, and then turn his attention back to Virgine's warehouse.

"Okay. Either he didn't see, or he's prepared to turn on her."

That seemed like a wild assumption to Burt. The boy might not be sure he saw anything or might think it was someone who belonged there. But he held his tongue. Either way, Beth and Terry were out of the line of fire. Burt didn't want to worry about how they happened to be here now.

"We have traced her call," came a voice Burt did not recognize. "She's talking to Ballista. We have the phone number confirmed, and voice recognition says ninety percent."

"You're recording?" Gibson asked.

"Of course. She's complaining that the ship came early, blaming it for the man who was killed, says her people were not prepared. Ballista isn't buying it."

"Let her finish, see how it ends."

A moment later it ended with Virgine angrily shutting her flip phone to end the call. She shoved it into her evening bag and said something to Mathieu. He nodded and turned toward the Cadillac. She squared her shoulders and strode into the warehouse.

"Go. Go. Go."

♪

"You two stay here," the armed man in a bullet proof vest said to Beth and Terry, raising his hand palm out in a "stay" gesture as if they were dogs.

"What's happening?" she asked, frowning. Both men stepped through the door of the warehouse as if reacting to a silent command.

"Ear pieces," Terry said quietly, tapping his left ear.

"Oh."

"I could see it in the one guy's ear. I think they're moving in on Virgine's warehouse."

Beth went to the warehouse door.

"We can't go out there Beth. We'll be in the way."

Beth knew he hadn't said what he was thinking—the men had weapons, and there was going to be shooting.

"I just want to see out," she said, stepping close to the open door, but staying in the shadows inside. Terry moved in beside her.

The two men who'd left them behind were moving quickly and quietly along the front of the building. They disappeared around the corner.

"They're going to the back entrance," Terry whispered.

"Look over there." Beth was looking across the drive toward a smaller warehouse building. The door stood open and there were two more armed figures running in a crouch toward Virgine's warehouse. One of them had an automatic rifle aimed at Virgine's Cadillac. The two from the small warehouse crossed behind it, out of the light. One of them continued to train his weapon on the car as they flattened themselves against the front of Virgine's warehouse.

Beth saw two more men coming from further into the shipyard. When they reached Virginie's warehouse, one of them grasped the handle on the door and raised his other fist. He raised one finger, another finger, and finally a third, then dragged the sliding door open. The other three rolled around the sides of the opening and into the dim interior.

Movement in the yard caught Beth's eye. There was another man coming from the same direction as last two. He walked confidently with no stealth in his gait. But Beth noticed that he avoided walking into the light projected by the parked car.

"He's got to be in charge," Terry murmured.

"Beth, Terry, get back."

Beth's heart skipped a beat and then pounded at the sound of Burt's voice from right outside. As he stepped through the door gunfire sounded from within Virgine's warehouse. Beth jump backward, slamming into Terry. Somehow he absorbed the energy of her move and tugged her away from the door. Burt took up their position looking out. There was more gunfire from next door, and screams of men, women, and children. A child continued to wail even after the shooting had stopped.

Beth's mouth had gone dry and her breathing came far more rapidly than during a bad squall.

"Are they shooting the people?" Suddenly tears were streaming down her cheeks. "They're killing them," she said, unable not to visualize people dressed in rags being mowed down by gunfire, like a scene from an awful World War II movie. Terry's hand on her shoulder steadied her some, but she couldn't stop the gasping. The tears. Those innocent people were dying, and she was involved.

"Beth, you don't know that. It's more likely our people shooting at the guards, and the guards shooting back. Our people would take out a guard who started shooting the captives."

Burt sounded so sure, so confident. Beth forced herself to breathe through her nose. She dashed at her cheeks and her brimming eyes with the back of her wrist. Terry squeezed her shoulder.

"How did you get here?" Burt asked. Trying to distract her, she knew. She appreciated it.

"We followed Virgine," she said between rough inhales. She saw him watching her. This was a test. An unplanned, but valuable test to assess how much she could handle. Something deep inside her wanted to pass. Her heart rate slowed. She made a final wipe at her eyes and looked straight at Burt.

"I'm okay," she declared. "It was just a shock."

He nodded. She realized he was waiting for more of an answer.

"She was competing in a black jack tournament. Remember Ori told me about it?"

"Yes. We expected her to be busy for a few more hours."

"Mathieu came into the casino and got her. She was winning. She had to drop out. She was livid."

Burt turned to look out the door, then he stepped out, gesturing that they could follow him. Beth took Terry's hand in hers and they stepped outside.

Mathieu and the driver were standing next to the Cadillac with their hands on its roof. A man—the one who'd come across the yard, Beth thought—was standing behind them with an automatic rifle aimed at them. Mathieu's head turned toward Burt, Beth, and Terry. She could see the whites of his eyes as he stared at her, and then she was certain she saw his head bob in acknowledgement of her presence.

"Mathieu is a victim," she said. "I'm sure of it."

"Yes, I know. We'll sort it out," Burt said.

Two of Virgine's guards came out of her warehouse with their hands on their heads. Virgine followed, stumbling in her heels as one of the team gave her an unnecessary shove.

"Easy there," the man holding the gun on the driver and Mathieu said with obvious authority.

"You want her to see you?" Burt asked Beth quietly, "or not?"

Beth couldn't take her eyes off of her former client. The woman became enraged as one of the team dragged her hands off of her head and behind her back, locking handcuffs around her wrists. The two guards were also in handcuffs. Beth became aware of a dissonant French siren getting closer.

"I want her to see me," she decided. "I want her to know I wasn't fooled."

"Let's go then." Burt said.

As she followed him toward the car she wondered if that had been a test and whether she'd passed or failed.

"Should I stay under cover?" She asked, even though Virgine had already noticed them. She watched them approach, and then her eyes widened, clearly recognizing Beth.

"Too late," Burt said with a hint of amusement. "It's okay. There wasn't more you could do 'under cover'."

"You!" Virgine hissed at her when they were within earshot.

"Hello Virgine," Beth heard herself say. She wished she could think of a cutting comment, but none came. So much for being the suave, clever secret agent.

The siren grew painfully loud and then stopped, the sound still echoing among the warehouses, as the ambulance drew to a stop behind the Cadillac. A police van pulled in next to it. Burt drew Beth and Terry out of the way.

"The man holding the gun on Mathieu and the driver is Charles Gibson. He's in command. The team is made up of officers from various organizations and nations."

"So they captured Virgine, but what about the rest of her ring?"

"She called her contact before they moved in. They traced the call and identified him. The recording of their conversation is sufficient evidence to take him. In fact, I believe that is happening now, somewhere in Central America."

"Wow, just like that?"

"As I told you, this investigation has been going on for a while. Months of boring surveillance and research went into this operation tonight. So no, not 'just like that'."

"What about Broadhead's money?"

Burt turned to stare at Beth, and then grinned. "Left at the casino, I believe," he said, "at least a large part of it. But it wasn't Broadhead's anyway. They were just the conduit."

"You mean, it was—"

"Supplied by the anti-trafficking task force. Yes."

"But weren't you supposed to guard it?"

"Unfortunately for the bookkeepers, I was summoned here, so I did not have an opportunity to prevent Madame Guesnon from going to the casino. It's all right. The successful capture of her and rescue of the victims makes up for the loss."

The crew from the ambulance had taken a stretcher into the warehouse. Now two emerged with one of Virgine's guards on it.

"You'll be relieved to know that in all the shooting, only the one guard was hit. Come on," Burt said, clearly listening to an earpiece like the other team members.

Beth and Terry followed him past the Cadillac and the captives toward the warehouse entrance.

The first thing she noticed was the pungent smell of dirty bodies, sweat, and sewage. It made the odor aboard *Trouble* from the broken head seem pleasant. Overhead lights and been switched on inside, but they failed to penetrate the dim corners. Burt led them around a wall of boxes a few feet back from the door and into an open space where tables were stacked with the boxes from China Beth had seen on the truck.

"Her craft operation," Burt said. "You were right about the counterfeit trade goods. That was a fine bit of investigation. Some of the task force are embarrassed that they didn't figure it out."

"Wow, really?" Beth said.

"Yes. This way," he guided them past the table and around another wall of boxes. The smell was much stronger back here.

About thirty men, women, and children were sitting on mats and blankets. Their clothing was filthy rags in shades of brown and black. Their faces were wary. Some were drinking cups of water being distributed by the darkly dressed team members and the ambulance crew. Shaking hands reached up to take the plastic cups. Beth realized one of the team members was a woman as she crouched before a wide-eyed child.

"Did they all just arrive?" Terry asked Burt.

"No. Twenty of them came on the ship tonight. The rest were here."

"What will happen to them?"

"They'll be fed and allowed to bathe, receive medical attention. Some may need to be admitted to the hospital. Others will be housed in a shelter while they're interviewed. Returning them home is sometimes the hardest part. Some of them come from remote villages. Sometimes the womens' families don't want them back."

"What about Kelvin, and Mathieu?"

"They're looking for Kelvin's family in South Africa. Mathieu will be interviewed, and they'll try to find his, too. I suspect he's not the only member of Virgine's household who came to her this way. The aftermath of this is not quick, nor easy. I wanted you to see them, though. To make sure you realized how important this work is."

"I already realized. But this is—" Beth shook her head. "I had already come to loathe Virgine. This just seals my opinion of her."

"She has her story too," Burt said. "She is the product of her society and her family. Unfortunately, she chose to exploit the darker aspects of it."

"I think she's a sociopath. No sense of empathy, completely selfish."

Burt nodded. "Could be. There will be a psychological assessment."

"I hope they don't find her mentally unstable," Terry said, drawing Burt and Beth's eyes. He'd been so quiet until now. "If she's insane, she won't be tried. She deserves to spend a lot of time in prison."

Fifty-seven

Fort Louis Marina, Marigot Bay, St. Martin

"*O*h no. This is bad."

Terry's legs were bent in a pretzel where they stuck out of the head compartment doorway. His upper body was on the floor where he was installing the replacement hose that had been delivered to the marina that morning. It had taken both his and Beth's assertions to convince the marina staff that they could install it themselves. Terry was already regretting it.

"What is it?" Beth leaned over his feet to look into the head.

"This," Terry said, awkwardly raising his right hand above the toilet to show her an oddly shaped piece of grayish plastic.

"What is that?"

"Hell if I know, but it's part of the pump mechanism, I'm sure. Umph," he grunted as he pushed himself into an awkward sitting position. With his left hand he dragged the pump handle upward and tried to push it down. The same grinding sound Beth had heard came from the mechanism. "Did you consider taking it apart before you diagnosed the hose?"

He regretted his accusatory tone when he looked up at her. He thought she might burst into tears. Not over the head, he knew.

She took care of her boat, made mistakes and corrected them, without breaking down. She might get upset or angry at herself, but she always approached it as a challenge, not a crisis. It was one of the things he admired about her. It was no wonder she didn't check further than the clogged hose when the head failed just as she learned about Virgine, Burt, and Broadhead. No wonder the broken pump was enough to push her over the edge of emotional stability when she—neither of them—had gotten over what they witnessed Saturday night.

"Hey, I'm sorry. That came out wrong. Bethy," he struggled to untwist and get to his feet. She stepped back to give him room, eyes on his hand holding the broken part. "Listen, it's an old head, they wear out."

"I can't believe I didn't look at it. I should have realized it being hard to pump wouldn't be from the clogged hose."

"Well, it could have been," he tried, even though he agreed with her. She shrugged, head tipping to one side, and met his eyes. Hers were clearing, the potential outburst past, or suppressed. He wanted to take her into his arms but having just gotten up from the floor beneath the toilet made him stop.

"I'd give you a hug, but …"

"Yeah, thanks—for the thought." She smiled with wry appreciation of his consideration. He loved that about her too. Then she turned away and went to the navigation station, flipping open the cruising guide.

"I think we should get it fixed," she said as she looked for something in the spiral bound book. "The engine has been running rough, too."

"You said 'we'," Terry said.

"Hum?" she glanced up at him.

"You said 'we' about a decision about *Trouble*."

"Yeah, I guess I did. Well, she is ours, not just mine. You've put a lot into her. What do you think about bringing her in to one of the boatyards here for some work? They could store her for us. I can't take the time to sail her back to St. Thomas now."

Never mind that his fiancé was proposing spending money to fix her—their—boat. She was thinking of it as theirs, not hers, at last. He felt himself nodding and grinning like an idiot.

"Yes," he said to conceal his overreaction.

"Good," she said, her eyes conveying amusement. He couldn't hide much from her. She refocused on the cruising guide, apparently having found the information she wanted. She picked up her phone and punched in a phone number. Still grinning, Terry dropped the broken part in the head sink and shut the door. He passed behind her to the galley and washed his hands, listening to her talk to someone at a boatyard, describing the work she wanted done and making arrangements to bring *Trouble* in.

He lifted the lid on the refrigerator and dug out two cold bottles of beer. There was one more left, he noticed. He removed the tops and pressed one to Beth's upper arm. She half turned, smiling, and took it, listening to the phone. Terry climbed the companionway ladder and sat down in the cockpit.

)

A few minutes later Beth followed him up and sat beside him.

"We can take her in tomorrow. He said to come at high tide, the work slip is shallow."

"They're hauling her?"

"Yes. I don't know when we'll be back. I made storage arrangements."

Terry nodded and sipped his beer.

"Are you going to ask how much?"

He couldn't help erupting in laughter, especially when she gently elbowed him, laughing herself.

"I didn't want to!" He said. "It doesn't matter anyway. We've got to leave her here, and on the hard is cheaper than in a slip and safer than anchored."

"Exactly."

They fell into companionable silence, sipping their beers, until a voice from the dock roused them.

"Permission to come aboard?" Burt asked.

"Yes, come on," Beth replied.

"We have one more beer." Terry started to rise.

"No need, I came prepared," Burt said as he stepped into the cockpit. He set a canvas tote on the seat and sat down beside it.

"How are you?" He looked from Beth to Terry.

"Still processing," Beth replied. "I spoke to my supervisor at Broadhead this morning. He already knew what happened. He told me how much—how little—I could share with the team. Then I spoke to them. They're disappointed that we've lost a client," she shook her head. "They have no clue."

While she was speaking, Burt drew a bottle of beer and an opener out of his bag. He popped the cap and took a sip.

"Go easy on them. As you said, they have no clue, and you can't tell them."

"They do know she was involved in human trafficking, but they don't know what it means. They didn't see the faces of her victims or smell that warehouse. I will never forget that smell."

"Good."

"It's why you do it, isn't it?"

Burt shrugged, his expression non-committal. "If you stick with this, Beth, you will find yourself conflicted sometimes. Not all operations have such clear and compelling victims. But yes, on the whole, I think the things I've done have been on the side of the good, which is why I do them."

They all sat quietly for a few minutes. Beth took two more gulps and drained her bottle. Seeing it, Burt withdrew another from his bag, opened it, and handed it to her.

"Thanks. We're both heading back to D.C. tomorrow."

"And *Trouble*?"

"Going on the hard here."

Burt nodded.

"What about you?"

"I have a charter lined up. I might stick around here for the rest of the season, if business continues. Americans are more comfortable flying to St. Martin than Guadeloupe, it seems. What about your friend Ori?"

"I don't know. She has not been in touch since Hunter found her in the casino on Saturday."

"That's going to be an interesting situation."

"Interesting is one word for it."

Burt chuckled, making Beth do the same.

"Well, I guess this is it until you have another excuse to come to the islands," Burt said after a few more sips of beer.

"I have a feeling it won't be very long," Terry said, looking at Beth.

"Don't look at me," she shrugged. "I don't know what's going to happen when I go back to the office."

"I have an idea," Burt smiled slyly, his eyes meeting Terry's.

"If I'm sent back here for another operation like this one, I want to know what I'm getting into going in. And Burt, next time I want an earpiece too."

Burt and Terry both burst out laughing, and Terry put his arm around Beth, squeezing her shoulders. She turned her head to smile at him, reveling in his affectionate gaze. With these two men in her life she felt a surge of confidence about taking a nine-to-five job that had turned out to be something else entirely.

About the Author

A Southern California native, S. Mia McCroskey started writing when she was in ninth grade. She took up sailing when she was in her twenties as an antidote to an unpleasant job. It was a toss-up between sailing lessons and pottery classes. She flipped a coin; the quarter was a lucky one. She moved from California to New York for a better job a couple years later and continued sailing in Long Island Sound and the Chesapeake Bay. Since stepping aboard that first soling in Marina del Rey she has become qualified to charter large, valuable sailboats in fascinating locales all over the world, and has gotten used to being called "the lady captain" by the locals. In her professional career she transitioned from a magazine and book editor to managing software development. She attributes most of her professional leadership skills to her experience handling crews of friends and acquaintances aboard sailboats. She has never owned her own boat, but she did eventually take pottery classes.

S. Mia McCroskey

The print edition of *Too Much Trouble* is set in a digital version of 12 point
Baskerville, designed by John Baskerville (1776 – 1775).

SUNSEA PRESS

New York